A TEXT BOOK OF

BUILDING TECHNOLOGY AND MATERIALS

FOR
SEMESTER - I
SECOND YEAR DEGREE COURSE IN CIVIL ENGINEERING

Strictly According to New Revised Credit System Syllabus of Savitribai Phule Pune University
(w.e.f June 2016)

Dr. R. K. JAIN
M.E. (Civil), Ph. D.
Principal,
Rajashri Shahu College of Engineering,
Tathawade, Pune .

V. R. PHADKE
M.E. (Civil)
Formerly Professor, Civil Engg. Deptt.,
Rajashri Shahu College of Engineering,
Tathawade, Pune .

Mrs. V.S. LIMAYE
M. Tech. (Civil –TP) M.P.M.
Associate Professor,
Civil Engineering Deptt.
Sinhgad College of Engineering,
Vadgaon (Bk), Pune.

P. R. MINDE
B.E. (Civil), M.E. (C & M),
Assistant Professor,
Civil Engineering Deptt.,
JSPM's PVPIT,
Bavdhan, Pune.

NIRALI PRAKASHAN
ADVANCEMENT OF KNOWLEDGE

N3527

BUILDING TECHNOLOGY & MATERIALS (SE Civil)   ISBN 978-93-86084-01-9

Second Edition : **June 2017**

© : **Authors**

The text of this publication, or any part thereof, should not be reproduced or transmitted in any form or stored in any computer storage system or device for distribution including photocopy, recording, taping or information retrieval system or reproduced on any disc, tape, perforated media or other information storage device etc., without the written permission of Authors with whom the rights are reserved. Breach of this condition is liable for legal action.

Every effort has been made to avoid errors or omissions in this publication. In spite of this, errors may have crept in. Any mistake, error or discrepancy so noted and shall be brought to our notice shall be taken care of in the next edition. It is notified that neither the publisher nor the authors or seller shall be responsible for any damage or loss of action to any one, of any kind, in any manner, therefrom.

Published By :   Polyplate

NIRALI PRAKASHAN

Abhyudaya Pragati, 1312, Shivaji Nagar,
Off J.M. Road, Pune – 411005
Tel - (020) 25512336/37/39, Fax - (020) 25511379
Email : niralipune@pragationline.com

☞ **DISTRIBUTION CENTRES**

PUNE

Nirali Prakashan : 119, Budhwar Peth, Jogeshwari Mandir Lane, Pune 411002, Maharashtra
Tel : (020) 2445 2044, 66022708, Fax : (020) 2445 1538
Email : bookorder@pragationline.com, niralilocal@pragationline.com

Nirali Prakashan : S. No. 28/27, Dhyari, Near Pari Company, Pune 411041
Tel : (020) 24690204 Fax : (020) 24690316
Email : dhyari@pragationline.com, bookorder@pragationline.com

MUMBAI

Nirali Prakashan : 385, S.V.P. Road, Rasdhara Co-op. Hsg. Society Ltd.,
Girgaum, Mumbai 400004, Maharashtra
Tel : (022) 2385 6339 / 2386 9976, Fax : (022) 2386 9976
Email : niralimumbai@pragationline.com

☞ **DISTRIBUTION BRANCHES**

JALGAON

Nirali Prakashan : 34, V. V. Golani Market, Navi Peth, Jalgaon 425001,
Maharashtra, Tel : (0257) 222 0395, Mob : 94234 91860

KOLHAPUR

Nirali Prakashan : New Mahadvar Road, Kedar Plaza, 1st Floor Opp. IDBI Bank
Kolhapur 416 012, Maharashtra. Mob : 9850046155

NAGPUR

Pratibha Book Distributors : Above Maratha Mandir, Shop No. 3, First Floor,
Rani Jhanshi Square, Sitabuldi, Nagpur 440012, Maharashtra
Tel : (0712) 254 7129

DELHI

Nirali Prakashan : 4593/21, Basement, Aggarwal Lane 15, Ansari Road, Daryaganj
Near Times of India Building, New Delhi 110002
Mob : 08505972553

BENGALURU

Pragati Book House : House No. 1, Sanjeevappa Lane, Avenue Road Cross,
Opp. Rice Church, Bengaluru – 560002.
Tel : (080) 64513344, 64513355,Mob : 9880582331, 9845021552
Email:bharatsavla@yahoo.com

CHENNAI

Pragati Books : 9/1, Montieth Road, Behind Taas Mahal, Egmore,
Chennai 600008 Tamil Nadu, Tel : (044) 6518 3535,
Mob : 94440 01782 / 98450 21552 / 98805 82331,
Email : bharatsavla@yahoo.com

niralipune@pragationline.com | www.pragationline.com

Also find us on ⓕ www.facebook.com/niralibooks

Dedicated to ...

Our Students

...Authors

PREFACE TO THE SECOND EDITION

We are glad and excited to announce that the First Edition of this book received an overwhelming response from the engineering student community, compelling us to release its **Second Edition** within a very short period of time.

This thoroughly revised **Second Edition** has been updated with additional matter, including **All Solved University Examination Papers December 2013 to May 2017**.

Special care has been taken to maintain high degree of accuracy in the theory and numericals throughout the book.

We take this opportunity to express our sincere thanks to Dineshbhai Furia of Nirali Prakashan, a reputed pioneer in the publication field. Our special thanks to Jignesh Furia and Mrs. Nirali Verma for their effective cooperation and great care in bringing out this revised edition. We also appreciate the efforts of M. P. Munde and the entire staff of Engineering Books Deptt. of Nirali Prakashan namely Mrs. Deepali Lachake (Co-ordinator) and Mrs. Shilpa Kale for bringing this book to the students in a timely manner.

We sincerely hope that this **"Second Edition"** will also be warmly received by all concerned as in the past.

Valuable suggestions from our esteemed readers to improve the book are most welcome and highly appreciated.

Pune –   **Authors**

PREFACE TO FIRST EDITION

It gives us great pleasure in publishing this text book on **"Building Technology and Materials"** for the Students of Second Year Degree Course in Civil Engineering. This book is strictly written According to New Revised Credit System Syllabus of Savitribai Phule Pune University (2015 Pattern).

As per the policy of the University, Engineering Syllabi is revised every five years. Last revision was in the year 2012. New revision is coming little earlier, as university has introduced **Online** system of examination from year 2012.

As per the New Credit System, the **In Sem (Online - 50 Marks) Examinations** (Combined Phase-I and Phase-II) will be conducted based on first, second, third and fourth units. The **Online** examinations will have objective types of questions with multiple choices. **End Semester Examination (Theory Paper 50 Marks)** will be based on all the six units and that will be conducted in traditional way and the theory course will have 4 credits.

Authors have tried to introduce the subject to the average students, with a large number of solved examples. The subject matter has been developed in a logical and coherent manner with neat illustrations along with a fairly large number of solved examples and exercises. Answers to many unsolved numerical problems are also given.

The Main Objectives of this Text are :

- To cover the basic principles of Building Materials.
- To develop a very good understanding of the subject matter.
- To give practice to solve the numerical examples in Building Technology and Materials.

We have given Free Separate book of Multiple Choice Questions (MCQ's) which will be very useful to the students, especially for Online Examinations.

We take this opportunity to express our sincere thanks to Shri. Dineshbhai Furia, Shri. Jignesh Furia, Mrs. Nirali Verma and Shri. M. P. Munde and entire team of Nirali Prakashan namely Mrs. Deepali Lachake (Co-ordinator), Mr. Bharat Jadhav who really have taken keen interest and untiring efforts in publishing this text.

Finally, we express our gratitude to our family members for their continuous support and encouragement, thanks to all.

We have no doubt that like our earlier texts, student's community will respond favourably to this new venture.

The advice and suggestions of our esteemed readers to improve the text are most welcomed, and will be highly appreciated.

24 June 2016   **Authors**

Pune

SYLLABUS

Unit I : Introduction to Building Construction and Masonry [8 Hrs]

(a) Introduction to building construction: definition, types of building as per National Building Code. Building components and their basic requirements i.e substructure and superstructure requirements. Superstructure: Concept and advantages of a framed structure, types: light framed structures, Timber framed, RCC framed structures. Substructure - shallow and deep foundations and their suitability. General procedure in foundation design, Failure of foundation and its causes, Foundation in black cotton soil, Foundations near existing adjacent old structures. Damp Proof Course, plinth filling and soling.

(b) Masonry: Stone masonry: Principal terms, types of stone masonry. Brick masonry: characteristics of good building bricks, IS specification and tests, classification of bricks: silica, refractory, fire and fly ash bricks. Brick work, types of bonds: English, Flemish, Header, Stretcher, construction procedure, supervision.

Unit II : Block Masonry and Form Work [8 Hrs]

(a) Block Masonry: Cellular lightweight concrete blocks, hollow blocks, concrete blocks, glass blocks, solid blocks, cavity wall construction. Requirement of a good partition wall: metal partitions, asbestos cement partition, wooden partition. Reinforced brick masonry: applications, advantages, materials required and construction procedure. Composite masonry: types, advantages, applications, materials required and construction procedure.

(b) Form work and casting procedure for reinforced concrete columns, R.C.C. beams and girders, R.C.C. slabs, curing methods, precast and pre-stressed concrete construction and joints in concrete work. Slip form work: component parts- design criteria, underpinning, Scaffolding: purpose, types and suitability.

Unit III : Flooring and Roofing Materials [8 Hrs]

(a) Flooring and Flooring Materials: Functional requirement of flooring, types of floor finishes and their suitability, construction details for concrete, tiles and stone flooring. Types of flooring: timber flooring, cement concrete flooring, mosaic flooring, ceramic flooring, terrazzo flooring, tiled flooring, rubber flooring, cork flooring, epoxy asphalt flooring, hollow block and rib floors, Industrial flooring: tremix or Vacuum Dewatered Flooring (VDF).

(b) Roofing Materials: galvanized iron pre-coated aluminum sheets, fiber sheets, and Mangalore tiles. Roof construction: types and their suitability, method of construction, types of trusses, types of shell structure:dome, translation shells, space and frame structure: pneumatic structures, grain storage structures, prefabricated structures, fixing details of roof covering.

Unit IV : Doors, Windows, Arches and Lintels [8 Hrs]

(a) Doors and Windows: definition of technical terms, installation of doors and window frames and their size specifications, fixtures and fastenings. Types of doors: glazed or sash doors, plastic doors, flush doors, louvered doors, collapsible doors, revolving doors, rolling steel doors, sliding doors, swing doors, folding doors. Types of windows: casement window, double hung window, pivoted window, sliding windows, louvered or venetian window, metal window, sash or glazed window, bay window, corner window, dormer window, gable window, skylight window, circular window, mosquito proof window, curtain wall window. Ventilators: purpose and types.

(b) Arches and Lintels: principle of arch action, types of arches, method of arch construction, centering and removal of centering. Lintels: necessity and types, chajja or weather shade necessity and types.

Unit V : Vertical Circulation and Protective Coatings   [8 Hrs]

(a) Vertical Circulation: Consideration in planning, design considerations, Staircase: types, and details of ramps. Ladders, lifts, and escalator. Types of staircase: straight stairs, open well stairs, quarter turn stairs, half turn stairs, turning stairs, dog-legged stairs, circular stairs, geometrical stairs, bifurcated stairs, and spiral stairs.

(b) Protective Coatings – plastering types: lime plaster, cement plaster, gypsum plaster used in spray fire proofing, plaster of Paris and application, pointing: purpose & types, mortar preparation and types, painting and varnishing, types and application, white washing, distempering, oil paints. Wall cladding: materials, method, wall papering and glazing work.

Unit VI : Miscellaneous Materials and Safety in Construction   [8 Hrs]

(a) Miscellaneous Materials: Properties, types and uses of following materials: lime, polymers, plastic types, mastic, gypsum, clay tiles and glazed wares, Timber: types and properties, advantages and applications of aluminum, stainless steel, fibrous, laminated, particulate, combinations of composite materials: laminated fiber reinforced polymers. Glass: uses, types and properties, application and ingredients, market forms, glass claddings, aluminum composite panel cladding. Ceramic products: ceramic sanitary application, water closet, urinals, washes basins, their common sizes, pipes and fittings. Eco-friendly materials: eco-friendly decorating materials, eco-friendly flooring, thatch, bamboo, linoleum, cork.

(b) Safety in Construction: safety on site, storage of materials, construction safety, prevention of accidents, fire proof construction. Repairs and maintenance: addition, and alteration, strutting and shoring.

CONTENTS

Unit III : Flooring and Roofing Materials

CHAPTER 1
INTRODUCTION TO BUILDING CONSTRUCTION

1.1 INTRODUCTION

- Man requires different types of buildings for his activities, stations, houses, bunglows and flats for his living; hospitals and health centres for his health; schools, colleges and universities for his educations etc.
- Fundamental requirements of these buildings are that they should fulfill the physical, emotional, social and biological needs of the person or persons who are going to occupy them.
- All the requirements can be grouped under two main headings - Form and Function.
- "Form" covers the emotional and aesthetic portion of the human requirements while "Function" covers the biological, social and physical needs.
- Both form and function are important and if possible should be achieved to the maximum extent. But in case of comparison, of the importance of the two "Function" out weighs "Form".
- Functionally, a building should be well satisfied before one can skip on to the importance of "Form". If a piece of architecture does not fulfill the basic requirements of function and all importance is stressed on "Form", then it reduces to mere piece of sculpture and ceases to be architecture.
- The building design has traditionally been the responsibility of the architect, though the building construction has been the responsibility of the civil engineer.

Office Buildings

Cottages

Residential buildings

Trade buildings

Fig. 1.1 : Different types of buildings

1.2 DEFINITION

- National Building Code of India (NBC) defines the building "As any structure for whatsoever purpose and of whatsoever materials constructed and every part thereof whether used as human habitation or not and includes foundation, plinth, walls, floors, roofs, chimneys, plumbing and building services, fixed platforms, verandah, balcony, cornice or projection, part of a building or anything affixed there to or any wall enclosing or intended to enclose any land or space and signs and outdoor display structures".
- Tents, shamian as and tarpaulin shelters are not considered as building.
- National Building Code for Residential Apartments in India National Building code is a document containing standardized requirement for the design & construction of most types of building in the country.
- A building can also be defined as enclosed space covered by roof.
- The building has to perform many functions such as utility of the buildings, structural safety, fire safety and it should also satisfy the requirement of sanitation, ventilation, day light.
- These requirements will vary from building to building and the design of building is dependent on the minimum requirements prescribed for each of the functions mentioned above.

1.3 TYPES OF BUILDINGS   (Nov. 16)

According to the National Building Code of India, Buildings are classified, based on occupancy in 9 groups, as follows :

1. Group A : Residential Buildings
2. Group B : Educational Buildings
3. Group C : Institutional Buildings
4. Group D : Assembly Buildings
5. Group E : Business Buildings
6. Group F : Mercantile Buildings
7. Group G : Industrial Buildings
8. Group H : Storage Buildings
9. Group I : Hazardous Buildings

1. Group A : Residential Buildings

These are those buildings, in which sleeping accommodation is provided for normal residential purposes, with or without cooking or dining or both facilities, except any building classified under category C. Buildings of group A are further sub-divided as follows :

- **Sub-Division A - 1 : Lodging or Rooming Houses**

  These include any building or group of buildings under the same management, in which separate sleeping accommodation for a total of not more than 15 persons, on either transient or permanent basis, with or without dining facilities, but without cooking facilities for individuals, is provided.

- **Sub-Division A - 2 : One or two Family Private Dwelling**
  These include any private dwelling which is occupied by members of a single family and has a total sleeping accommodation for not more than 20 persons.
- **Sub-Division A - 3 : Dormitories**
  These include any building, in which group sleeping accommodation is provided with or without dining facilities, for persons who are not members of the same family, in any one room or a series of closely associated rooms under joint occupancy and single management, for example, school and college dormitories, students and other hostels and military barracks.
- **Sub-Division A - 4 : Apartment Houses (Flats)**
  These include any building or structure in which living quarters are provided for three or more families living independently of each other and with independent cooking facilities, for example, apartment houses, mansions, chawls.
- **Sub-Division A - 5 : Hotels**
  These include any building or group of buildings under single management in which sleeping accommodation, with or without dining facilities, is provided for hire to more than 15 persons who are primary transient, for example, hotels, inns, clubs and motels.

2. **Group B: Educational Buildings**
These include any building used for school, college, or day-care purposes for more than 8 hours per week involving assembly for instruction, education, recreation and which is not covered by Group D.

3. **Group C : Institutional Buildings**
Buildings under group C are further sub-divided as follows :
- **Sub-Division C - 1 : Hospitals and Sanitaria**
  These include any building or group of buildings under single management, which is used for housing persons suffering from physical limitations because of health or age, for example, hospitals, infirmaries, sanitaria and clinics.
- **Sub-Division C - 2 : Custodial Institutions**
  These include any building or group of buildings under single management, which is used for the custody and care of persons such as children, convalescents and the aged, for example, homes for the aged and infants, convalescent homes and orphanages.
- **Sub-Division C - 3 : Penal Institutions**
  These include any building or group of buildings under single management which is used for housing persons under restraint, in which the liberty of the inmates is restricted, for example, jails, prisons, mental hospitals, mental sanitaria and reformatories.

4. **Group D : Assembly Buildings**
Buildings under group D are further subdivided as follows :

- **Sub-Division D - 1**

  This sub-division includes any building primarily meant for theatrical or operatic performances and exhibitions and which has a raised stage, proscenium curtain, fixed or portable scenery or scenery loft, lights, motion picture booth, mechanical appliances or other theatrical accessories and equipment and which is provided with fixed seats over 1000 persons.

- **Sub-Division D - 2**

  This sub-division includes any building primarily meant for use as described for sub-division D - 1 but with fixed seats for less than 1000 persons.

- **Sub-Division D - 3**

  This includes any building, its lobbies, rooms and other spaces connected thereto, primarily intended for assembly of people, but which has no theatrical stage or cinematographic accessories and has accommodation for more than 300 persons, for example, dance halls, night clubs, halls for incidental picture shows, dramatic, theatrical or educational presentation

- **Sub-Division D - 4**

  This includes any building primarily intended for use as described in D - 3 but with accommodation for less than 300 persons.

- **Sub-Division D - 5**

  This includes any building meant for outdoor assembly of people not covered by D - 1 to D - 4, for example, grand stands, stadia, amusement park structures, reviewing stands and circus tents.

5. **Group E : Business Buildings**

These include any building or part of a building which is used for the transaction of business (other than group F); for keeping of accounts and records and similar purposes, service facilities, such as news-stands, lunch counters serving less than 100 persons, barber shops and beauty parlours. City halls, town halls, court houses and libraries should be classified in this group.

6. **Group F : Mercantile Buildings**

These include any building or part of a building, which is used as shops, stores, markets, for display and sale of merchandise either wholesale or retail.

Office, storage and service facilities incidental to the sale of merchandise and located in the same building should be included under this group.

7. **Group G : Industrial Buildings**

These include any building or part of a building, in which products or materials of all kinds and properties are fabricated, assembled or processed, for example, assembly plants, laboratories, dry cleaning plants, pumping stations, smoke houses, gas plants, refineries, dairies and saw-mills.

8. **Group H : Storage Buildings**

These include any building or part of a building, used primarily, for the storage and sheltering of goods, wares or merchandise, vehicles or animals, for example, warehouses, cold storages, freight depots, transit sheds, store houses, truck and marine terminals, garages, hangers (other than air craft repair hangers), grain elevators, barns, stables.

9. Group I : Hazardous Buildings

These include any building or part of a building which is used for storage, handling, manufacture or processing of highly combustible or explosive materials or products which are liable to burn with extreme rapidity and/or which may produce poisonous fumes or explosions.

Examples of buildings in this class are those buildings which are used for :

- Storage under pressure of more than 1 kg/cm^2 and in quantities exceeding 70 m^3, of acetylene, hydrogen, illuminating and natural gases, ammonia, chlorine, phosgene, sulphur dioxide, carbon dioxide, methyl oxide and all gases subjected to explosions, fumes or toxic hazard.
- Storage and handling of hazardous and highly flammable liquids.
- Storage and handling of hazardous and highly flammable or explosive other than liquids.
- Manufacture of artificial flowers, synthetic leather, ammunition, explosives and fireworks.

1.4 COMPONENTS OF A BUILDING

A building has three basic parts:

(1) Super-structure.
(2) Plinth, and
(3) Sub-structure or foundations,

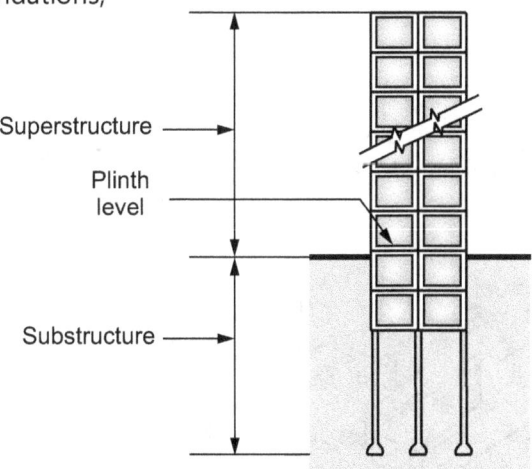

Fig. 1.2 : Basic parts of building

(1) Super-Structure :

It is that part of the structure which is above ground level and which serves the purpose of its intended use.

(2) Plinth :

- It is defined as the portion of the structure between the surface of the surrounding ground and surface of the floor, immediately above the ground.

- The level of the floor is usually known as the plinth level.
- The built-up covered area measured at the floor level is known as plinth area.

It has following functions,

- To avoid differential settlement.
- To maintain the plinth plane proper.
- To connect all the columns if depth of foundation is high.
- To avoid difficulties in construction of walls.
- Prevent leaking of water

(3) Sub-Structure or Foundation :

It is the lower portion of the building usually located below the ground level, which transmits the loads of super-structure to the supporting soil.

Components of building:

A building has the following components:

1. Foundations
2. Plinth
3. Masonry units : walls and columns
4. Floor structures
5. (A) Doors   (B) Windows and window frame
6. (A) Lintel etc.   (B) Window sill
7. Stairs [vertical transportation]
8. Roof slab
9. Roof terrace with flooring

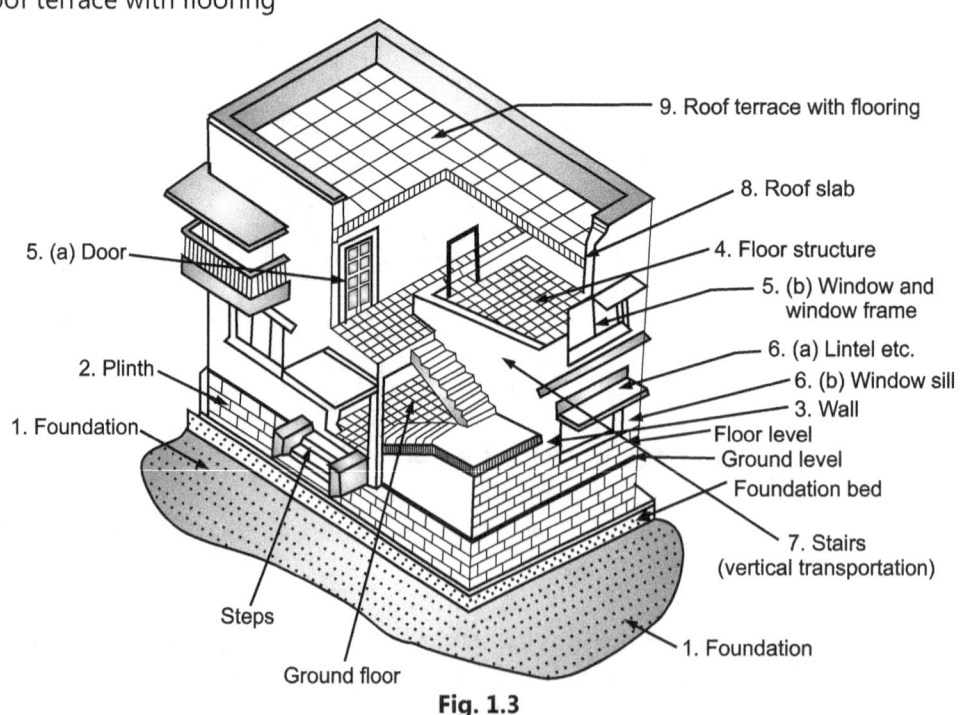

Fig. 1.3

1.5 FOUNDATIONS   (May 16, 17)

- It is the part of structure which is below ground level.
- Foundation is the part of sub-structure, which receives load of super-structure and transmits it to lower and firmer strata safely without causing excessive settlement or stresses or any damage to super-structure.
- It is very difficult and costly to carry out any repairs to foundation after it is constructed. Hence, it is essential to understand basic principles of foundations.

1.5.1 Definition and Purpose of Foundation   (Nov. 15, 16)

Definition: *It is the part of structure below ground level, which is directly in contact with subsoil to receive load of superstructure and to transmit it to firm strata below safely.*

Purpose: Foundation of a building is designed to achieve the following objectives:

- **It should Carry Loads Safely:** The soil strata, on which foundation is to rest, should be strong enough to safely bear the loads imposed on it.
- **Settlement of Structure should be Uniform and within Permissible Limits :** Due to loads imposed on foundation, structure is likely to settle. Foundation is so designed that, the settlement is as uniform as possible throughout and is within permissible limits.
- **Differential Settlement should be Less:** If a part of foundation settles more than the other part then, the difference between the two settlements is called as *'Differential settlement'.* This differential settlement induces heavy stresses and cracks appear in super-structure thereby endangering safety of structure.
- It should offer required stability to structure against uplift forces sliding, overturning.
- It should be strong enough to resist attack by harmful substances and strong undercurrents (if any) present in subsoil.
- Construction of foundation should not cause adverse effects on adjoining structures and on environment. e.g. Vibrations during pile driving or pumping out of ground water may cause large settlement of adjoining structures.

1.5.2 Settlement of Foundation

- Settlement is the vertical downward movement of a loaded base.
- Consider a ship floating in water. As load on ship is increased gradually and uniformly, ship sinks uniformly, without causing any damage to ship.
- Similarly, if load on foundation is designed in such a way that structure settles uniformly, and then it will not cause any structural damage. However, even excessive uniform settlement has the following disadvantages :
  (a) It will cause damage to water supply and drainage pipe connections.
  (b) Aesthetically, it may give bad appearance to the structure.
- Settlement of foundation on clayey soils is very gradual, continues for a long time, and is more whereas settlement of foundation in sandy soils is quick and less.
- However, clayey soil permits strain adjustment in structural members. Hence, more settlement of structures in clayey soil is permitted, than in sandy soils.

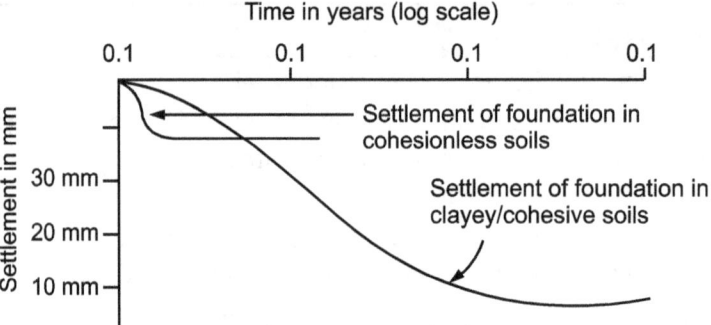

Fig. 1.4: Times-settlement curve

Causes of Settlement

A structure settles due to the following reasons:

- Reduction in volume of air in soil.
- Expulsion of water from soil i.e. consolidation.
- Increase in stresses due to lowering of water table.
- Excavation in adjoining area (especially excavation in sandy soil in nearby area, underground excavation for sewers, tunnels, mining).
- Dynamic loads : Vibratory loads during construction activity (such as vibrations during pile driving, vibrations of machines).
- Seasonal swelling and shrinkage of expansive soils.

1.5.3 Differential Settlement

- If a part of structure settles more than the other part, then difference between the two settlements is called as differential settlement.
- This differential settlement is far more harmful than settlement of structure, because it induces heavy stresses in structures leading to cracks in super-structure. It is therefore, essential to control differential settlement.
- As shown in Fig. 1.3, let footing of column A settle by amount δ_1 and column B by δ_2 from the original footing level. Then differential settlement $= \delta = \delta_2 - \delta_1$.

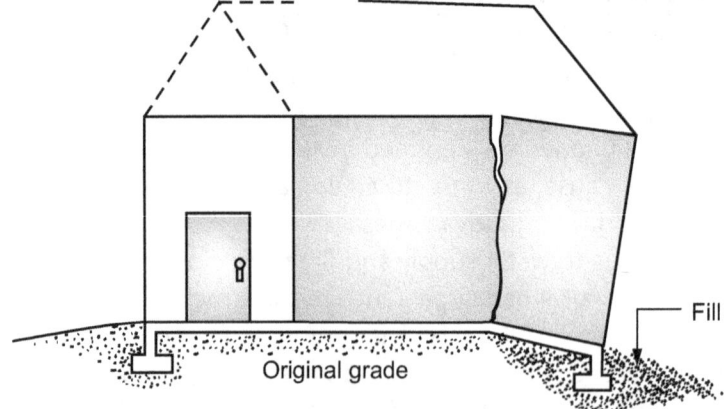

Fig. 1.5 : Example of differential settlement

- Ratio of differential settlement between the two footings and distance between the two columns is known as angular distortion.

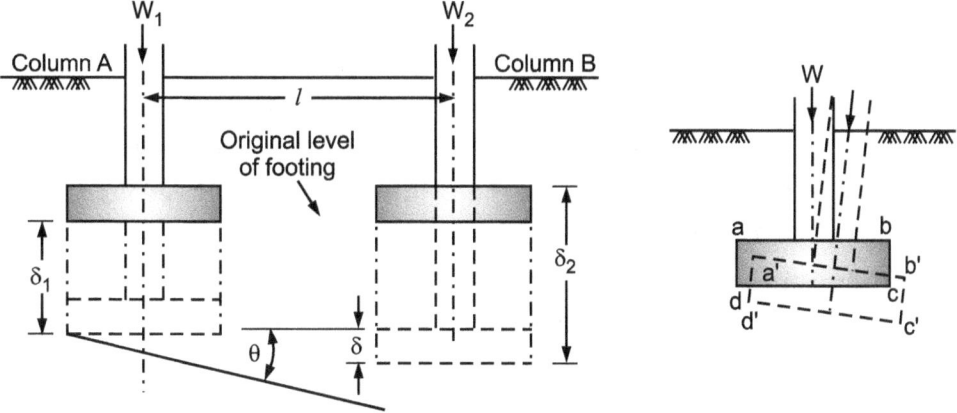

Fig. 1.6 : Differential settlement

$\therefore$ θ = Angular distortion = $\dfrac{\text{Differential settlement}}{\text{Distance between two columns}}$

$$= \frac{\delta_2 - \delta_1}{l} = \frac{\delta}{l}$$

This angular distortion causes more damage to structure.

Causes of Differential Settlement

- Small pockets of soft soil such as clay, peat, mud and organic matter.
- Unequal intensity of loading on foundation.
- Overlapping of stresses from adjoining structures.
- Unequal swelling, softening and drying of soil.
- Difference in compressibility of underlying soils.
- Tilting of rigid base.

1.5.4 Causes of Failure of Foundations

- **Differential Settlement of Foundation:** If a structure settles uniformly, then no damage is caused. However, if there is uneven settlement of foundation, then it may lead to serious cracks in super-structure. Unfortunately, it is very difficult to measure differential settlement. However, if total settlement is restricted, automatically, it reduces differential settlement.
- **Reduction in Water Table Level:** Due to drying of soil or due to pumping of water from nearby structure.

  The reduction in water table induces very heavy stresses on soil; which in its turn imposes heavy stresses on foundation. This leads to heavy settlement or differential settlement and thereby failure of foundation.

- **Heavy Floods:** During heavy floods, lot of soil is erroded. Removal of soil, especially in case of piers of bridges, may lead to undermining below foundation and thereby cause failure of foundation.
- **Heavy Lateral and Uplift Forces:** A structure may be subjected to heavy lateral forces due to wind, earth pressure of embankments. If the foundation is not designed to withstand excessive compressive and tensile stresses, then is likely to fail.
- **Liquification of Soil:** Due to shock waves during earthquake or vibrations caused due to pile driving or due to machines.
- **Sliding of Embankment:** due to shear failure of soft soil located at greater depth. The strata immediately below the structure may be firm; however, at a greater depth, a soft strata may be available.
- **Material Quality:** Failure due to poor quality of material used in foundation or failure of foundation material to resist harmful materials present in soil below.

1.6 TYPES OF FOUNDATIONS

Depending upon ratio of depth D and width W, foundation is classified as under :

1. Shallow Foundation $= \left(\dfrac{D}{W} < 1\right) = D < 5$ m

2. Deep Foundation $= \left(\dfrac{D}{W} > 1\right)$

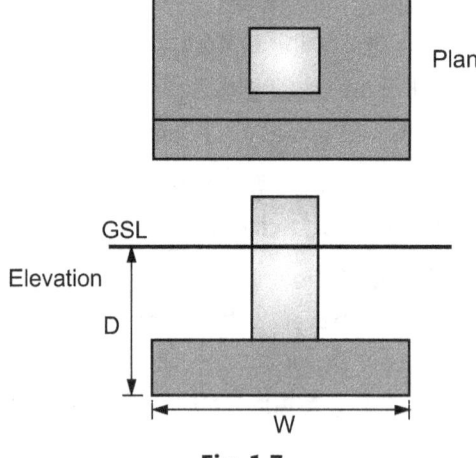

Fig. 1.7

1.6.1 Shallow Foundations   (Nov. 15, May 14, 16)

Shallow Foundation is further classified according to distribution of load on soil as shown in following chart and in Fig. 1.8.

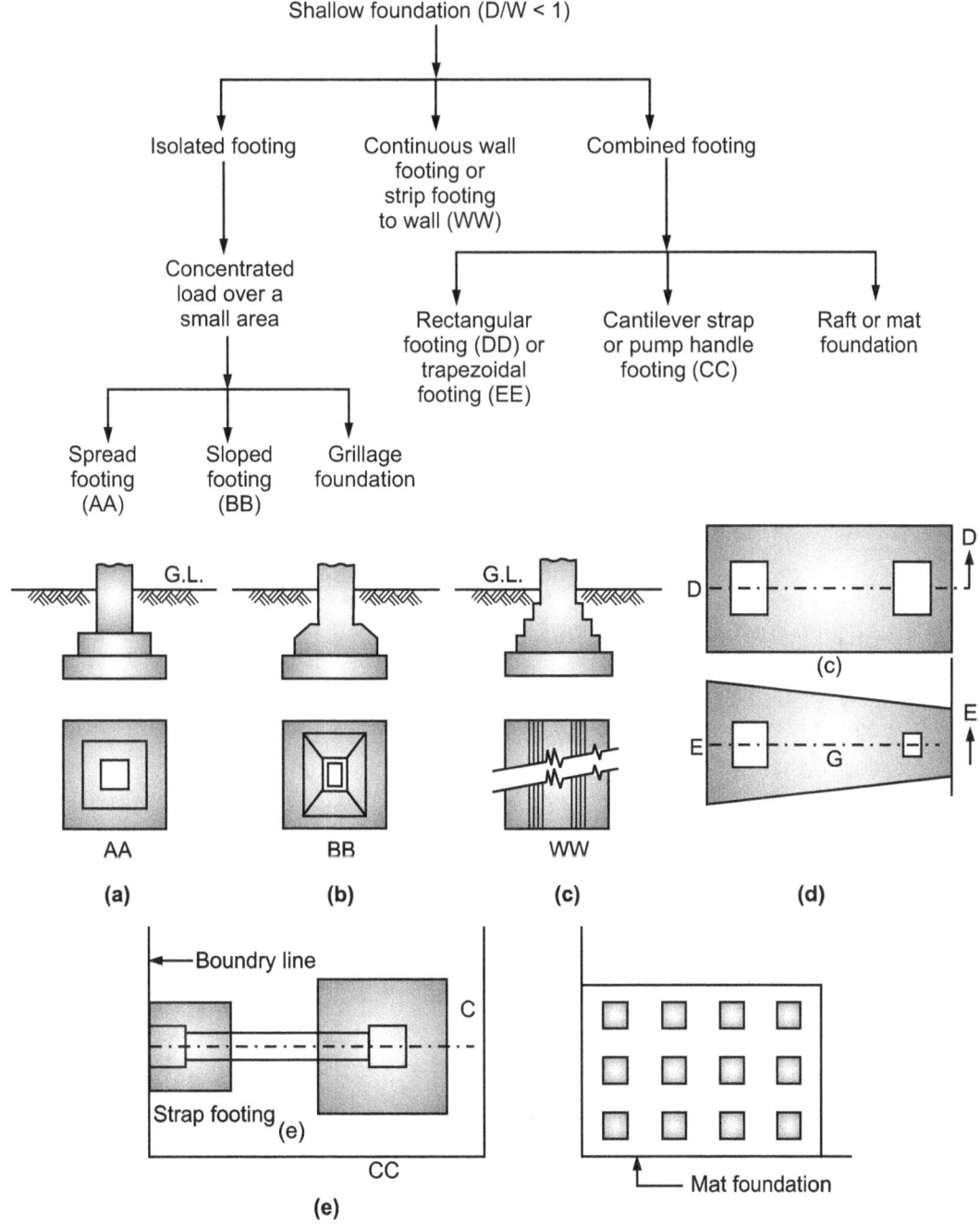

Fig. 1.8

(A) Spread Footing

- It is the most common type of shallow foundation used to transmit load of wall or isolated column. The base of wall of column is enlarged or spread to distribute load over a large area (to reduce intensity of load).

- Spread footing does not directly rest on soil. Usually, about 15 to 30 cm thick lean concrete of mix (1 : 4 : 8) called as foundation concrete is first laid, as a base course to cover small pockets in foundation and to provide level surface for laying spread footing.

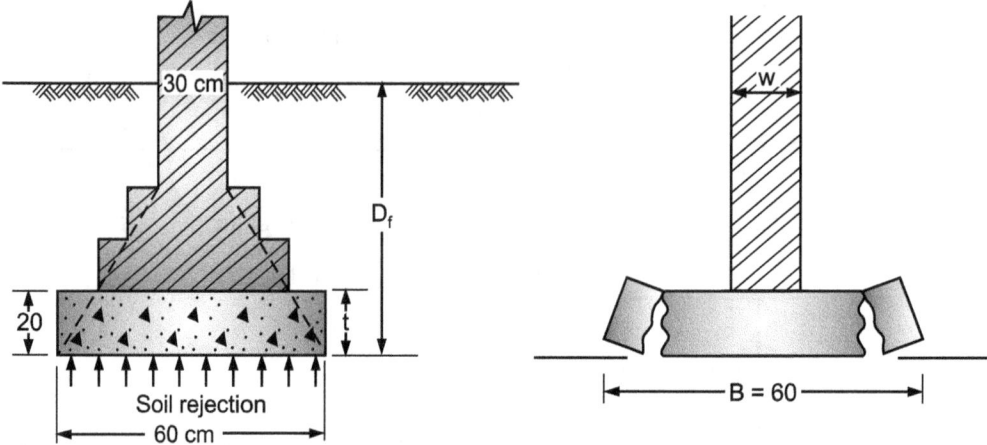

Fig. 1.9 : Spread stepped foundation

- Over this foundation concrete, spread footing rests. If load of wall footing is high and if there probability of differential settlement, then instead of providing plain foundation concrete, the foundation concrete is reinforced by providing steel reinforcement.

  1. If projection of footing beyond wall is excessive, the footing may crack due to soil reaction in the cantilever portion. Hence, stepped foundation is provided.

  2. If thickness " t " of footing is less, the wall may punch in the footing.

  3. Depth of foundation (D_f) should be adequate to give necessary safe bearing capacity. Minimum depth of foundation of 90 cm is provided.

(B) Grillage Foundation

- This type of foundation is used to transmit heavy loads from steel columns to soils having low bearing capacity over a large area. It consists of steel beams (called as Rolled Steel Joists) in one or two tiers.

- Beams in each tier are held in position by 20 to 25 mm diameter spacer bars. This type of foundation avoids deep excavation and provides large area to reduce intensity of load. Depth of excavation is limited to 1.2 to 1.5 m only. The space between beams is filled with concrete to protect steel beams from corrosion.

- In water logged area, sometimes, instead of steel beams, wooden logs are provided in 2 or 3 tiers. This eliminates possibility of corrosion of steel and foundation is economical. Since, total quantity of steel required is large, this type of foundation becomes costly and hence has become outdated.

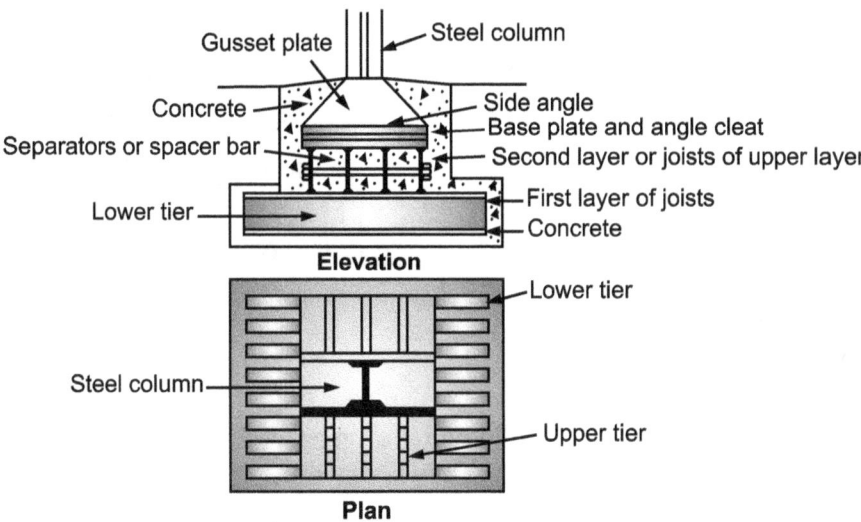

Fig. 1.10 (i) : Grillage foundation

- For continuous wall foundations (plain or reinforced) adequate reinforcement should be provided, particularly at places where there is abrupt change in load or variation in ground support.

- On sloping sites, the foundation should have a horizontal bearing and stepped and lapped at charges of levels for a distance at least equal to thickness of foundation or twice the height of step, which ever is greater. The steps should not be of greater height than thickness of the foundation.

The foundation of walls on sloping ground may be at one level or stepped as shown in Fig. 1.6 (ii).

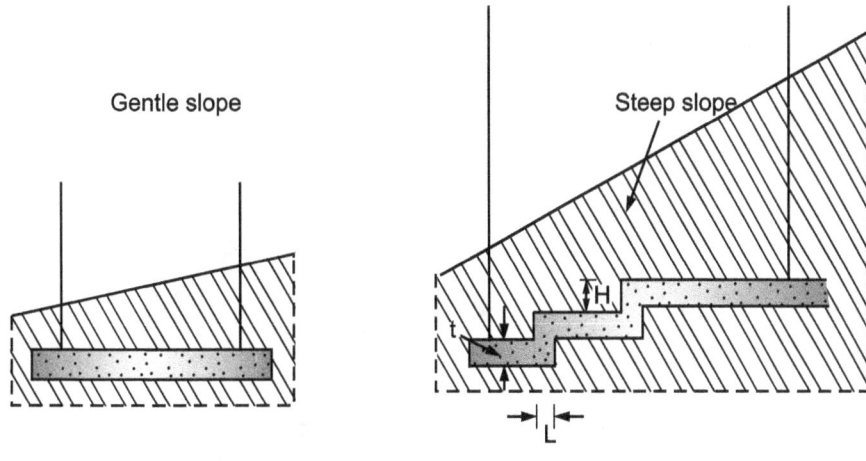

(a) Footing on gentle sloping ground   (b) Footing on steep sloping ground

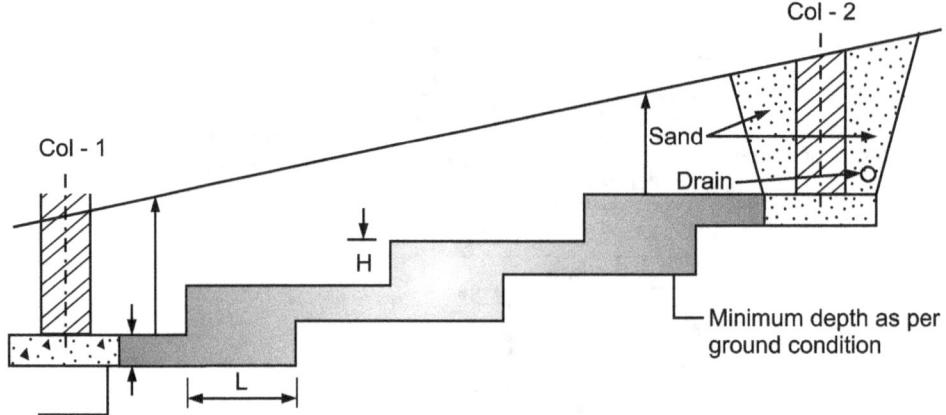

(c) Details of footing on sloping ground

Fig. 1.10 (ii)

Where the slope is gentle, the foundation may be at one level, but if the slope is steep, a portion of floor rests on filled up portion as a portion rests on excavated and levelled ground. Cutting is extended beyond the wall at the highest point and arrangements are made to drain out water, so that, the stability of ground at highest level is not in danger.

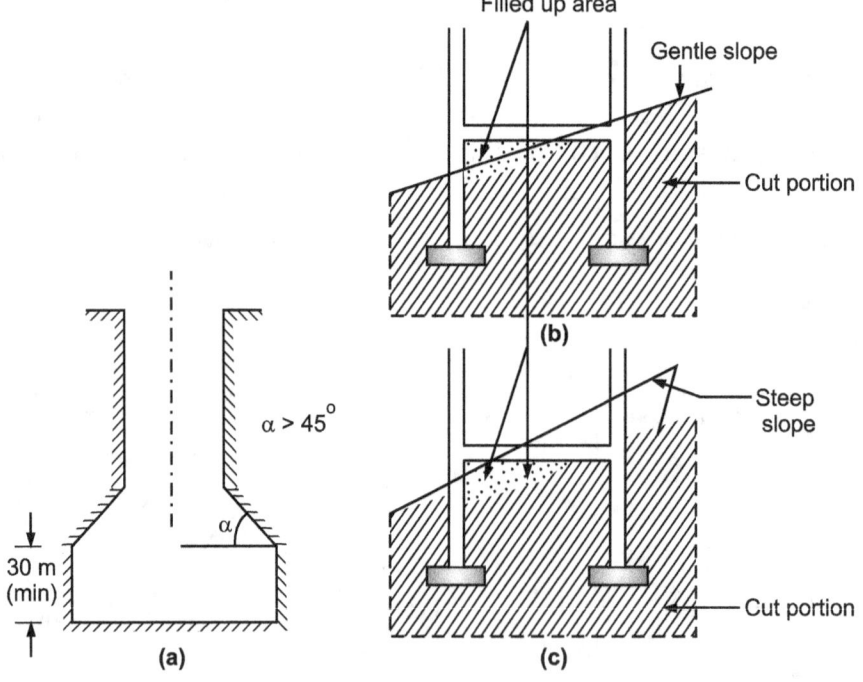

Fig. 1.11 : (a) Belling of footing to increase load carrying capacity

(b) Footing on sloping ground with gentle slope. Floor on filled up compacted soil

(c) Footing partly in cut section and partly in filled up section

If the bottom of footing is to be of bell shape, to increase load carrying capacity, then such bell should be atleast 30 cm thick at its edge. The sides should be sloped at an angle more than 45° with the horizontal. The least dimension should be 60 cm (circular, square or rectangular).

(C) Deep-Strip / Trench Fill Foundation

If the allowable bearing capacity is available only at a greater depth, the foundation can be rested at a higher level, for economic considerations and the difference between the base of foundation and the depth at which the allowable bearing capacity occurs can be filled up either with (a) concrete of allowable compressive strength, not less than the allowable bearing pressure or (b) non-compressible fill material such as sand, gravel etc., in which case, the width of fill should be more than the width of foundation by an extent of dispersion of load from the base of foundation on either side at rate of 2 vertical to 1 horizontal.

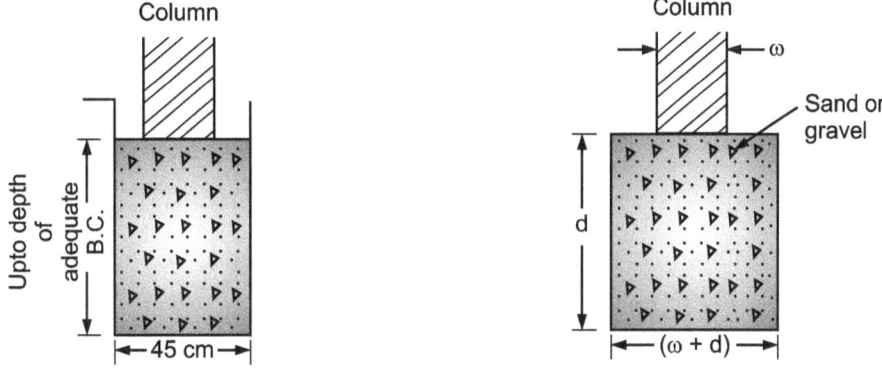

(a) Deep trench with PCC filling   **(b) Deep trench with sand filling**

Fig. 1.12 : Deep strip foundation

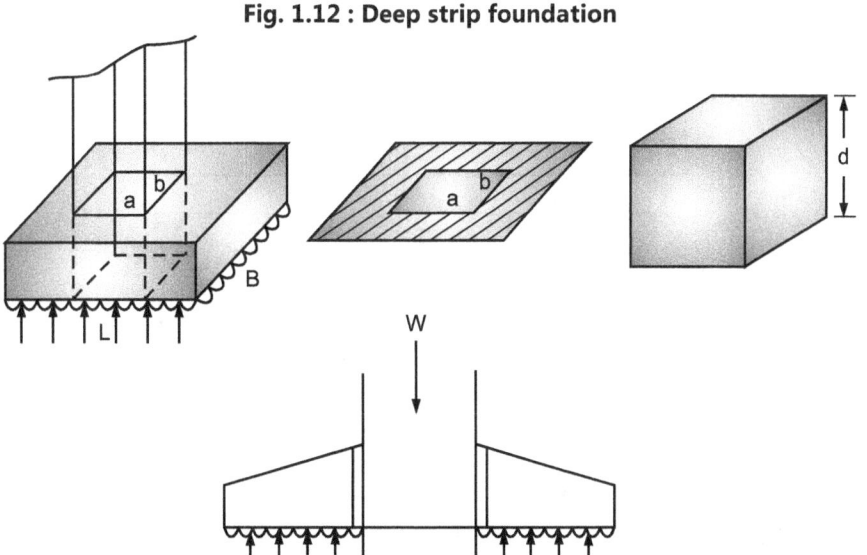

Fig. 1.13 : Assistance to punching shear

(D) Combined Footing

Combined footings are provided under the following situations :

- When loads on adjacent columns are very high.
- Bearing capacity of soil is relatively less and
- There is possibility of heavy differential settlement.

In combined footing, a common footing is provided for two or more columns. Combined footing is very rigid hence, the columns settle together and thereby eliminate possibility of differential settlement. Depending upon different loading conditions, following varieties of combined footing are provided :

(a) Rectangular Combined Footing : This type of footing is provided,

- When load to be carried by the two columns is high and is nearly same.
- Distance between two columns is less.
- Projection of footing beyond columns is permitted.

Considering the safe bearing capacity of soil, and total load to be carried, area of footing is worked as under :

$$A = \text{Area of footing} = \frac{\text{Total load } (\Sigma W)}{\text{Safe bearing capacity}} \cdot \bar{x} = \frac{W_1 \cdot l}{W_1 + W_2}$$

Knowing individual column loads W_1, W_2 and spacing of columns, C.G. of load is found out. Footing is arranged in such way that, C.G. of load coincides with C.G. of area of footing.

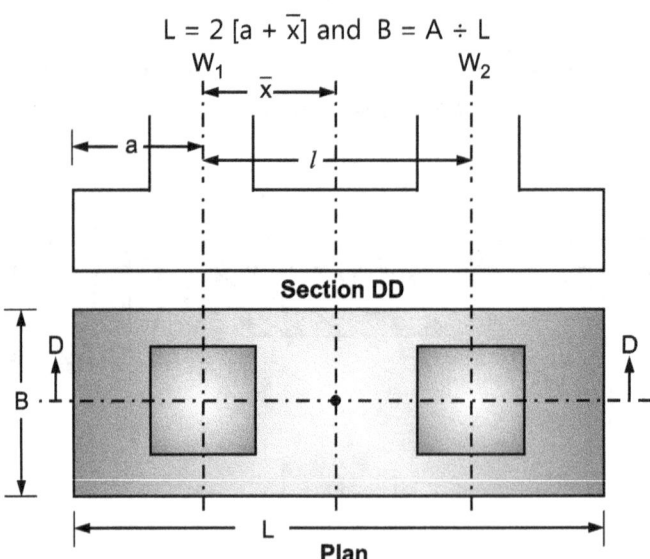

Fig. 1.14 (a) : Combined rectangular footing

(b) Trapezoidal Footing : This type of combined footing is provided when,

- Loads to be carried by two adjacent columns are high.
- Difference between the two column loads is large and

• Bearing capacity of soil is less.

Trapezoidal footing consists of proportionately more width near heavier column and less width near lighter column as shown in Fig. 1.14 (b).

If two column loads W_1 and W_2 spaced at a distance l, then total load $(W_1 + W_2)$ will act at a distance $\bar{x}$ from heavier column W_1.

$$\bar{x} = \frac{W_1 \cdot l}{W_1 + W_2} \quad W_1 > W_2$$

Footing width "a" near heavier column is more than footing width "b" near lighter column such that,

$$A = \text{Area of footing} = \frac{(a + b)}{2} \cdot L = \frac{W_1 + W_2}{\text{Safe bearing capacity}}$$

where, $L = $ Length of footing

C.G. of the trapezoidal footing from side "b" will be at a distance,

$$x' = \left(\frac{a + 2b}{a + b}\right) \cdot \frac{L}{3}$$

Projection of footing beyond column face is adjusted in such a way that $\bar{x}$, the C.G. of loads W_1 and W_2 coincides with x', the C.G. of footing.

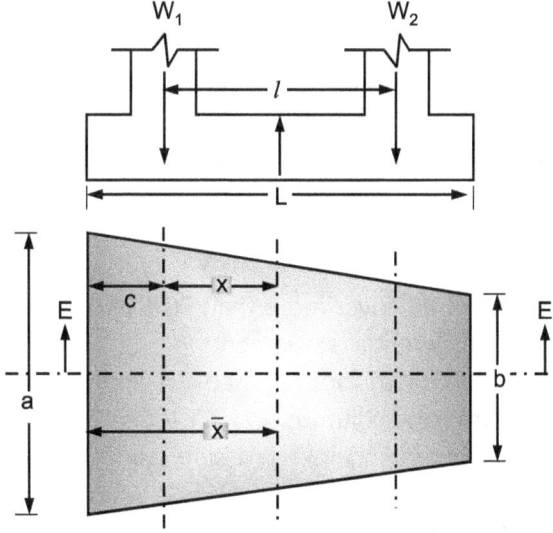

Fig. 1.14 (b) : Trapezoidal footing

(c) Cantilever Footing or Strap footing (May 16, 17) : This type of footing is provided when,

• Column footing is not permitted to project beyond column face as in case of a column near compound wall.

- When the distance between the two columns for which a combined footing is to be provided is more. In such a case, rectangular footing is not economical.

Individual Column Footing is provided in proportion to reaction R_1 and R_2 below column C_1 and C_2 (Refer Fig. 1.14 (c)). Two footings are connected together rigidly by a beam. Hence, the footings settle together and avoid differential settlement. Due to cantilever action, the reaction R_1 is more than cantilever load W_1.

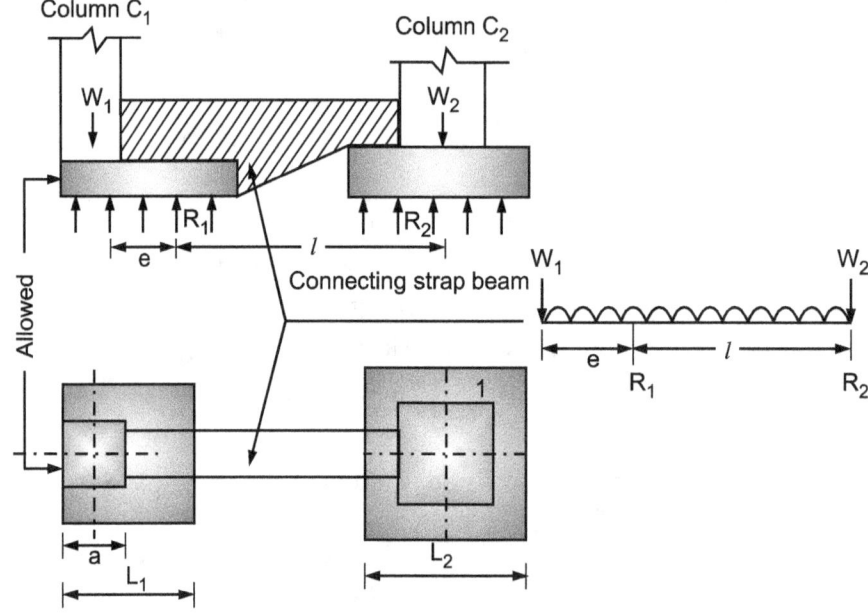

Fig. 1.14 (c) : Cantilever footing

Sometimes this footing is also called as pump handle footing.

(d) Mat or Raft Foundation : This type of foundation is provided when :
- Bearing capacity of soil is low or difficult to determine or is of doubtful nature or strata is highly compressible.
- Loads are heavy.
- Use of spread footing would cover more than 50% of the entire area.
- It is difficult to control differential settlement.

A mat or raft foundation is a combined footing. It covers entire area beneath a structure and supports all walls through beams and columns.

Raft consists of thick, heavily reinforced inverted slab using heavy beams from column to columns. Raft tends to bridge over erratic deposits and hence eliminate differential settlement. For this reason, total settlement of 75 to 100 mm is permitted for raft foundation. In case of highly compressible strata, raft foundation is taken to such a depth that,

Weight of excavated soil = Weight of structure and loads on structure.

Such type of foundation is called as **floating foundation**.

Sometimes, to reduce the self weight of thick raft, cellular foundation or reinforced basement walls serves as raft. A few types of rafts are shown in Fig. 1.14 (d).

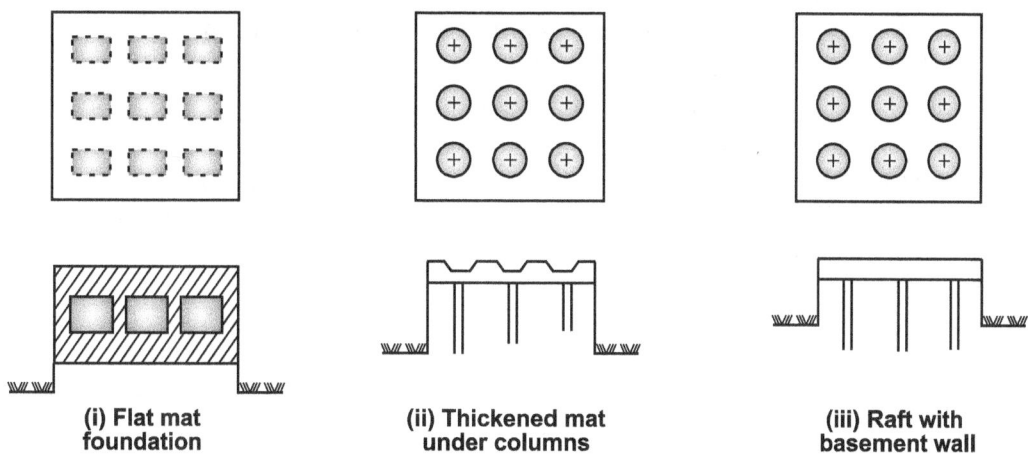

(i) Flat mat foundation   **(ii) Thickened mat under columns**   **(iii) Raft with basement wall**

Fig. 1.14 (d) : Mat/Raft foundation

1.6.2 Deep Foundation   (Dec. 14, Nov. 15, May 14, 16)

These foundations carry heavy loads from structure through weak, compressible soils or fills on stronger and less compressible soils or rock at depth.

Some of the types of deep foundations are mentioned below :

(1) Pile foundations, (2) Well foundations, (3) Caissons, (4) Pier foundations.

Pile Foundation

Pile foundation is preferred under the following situations :

- When open foundation is not possible or for structure such as in deep-sea, or river, or where there is heavy seepage.

- When open excavation upto firm strata is difficult and uneconomical or when water table is high or strata consists of expansive soils.

- When loads are heavy, non-uniform and there is possibility of differential settlement at shallow depth.

Classification of Piles :

Piles are classified based on :

- Mode of transmission of load such as end bearing or friction piles.
- Method of construction such as bored or driven piles.
- Material of construction such as timber, steel, concrete.

(a) End Bearing Piles : *When pile passes through poor, weak strata and its tip penetrates for a small depth into hard strata, and transfers load to hard strata, it is called as end bearing pile.* The hard strata should be available at a reasonable depth. Size of pile depends upon strength of hard strata.

(b) Friction Pile : *When a pile passes through deep strata of limited bearing capacity, the strata offers sufficiently higher frictional resistance along the surface of piles, then it is* *called as friction pile.* These piles derive support mainly from surrounding soil although a very small load is carried at the lower tip of pile.

This type of pile is provided when hard rock/hard strata is available to a great depth. Length and size of pile depends upon type of soil, load etc.

(c) Under Reamed Piles : These piles are provided in expansive soils such as black cotton soil, to resist tensile stresses due to changes in moisture content. By special equipment called under reamer, diameter of pile can be enlarged. The surface of enlarged bulb of pile helps in resisting tensile stresses.

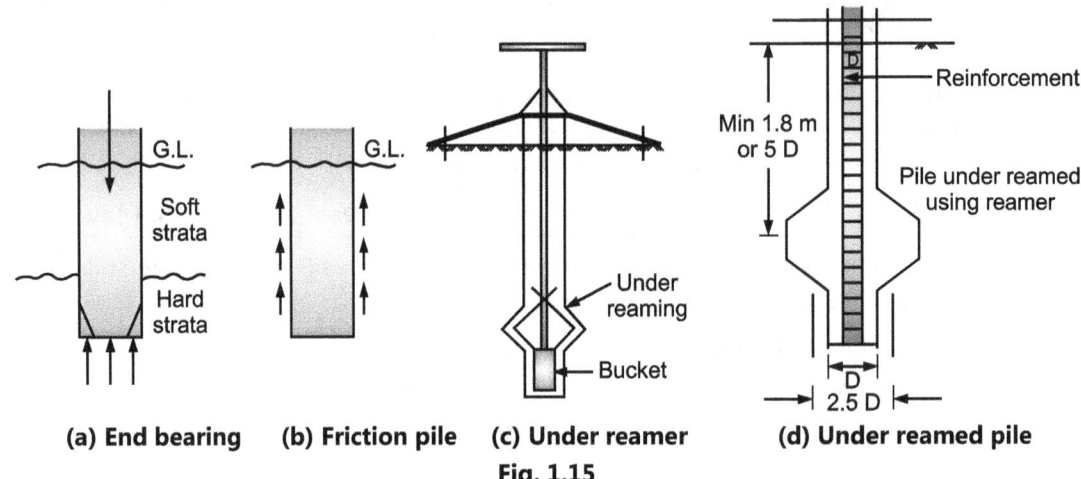

(a) End bearing   **(b) Friction pile**   **(c) Under reamer**   **(d) Under reamed pile**

Fig. 1.15

Foundation for Radar Antenna, Microwave and T.V. Towers

- Uplift load becomes an important governing criteria for selection and design of foundation of these structures. Uplift loads are assumed to be counteracted in case of shallow foundations by the weight of the footing *plus* the weight of an inverted frustum of pyramid of earth on the footing pad, with sides inclined at angle of upto 30° with the vertical (Ref. Fig. 1.16). A footing on rock, for uplift may be considered to develop strength by the dead load of the concrete and the strength of all bars anchored under the footing or embedded in concrete in drilled holes.

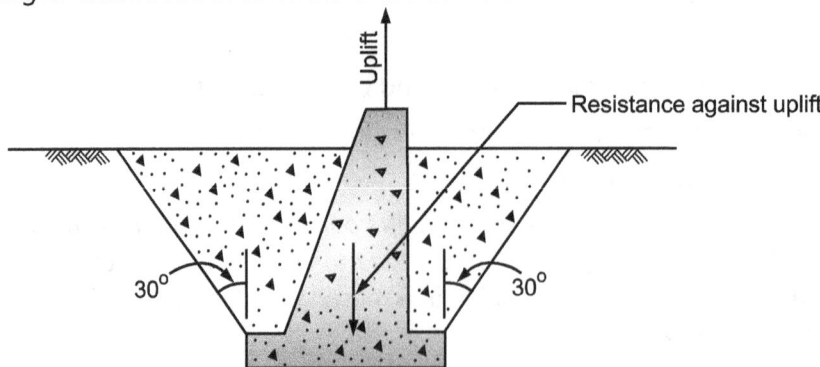

Fig. 1.16 : Conventional Assumption – Resistance against uplift by weight of frustum of earth plus weight of concrete

- Allowable settlement and maximum allowable differential settlement shall be as under :

Type of Tower	Allowable settlement	Allowable differential settlement
1. Radar antenna tower	12 m	6 mm
2. Microwave towers with dish antenna	16 mm	12 mm
3. T.V. towers.	50 mm	20 mm

- Raft foundations become good choice if
  (i) Basements are provided.
  (ii) Soils are weak with low settlement value.
- Isolated footings are provided in case of lattice towers resting on good soils with medium to high bearing capacity and when tower legs are spaced far apart.
- Bored piles with enlarged bases usually provide economical type of footing where under-reaming is possible.

1.6.3 Foundation Plan

It is the plan at footing level, showing the locations, sizes of various footings, centre lines of columns, walls, etc. such as that shown in Fig. 1.17.

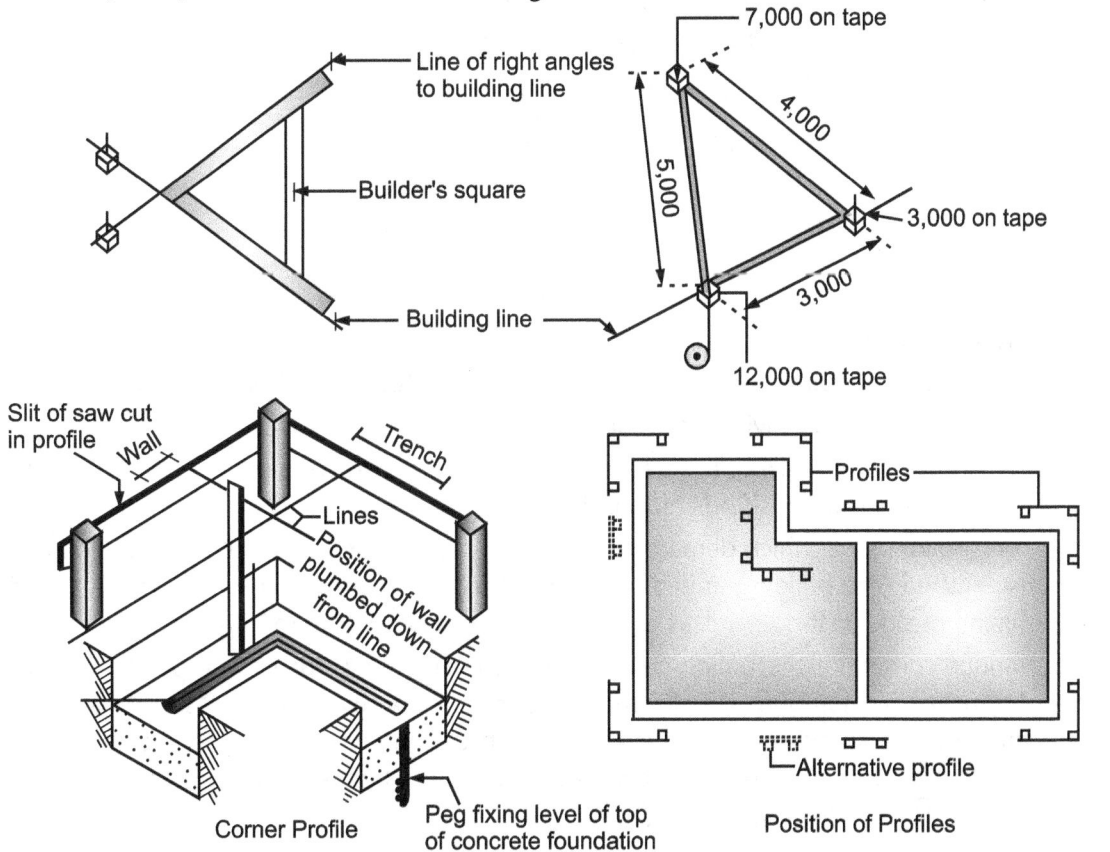

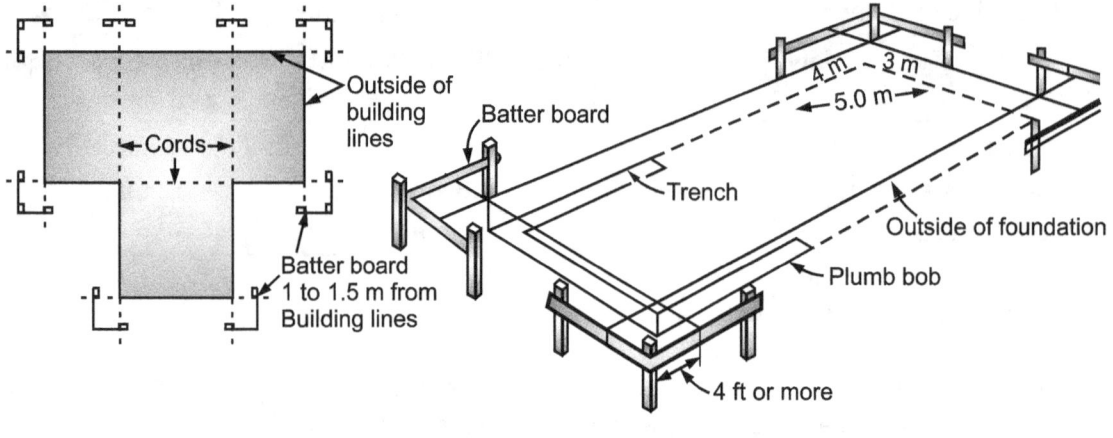

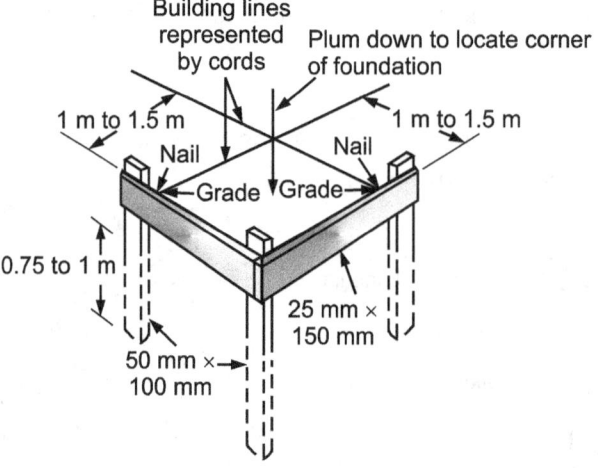

Fig. 1.17

(a) Setting Out Building

Before commencing of building operation, the following factors should be well studied :

- Site is cleared by removing tree stumps, loose soil and is levelled.
- Temporary bench mark from a known permanent bench mark is established to decide levels of various floors, footings etc.
- Then building line which demarcates the outer face of the front wall of the building is established. The building line is decided taking into account set back distances, and minimum side distances etc. as per bye laws prevalent in that locality.
- Various corners of the building are then fixed accurately. For this purpose, measure distances in multiples of 1.5 m along one side. By making use of builders square establish points at intervals of 2 m on the line which is perpendicular to the first line. If the lines are set accurately then, the distances between stakes will be $\sqrt{1.5^2 + 2^2}$ = 2.5 m or multiples of 2.5 m.

- After locating the corners, drive three 50 mm × 100 mm stakes into the ground about 1.5 m beyond each corner. Nail 25 mm × 150 mm batter boards horizontally to the stakes. The tops of these batter board must be at the same level.
- On these batter boards, saw cuts are made (or nails are driven) to demarcate the width of walls; and spread of foundations.
- Strong thin twine or wires are stretched across the tops of opposite batter boards.
- The centre of footing or excavation pit can be located by lowering plumb bob from the point where strings cross. Care must be taken to ensure that, stakes and batter boards (which serve as reference points) are protected/undisturbed throughout.

1.7 NECESSITY OF DAMP PROOFING IN BASEMENT CONSTRUCTION AND ROOFS

- The utility area provided below the ground is known as basement. This may serve the following needs : (i) Security, (ii) Storage, (iii) Parking, (iv) Commercial needs etc.
- As basement is constructed below ground level, it is subjected to water pressure from sides and from bottom, which may lead to dampness. This condition is harmful to occupant's health and building health as well.
- In order to render buildings damp proof, during construction a damp proof course (D.P.C.) is practically given to all the buildings. It is done by interposing a layer of damp proof material between sources of dampness and building.
- The major cause for dampness of basement is ground water table and other factors are seepage through walls, inadequate slopes for roofs, no (or less) protection to external walls against rains etc.

Fig. 1.18

Effects of Dampness
- Disintegration of materials i.e. efflorescence effect.
- Softening of plaster, weak concrete.
- Unsightly white patches.
- Promotion to termite growth.

- Corrosion of reinforcement, metallic fittings.
- Damage of electrical fittings.

Materials to be used for Damp Proofing

Hot bitumen, mastic asphalt, bituminous felt, cement - concrete, lime - cement concrete, metal sheets and felts alongwith good quality bricks and stones.

General Principles

- D.P. course is horizontal, vertical or sometimes inclined to connect to different levels of D.P.C.
- The horizontal D.P.C. runs throughout the thickness of the wall.
- Unbroken D.P.C. is to be provided throughout the length of the wall.
- Bitumen sealing for lap joints is essentially be provided.
- D.P.C. should not be kept exposed on the wall surface.

1.7.1 D.P.C. for Basement   (May 15)

In order to protect the basement, DP course is provided on the outside of the walls and below the floors of basements. The latter provides necessary support to withstand water pressure.

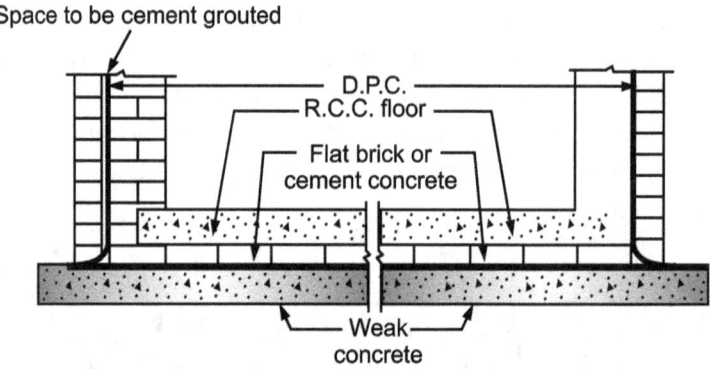

Fig. 1.19 : Damp proofing of a basement under normal conditions

This can be achieved by providing :

- Adequate dewatering arrangements i.e. pumping facilities.
- Strong and suitable shuttering to avoid collapse of excavation sides.
- A base slab (100 to 150 mm thickness) of weak cement concrete to be spread on excavated floor; with a projection of at least 150 mm beyond outer face of wall, throughout periphery of the building.
- The base slab is to be covered with two layers of mastic asphalt.
- A protective flooring of c.c. 1 : 3 : 6 (with water proof compound) or brick provides necessary support to D.P.C.
- Walls are then constructed with water proof cement plaster on outer side, which in turn receives the D.P.C.

- Outer side of the wall with D.P.C. and originally laid base slab with D.P.C. must ensure coherent action i.e. the joint between these must be provided with a smooth curved surface coat of D.P.C. again or the gap is to be grouted.

Damp Proof Course for Roofs

(A) Flat Roofs

- Suitable slope in the range of 1 : 40 to 1 : 60 for R.C.C. or R.B.C. roof.
- Down take rain water – 75 mm ϕ or outlet pipes that are projecting outward (minimum 300 mm) to be provided either in the centre or at corner.
- Provide coping to parapet walls.
- D.P.C. asphalt layer covering the roof should be turned on parapet wall (minimum 150 mm) and D.P.C. for parapet should be provided at this level with sufficient overlap if necessary.
- Provide hot bitumen - felt on roof top.

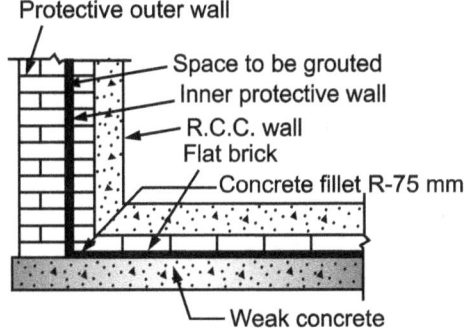

Fig. 1.20 : Damp proofing of a basement under heavy pressure

(B) Pitched Roof : Source of dampness are valley gutters :

- Provide sufficient water tightness and dimension to carry heavy rains.
- Roofing tile should remain suitably projecting beyond the edge of gutter.
- Lead flashing should be continued upto the vertical face of parapet wall and should stop inside the body of wall.
- Provide coping to protect parapet wall.

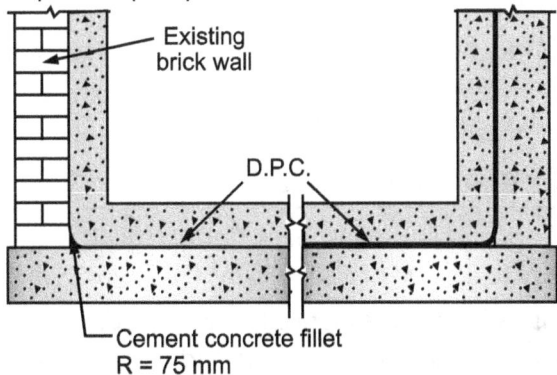

Fig. 1.21 : Damp proofing an existing basement

Water Stops : Are to be provided to check the entry of water inside the structure through joints.

- **Rubber W.S. :** Fixed in concrete directly.
- **Metallic W.S. :** Made from steel, copper, zinc etc., 14 to 16 gauge thick. Strips remain embedded half in concrete on either side of joint. Shape of M.W.S. is V or semi-circular.
- **Mastic type W.S. :** Not suitable for areas subjected to thrusts. Pouring of mastic into joints on site is possible.

1.7.2 Basement Repairs and Maintenance

(A) Damp proofing the existing basement subjected to heavy water pressure.

- When the wall is subjected to heavy lateral pressure, chances of development of cracks are increased, hence aroses the need for maintenance and repairs.
- In this situation D.P.C. has to be laid inside the existing basement. As the support to this D.P.C. is given by existing basement, proper bearing strength of the same is to be worked out and then second D.P.C. is to be laid. Its positioning reduces the volumetric content of basement.

Precautions :

- Keep the site free from water till the treatment is completed.
- Before application of D.P.C., inner coats of paint are to be removed.
- Surface is to be cleaned up by brush.
- Cement mortar rendering is carried out and then D.P.C. coat is provided.

(B) D.P.C. provision to existing wall above ground (close to G.L. and above) :

- Decide the level of D.P.C. (usually 150 mm above G.L. or floor level).
- Special saw is used to make a cut in the corner of the wall and brick layer above the cut is removed.
- Membrane : Bituminous felt membrane is laid.
- Cycle is repeated till entire periphery is covered.
- Relaying of removed bricks is carried out simultaneously and pointing or plaster finish is applied.
- Paint is applied between D.P.C. and floor or ground level from outer side.

1.7.3 Foundation in Black Cotton Soil   (Nov. 16)

- A classic example, of agricultural soil is Black Cotton soil. It is quite strong when dry but looses bearing capacity to a value of about $5t/m^2$ ($50 kN/m^2$) when wet.
- Also moisture content variation is responsible for volumetric change of the order of 30% of original volume. Alternate shrinking and swelling action lead to crack formation (width around 20 cm and depth around 2 to 4 m).

Precautions for Foundation Work
- **Depth of Foundation :** More than the depth of cracks formed usually.
- Avoid the entry of water at the bottom of the foundation by adopting suitable measures.
- Layer of granular material such as Sand, Boulder moorum is to be provided to avoid resting of foundation directly on B.C. soil.
- Removal of entire layer of B.C. soil if the depth is very less.
- Following methods are worked out for the construction of foundation if the depth of B.C. soil layer is more than 2 m.

1.8 PLINTH FILLING AND SOLING

- When the level of ground floor and plinth level are at same height with respect to the ground level, the space within four walls is to be filled with some material.
- This plinth filling is not just the filling to raise the level above ground but it has to support the flooring and distributing the load to natural ground.
- This plinth filling is analogous to road embankment as far as distribution of load is concerned. The concrete layer is supported on a hand-packed rubble and this layer either rests on ground or on other layer of less strong material like moorum or coarse grained soil.
- If the intensity of load is less entire plinth height may be filled with moorum. Top to bottom layers possess decreasing strengths.
- Basement floors and floors subjected to traffic or heavy loads need to be made of solid concrete core or a thick layer of concrete on hand packed rubble soling that directly rests on ground.
- Whenever, the plinth have to be filled with soil it should not be just the excavated earth but necessarily coarse grained non-cohesive soil; the consolidation of which is that way instant.
- Avoid use of clayey - silty soils. Sometimes suspended binder floor structure is used to support ground floor. In this situation, the space under the boarding should be well ventilated and dampness should be avoided.

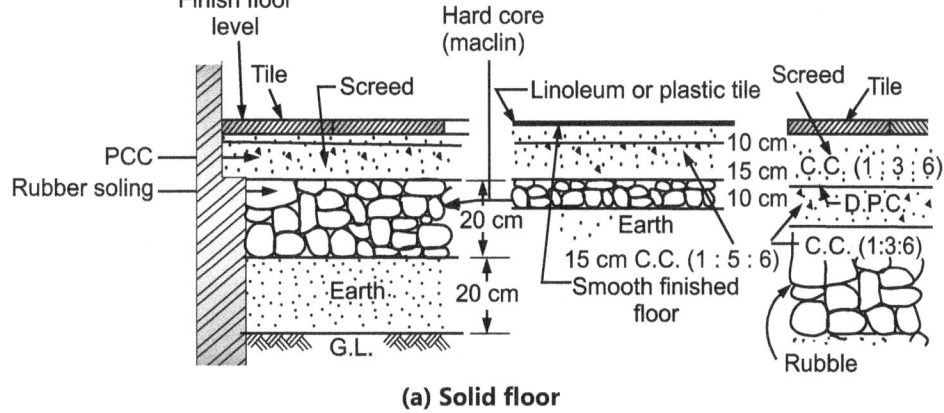

(a) Solid floor

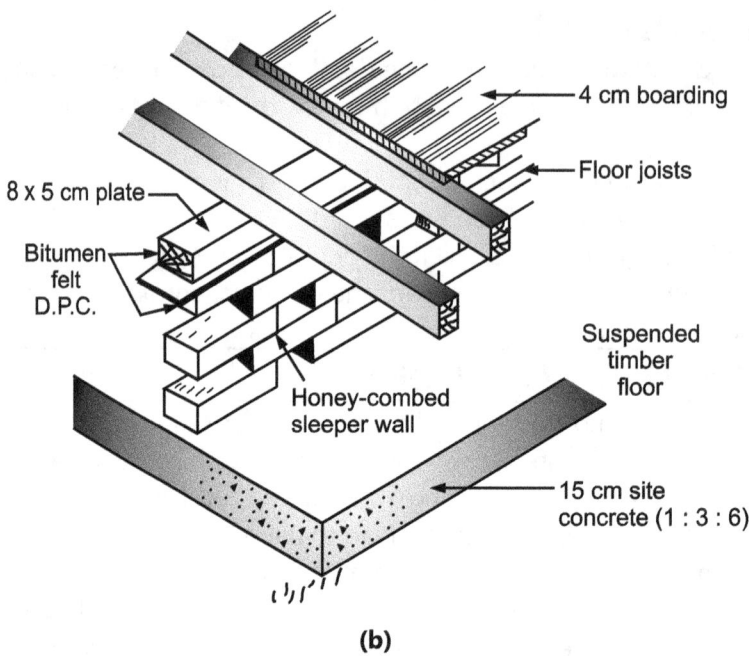

(b)

Fig. 1.22 : Ground floor structures

- Subgrade for the plinth shall be well consolidated and compacted. For soling overburnt bricks (Jhama) or second class bricks in dry condition shall be laid flat or on edge well packed and joints filled up with sand and surface blinded with thick earth and lightly rolled.

OR

- Split stone boulders 15 cm (6") thick laid well packed and surface blinded with earth and rolled with roller.

1.8.1 Earthwork in Filling

(a) Earth

- Earth used for filling shall be loose, free from brick-bat, stone, boulder not larger than 75 mm in any direction, salts, organic or other foreign matter.

- Excavated earth can be used for filling. If such earth contains deletorious material then the use is avoided.

(b) Filling

- The space around the foundations, pipes and drains in trenches shall be cleared of all debris, brick-bats etc. The filling shall be done in layers, not exceeding 20 cm each layer.

- Each layer shall be watered, rammed and consolidated before the succeeding one is laid. Earth shall be rammed with iron rammers where feasible and with the bull-ends of crowbars where rammer cannot be used.

- Special care shall be taken that no damage is caused to the pipes, drains and masonry in the trenches below. In case of filling under floors the finished level of filling shall be kept sloping, as intended to be given to the floor.

1.8.2 Sand Filling in Plinth

Sand : Sand used for filling shall be fine, free from dust, organic and foreign matter.

Filling : Sand shall be spread uniformly to a layer not exceeding 20 cm to the entire filling area. The sand shall then be thoroughly saturated in water.

Ramming

- Ramming shall be started by a number of rammers in a row for the space between the two plinth walls.

- The centre to centre positioning shall be 1.5 m and simultaneous ramming by all rammers in the row shall be done upto the end of other side of the area. Successive course of ramming shall be done in a transversed direction to the first course of ramming. After desired consolidation of first layer the second layer of sand to a thickness not exceeding 20 cm shall be spread uniformly over the first consolidated layer.

- The second layer of sand shall be thoroughly saturated with water as in of first layer and the process of ramming shall be continued. Before ramming the final layer the entire filled up area shall be flooded with water and the same process of ramming shall be continued till no further settlement can be appreciated.

- At the edges or corners consolidation shall be done with bull ends or crowbars. The finished surface shall be finally levelled longitudinally and transversely to the desired slope and kept open for inspection.

1.8.3 Brick Soling in Foundation Trenches

- Picked Jhama or second class brick in dry condition shall be laid on the foundation bed as headers with frogs upwards.

- All bricks shall be laid closely with break joints and the small gaps between them shall be filled up with local fine sand or dry loose earth.

- Brick-bats which are permitted to be used only to provide break joints, shall be placed at the edges of trenches.

- The finished surface shall be levelled both longitudinally and transversely.

REVIEW QUESTIONS

1. State the purpose of soil investigation and care to be taken in collecting data.
2. State the condition suitable for the following types of foundation :
   (a) Raft foundation
   (b) Trapezoidal combined footing
   (c) Under ream pile
   (d) Combined footing
   (e) Well foundation
   (f) Cantilever foundation
   (g) Trap footing
3. Explain the arrangement to avoid dampness from foundation in poorly draining soil.
4. State the purpose of site exploration and points to be observed along with their significance.
5. Enlist and classify materials commonly used for damp proofing course. Explain with a neat sketch, treatment to be provided to basements in damp soils to avoid dampness.
6. Explain the most suitable type of the pile for the following sub-soil condition :
   (a) Sand soil upto appreciable depth.
   (b) Foundation soil is weak but hard strata is available of reasonable depth.
7. Why black cotton soil is not suitable as foundation strata ? Draw a typical wall footing in black cotton soil. Explain provisions made to minimize problems.
8. State four important advantages of precast concrete piles.
9. Define building. State any four components of building and their major function.
10. Explain differential settlement with neat and detailed sketch.
11. State the detailed and step by step procedure of setting out building in the field.
12. Describe with sketch the following :
    (a) Bearing pile
    (b) Friction pile
    (c) Under reamed pile.
13. Explain cantilever footing with labelled sketch.
14. Describe the various causes for the failure of foundation.
15. Differentiate between shallow foundation and deep foundation.
16. Write detailed note on the treatments of building against dampness by interposing damp proofing courses in a building at the various positions.
17. Explain stage of plinth filling with sketch.

18. Compare bearing pile and under reamed pile with sketches.

19. Describe open test pit method of site investigation with sketch.

20. Write down the circumferences where strap footing is used. Give sketch of strap footing.

21. Describe settlement of foundation.

22. Describe design considerations for shallow foundations.

23. Explain with sketches :

    (a)   Bearing pile

    (b)   Framed structure

24. Explain plinth, a building component with neat sketch.

25. Differentiate between Bearing pile and Under reamed pile.

26. Define settlement. Write down the causes for differential settlement.

27. Write down the circumstances where the following types of foundations are used :

    (a)   Raft foundation

    (b)   Pile foundation

    (c)   Grillage foundation

    (d)   Inverted arch foundation

28. Describe with sketches :

    (a)   Under reamed piles

    (b)   Cantilever footing

SOLVED UNIVERSITY QUESTIONS

DEC. 2014

1. It is proposed to construct a residential building on black cotton soil. As a civil engineer; you have two choices, Isolated column footing and Pile foundation. Comment with reason, which you would select. **[6]**

   [**Ans.:** Refer Article 1.6.2(1)]

MAY 2014

1. With an appropriate figure any two types of Shallow Foundation and their suitability. **[6]**

   [**Ans.:** Refer Article 1.6.1 (a),(b)]

2. With an appropriate figure any two types of Deep Foundation and their suitability. **[6]**

   [**Ans.:** Refer Article 1.6.2]

MAY 2015

1. Discuss the need of Damp Proof course for roofs and basement. **[6]**

   [**Ans.:** Refer Article 1.7.1]

NOV. 2015

1. Define shallow foundation. State the functions of foundation.   **[6]**

   [**Ans.:** Refer Articles 1.5.1, 1.6.1]

2. Define the following : Deep foundation   **[6]**

   [**Ans.:** Refer Article 1.6.2]

MAY 2016

1. Explain strap footing.   **[6]**

   [**Ans.:** Refer Article 1.6.1(D)(C)]

2. Define foundation. Distinguish between shallow foundation and deep foundation with sketch.   **[6]**

   [**Ans.:** Refer Articles 1.5, 1.6.1, 1.6.2]

NOV. 2016

1. What do you understand by Foundation? Briefly explain Foundation in black cotton soil.   **[6]**

   [**Ans.:** Refer Articles 1.5.1, 1.7.3]

2. List any four types of building as per National Building Code 2005 ? Briefly explain commercial building.   **[6]**

   [**Ans.:** Refer Articles 1.3]

MAY 2017

1. Explain the general procedure of foundation dssign.   **[6]**

   [**Ans.:** Refer Articles 1.5]

2. Explain Cantilever footing with a labeled sketch.   **[6]**

   [**Ans.:** Refer Articles 1.6.1(D), (C)]

CHAPTER 2
STONE MASONRY

2.1 INTRODUCTION TO STONE MASONRY

- Stone is the oldest building construction material known to man.
- Beautiful structures have been constructed, with the help of this age old material.
- Out of seven wonders of the world, three wonders have been constructed using stone viz., The great wall of China, (2) "Pyramids" in Egypt, (3) The famous "Taj Mahal" in Agra.
- Apart from these historical buildings, forts, docks, harbours, dams, bridges, arches, rail tracks, plain and reinforced concrete works, beautiful statues, temples, thousands of kilometres of roads etc. have been constructed using stones.
- Stones are strong, durable, can take polish and are available not only in large quantity, but have variety of pleasing colours.
- In this section, characteristics of good building stones, natural bed, defects in stones, different types of tests carried on stone, etc. UCR and CR masonry, etc. are discussed.

Table 2.1 : Physical Properties and Engineering Uses of Familiar Stones

Sr. No.	Type of rock and classification	Properties and Engineering Uses	Locality where available	Physical Properties		
				Compressive strength kg/m^2	Sp. gravity G	Density γ, kg/m^3
1.	Sand stone (sedimentary)	Hard, strong, non-absorbent, easy to work. Can resist heat (if mica is absent). **Uses :** Ornamental work, floor, wall, columns, steps, road metal.	A.P., M.P., H.P., U.P., Gujarat, Karnataka, T.N., Maharashtra	650	2.6 to 2.9	2200
2.	Deccan trap (Igneous)	Hard, tough durable difficult to work. Not suitable for ornamented work. **Uses :** Suitable for rubble masonry work, road metal, paving stone, flay stone.	Maharashtra, Gujarat, Bihar, M.P.	1500 – 1900	2.9	2800 – 2900

...Conti.

3.	Granite (Igneous)	Very strong available in pleasing colours, difficult to work with highly durable (in absence of feldspar and mica). **Uses :** Bridge piers, walls, columns, steps, sills, road metal, ballast.	Karnataka, M.P., U.P., Gujarat, Punjab, Rajasthan, Bihar, Orissa, Kashmir	700 – 1300	2.6 – 2.7	2600
4.	Lime stone (sedimentary)	Soft, liable to be affected by acid, easy to work. **Uses :** Walls, floors, steps, road work, manufacture of cement, as a flux	A.P., M.P., U.P., Gujarat, Maharashtra, Rajasthan	550	2 to 2.7	1700
5.	Marble (metamorphic)	Easy to work, taken polish, available in pleasing colours. Can be easily swan and carved. **Uses :** Ornamental work, columns, floors, steps.	Rajasthan, Gujarat, Maharashtra, A.P., M.P., U.P.	720	2.65	2700
6.	Laterite (metamorphic)	Porous, cellular structure, can be quarried in blocks, available in different colours. **Uses :** Building stone, road metal.	Bihar, Orissa, A.P., M.P., Maharashtra, T.N.	20 to 30	2.2 to 2.5	1200 – 1600
7.	State (metamorphic)	Non-absorbent, splits along natural bedding plane.	Flooring, roofing, sills, damp-proofing.	750 – 2100	2.9	2600

2.2 MASONRY

- Masonry is defined as assemblage of masonry unit properly bonded together with mortar.
- Masonry units are individual units which are bonded together with the help of mortar to form a masonry element such as wall, column, pier, buttress etc.

2.2.1 Types of Masonry

Masonry units may be of the following types :

- Stones
- Common burnt clay bricks, sand-lime bricks
- Concrete/lime based blocks
- Burnt clay hollow blocks
- Autoclaved cellular concrete blocks
- Gypsum partition blocks; which are used only for construction of non-load bearing walls.

A wall is a continuous vertical structure of stone, brick, concrete etc. thin in proportion to its length and height, which encloses a building,

- to carry designed vertical and horizontal load, on it,
- to protect it from rain, dampness, heat and
- to divide building in suitable rooms.

2.3 TERMS USED IN STONE MASONRY

Some of the terms used in stone masonry are explained as follows :

1. **Bed / Bed Surface / Bedding Plane :** It is the surface of a stone perpendicular to the line of pressure.

2. **Quoins :** These are the stones used at the corners of wall. In order to give better appearance, these are properly dressed and selected from larger stones having better appearance. Where good stones are not available, precast concrete blocks of suitable size are provided.

3. **Cornice and Corbel**

   (a) **Cornice :** It is a moulded stone, with ornamental treatment, having large projection and is placed at the junction of wall and ceiling and is finished so as to throw rain water.

   (b) **Corbel :** It is also a stone projecting outside to support a structural member to serve as support to wall plate. Thus,

   - Although both cornice and corbel are stones projecting, cornice has ornamental appearance whereas corbel may not have ornamental treatment;
   - Cornice is exposed to atmosphere and is having slope to drain off rain water, whereas corbel is not exposed to weather and is intended to support structural member.

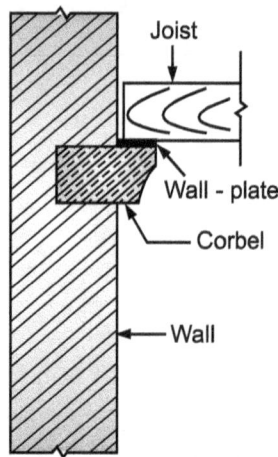

Fig. 2.1 : Corbel

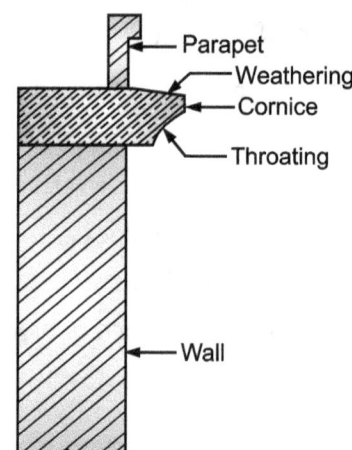

Fig. 2.2 : Cornice

4. **String Course, Drip Stone and Throating**
   - **String Course :** It is a continuous horizontal course, projecting from the face of wall and is intended to throw off rain water. It is provided at floor level. It may or may not have groove at the underside to drain off water.
   - **Drip Stone :** It is a projected stone moulding having throating under surface to drain out rain water off wall.
   - **Throating :** These are the grooves cut on the under surface of sills, copings, string courses to drain off rain water trickling from walls.

5. **Through Stone :** These are non-porous strong, and thick stones (or precast concrete block) extending throughout the thickness of wall, (i) to reduce ingress of moisture and (ii) to increase stability of wall. Even if a wall settles, these stones being strong will not crack.

6. **Heads and Header**
   - **Heads :** These are the stones provided at the top of openings of doors, windows, etc. with sufficient bearing on either side of the opening. This is another name to stone lintel.
   - **Header :** It is a brick or stone which lies in its greatest length at right angles to the face of the work. In stone masonry, it is sometimes called as through stone. In case of brick masonry, the course, in which all the bricks are laid as headers is known as header course.

7. **Jambs and Reveals**
   - **Jambs :** These are the vertical surfaces of an opening for doors and windows. These may be (i) plain or (ii) splayed or (iii) rebated to receive the frames of doors and windows.
   - **Reveals :** These are the exposed vertical surfaces left on the sides of opening, after the door or window frame has been fitted in the position.

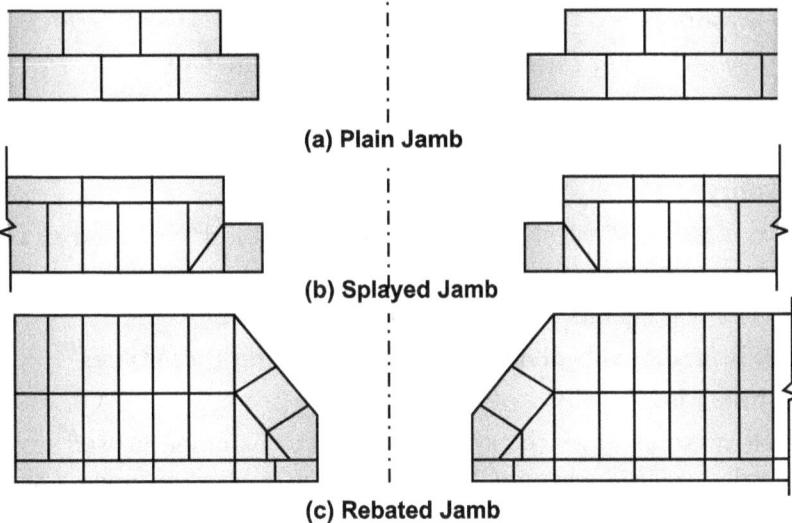

(a) Plain Jamb

(b) Splayed Jamb

(c) Rebated Jamb

Fig. 2.3 : Jambs

8. **Buttress, Pier, Pilaster**

   - **Buttress :** It is sloping or stepped masonry projection from a tall wall intended to strengthen the wall against the thrust of a roof or arch or pressure of wind or soil.
   - **Pier :** It is an isolated vertical mass of stone or brick masonry to support beams or lintels. If it is made monolithic with the wall and project from wall (to support concentrated load) it is called as pilaster.

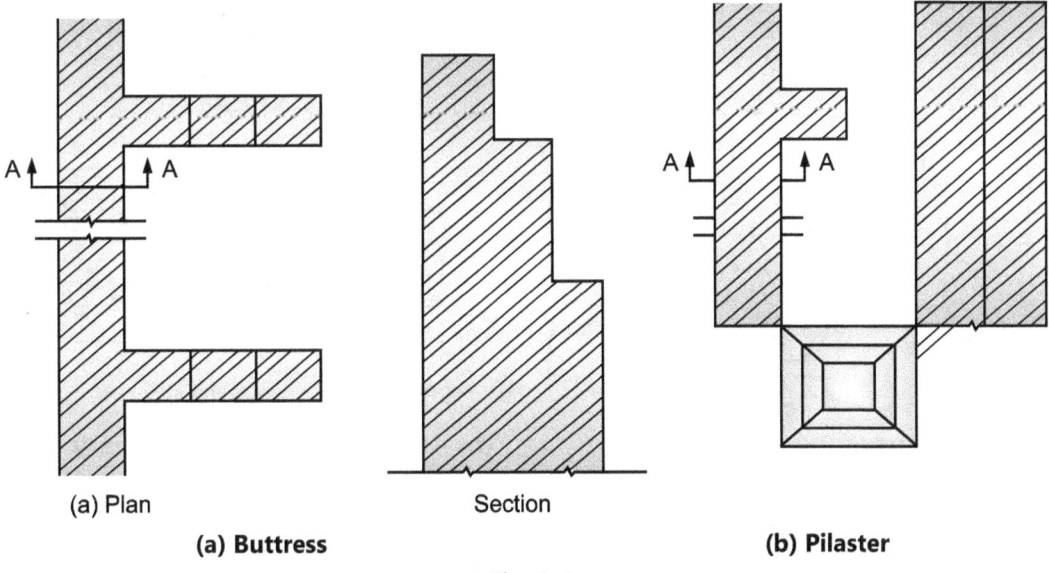

Fig. 2.4

9. **Dowel :** It is a pin or peg let into two pieces of stone or wood for joining.
10. **Spalls :** These are small pieces of stones, placed vertically and embedded in the mortar in the central portion of wall, to fill the voids.

Types of Stone Masonry

Stone masonry may be broadly classified into the following two types:

(a) Rubble Masonry

(b) Ashlar Masonry

(a) Rubble Masonry

- The stone masonry in which either undressed or roughly dressed stone are laid in a suitable mortar is called rubble masonry.
- In this masonry the joints are not of uniform thickness.

Rubble masonry is further sub-divided into the following three types

1. Random Rubble Masonry

- The rubble masonry in which either undressed or hammer dressed stones are used is called random rubble masonry. Further random rubble masonry is also divided into the coursed & uncoursed types.
- In coursed type of masonry, the stones used are of widely different sizes. This is the roughest and cheapest form of stone masonry. The masonry work is carried out in courses such that the stones in a particular course are of equal height.
- In uncoursed random rubble masonry, the stones used are of widely different sizes. This is the roughest and cheapest form of stone masonry. The coarses are not maintained regularly. The larger stones are laid first and the spaces between them are then filled up by means of spalls or sneeks.

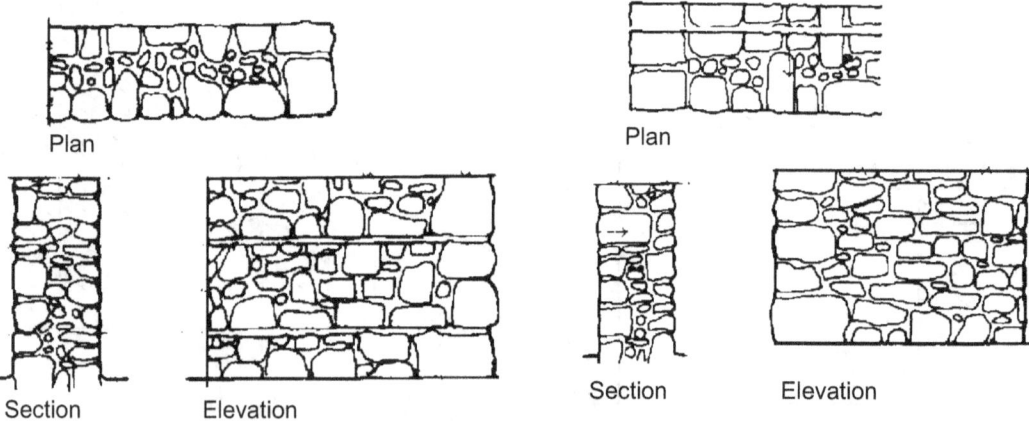

(a) Coursed Rubble Masonary   (b) Uncoursed Rubble Masonary

Fig. 2.5

2. Squared Rubble Masonry

- The rubble masonry, in which the face stones are squared on all joints and beds by hammer dressing or chisel dressing before their actual laying, is called squared rubble masonry.
- It is also divided in course and uncoursed type

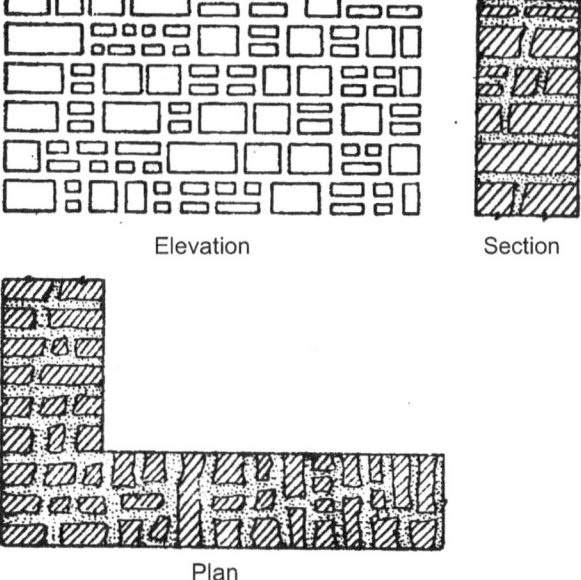

Elevation   Section

Plan

Fig. 2.6

3. Dry Rubble Masonry

- The rubble masonry in which stones are laid without using any mortar is called dry rubble masonry or sometimes shortly as "dry stones".

- It is an ordinary masonry and is recommended for constructing walls of height not more than 6m. In case the height is more, three adjacent courses are laid in squared rubble masonry mortar at 3m intervals.

Fig. 2.7

(b) Ashlar Masonry

The stone masonry in which finely dressed stones are laid in cement or lime mortar is known as ashlars masonry. In this masonry are the courses are of uniform height, all the joints are regular, thin and have uniform thickness. This type of masonry is much costly as it requires dressing of stones.

Suitability: This masonry is used for heavy structures, architectural buildings, high piers and abutments of bridges.

Ashlars masonry is further sub divided into the following types:

1. Ashlar Fine or Coarsed Ashlar Masonry

In this type of stone masonry stone blocks of same height in each course are used. Every stone is fine tooled on all sides. Thickness of mortar is uniform throughout.

It is an expensive type of stone masonry as it requires heavy labor and wastage of material while dressing. Satisfactory bond can be obtained in this type of stone masonry.

Fig. 2.8

2. Rough Tooled Ashlar Masonry

This type of ashlar masonry the sides of the stones are rough tooled and dressed with chisels. Thickness of joints is uniform, which does not exceed 6mm.

Fig. 2.9

3. Rock or Quarry Faced Ashlar Masonry

In this type of ashlar masonry, a strip about 25mm wide and made by means of chisel is provided around the perimeter of every stone as in case of rough-tooled ashlor masondry. But the remaining portion of the face is left in the same form as received from quarry.

Fig. 2.10

4. Chamfered Ashlar Masonry

In this type of ashlar masonry, the strip is provided as below. But it is chamfered or beveled at an angle of 45 degrees by means of chisel for a depth of about 25mm

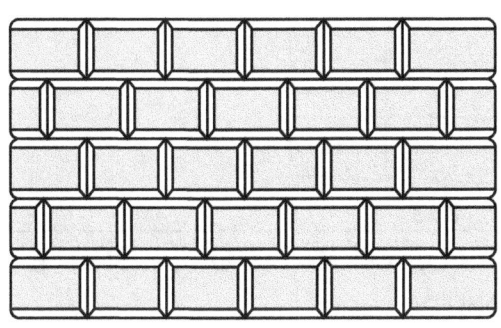 

Fig. 2.11

5. Block-in Course Masonry

This is combination of rubble masonry and ashlar masonry. In this type of masondry, the face work is provided with rough tooled or hammer dresses stones and backing of the wall may be made in rubble masonry

Fig. 2.12

6. Ashlar Facing

Ashlar facing is the best type of ashlars masonry. Since this is type of masonry is very expensive, it is not commonly used throughout the whole thickness of the wall, except in works of great importance and strength. For economy the facing are built in ashlars and the rest in rubble.

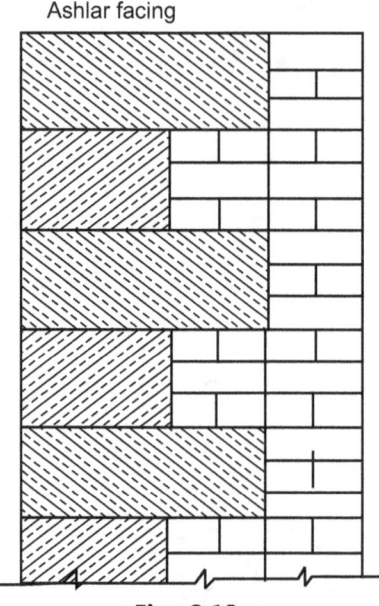

Ashlar facing

Fig. 2.13

2.3 DIFFERENCE IN DIFFERENT TYPES OF RANDOM RUBBLE AND SQUARE RUBBLE MASONRY

Difference in different types of random rubble and square rubble on important aspects is as follows.

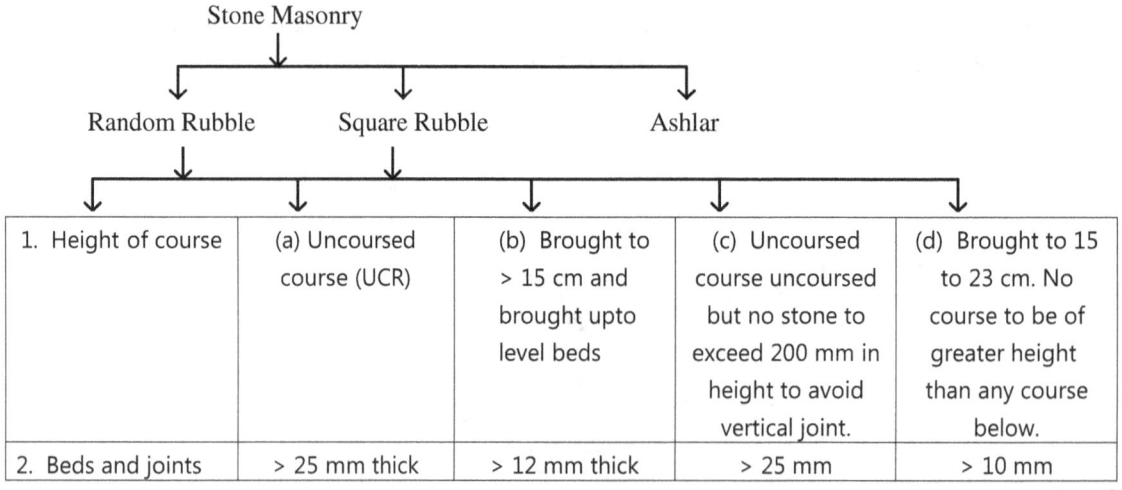

	(a) Uncoursed course (UCR)	(b) Brought to > 15 cm and brought upto level beds	(c) Uncoursed course uncoursed but no stone to exceed 200 mm in height to avoid vertical joint.	(d) Brought to 15 to 23 cm. No course to be of greater height than any course below.
1. Height of course				
2. Beds and joints	> 25 mm thick	> 12 mm thick	> 25 mm	> 10 mm

...Conti.

3. Dressing	Hammer dressed on face, sides and beds so that the stones will come close with neighbouring stones.	Same as UCR. No face to be shorter than height. At least 33% of face stones shall tail into wall for twice their height	Hammer dressed on face and sides. Face beds to be squared back at least 100 mm and joints 65 mm.	Chisel dressed so that no portion of dressed face is more than 6 mm from the edge a straight edge laid along face of stone.
4. Quoins or corner stones	Face beds to be squared back carefully at least 100 mm and joints 65 mm.	Same as (a) and (b) but, corner of each quoin to have chisel drafted margin of 25 mm on each side to facilitate plumbing.		
5. Bonds or through stones	One bond stone for every 0.5 sq. m. of wall surface and staggered.	In the interior thickness of wall, 45 cm long bond stone shall be provided 150 cm.	Same as (a)	Same as (b) 150 cm apart in every course and to be staggered.
6. Hearting	Stones not to be less than 15 cm in any direction, carefully laid and hammered down with wooden mallet into place and solidly beaded with mortar. Chips and spalls being wedged into to avoid thick beds of joints and mortar.	Same as (a) but vertical plums to be placed wherever possible, projecting not less than 150 mm to form bond between successive courses.		

2.5 SPECIFICATION FOR UNCOURSED RUBBLE MASONRY

- **Stone :** Stone should be tough, hard, dense, durable and of uniform colour; should be free from flaws, veins, etc. When immersed in water for 24 hours, should not absorb more than 5% of its dry weight.
- **Size of Stone :** Width and height shall not be less than 15 cm and length shall not be less than 1.5 times its height.
- **Dressing :** Stones shall be hammer dressed, weak corners and edges shall be removed.

- **Face Stones :** Stones with larger sides, having good beds shall be used for face work. At least 50% of them shall be more than 10 litres in volume. The beds and joints shall have a minimum bearing of not less than 2 cm. Face stones shall be dressed in straight lines and these sides shall be in one plane.
- **Through Stones :**
  - Through stones shall be about 0.03 m^2 in face area and shall occupy full width of wall, if thickness of wall is upto 60 cm.
  - If thickness of wall is more than 60 cm, a line of headers over lapping each other by at least 15 cm shall be provided.
  - Through stones shall be marked on their faces by paint.
  - Through stones / headers shall be laid @ 2 stones / m^2. Each stone shall break joint with the stone in course below or above by at least 8 cm.
- **Hearting and Backing Stones :** 30% of stones used in hearting and backing shall exceed 10 litres in volume.
- **Quoins :** Quoins shall be of size 30 cm $\times$ 15 cm $\times$ 15 cm. The faces of quoins shall be hammer dressed. Each side of exposed corner shall be chisel drafted to a width of 40 mm. The quoins shall tail into wall to a length not less than 20 cm and 10 cm measured at right angles to the shorter and longer face respectively.
- **Thickness of Joint :** No face joint shall exceed 16 mm in thickness; and all joints shall be raked to a depth of 16 mm.
- **Raising of Masonry :** Face work and hearting shall be brought up evenly, but top of each course shall not be levelled. The rate of raising masonry shall not exceed 60 cm per day.
- **Laying Stones :** All stones shall be laid full in the mortar, both in bed joints and side joints. Clean chips and spalls shall be wedged into the mortar joints in hearting.
- **Quantity of Mortar :** The volume of mortar used per cubic metre of masonry shall be between 0.30 to 0.35 cubic metre.

2.6 SPECIFICATION FOR COURSED RUBBLE MASONRY [FIRST SORT]

- **Stones :** Same as that for uncoursed rubble masonry.
- **Size of Stones :** Height of stone shall be 15 cm. Breadth shall be more than height and shall tail back into the masonry 1.5 times the height.
- **Scaffolding :** It shall be double scaffolding and shall be sufficiently strong.
- **Face Stones :** Bushing on the face of stone shall not be more than 4 cm. The beds and tops shall be rough tooled to atleast 8 cm from face and the vertical faces shall be rough tooled to at least 4 cm from face.
- **Through Stones :** The height of the through stones shall be the full height of the course and the width shall not be less than height. Rest same as that for UCR.

- **Hearting and Backing Stones :** Same as that for UCR.
- **Quoins :**
  (i) The faces of quoins shall be rough tooled and the sides of exposed corner shall be provided with a chisel draft of about 4 cm from the face.
  (ii) These shall be of the same height as that of the course.
  (iii) The length (L) of Quoins on the longer face shall not be less than twice their height (H) and on shorter face not less than height.

  The quoin shall tail into the wall to length of not less than 20 cm and 10 cm measured perpendicularly to the shorter and larger sides respectively.
- **Joints :** The thickness of joint shall not exceed 10 mm. Horizontal joints shall be truely horizontal and vertical joints shall be truely vertical.
- **Raising of Masonry :** Same as that for UCR masonry.
- **Laying :** The stones shall be laid in horizontal course of 15 cm height. All courses shall be of equal height.
- **Quantity of Mortar :** The volume of mortar used per cubic metre of masonry shall be between 0.25 to 0.30 cubic metre.

Notes :
- In Course Rubble Masonry of second sort, each course need not be of the same height but not more than two stones are used in the height of the course.
- In Course Rubble Masonry of third sort not more than three stones are used in the height of the course.

Thus, in Course Rubble of first sort, second sort and third sort, one stone, two stones and three stones are used respectively in the height of course.

2.7 GENERAL POINTS TO BE OBSERVED DURING THE PERVISION OF STONE MASONRY WORK

Various points as regards thickness of joints, quoins, through stones, dressing, height of course, hearting have been summarized and given in the chart for Random Rubble and Square Rubble Masonry and in the specifications for DCR and CR masonry. In addition to this, the following points should be observed :

- The stones should be properly wetted so that stones do not absorb moisture in mortar.
- The stones should be dressed as per requirement, before placing in position.
- Positioning, spacing of centre line of walls must conform as per drawings; during the entire construction of the wall. The same must be checked with the help of reference points located outside.
- Verticality of the wall should be checked from time to time, with the help of plumb bob. This is to ensure that, the loads acting on the wall is concentric.
- The various courses should be brought to level with the help of thin string stretched between the ends of walls.

- Construction of stone masonry should commence at prominent corners of walls. Masonry between corners should be raised gradually, uniformly and in plumb.
- Good and bad examples of (i) Stretcher stone, (ii) Quoins, (iii) Through stones and (iv) Faulty construction are shown in the following sketches. Faulty materials and methods should be avoided.
- All surfaces should be kept wet while the work is in progress. After completion of work, the masonry should be cured in 2 to 3 weeks.

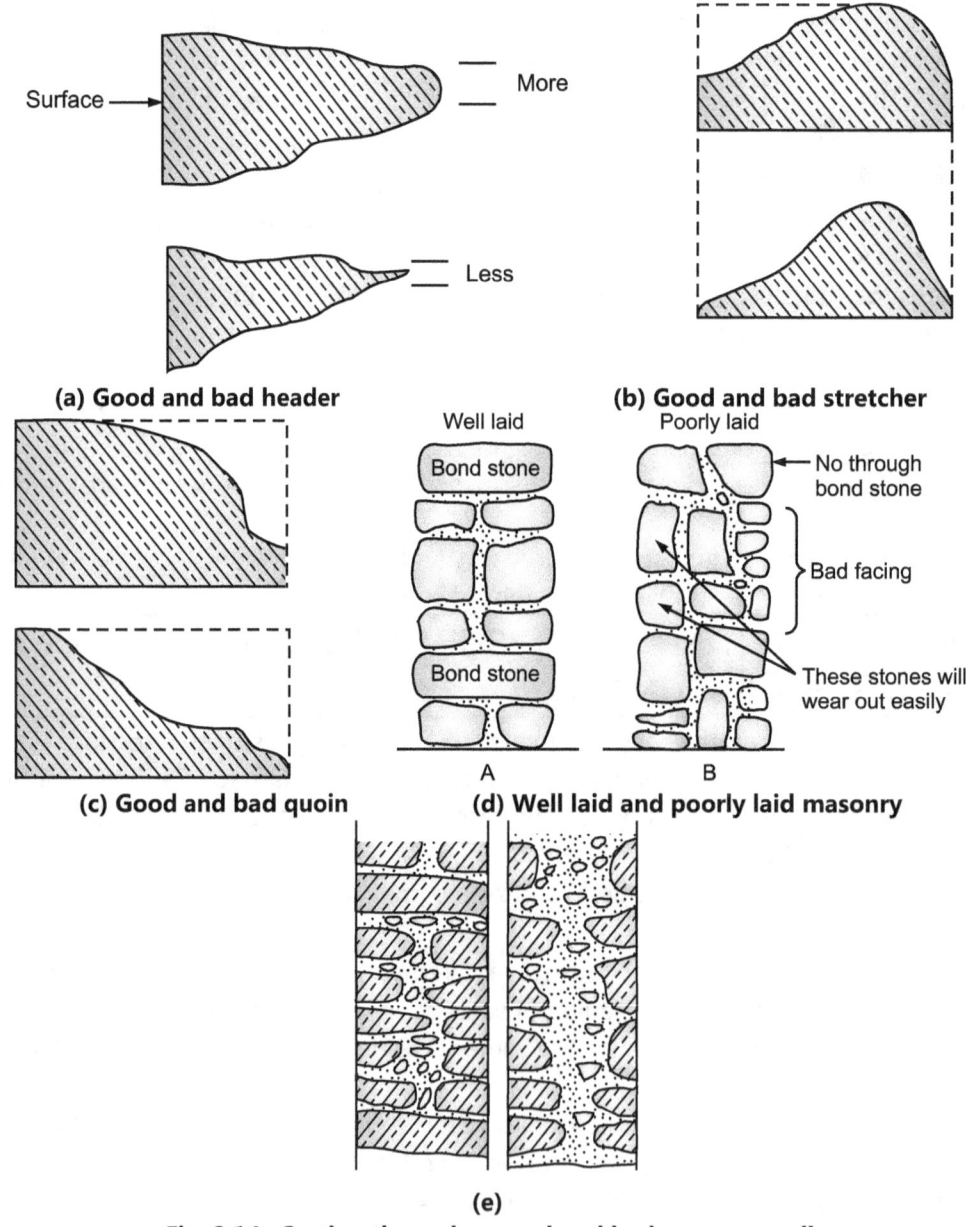

(e)
Fig. 2.14 : Section through a good and bad masonry wall

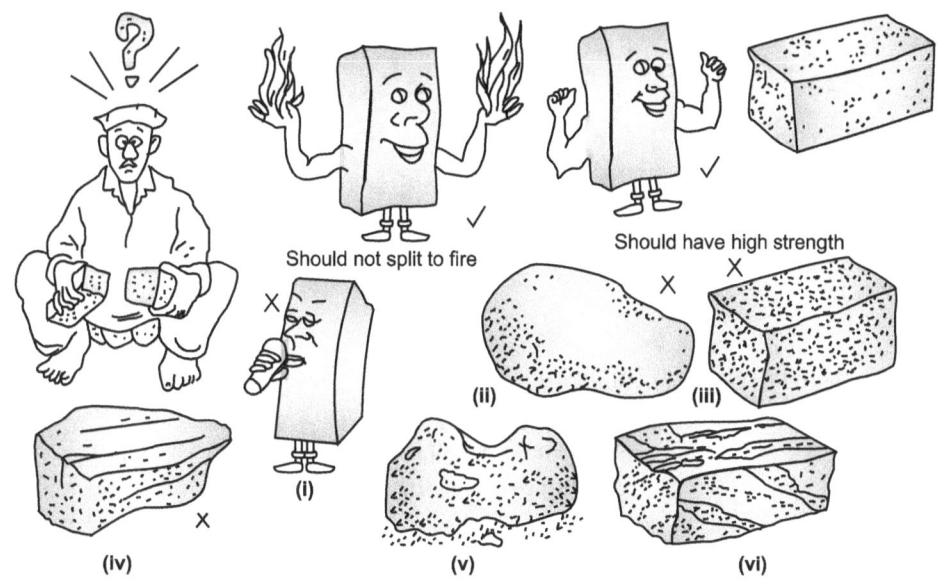

Fig. 2.15 : Avoid (i) Stones absorbing more water (ii) Rounded (iii) Soft and stone composed of sand and soil (iv) Irregular flat pointed (v) Likely to affected by weather (vi) With dark spots and bonds of different colours

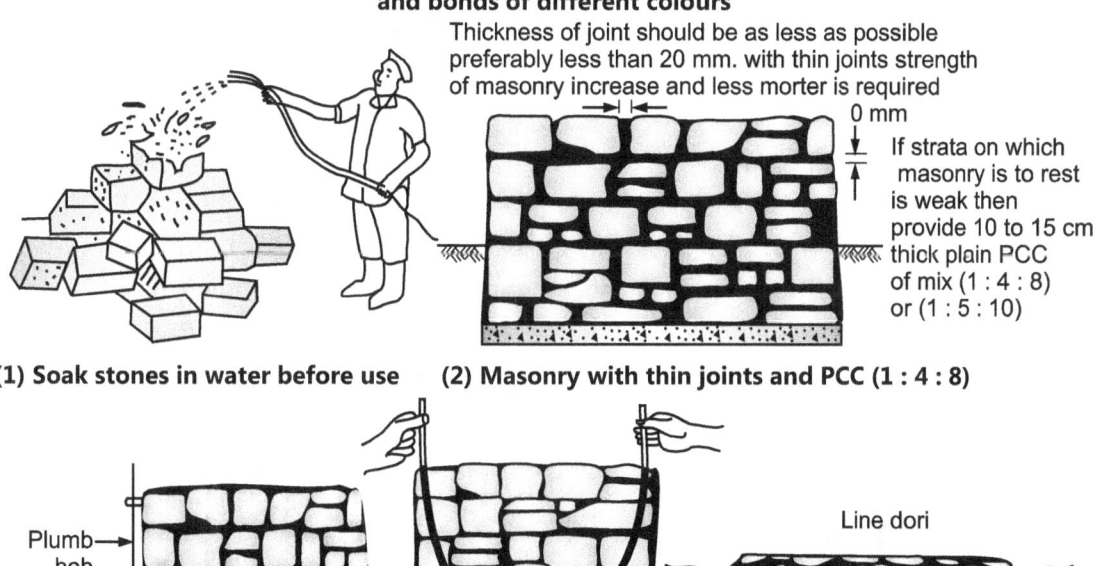

(1) Soak stones in water before use   (2) Masonry with thin joints and PCC (1 : 4 : 8)

(3) (a) Check frequently with plumb bob whether masonry is in plumb   (b) With level tube masonry should be brought to level   (c) Masonry should be raised in line and level

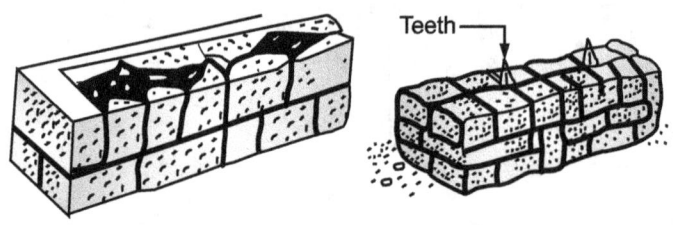

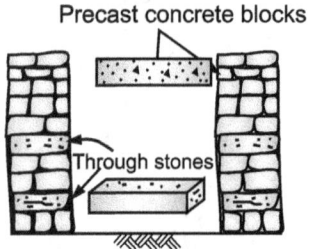

(4) (a) Fill voids between stones using spalls in hearing

(b) At the end of day's work, provide pointed stones as shown. This will help in providing grip in further work

(c) Provide through stones for full width of wall. Sometimes precast concrete blocks are provided, in place of through stones

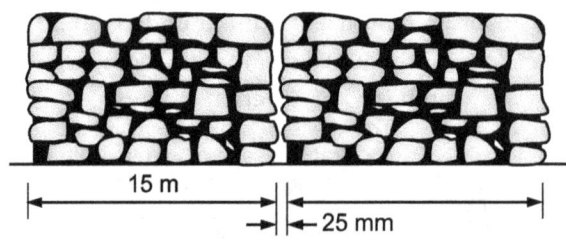

(5) If the length of compound wall exceeds 15 m, then provide a gap of 25 mm throughout width and height to serve as expansion joint

Fig. 2.16 : Seven commandments for good stone masonry (continued)

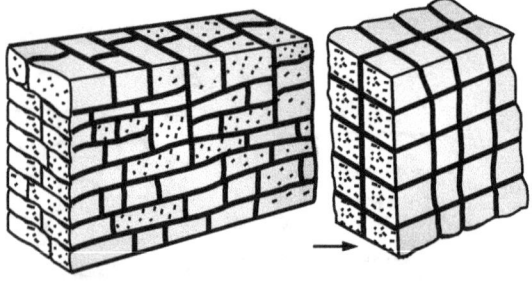

(c)

(6) (a) In one day masonry should not be raised to height more than 0.6 m

(b) The joints should break and should not be vertically one above other, as in (c)

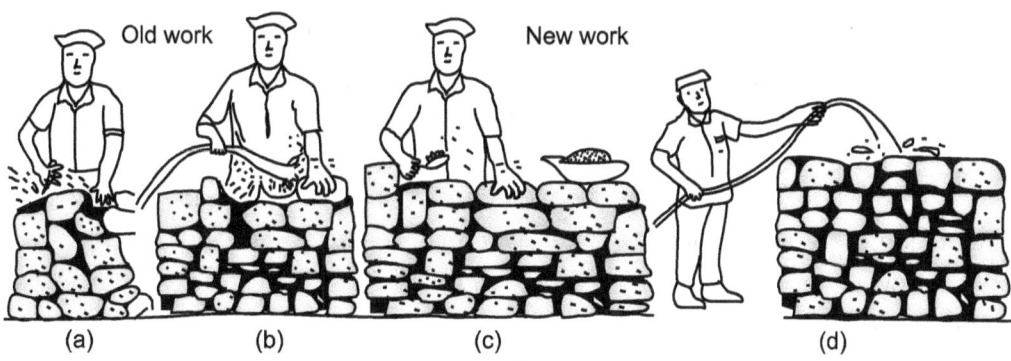

(7) (a) **Before starting new work, the old mortar should breaked out to sufficient depth and**

(b) **Then masonry work is soaked with water**

(c) **Provide fresh mortar "into the masonry" and not on the previous levelled surface to obtain good grip. Keep mortar just near the work (and not at far away and too low level) to speed up construction.**

(d) **After completion of work, it should be cured atleast for 15 days.**

Fig. 2.17 : Seven commandments for good stone masonry

REVIEW QUESTIONS

1. Explain properties expected in a good building unit for a masonry construction. Compare conventional brick, IS brick. Compare rubble, Khandki and Ashlar.

2. State your choice of stone type of masonry and reasons for the following situations :

   (a) Foundation of load bearing structure.

   (b) Monumental work in industrial township.

   (c) External wall of a bungalow in Kokan area.

3. State six important points regarding laying of coursed rubble masonry.

5. Describe the following terms with sketch :

   (a)   Coping   (b)   Throating

   (c)   Sill   (d)   Cornice

   (e)   String course   (f)   Frieze.

6. Compare the stone masonry with brick masonry with regards to the different points.

7. Explain with neat sketch :

   (a)   Through stone   (b) Throating

8. Explain the following terms used in masonry :

   (a)   Corbel   (b)   Template   (c)   Cornice

   (d)   Spalls   (e)   Header   (f)   Bevelled closer

   (g)   Queen   (h)   Throating.

9. Write down the characteristics of a stone which should be observed in case of monumental building.

10. Describe the following terms with sketches :

    (a)   Corbel   (b) Cornice   (c) Mitred closer

    (d)   Toothing   (e) Bed joint   (f) Lap

11. State different stones available in India, with their characteristics and one uses.

12. Write down the characteristics of the stones which should be observed in case of educational building.

13. Describe masonry. Enlist the different units of masonry.

14. Describe the following with sketches :

    (a)   Header stone   (B) Through stone

15. What general principles would you keep in mind while supervising a stone work ? What points would you apply to ensure strength, pleasant and comfort in stone masonry construction ?

CHAPTER 3
BRICK MASONRY

3.1 INTRODUCTION TO BRICK MASONRY

Although beautiful structures can be constructed using naturally available stones, it has its limitations; such as :

- Availability of stones of desired quality and quantity at economically viable cost.
- Stones are required to be dressed to attain desired finish.
- Stones are required to be quarried and transported.
- Usually stones are heavy and wall thickness is more whereas bricks are light, wall thickness is less hence, dead weight of wall is less.
- Speed of construction of stone masonry is less and more quantity of morter is required.

In view of above, many times it is advantageous to use light bricks of regular shape and size. Usually mouldable earth, suitable for manufacture of bricks is easily available.

The advantages and disadvantages of bricks as compared with stone as a building material are given below :

- Bricks are lighter in weight and can be more easily handled. The size and shape of bricks are such that the brick layer can continuously lay them for hours together without fatigue.
- Bricks may be easily moulded from clay into required size and shape at a moderate cost. But stones are usually more costly than bricks, difficult and expensive to quarry and dress down the required size and shape and plaster does not stick well to stone as it does to bricks.
- Bricks do not absorb as much heat as stones and are also more fire-resisting than stones.
- Good bricks stand the effects of weather and of chemicals in the atmosphere better than stones. Under certain atmospheric conditions, stones are not suited.
- Walls with bricks can be easily constructed to the required thickness viz. 100 mm, 200 mm, 300 mm, and above, whereas walls with stones are to be constructed to a thickness of 400 mm or above for ease of construction and strength.
- Bricks are not so strong or durable as stones. For public buildings and works of monumental nature bricks are not so suitable as stones; as a better architectural effect can be obtained in stones than in bricks.

- Bricks absorb more water than stones and are not heavy as stones. Hence, bricks are not suitable for heavy engineering works.
- In walls, the faces of bricks are generally to be covered by means of lime or cement plaster in order to prevent the absorption of moisture. But stones do not require plastering.

3.2 CHARACTERISTICS OF A GOOD BRICK

Good bricks which are to be used for the construction of important structures should possess the following qualities :

- Bricks should be well-burnt in kilns, copper coloured, free from cracks, with sharp and square edges.
- Bricks should be uniform in shape and should be of standard size.
- Bricks should give clear ringing sound when struck with each other.
- Bricks when broken should show homogeneous and compact structure.
- Bricks should not absorb water more than $1/8^{th}$ to $1/6^{th}$ of its weight, when soaked in water for a period of 24 hours.
- Bricks should be sufficiently hard. No impression should be left on brick surface, when it is scratched with finger nail.
- Bricks should not break *when droped on hard* ground from a height of about one metre.
- Bricks should have low thermal conductivity and they should be sound proof.
- Crushing strength of brick varies from 4 N/mm² to 7 N/mm² depending upon type or class of bricks.

Types of Bricks

There are two types of bricks.

1. Conventional or Traditional Bricks
2. Standard or Modular Bricks

1. Conventional or Traditional Bricks

- These types of bricks have not standardized in size.
- Their length varies from 200 mm to 250 mm
- Their width varies from 100 mm to 130 mm
- And thickness varies from 50 mm to 75 mm
- The nominal size of these types of brick is 230 × 114 × 75 mm
- The nominal size means the size of brick plus the mortar thickness.

Fig. 3.1

2. Standard or Modular Bricks

- In different countries, the size of brick is different.
- In India, the Bureau of Indian Standard has suggested a fix size of brick.
- Any brick which is of that size is known as modular brick or standard brick.
- The actual size of these types of brick is 190 x 90 x 90 mm and nominal size of brick is $200 \times 100 \times 100$ mm.

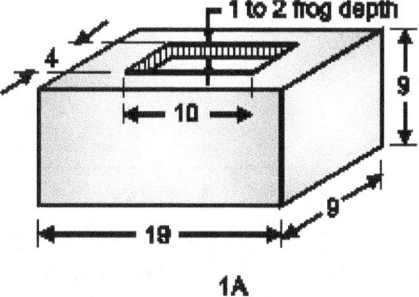

1A

Fig. 3.2

Constituents of Brick Earth

1. Silica

- It is main constituents of brick earth.
- For good brick earth, the presence of silica is about 50- 60% of clay
- Silica helps the brick to retain its shape, to give durability and to prevent shrinkage.
- Excess of silica makes the brick brittle and weak on burning.

2. Alumina

- It is another main constituents of brick earth
- The percentage of alumina in good brick earth is 20-30 % of clay
- Alumina absorb the water and renders the clay plastic
- If alumina is available in excess then it creates cracks in brick while drying.

3. Lime

- The presence of lime is less than 10% of clay
- It reduces the shrinkage on drying

- Lime causes silica to melt during burning process and thus it helps to bind it.
- If lime is available more than 10% of clay then it cause the brick to melt and the brick loses its shape.

4. **Iron Oxide**
   - It constitute less than 7% of clay
   - It gives the red colour to brick on burning
   - If excess of iron oxide is available in clay then it makes brick dark blue.

5. **Magnesia**
   - Magnesia rarely exceeding 1 % of clay.
   - The more percentage of magnesia affects the colour and makes the brick yellow.

3.3 PROPERTIES OF BURNT CLAY BRICKS   (May 15)

The standard properties of burnt clay bricks have been discussed by IS : 1077–1976 under the following sub headings :

- General quality of bricks.
- Dimensions and tolerances.
- Water absorption by bricks.
- Strength of bricks.
- Efflorescence.

3.3.1 General Quality of Bricks

- According to IS : 1077–1976, hand moulded or machine moulded bricks should be free from cracks, flaws and from nodules of free lime.
- Bricks of 9 cm height may be moulded with a frog 1 to 2 cm deep on one of its flat sides (Fig. 3.9) but bricks of 4 cm height and those made by the extrusion process may not be provided with frogs.

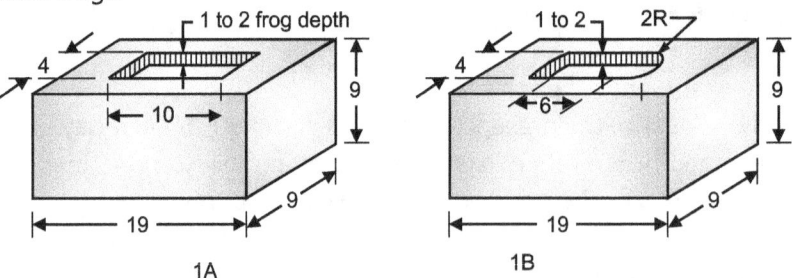

All Dimentions in Centimeters

Fig. 3.3 : Shape and size of frogs in bricks

- Bricks having smooth rectangular faces and sharp corners, and emitting a clear ringing sound when struck against each other, are classified under sub-class A.
- Bricks having a slight distortion and rounded edges, provided no difficulty arise on this account in laying of uniform courses, have been classified under sub-class B.

3.3.2 Water Absorption Test (IS – 3495 Part II 1976)

• For this test, five samples of bricks at random are selected and oven dried at temperature 105°C to 115°C till they substantially attain constant weight (W_1).

• The specimen are cooled to room temperature and then immersed in a water tank with temperature of 27°C ± 2°C for 24 hours.

• Each specimen is then removed, wiped with a damp cloth and weighed (W_2).

$$\% \text{ Absorption water} = \frac{W_2 - W_1}{W_1} \times 100$$

3.3.3 Compressive Strength Test (IS 3495 Part – I 1976)

• Fire brick samples at random are taken and immersed in water tank at room temperature for 24 hours.

• Bricks are taken out of water tank and wiped of surplus moisture.

• Frogs and all voids in the bed are filled with cement morter (1 : 1) using coarse sand passing 3 mm sieve and cured for 24 hours under moist conditions such as damp sack for 72 hours.

• The bricks are wiped, dry and placed on the compression testing machine facing upwards. Two plywood sheets of about 3 mm thickness are placed both below and above the brick.

• Compressive load of 140 kg / sq. cm per minute is applied till failure.

$$\text{Compressive strength of brick} = \frac{\left(\begin{array}{c} \text{Average compressive load of} \\ \text{5 brick samples} \end{array} \right)}{\text{Area of brick (i.e. } l \times b)}$$

It may be noted that, compressive strength of any brick should not be less than 20% of the specified compressive strength of the class of the brick.

Table 3.2 : Permissible water absorption percentage and compressive strength, etc.

Type of Brick	Class Designation	Compressive strength in kg/cm^2	% Water absorption (Max.)	Efflorescence (not more than)	20 Bricks Dimensional tolerance (in mm)	
		(1)	(2)	(3)	(4)	
					Length	Width
I. Common burnt clay Building Bricks (IS 1077 – 1976)	35, 50, 75 100, 125	35, 50, 75, 100, 125	< 20%	Moderate	Class A 350 ± 12 mm	180 ± 6 mm
II. Class B Burnt clay facing bricks (IS 2691 – 1972)	150, 175, 200, 250, 300, 350	150, 175, 200, 250, 300, 350	< 15%	Slight	Class B 380 ± 30 mm	180 ± 15 mm
	Class I	100, 75	< 15%	NIL	± 3 mm	± 2 mm
	Class II				± 5 mm	± 3 mm

...Conti.

III. Heavy Duty Burnt clay bricks (IS 2180 – 1970)	400, 450	400 450	< 10%	NIL to Moderate	± 7 mm	± 4 mm
IV. Paving bricks IS 3583 – 1975	–	400	< 5%	–	195 ± 6	4 ± 1.5 9.5 ± 3
V. Soling bricks IS 5779 – 1970	–	50	< 20%	Slight	380 ± 30	180 ± 15 80 ± 6
VI. Sewer bricks IS 4889 – 1968	–	175	< 10%	Slight	19 ± 5	90 ± 2 40 ± 1.5

3.3.4 Efflorescence Test (IS 3495 Part III 1976)

This test is carried out to know whether any alkaline matter, which disfigures plastered / white washed surfaces is present in bricks.

- Five sample bricks taken at random are selected and are placed on end in a dish containing distilled water, so that the depth of immersion of brick is not less than 2.5 cm. The dish is kept in a well ventilated room, till brick absorbs water completely. The dish is refilled with distilled water to the same depth and the brick is allowed to absorb water/evaporate water.
- The disk is kept in a ventilated room, till bricks absorbs water completely.
- The disk is refilled.

Due to absorption of water, alkalies present in the brick get dissolved and cause efflorescence.

The efflorescence is recorded as under :

- **Nil :** When there is no perceptible deposit of efflorescence.
- **Slight :** When not more than 10% of the area of the brick is covered with a thin deposit of salts.
- **Moderate :** When there is a heavier deposit covering upto 60% of the brick surface but unaccompanied by powdering or flaking of the surface.
- **Heavy :** When there is heavy deposit of salts covering 50% or more of brick surface but accompanied by powdering or flaking of the surface.
- **Serious :** When there is heavy deposit of salts accompanied by powdering or flaking of the surfaces and tending to increase with repeated wetting of the specimen.

The bricks subjected to heavy or serious efflorescence should not be used for engineering works.

The rating of efflorescence shall not be more than "moderate" upto class 125 and slight for higher classes.

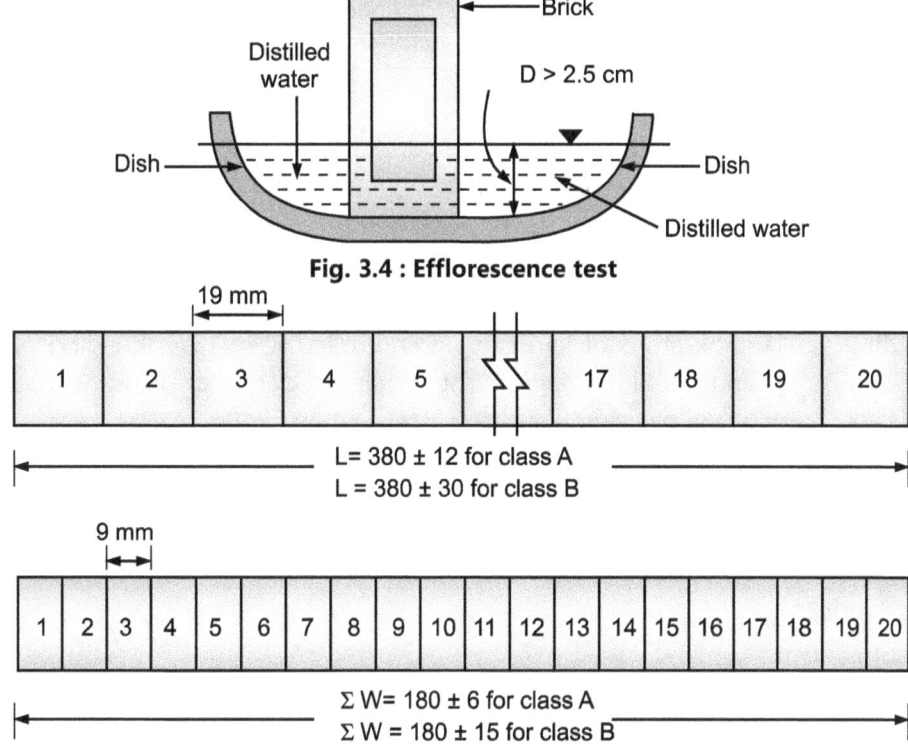

Fig. 3.4 : Efflorescence test

Fig. 3.5 : Dimensional tolerance test on 20 bricks

- **Dolomite Bricks :**
  - Use of Dolomite rock floor is used in manufacture of these bricks. Dolomite rock is broken into pieces, heated at high temperature and then powdered.
  - Such powdered dolomite, is mixed with magnesium carbonate, lime water and bricks are moulded. On drying, the bricks are burnt at temperature less than 1800°C.
  - Comparatively these bricks are less fire resistant than magnesite bricks and contract at high temperature.

3.4 REFRACTORY BRICKS OR FIRE BRICKS

These are the bricks which resist high temperature such as that in the lining of Bessemer converter, open hearth furnaces, copper furnaces, flues of chimnies etc. without softening or melting.

Difference between Ordinary Building Bricks and Refractory Bricks :

1.	Compressive Strength	Maximum compressive strength of ordinary building bricks is about 350 kg/cm², whereas that of fire bricks is upto 1500 kg/cm².
2.	Resistance to Fire	Ordinary bricks resist temperature upto 1200°C, whereas fire bricks can with stand temperature upto 1700°C.

...Conti.

3.	Water Absorption	It is about 15 to 20% for ordinary bricks, whereas that for fire clay bricks is about 4 to 10%.
4.	Brick Size	Standard brick size of Ordinary bricks is $190 \times 90 \times 90$, whereas that of fire clay bricks is $230 \times 65 \times 113$ mm.
5.	Composition	Brick earth suitable for ordinary brick differs from that required for fire clay brick and is given in Table 3.4. Fire resistance increases with increase in percentage of Alumina (in proportion to silica).
6.	Burning and Moulding	Fire clay bricks are always machine moulded and burnt in kiln where temperature of kiln can be controlled. Generally, building bricks are hand moulded and burnt either in clamp or kilns, without much control over temperature.

3.4.1 Classification of Refractory Bricks

Refractory bricks are classified as :

(1) Acid bricks.

(2) Basic bricks.

(3) Neutral bricks.

(1) Acid Bricks :

(a) Fire bricks have the following composition :

- Silica 55 to 75%.
- Alumina 20 to 35%.
- Oxide of iron 2 to 5%.
- Magnesium, Lime 1%.
- Soda, Potash, Alkalis $2\frac{1}{2}$ %.
- Fire Bricks
- Alumina present in brick is responsible for making it fire resistant. However, Alumina is difficult to fuse. Optimum presence of magnesia, lime and alkalis, help in fusing alumina and silica easily, however, excess of the same makes the brick fusiable, and hence unsuitable.
- Fire clay with uniform texture, coarse open grains having greasy feel is more fire resistant.
- Fire bricks are manufactured in the same way as ordinary bricks are manufactured, except the following :
- The bricks are machine moulded and burnt in kiln or a furnace, where temperature can be controlled. The bricks are uniformly burnt at furnace lining temperature of about 1800°C and thereafter allowed to cool gradually. The properties of fire bricks are already covered in last para.

- The best fire clay is available in the seams of coal field of Raniganj and RajMahal in Bihar, Jabalpur, Manglore, Calicut etc.

(b) Silica Bricks

- Silica bricks have comparatively less compressive strength ($= 150$ kg/cm^2) when compared with that of fire bricks
- For manufacture of these bricks, pure silica is obtained from sand stone or quartzite rock. 95% of such finely ground silica is mixed with 2 to 3% of lime or milk of lime.
- The mixture is compressed in mould and allowed to dry and then burnt in furnace. Such bricks are used in the lining of Bessemer converter or Siemen's furnace to resist action of acidic slags or silicous slags.

(c) Sand Lime Bricks : (IS 4139 – 1976)

- These bricks have high compressive strength and low drying shrinkage. Depending upon compressive strength, the bricks are classified in four classes.
- Dimensional requirement and physical characteristics are given in the following tables.

The bricks come in two sizes. The dimensional requirement and tolerances are as under

	Length	Breadth	Height
1.	190 ± 3 mm	90 ± 3 mm	90 ± 2 mm
2.	190 ± 3 mm	90 ± 3 mm	40 ± 2mm

Physical Characteristics

Class	Average compressive strength in kg / cm² (Not less than)	Drying shrinkage % of wet length
75	75	0.025
100	100	0.025
150	150	0.035
200	200	–

(2) Basic Bricks

Magnesite, dolomite bricks come under this category and are used in the lining of furnaces to resist slags having basic properties, such as that in open hearth furnace, blast furnace, copper furnace, cement kiln and other furnaces.

Magnesite Bricks

- As the name suggests, the chief constituent of brick is magnesium oxide. Other oxides such as iron, lime etc. amounting to 10% to 12% are added with it to act as flux.
- The bricks are machine moulded under high pressure and burnt at high temperature.
- Initially, at about 800°C, CO_2 is driven out of magnesium carbonate. On further heating, when it is about to fuse, about 5% of powdered magnesia, small quantities

of magnesium chloride or tar is added, so that the bricks become mouldable. The bricks are then dried and burnt.

(3) Neutral Bricks

These bricks are more inert to action of slags or acidic fumes. Bauxite, chromite and chrome magnesite bricks come under this category.

(a) Bauxite Bricks

- Although these bricks are many times classified as basic bricks, these are actually neutral bricks capable of withstanding action of acid and basic oxides.
- Composition of these bricks resemble that of bauxite rock, hence name bauxite bricks which is Alumina 71%, silica 16%, iron oxide 03%.
- Alumina and iron oxide in above proportion is mixed and heated and then ground to fine powder. To this mixture, about 15 to 30% of fire clay and water is mixed and bricks are moulded.
- On drying, the bricks are burnt at high temperature. However, the burning temperature is less than that in magnesite bricks.

(b) Chromite Bricks and Chrome Magnesite Bricks

Chromite bricks consists of :

- Chromium oxide 50%
- Iron oxide 30%
- Bauxite and Silica 20%.

Chrome magnesite bricks consist of burnt magnesite and chrome ore. These bricks are used in lining of furnaces, flues subjected to either basic or acidic reaction.

3.5 BRICK MASONRY

- Stone masonry has certain limitations and drawbacks such as availability of suitable stones at a economically viable cost, weight, necessity of dressing the stones and resistance to fire.
- Some of these limitations and disadvantages of stone masonry can be overcome by using small sized, light bricks having regular shape and size.
- Strong and beautiful structures have been built using bricks. Brick masonry has certain over-riding advantages over stone masonry, especially where stones of desired quality and quantity can not be made economically available and where bricks can be manufactured easily by making use of locally available clayey soils (with certain modifications).

3.5.1 Comparison of Brick Masonry with Stone Masonry

Following are the advantages of Brick Masonry over Stone Masonry

- **Labour :** Comparatively more number of highly skilled labourers are required to quarry stones, dress them to required size and shape. Further special tools and tackles are required to lift heavy stones; whereas bricks being small, of regular size and shape and light in weight, no dressing is required and no special tools are required for lifting.

- **Time :** Bricks being of regular size and shape, construction of brick masonry is fast.

- **Quantity of Mortar :** Thickness of joint in Ashlar masonry is less; but voids in respect rubble masonry in hearting are more. Hence, more quantity of mortar is required for stone masonry than for brick masonry. For one cubic metre of random rubble masonry about 0.35 to 0.45 cu. m of mortar is required whereas for one cu. m of brick masonry only 0.23 to 0.27 cu. m of mortar is required.

- **Thickness of Wall :** Comparatively thickness of stone masonry wall is more than that of brick masonry. As a result, dead weight of stone masonry is more and lesser carpet area is available.

- **Resistance to Fire :** Brick masonry is comparatively more fire resistant than stone masonry.

However, the brick masonry has the following disadvantages.

- **Strength :** Strength of stone masonry is more than that of brick masonry.

- **Water Tightness :** Stone masonry absorbs less moisture than brick masonry. Therefore, to protect brick masonry from weathering action, external surfaces are required to plastered / pointed.

- **Aesthetical Effects :** Aesthetical effects which can be obtained due to availability of variety of pleasing colours, due to dressing and polishing of stones can not be attained by use of brick masonry.

- **Resistance to Weathering and Maintenance :** Stone masonry is more weather resistant and requires very less maintenance when compared to brick masonry.

1 Size of Brick

Bricks of different sizes are available in market. I.S. advocates use of modular sized bricks, i.e. bricks of size $19 \times 9 \times 9$ cm with a thickness of joint of 1 cm, the nominal dimension would be $20 \times 10 \times 10$ cm. However, despite of advantages of modular size, still in many places use of old sized bricks is continuing.

Standard sizes for 9" bricks as prescribed in various PWDs in India are :

$$9" \times 4\frac{1}{2}" \times 2\frac{1}{2}" \,, \quad 9" \times 4\frac{1}{4}" \times 2\frac{3}{4}" \,, \quad 9" \times 4\frac{3}{8}" \times 2\frac{3}{4}" \,, \quad 8\frac{7}{8}" \times 4\frac{1}{4}" \times 2\frac{3}{4}" \,, \quad 8\frac{7}{8}" \times 4\frac{1}{4}" \times 3" \,,$$

$$8\frac{3}{4}" \times 4\frac{1}{4}" \times 2\frac{3}{4}"$$

Now-a-days, wider bricks popularly known as "Thokala Bricks" of size $8\frac{1}{2}" \times 6" \times 3\frac{1}{2}"$ are also available in market.

3.6 CLASSIFICATION OF BRICKS

I.S. does not classify bricks into first class brick, second class brick and third class brick. However, in many organizations such as PWD, MES etc. bricks are classified as first class, second class and third class bricks. The difference between these three bricks and three classes of brick masonry is summarized as under.

No.		1st Class Bricks	2nd Class Brick	3rd Class Brick
1.	Burning	Well burnt	Slightly over burnt but not vitrified	Under burnt
2.	Colour	Uniformly reddish	Non - uniform	Yellowish
3.	Shape and size	Regular, sharp, straight and right angled edges	Somewhat irregular with rough surface	May be distorted with round edges.
4.	Sound when struck	Clear ringing	Clear ringing	Dull sound
5.	Water absorption %	< 20%	< 22%	< 25%
		When soaked in water for 24 hours		
6.	Efflorescence	Not appreciable when dried in shed	Not appreciable either in wet or dry state	Moderate signs of efflorescence
7.	Curshing strength	$\geq 105 \text{ kg / cm}^2$	$\geq 70 \text{ kg / cm}^2$	–
8.	Flaws	Free from flaws, cracks, chips, nodules of lime or kankar	Slight chips or flaws or surface cracks but free from lime.	–
9.	Uses	All masonry works, Floaring, Face work, reinforced brick work	In unimportant works interior walls	Inferior and temporary buildings if not subjected to heavy rains, scaffolding and centering.
10.	Thickness of joint	For 1st class brick masonry thickness of joint should not be more than 10 mm	< 12 mm	–

3.7 TERMS USED IN BRICK MASONRY　　　　　　(Nov.15)

Various terms used in brick masonry are explained as follows :

- **Arrises :** The edges formed by the intersection of plane surfaces of a brick are called the arrises and they should be sharp, square and free from damage.
- **Quoin :** A corner or external angle on the face side of a wall is called as Quoin.

- **Course :** It is a complete layer of brick or stone, laid on the same bed. A header course consists of only headers whereas stretcher course consists of stretchers only as seen in elevation. In general, the courses are of the same height.
- **Bond :** It is the method of arranging bricks in courses so that the individual units are tied together. Bonds are distinguished by their face appearance or elevation.
- **Bed Joint :** The horizontal layer of mortar upon which bricks are laid is known as a bed joint.
- **Lap :** The horizontal distance between the vertical joints in successive courses is termed as a lap and for a good bond, it should be one-fourth of the length of a brick.
- **Stretcher :** This is a brick laid with its length parallel to the face or front or direction of a wall. The course containing stretchers is called a stretcher course.
- **Header :** This is a brick laid with its breadth or width parallel to the face or front or direction of a wall. The course containing headers is called a header course.
- **Perpends :** The vertical joints separating the bricks in either length or cross directions are known as perpends and for a good bond, the perpends in alternate courses should be vertically one above the other.

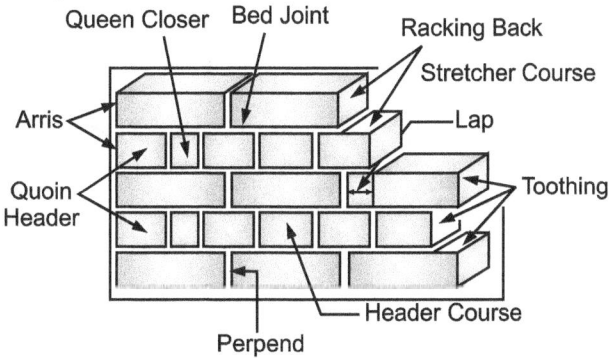

Fig. 3.6 : Brick terms

3.8 CLOSERS

- If joints of successive courses come in one line, then the strength of joint will be reduce. To prevent this, a piece of brick which is used to close up the bond at the end of course is called a closer.
- These are usually prepared by cutting brick. (i.e. usually these are not specially moulded). Sometimes, bricks are cut using trowel. However, with trowel accurate surface is not obtained. Bricks cut using bolster chisel give accurate surface.

Types of Closers

Following are the types of closers :

1. King closer
2. Queen closer
3. Bevelled closer and
4. Mitred closer.

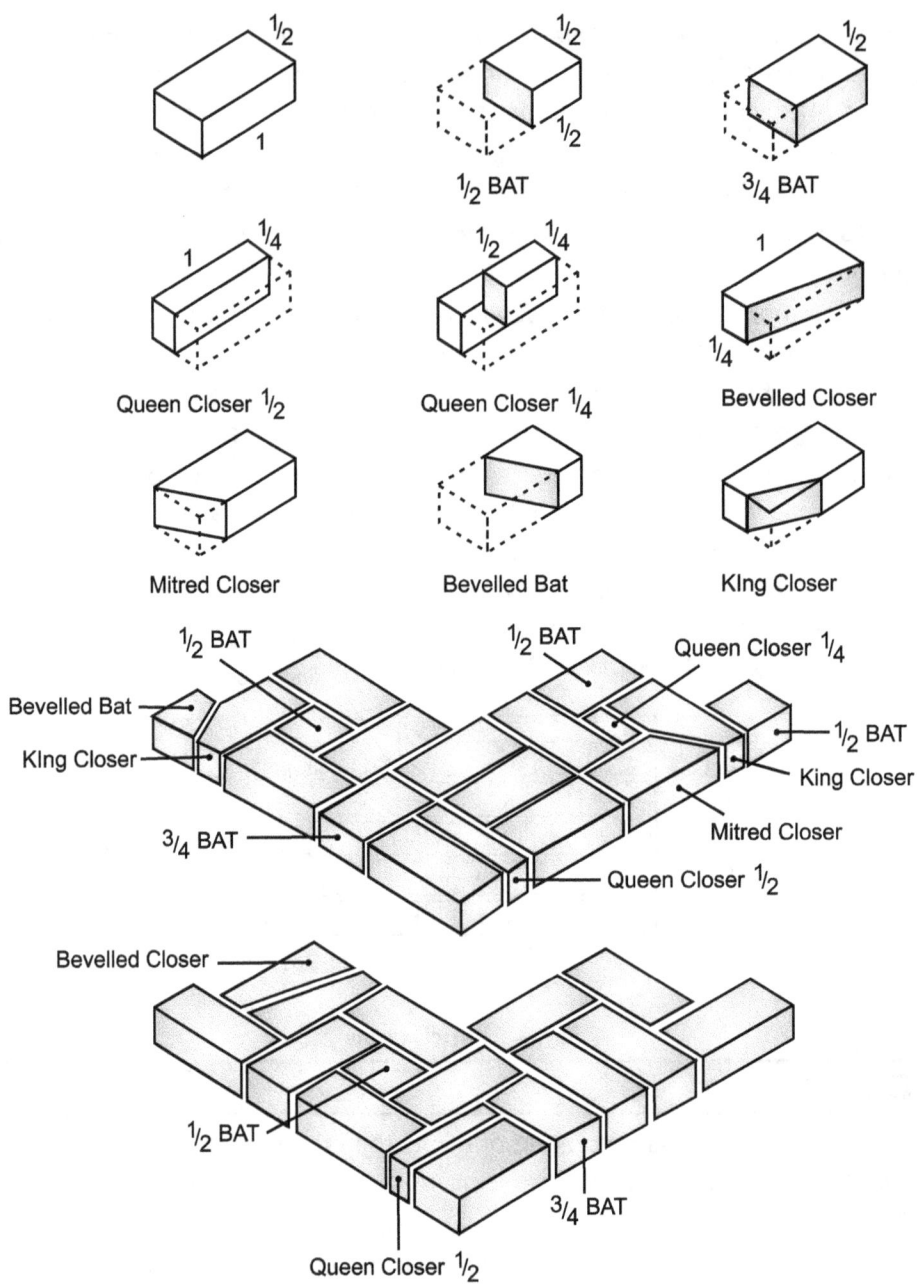

Fig. 3.7 : Types of closers

King Closer : As shown in adjoining Fig. 3.7, it is formed by removing / cutting triangular portion of brick at its half length and half width. The volume of portion removed will be $\frac{1}{16}$th of the volume of brick. King closer is more useful near door and window openings to get proper joints.

Queen Closer $\frac{1}{2}$: It is formed by cutting a brick longitudinally into placed near Quoin header to close the bond. It differs from half bat. In case of bat, brick is cut width-wise, whereas queen closer is formed by cutting brick length-wise. [Size = $L \times \frac{w}{2} \times h$]

Mitred Closer and Bevelled closer : Mitred closer is formed by cutting a triangular portion of brick, across width, and at an angle ranging from 45° to 60°, with the length of brick to suit joint at corner or junction, whereas bevelled closer is formed by removing a triangular portion of brick of size $\left(L \times \frac{w}{2} \times h \right)$.

It may be noted that, volume of brick cut and removed in case of queen closer is double the volume of brick cut and removed in respect of bevelled closer.

Half Bat and Three Quarter Bat : Half bat is formed by cutting brick into two equal parts width wise. Three quarter bat is formed by removing 25% of brick by cutting brick widthwise as shown in Fig. 3.7.

$$\text{Half bat} = \left(\text{size} = \frac{L}{2} \times w \times h \right)$$

$$\text{Three quarter bat size} = 3\,\frac{L}{4} \times w \times h$$

Queen Closer $\frac{1}{4}$: It is a cut brick having length and width equal to half length and half width of full brick i.e. $\frac{l}{2} \times \frac{w}{2} \times h$.

Volume of brick removed from the full size brick (of dimension $l \times w \times h$) in respect of King closer, bevelled closer, queen closer $\frac{1}{2}$, queen closer $\frac{1}{4}$, is $6\frac{1}{4}$ % , 25%, 50% and 75% respectively.

3.9 SPECIALLY SHAPED BRICKS

- In order to obtain architectural effects, bricks having special surfaces are moulded. These are used in face work, such as that in side walks, steps, copings, garden walls.

- A moulded brick with single rounded angle is called as bull-nose, whereas a moulded brick with double angle is called as cow-nose. Some of specially shaped bricks are shown in Fig. 3.8.

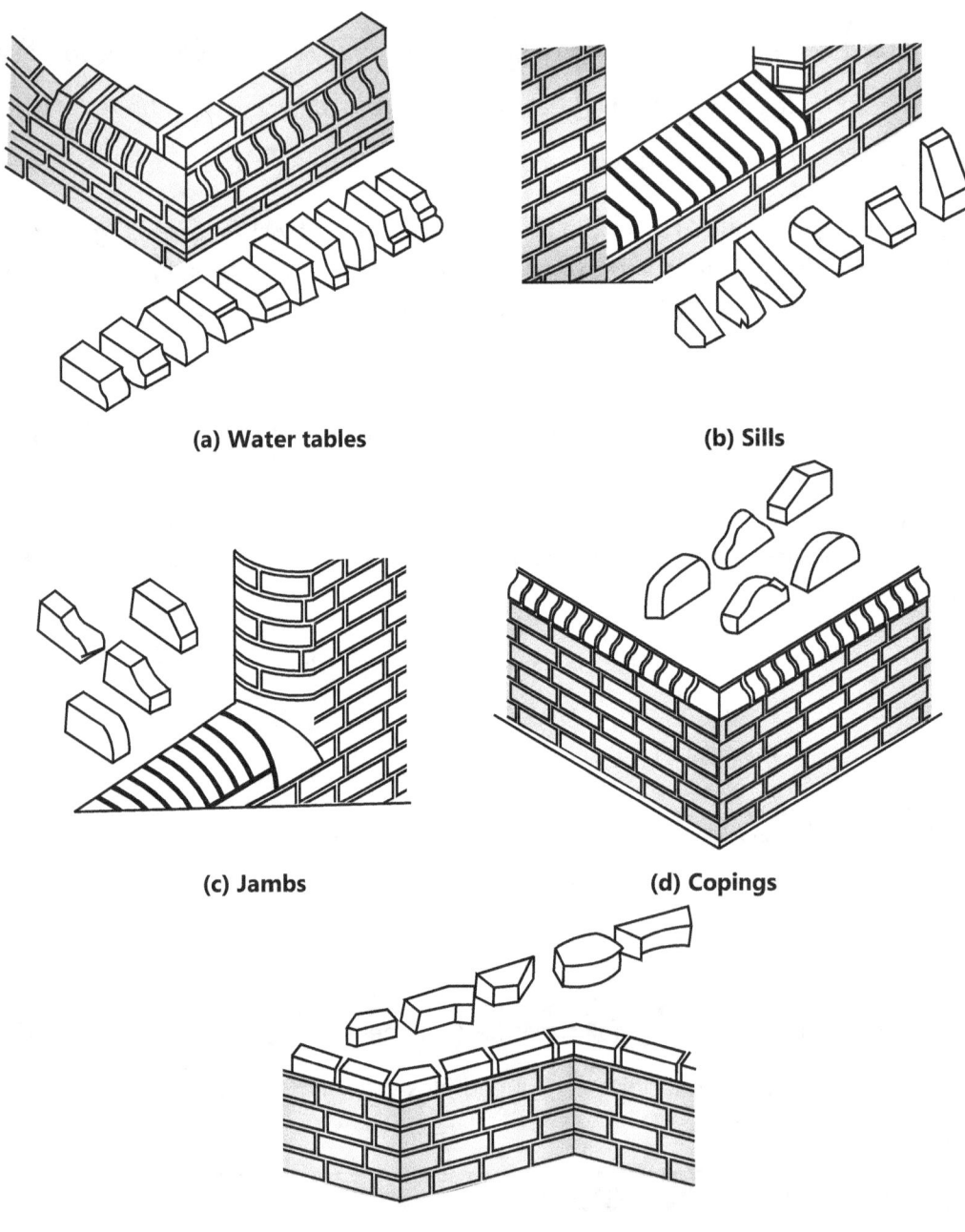

(a) Water tables   **(b) Sills**

(c) Jambs   **(d) Copings**

(e) Angles and radials

Fig. 3.8 : Some commonly used custom brick shapes. Notice that each water table, jamb and coping brick shape requires special inside and outside corner bricks as well as the basic row lock or header brick. The angle bricks are needed to make neat corners walls that meet at other than right angles.

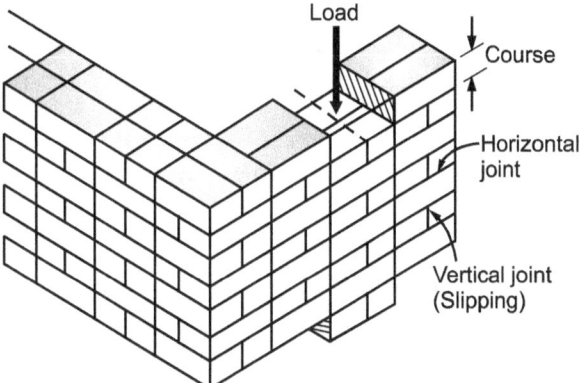

(a) Brick wall with continuous vertical joint

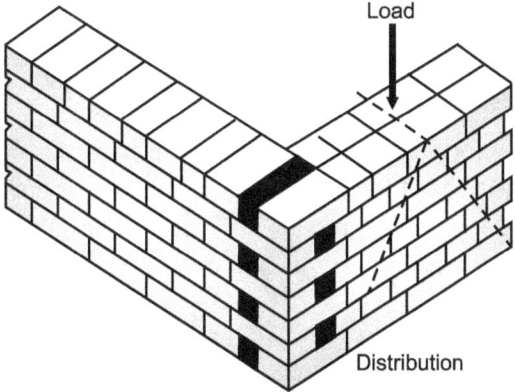

(b) Brick wall with staggered vertical joint

Fig. 3.9

Bond In Brick Masonry

- It is arrangement of bricks in courses so that various units in horizontal and vertical layers are interlocked properly so as to make brick work as good, strong and pleasing as possible.
- If continuous vertical joint as in Fig. 3.9 (a) is present, then the bricks will separate from each other by shearing mortar. However, with vertical joints as shown in Fig. 3.9 (b) the load gets distributed.

How good bonding is achieved ?

Good bonding can be achieved by observing the following :

- Length of brick should twice the width plus one joint thickness and all bricks should be of uniform size and shape.
- Vertical joints in alternate courses should be in plumb.
- Bricks in one course should overlap those in the course below by 1/4th brick along length of wall; and by 1/2 brick across thickness of wall. This achieved in English bond by using Queen closer.
- Least number of brick bats should be used.

3.9.1 Mortar Selection

Requirements of a good mortar for masonry are :

- Strength
- Workability
- Water retaintivity and
- Low drying shrinkage.

- Mortar strength should not be in general greater than that of masonry unit. Mortar should harden to such an extent that it can carry the weight of masonry unit, without crushing and it should be plastic enough to take varying sizes of bricks, stones etc.
- Mortar should not deteriorate due to weathering action of rain and atmospheric changes.
- A mortar of sand and cement is durable and is used for all masonry work below ground level and all masonry work exposed to weather. Cement mortar has greater compressive strength than required, and is not very plastic. Hence, many times mixture of lime and cement with sand is used.
- Richer the mix of the mortar, greater is the compressive strength and weaker the mix, greater is the ability of mortar to accommodate moisture or temperature movements.
- The following Table 3.3 gives compressive strengths of some of commonly used mortars, optimum mortar mixes for maximum masonry strengths and locations, where the mix can be used.
- The mortars recommended exhibit creep and plastic flow, which will undoubtedly relieve high stresses and reduce risk of cracking in the masonry work.

Table 3.3 : Showing mix of mortar, minimum compressive strength of mortar and matching masonry unit strength

Sr. No.	Mortar mix by volume Cement lime sand			Minimum compressive strength of mortar [in N/mm^2]	Suitable for masonry unit strength	Situation where to be used
1.	1	0	3	10	25 or above	Sills, copings and retaining walls
	1	0. 25	3			
2.	1	0	4	7.5	15 to 24.9	Parapets and chimneys
	1	0.5	4.5	6		
3.	1	0	5	5	5 to 14.9	Walls below damp proof course
	1	1	6	3		
4.	1	0	6	3	below 5	Walls above D.P.C
	1	2	9	2		
5.	1	0	8	0.7		Internal walls and light weight block
	1	3	12			

- In conclusion, it can be said that, although mortar forms only a small proportion of brickwork as a whole, its characteristics, nevertheless, do have a significant effect, particularly in relation to movements, both within the wall itself and with adjacent parts of the structure.

- It is not only uneconomical but also very unwise to specify mortars stronger than necessary. This is particularly so with low strength units, which have been known to show signs of distress due to such practices.

- Fig. 3.10 shows permissible compressive stress in tons/m² for different types of masonry. From this Fig. 3.10 it will be seen that, (except for Ashlar masonry) strength of cement concrete masonry with mix 1 : 4 : 8, is more than any other masonry. The advantages that brick masonry has over other stone masonry are also evident.

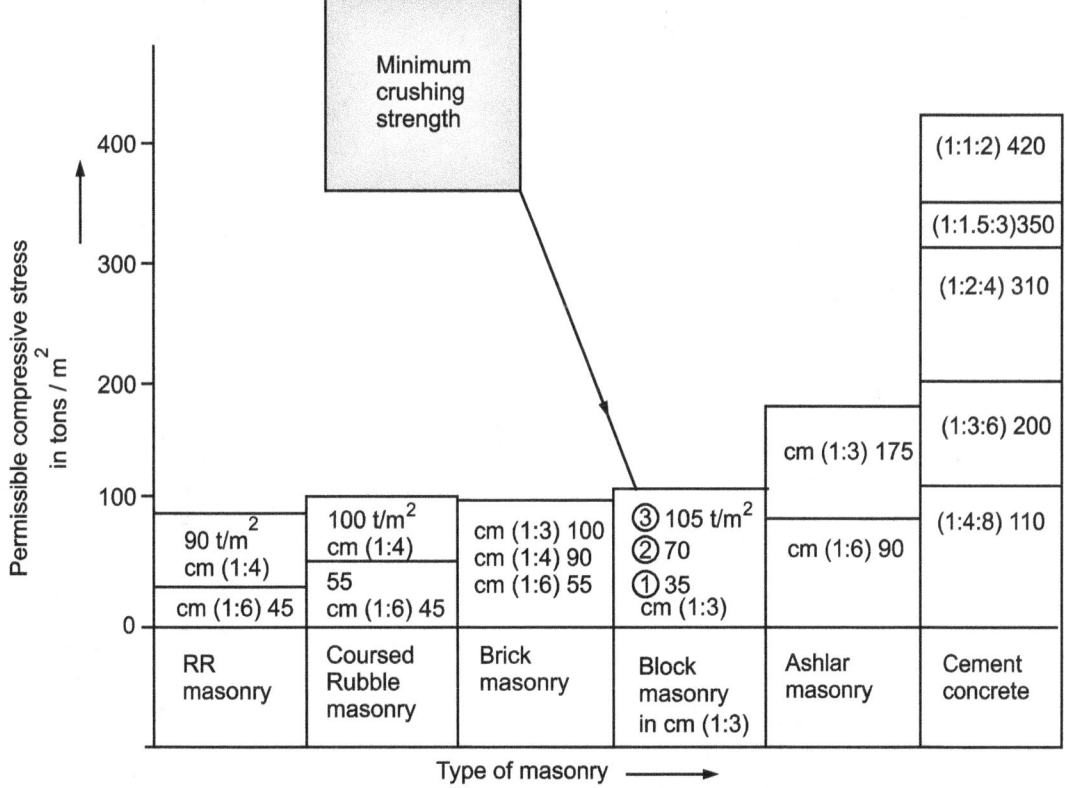

Fig. 3.10 : Permissible compressive stress in different types of masonry

3.10 TYPES OF BOND   (May 17, Dec. 13)

Following are some of the types of bonds used in brick masonry :

1. English bond
2. Single and double Flemish bond
3. Header bond
4. Stretcher bond
5. Herring bone bond
6. Diagonal bond
7. Garden wall bond.

3.10.1 English Bond   (May 17, Dec. 14, May 15)

This bond is considered as the strongest in brick work and is used extensively. Following are the features of English bond. (Refer Fig. 3.11 and 3.12).

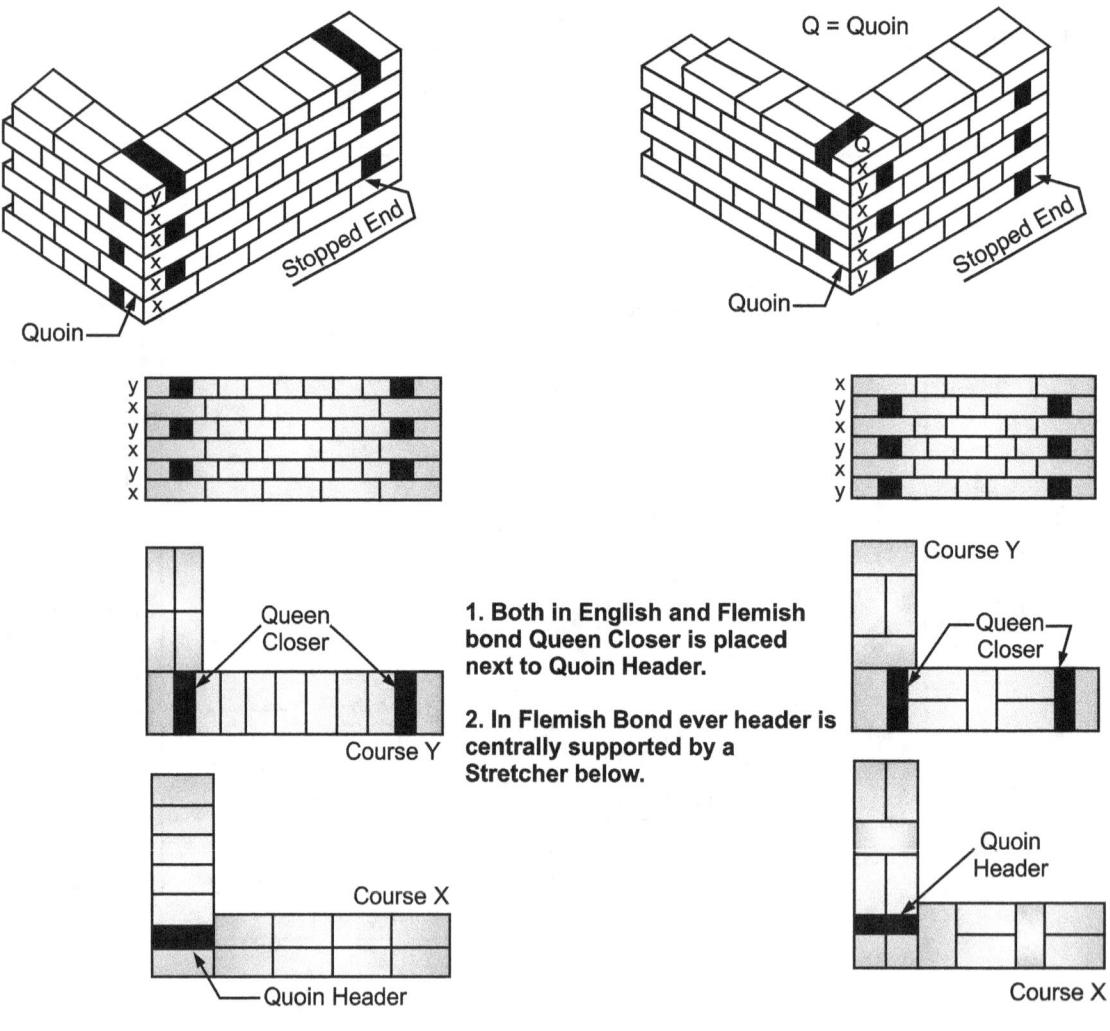

1. Both in English and Flemish bond Queen Closer is placed next to Quoin Header.

2. In Flemish Bond ever header is centrally supported by a Stretcher below.

English Bond   **Flemish Bond**

Fig. 3.11 : Brick wall with corner and stopped end

- Queen closer is placed next to Quoin header and Queen closer is not required in stretcher course.
- In alternate courses headers and stretchers are provided.
- No continuous vertical joint is formed.
- Lap between header and stretcher course in successive courses is not less than $1/4^{th}$ of length of brick.
- For 1, 2 and 3 brick thick wall in both front and rear elevation, the same course shows headers or stretchers.
- However, for $1\frac{1}{2}$, and $2\frac{1}{2}$ thick brick wall, if header is in front elevation, stretcher will be seen in rear elevation for the same course.
- Since, the number of joints in header courses are double than that in stretcher course, these joints should be thin, so that desired lap is maintained.

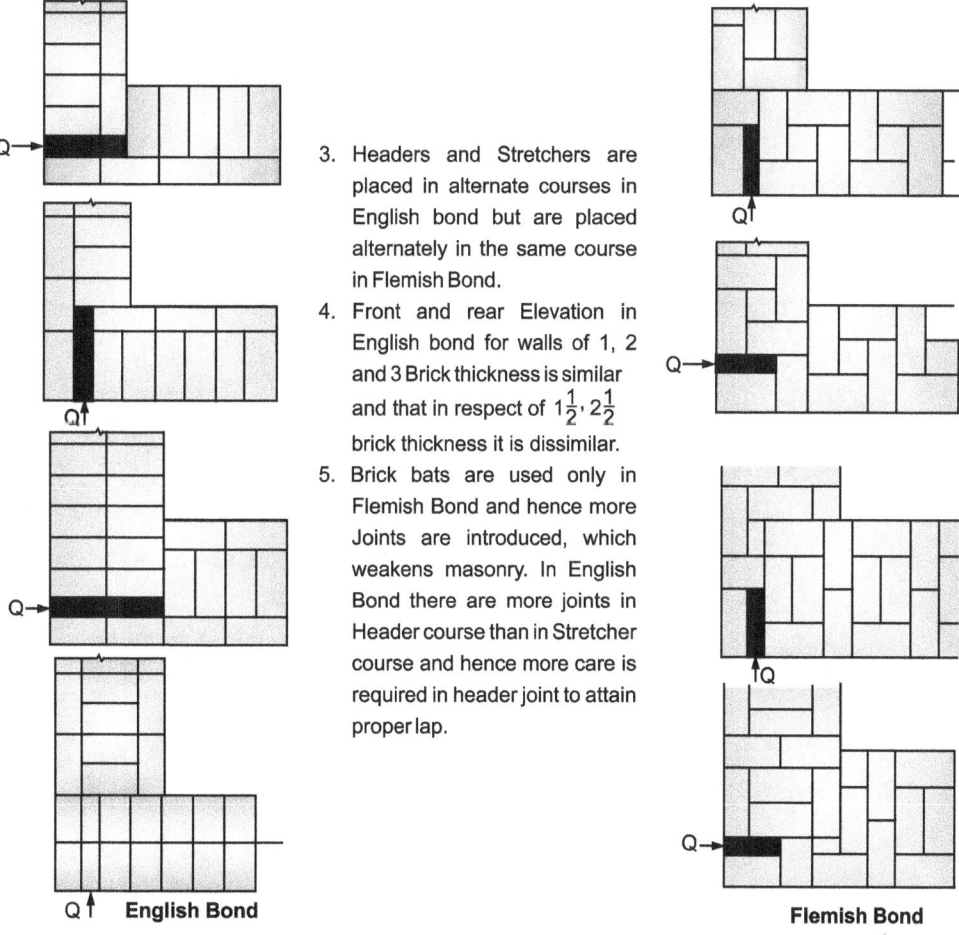

3. Headers and Stretchers are placed in alternate courses in English bond but are placed alternately in the same course in Flemish Bond.

4. Front and rear Elevation in English bond for walls of 1, 2 and 3 Brick thickness is similar and that in respect of $1\frac{1}{2}, 2\frac{1}{2}$ brick thickness it is dissimilar.

5. Brick bats are used only in Flemish Bond and hence more Joints are introduced, which weakens masonry. In English Bond there are more joints in Header course than in Stretcher course and hence more care is required in header joint to attain proper lap.

English Bond   **Flemish Bond**

Fig. 3.12 : Plans of alternate courses in English and Flemish bond for $1\frac{1}{2}$ and 2 brick thick walls

3.10.2 Flemish Bond

The Following are the Main Features of this Bond

- In this bond, in the same course, headers and stretchers are placed alternately.

- As in English bond, Queen closer is placed next to Queen header.

- Every header is centrally supported by a stretcher below; and hence gives pleasing appearance in elevation.

- In English bond, in case of walls of thickness of 1, 2 or 3 bricks, only front and back elevation is similar; and is dissimilar in case of $1\frac{1}{2}$, $2\frac{1}{2}$ thick walls. However, in Flemish bond, walls of all thickness have similar elevation both in front elevation and rear elevation. Only difference is that, for walls of thickness of $1\frac{1}{2}$, $2\frac{1}{2}$ bricks, quarter bat is used in the hearting portion, whereas no such bats are required in respect of 2 or 3 brick thick wall.

Comparison between English and Flemish Bond

- Brick work in English bond having thickness 2 bricks and more, is stronger than that in Flemish bond.

- In general more care is required to be taken while using Flemish bond. Pleasing appearance which can be had in Flemish bond is lost, if thickness of joint is not maintained. In case of English bond, more care is required to taken while laying header course, since number of joints in header course are double that in stretcher course.

- While constructing $1\frac{1}{2}$, $2\frac{1}{2}$ walls, use of bats is made in Flemish bond. As such, material cost is less in Flemish bond. But strength is reduced due to increase in number of joints in Flemish.

- Walls in English bond are monotonous bond have pleasing appearance. However, unless bricks have regular size, shape and sharp edges, Flemish bond should not be used.

- If brick work is to be plastered, it is advisable to use English bond than Flemish bond.

3.10.3 Stretcher Bond For 1/2 Brick Walls

As name implies, all courses are laid as stretchers only; and that there are no headers. From plan and elevation, it is clear that, with this bond only 1/2 brick thick walls, (as in partition walls) can be constructed.

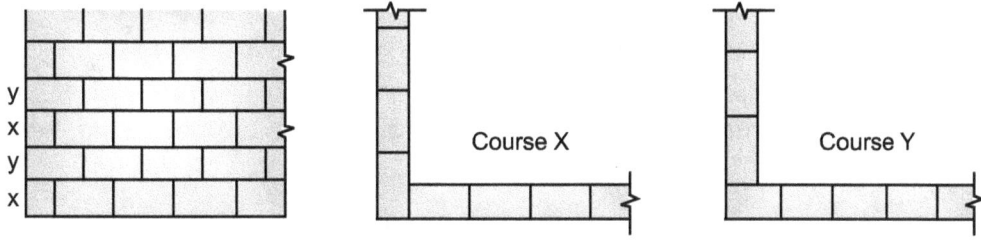

Fig. 3.13 : Stretcher bond

3.10.4 Header Bond For 1 Brick Wall   (Dec. 13

In this bond, as the name implies, the bricks are laid with their ends towards the face of wall (like headers). There are no stretchers; and hence, wall of 1 brick thickness only can be constructed. The bond does not possess sufficient strength to transmit load, in the direction of the length of wall. However, with this bond, walls having curvature can be constructed as headers can be cut to suit curvature; whereas cutting of stretchers is quite inconvenient.

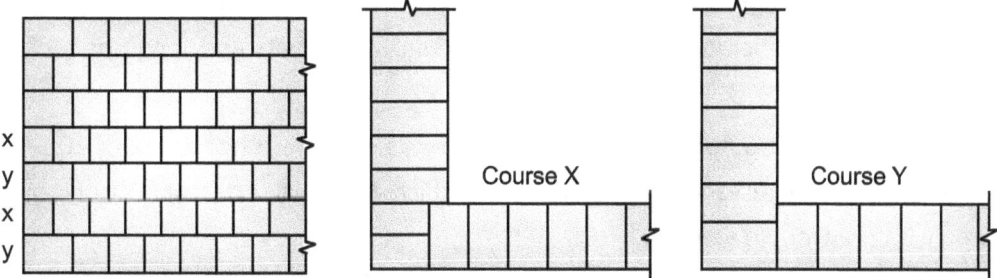

Fig. 3.14: Header bond

3.11 COLUMNS IN ENGLISH AND FLEMISH BONDS

Following are the features of square columns in English and Flemish bond :

(a) One Brick Thick Column :

(i)   In English bond, it can be constructed by laying two bricks side by side. Each of the next course is laid at right angles to the previous course.

(ii) It may be noted that one brick pier in flemish bond is not possible.

(b) $1\frac{1}{2}$ Brick Thick Column :

(i)   In English bond, it can be constructed either by laying 2 numbers of 3/4th bat side by side and 3 numbers of full bricks. It can also be constructed by using 6 numbers of 3/4th bats.

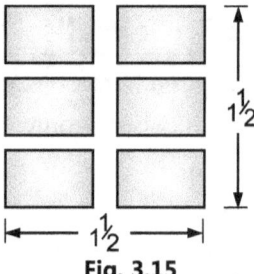

Fig. 3.15

However, columns constructed by using this second alternative, are not strong, hence are avoided.

(ii) In Flemish bond, $1\frac{1}{2}^{th}$ brick columns can be constructed by using 4 numbers of 3/4th

bat and centrally placed half bat. This column in Flemish bond is comparatively weaker than that in English bond, since, more number of joints are introduced.

(c) 2 Brick Thick Column in English Bond :

- Here use of 6 bricks of full length and 4 Queen closers is made 2 brick thick column. Each of the next course is laid at right angles to the previous course.

- Two brick columns in Flemish bond are constructed by making use of 10 pieces consisting of 4 brick of full length, 4 numbers of 3/4th bats and 2 numbers of queen closers.

It is clear that, as against 6 numbers of full length bricks, in English bond, use of 10 pieces in flemish bond is made. As a result, work with English bond is faster and stronger, when compared with the work in Flemish bond.

3.12 JUNCTIONS

Special care is required to be taken when two walls of same thickness or different thickness either meet or cross each other at right angles. Cracks are likely to be developed, if proper bond is not provided.

- Use of tie brick is made, which header course of cross wall enters into stretcher course of main wall. There is no difference in tie brick and full brick. Only difference is in method of laying. Half of tie brick enters into main wall, half of tie brick projects outside main wall, thereby strengthening locking between main wall and cross wall.

- No tie brick is required, when stretcher course of cross wall meets cross wall. It merely abuts the main wall.

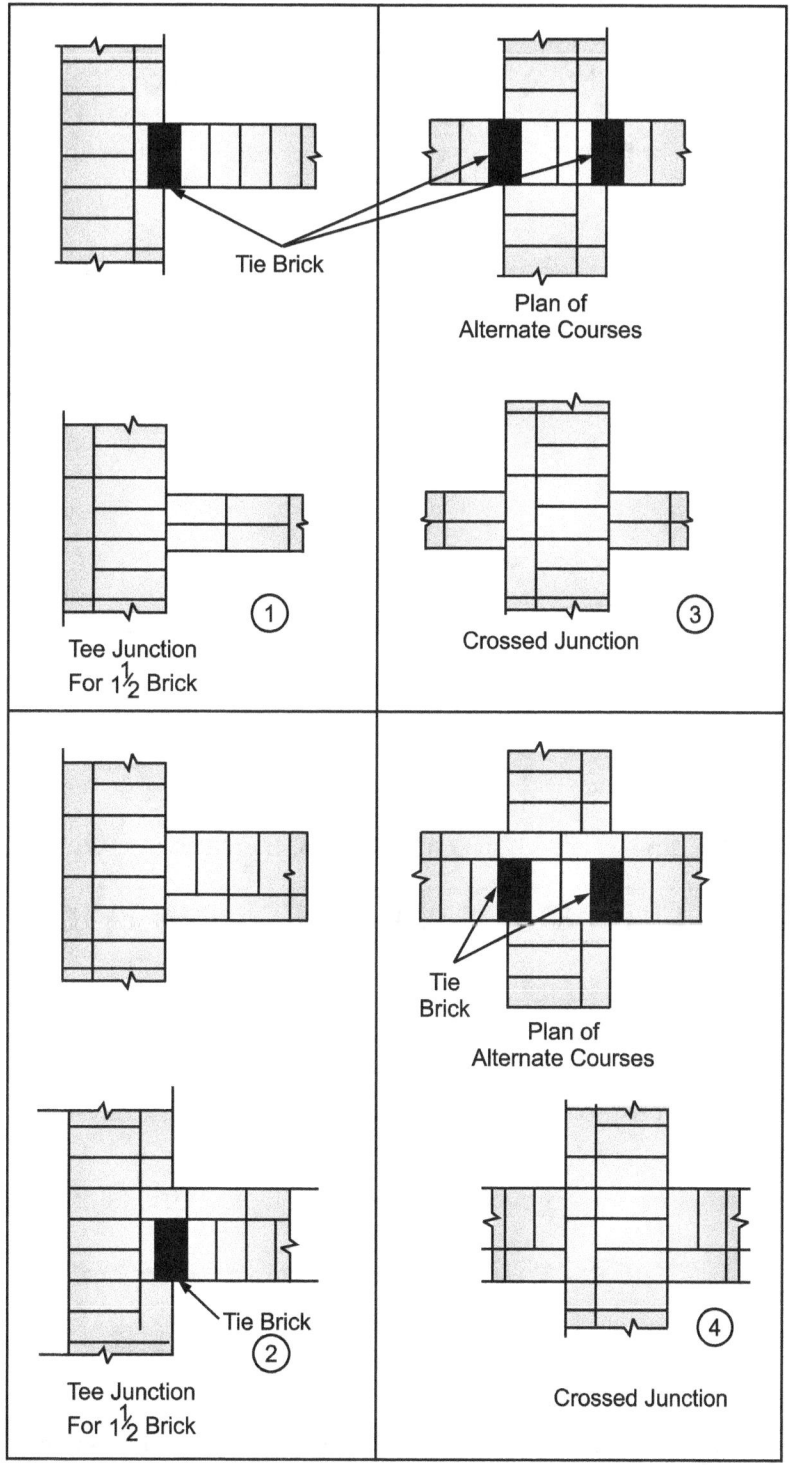

Fig. 3.16 : Tee junction and crossed junction for $1\frac{1}{2}$ brick walls

3.12.1 Squint Junction

When two walls meet each other at an angle other than right angle, the junction formed is called as squint junction. These are difficult to construct. Alternate course of (a) acute and (b) obtuse squint junctions both in English bond and Flemish bond are shown in Fig. 3.21.

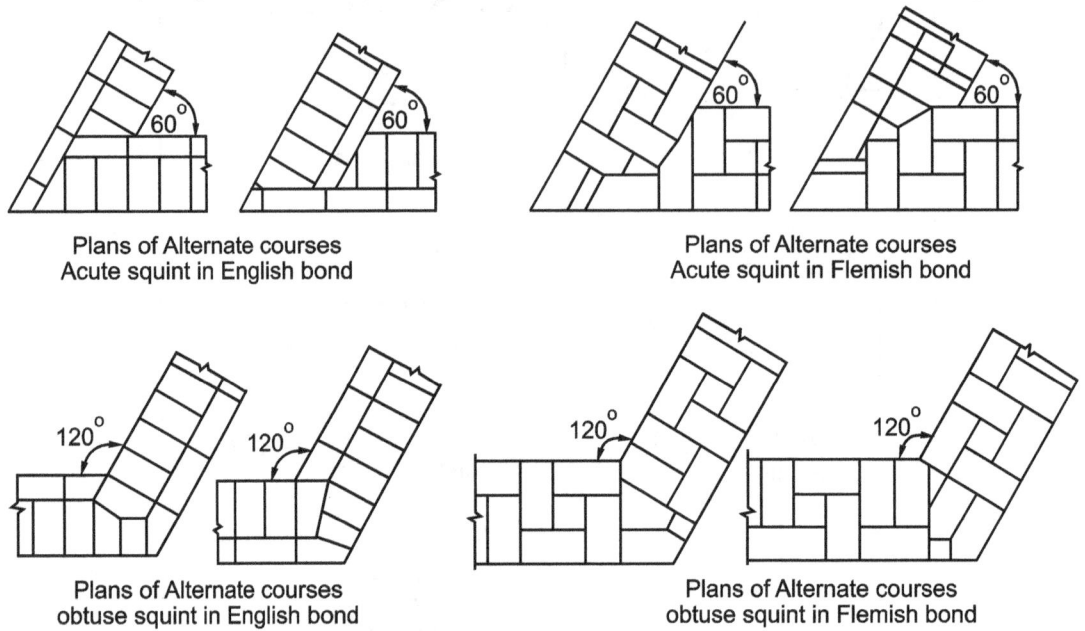

Plans of Alternate courses
Acute squint in English bond

Plans of Alternate courses
Acute squint in Flemish bond

Plans of Alternate courses
obtuse squint in English bond

Plans of Alternate courses
obtuse squint in Flemish bond

Fig. 3.17 : Squints in English bond and Flemish bond for $1\frac{1}{2}$ brick wall

3.13 COPINGS, SILLS, JAMBS AND CORBELS IN BRICK WORK

3.13.1 Copings

These are the coverings provided on the top of parapet and are designed to throw off rainwater etc. efficiently. To make coping attractive, different shapes such as saddle back, semi circular, bull nose chamfered stone creasing etc. are shown in Fig. 3.19 (A) and Fig. 3.19 (B). The following points should be noted.

The bricks used in copings should be strong, durable and non absorbant and should be laid in cm (1 : 4).

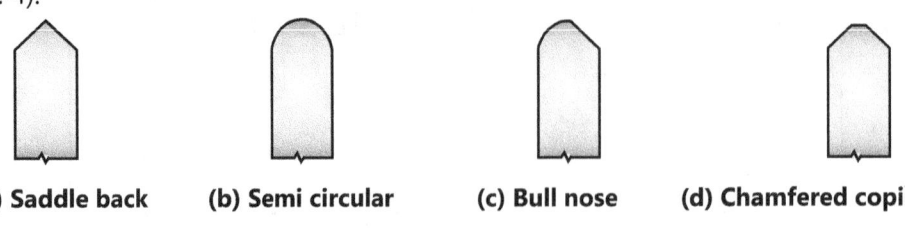

(a) Saddle back   **(b) Semi circular**   **(c) Bull nose**   **(d) Chamfered coping**

Fig. 3.18 : Types of copings

3.13.2 Sills

Sills are provided in window openings to give pleasing appearance and to protect wall below from direct rain. The projection of sill beyond wall should be more than 5 cm and should be properly throated. To prevent ingress of dampness, Damp-proof course is provided below sill.

3.13.3 Jambs

These are the vertical sides of openings left in walls to receive doors, windows, fire places etc.

(a) Square Jambs : Here bricks are bonded suitably as in case of dead ends. These are relatively easy to construct, but in due course of time when plaster or pointing becomes defective, allow free passage to rain and wind, and therefore are not desirable. They are provided, when opening is sheltered.

(b) Recessed or Rebated Jambs : These consist of recesses in which doors and window frames can fit. Rebated jambs provide an effective means of preventing entry of water. Depth of recess may be 5 or 10 cm.

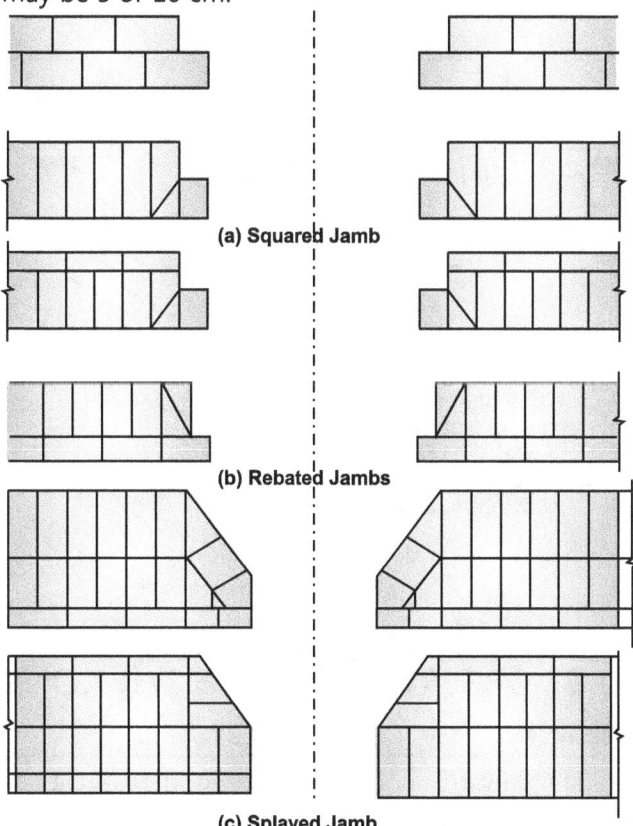

(a) Squared Jamb

(b) Rebated Jambs

(c) Splayed Jamb

Fig. 3.19 : Types of jambs

(c) Splayed Jambs : Splayed jambs are provided in thick walls. Aesthetically not only they are better, but also allow more light in rooms; and strong to withstand forces from arches and lintels. Fig. 3.20 shows alternate courses of the three types of jambs mentioned above.

3.13.4 Corbels

- These are the projections from a wall to serve as end support to beams, lintels etc. However, if these projections are too large and if there is not sufficient counter weight, it may cause instability. Hence, maximum projection is limited to the thickness of wall and projection of each corbel course is limited to $\frac{1}{4}$ th brick thickness.

- Lesser the projection, better is stability. Corbels may be either isolated or continuous.
- More care is required to taken if corbel is isolated. To distribute load effectively, wall plate in the form of strong stone block or concrete block is provided, on topmost corbel, which receives load from beam.
- Headers provide better bonding, hence, they are used to form corbel courses. The work should be closely supervised, since bad workmanship is likely to lead to cracks and instability.

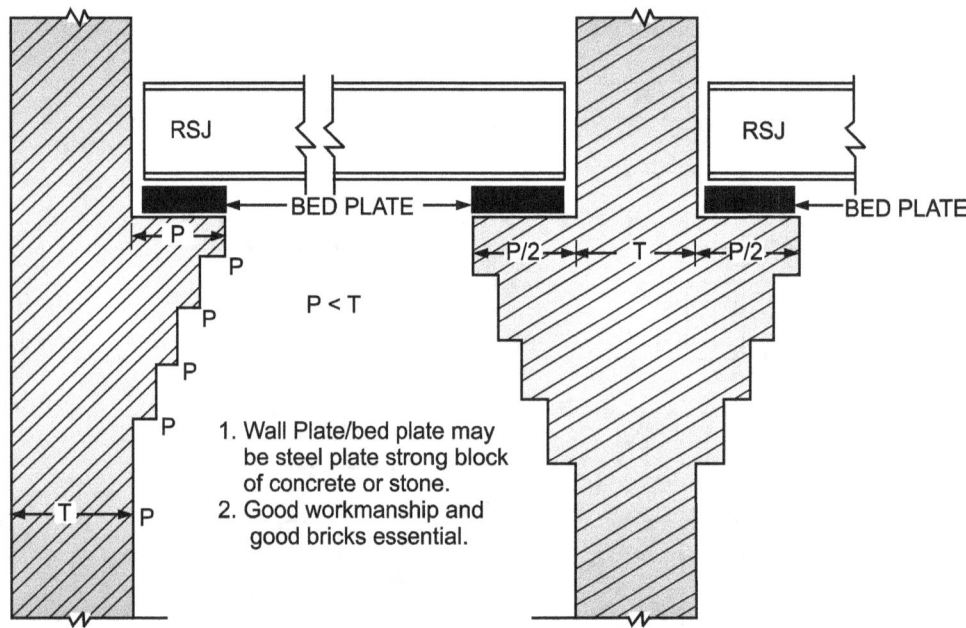

Fig. 3.20 : Types of corbels

3.14 POINTS TO BE OBSERVED DURING THE CONSTRUCTION OF BRICK MASONRY   (May 14)

- The bricks to be used in the work should be of appropriate quality as regards size, shape, burning, strength, efflorescence etc.
- In order that brick do not absorb water from mortar, bricks should be soaked in water at least for 2 hours before use. This also helps in spreading of mortar uniformly, washing of kiln dust and proper adhering of mortar to bricks.
- Next to quoin header, queen closer is placed.

- Mortar is spread over the first course to a thickness of 1 cm. End stretcher is placed in position and hammered down till thickness of joint is one cm.
- Corners of wall are built upto certain height first, and then by making use of reference monuments, "line dori" and "plumb bob", wall are constructed in line, level and in plumb.
- When wall is built upto the height of wall near corner, brick work near the corner is raised further and construction is raised further and work proceeds further.
- All the walls should be raised uniformly and difference between levels of any two portions of walls, should not be more than 1 metre. This will ensure uniform distribution of load and will avoid uneven settlement.
- As work proceeds, joints in the brick work should be raked out to depth of about 1 cm. This will help in having proper key to plastering or pointing.
- As far as possible double scaffolding should be provided, so as to avoid making holes in masonry to support cantilever scaffolding.
- In order to have proper grip with previous brick work, either steps are provided or toothing is provided.
- Previous days work is roughened and cleaned, while starting next day's work.
- Brick work should be cured for 2 to 3 weeks.

REVIEW QUESTIONS

1. Compare English bond and Double flexmish bond with suitable sketch.
2. State the precautions to be taken in brick masonry construction.
3. State four important advantages of usng hollow concrete block masonry.
4. State four important tests and significance of each test for bricks.
5. Illustrate neat sketch of successive courses in plan and elevation to illustrate construction of brick wall $1\frac{1}{2}$ brick thick in Flemish Bond.
6. Compare the stone masonry with brick masonry with regards to the different points.
7. Draw neat sketches in plans and elevation to illustrate the construction of $2\frac{1}{2}$ brick thick wall in English bond at a right angled corner.
8. Illustrate neat sketch of successive courses in plan and elevation to illustrate construction of brick wall $1\frac{1}{2}$ thick in English bond.
9. Write down detailed test procedure to test efflorescence test of brick.
10. Compare English bond and Flemish bond.
11. Describe the compressive strength test on brick.
12. Define bond. Give the detailed sketch of stretcher bond. State the uses of stretcher bond.
13. Describe masonry. Enlist the different units of masonry.

14. Describe the following with sketches :
    (a)   Header stone   (b) Queen closer
    (c)   Mitred closer   (d) Through stone
15. Write down detailed test procedure to test efflorescence test of bricks.
16. What is the significance of bonding in brick work ? Explain by sketches the difference between English bond and Flemish bond.
17. Explain in short 'Defects in Brickwork'.
18. Explain the method of construction of reinforced brick wall and state situation where its use is recommended.
19. Describe the construction of reinforced brick lintels.
20. Explain the situations in which reinforced brick masonry is used.
21. Describe the construction of reinforced brick column.

SOLVED UNIVERSITY QUESTIONS

DEC. 2013

1. Define bond. State different types of bonds. Explain header bond with sketch.   **[6]**
   [**Ans.:** Refer Article 3.10, 3.10.4]

MAY 2014

1. Explain the construction procedure for Reinforced Brick Masonry.   **[6]**
   [**Ans.:** Refer Article 3.14]

DEC. 2014

1. Write short notes on: (ii) English bond.   **[6]**
   [**Ans.:** Refer Article 3.10.1]

MAY 2015

1. Discuss the properties of a good brick used in construction.   **[6]**
   [**Ans.:** Refer Article 3.3]
2. Write a short note on English bond with a neat labelled diagram.   **[6]**
   [**Ans.:** Refer Article 3.10.1]

NOV. 2015

1. Define the following : (iii) Bond.
   [**Ans.:** Refer Article 3.7]

May 2017

1. Enlist various types of Bonds Explain any one with a neat figure.   [6]
   [**Ans.:** Refer Articles 3.10, 3.10.1]

CHAPTER 4
BLOCK MASONRY

4.1 INTRODUCTION

- Block masonry units, whether solid or hollow, are becoming increasingly popular in construction industry. Various materials are in use for manufacturing of blocks.
- Concrete masonry units are manufactured by vibrating a stiff concrete mixture into metal moulds, and then immediately the wet blocks are turned out on a rack, so that, the mould can be reused.
- The concrete masonry units on rack are then cured at accelerated rate by subjecting to steam at atmospheric pressure or at higher steam pressure. The blocks can as well be cured immersing them in water tank.

4.2 BLOCK MASONRY UNITS

The concrete masonry units can be used in the construction of load bearing and non-load bearing walls. The concrete masonry units may be :
- Hollow open or closed cavity blocks
- Solid load bearing concrete blocks.

4.2.1 Advantages

Hollow concrete block masonry is much more economical than solid stone or brick masonry because of the following reasons :
- Volume of standard concrete block occupies volume of 12 modular bricks. Therefore, speed of construction is high.
- Less quantity of mortar is required.
- Finish of block is nice.
- Concrete blocks of required quality can be manufactured.

4.2.2 Terminology

Hollow (open or closed cavity) block : It is a block having one or more large holes or cavities, which either pass through the block (open cavity) or do not effectively pass through block (closed cavity) and it has solid material between 50 to 75% of the total volume of block calculated from the overall dimensions. The cores in the block should be at least two in number and preferably should be oval shaped. The face thickness of these blocks should not be less than 5 cm.

Solid Block : A block has solid material not less than 75% of the total volume of the block.

4.2.3 Dimensions

Actual dimensions of the block are 10 mm short of the nominal dimensions given below.

Length	:	400, 500 or 600 mm
Height	:	200 or 100 mm
Width	:	50, 75, 100, 150, 200, 250 or 300 mm.

The following table gives details of physical requirements and classification/grading of concrete masonry units.

Classification and physical requirements of concrete masonry units

Type	Grade		Density kg/m^3	Minimum compressive strength @ 28 days N/mm^2	Water Absorption	Drying shrinkage %	Moisture movement
Hollow load bearing unit	A	(4.5)	> 1500	4.5	< 10% by mass		
		(4.5)		4.5			
		(5.5)		5.5			
		(7.0)		7.0			
	B	(2.0)	> 1000	2.0		< 0.1%	< 0.09%
		(4.0)	< 1500	4.0			
		(5.0)		5.0			
Hollow non load bearing unit	C	(1.5)	> 1000 < 1500	1.5			
Solid load bearing unit	D	(5.0)	> 1800	5.0			
	D	(4.0)		4.0			
Load bearing light weight conc. blocks*			> 1000 < 1600	2.8	< 250 kg/m^3	< 0.06%	< 0.05%

* Light weight concrete blocks are made by using the following light weight aggregates :
Granulated blast furnace slag, foamed slag, or light weight aggregates by expansion of slates, etc.

Natural sand or crushed sand is added to above aggregate, which shall pass through IS 1.2. mm sieve. Mix not richer than 1 cement : 6 combined aggregate by volume is used.

4.2.4 Cellular Lightweight Concrete Blocks   (Dec. 13)

- Burnt Clay Brick is the predominant construction material in the country. The CO_2 emissions in the brick manufacture process have been acknowledged as a significant factor to global warming.
- The focus is now more on seeking environmental solutions for greener environment. The usage of Cellular Light-weight Concrete (CLC) blocks gives a prospective solution to building construction industry along with environmental preservation.
- The energy consumed in the production of CLC blocks is only a fraction compared to the production of red bricks and emits no pollutants and creates no toxic products or by products.

- It is produced by initially making slurry of Cement + Fly Ash + Water, which is further mixed with the addition of pre-formed stable foam in an ordinary concrete mixer under ambient conditions.
- Based on the trial mixes, it is found that compressive strength of CLC blocks is more than the compressive strength of conventional clay bricks. The addition of foam to the concrete mixture creates millions of tiny voids or cells in the material, hence the name Cellular Concrete.

Fig. 4.1 : Cellular light weight concrete block

Classification of CLC Blocks : The cellular light weight concrete blocks are classified into the following grades :

GRADE - A : These are used as load bearing units and have a block density in the range of 1250 kg/m^3 to 1850 kg/m^3.

GRADE - B : These are used as non-load bearing units and have a block density in the range of 850 kg/m^3 to 1100 kg/m^3.

GRADE - C : These are used for providing thermal insulation and have block density in the range of 450 kg/m^3 to 650 kg/m^3. Therefore, CLC can be produced in a density range of 450 kg/m^3 to 1850 kg/m^3. In cellular light weight concrete, the density is controlled by introduction of gas or foam by foam generator.

Advantages of Cellular Light Weight Concrete Blocks

- The most significant property is of CLC is reduced weight at no sacrifice in strength. This enables reduction of dead load. Weight reduction becomes highly beneficial for structural reasons, for reduced dimensions and substantial saving of steel reinforcement in the foundation.
- Fly-ash is considered as one of the industrial waste product that cannot be easily disposed. It solves the problem of disposal of fly-ash and at the same time it reduces the cost of the construction.
- Fly-ash based CLC is considered as environment friendly sustainable material produced with least energy demand.

Hollow Concrete Blocks

- Hollow masonry units are those having a specified net cross-sectional area less than 75 per cent of their corresponding gross cross-sectional area. Where the specified net cross-sectional area is equal to or greater than 75 per cent of the gross cross-sectional area, the unit is considered to be solid.

- Hollow units shall be placed such that face shells of bed joints are fully mortared. Webs shall be fully mortared in all courses of piers, columns, pilasters, in the starting course on foundations where adjacent cells or cavities are to be grouted, and where otherwise required.

- Head joints shall be mortared a minimum distance from each face equal to the face shell thickness of the unit.

Solid Concrete Blocks

- Solid masonry units have a specified net cross-sectional area 75 per cent or greater of their corresponding gross cross-sectional area. Where the specified net cross-sectional area is less than 75 per cent of the gross cross-sectional area, the unit is considered to be hollow.

- Unless otherwise required or indicated on the construction documents, solid units shall be placed in fully mortared bed and head joints. The ends of the units shall be completely buttered. Head joints shall not be filled by slushing with mortar.

- Head joints shall be constructed by shoving mortar tight against the adjoining unit. Bed joints shall not be furrowed deep enough to produce voids.

4.2.5 Manufacturing of Concrete Blocks

Following points should be observed during manufacture of concrete blocks :

- 40% of coarse aggregate should be mixed with 60% fine aggregate. Very fine sand should not be used. Fineness modules of the combined aggregate should be less than 4.6.

- Machine moulding should be preferred to hand moulding, since with former proper compaction, finish can be obtained and stiff mix can be used.

- Concrete blocks should be released from the mould, only after it has well set and hardened.

- The blocks should not be disturbed from the moulding platform, at least for one day; and thereafter, should be either steam cured or immersed in water tank.

- After curing, the blocks should stacked horizontally and not vertically.

- Minimum compressive strength of the block at the age of 28 days should be as given in the above table.

4.2.6 Laying of Concrete Blocks   (Dec. 14)

Mortar used for laying brick masonry is used. Only on face of blocks thick mortar is applied. No mortar is applied to the web portion.

- To start with a bed of mortar is spread,
- Mortar for the head joint is applied to each block with trowel.
- The block is then lifted and then placed on the bed of mortar.
- Further, units in the lower most course are placed in similar fashion.

- Second course of blocks is laid over the bottom course mortar is applied on the face shell of the block and not on the webs.
- While laying second course, height, level breaking of bond etc. is carefully checked with spirit level, plumb bob.
- The joints of the lead are tooled.
- A mason's line is held taught between the leads on the line blocks.
- The courses of the block between the leads are laid rapidly and are aligned only with the mason's line. No spirit level is necessary.

4.3 REINFORCED BRICK WORK

- Plain brick masonry is unable to resist tensile and shear stresses, and if the brick work is founded on weak soil, where there is probability of unequal settlement, bricks get pulled apart.
- Under such circumstances, and where loads are not uniform, it is desirable to increase load carrying capacity of brick work by providing steel fabric or steel reinforcement in between mortar joints.

Advantages :
- Reinforced masonry does not require shuttering and eliminates use of cement concrete.
- Easy to construct.
- It has higher fire resistance.
- It is cheap, especially when loads are not unduely high.

Applications :
Reinforced brick work can be used for construction of walls, slabs, lintels, columns, construction of retaining walls upto 6 m height.

4.3.1 Reinforced Brick Walls

Brick walls can be reinforced by providing :
- Steel fabric in the form of expanded steel mesh (XPM sheets).
- Hoop iron in the form of M.S. flat of 25 mm or 30 mm in width and 1.5 mm to 3 mm in thickness. These are dipped in tar and sanded to prevent rusting.
- M.S. round bars of suitable diameter.

Construction of Reinforced Brick Walls
- Cement mortar is spread over the brick course; and while the mortar is in plastic state, steel fabric (XPM) or hoop iron is laid on the mortar and pressed in the mortar. Next course of bricks is laid. Steel fabric reinforcement is placed at every 3rd or 4th course of brick.
- One strip of hoop iron is provided for every thickness of half brick and every sixth course of brick is reinforced.
- If vertical reinforcing bars are to be provided as in case of retaining walls, then specially moulded bricks as shown in Fig. 4.2 are used. Vertical reinforcement of 6 to 8 mm diameter passes through the slot provided in special type of brick and is tied at suitable intervals with fine wire.

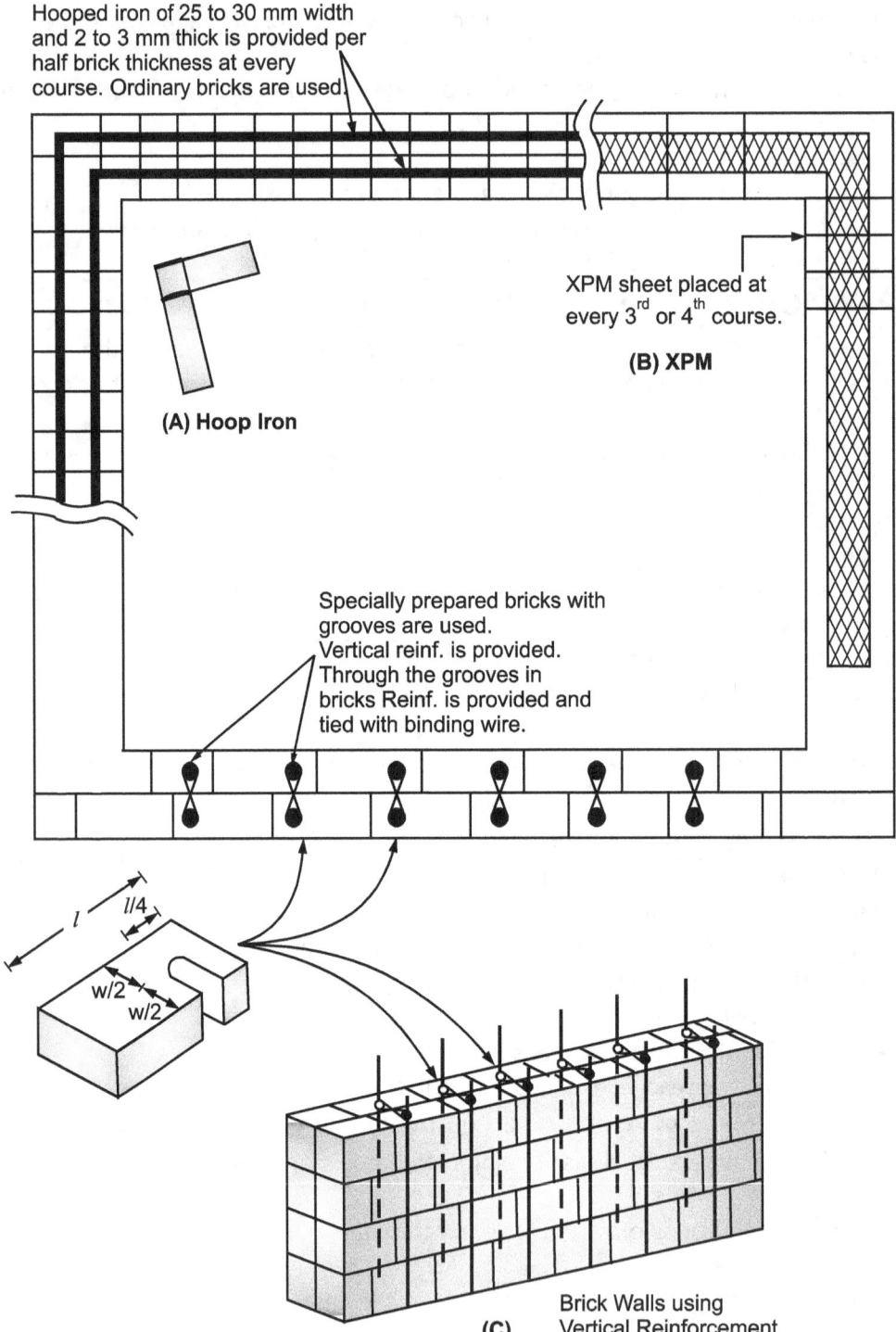

Hooped iron of 25 to 30 mm width and 2 to 3 mm thick is provided per half brick thickness at every course. Ordinary bricks are used.

(A) Hoop Iron

XPM sheet placed at every 3rd or 4th course.

(B) XPM

Specially prepared bricks with grooves are used. Vertical reinf. is provided. Through the grooves in bricks Reinf. is provided and tied with binding wire.

(C)

Brick Walls using Vertical Reinforcement

Fig. 4.2 : Reinforced brick wall (A) Hoop iron, (B) XPM sheet, (C) Vertical reinforcement

4.3.2 Construction of Columns   (Dec. 13)

- For construction of columns, special purpose bricks as shown in Fig. 4.3 are used, to allow provision of vertical reinforcement.

- 6 mm thick plates or XPM cut to suitable size are provided at every 4th course. Vertical reinforcement is anchored in foundation concrete adequately.

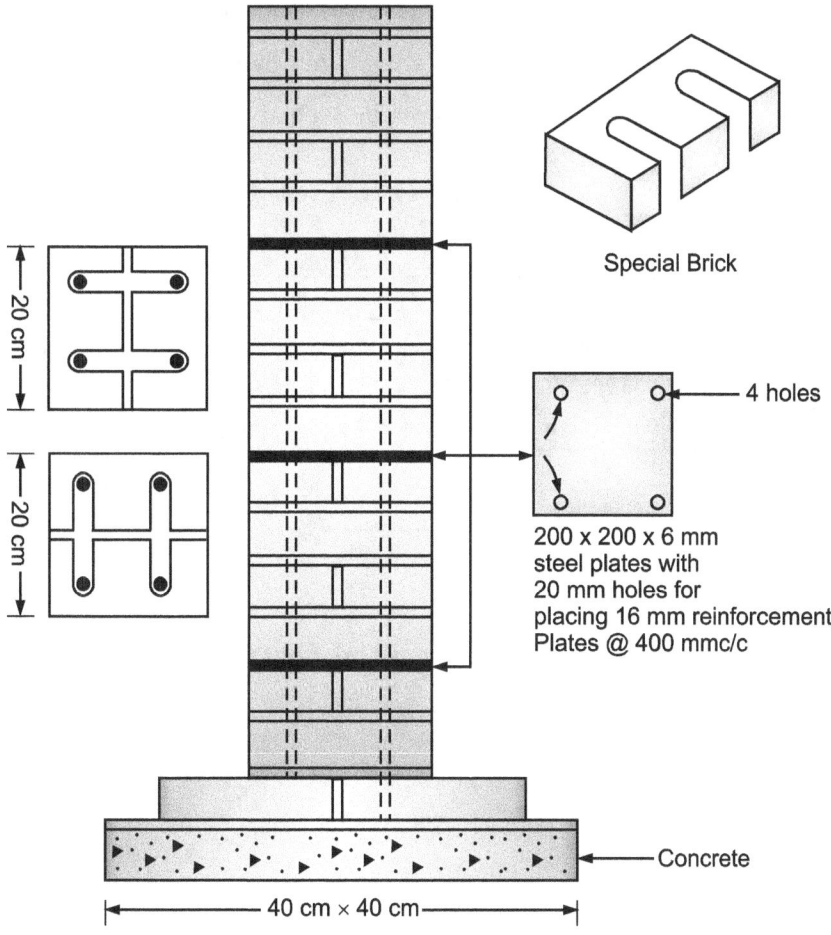

Fig. 4.3 : Reinforced brick column

4.3.3 Construction of Reinforced Brick Lintels

- For construction of lintels, bricks of special shape are not required. Longitudinal reinforcement (comprising of 6 to 12 mm diameter bars) is provided between vertical joints. If required, 6 mm diameter vertical stirrups are provided at every third vertical joint.

- To support the lintel during construction, centering consisting of supported platform is used. On this platform thick, dense layer of earth is laid, which is finished with fine sand. Longitudinal reinforcement is positioned. On either side of and also in between reinforcing bars, bricks are placed.

- The gap between the bricks i.e. vertical joints is filled with rich mortar. Vertical stirrups are provided at every third vertical joint. Centering is removed only when brick work attains sufficient strength. In elevation, the bricks will be seen as placed vertically.

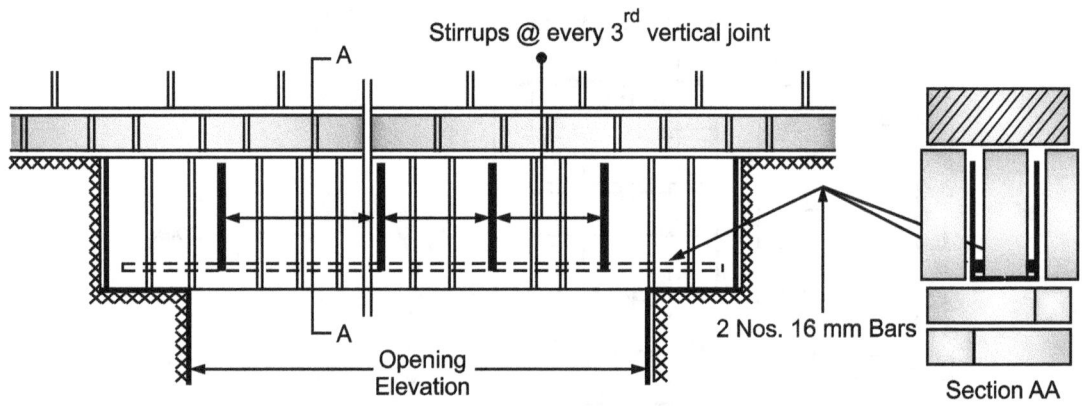

Fig. 4.4 : Reinforced brick lintel

4.3.4 Construction of Reinforced Brick Slab

- Construction of slab is similar to that of lintel, except that, slabs of definite depths i.e. 10 cm, 20 cm etc. can only be constructed. Bricks are laid flat, one above other or are laid on edge.

- Reinforcement is placed at such spacing that, it is in multiples of brick units. In order to keep thickness of joint small, reinforcement not greater than 12 mm diameter is used. To provide sufficient anchorage, reinforcement is bent in the form of semicircular hooks. Centering, curing etc. is similar to that for lintel.

4.3.5 Cavity Wall   (Nov. 15, May 16)

- Cavity wall is a wall comprising of two parallel walls, (separated by a continuous air cavity) interconnected at intervals by ties.

- Outer wall (also called as outer leaf) of the cavity wall is usually thinner than the inner wall or may be of same thickness as inner wall. Thickness of outer leaf is 10 cm or more; and is constructed using bricks of high quality.

- Outer wall is constructed to protect from heat, rain, sound etc., whereas inner wall is constructed using ordinary bricks and is designed to serve as load bearing wall.

- Usually, wall upto depth of 10 to 30 cm below damp proof course, no cavity wall is provided, but is constructed as solid wall, since cavity wall does not serve any purpose.

During construction of cavity wall, the following points are observed :

- For cavity wall to be more effective, the contact between outer and inner leaf should be least.

- Measures are taken to prevent dropping of brick bats, mortar in the hollow space by providing movable screens to collect the same or by providing small openings at bottom, where from droppings like brick bat, mortar etc. can be removed. Later on, when work is completed, the openings are sealed with bricks.

- The outer and inner leaf should be inter connected by providing metal ties which are placed @ 1 m c/c horizontally and vertically @ 0.5 m c/c in staggered fashion.

- Outer leaf being thin, is constructed using high quality bricks in stretcher bond.

- To prevent rusting, metal ties are coated with tar or are galvanized before placing in position.

- Separate damp proof course is provided for inner leaf as well as for outer leaf. Cavity wall is constructed upto bottom of parapet wall. A damp proof course is provided below bottom of parapet wall; and thereafter solid parapet wall with coping is provided.

Advantages of Cavity Wall :

- Cavity wall prevents transmission of heat, dampness and sound. A cavity wall with 10 cm thick inner and outer leaf with **a cavity of 5 to 7.5 cm is 25% more efficient as regards dampness** than solid wall of 20 cm thickness.

- Cavity wall tend to reduce nuisance of efflorescence.

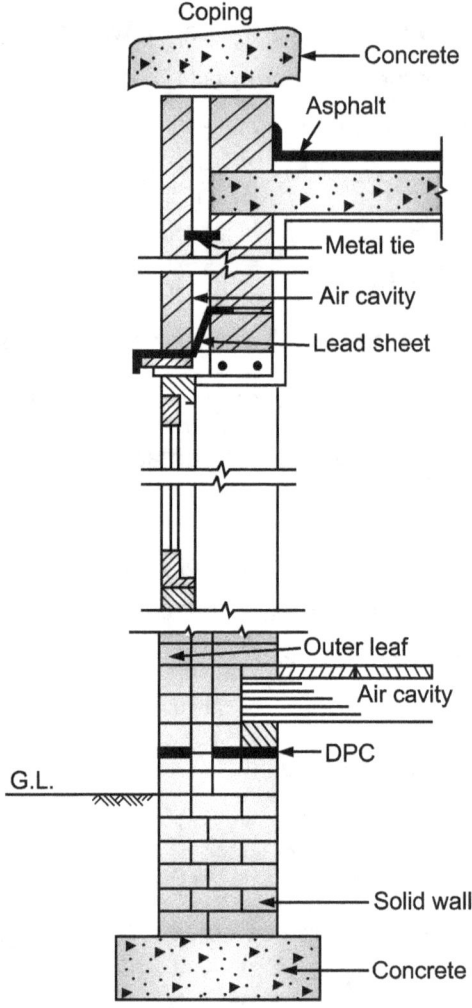

Fig. 4.5 : Cavity walls

4.4 COMPOSITE MASONRY   (Nov. 16, May 16)

It is a masonry, in which facing wall and backing wall are constructed using two different types of masonry. Composite masonry is intended to

   (i)   Reduce overall cost of construction.

  (ii)   Provide maintenance free, durable and asthetically sound masonry.

Different varieties of composite masonry as listed below can be obtained :

  (a)   Facing of stone slab and backing of concrete

  (b)   Facing of brick work and backing of rubble masonry

  (c)   Facing of brick work and backing of concrete

(d) Facing of brick work and backing of hollow concrete

(e) Facing of ashlar masonry and backing of rubble masonry of brick masonry.

Unless proper care is taken, composite masonry is likely to lead to unequal settlement, because number of mortar joints in the inside / backing masonry are more than those in facing masonry.

To guard against these defects, following measures are required to be taken :

- Facing and backing masonry should be constructed simultaneously.
- Backing work should be constructed using rich mortar.
- Connection joints between front and rear masonry can be obtained by use of cramps.
- Large sized tough stones should be provided.

Advantages :

- New aesthetic possibilities : An ability to mould complex, fluid and creative forms and produce more efficient geometric shapes.
- The ability to integrate special surface finishes and a wide variety of unusual effects including simulating traditional materials.
- Hugely significant weight savings – an advanced composite cladding model can typically weigh as little as 10% of its concrete equivalent.
- Rapid installation enabling time and cost savings on site – composite structures can cover much larger spans between support points, reducing the need for substructures dramatically. This has a positive effect on the cost and weight of the completed structure, as well as a significant reduction in installation time.
- Superior durability with reduced through life costs and less degradation.
- Improved thermal insulation and lack of cold bridging.

REVIEW QUESTIONS

1. Draw neat sketches of hollow concrete blocks.
2. Write a short note on cavity wall construction.
3. Describe masonry. Enlist the different units of masonry.
4. Describe the construction and procedure of composite masonry.
5. What is the purpose of providing cavity walls ? What advantages of cavity walls have over the solid wall construction ?
6. Explain what do you understand by the term 'Composite Masonry'. Draw neat sketches wherever necessary to support your answer.

7. Write short notes on :

   (a)   Glass block masonry

   (b)   Cavity wall

8. Enlist advantages of hollow concrete block masonry over the stone masonry.

SOLVED UNIVERSITY QUESTIONS

DEC. 2013

1. Define hollow concrete blocks. Explain reinforced brick column in detail.   **[6]**

    [**Ans.:** Refer Articles 4.2.4, 4.3.2]

DEC. 2014

1. Write short notes on: Laying of block   **[6]**

    [**Ans.:** Refer Articles 4.2.6]

NOV. 2015

1. Write short notes on : Cavity wall construction   **[6]**

    [**Ans.:** Refer Articles 4.3.5]

MAY 2016

1. Write short notes on : Cavity wall construction.   **[6]**

    [**Ans.:** Refer Articles 4.3.5]

2. State different types of composite masonry. Explain form work for plinth beam.   **[6]**

    [**Ans.:** Refer Articles 4.4]

NOV. 2016

1. Explain briefly composite masonry with respect to materials and types.   **[6]**

    [**Ans.:** Refer Articles 4.4]

CHAPTER 5
FORM WORK

5.1 INTRODUCTION (Dec. 13, Nov. 15)

- Forms are the moulds and dies for concrete construction.
- Forms mould the concrete to the desired size and shape and control its alignment and position.
- Form work also carries the weight of freshly placed concrete besides live load due to materials, equipment and workmen.
- The objectives of Form work are quality, safety and economy. Economy is a major concern since form work cost may range anywhere from 25 to 60% of the cost of the concrete structure.
- Judgment in selection of materials and equipment, in planning fabrication and erection procedures, in scheduling reuse of forms and in deployment of trained and experienced man power helps to save form work cost and at the same time expedite the job.
- The economy measures which may lead to form work failure; also defeat the very purpose as the costs due to loss of human lives and materials will totally out weigh the savings due to economic measures.
- It is necessary to understand the requirements of form work before going into the details of materials, erection, inspection and other essential steps for successful and proper job.

Forwork for Column

Forwork for Staircase

Fig. 5.1

5.2 REQUIREMENT OF FORM WORK (Dec. 13)

The following are essential requirements:

- To obtain the required shape, size, finish, position and alignment of concrete members.

- To have design for quick erection and removal (stripping).
- To handle easily using available equipment or man power.
- Joints between form work must be tight enough to prevent leakage of grout.
- To provide easy and safe access for concrete handling and placing.
- To avoid damage to concrete or form work itself while stripping.

Types of Form Work Based on Material

1. Wooden Materials

- Timber and plywood are the most commonly used materials for form work because these can be cut or assembled easily on site.
- Use of wooden props and bamboo props is still persisting in many construction works.
- Even large floor heights are constructed using these props without proper interconnection for the extended length or without proper bracing. These often result in serious failures.
- It is not recommended to use wooden props especially when floor heights are large requiring connecting one prop over the other using inadequate method of connections.
- In any case, the load carrying capacity of any wooden or bamboo prop is often not known and difficult to ascertain, depending on the type and quality of wood, its moisture content, size and shape.
- Plywoods of different types and quality are used. It is usual to frame up the materials into largest size panels that can be handled by the available equipment on the site or is convenient for manual handling.
- The size will also depend on the shape of the structural member being cast.
- The plywood panels are suitable for large smooth areas like walls and floors.
- For complicated shapes, timber frames with plywood face are usually more economical than timber boards or other materials especially when high numbers of reuses are required.
- Ply surfaces get easily damaged, hence adequate care has to be taken during assembly, erection, casting, (removal) and storage.
- The soft surfaces and edges are more prone to damage than other surfaces and therefore, they need to be protected.
- The cut edges of ply and tie holes should be sealed and protected to prolong the life of the plywood panels so that more number of usages are obtained.

2. Steel

There are two way in which steel is used in form work and false work :

(a) In proprietary form work.

(b) Purpose made from work.

(a) Proprietary Form Work : These system are available in different forms, some of which are listed as follows :

- Steel framed panels with either steel plate or plywood facing.
- Telescopic supporting trusses.
- Adjustable props (tubular).
- Yokes and fastening devices.
- Tie rods and spacers.
- Clamps and bracings (tubular).

(b) Purpose Made Form Work : These form works are specially designed for a particular type of job work as in case of linings inside tunnels, culverts, slip form work for tall structures curved surfaces of water tanks, shells, domes, parabolieds and other jobs which have unusual shape.

3. Other Materials

- There are several other types of materials used in form work such as glass reinforced plastics, vacuum formed plastic facings etc.
- Although these types of form work offer many uses, additional care has to be taken while placing and vibrating concrete to avoid damage to the form face.
- Scrapers cannot be used when concrete is being poured into these form works.
- Cleaning also needs to be done immediately after deshuttering.
- Wet cloth cleaning is necessary to remove dust and cement concrete paste sticking to the surface.

5.2.1 Propping Form Work

- Collapses of Form work have been mostly attributable to incorrect propping system. This can be due to inadequate quality of propping material or improper application.
- It is preferable that wooden props are not used. Steel props are safer and their load carrying capacity is more predictable than that of wooden props.
- It is very important that steel props are also to be used in correct way and props having defects not used in supporting system.

The following essential tips are required to be followed at site :

- Defective props should not be used. Props must be properly inspected piece by piece prior to erection. Steel tube props having a bend or crease, extensive surface corrosion, bent or damaged head and/or pin and /or base plate should not be used.
- Correct setting up of props is vital. The load carrying capacity of adjustable steel props is considerably reduced if they are erected out of plumb and/or if the load applied is eccentric. This is also applicable to plain tubular props or wooden props. No prop should be more than 1 in 40 out of plumb.

- Holes made in the form work on site should be neat so that plugging is easier. Timber form work must be drilled from the face to avoid splintering.
- Make sure that inserts, blocking out pieces, boxes and battens are securely fixed.
- Ensure that dirt, wooden shavings, tie wire clippings, nails etc., from the form work are removed prior to commencement of concreting.
- Ensure that proper walkways, working platforms and approaches are available for free and safe movement of work force.
- Sloping or horizontal top forms are subjected to uplift pressure from freshly placed concrete and therefore, need to be firmly restrained.
- Large prefabricated Form work panels must be provided with a spreader or lifting beam to prevent damage or distortion.
- Bracings should be provided in both directions and securely clamped.
- Props at ends must be checked for verticality in each row and the rest can be inspected by visual inspection.
- Runners supported by props should not be off centre. Maximum of 25 mm off centre can be permitted.
- Props should have a firm bearing. Spreaders must be used if the supporting sub-grade or base is weak in taking bearing pressures. Spreaders will not be required if bearing is directly on concrete.

5.2.2 Erecting Form Work

Form work is a temporary structural arrangement which is removed as soon as concrete is capable of taking adequate load.

Some general tips which may help avoid serious problems are as follows :

- All fixtures, fittings and fastenings must be in the right place and each panel to avoid mistakes.
- All tie bolts or wall ties must be tightened.
- Temporary distance pieces must be removed.
- Form work must be cleaned and checked to ensure that nothing has fallen within.
- Avoid drilling holes or cutting standard panels.
- Any make up or fill-in pieces or closure panels should marry with the main form work. They should be so designed that they can be easily fixed and stripped without causing any damage to themselves and the neighbouring panels.

Props and Shorings

Beams and slab forms carry a heavy load of concrete on slender props one or more stories high. Bracings of this support are of utmost importance and it is vital that these provide proper stability to the vertical props.

- Bearing value of soil, suitably of mud still sizes for load distribution below the props.
- Compaction of soil under the mud sills and proper drainage to prevent ponding of water in the area.

- Soil, if soft and unsuitable, is removed and replaced with stabilized materials under the sills.
- Ground level slab is completed wherever possible before props are erected for supporting the slab above.

5.3 CLEANING AND STORAGE OF FORM WORK

5.3.1 Cleaning of Form Work

- Form work must be cleaned as soon as it is removed. Timber and ply forms should be cleaned with a stiff brush to remove dust and grout.
- A timber scraper should be used for stubborn bits of concrete or grout. Steel scrapers on ply or faced ply are not to be used.
- Timber and untreated ply should be given a coat of release agent when it is required to be stored for a longer period. Steel form if required to be stored for a longer period will also need a light coat of oil to prevent rusting.
- If any repairs are necessary should be done immediately. Any depressions, splits and nail holes should be repaired with suitable material followed by light rubbing down.
- Unwanted holes should be over filled with suitable filler and then sanded down to a smooth surface.

5.3.2 Storage

- Storage of form work is extremely important. Most of the form work material deteriorates very fast if not repeatedly used and not preserved and stored properly.
- The main aim for good storage is to avoid doing any damage when form work is not in use.
- If immediate reuse of form work materials is not required, form work must not be allowed to lie on site unprotected.
- Panels and plywood sheets after cleaning and oiling must be stored horizontally on a flat levelled base so that they lie flat without twisting and should be stacked face to face to protect the face.
- Large panels are best stored on edge in specially designed racks. Loose wailings, soldiers, struts etc. are best stored with their respective panels after numbering them so that they can be easily matched at a later stage.
- Small components such as bolts, clamps, keys, pins, wedges and ties should be kept in boxes. Props should be stacked off the ground to prevent them from deterioration due to contamination, mud and moisture.
- Fire extinguishers in working condition should always be made available in easily accessible areas.

- The storage area should be properly protected from rain and moisture. It should also be well ventilated and kept in a tidy condition so that it is easy to get any material required for reuse.

5.4 DEFECTS COMMONLY OBSERVED IN USE OF THE PROPRIETARY FALSE WORK   (Dec. 14)

1. **Beam, Column and Wall Clamps**

   - Bolts and wedges over tightened causing crushing in the timber packing members and resultant loss of strength.

   - Locking devices such as nuts, bolts, brackets and podger eyes are not positioned correctly.

2. **Form Ties**

   - Inadequate bearing area or thickness. Maximum loading is governed by the size of washer plate and its thickness.

   - Damage/deformation of threaded portion and excessive wear on threads.

   - Unequal depth of double struts or wallings causing uneven bearing on washer plate.

   - Incorrect positioning of 'left in' portions resulting in protrusions from the finished wall face.

3. **Adjustable Steel Props**

   - Nails, bolts or mild steel reinforcement used in place of standard pins.

   - Top and bottom plates deformed and not at right angles to the prop axis.

   - Inner and outer prop tubes deformed. This defect is particularly important when the prop is used at its maximum extension.

   - Inadequate lateral bracing to rops, particularly when they are used at their maximum extension.

   - Eccentric loading.

   - Inadequate bearing at top or bottom plate.

   - Inadequate lateral stability and transfer of load on settlement. One prop is placed on top of another. The method of using props is in any case not recommended.

   - Non-vertically or out of plumb.

4. **Pipe Bracing**

   - Not clamped at correct location and spacing.

   - Not provided both ways for proper lateral stability.

   - Often used to transfer vertical loads. This causes excessive deflection as horizontal pipe bracings are not supposed to carry vertical load.

5. **General Notes**

   - Proprietary form work should not be used without reference to the loaded pipe bracing.
   - Periodic maintenance and inspection is necessary.
   - The above list is only for guidance and should not be considered exhaustive or complete.

5.5 CHECKS ON FORM WORK TO BE CARRIED DURING CONCRETING

- Presence of an experienced supervisor.
- Supply of spare drops, clamps, bolts, wedges with skilled workers should be available at the site.
- Continuous checks on alignment, camber and plumpness while concrete is being placed is essential.
- Grout loss is an indication that joints between the panels were not tight initially or that some movement has occurred during placing.
- Vibrations transmitted to the form work if are considerable, then results in loosening of wedges and fixings.
- All wedges, fastenings, bolts should be continuously observed and tightened if and when necessary.
- Split concrete or grout leakage should be cleaned from the form work immediately after concreting.
- Wooden spreaders to hold form work (used in walls and beams) should be removed as concreting proceeds.
- Wooden members used for creating pockets in concrete should be eased before the concrete sets and removed gently as soon as possible afterwards. If wooden members or pocket Form work is left overnight it will be difficult to remove them without damaging the concrete.
- The form work should be designed in such a manner that it can be struck easily without damaging the concrete or the form itself.
- Form work must be struck when the concrete has gained enough strength to be self supporting and also be able to carry any other loads that may be put on it.
- The removal time of form work is generally specified in the drawings or specification. This time will depend on the following factors :
  - Size and shape of the member span of the member (beams).
  - The concrete mix used.
  - The type of cement used.

- The ambient temperature and weather conditions. Curing of concrete prior to removal.

- For walls, columns, beams, sides, the forms can be usually removed within 12 to 24 hours of placing the concrete. However, care should be exercised as concrete will still be green and therefore easily prone to damage.

- During cold weather forms should be left for a longer period of time.

- At the time of removal, ties, clamps and wedges should be loosened gradually to prevent the last tie from bending.

- All bolts, nuts, clamps, wedges removed should be collected in a box and not dropped down.

- When lowering large panels of form work care should be taken to see that they are not damaged by scaffolding or any other projection.

- The panels should be rested on levelled surface so that they are not twisted or misshapened.

- If cranes are used to handle to form work the person controlling the operation should know where to sling the form work and should be aware of correct signal codes to direct the operator.

Bureau of Indian Standards (IS)-456 has given certain guidelines for Form work removal; the same are reproduced below :

- **Stripping Time :** Forms shall not be struck until the concrete has reached a strength of at least twice the stress to which the concrete may be subjected at the time of removal of form work. The strength referred to shall be that of concrete using the same cement and aggregates, with the same proportions and cured under conditions of temperature and moisture similar to those existing on the work.

  - While the above criteria of strength shall be the guiding factor for removal of form work, in normal circumstances where ambient temperature does not exceed 15°C and where ordinary portland cement is used, forms may generally be removed after the expiry of the periods mentioned in the Table 5.1.

  - The number of props left under, their sizes and disposition shall be such as to be able to safely carry the full dead load of the slab, beam or arch as the case may be together with any live load likely to occur during curing or further construction.

  - Where the shape of the element is such that the form work has re-entrant angles, the form work shall be removed as soon as possible after the concrete has set, to avoid shrinkage cracking occurring due to the restraint imposed.

Table 5.1

Type of Form Work	Minimum Period Before Striking Form Work
Vertical form work to columns, walls, large beams	16 – 25 hours
Soffit form work to slabs (Props to be refixed immediately after removal of form work)	3 days
Soffit form work to beams (Props to be refixed immediately after removal of form work)	7 days
Props to Slabs : (1) Spanning upto 4.5 m (2) Spanning over 4.5 m	 7 days 14 days
Props to Beams and Arches : (1) Spanning upto 6 m (2) Spanning over 6 m	 14 days 21 days

For other cements and lower temperature the stripping time recommended above may be suitably modified.

Release Agents

The main purpose of treating form work with a release agent is to make it easy to strike and release the form work away from the concrete face. It is often observed that burnt transformer oil and other cheap oils are used as release agents. They can cause severe stains and also result in inefficient removal of form work from the concrete surface. It is therefore extremely important to select the right type of release agent. Some commonly used release agents are as follows :

- Neat oils with surfactants. They can be used on steel, timber or ply faces of the form work.
- Mould cream emulsions. The most general purpose release agent used on all types of form faces.
- Chemical release agents. Recommended for all high quality form finished concrete works.

An unused and untreated plywood and timber surfaces have tendency to absorb the coating of the release agent, the surface should be given a primary coat of release agent 36 hours before being used and a secondary coat of release agent should be applied just before using it for the first time.

It is important to apply the right amount of release agent in the form of a thin film. Application can be made uniformly either by brush, roller or best of all by spraying. Too thick or too much application of release agent can stain the concrete while too less release agent can cause difficulty in striking of the form work.

In case excess mould oil is put on the form work surface, by mistake, then the excess amount can be wiped off using a clean rag.

5.6 CAUSES OF FAILURES

Some general causes of the form work failures are as follows :

- A system of form work filled with wet concrete has its weight at the top and is not basically a stable structure. Many a times unexpected events may cause one member to get overloaded. This causes a failure of the member which results in overloading and misalignment of other members and the whole form work structure collapses.

- Sometimes form work is not well braced diagonally and due to some reason strong lateral loads occur creating imbalance and subsequent failure.

- Minor differences in the assembly results in localised weakness and overstress causing failure.

- Human error on the job whether due to indifference, hurry or lack of knowledge causes failures.

- Premature stripping of forms resulting from a desire for economy or speed can cause a failure.

- Premature removal of props and careless practices of repropping (reshoring) have caused numerous failures or defects in the completed concrete structure.

- Inadequate size and spacing of props may lead to a form work collapse during construction as well as damage to the concrete structure due to excessive deflection.

- Use of wooden or bamboo props of inadequate strength and out of plumb fixing can also cause serious failures specially when floor heights are more than normal (over 3 m height).

- Concentration of load due to heaping up of concrete or concentration of equipment and manpower more frequently causes lateral forces or induces displacement of the supporting members. This can cause failures.

- Inadequate cross bracing and horizontal bracing of props is one of the factors more frequently involved in causing form work failures. One major objective of bracing is to prevent such a minor accident or failure from becoming a disaster.

- Forms sometimes collapse when the supporting shores or jacks are displaced by vibration caused by passing traffic, movement of men and equipment on the form work and/or effect of vibrating concrete.

- Unstable soil or support under shoring will allow settlement that overloads or shifts the form work.

- If temperature drops during concreting operations and the rate of concrete is not slowed down then build up of lateral pressure can overload the forms and cause in failure.
- Steel channels or I beams, if used, should be correctly placed as given.
- There have been several failures of propping systems below prestressed girders or beams. Initially, that is, prior to prestressing the beam will be resting uniformly on all props placed below. As prestressing is done in stages the girder hogs and the load at two supporting ends increase, while load on props placed in between gets released. This causes complete load transfer onto the end supports and intermittent supports.
- It is not always the fault of form work when forms and slabs collapse during concreting. The existing structure below may settle under additional load or may fail due to overloading. Hence, failures should be carefully examined before drawing any conclusion as to the cause of the failure.

Form work cannot be neglected by any means. Safety should be given the top priority while planning and designing form work. The best way to inspect form work is to check from the bottom upwards inspecting all members which take part in load transfer. Inspection of form work is easy if it is properly planned, designed and executed as per drawing.

Most of the form work failures can be prevented if the Architects and Consultants insist on proper engineering designs and drawings before its implementation. Systematically and uniformly made form work as per approved drawings is always safe and gives a good finish to the concrete surfaces.

5.7 COLUMN FORMS   (Nov. 16)

- Forms for columns usually are made of vertical planks/plywood. The parts are prefabricated and assembled in the location where they will be used. Adjustable steel clamps are used to resist the pressure from the concrete.
- Forms shall be designed to resist the high pressure resulting from quick filling. If forms are filled in 30 minutes or less, concrete may exert the full hydrostatic pressure based on a weight. Density being approximately 2400 kg/m^3.
- Column forms require 0.06 to 0.09 cubic metres of timber per square metre of contact. The larger the column less the timber required per square.
- It is usual practice to prepare form of all columns on the lowest floor and to use the same forms again on the upper floors.
- Column forms more than 4 m height, should be braced at intermediate points to give them sufficient rigidity. Yokes are generally used to stiffen them.
- Yokes are comparatively of heavier section and are connected together by two long bolts of 6 mm diameter. Four wedges, one at each corner, are inserted between the bolts and the end yokes. The sheathing is nailed to the yokes.
- Wooden forms for round column are seldom used. Steel forms are generally used for round columns. Plywood can be used for it.

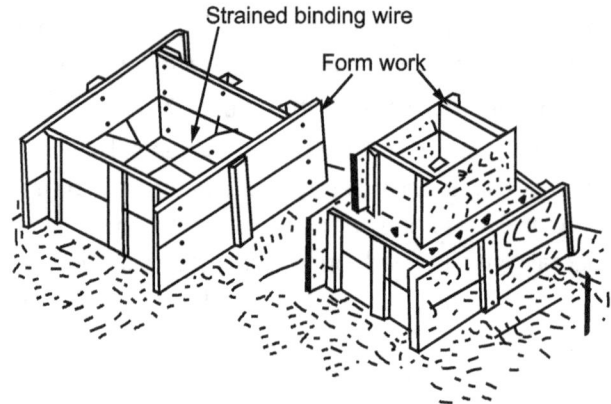

Fig. 5.2 : Form work for stepped footing

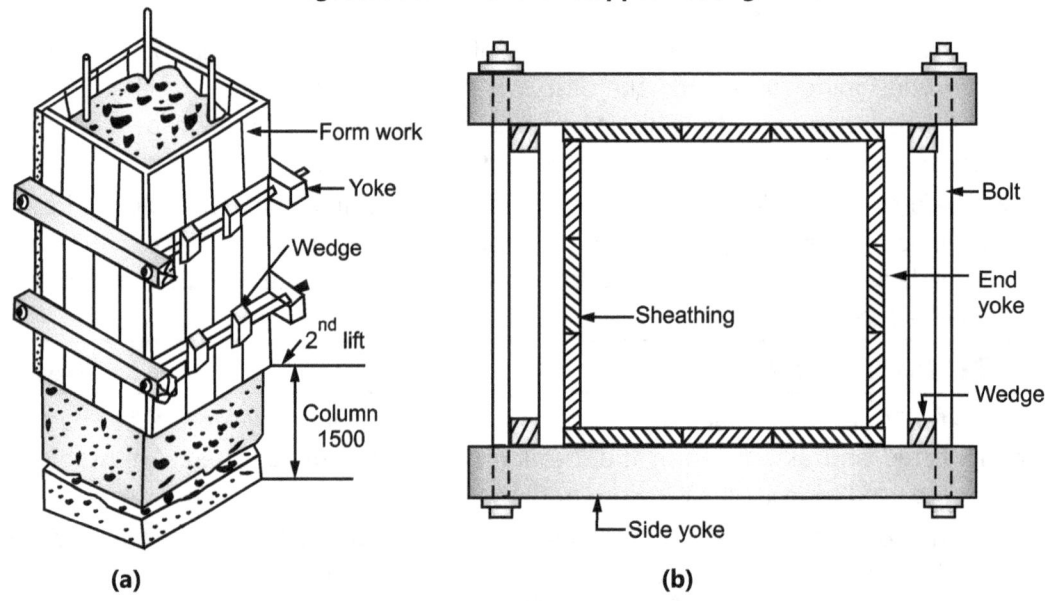

(a)   **(b)**

Fig. 5.3 : Form work for column

5.8 SHUTTERING FOR BEAM AND SLAB FLOOR   (Nov. 15)

- Fig. 5.4 shows the form work for beam and slab floor. The slab is continuous over a number of beams.

- The slab is supported on thick sheathing laid parallel to the main beams. Sheathing is supported on wooden battens which are laid between the beams, at suitable spacing.

- In order to reduce deflection, the battens are propped at middle of the span through joists. The side and bottom forms of the beam form may be 5 to 7 cm thick. The ends of the battens are supported on the ledger which is fixed to the cleats throughout the length.

- Cleats are fixed to the side forms at the same spacing as that of battens, so that battens may be fixed to them. The beam form is supported on a head tree.

- The shore or post is connected to head tree through cleats. At the bottom of shore, two wedges of hard wood are provided over a sole piece.
- Plywood is installed more rapidly and has a higher salvage value, which may offset its higher cost compared to planks.

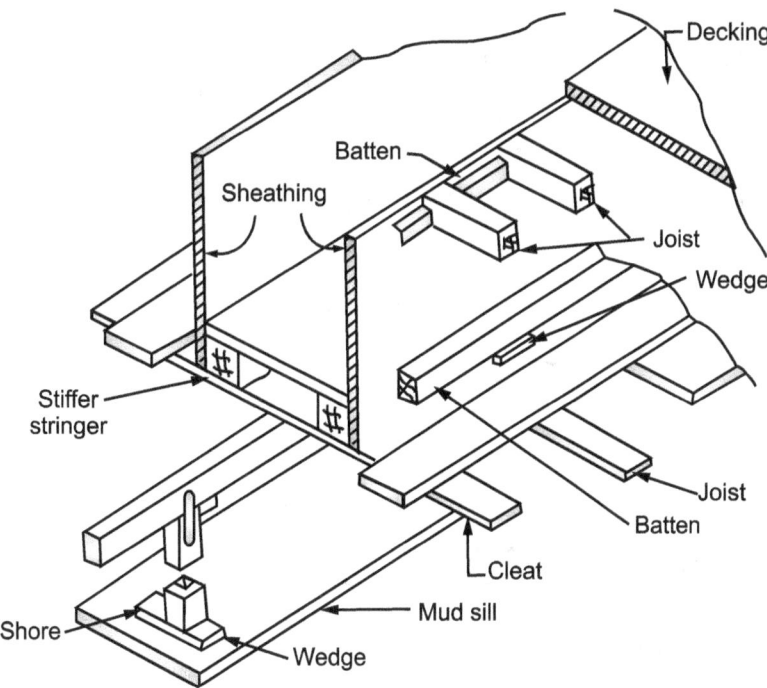

Fig. 5.4 : Wood forms for beam and slab concrete floor

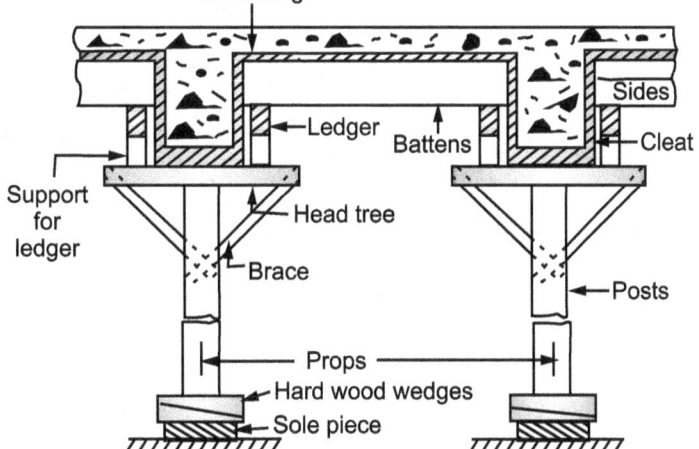

Fig. 5.5 : Wood forms for beam and slab concrete floor

The maximum spacing of shores, stringers and joists under the stringers will be limited by the strength or the permissible deflection of the **stringers, joists and decking respectively**.

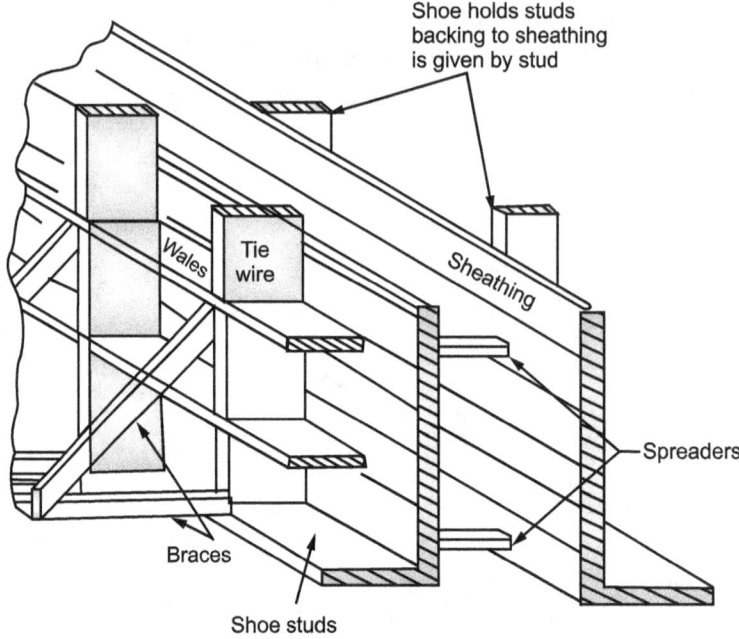

Fig. 5.6 : Forms for a concrete wall

5.9 FORM WORK FOR STAIRS

- Refer Fig. 5.7. The sheathing for the deck slabs is carried on cross-joists which are in turn supported on raking ledgers.

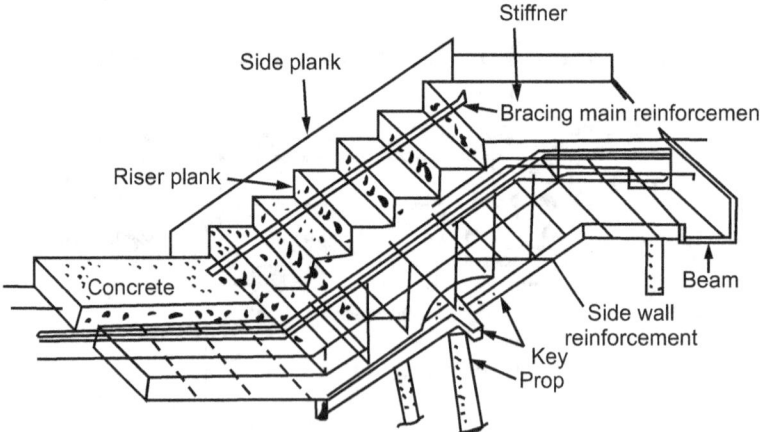

Fig. 5.7 : Form work for stair case

- The risers planks are bevelled at the bottom to permit the whole of the tread faced to be trovelled.
- The riser planks are placed only after the reinforcement has been fixed in position. The cut string is strutted to the cross-joists by struts.
- The wall ends of the riser planks are carried by hangers secured to board fixed to or strutted against the wall.

- The treads are left open to permit concreting and thorough vibration. A stiffener joist is placed along the middle of the riser planks. The stiffener is wired to cross-joists through decking.

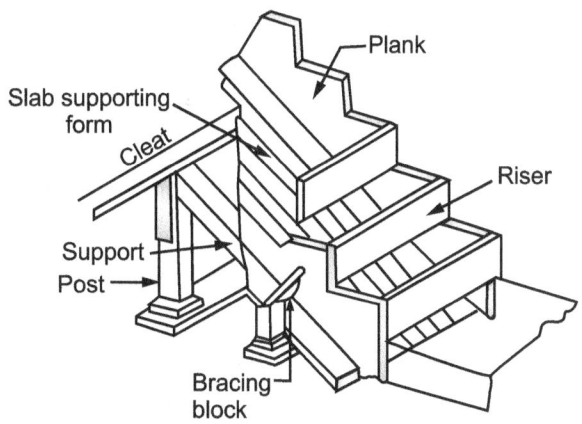

Fig. 5.8 : Form for concrete steps

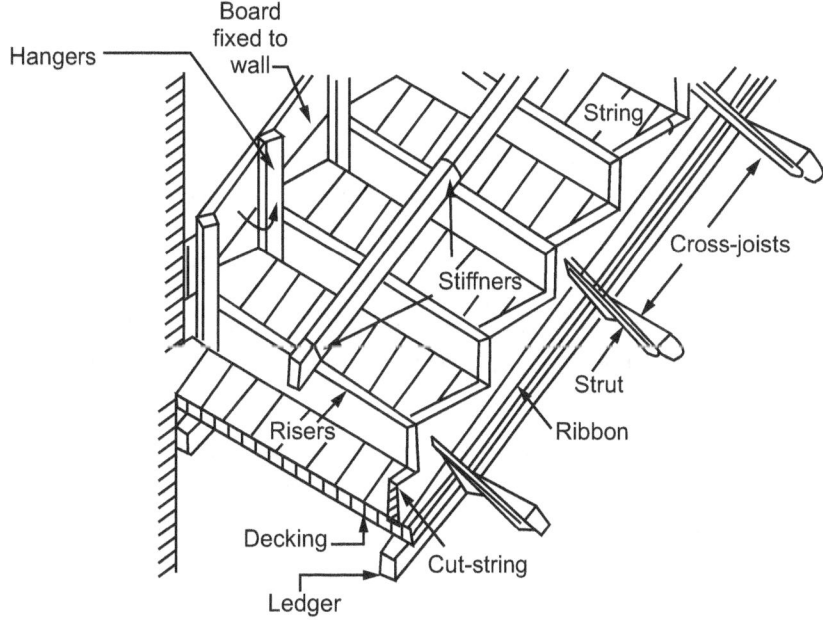

Fig. 5.9

5.10 CURING

- The chemical action between cement and water, results in the setting and hardening of concrete or mortar. Duplication for cement + water, presence of water.
- Although there is normally adequate quantity of water for full hydration when the concrete or mortar mix is prepared, it is important to ensure that the water is either retained or replenished to enable the chemical action to be continued till such time the required strength is gained.

- A significant loss of water due to evaporation from the concrete or mortar surface may result in slowing down or stopping the hydration process and resulting in consequent reduction of strength and durability.

- To help the hydration process to continue, water in the capillaries should be prevented from evaporating. It is, therefore, necessary to maintain an environment of high humidity around the freshly placed concrete or mortar till it attains reasonably good strength. This process is called curing of concrete.

- Curing of concrete or mortar is the last step required to be taken in the process of concrete or masonry construction.

- Curing has a strong influence on various properties of concrete and therefore, it should not be taken lightly.

- Strength, durability water, tightness, wear resistance, volume stability, chemical attacks and resistance to freeze-thaw cycle are much superior of a well cured concrete or mortar than that of a concrete wherein, curing was neglected, all other parameters being identical.

1. There are two general ways by which concrete can be kept moist and humid or kept at a favourable temperature.

- By maintaining the presence of mixing water in the concrete during the early hardening period. Methods generally deployed are ponding or immersion, spraying, sprinkling or fogging, wet covering using hessian cloth, gunny bags etc.

- By preventing loss of mixing water from the concrete by sealing the exposed surfaces of concrete. The exposed surfaces can be generally covered by membrane formed by a curing compound, impervious paper, plastic sheets or even by leaving form work in place.

2. However at times, there is a need to accelerate curing or there is necessity to expedite gain of strength due to adverse weather conditions or if it is required to handle or put to use the concrete structure earlier. This is achieved by using live steam, heating coils or electrically heated forms or pads.

3. The curing method or combination of curing methods are generally selected depending on some of the following factors :
   - Specifications
   - Availability of curing materials
   - Economics
   - Type of concrete structure (precast/cast-in-situ)
   - Shape and size of concrete surface
   - Aesthetic appearance.

5.10.1 Ponding or Immersion in Water

The best curing method is total immersion of concrete in water. However, following precautions are necessary :

- Ponding water lost due to evaporation should be continuously replenished.
- Ponding water should also cover the corners and edges and should be able to cover the entire surface uniformly to avoid dry spots wherein curing would be deficient.
- Water used for curing should have identical properties as that of water used for manufacture of concrete.
- Water and the materials used for bunding should be free of substances that will stain or discolour the concrete surfaces.
- The difference in the curing water temperature and the concrete temperature should not be more that 11°C to prevent thermal stresses that could result in cracking.
- Adequate water should be available at the site throughout the curing period.
- Bunds of impervious earth or cement mortar to retain water should be maintained throughout the curing period.
- The height of the bunds and area of concrete surface to be ponded must be so selected that there is at least about 25 mm of water ponded on the highest surface.

5.10.2 Fogging or Spraying Water

This method can be applied to both horizontal and vertical concrete/mortar surfaces. However, ample water is necessary throughout the curing period and round the clock. The following precautions are necessary :

- There should be continuous water supply available in adequate quantity.
- Covering the surface with gunny bags, hessian or plastic sheets may help in retaining the water for a longer period. However, there are chances that surfaces may not be uniformly moistened hence, care is to be taken to replenish the water before any part of the concrete surface starts drying.
- Continuous supervision is necessary, if this method is employed as there are good chances that during certain intervals of time, within the curing period, some surfaces will dry off and start cracking or crazing. Concrete or mortar will crack faster, if it is allowed to dry off between the alternate wetting applications.
- In this method, precautions have to be taken so that water sprayed on old concrete or mortar does not fall on to the freshly laid concrete or mortar causing erosion of the top surface.
- This system should be generally avoided when ambient temperatures are close to the freezing point.

5.10.3 Moist Fabric Covers

This method of curing is not quite observed in our country wherein different types of covers soaked with water are used on both vertical and horizontal concrete surfaces.

The different types of fabrics or materials used are :

- Burlap
- Cotton mat
- Rugs
- Hessian cloth (multiple layers)
- Other moisture retaining fabrics/materials such as soil, sand, saw dust or hay.

The precautions required in this curing process are as follows :

- The concrete should be covered with the fabric as soon as it has hardened sufficiently to prevent surface damage.
- The entire surface including the edges of slabs and joints should be kept covered so that parts of the structure are not inadequately cured.
- The fabric helps in retaining water for a greater period of time than otherwise. However, the fabric must be continuously kept wet or most so that concrete surface is in contact with water or moisture throughout the curing period.
- If wet burlap is used, it should be free of sizing or any substance that is harmful to concrete and would cause discolouration.
- Burlap if used should be first rinsed with water to remove soluble substances and to make the burlap more absorbent.
- On flat surfaces a layer of earth, sand, sawdust (50 mm thick) or hay (15 mm thick) can be used as an effective medium to retain moisture for a longer period than the surfaces kept totally exposed. However, these materials will have to be kept continuously wet and prevented from blowing away or erosion.
- There are also good chances of discolouration of the concrete in this method and hence precautions must be taken while selecting the different cover materials.

5.10.4 Plastic Sheets

Plastic sheets made from polyethylene film comes under the category of effective moisture barriers and can be used on horizontal, vertical surfaces as well as on surfaces of different shapes and sizes. The following precautions are necessary when this method is used :

- All edges and corners must be kept well covered and sheets firmly placed on the concrete surface. Wind blowing away the sheets at the edges and corners and drying the concrete in these areas.
- Lap joints should be minimum 300 mm between the sheets.

- The sheets should be in close contact with the concrete surface. Wind should not be allowed to blow between the concrete surface and the sheets, causing rapid drying of the moisture in the concrete top surface.
- The vertical surfaces must be firmly fixed with tapes or strings.
- Place and fix plastic sheets within half an hour of removal of form work from vertical surfaces. On slabs the sheets should be placed as soon as concrete has hardened enough to prevent surface damage.
- Avoid plastic sheets from wrinkling while spreading on the horizontal surfaces, wrinkling may cause discolouration in patches.
- The polyethylene film should be of at least 0.10 mm thickness and preferably be transparent or white opaque in colour when used in warm weather. Black sheets can be used during cool weather.

The polyethylene film/sheet can be ideally used in combination with other methods as stated below to give excellent curing to the concrete surface and totally eliminating any defects due to in adequate curing.

- After placing the sheet firmly on the concrete surface water is allowed to flow between the concrete and the sheet.
- After layers of soaked hessian cloth or burlaps are placed on the concrete surface they are covered with plastic sheets which help in retaining moisture for a very long time as evaporation is virtually prevented as condensation of water vapour takes place on the internal sheet surface. The above combinations are strongly recommended at site where drying shrinkage cracks and crazing are repeatedly observed.

5.10.5 Curing Compounds

- Curing compounds are now easily available in our country.
- They generally consist of waxes, resins, chlorinate rubber and solvents of high volatility and form a thin liquid membrane on the concrete surfaces and result in preventing to a certain extent evaporation losses.
- The curing compounds are generally available in two types, clear or translucent and white pigmented.
- The clear or translucent curing compounds may contain a fugitive dye to assure complete coverage of the concrete surface by visual inspection. This dye fades away as soon as the application is few hours old.

The following precautions are necessary when curing compounds are used :

- Pigmented compound should be stirred in a container before use as there is a tendency for the dye to settle down.
- Curing compound should be applied soon after final finishing of the horizontal surface is completed or soon after the form work of vertical surfaces is removed.

- Curing compound should be sprayed uniformly on the concrete surface. Brush application may not give the desired coverage or performance.
- Curing compound must be sprayed on moist concrete surface. If coating is sprayed evenly the curing compound will cover nearly 3.5 to 5 sq. m per litre.
- Curing compound must be preferably sprayed in two layers. The second layer must be sprayed at right angle to the first layer.
- Curing compounds can prevent proper bonding between hardened concrete and subsequent fresh concrete or bonding between steel and concrete.

Proper precautions are necessary while spraying so that the curing compound is not accidentally sprayed onto reinforcement steel or construction points.

- Curing compounds must be uniform and easy to maintain in a thoroughly mixed solution. The layer must not sag, run-off, peak or collect in grooves.
- The film formed by curing compounds should be tough to withstand early construction traffic without wear or tear.
- The curing compound film should be non-yellowing and should not stain the concrete surface.
- Above all, the curing film should have good moisture retention property.
- The spray nozzle must be held about 300 to 500 mm from the surface especially during windy conditions.
- Make sure that the cleaning solvent is available for cleaning the spraying equipment, the nozzle and the hose whenever there is break in usage for more than half an hour.
- Do not use curing compound on surfaces which are to receive renderings, screeds or paints. The resin film generally breaks down and flakes off after 28 days exposure to bright sunlight but if any is left on the surface, it will prevent bonding of any surface applications which may come on the concrete surface subsequently.
- As a safety precaution, the person spraying the curing compound must wear goggles.

5.10.6 Forms Left in Place

Forms provide good protection against loss of moisture, if the top exposed surface of concrete is kept moist. It is only after stricking the form work that further curing may be necessary.

The following precautions are necessary for form curing :

- Balance exposed surfaces should be kept continuously wet using a soaker hose.
- Wood forms left in place should be kept moist by sprinkling especially during hot and dry weather.
- Steel form work left in place should be kept covered with soaked hessian and kept wet.
- If form work cannot be kept moist than it is preferable to remove them and use alternative curing methods.

The present generation of cements are finer than those available earlier, due to which they gain strength quite rapidly and therefore, need good curing at an early period of time. Adequate strength when curing can be started is often developed within less than a couple of hours of compaction and finishing operations.

It is often observed that at high ambient temperatures and windy conditions freshly placed concrete develops plastic shrinkage cracks and crazing within few hours of its finishing. These cracks, are often through the entire slab thickness, result in permanent defects in the concrete structure causing leakages and subsequent loss of durability.

- Concrete placed with pumps have much higher workability than the conventional concrete, hence there is a tendency of over vibration of the placed concrete and resultant segregation causes fines to surface at the top and coarser materials to settle below. The top layer of finer fines have tendency to shrink and crack. To avoid this it is advisable to plough up the coarse aggregates using a fork (punja) prior to trowelling or finishing.

- Concrete slab surfaces, exposed in the preliminary stages (at the time when initial setting or hardening is taking place) to high velocity winds and high temperatures, shrink due to rapid drying of the surface moisture. It is, therefore, very essential to protect such surfaces from wind with a plastic sheet or other types of covers and prevent the drying of concrete surface. Drying due to high ambient temperatures is prevented by placing moist (not very wet or soaked) hessian or allowing the water to flow gradually on the surface between the concrete and the plastic sheet after concrete has gained the initial set. In certain cases drying is so rapid that before the slab at one end is placed and finished, the concrete placed at the earlier end starts showing signs of shrinkage cracks. Trowelling over the cracked concrete surface when it is in plastic stage can also help reduce cracking of the surface.

- Depending on concrete materials, their temperatures and ambient conditions, plastic shrinkage cracks often appear within 30 minutes to 6 hours of concrete placing, compacting and finishing. Generally, these cracks appear at random locations in slabs or over slab reinforcement. The cause for such cracking in slabs is due to rapid-early-drying or due to location of steel near the top slab surface where settlement of concrete mix due to bleeding (non-cohesiveness) has taken place. Early improvement in concrete as suggested above can help to reduce such cracking.

- Crazing or cracking of concrete in a close crazy pattern on the surface is often observed within one to seven days, and at times even later.

  Rich concrete mix, cast in impermeable form work to give fair faced smooth finish, often displays crazing which can be avoided by improving curing. Floated concrete in slabs, due to poor curing and over trowelling, also display crazing. This too can be improved by proper curing and finishing.

- At some sites the following procedures were followed successfully to avoid plastic shrinkage cracks :
  - The concrete of high workability after placing is first compacted properly in the deeper areas (beams) and lightly in the shallow areas (slabs) and left without finishing for sometime. After about 30 minutes lapse of time (depending on the concrete mix and ambient conditions), the stiffer concrete is once again compacted this time perfectly and finished thereafter.
  - The top surface, if not required to be finished trowel smooth, should be broomed, so that the surface tension on the thin finished layer is reduced, thereby reducing the chances of cracking at the surface.

It is essential to relate temperature of concrete and curing. During curing, adequate warmth is necessary. It is observed that temperature around 15°C is considered optimum for normal curing. However, for ambient temperatures in the range of 10°C to 40°C, normal curing methods as explained earlier are suitable. Additional precautions for curing are necessary, if the temperatures are outside the normal curing temperature range as stated above.

5.10.7 Precautions Above 40°C

The following precautions are necessary, if the ambient temperatures are above 40°C :

- Higher the ambient temperature, the greater is the chance for concrete to dry out if curing and surface protection are not done. It is therefore, necessary, that curing and protection of concrete surface from loss of water is done immediately after compaction and finishing.
- All concrete surfaces are required to be covered with wet (moist not soaked) hessian or other types of covers as soon as finishing is over. The covers should be kept moist for at least few hours untill the concrete can take wetter cutting without surface damage.
- Cold water for ponding or sprinkling on the covers will help in cooling the concrete surface to temperature below 40°C. However, precautions are necessary that after the concrete surface has hardened, cold water used for curing should not have temperature which is far less than temperature of the concrete at its surface.
- Ponded curing water should be adequate enough and replenished before the surface dries up. Alternate wetting and drying is undesirable, because it cracks the concrete surface.
- In very hot climate, form curing is undesirable. The form work should therefore, be removed and wet curing commenced immediately thereafter.
- In hot weather, continuous wet curing is a must in the first 24 hours. Further, curing must be continued depending on availability of water or other curing materials/ methods. Curing must be uninterrupted and continued for as long a time as practicable. The duration of curing should definitely be more than, in case of normal temperature range.

- Curing compounds should be applied only after wet curing for 24 hours is completed.
- Concrete surface should be allowed to dry out gradually at the end of the curing period to avoid chance of cracking or caking.

5.10.8 Precautions Below 10°C

- Generally, precautions are necessary in cold climate to protect the concrete adequately so that the concrete temperatures due to the exothermic reaction are retained significantly within the concrete mass. The lower the ambient temperature, slower is the rate of hydration which results in slower rate of gain of strength.
- It is observed that very little hydration occurs below a temperature of 4°C. Adequate care has to be taken so that water in freshly placed concrete does not freeze at any time till adequate strength gain has occurred. It is, therefore, essential to keep the temperature around and within the concrete to as high as possible (at least 10°C) so that, at no stage, the water mixed in concrete gets converted to ice.
- In ambient temperatures below 0°C, chemical additives (antifreeze) are used to lower the freezing temperature of water in the concrete. Due to this, the water remains in a fluid form and reacts with cement without creating problems in the hydration process. As the hydration process continues, the temperature within the concrete mass rises, due to which freezing of the water in concrete is further prevented till such time concrete has sufficiently hardened. Once water freezes in fresh concrete, concrete can lose about half of its potential design strength.
- In cold climate, temperature of concrete at the time of placing is kept as high as possible, so that concrete after it is cast does not suffer volume changes or lack of hydration due to freezing water within the mix.
- Form work and concrete, in cold climate, are covered with thick blankets during the curing period, so that due to the heat of hydration the concrete temperature rises and hydration process improves which in turn improves the rate of gain of strength of concrete.

5.11 PRECAST (PREFABRICATED) CONCRETE

Precast (Prefabricated) concrete is getting popular day-by-day.

Advantages :
- Economy in form work.
- Possibility of standardization and employment of machinery for manufacture.
- Controlled weather conditions.
- Use of experienced and skilled workmen.
- Temperature effects in the structure are negligible due to many construction joints.
- Defective components can be easily rejected.

Disadvantages :

- Repeated handling may break the unit.
- The problem of connecting various units properly is difficult.

Requirements :

Precast concrete units must be strong at the same time light. It is, therefore, necessary to use light weight concrete in case of non-structural units. Structural units are made either hollow or flanged or are in prestressed concrete so as to cut down the quantity of concrete. It is also necessary to use special methods of consolidation and curing such as vibration, shocks, spinning, steam or electric curing etc. The concrete also is very carefully designed and made. Typical sections of structural precast concrete units are shown in Fig. 5.10.

Applications :

Precast concrete is used for numerous purposes, the following being only a typical list of most important items :

Floors	Sockets for wooden or steel column plates — do — pedestals — do — piles etc. — do — etc.
Building frames	Portals, gabled, frames etc.
Building units	Hollow and solid blocks, lintels, wall panels (hollow or solid), window and door stills, cornices, string courses, chimneys, trusses, roofing tiles etc.
Bridges	Bridge girders, slabs, arch voussoirs.
Miscellaneous	Pipes, transmission line poles, garden furnitures, drains, silos, tanks, railway sleepers etc.

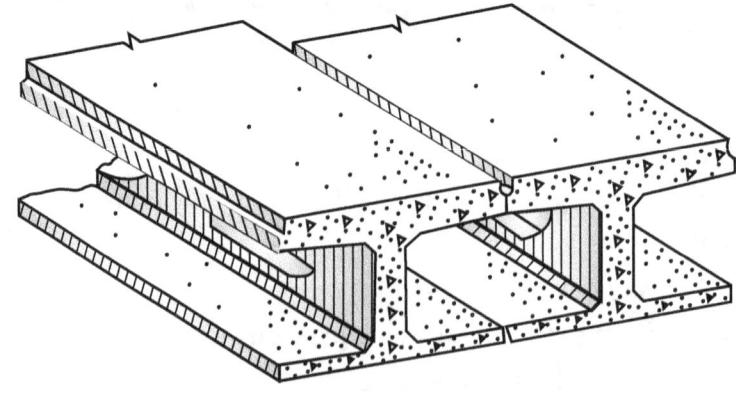

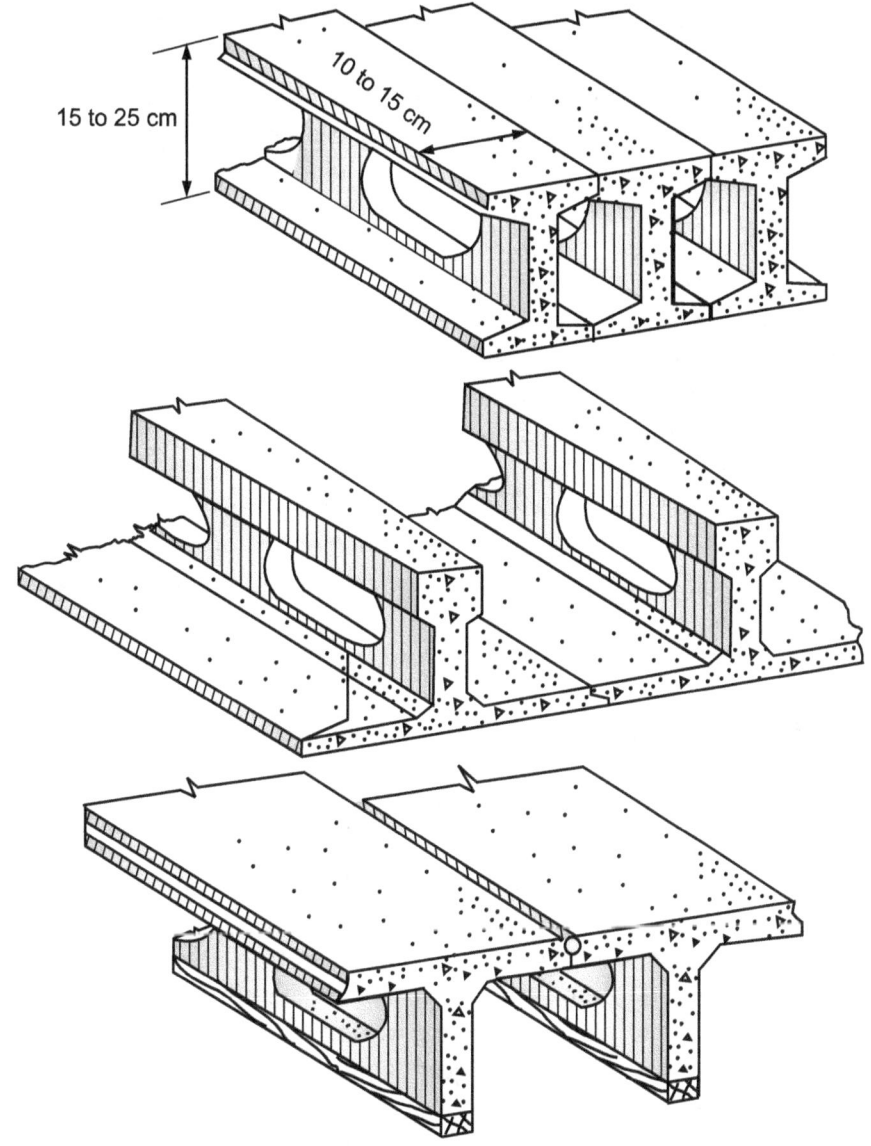

Fig. 5.10 : Precast floor systems

5.12 JOINTS IN CONCRETE STRUCTURES

Following are the two types of joints which are to be provided in the concrete structures :

1. Construction joints.
2. Expansion and contraction joints.

(1) Construction Joints

- The construction joints are provided at locations where the construction is stopped either at the end of day or for any other reason.

- The provision of a construction joint becomes necessary to ensure proper bond between the old work and the new one.
- If the construction activity is arranged in such a way that the work is stopped at expansion or contraction joint, the necessity of a construction joint will not arise.
- However, it is often difficult to complete the concreting for large work in one operation. It then becomes necessary to take special measures to achieve perfect continuity between the previously laid concrete that has already set and hardened and the new concrete.
- The construction joints may be horizontal (Fig. 5.10 (a)) or vertical (Fig. 5.10 (b)). For an inclined or curve member, the joint should be at right angle to the axis of the member. It is necessary to determine the locations of the construction joints well in advance from the view point of structural stability.

Following points should be kept in view, in case of the construction joints :

- The columns should be filled with concrete to a level few centimeters below its junction with the lowest soffit of the beam or bottom of the haunching, if any. The operation of concreting above the construction joint should be taken up after an interval of at least 4 hours.
- The construction joints should be located along or near the planes of the least bending moment and shear force.
- In case of T-beams or L-beams, the ribs should be filled with concrete first and then the slabs forming the flanges can be filled upto the centre of the rib, as shown in Fig. 5.11 (c). If a construction joint between slab and beam becomes unavoidable especially as in the case of long and deep beams, the rib of the beam can be concreted upto 25 mm below the level of soffit of the slab and the construction joint should be located at that level.
- For water tanks and other structures which store water, the strips of copper, aluminium, galvanized iron or other corrosion resistant material, known as the *water stops* or *water bars*, are placed in a construction joint as shown in Fig. 5.11 (d). The function of water stop is to seal the joint against passage of water. The water stop, may also be of natural and synthetic rubber or polyvinyl chloride (PVC). One-half of the water stop is inserted when the concrete is placed and the other-half is left projecting to be covered up by the next stage of concreting.
- For slabs supported on two sides, the construction joints should be vertical and parallel to the main reinforcement. Alternatively, the construction joint can also be provided at the middle of span at right angle to the main reinforcement. For two way slabs, the construction joint can be provided near the middle of the either span.
- For R.C.C. walls, the location of horizontal construction joints is governed by the convenience in placing the form work and the ease of access for compaction of concreting. The continuity at the joint is achieved by the formation of key as shown in Fig. 5.11 (e). The bevelled edged planks are placed on the inner face of the wall shuttering and they are removed before the pouring of concrete above the joint

Fig. 5.11 (e) (i) shows the arrangement of planking and Fig. 5.11 (e) (ii) shows the shape of joint after casting.

- The curing of horizontal construction joint should be suspended a few hours before new concreting is started. If the new concrete is to be laid within 48 hours, the surface of construction joint should be thoroughly cleaned with wire brush and water and treated with cement mortar of the same proportion as that of concrete. However, if the new concrete is to be laid after 48 hours or more, the surface of the construction joint should first be roughened by chiselling. It should then be cleaned of scum, loose aggregates and other foreign matter, wetted and a coat of cement mortar of the same proportion as that of the concrete is applied before placing new concrete.

(2) Expansion and Contraction Joints : These joints are provided in all the concrete structures of length exceeding 12 metres, mainly for two purposes :

- To allow for changes in volume of concrete due to temperature, and
- To preserve the appearance and the original shape of the concrete structures.

These joints generally consists of some elastic material, known as the *joint filler* and *dowels* or *keys*.

- The joint filler should be compressible, rigid, cellular and resilent. In cold weather, it should not become brittle and it should be easy to handle.
- The usual joint fillers are built-in strips of metal, bitumen-treated felt, cane fibre-board, cork bound with rubber or resin, dehydrated cork, natural, cork, soft wood free from knots etc.
- The dowels or keys are provided in these joints to transfer the load.
- The contraction joints are installed to allow for shrinkage movement in the structure. It may either be a complete contraction joint as shown in Fig. 5.10 (f) or a partial contraction joint as shown in Fig. 5.11 (g). In the former case, there is complete discontinuity of both concrete and steel.
- In the latter case, there is discontinuity of concrete, but the reinforcements continue across the joint. In both the cases however no gap is provided for the joint. But only complete or partial separation of the adjacent sections is made.
- Fig. 5.11 (h) shows another form of the contraction joint. It is also known as the *dummy joint* and in this case, a groove of about 3 mm width is created in the concrete member to act as joint. The groove is filled with joint filer and its depth is about one-third to one-fifth of the total thickness of the member.

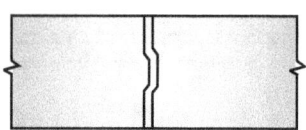

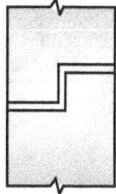

(a) Horizontal construction joint   **(b) Vertical construction joint**

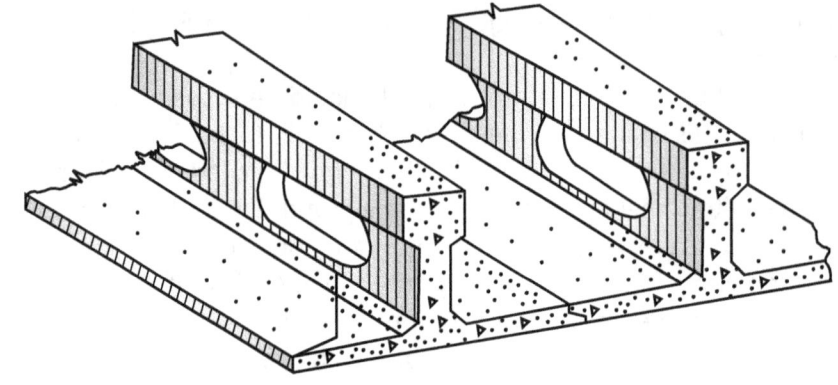

(c) Construction joint

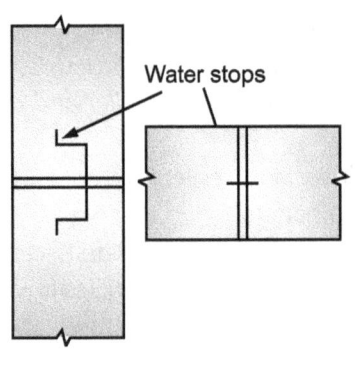

(d) Side floor of a water tank

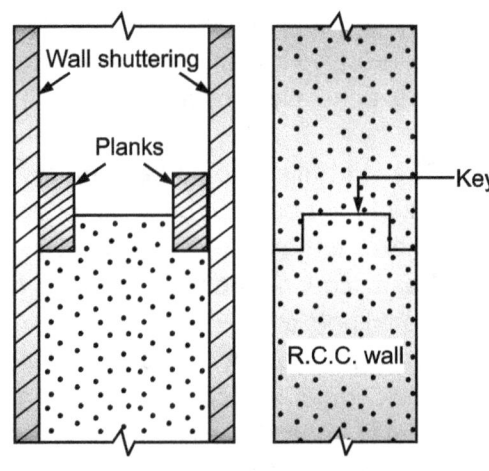

(i)   **(ii)**

**(e) Horizontal construction joint
for R.C.C. wall**

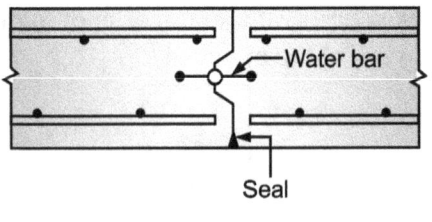

(f) Complete contraction joint

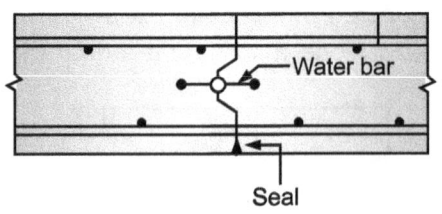

(g) Partial contraction joint

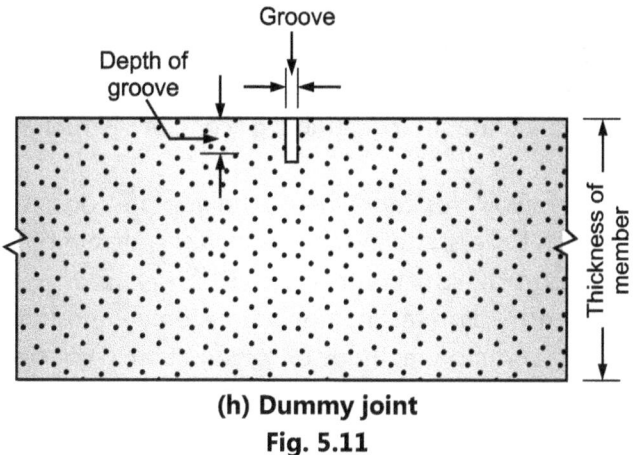

(h) Dummy joint

Fig. 5.11

If for any reason a joint has to be made between the slab, and the beam, it is then necessary to provide some form of key and to add shear reinforcement to meet any weakness at the joint.

The position of joint in column and beam construction should be as illustrated in Fig. 5.12.

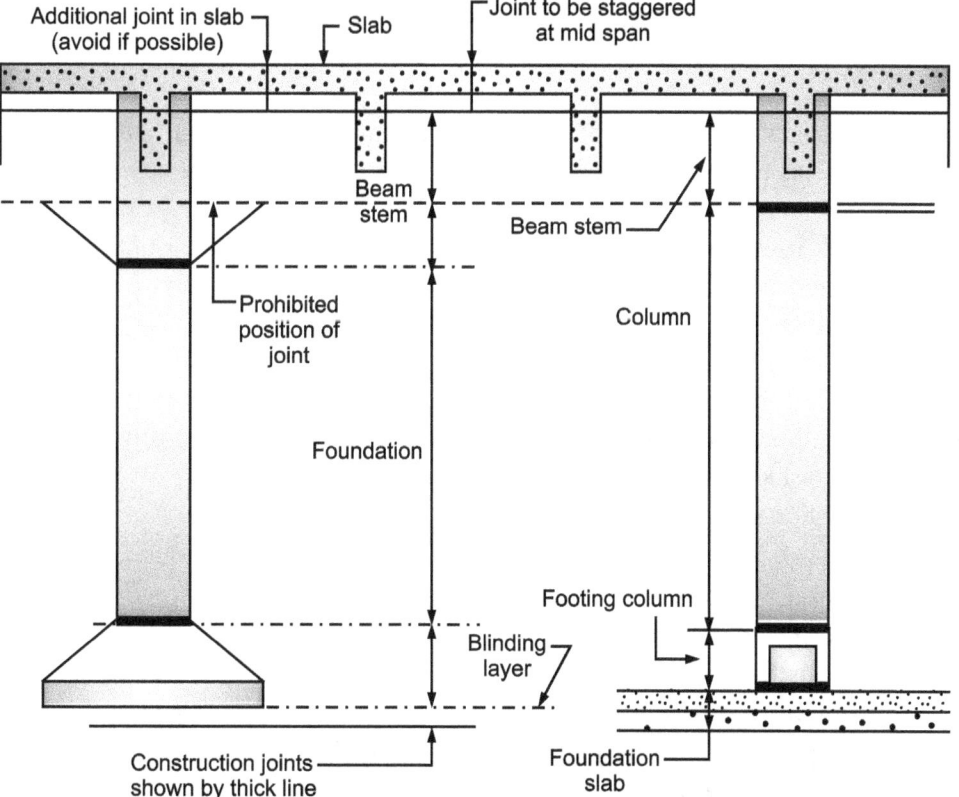

Fig. 5.12 : Construction joints in column and beam construction

Horizontal joints in walls are usually made at such position at the top of a plinth or the top or bottom of a window opening.

5.13 SLIP FORM TECHNIQUE

- Because of superior speed and productivity, slip forms were extensively utilized as a potential formwork candidate in constructing concrete structures for the past few decades.
- Typical projects that employ this formwork technique are: Core of high-rise buildings, silos, telecommunication towers, cooling towers, heavy concrete offshore platforms etc.
- Slip form is a sliding form construction method, which is used to place vertical concrete structures. Slip-form construction technology has become important in high rise concrete structures and the most common methods of construction in concrete silos.
- It differs from conventional concrete forms because it moves semi continuously with respect to the concrete surface in which form ties are not used.
- Recent improvements in larger yoke capacities and better laser guidance result in more efficient and faster slipping rates.
- Slip form is similar in nature and application to jump form, but the formwork is raised vertically in a continuous process.
- It is a method of vertically extruding a reinforced concrete section and is suitable for construction of core walls in high-rise structures such as lift shafts, stair shafts, towers, etc.
- It is a self-contained formwork system and can require little crane time during construction. This is a form work system that can be used to form any regular shape of core.
- The form work rises continuously, at a rate of about 300 mm per hour, supporting itself on the core and not relying on support or access from other parts of the building or permanent works.
- Commonly, the form work system has three platforms. The upper platform acts as a storage and distribution area while the middle platform, which is the main working platform, is at the top of the poured concrete level. The lower platform provides access for concrete finishing.

The basic construction sequence using in this form work is as follows:

- The formwork and the access platform are assembled on the ground.
- The assembly is raised using hydraulic jacks.
- As the formwork rises continuously, continuous concrete and rebar supply are needed until the operation is finished.
- At the end of the operation the formwork is removed using a crane.
- The entire process is thoroughly inspected and highly controlled.

Advantages of Slip Form Technique :

- Prudent and careful planning of construction can achieve high rates of production.
- The slip form does not require a crane to move upwards so the need for crane time is reduced.

- Concrete supply, on the other hand, can be heavily dependent on crane time or lift availability since volumes required are well below the capacity of normal concrete pumps.
- As this formwork operates independently, formation of the core in advance of the rest of the structure takes it off the critical path. This can help to provide stability to the main structure during its construction.
- The availability of the different working platforms in the formwork system allows the exposed concrete at the bottom of the rising formwork to be finished, making it an integral part of the construction process.
- Certain formwork systems permit construction of tapered cores and towers.
- Slip form systems require a small but highly skilled workforce on site.
- The repetitive uniform nature of the work, combined with the engineered nature of the formwork, allows fine tuning of the construction operations, which in turn leads to reduced concrete wastage.
- The form work system is reusable with little waste generated compared to traditional form work.
- Slip form systems can offer safe and cost effective solutions for certain high-rise building structures.

Fig. 5.13 : Photograph showing arrangement required for concreting in slip form work.

Various Steps for Slip Form

A slip-form passes through several steps in order to build one floor of the core or 1 m of silo height as follows :

Step 1 :

- Slip form starts from the bottom level where the building structure connects to the concrete core. If the rest of the building is made of steel typical high-rise structures, steel beams have to be welded to embedded plates that should be installed during slip-form operation in the core.

- Specific form works for the openings of elevators, mechanical, and electrical should be constructed during stoppage duration.
- Usually at this stage, vertical reinforcements are installed with the appropriate lengths to cover one floor.
- For silos, slip form starts from a specific level in its height based on foundation design. In this step, a tower crane lifts reinforcements and embedded plates to the platform.

Step 2 : One-step jacking is done where the slip form is driven up one jacking step = 2 inches = 5.08 cm.

Step 3 : A horizontal rebar will then be installed and concrete will be pumped to fill the empty form. Concrete will be cured and finished in order to be ready for the next step.

Step 4 : Repeat Step 2 four times where 20 cm of form is raised. Horizontal rebar will be installed for the next 20 cm of floor or silo height.

Step 5 : Repeat the above four steps until the completion of one floor bottom of the slip form reaches the following upper floor level or 1 m of silo height.

Step 6 : Repeat the above five steps until the completion of the building core or silo.

Fig. 5.14 : Slip form core for the O2 Arena, Millennium Dome, London
(courtesy Byrne Bros)

Various components to be used for the slip form technique are explained below :

1. Yokes

- A set of yoke leg placed at required alignment and connected by means of yoke beams at the top wherein climbing jack mounted, provides key members for fixing the Form Panel for inner and outer faces.
- Requirements of total number of yoke sets depend on the sizes of the structure and the capacity of hydraulic jack. Spacing of the jack would be around 2.0 m.

2. Slip form Hydraulic Jacks

- We shall be using 75 nos. 6.5 T capacities "Inter form" type hydraulic jacks which climbs on bright steel rod of 32 mm diameter and operates with two sets of ball grip. Jacks can only move upward direction when hydraulic pressure is applied.

- The upper movement of the slip form will be as per set criteria provided by the manufacturers of the Jacks or minimum of 100 mm / 150 mm per hour.

3. **Consoles**

- Consoles shall be provided on to the yokes meant for support of the working platform both inside and outside.
- This working platform shall be used for concreting, reinforcement binding and operation of the hydraulic pumps. Consoles will be fabricated members in combination with structural angles and tubular pipes / reinforcement rod.

4. **Hanging Scaffolding**

- These members are suspended from consoles both inside and outside for the purpose of inspection and finishing work of the exposed concrete after slipping.
- These hanging scaffolds will be of rigid frame structural members.

5. **Waler**

- These member spans within the two yokes and provide support for the Form Panel against lateral force due to green concrete.

5.14 UNDERPINNING   (May 15, 16)

It is a method of providing new foundation below the existing foundation without damaging the stability of existing structure to meet the following requirements :

- If deep foundation is to be constructed adjoining to a building having shallow foundation; the shallow foundation may face some problems, and may need strengthening.
- If height of existing building is to be increased, and existing foundation, if unable to bear increased load, may require strengthening.
- If basement is to be provided to the existing building and if depth and strength of existing foundation is insufficient, then existing foundation may need strengthening.

5.14.1 Methods of Underpinning

Of the various methods, the following methods are commonly used for underpinning :

- Alternate pit method
- Cantilever beam method
- Micropile method.

(a) Alternate Pit Method

- Pits of size 1.2 × 1.2 m or 1.5 × 1.5 m and to a depth greater than the depth of existing foundation, are excavated on either side of the existing wall.
- To start with, pits are excavated at mid length of wall; and further pits are excavated in alternate bays spaced at 3 to 4 m c/c.
- Holes are made in the existing wall at desired level, so that, steel joists (RSJ) called as needle beam with bearing plate on the top can be inserted. Bottom and top of the

hole is levelled and RSJ with bearing plate is inserted and RSJ is supported at either ends. With this arrangement, load of wall above the needle beam is transferred on needle beam, and no damage will be caused for a short period, if soil below the existing foundation is removed.

- As soon as soil below the foundation is removed it is replaced by new, stronger foundation on an unyielding strata.
- Same process is continued in alternate bays; and new foundation is provided using rich cement concrete.
- Later on balance pits are excavated and new foundation is provided in similar manner.
- Needle beams and vertical supports are removed and load is transferred to the new foundation.

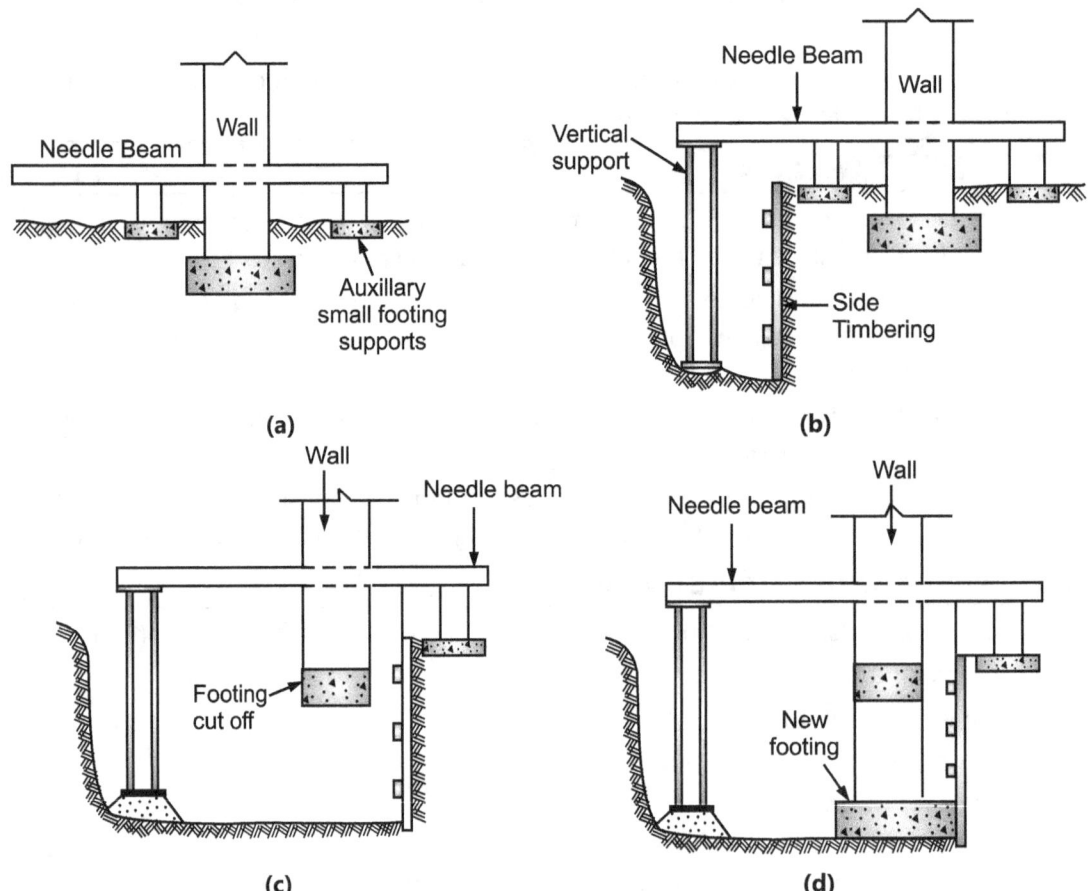

Fig. 5.15 : Alternate pit method

(b) Cantilever Needle Beam Method

If sufficient space is not available to support the needle beams, outside the existing building, then the needle beam is supported on a fulcrum inside building. At the end of needle beam, load is placed on the needle beam. Due to cantilever action, load of the wall is transferred on the needle beam; and soil below existing foundation can be removed without causing any damage to existing building and new stronger foundation can be provided.

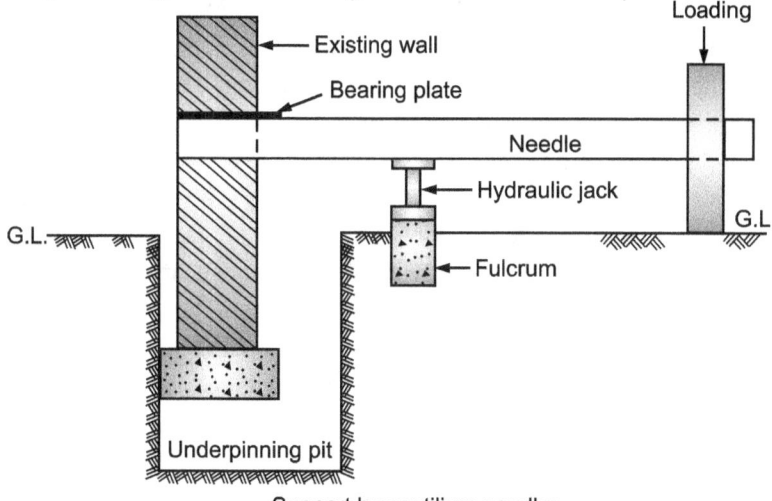

Support by cantiliver needles
Fig. 5.16 : Cantilever needle beam method

(c) Pile Method

Pit method is used with strong strata at a shallow depth and without any ground water problem pits can be excavated. However, if ground water table is met at shallow depth and unyielding strata is available at greater depth, then bored piles are provided on either side of existing wall; and the piles are interconnected by providing pile cap through existing wall.

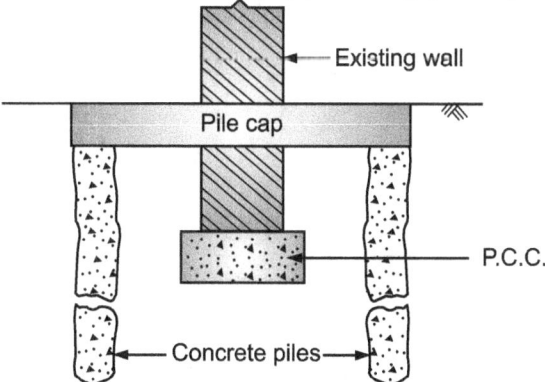

Fig. 5.17 : Pile method

5.15 SCAFFOLDING

When the height of construction is more than 1 m, workmen need some platform on which they can stand safely, keep necessary materials of construction, tools such as bricks, mortar, trowel, plumb bob, hammers etc. Temporary platform made out of timber or steel, to facilitate construction, repairs, maintenance or demolition is called as **scaffolding**. As work progresses, height of scaffolding is increased suitably.

5.15.1 Types of Scaffolding   (May 17)

Different types of scaffolding commonly used are described below :

(a) Single Scaffolding or Brick Layer's Scaffolding : (Ref. Fig. 5.18 (a))

In this type, only one row of vertical members (mostly of timber, bamboo or hollow steel tubular sections) called as standards are erected at a distance of about 1 m from the wall to be constructed. The standards are spaced at a distance of 1.5 to 3 m c/c. Standards "S" are fastened to ledgers "L" by rope or other means. Ledgers are the horizontal members, parallel to the wall and at right angles to standard. Putlogs "P" are placed on ledgers, at right angles to the walls, one end of which is held firmly in wall and are spaced at 1.2 m to 1.5 m c/c. Planks are placed on the putlogs. Guard boards "G" are placed at working level, whereas toe boards are placed slightly above planks to guard against material. Diagonal braces "D" are placed diagonally, to increase stability of standards against lateral movement. This type of scaffolding is slightly weaker than double scaffolding and is used while laying bricks, hence is known as Brick Layer's scaffolding.

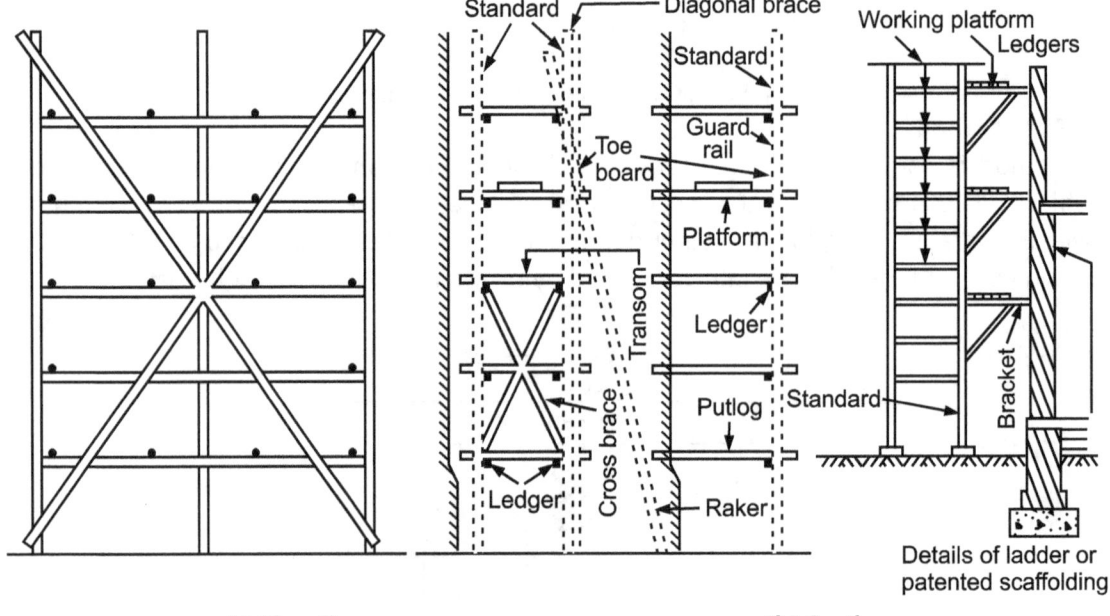

(a) Elevation   **(b) Section**

Fig. 5.18 : Brick layer's scaffolding

(b) Double Scaffolding or Mason's Scaffolding

Frame work of this scaffolding is similar to single scaffolding, except that as against one row of standards provided in single scaffolding, *two rows of standards* are provided in Double scaffolding, and hence it is stronger than single scaffolding. It is used by Mason in construction of stone masonry, hence is termed as Mason's Scaffolding. As shown in Fig. 5.19 (b), one row of standards is placed about 20 cm away from wall, and the other row is about 1.2 to 1.5 m away from wall. Putlogs are not required to be embeded in the wall, and are supported on the two rows of ledgers. Thus, this type of scaffolding is independent of wall.

(c) Cantiliver Scaffolding or Needle Scaffolding : (Ref. Fig. 5.19)

This type of scaffolding is provide under the following conditions :

- Single scaffolding as well as double scaffolding rests at ground level. Such scaffolding may obstruct traffic on busy street.
- If repairs are to be carried out only in few floors at higher elevation in tall building, then it is uneconomical to provide scaffolding from ground floor.

This type of scaffolding is required to be erected with great care, to avoid damages to other parts of building.

At floor level holes are made @ 0.5 to 1 m interval, through which steel joists called as **'needles'** are inserted and projected outside. To provide necessary reaction for the cantiliver outside struts are provided over these joists, which will butt against upper floor slab. On the projected end of Needle, standards are provided. Thus, needle beams provide necessary support to standards. Ledgers, putlogs, planks etc. are provided similar to those in single scaffolding. The strut ends are secured to the floors by wedges.

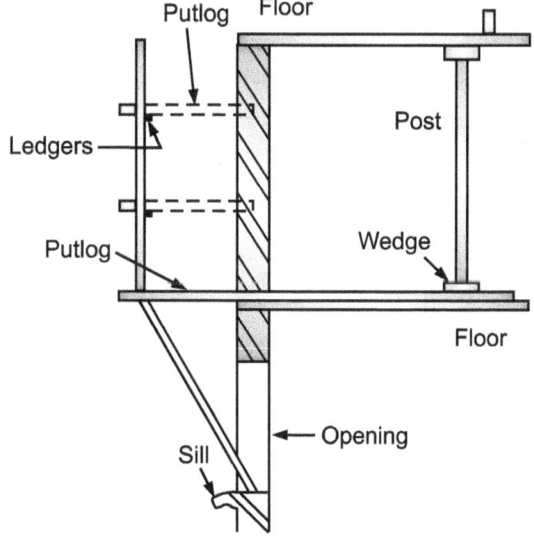

Fig. 5.19 : Cantiliver scaffolding

(d) Suspended Scaffolding

In this type of scaffolding, working platform is suspended from roof (or top of upstream of dam or bridge) by means of ropes or chains. Arrangements are made to raise or lower the platform, so that work can be carried out at desired level. This scaffolding is light in weight and is used to carry occasional maintenance and repairs such as white washing, painting, removing obstacles etc. In this type of scaffolding, standards are not required to be erected. This type of scaffolding does not create any obstruction to traffic etc. at lowerer level.

(e) Steel Scaffolding : (Ref. Fig. 5.20)

Now-a-days, steel scaffolding is being used in preference to timber scaffolding, as it has the following advantages :

* These are simple to erect, as only few sizes and fasteners are to be dealt with.
* It can be used to support vertical loads of all types.
* The scaffolding can be used for form work as well. Hence, its versatility increases.
* Compared to timber scaffolding it is light, strong, fire resistant, durable and has higher scrap value.

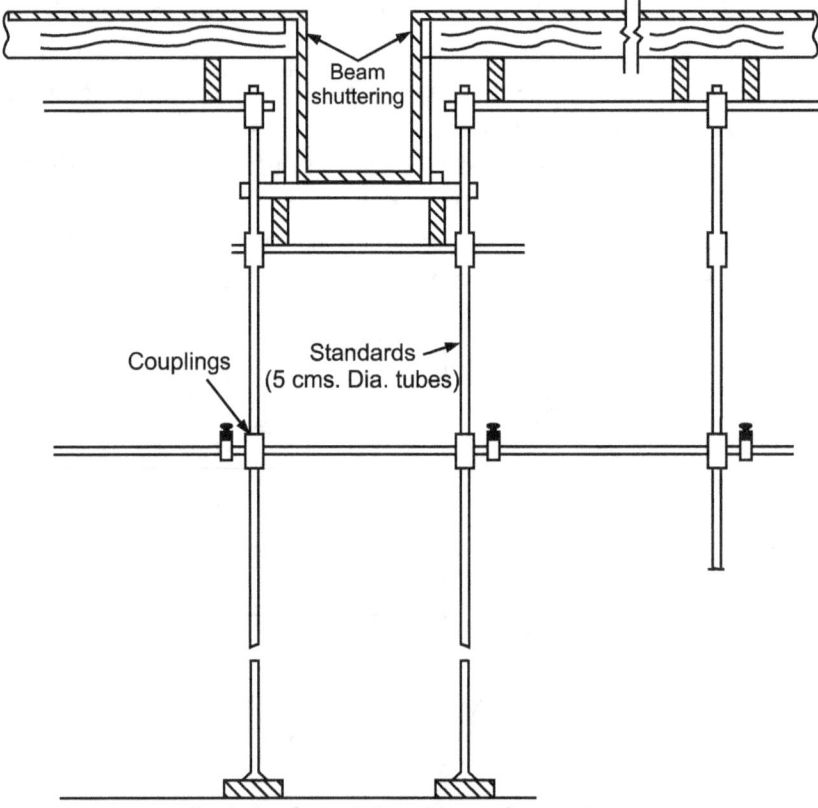

Centering for a slab and beam formwork

Fig. 5.20 : Steel scaffolding

However, it has the following disadvantages :

* Initial investment is high. But in long run it is cheap.
* Small fittings, if lost, becomes difficult to replace. Proper care is required to be taken for storing and handling.
* To guard against corrosion, scaffolding is required to be cleaned, and painted periodically.

Steel tubes used for scaffolding are of 5 mm thickness and are of 40 to 60 mm diameter. Scaffolding can be erected speedily by using special couplings and set screws

REVIEW QUESTIONS

1. What is approximate percentage cost of form work with respect to cost of concrete.
2. State the requirements of form work.
3. State the aspect that should be considered, while selecting material for form work.
4. Compare advantages and disadvantages of steel form work and wooden form work.
5. Make a list of checks that should be carried out on form work :
   (a)   Before concreting   (b) During concreting   (c) After concreting.
6. Fill in the blanks in the following table, indicating the period, before which form work should not be striked :

Column		Removal of Soffit		Removal of Props			
		Slabs	Beams	Slabs		Beams	
				Slabs Span < 4.5 m	Span > 4.5 m	Span < 6 m	Span > 6 m
Period in Days							

7. What is the purpose of releasing agent in connection with form work ? Compare performance of various releasing agents.
8. Make a list of causes of failure of form work and steps to be taken to avoid the same.
9. Explain with a sketch the arrangement of form work made to cast R.C.C. (i) Column footing, (ii) Column.
10. State the precaution that should be taken while concreting of heavily reinforced column so as to avoid honey combing.
11. Draw typical labelled sketch of form work for concreting of beam and slab. Explain functions of shores, stringers, joists. On what, spacing of these componants is based ?
12. Draw a sketch of form work for concreting of staircase and label the following parts :
    (a)   Decking i.e. slab supporting form   (b)   Riser
    (c)   Stiffner   (d)   Side planks
    (e)   Ledger and   (f)   Cross joists.
13. What is the purpose of curing ? Make a list of various methods of curing and explain in detail the followings :
    (a)   Fogging,   (b) Curing compounds.
14. When black polythene sheets and white polythene sheets are used for curing ?
15. Make a list of cautions to be taken while applying curing compounds, as regards :
    (a)   Method of spraying,   (b)   Health of person spraying the compound,
    (c)   Reinforcement,   (d)   Construction joints,
    (e)   If surface is to be plastered/painted after curing.
16. As regards concreting at temperature, (a) more than 40°C and (b) less than 10°C. Explain the followings :
    (a) Defects likely to develope and reasons therefore,
    (b) Precautions to be taken.

17. In a tabular form draw illustrative sketches and explain the following types of joints :
    (a) Horizontal and vertical joint,   (b) Contraction and expansion joint.
18. Indicate by suitable sketch and give reasons for avoiding locations, where joints should not be provided.
19. What are the cutting methods of concrete ? Explain any one in detail.
20. Describe the formwork costing procedure for reinforced concrete column.
21. State the different types of joints provided in concrete work.
22. Name the various temporary structures used in the building construction works. State the objectives of using each.
23. What are the essential requirements of a good form work ?
24. Write a short note on form work for columns.

SOLVED UNIVERSITY QUESTIONS

DEC. 2013

1. Define formwork. State any four component parts of formwork. Explain ideal requirements of formwork. **[6]**
[**Ans.:** Refer Article 5.1, 5.2]

DEC. 2014

1. Write short notes on: Form-work for beam. **[6]**
[**Ans.:** Refer Article 5.4]

MAY 2015

1. Discuss the method underpinning. **[6]**
[**Ans.:** Refer Article 5.14]

NOV. 2015

1. Write short notes on : Form work for slab.
[**Ans.:** Refer Article 5.8]
2. Define the following : (Form work
[**Ans.:** Refer Article 5.1]

MAY 2016

1. Discuss the method underpinning. **[6]**
[**Ans.:** Refer Article 5.14]
2. Write short notes on : Formwork for trapezoidal footing **[6]**

NOV. 2016

1. Draw neat sketch of wooden formwork for a steeped column footing. **[6]**
[**Ans.:** Refer Article 5.7]

MAY 2017

2. Enlist types of Scaffolding. Explain any two in detail. **[6]**
[**Ans.:** Refer Article 5.15.1]

CHAPTER 6
FLOORING MATERIALS

6.1 INTRODUCTION

- The horizontal members of the building which divide vertical space into different parts at different level are called as **floors**.
- Floor supports the occupants, furniture and equipments. A building may be single storeyed or multi storeyed.
- Single storeyed building has only one floor which is called as ground floor. In multi-storeyed structures, there are additional floors which are called as upper floors.
- The floors which are constructed below ground floor are called as **basement floor**.

A floor consists of two components:

- Sub-floor or base course or sub-grade which imparts strength, stability and support floor covering and all other super imposed loads.
- Floor covering which provides a hard, durable, clean, smooth, impervious and beautiful surface to the floor.

Fig. 6.1 : Tile flooring

6.2 FUNCTIONAL REQUIREMENT OF FLOORING MATERIAL
(Dec. 13, Nov. 15)

The floor is intended to serve the following functions:

- It should be strong though to sustain safely the intended to the applied.
- It should resist wear and tear.
- It should sustain impact load.
- It should be easy to clean and maintain.
- It should have pleasing appearance.

- It should be impermeable.
- It should take polish.
- It should not be slippery.
- It should be easily available and economical.

6.3 VARIETIES OF FLOOR FINISHES AND THEIR SUITABILITY

(Dec. 13)

Flooring materials can be broadly classified as :

- **Hard Floor :** Natural stone, clay/ceramic tiles and cement/cement based floors.
- **Wooden Floors :** Hardwood, softwood.
- **Soft Floors :** PVC (vinyl), coir, cork, linoleum.
- **Floor Coverings :** Carpets, rugs and other floor furnishings.
- **Specialised Floors :** Mild steel/iron tiles, plastics, seamless, aluminium.

Note : "All purpose" referes to the human activities confined to domestic houses, flats etc. commercial offices, shops, schools and public buildings.

Light Foot Traffic : Seldom used areas i.e. floors in houses, executive cabins etc.

Medium Foot Traffic : Moderately used areas i.e. floors in commercial establishments.

Heavy Foot Traffic : Much used areas i.e. floors in public buildings and reception room of offices.

Table 6.1 : Different types of flooring materials and their applications

Sr. No.	Material	Usage	Remarks
(1)	**Hard floors**		
1.	**Natural stone**		
	(a) Cuddapah	All purpose	Economical, available only in black. Not commonly used in bathroom, main room.
	(b) Granite	All purpose	Expensive, elegant and durable.
	(c) Marble	All purpose	Expensive, elegant and durable.
	(d) Quartzite	All purpose	Economical
	(e) Slate	All purpose	Economical
	(f) Sand stone	Light traffic areas	Economical
	(g) Shahabad	All purpose	Economical
	(h) Kotah, limestone	All purpose	Available in black colour only.

...Conti.

2.	**Clay/ceramic tiles**		
	(a) Sintered clay/ceramic glazed tiles	All purpose	
	(b) Unglazed or quarry tiles	All purpose	
3.	**Cement/cement based**		
	(a) Cement concrete (in-situ)	All purpose includes industrial floor	End use governs mix properties.
	(b) Terrazzo floors (in-situ)	All purpose	Frequently laid where a high standard of appearance and cleanliness is required.
	(c) Mosaic tiles	All purpose	Used where high cleanliness is not required.
	(d) Other cement based tiles	All purpose	Available in various designs and shapes.
(2)	**Wooden floors (Timber flooring)**		
1.	Hard wood	Heavy foot traffic areas	It can be painted with polyurethane points. It is often covered by carpet. Durability can be improved by good seal.
2.	Parquet	Light medium foot traffic areas	It is not used in damped areas.
3.	Softwood	Light foot traffic areas	Painted with polyurethane paint. It is covered by carpet.
(3)	**Soft floors**		
1.	Coir tiles	Light medium foot traffic areas	
2.	Cork tiles	Light-heavy foot traffic areas	Avoid its use in damp areas.
3.	Linoleum	Light-heavy foot traffic areas	Available with anti-static properties.
4.	PVC (vinyl) with Asbestos	Light-heavy foot traffic areas	Available with anti-static properties.

6.4 CONSTRUCTION DETAILS OF CONCRETE FLOOR   (May 16)

This flooring is called as artificial stone flooring. It's constructional details are explained as follows :

(i) Preparation of Ground
- It should be well compacted. It should be watered properly to gain considerable strength to offer support.
- It should not contain pockets of loose soil.

(ii) Preparation of Sub-grade
- If sub-grade is of concrete it's proportion will be 1 : 2 : 4. It should be mixed thoroughly by any means i.e. manually or mechanically.
- It should be provided with proper slope. It should be coated with cement slurry to get a good bond between the sub-grade and concrete floor.
- The surface of subgrade should be roughened with steel wire brushes without disturbing the concrete. The sub-grade may be R.C.C. slab.

(iii) Laying of Flooring
- The concrete should be placed gently and evenly spread within the panel of area 2 m^2.
- The panel should be of uniform size. Its dimension should not exceed 2 m.
- The operation of laying of concrete for each panel should be finished within half an hour.
- To ensure uniformity of colours and straightens in all the panels it should be laid in one operation using plain asbestos sheet stripes at the junction of the panels.
- The panels should be bounded by wooden battens. The depth of the battens should be same as that of the concrete flooring surface of the flooring which should be smoothed with wooden floats.
- The battens should be removed after 24 hours once laying of concrete is finished.
- If ends are damaged, it should be repaired with cement mortar 1 : 2.

(iv) Finishing of Flooring
- Once moisture is varnished cement slurry should be prepared.
- It should spread over flooring. It should be properly pressed and finished smooth.

(v) Curing
- Once the top layer has hardened, curing should be done for minimum ten days.

Casting Large Floors
- For large industrial and commercial buildings it is not feasible to cast floor of the size required in one section.
- There are two methods of casting large floors to remove this difficulty.

These are explained as follows :

(1) The Chequer Board Method
- In this method, floor can be subdivided into a series of sections of restricted width and length. Alternate sections of the floor can cast in a chequer board arrangement.
- This method is not easy. It requires to put many structural joints running along and across the floor. It does not offer speedy construction.

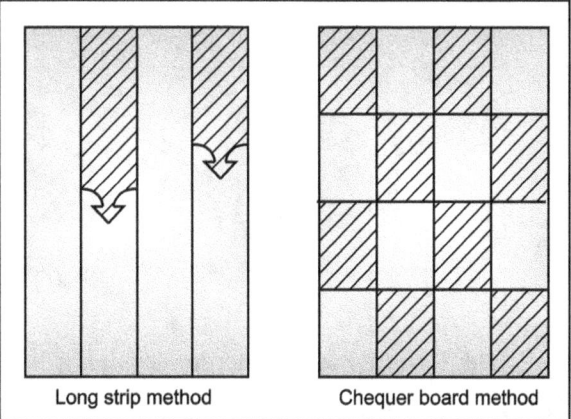

Fig. 6.2 : Long strip and chequer boad options

(2) The Long Strip Method
- It is based on the division of floor into a series of long strips. It is around 4.5 m in width, running the full length of the building or upto a selected movement joint.
- The strips can be cast in two phases, initially with alternate strips and the in-fill joints cast after some days.
- Narrow edge strips (630 – 1000 mm wide) are formed near the walls to allow ready access for the compacting beam across full width strips.
- There is possibility of development of cracks. To control it strips are normally divided into bays. The need of the joints is related to the length of the strips and the presence of reinforcement.

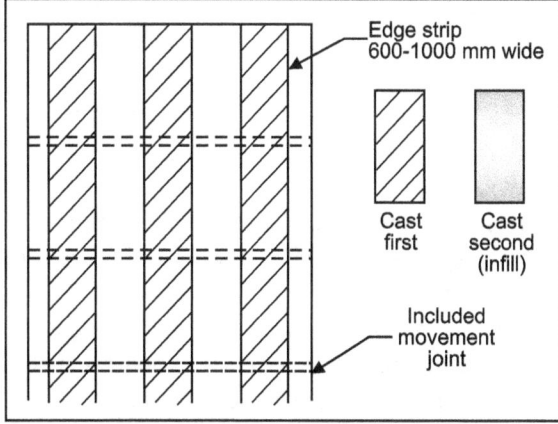

Fig. 6.3 : Long strip floor layout

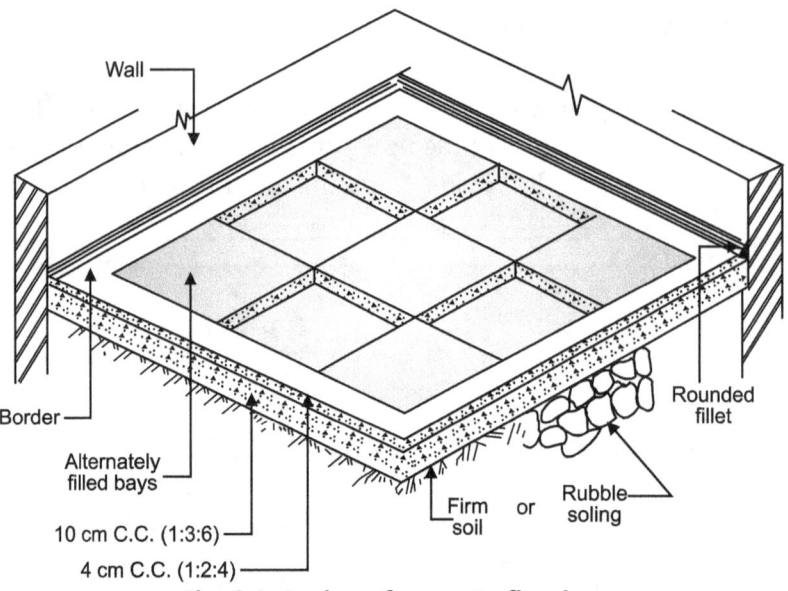

Fig. 6.4 : Laying of concrete flooring

6.5 CONSTRUCTION DETAILS FOR TILE FLOORING   (Dec. 13)

It can be divided into the following types :

(i) Levelling of Ground
- The ground should be levelled properly.
- It should be properly watered and rammed so that it can offer good base to different components.

(ii) Preparation of Subgrade
- It should be of mortor cement concrete or R.C.C. of 15 to 20 cm thickness as per requirement.
- The top surface should be kept slightly rough. The required slope should be provided to the subgrade.

(iii) Laying of Tiles
- The surface of the subgrade should be cleaned of all loose materials. The mortor bedding of thickness 12 mm to 20 mm should be placed in any one place. The cement slurry should be spread.
- Tiles fixed in the adjoining wall should be arranged that the surface of the round edge tiles should correspond to skirting or dado. Each tiles should be well pressed and gently tapped with mallet (wooden).
- The joints should be kept as close as possible and in straight lines. It should not be more than 1.5 mm. After two days it should be polished as per the requirement. After polishing it should be washed with solution.

[**Note :** For Makrana/coloured and veined Pepsu/Baroda marble slabs.
Slabs should be hard, dense uniform and homogeneous in texture. It should have even crystalline grain and free from defects and cracks. It's edges should be machine cut true and square. The rear surface should be rough enough to provide a key for the mortar.]

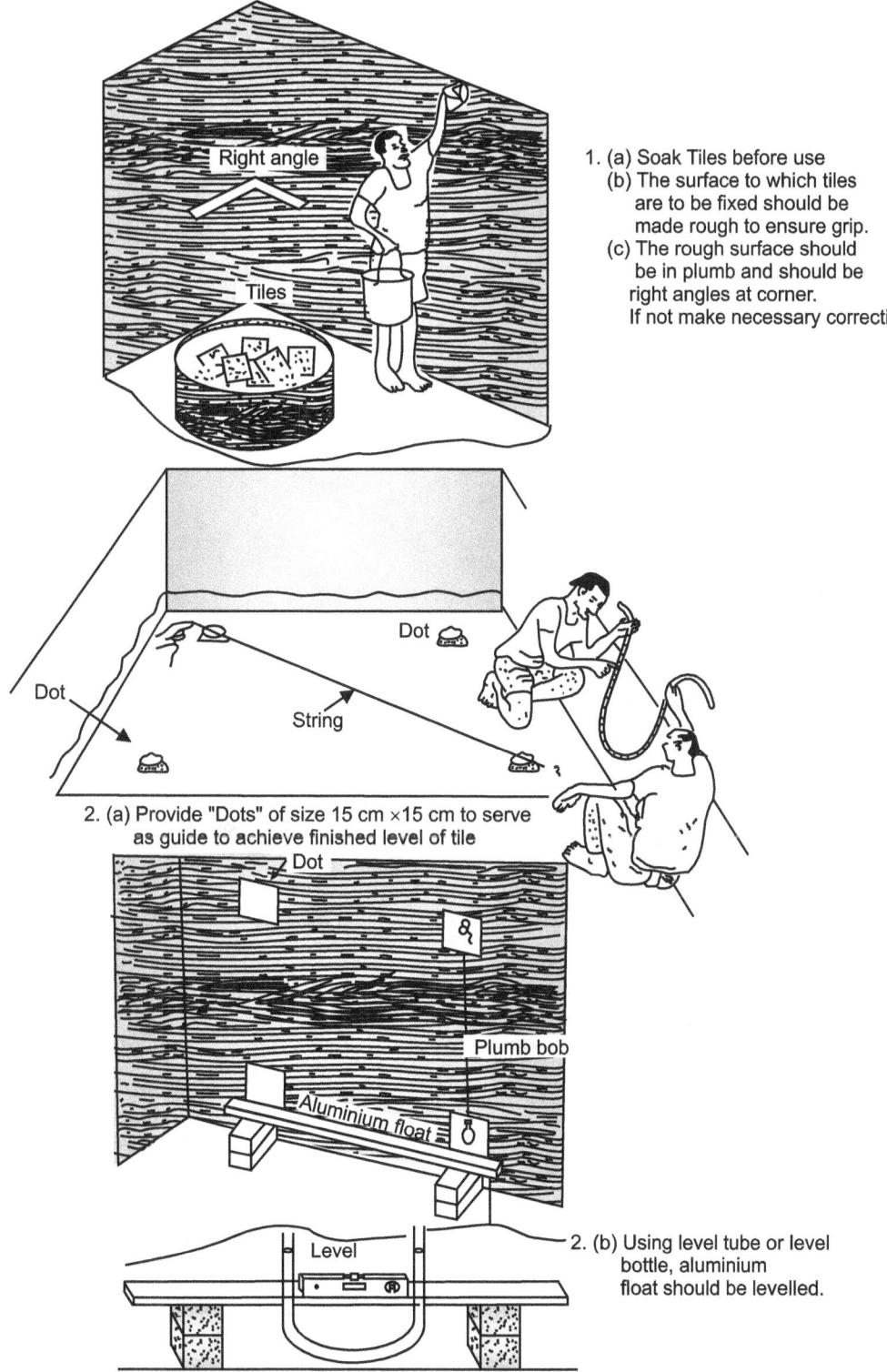

1. (a) Soak Tiles before use
   (b) The surface to which tiles
       are to be fixed should be
       made rough to ensure grip.
   (c) The rough surface should
       be in plumb and should be
       right angles at corner.
       If not make necessary corrections.

Right angle

Tiles

Dot

Dot

String

2. (a) Provide "Dots" of size 15 cm ×15 cm to serve
       as guide to achieve finished level of tile

Dot

Plumb bob

Aluminium float

Level

2. (b) Using level tube or level
       bottle, aluminium
       float should be levelled.

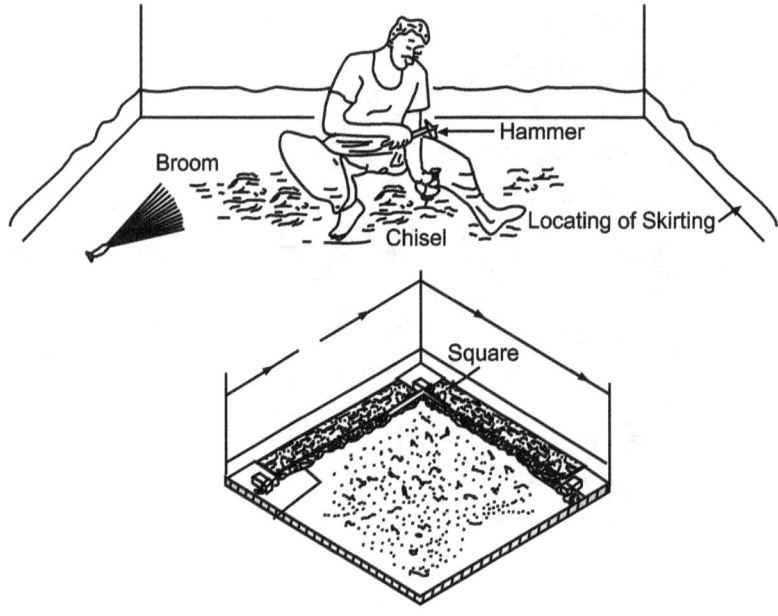

3. (a) Reference lines are set up using level tube
   (b) Using the reference lines, tiles are placed in line, level and at right angles.

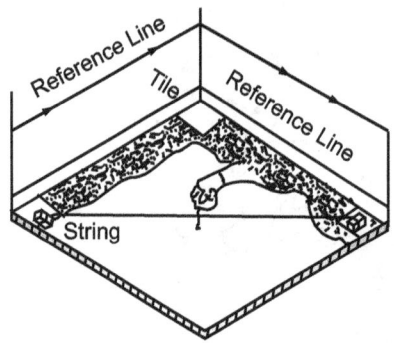

5. Laying cement morter below tiles

4. (a) Using line "Dot" and tape, accuracy of tiling work is checked.
   Tiles near wall should be about 12mm away from the wall.

7. After laying tile, it is levelled by a tamping light with wooden mallet.

Polishing of tiles in skirting is done manually

6. Placing tile over cement morter

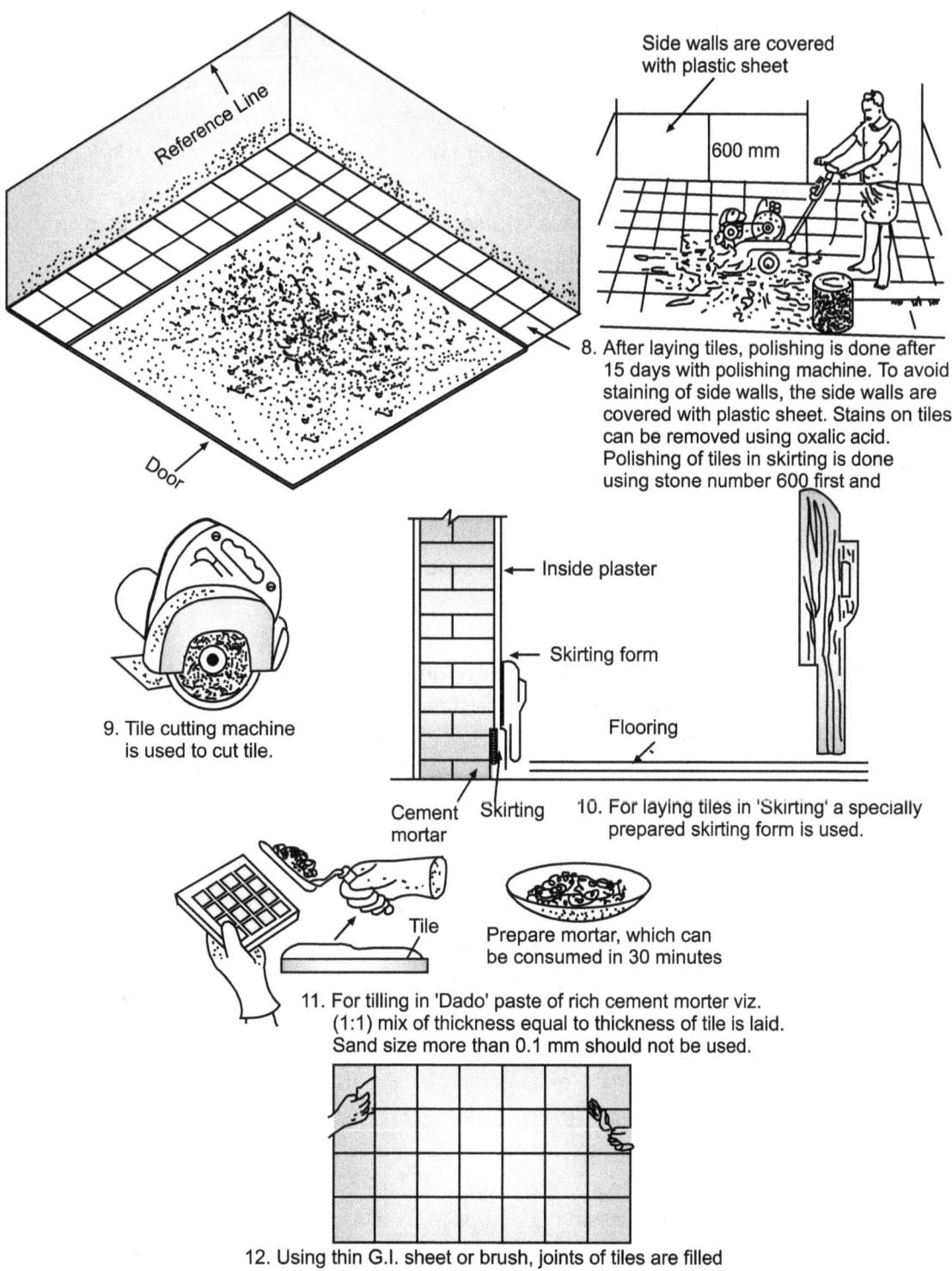

8. After laying tiles, polishing is done after 15 days with polishing machine. To avoid staining of side walls, the side walls are covered with plastic sheet. Stains on tiles can be removed using oxalic acid. Polishing of tiles in skirting is done using stone number 600 first and

9. Tile cutting machine is used to cut tile.

10. For laying tiles in 'Skirting' a specially prepared skirting form is used.

11. For tilling in 'Dado' paste of rich cement morter viz. (1:1) mix of thickness equal to thickness of tile is laid. Sand size more than 0.1 mm should not be used.

12. Using thin G.I. sheet or brush, joints of tiles are filled with white cement or matching coloured cement.

Fig. 6.5

6.6 CONSTRUCTION FOR STONE FLOORING

Stone flooring construction details are governed by purpose of flooring, thickness of stone, type of mortar specified in the defined specifications.

The method of construction of stone flooring can be divided into the following steps :

(1) General Preparation

- To offer proper support to base course and wearing surface and also to distribute load evenly to the ground, it should be compacted properly.
- It should obtain maximum strength by reasonable spraying of water.

(2) Preparation of Bare Course or Bedding

- Before spreading the mortar the floor or base should be cleaned of all dirt, scum or laitance and of loose material.
- It should be evenly and smoothly spread over the base by the use of screed battens. The thickness of the mortar bedding should not be less than 12 mm and not more than 25 mm.
- The required slope shall be given to the bed. When sand bed is provided, it shall spread upto a thickness of 12 mm. The sand shall not contain more than 10% of clay. Sand used shall be coarse.

(3) Fixing the Stones

- Before placing/laying, it should be thoroughly wetted with clean water. Neat cement grout or cement slurry of required consistency should be spread on the mortar bed.
- If sand bed is provided there is no need of cement grout.
- The specified stone should be placed on the neat cement float. It should be evenly and firmly bedded to the required level and slope in the mortar bed. It should be gently lapped with wooden mallet.
- If there is hollow sound or gentle tapping, the stone should be removed and reset again properly. No hollow spaces should be left.
- The joints should be of uniform thickness and in straight lines. The joints should be 6 mm to 10 mm thick. It should be filled solidly with mortar for their required full depth.
- It should be struck smooth. The stones should be placed such as to give continuous parallel long joints with cross joints at right angles to them.
- For polished stone flooring thickness of joints should not exceed 1.5 mm. Joints should be grouted with neat cement slurry.
- The flooring joints have completely set, the surface should be machine polished to give smooth finish and pleasing appearance.
- After this activity the flooring should be thoroughly cleaned and free from any mortar strains.

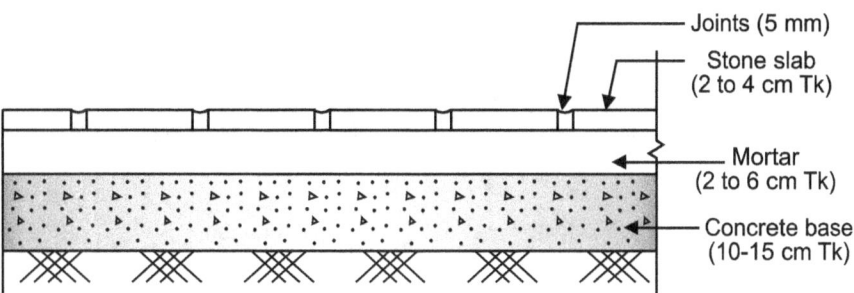

Fig. 6.6 : Cross-section of stone flooring

6.7 JOINTS IN LONG SPAN FLOORS

- Large span floors are used for industrial and commercial buildings. For these floors there may be possibility of expansion and contraction process.
- To accommodate the movements due to these processes, there is requirement of joints. The design of joint is important to resist the vertical movement between bays.

The joints are classified into four categories as below :

(1) Longitudinal Joints
- It is main construction joint in the floor. It separates the slab into the long strip pattern. It consists of tie bars. If tie bars are debonded, it will allow a degree of contraction in the slab across the joint.
- If tie bars are bended the contraction will be restricted.
- In both conditions vertical loads are transferred between adjacent bags through the bars.
- If tie bars are bonded the contraction will be restricted. In both conditions vertical loads are transferred between adjacent bays through the bars.

(2) Induced Joints
- These are used to control the bay length. It can be obtained through a mechanism for controlled cracking of the slab as it cures.
- This joint is depending upon the friction between the sides of the joint for restriction of vertical movement.
- It can be accomplished by sufficient interlocking of the exposed aggregate at the crack faces.

(3) Movement Joints
- It is included within the slabs. Due to variation in temperature there is natural movement of the material.
- Due to shrinkage of concrete, contraction joint is becoming more common. Sometime expansion joint is also required.

(4) Isolation Joints
- It is sub-group of movement joint. Its purpose is to allow movement of slab around fixings.
- In framed structures it is mainly common around the bases of columns or stanchions.

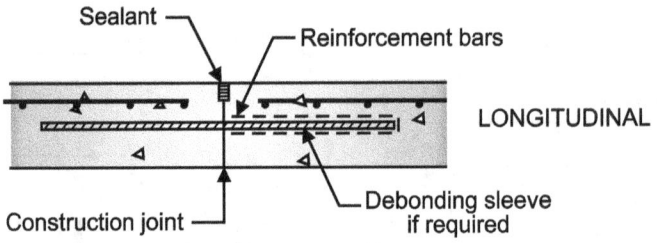

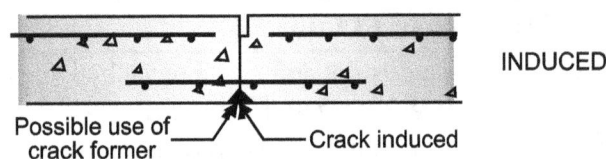

EXPANSION

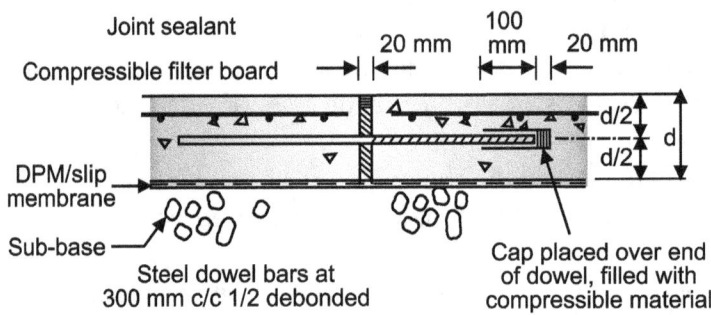

CONTRACTION

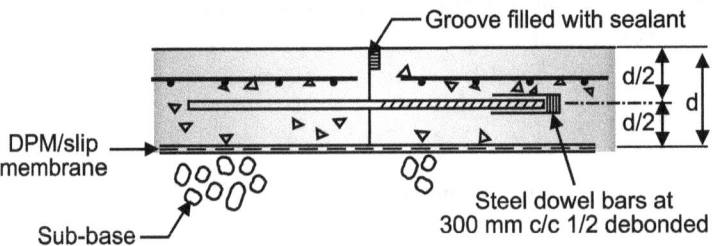

Fig. 6.6 : Joint details

6.8 TYPES OF FLOORING　　　　(Nov.16, May 14, 15)

(1) Filler Joist Floor

- Small sections of rolled steel joists, resting on wall or on steel beams, are placed within concrete. The centre to centre distance is 600 to 900 mm.

- These joists serve the purpose of reinforcement.
- A concrete cover of the minimum 25 mm is to be provided to avoid corrosion. Flooring is laid over concrete surface.

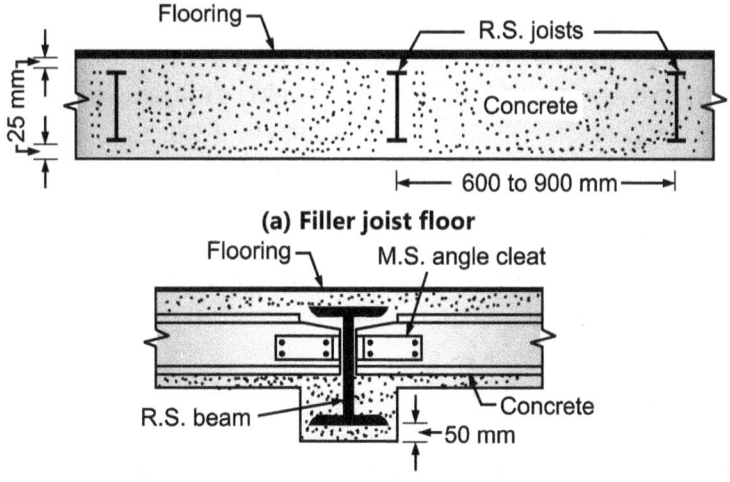

(a) Filler joist floor

(b) Connection of R.S. beam with R.S. joists

Fig. 6.7

(2) Jack Arch Floors

- Arches made up of bricks or concrete are so laid as to rest on lower flanges of M.S. joists.
- The joist in turn rests either on wall or a beam; with centre to centre distance ranging within 800 to 1200 mm.

(a) Brick Jack Arch Flooring

- Laying of bricks starts from edges of joists. Bricks to be used are well burnt and to be saturated with water.
- Joints are to be filled with rich mortar for proper binding and transfer of load from key brick to springer brick and finally to the support.
- Curing of brick work is to be carried out for 15 days minimum. On the top of concrete (above the arch) floor tiles are placed.

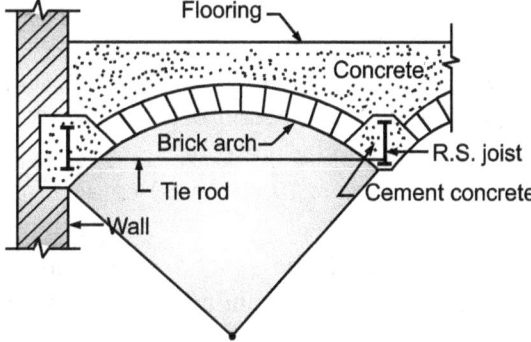

Fig. 6.9 : Brick jack arch floor

(b) Concrete Jack Arch Floor

- **Centering :** Made up of steel plate of about 3 mm thickness, hence can be moulded to take the required shape. It has pair of holes (centre to centre distance 750 mm) to hold steel bars which keep the arch at its position.
- Concrete is laid to required thickness and curing for ten days is carried out. Shuttering is to be removed after concrete attains sufficient strength.
- Rolled steel joists are embedded within concrete if the span is more than 3.6 m for the arch. Tie rods are to be provided between the joists to resist horizontal thrust in extreme pair of steel joists.

(3) Hollow Block and Rib Floor

- As the name suggests the hollowness for the blocks is responsible for reduction in overall weight of the floor and to achieve economy. This is preferred in case of hospitals, hotels, schools, offices etc.
- The blocks are placed at about 100 mm gap in between to facilitate position of M.S. bars.
- A cover of 80 mm or more is to be employed for this roof flooring on the top of which suitable flooring can be laid.

Advantages : Economical, fire proof, sound proof, light in weight, installation of electrical and plumbing accessories through hollow portions can be conveniently carried out.

Tiles Used : Hollow concrete or hollow clay floor tiles.

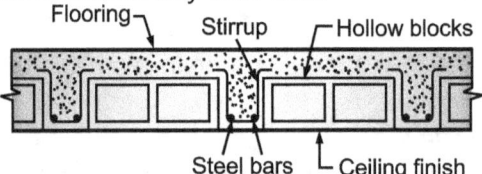

Fig. 6.10 : Hollow block and rib floor

(4) Cork

- Natural, flame retardant, made from bark of cork oak tree (bark being peeled after every 9 to 14 years with average life of 500 years).
- The flooring do not react to any fluid, supple under your feet but with a drawback that impact load creates a depression mark on it.
- The other characteristics of cork are as follows : Insect repellent, scratch resistant, fire resistant, sound absorbent, heat insulation qualities, non-slippery.
- The cork tile or carpet is made by heating or baking cork granules with linseed oil, phenolic or other resin binders under pressure.
- Sizes of tiles available are 10 cm × 10 cm to 30 cm × 90 cm and thickness ranging between 5 to 15 mm.
- Cork tile with natural finish should be sanded, sealed and waxed immediately after installation. Cork floors must be maintained with sealers and protective coatings to prevent soiling.

Applications : Libraries, Theatres, Art galleries, Broadcasting stations etc.

(5) Terrazzo Flooring

- Terrazzo topping i.e. terrazzo mix of broken marble chips, stones, ceramic articles is laid on concrete sub-base. Cement and epoxy resins are used as binders.
- Normally, it can be used anywhere in residential, public buildings as the look is effective. It also takes high polish and seamless laying of the mix makes the layer water proof.
- Normal thickness of topping PS 6 mm with marble chips 3 to 6 mm.

6.9 MATERIAL, TESTS AND IS SPECIFICATION

Various types of tiles are available. The following are types of tiles:

- Clay Flooring Tiles - IS 1478 – 1969.
- Flat Burnt Clay Tiles for Terracing – IS 2690 Part I and II.
- Flat Burnt Clay tiles for Irrigation, Drainage Work - IS 3367 – 1975.
- Manglore Tiles - IS 654 – 1972.
- Roofing Slate Tiles - IS 6250 – 1981.
- Tiles of Lime Stone - IS 1128 – 1974.
- Tiles of Sand Stone - IS 6250 – 1981.
- Tiles of Marble - IS 3622 – 1977.
- Glazed Earthen Ware Tiles - IS 777 – 1970.
- Cement Concrete Flooring Tile - IS 1237 – 1980.

6.9.1 Clay Flooring Tiles

- These tiles are flat, square and are available in many colours.
- These should be uniform in size, shape and free from irregularities and foreign materials either on the surface or on the fractured surface.

Dimensions and permissible tolerances are :

Length	Width	Minimum thickness
150 mm	150 mm	15 / 20
200	200	20 / 25
250	250	30
Tolerances ± 5 mm	± 5 mm	± 2 mm

The tiles are classified in three classes, the physical requirements of which are as under :

	Characteristics of Clay Flooring Tile	Class I	Class II	Class III
1.	Water Absorption (maximum)	10%	19%	24%
2.	Flexural strength kg/cm^2	6	3.5	2.5
3.	Impact Test : Max. height (in mm) drop of steel ball of 35 mm diameter and mass 170 gm.			
	Thickness of tile 15 mm	25	20	15
	20 mm	60	50	40
	25 mm	75	65	50
	30 mm	80	70	60

6.9.2 Flat Burnt Clay Tiles

- Usually, these are available in rectangular shape in various sizes available for terracing. These may be hand made or machine made.

- Burnt clay tiles are also used for lining irrigation and drainage work. However, these tiles differ from those used in roofing, as detailed in the following table.

Type of Tiles	IS No.	Dimensions with tolerances	Physical properties			
			Compressive strength kgf /cm^2 min	Water Absorption % (max.)	Transverse strength kgf/cm^2	WrapMax (mm)
1. Tiles for lining irrigation and drainage works.	3367 – 1975	l = 300 ± 10 mm b = 150 ± 5 mm t = 50 mm ± 1.5 mm	105 75	15% (for class 105) 20	15 12	3 mm 3
	2690 Part II (Hand made)	l = 150 to 250 in stages of 25 mm. b = 100 to 200 mm in stages of 25 mm	75	20% by weight	–	2%
2. Burnt clay flat terracing tiles.	2690 Part I (machine made)	Thickness = 25 to 50				
		l and b same as above t = 15 and 20 mm		15% by weight	15	

6.9.3 Cement Concrete Flooring Tile   (May 15)

According to IS : 1237 – 1980 followings are definitions of some types of tiles :

- **Plain Cement Tiles :** Tiles in the manufacture of which no pigments and stone chips are used in the wearing surface.

- **Plain Coloured Tiles :** Tiles having a plain wearing surface where pigments are used but no stone chips.

- **Terrazo Tiles :** Tiles at least 25% of whose wearing surface is composed of stone chips in a matrix of ordinary or coloured portland cement mixed with or without pigments and mechanically ground and filled.

Materials

(1) Cement

- Cement used in the manufacture of tiles shall be ordinary portland cement conforming to IS : 269 – 1976 or rapid hardening portland cement conforming to IS : 8041 – 1978 or white portland cement conforming to IS : 8041 –1978 or Port land cement conforming to IS : 1489 – 1976.

(2) Aggregate

- Aggregate used in the backing layer of tiles shall conform to the requirements of IS 383 – 1970.
- For the wearing layer aggregates shall consist of marble chips or any other natural stone chips of singular characteristics of hardness, marble powder or dolomite powder, or mixture of two.

(3) Pigments

- Pigments, synthetic or otherwise, used for colouring tiles shall have durable colour. It shall not contain any detrimental matter.
- The pigments should not contain zinc compounds or organic dyes. Lead pigments should not be used unless otherwise specified by the purchaser.

Pigments	I.S.
(i) Black/red/brown	IS : 44 – 1969
(ii) Green	IS : 54 – 1975
(iii) Blue	IS : 55 – 1970
	IS : 56 – 1975
(iv) White	IS : 411 – 1968
(v) Yellow	IS : 50 – 1979

Dimensions

The size of cement concrete tiles are as follows :

Length (mm)	Breadth (mm)	Thickness (mm)
200	200	20
250	250	22
300	300	25

Physical Requirements

- **Flatness of the Tile Surface :** It can be tested by means of a metal ruler. The length of it is not less than the tile diagonal. The amount of concavity convexity should not exceed 1 mm.
- **Perpendicularly :** It can be tested by square. The longest gap between the arm of the square and the edge of the tile shall not exceed 2% of the length of the edge.
- **Wet Transverse Strength :** According to IS : 1237 – 1980, for this test the span between the supports shall be follows :

Size of tile (mm)	Span (mm)
200 × 200	150
250 × 250	200
300 × 300	250

The load shall be applied gradually and at a uniform rate not exceeding 2000 N per minute, until the tile breaks.

The average wet transverse strength shall not be less than 3 N/mm².

- **Straightness :** The gap between the fine thread and the plane of the tile cannot exceed 1% of the length of the edge.
- **Water absorption :** The average percentage of water absorption shall not exceed 10%.
- **Resistance to Wear :** The wear shall not exceed the following value :
  - (a) For general purpose tiles :
    - Average wear 3.5 mm
    - Wear on individual specimen 4 mm.
  - (b) For heavy duty floor tiles :
    - Average wear 2 mm
    - Wear on individual specimen 2.5 mm.

Other than cement concrete flooring tiles, based upon purpose and materials, followings are types of tiles :

- **Common Tiles :** These are having different shapes and sizes. They are used for paving, flooring etc.
- **Encaustic Tiles :** These tiles are mainly used for decorative purposes in floors, walls ceilings etc.
- **Clay Flooring Tile (CBRI) :** It is based upon type of raw material used for it's preparation. It contains alluvial soil mainly. It represents high water absorption but poor impact and abrasion resistance. It possess uniform texture and colour, a metallic sound and good finish. It is available in three sizes   15 × 15 × 1.5 cm, 20 × 20 × 2 cm, 25 × 25 × 2.5 cm etc.
- **Cinder Flooring Tiles :** Cinder i.e. coal ash is an industrial waste. It is effectively used to manufacture semi-vitreous unglazed tiles. It is economical and cheaper. It can be used in school, hospital, public buildings, industrial sheds, railway platforms, roads etc.
- **Terracota Flooring Tiles :** It is unglazed clay flooring tiles of semi-vitreous type. It is widely used in various public buildings.
- **Matt Glazed Flooring Ceramic Tiles :** It was manufactured traditionally by use of twice fired earthenware body glazed tiles. Due to advanced technology it is available in various types of shades. It has a strength of 44 N/mm², 0.5 – 1% water absorption.

In the market various companies like NITCO etc. offering tiles in various shapes, sizes, categories. Tiles are generally available in 30 cm × 30 cm, 40 × 40 cm, 10 × 40 cm. These are categorised as exotica, elegant, prime plus, super exclusive, rustic etc.

6.9.4   VDF Flooring   (May 17)

- VDF (Vacuum Dewatered Flooring) is a special type of Flooring Technique to achieve High Strength, Longer Life, Better Finish and Faster Work. This type of floor is suitable for high abrasion & heavy traffic movement.

- The Vacuum Dewatered Flooring or VDF Flooring is a system for laying high quality concrete floors where the key is Dewatering of Concrete by Vacuum Process wherein surplus water from the concrete is removed immediately after placing and vibration, thereby reducing the water: cement ratio to the optimum level.

Fig. 6.11

Procedure

- In this system of VDF , concrete is poured in place & vibrated with a poker vibrator especially to the sides of the panel for floor thickness more than 100mm.
- Then surface vibration is done using double beam screed vibrator running over the surface, supported on channel shuttering spaced 4.0 meters apart.
- The screed vibrator is run twice to achieve optimum compaction & levelling. The vibrated surface is then leveled using a straight edge.
- After this a system of lower mats & top mat is laid on the green concrete & this is attached to a vacuum pump. This draws out surplus water if any.
- The concrete is left to stiffen. When the base concrete has stiffened to the point when light foot traffic leaves an imprint of about 3-6 mm, Floor Hardener is applied at an even application rate of between 3-5 Kg/Sqmt.
- Any bleed water should now have evaporated, but the concrete should have a wet sheen. The concrete is then further compacted and levelled using Power Floater followed by finishing as per the requirement using Power Trowel.

Benefits of VDF Flooring

- Increased Compressive strength of floor
- Increased Tensile strength
- Reduced Cement consumption (No cement is required for finishing the surface)
- Increased Abrasion resistance
- Reduced water / cement ration
- Increased Impact strength
- Reduced number of joints

- Less wear and tear of floor surface
- Reduced Shrinkage of concrete

Typical Application Areas of VDF Flooring

- Warehouses, Godowns
- Roads, Sports Courts
- Cellars, Parking Areas
- Production Areas,
- Pharmaceutical Companies
- As the base floor for Epoxy & PU Floorings

REVIEW QUESTIONS

1. State any four flooring materials. State the advantages and limitations of each.

2. State step-by-step procedure to construct concrete flooring for an industrial building.

3. Explain the construction of flat slab floor for commercial buildings. State the advantages of it. State recent technology used to reduce thickness of it.

4. A hall of size 7.50 m and 10.0 m is to be provided with two way ribbed floor construction. Explain process of construction with the help of neat sketches. State the grade of concrete and steel used for the construction.

5. State with reason, most suitable type of flooring material for the following situations :

   (a) A drawing room of a high specification bungalow.

   (b) Car parking of a residential flat building.

   (c) Ware house where heavy articles are stored.

   (d) Kitchen flooring for middle income group housing.

6. State step-by-step procedure of providing vacuum processed concrete flooring for industrial sheds. What type of coating is provided to make floor more resistant to abrasion and avoid dusting ?

7. Draw a labelled sketch of flat slab floor and show the following :

   (a) Capital, (b) Drop panel, (c) Flat slab.

   State two important advantages of the flat slab flooring.

8. Name the type of flooring materials available in the market. State advantages and limitations of each.

9. Write down the I.S. codes for any four tiles. Draw detailed sketch for tile impact test.

10. Describe the construction of concrete flooring.

11. What do you understand by the following types of floors :

(a) Basement floors, (b) Suspended floors.

12. Explain the following by means of neat sketches :

   (a) Brick jack arch floor,

   (b) Hering bone strutting in timber floors.

13. What types of flooring do you recommend for the following ? Discuss justifying your selection :

   (a) Dancing hall,   (b) Public W.C. and bath rooms,

   (c) Grain storage godowns,   (d) Chemical laboratories,

   (e) Recreation hall of a high class hotel,   (f) Garage

14. Explain the detailed procedure of construction of marble tiles flooring. Give sketch also.

15. State the functional requirements of flooring materials. Give the I.S. codes for any four tiles.

16. What do you understand by mosaic flooring ? Describe in detail the construction of such a floor.

17. State essential requirements of good flooring material.

18. What types of floorings would you recommend for the following :

   (a) Lecture hall of a Modern College,   (b) Drawing hall,

   (c) Laboratories,   (d) Hostels,

   (e) Dance halls.

19. Describe briefly the type of floor finishing used for different types of buildings and state the reasons for their choice.

20. What are relative advantages and disadvantages of pre-cast concrete floor ?

21. Enlist the various flooring tiles available in the market. Write advantages and disadvantages of any two.

22. What are the relative advantages and disadvantages of concrete floor.

23. Enlist the factors to be considered for the selection of flooring and state four types of tiles based on materials and I.S. specification.

24. Explain the procedure of construction of cement concrete flooring.

25. Explain the procedure of construction of concrete floor, giving its relative merits and demerits.

26. Explain the following by means of neat sketches :

   (a)   Floor ceilings   (b) Herring - bone strutting in timber floors.

27. Differentiate between the following :

   (a)   Floors and Flooring   (b) Basement Floors and Suspended Floors

   (c)   RCC Slab Floor and Flat Slab Floor.

SOLVED UNIVERSITY QUESTIONS

DEC. 2013

1. State functional requirements of flooring. **[3]**
   [**Ans. :** Refer Article 6.2]
2. State four market names of flooring tiles. **[3]**
   [**Ans. :** Refer Article 6.3]
3. State different brand names of flooring tiles. Explain detailed construction procedure of vitrified tiles flooring. **[6]**
   [**Ans. :** Refer Article 6.5]

MAY 2014

1. Explain any two types of flooring with their suitability **[6]**
   [**Ans. :** Refer Article 6.8]

MAY 2015

1. With a figure explain the Chequer board method of construction of floors. **[6]**
   [**Ans. :** Refer Article 6.8]
2. Explain the IS specifications for Cement concrete flooring tiles. **[6]**
   [**Ans. :** Refer Article 6.9.3]

NOV. 2015

1. State functional requirements of flooring materials.
   [**Ans. :** Refer Article 6.2]

MAY 2016

1. Explain with neat sketch construction of concrete flooring. **[3]**
   [**Ans. :** Refer Article 6.4]

NOV. 2016

1. Enlist any four types of flooring. Explain with neat sketch ceramic flooring? **[7]**
   [**Ans. :** Refer Article 6.8]
2. Write a short note on epoxy asphalt flooring. **[6]**
   [**Ans. :** Refer Article 6.8]

MAY 2017

1. Explain Vacuum Dewatered Flooring. **[6]**
   [**Ans.:** Refer Article 6.9.4]
2. Explain with reason which type of flooring is recommended for the following : **[6]**
   (i) Lecture hall of a college. (ii) Laboratories of a college
   (iii) Garage   (iv) Auditorium
   (v) Machine shop   (vi) Canteen

CHAPTER 7
ROOFING MATERIALS

7.1 INTRODUCTION

A **roof** is the covering on the uppermost part of a building, which protects the building and its contents from the effects of weather.

A roof form important part of superstructure and serves the following functions:

- It should offer adequate protection against natural forces like heat, sound, rain, etc.
- It should sustain various stresses due to dead load, wind load, etc.
- It should also enhance aesthetic sense of building.
- It should be easy to maintain and durable.
- It should be economical.

Fig. 7.1

7.2 VARIOUS ROOFING MATERIALS

- G.I. Sheets (Galvanized Corrugated Iron Sheets)
- A.C. Sheets (Asbestos Cement Sheets)
- Tiles
- Slates
- Slab Itself

7.3 GALVANIZED CORRUGATED IRON SHEETS

- These sheets are extensively used as a roof covering material in factories, workshops, sheds, cheap buildings etc.

- Actually, these sheets have been superseded, particularly for superior work, by asbestos cement sheets. Though galvanized corrugated iron sheets do not have an attractive appearance but still they are widely used as they are very durable, fire-proof, light in weight and require no maintenance.
- These sheets are manufactured in a form which has the corrugations (i.e. a series of parallel depressions) from one end to another. These sheets are laid with corrugations running down the slope of the roof.
- The purpose of corrugations is to impart additional strength to thin iron sheets and to discharge the water quickly away from the sheet. The iron sheets are galvanized with zinc to protect them from the rusting action of wet weather.
- Sometimes, these sheets are covered with ordinary half-round country tiles so as to maintain the inside coolness of the building by preventing the transmission of heat through roofing.

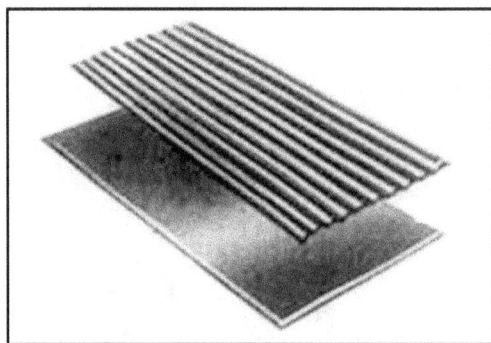

Fig. 7.2

7.3.1 Laying and Fixing of Galvanized Corrugated Iron Sheets

It is explained as follow :
- These sheets are light in weight so it can be fixed easily.
- It is generally 0.6 to 0.76 m wide, 1.37 m to 3.6 m long and of 1.625 to 6.559 mm gauge.
- The sheets are fixed to timber purlins at intervals about 0.8 m apart with special galvanized screws and washers driven through holes drilled in the crowns of corrugations.
- The sheets may also be fixed to steel angle purlins by means of hook bolts.
- All bolts should be in white lead.
- The lap of 15 cm in its length should be provided. The side lap should extend one and a half corrugations.
- Wind ties should be fixed along the eaves of the roof and the ventilators. Slot holes should be provided for expansion and contraction.

Special sections are available for covering hips, ridges and valleys.

It is shown in the Fig. 7.3.

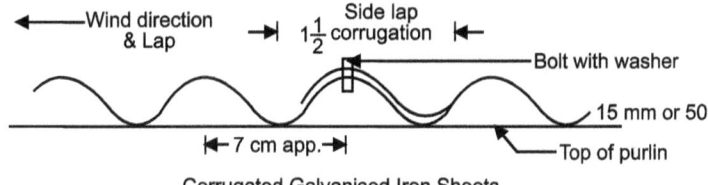

Corrugated Galvanised Iron Sheets

Fig. 7.3 : Fixing of CGI sheets

7.4 A.C. SHEETS (ASBESTOS CEMENT SHEETS)

- These sheets are light in weight, tough, durable, fire resistant, not susceptible to the attack of vermin, easy to cut, low maintenance, easy to fix, high speed of construction and cheap.

- On account of these advantages A.C. sheet roof covering is adopted for workshop, factories, garages, offices, temporarily sheets etc. A.C. sheets consists of Asbestos fibres (@ 15%) bonded together by cement.

- Asbestos cement roof coverings are supplied in flat, corrugated and ribbed sheets in various sizes. Ribbed sections are available with ribs at a spacing of 30 to 40 cm.

- The A.C. sheets are fixed at a very low cost as they can be cut, sawn or screwed easily where desired. A.C. sheets are obtained in the following three types, but in various lengths 1 to 3 metres, rising in 15 cm increments:

  (i)   Everite big six corrugated A.C. sheets.

  (ii) Everite standard A.C. sheets.

  (iii) Turnall trafford A.C. tiles.

The particulars of these three types are given in the following Table 7.1.

Table 7.1 : Showing Particulars of Asbestos Cement Sheets

Types of A.C. sheets	Standard lengths in metres	Laid width in metres	Thickness in mm	Side laps in cm	No. of corru-gations	Pitch in cm	Depth in cm
(i) Everite big six corrugated A.C. sheets.	1 to 3 m in 5 cm rises	1.05 m	6 mm	5 cm or 0.5 corrugation	$7\frac{1}{2}$	13 cm	5.5 cm
(ii) Everite standard A.C. sheets	1 to 3 m	1.05 m	6 mm	10 cm or 1.5 corrugations	$10\frac{1}{2}$	5.5 cm	2.5 cm
(iii) Turnall Trafford A.C. tiles	1.2 to 3 m, in 15 cm rises	1.09 m	6 mm	10 cm or 1 corrugation	'4' but with alternate flat portions	34 cm	5.0 cm

Table 7.2 : Dimensional and tolerances for corrugated and semicorrugated sheets appear IS 459 – 1970 are as under.

(All dimensions in mm figures in bracket indicate tolerances)

Type of sheet	Depth of corrugation	Pitch of corrugation	Overall Width	Effective Width	Thickness Nominal	Length of Sheet
Corrugated sheet	48 (+ 3)	146 + 6	1050 + 10	1010 + 10	6 mm (+) Free	1750, 2000
Semi-corrugated sheet	45 − 5	338 − 2	1100 − 2	1014 − 5	6 mm (− 0.5)	2500 or 3000

Fig. 7.4

7.4.1 Laying and Fixing of A.C. Sheet

It is explained in the following steps :

- Asbestos cement sheets are fixed to either timber or steel purlins directly.
- A.C. sheets are laid from right to left starting at eaves.
- The sheets are always fixed through the crowns of the corrugations.
- To connect the purlins and the sheets 8 mm diameter galvanized hook bolt is generally used. The length of this bolt is governed by the size of the purlins.
- The hook is engaged to the edge of the purlin and is secured by a nut. To ensure water tight joint, lead cupped and ashestos washers are also provided.
- The minimum overlap for lengthening is 15 cm and for widening the overlap is 60 to 100 mm or one and half corrugations.

- The unsupported overhang sheets should not be more than 30 cm.
- The ridge is formed with the aid of a pair of ridge capping. In this process, normally mitered joint is used for connection.
- An eaves filler piece is used to fill in the underside of the corrugations.

The details are shown in the Fig. 7.5.

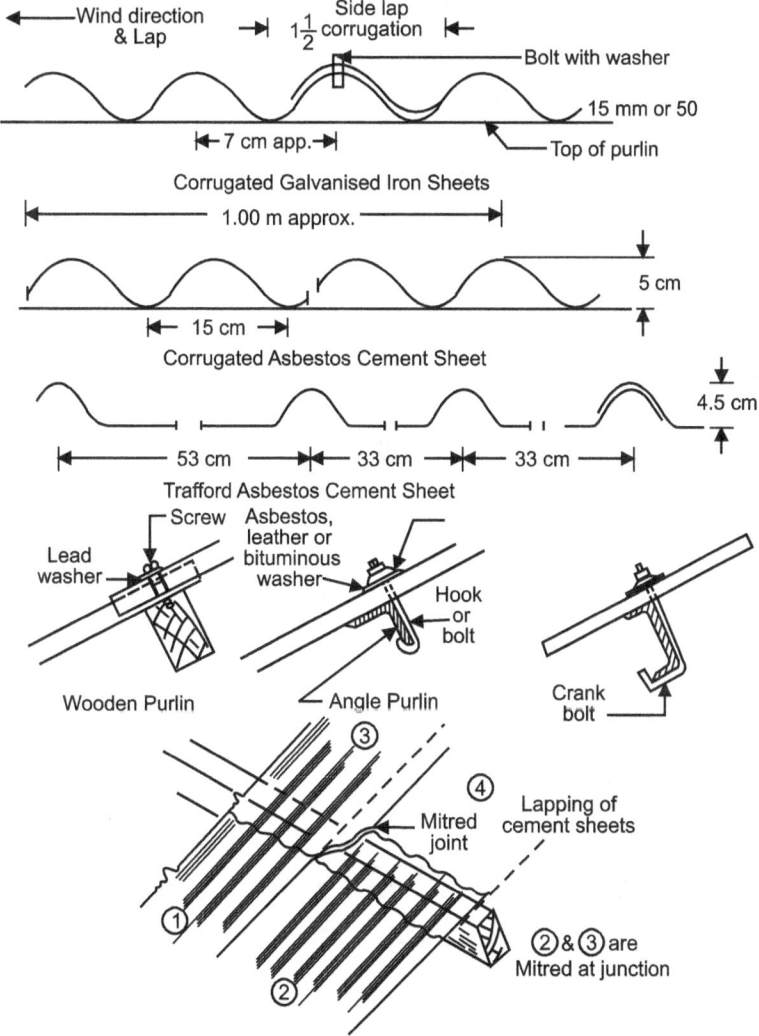

Fig. 7.5 : Details of laying and fixing of A.C. sheet

7.4.2 Asbestos Cement Products

The basic stages in the manufacture of asbestos cement are as follows :

- Preparation of the raw stuff consisting of several grades of fibre;
- Crushing of the mixture into finer fibres;
- Mixing with portland cement (by the dry, wet, or dry/wet process);
- Forming and pressing (for some sheet products);

- Preliminary hardening;
- Mechanical working (cutting corrugation, etc.);
- Final hardening;
- Surface finishing (if required).

With the wet process which is most commonly used in the industry, a liquid suspension of asbestos cement is formed into a thin layer on a wire-mesh cylinder, dehydrated, and compacted.

Corrugated sheets are made by shaping a semi-finished product. Finishing sheets are additionally compressed on hydraulic presses under a pressure of 25 to 40 MPa. Formed sheets are heat treated in steam curing chambers. The combination wet/dry process and continuous rolling of large sheets can be almost completely automated (in fact, 98% of all process operations are carried out automatically) and are, therefore, the most promising technologies.

Owing to the presence of reinforcing asbestos fibres, sheets 5 to 10 mm thick can be formed to various shapes before the cement has set. Hardened asbestos cement exhibits a considerable mechanical strength (its compressive and bending strength being as high as 90 MPa and 30 MPa, respectively), weather resistance, resistance to freezing (it can sustain upto 50 cycles of alternate freezing and thawing), durability, fire resistance, impermeability to water, alkali resistance and low thermal conductivity. It has a lower density (1500 to 1950 kg m^{-3}) than plain concrete and ferrocement.

On the other hand, asbestos cement has a poor impact strength (its toughness ranges between 1.5 and 2.5 kJ m^{-2}, being by about 30% lower for non-compressed materials) and can readily warp in service. Fortunately, this can be rectified by using more fibre or by giving the material a water repellency treatment.

Asbestos cement products include roofing and facing tile, and sheets (plain, corrugated, or otherwise patterned), pressure and non-pressure pipes and sleeve couplings, ventilation skips, window sills, electrical insulating boards, wall cladding, special purpose products, vases, flower pots and tubes, etc.

7.5 MANGALORE TILES (IS 654-1972)

These are flat roof tiles of special pattern with suitable keys and projection for fixing to roof.

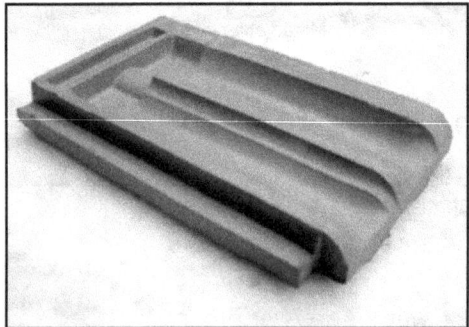 

Fig. 7.6

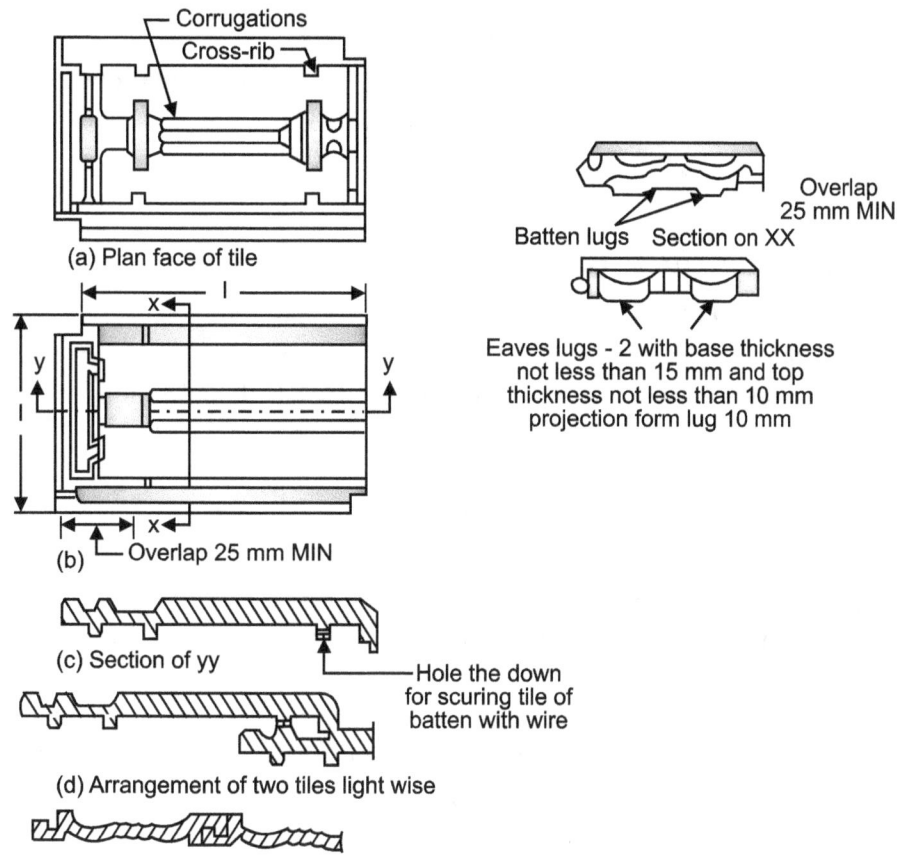

(a) Plan face of tile

(b) Overlap 25 mm MIN

(c) Section of yy

(d) Arrangement of two tiles light wise

(e) Arrangement of two tiles breadth wise

Fig. 7.7 : Mangalore tiles

On the basis of percentage of absorption, breaking load, etc. the tiles are classified as class AA and class A as detailed below :

Table 7.3

Size of Tile	Min. Breaking load kgf		Maximum water absorption %	
	Class AA	Class A	Class AA	Class A
410 × 235 mm	100	80	19	24
420 × 250	110	90	19	24
425 × 260	110	90	19	24

Minimum overlap is 60 mm lengthwise and average weight of tile should be between 2 to 3 kg, 1.6 to 2 mm diameter. Tie down holes are provided, to fix tile with galvanized wire. The tiles are well burnt and uniform in texture.

2 battern lugs and 2 eave lugs of thickness more than 15 mm are provided at bottom. The two lugs provided at top have thickness of 10 mm. The projections of batten lug shall be 7 to 17 mm and that of eave lug shall be 10 mm. For better understanding these are tabulated below.

Table 7.4

	Nos.	Thickness (mm)		Projection (mm)
		At top	At bottom	
Batten lug	2	> 10	> 15	> to 12
Eave lug	2	> 10	> 15	> 10

7.5.1 Roofing Slate Tiles : (IS 6250 – 1981)

In regions, like Himachal Pradesh slate tiles are used as roofing material.

The slate should have reasonably straight cleavage and grains should be longitudinal. The tiles should have uniform thickness, which should not be less than 15 mm. The tiles should be rectangular in shape, with reasonably full corners and edges shall be true. The standard sizes of tiles are :

600 × 300 × 15 mm thickness (minimum) or

500 × 250 × 15 mm thickness

The other physical requirements of tile are :

- Water absorption < to 2% by weight and should have low permeability so that, water does not ooze from the bottom.
- **Sulphuric acid immersion test :** During this test, the tile should not show any sign of delamination clay, and shall not show gaseous evolution during immersion.
- **Modulus of rupture :** It should not be less than 60 N/mm^2 (dry) and 40 N / mm^2 (wet).

7.5.2 Lime Stone Slabs and Tiles : (IS 1128 – 1974)

These are used in flooring and face work. These absorb very less water, have high strength and are quite durable. The physical requirements are given in the following Table 7.5.

Table 7.5

Characteristics	Requirement
1. Water absorption	< 0.15% by weight
2. Transverse strength	> 70 kgf/cm^2
3. Durability	Should not develop signs of spalling, disintegration of cracks.

These are available in lengths and breadths ranging from 15 to 150 cm and thickness from 15 to 95 mm. Stone used for the tiles should be without soft veins, cracks, flaws, shall have uniform texture, and curvature in any direction shall not be more than 5 mm.

7.5.3 Sand Stone Slabs and Tiles : (IS 3622 – 1977)

These can be used in flooring, roofing and face work. The slabs and tiles can be of (i) rough cut or (ii) machine cut. Tolerance of ± 1 mm only is allowed in length and breadth in respect of machine cut slabs and tiles.

The dimensions of slabs and tiles are :

Table 7.6

Length	Breadth	Thickness
15 to 360 cm	15 to 90 cm	15 to 100 mm
In stages of 5 cm	5 cm	5 mm
Tolerance ± 1 mm	± 1 mm	± 3 mm

7.5.4 Marble Tiles (IS 1130 – 1969)

Two classes of tiles viz white and coloured are available. The beauty of the tile can be enhanced by adopting different finishes such as :

- Sand or Abrasive finish : A flat non-reflective finish.
- Hone finish : Velvety finish with little or no gloss.
- Polished finish : Highly polished glossy surface. Square tiles of size 10×10 cm upto 60×60 cm in stages of 10 cm are available. (Tolerance + 4%). Thickness ranges between 18 to 24 mm.

Other physical requirements of tile are :

- Moisture absorption (after 24 hours) < 0.4%.
- Hardness (Mhos Scale) 3 min.
- Specific gravity 2.5 min.

7.5.5 Earthen Ware, Stone Ware and Glazed Wares

- Earthen stone ware is a clay product, manufactured from clay mixed with sand, crushed pottery, and is burnt at low temperature.
- Stone ware is also a clay product manufactured by mixing refractory clay with crushed potter and powdered stone and is heated it to high temperature.
- Glazing is a process of formation of thin, transparent layer at the surface, which becomes integral part of the article and protects the article from corrosive sewage water, sewer gases or weathering.

Articles such as stone ware pipes, sewer pipes, sanitary appliances, in bathrooms, toilets, floor tiles etc. are examples of glazed articles.

Following two methods are used for glazing :

- (a) Opaque or slip glazing
- (b) Salt glazing.

(a) Opaque or Slip Glazing :

A thin paste materials like quartz, basic oxide, oxides of zinc lead, tin, china clay, feldspar etc. is made.

The article to be glazed is dried, and above mentioned paste is evenly applied, and the article is heated in furnace to a high temperature of 1300°C to 1400°C when the paste gets fused with the article and forms thin, transparent protective layer at the surface. Depending upon the contents of the paste, different beautiful colours are obtained. In this process, burning and glazing of article is achieved simultaneously.

(b) Salt Glazing :

The clay product to be glazed is heated at temperature of 1300° to 1400°C in kiln and common salt (sodium chloride) is thrown on the article to be glazed 2 or 3 times at an interval of time. Sodium salt melts, and vapourises. The vapour of sodium salt combines with the clay product and forms transparent protective layer.

SWG pipes (Stone Ware Glazed pipes) are glazed in this manner. Relatively, salt glazing is inferior to opaque glazing.

7.5.6 Glazed Earthen Ware Tiles : (IS 777 – 1970)

Where cleanliness is very important such as in kitchen, hospitals, bathrooms, toilets etc. glazed earthen ware tiles and its associated fittings are used. The top surface to the tiles is glazed, whereas the under surface is unglazed to facilitate fixing of the tile to wall/floor. The tiles are available in the two sizes. With joint thickness of 1 mm the overall size becomes 100×100 mm and 150×150 mm. Dimensional requirements are as under :

Table 7.7

1.	Dimensional requirement tolerance	99×99 mm ± 0.8 mm	149×149 mm ± 0.8 mm
2.	Thickness tolerance	5, 6, 7 mm ± 0.8 mm	5, 6, 7 mm ± 0.8 mm
3.	Warpage	+ 0.5 mm, – 0.3 mm	+ 0.7 mm – 0.4 mm

Performance requirements are as under :

- Water absorption < 10%.
- Impact strength 0.02 kgf m/cm.
- Crazing (i.e. formation of fine cracks on the surface). Should not show any sign of crazing after two cycles of test in an autoclave.
- Glazed surface should be chemical resistant i.e. should not show any deterioration.

7.5.7 Testing of Tiles

Following three tests are carried out on tiles to assess its suitability :

- Water absorption test.
- Efflorescence test.
- Impact test.

Water absorption test and efflorescence test is similar to that carried for bricks. In case of efflorescence test, tile is immersed on its end, in a dish containing distilled water to a depth not less than 2.5 cm.

Impact Test :

In this test, tile to be tested with face upward is placed on 25 mm thick rubber sheet. The sheet is placed on a hard smooth and level surface such as steel plate or concrete floor.

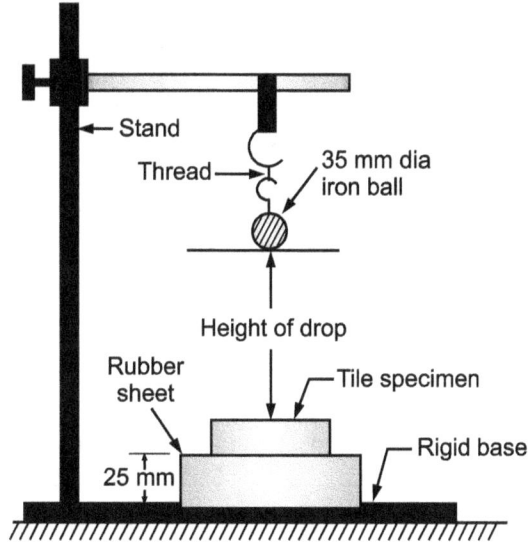

Fig. 7.8 : Impact test

A steel ball of 35 mm diameter and mass 170 gm is taken and tied to a hook by means of thread. Tile is centred, so that, on burning the thread, the ball is released and it falls exactly at the centre of the tile. The height of ball is raised from 10 cm, in steps of 5 cm, until tile specimen fractures. Average height of three specimen (taken at random from 500 tiles) is taken as resistance value of impact of tile. The specimen to be tested should be oven dried to temperature of 100 to 110°C, allowed to cool at room temperature.

By this test, toughness of tile is determined. The maximum height of drop of 53 mm diameter steel ball of mass 170 gm for class I, class II and class III tiles of different thickness shall be as under :

Table 7.8

Size of tile (mm)	Max. height of drop of steel ball of 35 mm dia. × 170 gm (cm.)		
	Class I tile	Class II tile	Class III tile
1. 150 × 150 × 15	25	20	15
2. 150 × 150 × 20 and 200 × 200 × 20	60	50	40
3. 200 × 200 × 20	75	65	50
4. 250 × 250 × 30	80	70	60

7.6 COMPARISON BETWEEN ASBESTOS CEMENT SHEET AND GALVANISED IRON SHEET

Point of Comparison	A.C. Sheets	G.I. Sheets
1. Materials	These are made from a mixture of asbestos fibres and cement.	These are made of galvanized wrought iron.
2. Thickness	These sheets cannot be made as thin as G.I. sheets.	Light in weight.
3. Weight	Heavy in weight.	Light in weight
4. Care in handling and fixing	Sheets are fragile. Much care is required in handling during transportation and fixing.	Sheets are not liable to break and can be handled with little care.
5. Durability	Durable and do not corrode.	Durable, but gets corroded by atmospheric actions
6. Effect on acids and fumes	Not affected by acids and fumes.	Affected by acids and fumes
7. Sound insulation	More or less sound insulating and do not produce much noise during rainfall over the sheets.	Not at all sound insulating and produce noise during rainfall over the sheets.
8. Resistance to fire	These are fire resisting.	These sheets become deformed when a fire occurs.
9. Possibility of damage	There is every possibility of sheets getting damaged due to external causes.	Possibility of getting damaged due to external causes is less.
10. Workability	Care is required in working with A.C. sheets.	One can easily work with G.I. sheets.
11. Initial cost	High initial cost	Initial cost is low.
12. Maintenance	Maintenance cost is nil, if not damaged. No painting is required	Maintenance cost is due to periodic painting against corrosion.
13. Appearance	Neat and pleasing appearance can be achieved.	The appearance is not pleasing even if a neat finish is made.

7.7 TYPES OF ROOF AND THEIR SUITABILITY

7.7.1 Types of Roof

Roof types are governed by slope of the roof, material used for roof, span of it etc.

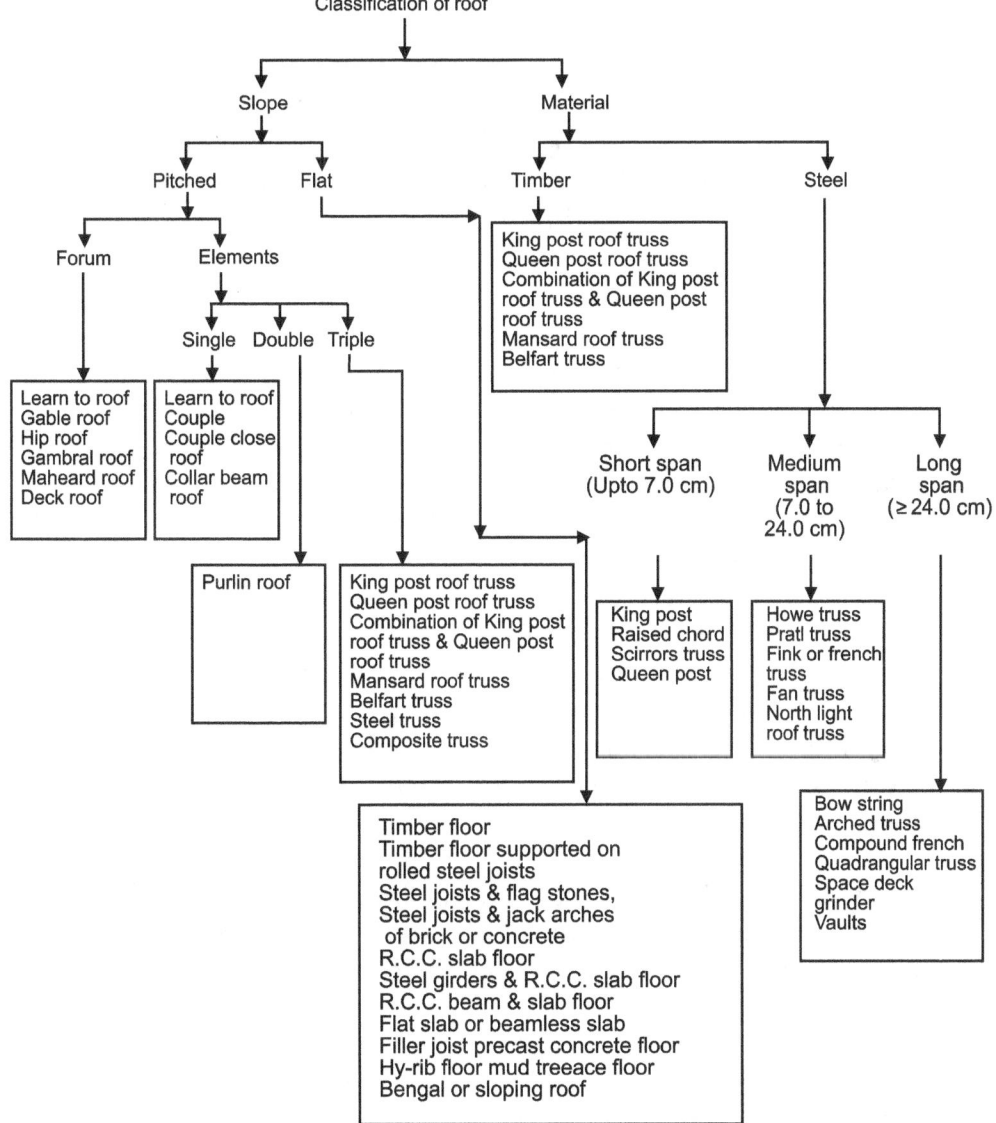

Chart : Classification of Roof

7.7.2 Technical Terms in Sloping Roof and Roof Trusses   (May 14)

Fig. 7.9 and shows various elements of sloping roof and roof trusses. These elements are defined below.

- **Ridge :** It is the apex line of the sloping roof.
- **Span :** It is the clear distance between the supports of an arch, beam or roof truss.

- **Pitch of Roof :** It is the inclination of sides of a roof to the horizontal plane. The pitch of the roof is usually expressed either in terms of degrees (angle) or as a ratio of rise to span.

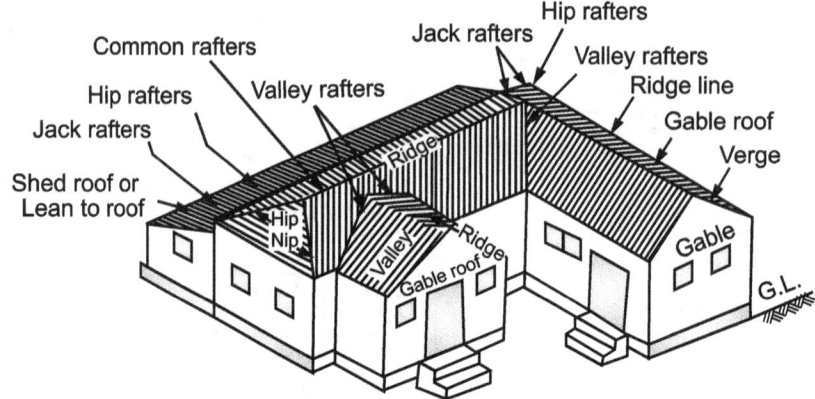

Fig. 7.9 : View of a building with basic sloping roofs.

- **Rise :** It is the vertical distance between the top of the ridge and the wall plate.
- **Eaves :** The lower edge of the inclined roof surface is called eaves. From eaves, the rain water from the roof surface drops down.
- **Hip :** It is the ridge formed by the intersection of two sloping surfaces, when the exterior angle is greater than 180°.
- **Valley :** A valley is the reverse of a hip. It is formed by the intersection of two roof surfaces having external angle, which is less than 180 degrees.
- **Hip Rafters :** These are the wooden members which form the hip of a pitched roof. These rafters run diagonally from the ridge to the corners of the walls to support roof covering. They receive the ends of purlins and ends of jack rafters.
- **Jack Rafters :** These are common rafters shorter in length which run from a hip to the eaves or from a ridge to a valley. A hip or valley is formed by the meeting of jack rafters.
- **Common Rafters or Spars :** These are the inclined wooden members supporting the battens or boarding to support roof coverings. They run from a ridge to the eaves. They are normally spaced at 30 to 45 cm centre to centre, depending upon the roof covering material.
- **Valley Rafters :** These are sloping rafters which run diagonally from the ridge to the eaves for supporting valley gutters. They receive the ends of the purlins and ends of jack rafters on both sides.
- **Hipped End :** It is the sloped triangular surface formed at the end of a roof.
- **Verge :** This is the edge of sheets, slates or tiles which projects beyond the gable end of the sloped roof.
- **Ridge Piece, Ridge Beam or Ridge Board :** It is the horizontal wooden member, in the form of a beam or board, which is provided at the apex of a roof truss. It supports the common rafter fixed to it.

- **Purlins :** These are the horizontal wooden or steel members, used to support common rafters of a roof when span is large. Purlins are supported on trusses or walls.

- **Eaves Board or Facia Board :** It is a wooden plank or board fixed to the feet of the common rafter at the eaves. It is usually 20 - 25 mm thick and 20 - 25 cm wide. The ends of the lower most roof covering material rest upon it. The eaves gutter can also be secured against it.

- **Barge Board :** It is the timber board used to hold the common rafter forming verge.

- **Wall Plates :** These are long wooden members which are provided on the top of stone or brick wall, for the purpose of fixing the feet of the common rafters. These are embedded from sides and bottom in masonry of walls, almost at the centre of their thickness. Wall plates actually connect the walls to the roof.

- **Post Plate :** This is similar to wall plate except that they run continuous, parallel to the face of wall, over the tops of the posts and support rafters at their feet.

- **Battens :** These are thin strips of wood, called scantlings which are nailed to the rafters for lying roof materials above.

- **Boardings, Sheeting or Sarking :** This consists of boards which are nailed to the upper edges of common rafters and to which tiles and other roofing materials are secured.

- **Truss :** A roof truss is a frame work of triangles designed to support the roof covering or ceiling over rooms.

- **Template :** This is a square or rectangular block, about 10 to 15 cm thick, which is placed below a beam or a truss, so as to spread the load over a larger area. It may be made of fine dressed flat stone, squared wood, concrete block or R.C.C. block.

- **Cleats :** These are short sections of wood or steel [angle iron], which are fixed on the principal rafters or trusses to support the purlins.

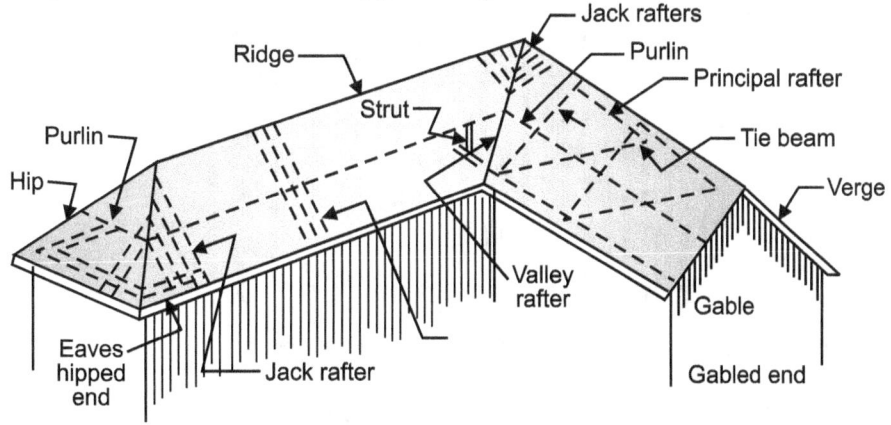

(a) Pitched roof, common terms

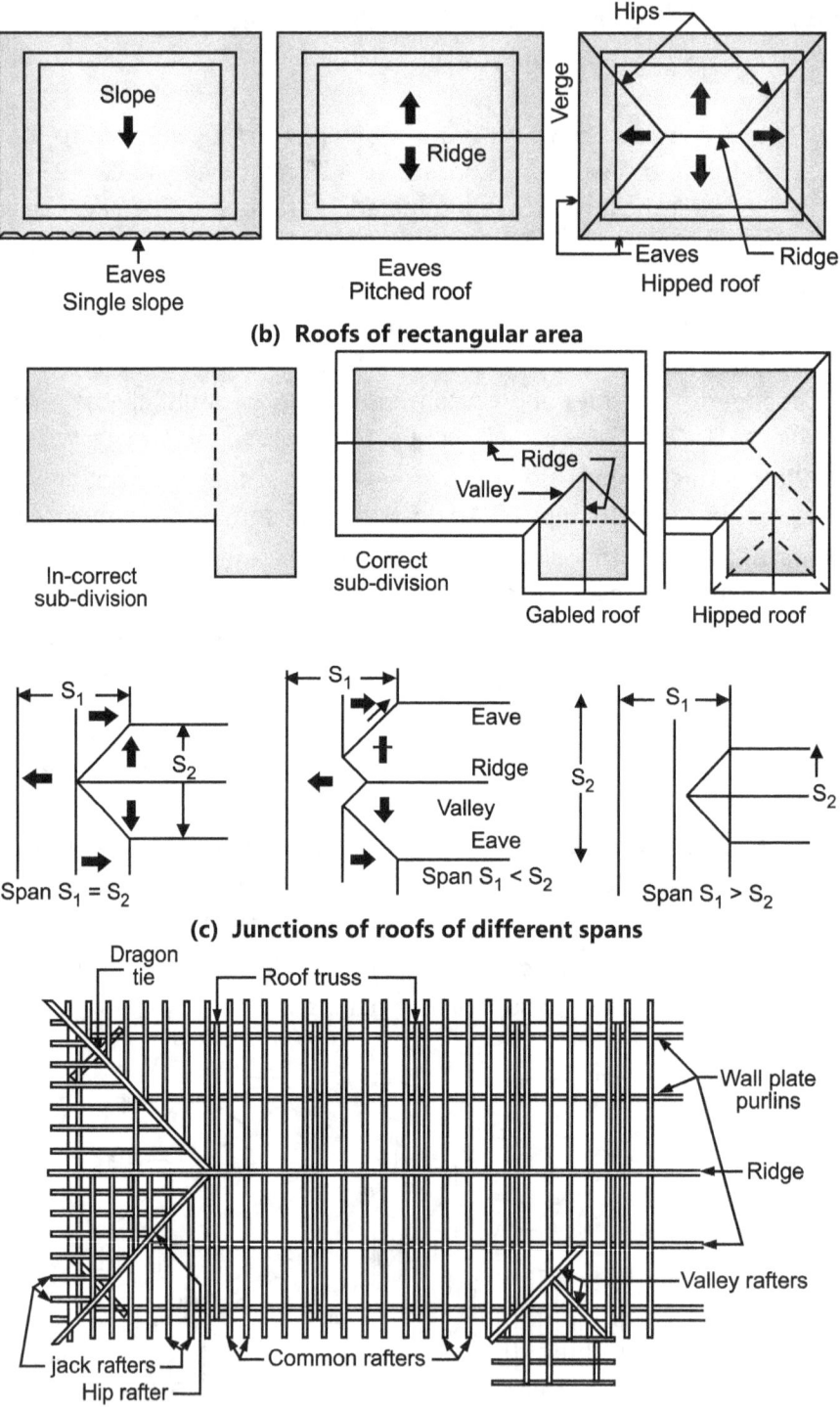

(b) Roofs of rectangular area

(c) Junctions of roofs of different spans

(d) Wood works for pitched roof

Fig. 7.10

7.7.3 Suitability of Roof

As per classification these are various types of roofs. Suitability of roof is governed by various factors like climatic conditions of the locality, slope of roof, durability, maintenance cost, appearance etc.

- **Mud Terrace Roof :** It is the cheapest and fiarly water tight. It is mainly used at places of light rainfall.

- **Bricks Concrete Terrace Roof :** It offers considerable water tight surface. It is mainly used in heavy rainfall region.

- **Madras Terrace Roof :** It is also called as "Brick Jelly or Composite Roof". It offers heat insulation and water tightness.

- **Jack Arch Flat Roofs :** It bears the load either from reinforcement or by arch action. It is not widely used. It does not offer pleasing appearance.

- **Bengal Terrace Roof :** It is mainly used in Bengal. It acts as porch. It covers verandah.

- **Shell :** It is three dimensional structures. It transfers the load on points of supports. It is mainly used for big area like factories, theatres, airport hangers.

- **Steel Structures :** It is economical. It is used from small span to large span. It offers good fire resistant. It is used for factories, sheds, etc.

- **Timber Roof :** It is less fire resistant. It is mainly used for small span structure. It is used in hilly and forest areas.

7.8 TYPES OF TRUSSES   (Dec 14, Nov. 15 May 16)

The function of any roof is to provide a protective covering to the upper surface of the structure. As it subjects to various types of imposed loadings, durability of the covering is very much important.

Based on span roof can be considered as :

(1) Short Span :

- Span is upto 7.0 m.
- It is of traditional timber construction with flat or pitched profile.
- Flat roofs are covered with a flexible sheet material generally.
- Pitched roofs are covered with small units such as slates or tiles.

(2) Medium Span :

- Span is varying from 7 m to 24 m.
- The usual roof structure is a truss or lattice of standard steel sections.
- Covering/sheeting may be corrugated asbestos cement or structural decking system.

(3) Long Span :

If span is greater than 24 m, it is considered as large span. Roofs for it are generally designed as girder, space deck or vaulting techniques.

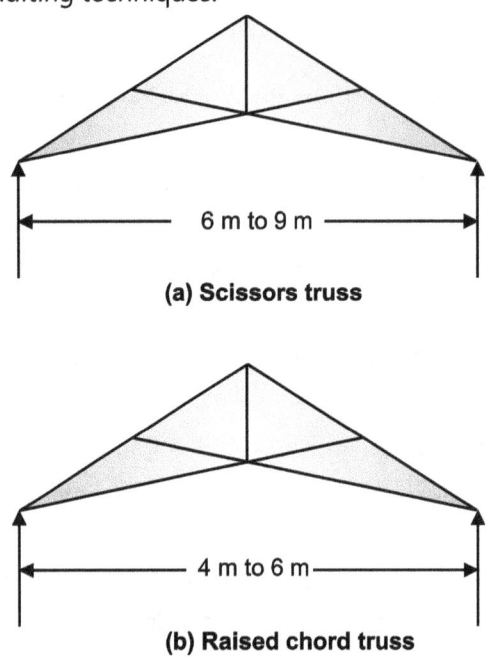

(a) Scissors truss

(b) Raised chord truss

Fig. 7.11 : Short span trusses

North light roof trusses are used for factories, workshops, etc. where natural light and ventilation are desired (Fig. 7.12 (a), (b), (c)).

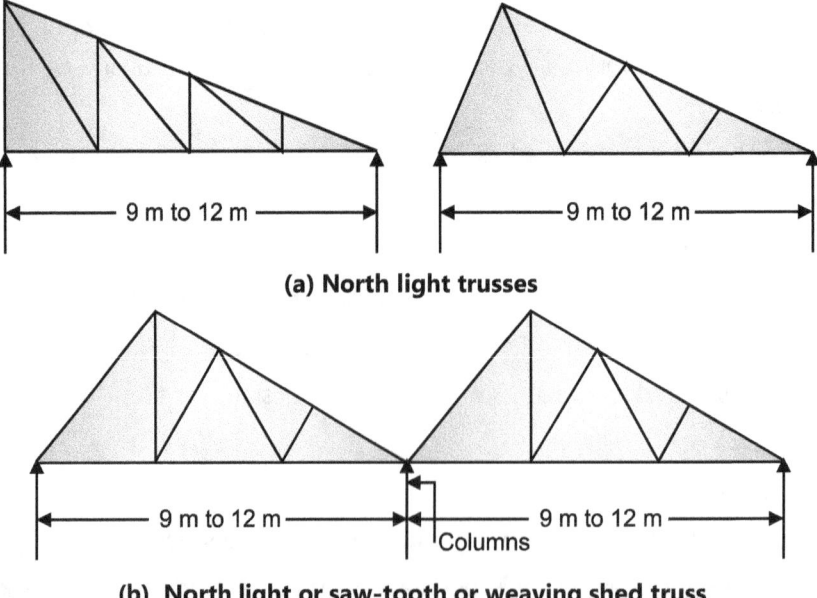

(a) North light trusses

(b) North light or saw-tooth or weaving shed truss

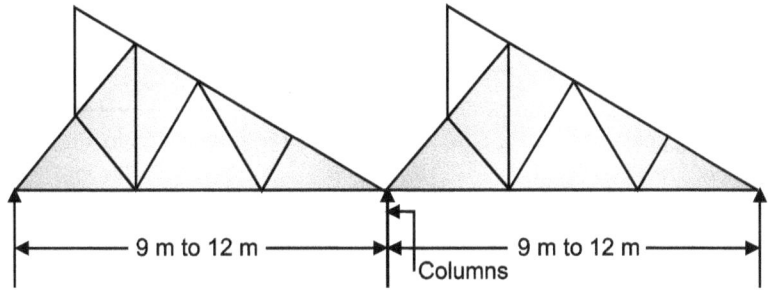

(c) Modified north light truss

Fig. 7.12 : Medium span north light steel trusses

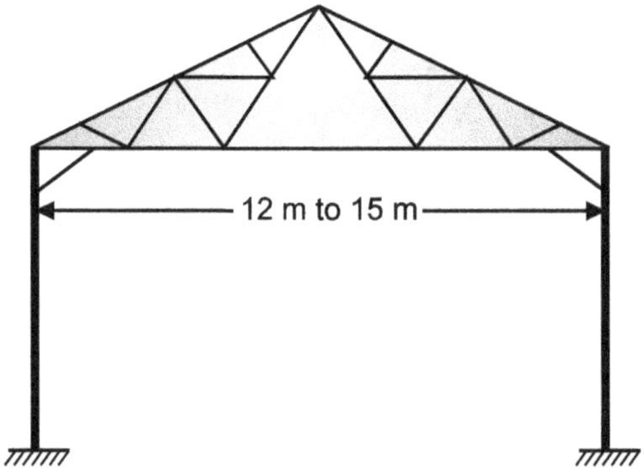

(a) Frame with fink truss

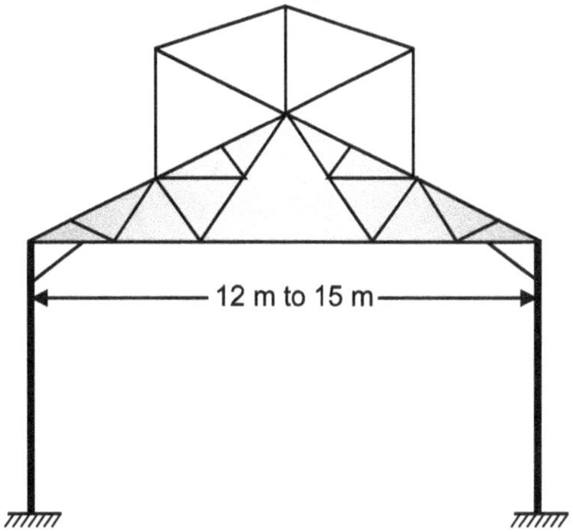

(b) Sky light on fink truss

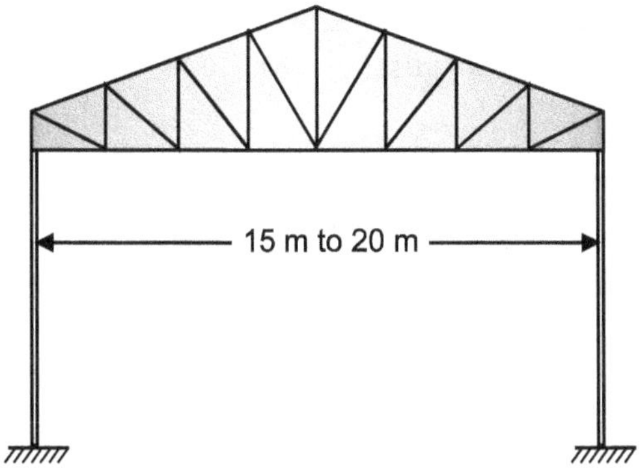

(c) Frame with pratt truss

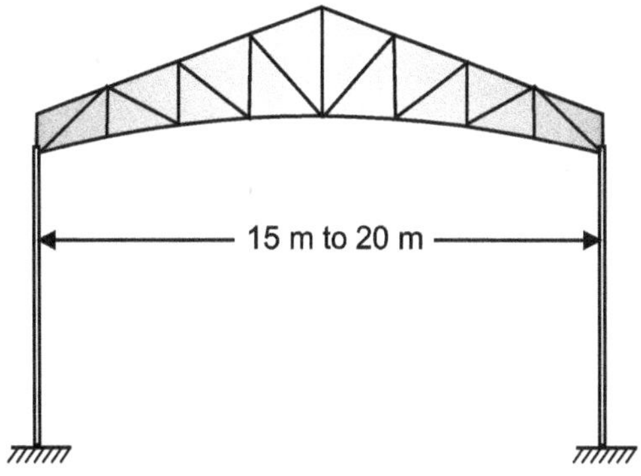

(d) Frame with arched truss

Fig. 7.13 : Industrial building bents

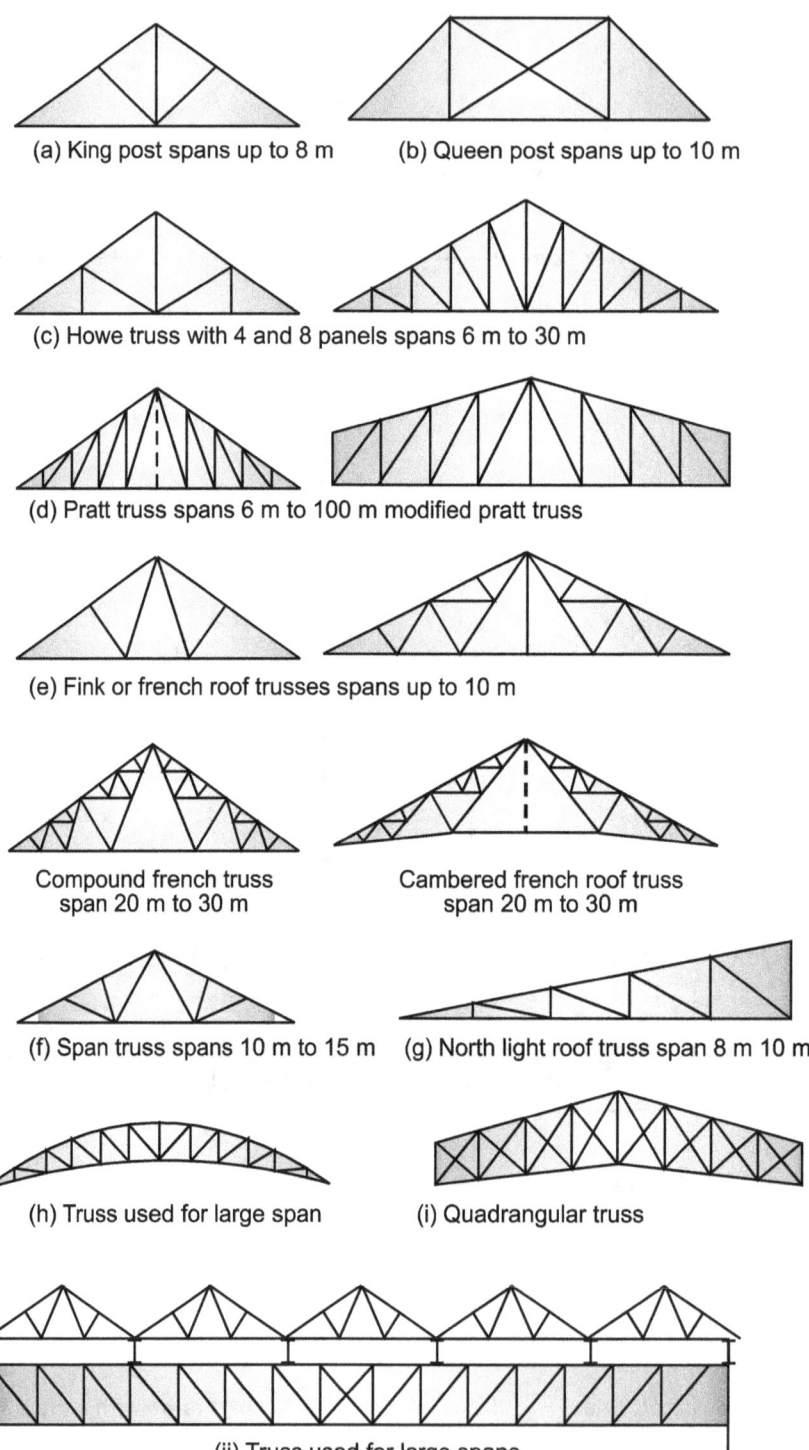

(a) King post spans up to 8 m   (b) Queen post spans up to 10 m

(c) Howe truss with 4 and 8 panels spans 6 m to 30 m

(d) Pratt truss spans 6 m to 100 m modified pratt truss

(e) Fink or french roof trusses spans up to 10 m

Compound french truss   Cambered french roof truss
span 20 m to 30 m   span 20 m to 30 m

(f) Span truss spans 10 m to 15 m   (g) North light roof truss span 8 m 10 m

(h) Truss used for large span   (i) Quadrangular truss

(ii) Truss used for large spans

Fig. 7.14 : Various types of steel roof trusses

7.8.1 Requirements of Roofing Material for Steel Structure

The basic requirements for covering materials to steel roof trusses are :

- It should be durable so that throughout the life of the roof there will be less maintenance.
- Fire resistance should be acceptable.
- It should have less self-weight, so that supporting members of an economic size can be used.
- Sufficient resistance to the penetration of rain, wind and snow.
- It should provide considerable thermal insulation.

7.8.2 Lean to Roof   (Nov. 15)

- It is the simplest form of pitched roof. In this type rafters slope to one side only.
- It's components are common rafters, wall plate, corbel stone, battens, roof covering, eaves board, string course etc.
- Inclination of common rafter is limited to 30°.
- The knee straps and bolts are used to connect the rafters with the posts.
- It is used for sheds, out-houses, verandah etc.

It is shown in the Fig. 7.15.

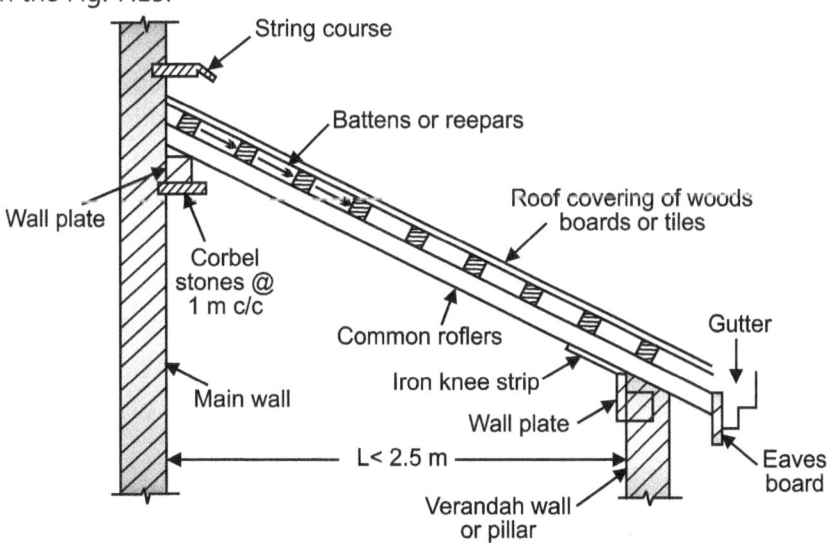

Fig. 7.15 : Lean to roof or verandah roof

7.8.3 King Post Truss Roof (Refer Fig. 7.16)   (Dec. 14)

- It is suitable for short span.
- It consists two principal rafters or principals, a tie-beam, a king post and two struts.
- It can be made sufficiently strong. Dimensions of different parts of it are defined with reference to the load they can carry.

- Under various load combinations each member of this truss is subjecting to the following stresses.

Principal rafter	– Compressive stress
Struts	– Compressive stress
King post	– Tensile stress
Tie-beam	– Tensile stress
Common rafters	– Transverse stress
Purlins	– Transverse stress.

The functions of various elements of this truss are given below :

- **Principal Rafter :** It supports the framework of roof.
- **Tie Beam :** It receives the ends of the principal rafters. It prevents the walls from being thrust outwards.

  It should be in as long length as possible.
- **Cleats :** It is fixed on principal rafters to prevent the purlins from tilting. It is usually spiked.
- **Pole Plates :** It is horizontal timber piece. It runs across the top of tie beam at their ends or on principal rafters near their feet.
- **Common Rafter :** It is usually rest on the purlin. Its upper end is supported by ridge piece, its middle by the purlins and its lower ends by pole plates.
- **Reepers :** It is nailed across the common rafter. It supports roof covering. The ends of the tie beam should not built into walls. The loads at the ends of a tie-beam should not be concentrated type. So it should be placed on bed plates.
- **King Post :** It is a vertical member. It prevents the tie beam from sagging at its centre.
- **Bed Plates :** It is called as bed blocks truss plates or templates. It receives ends of tie beam and principal rafter.
- **Struts :** It supports centres of principal rafters. It prevents sagging of it.
- **Purlins :** It is stout piece. It is usually placed over the principal rafters. It supports the common rafters.

Following joints are used at various junctions in king post truss.

- Joint between principal rafter and king post – mortice and tenon joint.
- Joint between principal rafter and tie beam – mortice and tenon joint or briddle joint or an oblique joint.
- Joint between principal rafter and strut – an oblique mortice and tenon joint.
- Joint between king post and tie beam – tenon joint. It is strengthened by a wrought iron or mild steel stirrup strap.

Joints of King post truss are shown in the Fig. 7.17.

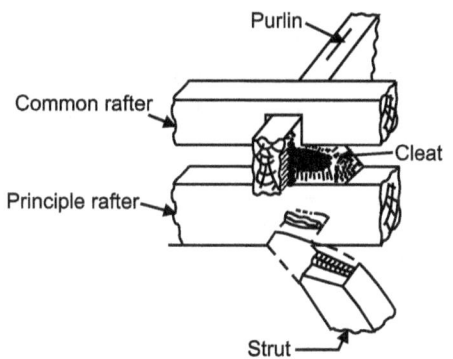

Fig. 7.16 : Joint of strut and principal rafter

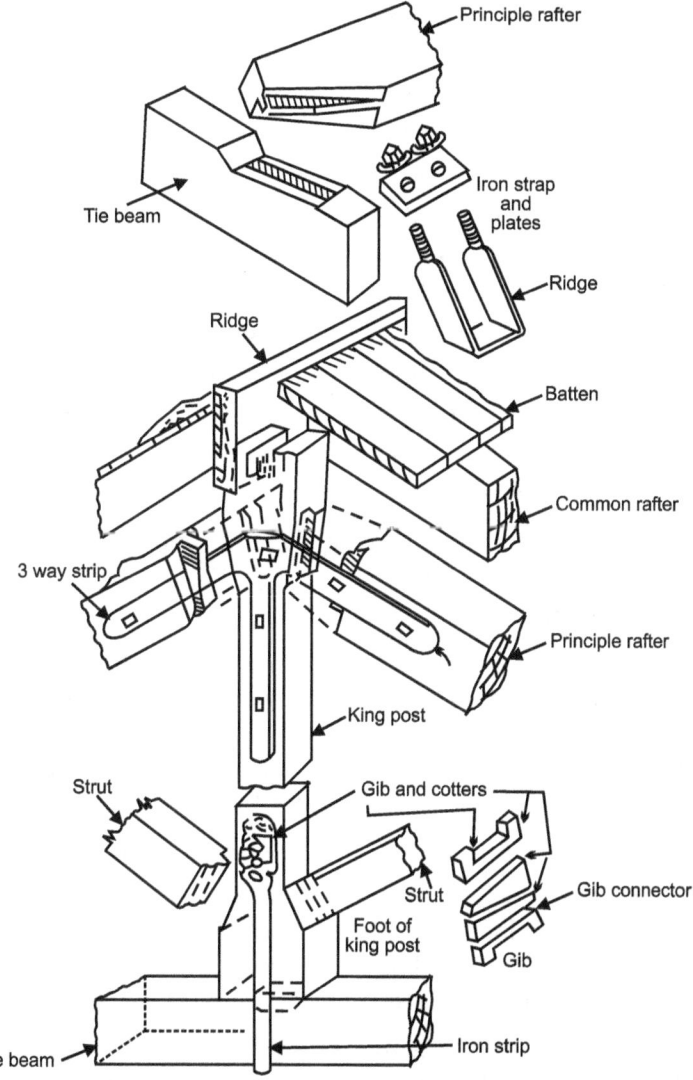

Fig. 7.17 : Details of king post truss

The ridge piece or ridge board is held in position by slotting the head of the kind post.

In combined members at a joint and that at the support it is essential to observe that the centre lines of various members intersect at the point and at the support in the joint through which the load line or reaction line passes.

7.8.4 Design and Construction of Steel Roof Trusses

The following points regarding design and construction of steel roof trusses should be noted :

- All the members of steel roof trusses are either designed for compression or for tension, and no bending stresses are allowed in them.

- Size of various members of the truss and their arrangement depend upon the roof slope, span, loading, wind pressure and centre to centre distance of the trusses.

- The compression members such as struts should be as short as possible to avoid buckling and the principal rafters subjected to transverse stresses should not be longer than 3 metres maximum. The tension members should be braced together.

- Normally, angles irons or channel sections are used as struts, whereas T-sections are best suited for use as principal rafters. Round or flat section can be used for tension members. In an ideal design all the members of structure should fail simultaneously. In practice, angles less than $50 \times 50 \times 6$ mm are not used.

- All the members of the truss should be arranged to form triangles so that the truss will not deform to a greater extent.

- The distance between the steel roof trusses should not exceed 3 metres. This distance or spacing is more for light roofs.

- Small trusses are fabricated (riveted or bolted together) at the factory or workshop and transported to the working site, whereas larger trusses are usually fabricated and assembled together at the job site.

- The joints or connections of members to each other are called noded or panel points are made by means of thin flat plates called gusset plates. Though the thickness of gusset plates depends upon the bearing value of the rivets employed, but usually, thickness of 6 mm and 10 mm are provided for small and large roof structures, respectively.

- In riveting, the pitch of the rivets should not be less than 3 times the diameter of the rivets. The maximum pitch is 15 cm for compression members and 20 cm for tension members. Further, a minimum distance from the centre of the rivet to the edge of the member must not be less than 25 mm for 15 mm diameter rivets. Minimum two rivets should be used for all connections.

- For small span, the ends of the trusses are fixed. In case of long span trusses, one end should be fixed and the other end is mounted on steel rollers.

- For a series of trusses, wind tie, diagonal braces between the two end trusses should be provided on either side to prevent the general distortion of the roof due to wind action.

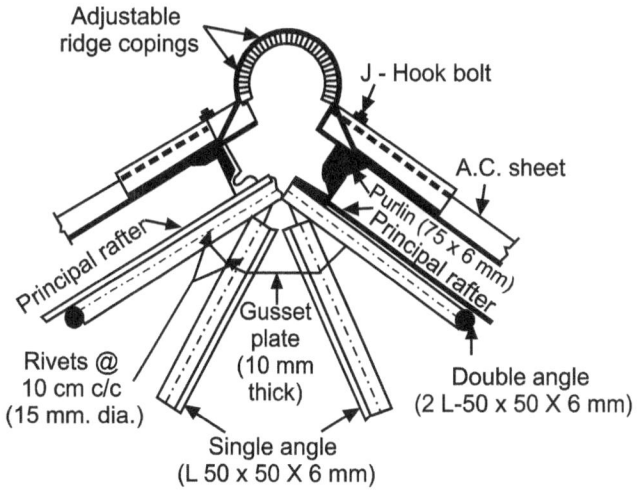

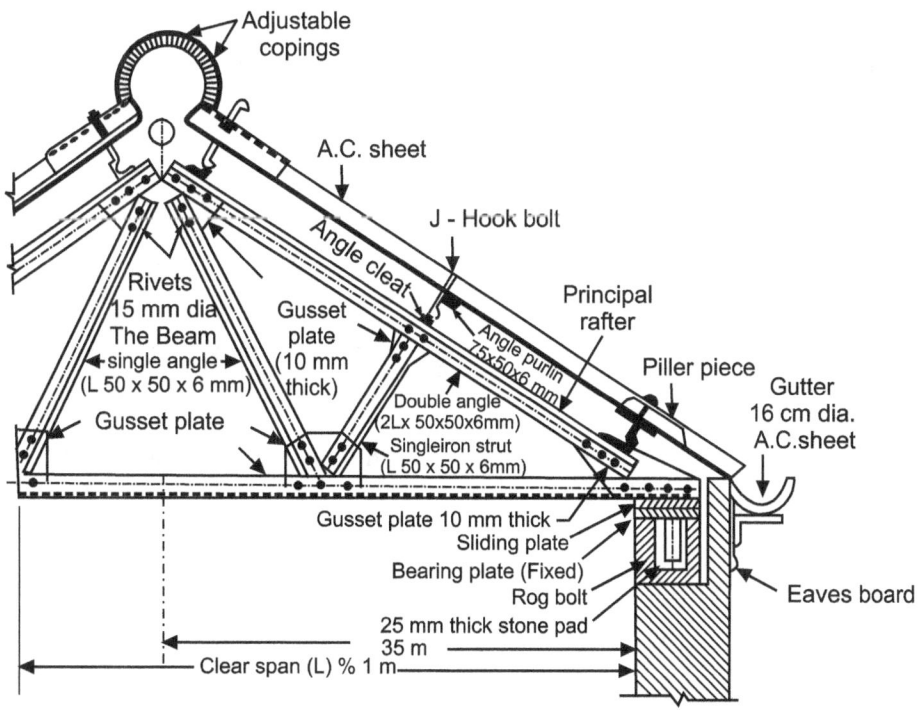

Fig. 7.18 : Simple steel fink roof trusses – details

[for span, i.e. L = 6 to 10 metres]

7.9 TYPES OF SHELL STRUCTURES [IS : 2210 – 1988]

- **Asymmetrical Cylindrical Shells :** Cylindrical shells which are asymmetrical about the crown are called asymmetrical cylindrical shells.

- **Barrel Shells :** Cylindrical shells which are symmetrical about the crown, are called as barrel shells.

- **Cylindrical Shells :** Shells in which either the directrix or generatrix is a straight line. The common curves used for cylindrical shells are arc of a circle, semi-ellipse, parabola, catenary and cycloid.

The moving curve is called as the generatrix. The stationary curve is called as the directrix.

- **Multiple Cylindrical Shells :** A series of a parallel cylindrical shells which are transversely continuous.

- **North Light Shells :** Cylindrical shells with two springing at different levels and having provisions for north-light glazing.

Important terms regarding shell :

- **Edge Member :** A member provided at the edge of a shell.

- **Gauss Curvature :** The product of the two principal curvature, $\dfrac{1}{R_1}$ and $\dfrac{1}{R_2}$ at any point on the surface of the shell.

- **Junction Member :** The common edge member at the junction of two adjacent shells.

- **Radius :** Radius at any point of the shell in one of the two principal directions. If cylindrical shell of a circular arc is used, the radius of the arc is radius of the shell. In other cases, the radius R at any point is related to the radius R_0 at the crown by

$$R = R_0 \cos n\phi$$

∴　　　　　ϕ = angle of inclination of the tangent to the curve at that point.

　　　　　n = 1 – for cycloid

　　　　　　= – 2 – for catenary

　　　　　　= – 3 – for parabola.

For an ellipse,　　$R = \dfrac{a^2 b^2}{(a^2 \sin^2 \phi \ + b^2 \cos^2 \phi)^{3/2}}$

∴　　　　　a = semi-major axes.

　　　　　b = semi-minor axes.

- **Rise :** The vertical distance between the apex of the curve representing the centre line of the shell and the lowermost springing.

- **Span :** The span of a cylindrical shell is the distance between the centre lines of two adjacent end frames of traverses.

- **Ruled Surfaces :** Surfaces which can be generated entirely by straight lines. The surface is to be 'singly ruled' if at every point, a single straight line only can be ruled. 'Doubly ruled' if at every point, two straight lines can be ruled.

  Cylindrical shells, conical shells, conoids are best examples of singly ruled surfaces.

  Hyperbolic, paraboloids and hyperboloids of revolution of one sheet are good examples of doubly ruled surface.

- **Shells :** Thin shells are those in which the radius to thickness ratio should not be greater than 20.

- **Shells of Revolution :** Shells which are obtained when a plane curve is rotated about the axis of symmetry.

  e.g. segmental domes, cones, paraboloids of revolution, hyperboloids of revolution etc.

- **Shells of Translation :** Shells which are obtained when the plane of the genetrix and the directrix are at right angles.

  e.g. cylindrical shells, elliptic paraboloids, hyperbolic paraboloids etc.

- **Edge Member :** A member provided at the edge of a shell. It increases rigidity of the shell edge and helps in accommodating the reinforcement.

7.9.1 Classification of Shells

Shells may be broadly classified as 'singly-curved' and 'doubly curved'. It is based on Gauss curvature. The gauss curvature of singly curved shells is zero because one of their principal curvatures is zero. So they are developable.

Doubly curved shells are non-developable. Based on their Gauss curvature is positive or negative it is classified as synelastic or antielastic.

7.9.2 Design of Reinforcement for Shell

The minimum reinforcement must be according to IS 456-1978. Diameter of reinforcement bar is varying from 8 mm to $\frac{1}{4}$ of shell thickness or 16 mm whichever is smaller.

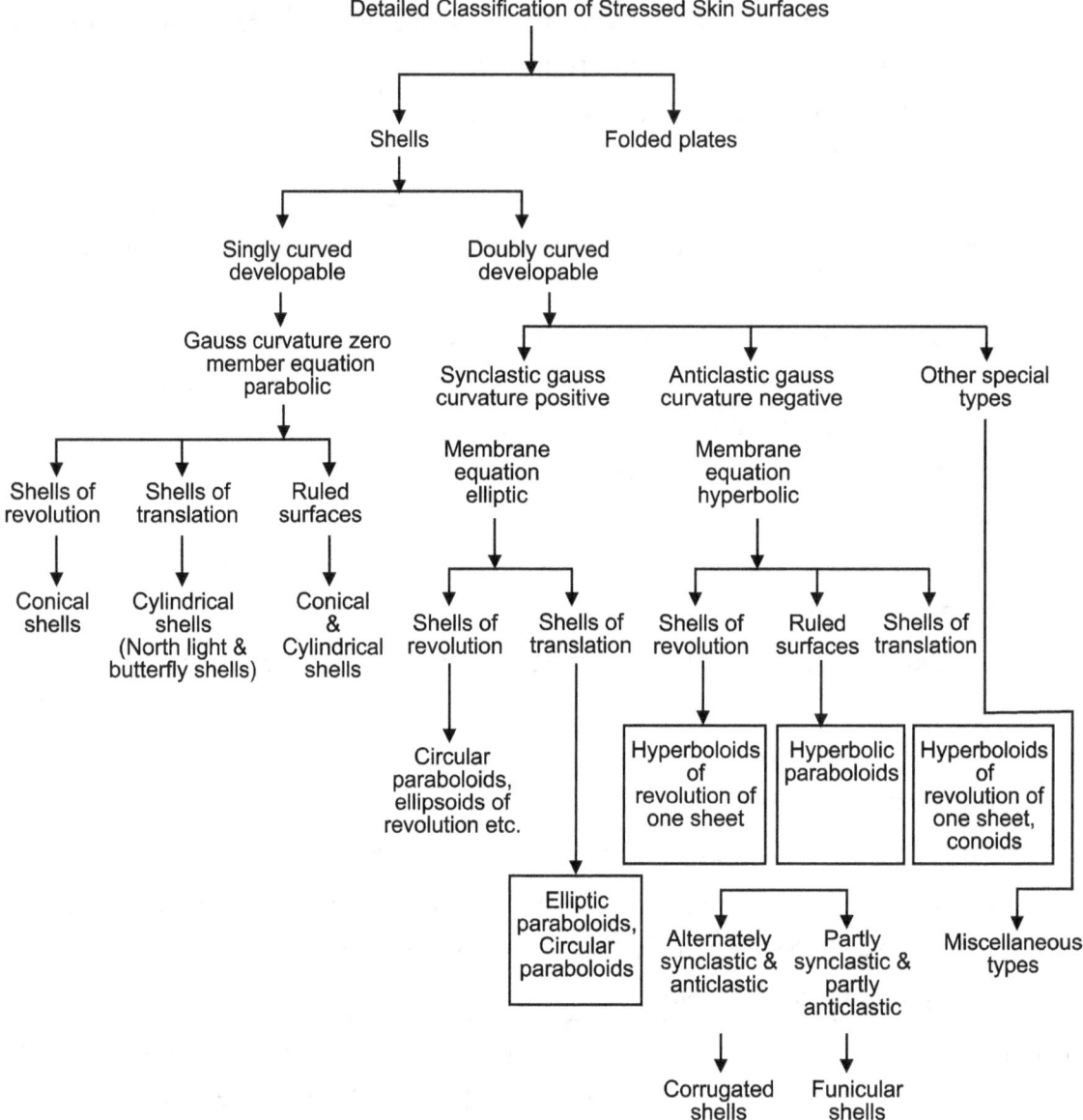

Chart : Detailed Classification of Stressed Skin Surfaces

For analysis purpose, Finite Strip Method (FSM) of analysis is commonly used. It is easy to apply and more economical than the finite element method. Following complexities may occur in shell structures :

- Material non-homogeneity.
- Irregular surface geometry.
- Sudden changes in curvature.
- Shells under dynamic wind action.
- Possibility of settlement and it's effects.
- Thermoelastic strains.

- Heavy and eccentric stiffness.
- Large deformations.
- Branching shell.
- Irregular surface geometry.
- Highly variable or localized loads.
- Complex supports or boundary conditions.

If shell is not subjecting to any complexities common classical methods for analysis are as follows :

- Membrane analysis, Edge disturbance analysis – for cylindrical shells.
- Beam method – for continuous cylindrical shell.
- Membrane analysis – Doubly curved shells.

d = Thickness of shell
B = Chord width
H = Semicentral angle of a symmetrical circular cylindrical shell
R = Radius
L = Span

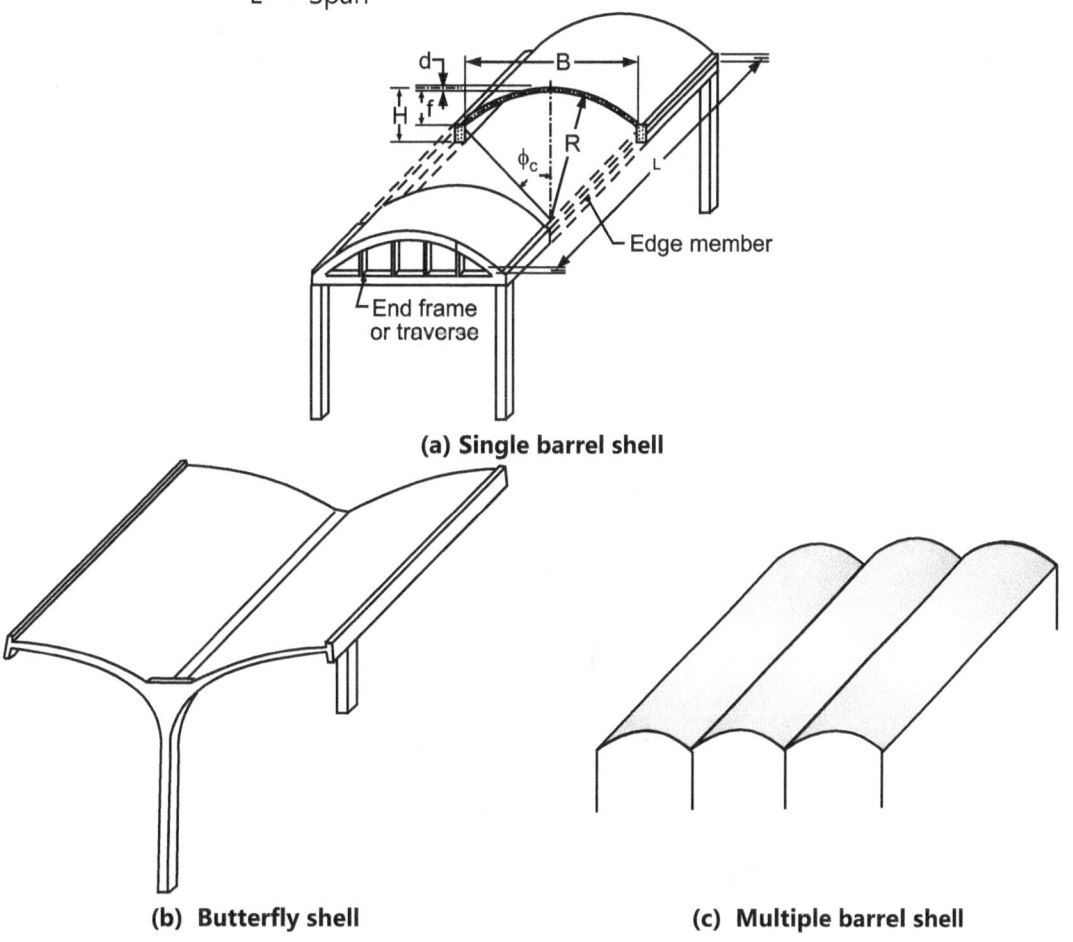

(a) Single barrel shell

(b) Butterfly shell   **(c) Multiple barrel shell**

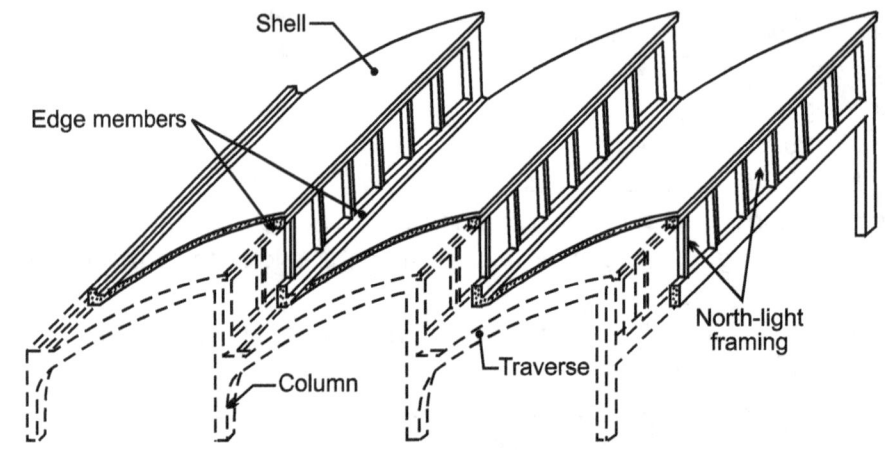

(d) North-light cylindrical shells

Fig. 7.19 : Various types of shells

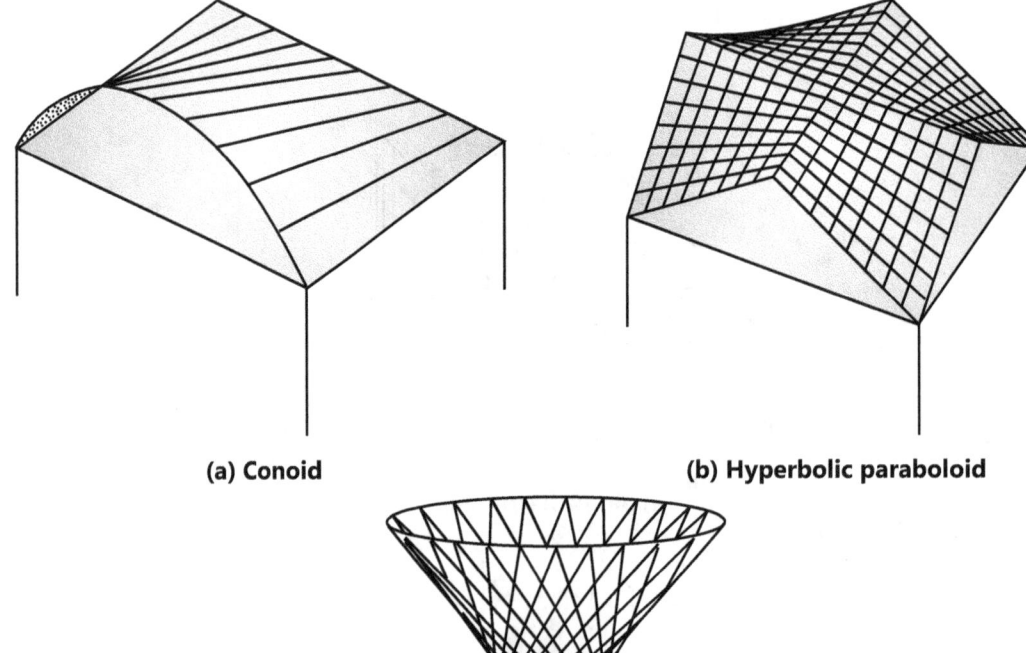

(a) Conoid　　　　　　　　　**(b) Hyperbolic paraboloid**

(c) Hyperboloid of revolution of one sheet

Fig. 7.20 : Ruled surfaces

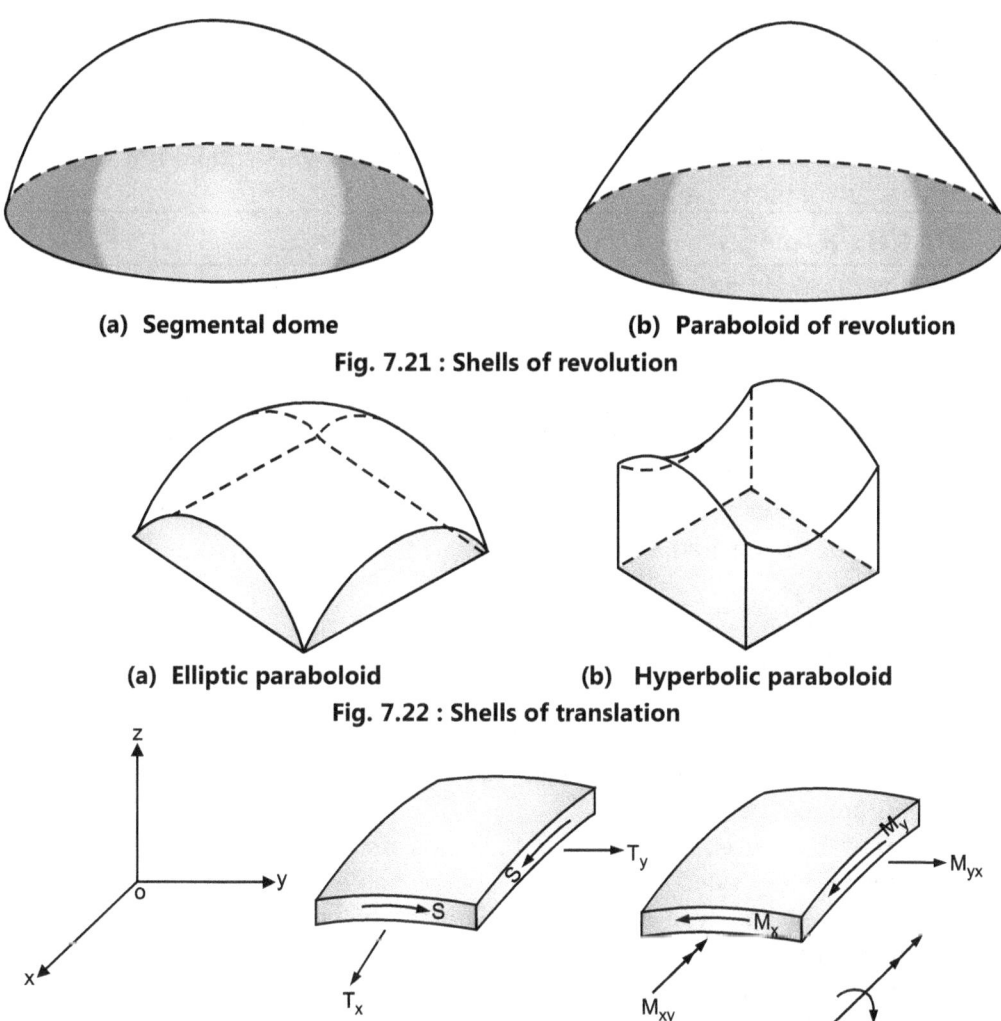

(a) Segmental dome   **(b) Paraboloid of revolution**

Fig. 7.21 : Shells of revolution

(a) Elliptic paraboloid   **(b) Hyperbolic paraboloid**

Fig. 7.22 : Shells of translation

Fig. 7.23 : Sign convention for stresses and moments in a shell element

S = Shear Stress

T_X = Normal Stress in X-Direction

T_Y = Normal Stress in Y-Direction

M_X = Bending Moment in the Shell in X-Direction

M_Y = Bending Moment in the Shell in Y-Direction

M_{XY}, M_{YX} = Twisting Moment in the Shell

Large diameter should be provided in the thickened portions, transverse and beams. The direction of the reinforcement should follow the direction of the principal stresses. To ensure monolithic joint between the shell and the edge members, the shell reinforcement shall be adequately anchored into the edge members.

In case of cylindrical shell the reinforcement should be divided into the following groups :

- Longitudinal reinforcement to take longitudinal stress M_X or M_Y.

- Shear reinforcement to resist principal tension caused by shear N_{XY} and
- Transverse reinforcement to resist N_Y and M_Y.

The maximum spacing of reinforcement in any direction in the body of the shell should be 5 times the thickness of the shell. The area of unreinforced panel should not be more than 15 times the square of thickness.

7.10 SPACE FRAMES

It is used for extremely large span buildings. It is economical. It is easily available off the shelf. It is having excellent span to depth ratio. It offers adjustable cambering facilities. It is easy to transport, handle and stack. It is easy to erect. No purlins are required. It is suitable for structures those are having irregular plan shapes. The space frame can be simply supported. It can be cantilevered. The maximum and minimum lengths of the cantilever depends upon the modular size of the pyramids. These pyramids are of prefabricated welded construction using a square mild steel angle section forming the top, with steel diagonals welded each corner of the frame and to the steel node followings are few examples of standard sizes.

$$- 1200 \times 1200 \times 750 \text{ mm deep}$$
$$- 1200 \times 1200 \times 1200 \text{ mm deep}$$
$$1500 \times 1500 \times 1500 \text{ mm deep}$$
$$1500 \times 1500 \times 1200 \text{ mm deep etc.}$$

Space frames are used for large span buildings, it may subject to movement and hence expansion joints are required.

The major types of frame used for large span buildings are as below.

(1) Plane Frames : It is fabricated in a flat plane.

According to their elevation type it is called as trusses or girders. It's main use is for roof construction and long span beams of light loading.

(2) Space Frames : It spans in two directions as opposite to the single spanning. To form lightweight roof structure it can be used in variation of the plane frame as a series of linked pyramid frames.

(3) Structural Frames : It can be used for industrial or commercial purpose. It is used when large uninterrupted floor spaces are required. It can provide large floor to ceiling heights.

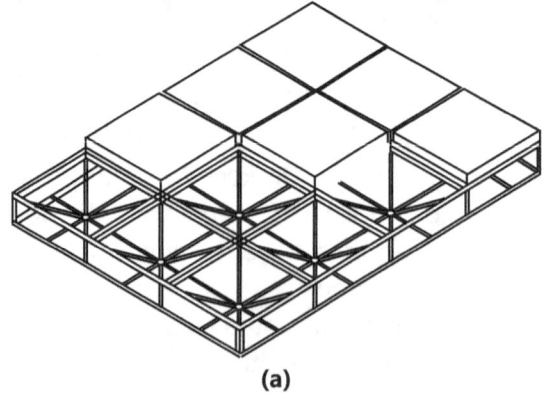

(a)

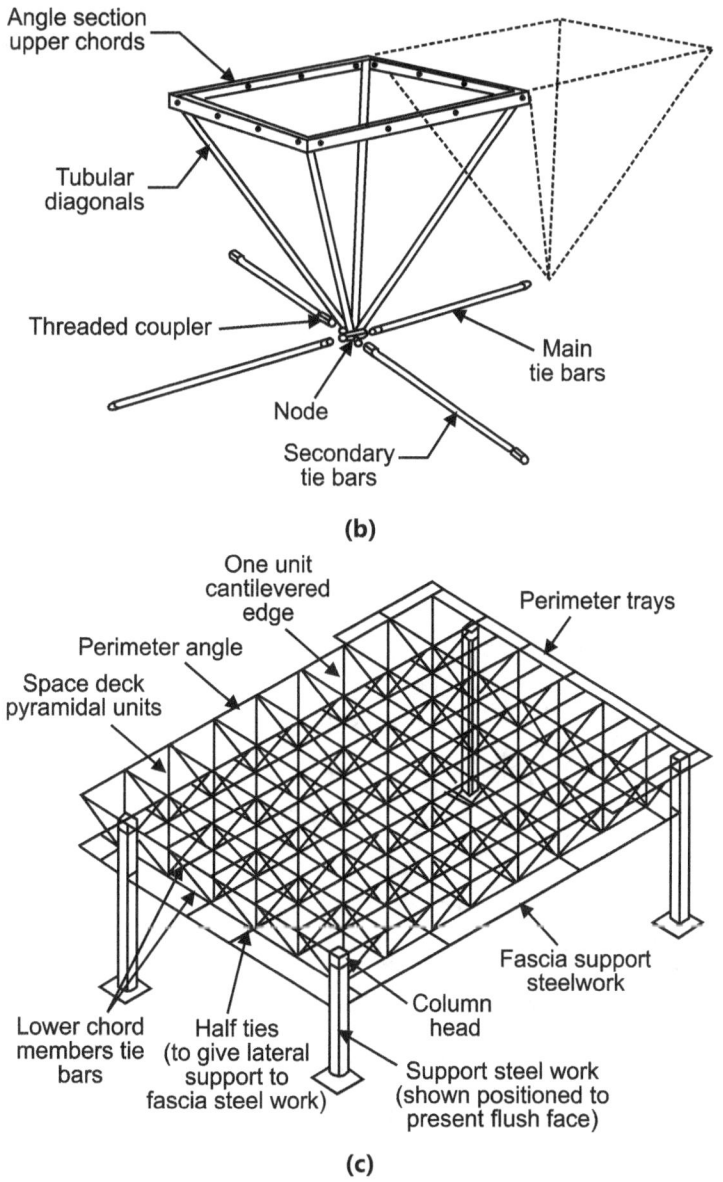

Fig. 7.24 : Details of space structure

7.11 FOLDED PLATES

It is competitive with shells. It is used to cover large column free areas. It consumes more material compared to material required for shell.

Folded plates consists of series of thin plates. These are joined monolithically along their common edges and supported on diaphragms. It is also called as hipped plates. In the following table different shapes of folded plates and their uses are given.

Sr. No.	Different shapes of plates	Uses/applications/disadvantages
1.	V-shaped plate.	For small span, does not provide enough area of concrete at top and bottom to resist compressive stresses.
2.	Trough shaped or trapezoidal shape	Eleminates the above mentioned disadvantages.
3.	Z-shaped plate	Serves as north-light roofs for factory building.
4.	Butterfly type plate	To cover factory roof and offers provision for window glazing.
5.	Tapering plates	For aesthetic reason.
6.	Hipped plates of the pyramidal types	Used for tent shaped roofs, cooling towers etc.

The thickness of the folded plates shall not be less than 75 mm. For preliminary designs the depth of the plate shall be taken as $\dfrac{1}{15}$ of the span.

The angle of inclination to the plates to horizontal shall be limited to 40° for in-site construction.

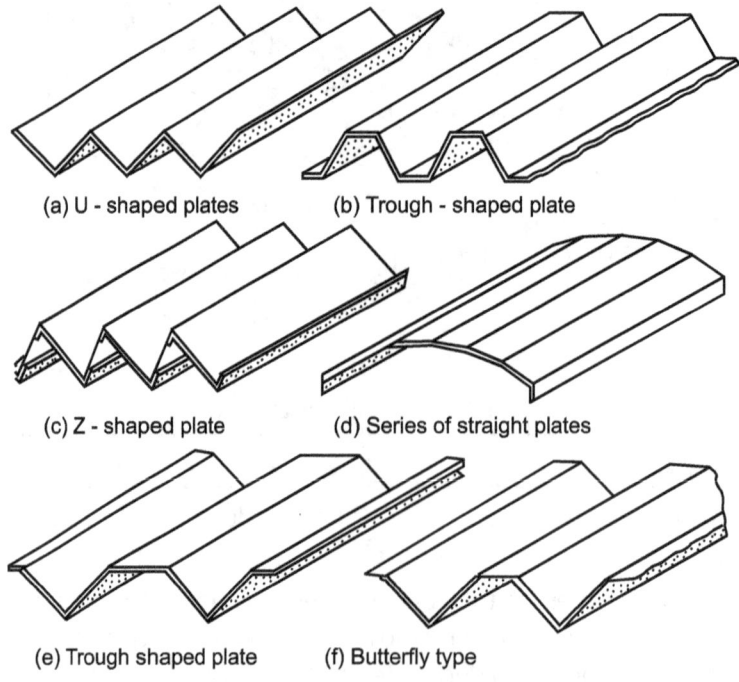

(a) U - shaped plates   (b) Trough - shaped plate

(c) Z - shaped plate   (d) Series of straight plates

(e) Trough shaped plate   (f) Butterfly type

Fig. 7.25 : Folded plates

To analyse structural behaviour of plates their are two methods as below :

(1) Transverse slab action analysis. (2) Plane plate action analysis.

The expansions joints shall conform to provisions laid down in IS : 456 – 1978. It should be located in the ridge slab. For large span, it should not be provided.

Transverse reinforcement should be provided along the cross section of the folded plate. It should be designed to resist the transverse moment.

Longitudinal reinforcement should carry the longitudinal tensile stresses in individual slabs.

To distribute the steel neatly reinforcement should be placed in that manner. In the compression zone nominal reinforcement of consisting of 8 mm diameter bars should be provided at about 200 mm centre to centre.

REVIEW QUESTIONS

1. State the points to be observed while providing A.C. sheet roofing to steel angle purlins.

2. A hall of size 7.50 mm and 10.0 m is to be provided with pitched roof of A.C. sheet roofing using steel trusses and angle purlins. Draw the arrangement of supporting structure, type of roof truss, purlin cleat angle junction details and fixing arrangement of A.C. sheet roofing to purlin.

3. Draw a typical arrangement for pitched roofing for L-shaped building with internal clear dimensions 7.50 m × 15.0 m for a long side and 7.50 m and 5.0 m for short side. Draw a labelled sketch and show the following :
   (a)   Ridge   (b) Eaves   (c) Valley
   (d)   Hip   (e) Gable end   (f) Hip end.
   State the type of truss and c/c spacing. State spacing of purlins for C.G.I. sheet roofing. Draw typical connection of fixing of C.G.I. sheet to angle purlin.

4. State the types of shell structure. What is butterfly shell ?

5. Give neat and labelled sketch of king post truss.

6. What are the advantages of constructing steel roof trusses over timber trusses ?

7. State circumstances under which each of the following is adopted :
   (a) Pitched roof,   (b) Flat roof,
   (c) Dome,   (d) Shell roof.

8. What are the relative advantages and disadvantages of flat roofs over other roofs ?

9. Draw neat and labelled sketch of queen post truss.

10. Name the types of roofing material available in market. State advantages and limitations of each.

11. Describe lean to roof in detail, with neat and labelled sketch.

12. Give neat and labelled sketches of the following structural steel sections. Write their min. sections available in market :
    (a)   Angle   (b)   Channel.

13. What are the relative advantages and disadvantages of flat roof over other types ?

14. Write short notes on :
    (a) G.I. sheets   (b) A.C. sheets
    (c) Laying and fixing of G.I. sheets   (d) Laying and fixing of A.C. sheets
    (e) Mangalore tiles   (f) Roofing tiles
    (g) Marble tiles
15. Explain in detail testing of tiles.
16. Compare asbestos cement sheet and G.I. sheet.
17. Explain in detail fixing of A.C. sheet
18. Explain with sketches :
    (a) Ridge cover   (b) Purlin   (c) Principal rafter
19. Enlist the forms of roof trusses and explain king post roof truss
20. Write a short note on space frame structures.
21. Define the following terms as used in pitched roof constructions :
    (a) Template   (b) Post-plates
    (c) Pitch of a roof   (d) Jack rafters
22. Discuss the various factors which require due consideration while selecting a roof - covering for a building.
23. Write notes on : (a) Shell structures   (b) Folded plate structures

SOLVED UNIVERSITY QUESTIONS

DEC. 2014

1. Draw sketch of King post truss.   [3]
   [**Ans.:** Refer Article 7.8.3]
2. Draw sketch of Queen-post truss.   [3]
   [**Ans.:** Refer Article 7.8]

MAY 2014

1. Draw sketch of sloping roof truss and show on it principal rafter, common rafter, Ridge cover, Effective span.   [6]
   [**Ans.:** Refer Article 7.7.2]

NOV. 2015

1. Write short notes on : Lean to roof   [3]
   [**Ans.:** Refer Article 7.8.2]
2. Draw sketch of queen-post truss.   [3]
   [**Ans.:** Refer Article 7.8]

MAY 2016

1. Draw sketch of queen post roof truss.   [3]
   [**Ans.:** Refer Article 7.8]

◈ ◈ ◈

CHAPTER 8
DOORS AND WINDOWS

8.1 INTRODUCTION

- To enter into a volumetric space of a room what we need is an openable barrier known as a **Door**.
- To provide light and ventilation and better vision what we need is a **Window** and when these are closed for partial or full privacy what we need is a **Ventilator**.
- Location, positioning and total number of doors and windows have a great impact on planning of a building.

General Guidelines for Location and Number of Doors

- The number of doors should be kept minimum so as to increase the circulation area thereby increasing utility of space.
- Normally (preferably) the door be located near the corner of the room, at around 20 cm from it.
- If it is customary to have two doors for a room, place them in opposite walls, facing each other for good ventilation and free circulation within the room.
- Other governing factors for location, number and size are desired day light, desired vision of surrounding privacy, natural ventilation, heat loss and other local climatic factors etc.
- Also in today's context interior decoration is to be considered while positioning the doors.

For locating the windows and for deciding their number one must concentrate upon the following factors; climatic condition, floor area, distribution of light within the room, ventilation control, privacy, interior decoration, outside vision etc.

General Guidelines

- The windows should preferably located in opposite walls, facing each other.
- Fresh air and continuous diffused daylight entry is achieved if northern side placement is worked out for windows.
- Windows should be located in prevalent wind direction.

Thumb Rules

- For residential buildings the sill height ranges from 0.7 to 1.0 m from floor level.
- $B_W = \dfrac{1}{8}$ (Width of room + Height of room).
- Total area $- \dfrac{1}{10^{th}}$ (min.) to $\dfrac{1}{5^{th}}$ of floor area (max. in case of public buildings).

- Area of opening = Residential 1 sq. m for 30 to 40 cu. m of inside volume.
- For admittance of light → glazed panel area = 8 to 10% of floor area.

8.2 DOORS AND WINDOWS

(A) Doors :

- A door may be defined as an openable barrier secured in a wall opening OR
- It can also be defined as a movable barrier, secured in an opening, known as doorway through a building wall or partition, for the purpose of providing an access to the building or rooms of a building.

Purposes Served :

- Access,
- Connecting link for various sections specially in case of commercial buildings,
- Security and privacy as and when needed.

(B) Windows :

A window is a barrier secured in a wall opening.

Purposes Served :

- Admittance of natural light and air.
- For viewing outside scenario.

Materials Used : Wood, Glass, Steel, Plastic and combinations of these etc.

Designation of Door, Window and Ventilators : Frames are designated by symbols denoting width, type and height in succession.

Width : It is indicated by the number of modules of 10 cm; (initial number in the designation - Refer examples a, b, c).

Type : It is indicated by an abbreviated letter/alphabet (middle term).

Height : It is indicated by number of modules of 10 cm (final number).

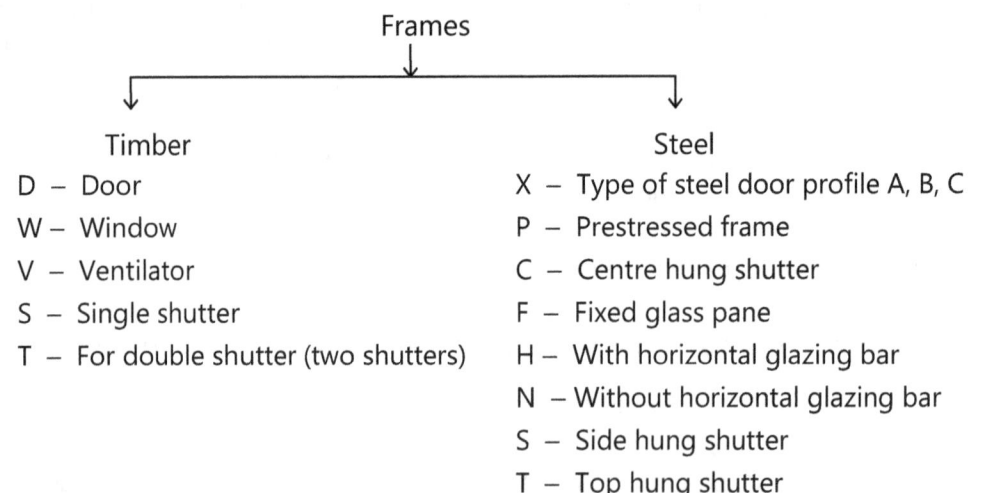

Frames

Timber	Steel
D – Door	X – Type of steel door profile A, B, C
W – Window	P – Prestressed frame
V – Ventilator	C – Centre hung shutter
S – Single shutter	F – Fixed glass pane
T – For double shutter (two shutters)	H – With horizontal glazing bar
	N – Without horizontal glazing bar
	S – Side hung shutter
	T – Top hung shutter

Examples :

(a) 8 DS 20 indicates single shutter door with;

$$\text{Width} = (8 \times 10) - 1 = 79 \text{ cm}$$
$$\text{Height} = (20 \times 10) - 1 = 199 \text{ cm}$$

(b) 10 P X 20 indicates prestressed steel frame with, profile X (i.e. X – A, X – B or X – C).

$$\text{Width} = (10 \times 10) - 1 = 99 \text{ cm}$$
$$\text{Height} = (20 \times 10) - 1 = 199 \text{ cm etc.}$$

(c) 6 WS 12 indicates single shutter window with 60 cm as width and 120 cm height for opening.

$$\therefore \qquad \text{Clear width} = (6 \times 10) - 1 = 59 \text{ cm}$$
$$\text{Clear height} = (12 \times 10) - 1 = 119 \text{ cm}$$

Table 8.1

Designation	Size of Opening	Frame Size	Shutter Size (Total)	Remark
8 DS 20 9 DS 20 10 DS 20 12 DT 20	80 × 200 90 × 200 100 × 200 120 × 200	79 × 199 89 × 199 99 × 199 119 × 199	70 × 190.5 80 × 190.5 90 × 190.5 110 × 190.5	→ Each shutter 56 cm wide with 2 cm overlap.
8 DS 21 9 DS 21 10 DS 21 12 DT 21	80 × 210 90 × 210 100 × 210 120 × 210	79 × 209 89 × 209 99 × 209 119 × 209	70 × 200.5 80 × 200.5 90 × 200.5 110 × 200.5	→ Each shutter 56 cm wide with 2 cm overlap.
6 WS 12 10 WT 12 12 WT 12	60 × 120 100 × 120 120 × 120	59 × 119 99 × 119 119 × 119	50 × 110 90 × 110 110 × 110	Shutter width 46 and 56 cm respectively with 2 cm overlap.
6 WS 13 10 WT 13 12 WT 13	60 × 130 100 × 130 120 × 130	59 × 129 99 × 129 119 × 129	50 × 120 90 × 110 110 × 120	Shutter width 46 (1st case) and 56 cm (2nd case) respectively with 2 cm overlap.
6 V 6 10 V 6 12 V 6	60 × 60 100 × 60 120 × 60	59 × 59 99 × 59 119 × 59	50 × 50 90 × 50 110 × 50	

Nominal sizes adopted – (Residential buildings) :

External door   – 1.0 × 2.0 m

Internal door   – 0.9 × 2.0 m
Bath/W.C. doors   – 0.7 × 2.0 m/0.9 × 2.0
Public buildings   – 1.2 × 2.25 m
Garages etc.   – 2.5 × 2.25 m

Note : Minimum height should not be less than 1.8 m.

8.3 TECHNICAL TERMS   (Nov. 16)

(A) Frame

An assemblage of vertical members (post/upright/jambs/gramps) and horizontal members (Top - head, Bottom - sill) forming an enclosure, to which shutters are attached.

Materials Used : (a) Timber, (b) Steel sections, (c) Aluminium sections, (d) Concrete, (d) Stone.

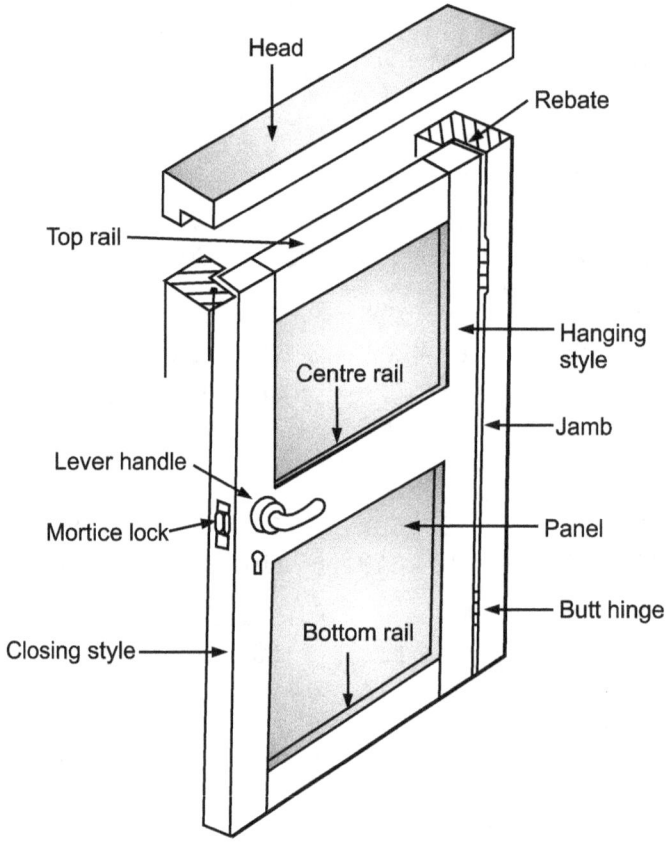

Fig. 8.1 : Parts of standard door

Details :

- **Head :** The top horizontal member to be connected with vertical posts with horns on either side (15 cm in length beyond vertical members) for securing the frame with masonry.

- **Sill :** The bottom horizontal member to be connected with vertical posts (in case of window).

- **Jambs or Posts :** The vertical parts of the frame attached to head (and sill of window) with tenon and mortise joint. The shutter rests on jambs (inner side).

- **Reveal :** The external jamb or right angles to the face of the wall. Hence, it represents a narrow cross surface of the wall on both sides of the opening on the outside of the frame.

- **Rebate :** A cut or a recess made inside a frame all around on one side to which the shutter is attached through rivets/hinges.

- **Holdfasts :** To provide additional fixity to the frame, M.S. flats 30 mm × 6 mm and 20 cm in length are provided, which remain embedded in the masonry.

- **Threshold :** Wooden fixture, fixed to the floor under door frame, thereby enabling the door to be cut short enough to clear floor coverings on the inside.

(B) Shutters :

A movable barrier of the door or window attached to the frame with assembly of styles, rails, panels or planks or otherwise.

Materials Used : Timber, Plywood, Plastic, Decorative or plane glass, Pressed boards, Hard boards and combinations of above.

Details :

- **Styles (Style/Stile) :** These are outer vertical members of shutter :

  (a) Hanging Style : Attached with the frames with hinges, the door hangs on it.

  (b) Closing Style : Which holds the latch.

  (c) Meeting Style : Provided for two shutter doors, where they meet.

- **Rails :** These are the horizontal members attached with styles at different levels and are classified depending upon the positions or functions. They are going to serve :

  Types : (a) Top rail, (b) Intermediate rail, (c) Frieze rail, (d) Lock rail, (e) Bottom rail.

- **Sash Bar or Glazing Bar :** Light weight member of shutter receiving or holding the glass.

- **Mullion :** It is the vertical member used to subdivide door or window shutter vertically.

- **Transom :** It is the horizontal member used to subdivide the window or door shutter horizontally.

- **Panel :** It is the area enclosed between the rails and styles. Glass or timber is usually used.

- **Louver :** An inclined piece of wood or glass positioned in such a way to maintain privacy but ventilation is possible through number of louvers.

- **Architrave :** This is a strip of wood, usually moulded or splayed, which is fixed round a door frame to improve its appearance at the joint with masonry, without leaving any reveal.
- **Putty :** This is a mixture of linseed oil and whiting chalk. It is used for fixing glass panels.

8.4 INSTALLATION OF DOOR AND WINDOW FRAMES

- The usual trend of materials used is mentioned earlier. Timber is most popular material of all as it can be moulded to required shape, size and made attractive.
- The drawback associated is attack by vermines, scarcity and thus costlier. Plywood can be used as covering material for flushed doors.
- Glass is invariably used where ornamental effect is essentially to be obtained and for admittance of more light. Steel confirming to IS 513, IS 1079 is in demand specially for windows but it can be easily subjected to dampness.
- Hence, at places where above conditions are prevalent such as attack of vermines on timber and dampness, R.C.C. or dressed stone frames can be used.

Methods of Installation :

1. **Built in Method**
   - The frame is installed either before or during the construction of the wall. For the door frame three holdfasts on either side of the posts are provided whereas in case of window frame two holdfasts are provided.
   - Horns are provided at the top and metal pins or wrought iron dowels are used to fix the frame to the floor.
   - The frames are coated with thick coal tar or any such water proofing paint. The cross battens hold the frame in rectangular shape during construction.
   - In case of positioning, the windows, chalk line marking for head and sill levels is essential as against only head in case of door.
   - Plumb line check for the posts is done to secure the frame exactly in vertical way.

2. **Prepared Opening Method**
   - The frame is installed after the construction of wall.
   - The frame is less liable to distortion and moisture change as the opening is in finished state, hence superior type of frames can also be easily installed in this case.
   - The frames can be nailed to the already driven plugs which are flushed with jambs.
   - In the end holdfast openings and the bottom pins are grouted with water proof grouting material.

8.5 FIXTURES AND FASTENINGS   (Dec. 13, 14, May 15)

- To ensure the gripping of frame to the wall, shutter to the frame and to close the door or window various fixtures and fastenings are used.
- Material for them may be iron, brass or aluminium. Sharp edges for such items are to be avoided and the screws to be used are counter sunk.

- Iron items are black enamelled or copper oxidized whereas brass fittings are oxidised, chromium plated with bright lustre. Aluminium fittings are normally anodised. Depending upon type, size, positions of different doors and windows different shapes are suitably promoted.

(A) Hinges

- **Butt Hinges :** These are screwed to the edges of doors/windows and rebates in frame. Length is 1 to 20 cm. One flange is screwed to edge of shutter and other to rebate of frame with counter sunk holes.
- **Back Flap :** When shutters are thin these are placed on the backside of shutter and frame.
- **Counter Flap :** As it is formed in three parts and two centres it allows folding of two leaves back to back.
- **Rising Butt Hinge :** To clear the obstructions like carpets, mats these butts are used. The shutter is raised about 10 mm from floor level as they are provided with helical joint. Closing operation is automatic.
- **T-shutter or Garnet Hinge :** Long arm is screwed to shutter, short plate to the frame. It can be used for heavy doors, gates, stable doors etc.

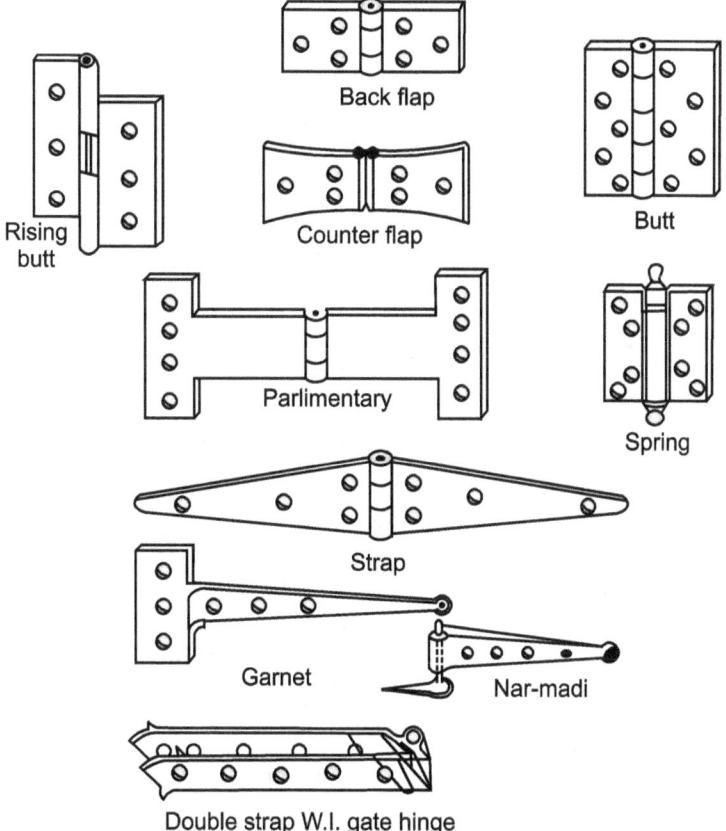

Fig. 8.2 : Various types of door hinges

- **Nar-madi Hinge :** Used for heavy doors. The flange or strap is fixed to shutter and the pin on which strap rotates is fixed to frame.
- **Parlimentary Hinge :** Shutter rotates through 180° and leans against wall. Opening remains free i.e. with minimum obstruction.
- **Pin Hinge :** This is to be used for heavy doors. The centre pin can be removed and two straps or leaves can be fixed separately.
- **Strap Hinge :** A substitute to garnet hinge, it can be used for heavy doors.
- **Spring Hinge :** Single or double acting hinges to be used in case of swinging doors. Single action indicates that the swing is only on one side whereas double action indicates swing is on either side. Closing operation is automatic.

Bolts

- **Hook and Eye :** When the window is open it remains at its place using hook (fixed to the sill of the frame) which is inserted in the eye fixed to the bottom rail of the shutter. It may be provided in case of doors as well.

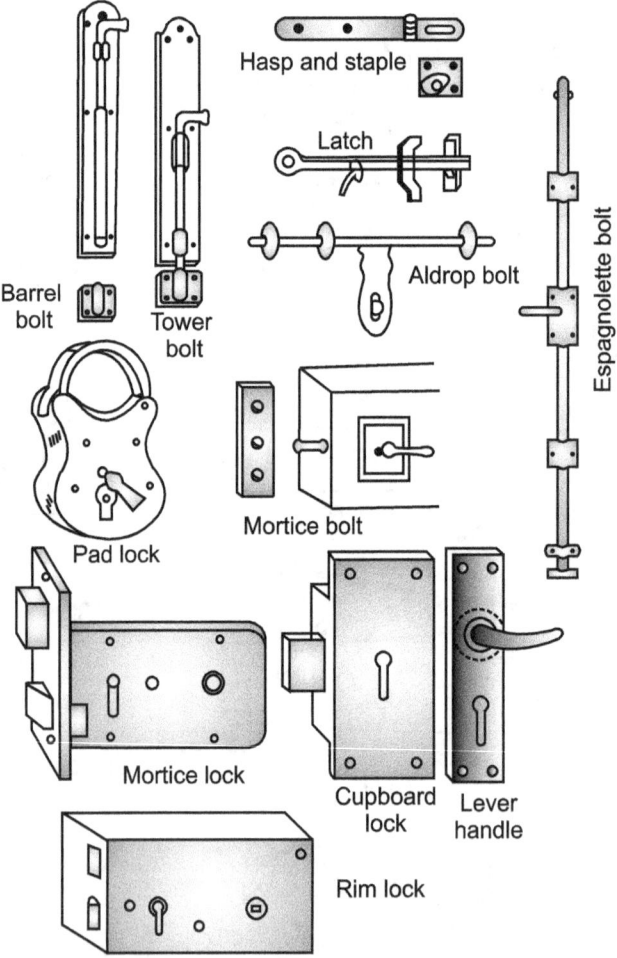

Fig. 8.3 : Various types of bolts, staples, latches, aldrops and locks

- **Barrel Bolt :** Used for fixing back faces of external doors. Plate is screwed to the inside of shutter and the bolt engaged in barrel or socket fixed to the frame. Length varies between 10 to 40 cm.

- **Tower Bolt :** Similar to barrel bolt with two or three steples provided with door frame instead of barrel.

- **Flush Bolt :** When it is desired to keep the bolt flush with the face of the door this is used. Hence, it is let into the doors either upon a face or on the edge.

- **Aldrop :** It is provided on external doors where padlocks are to be used. It is made up of iron.

- **Norfold Latch or Thumb Latch :** Made up of malleable iron or bronze, consisting of lever pivoted at one end. Lever can be actuated by trigger passing through door and pivoted in upper part of a vertical bow handle. The latch can be released by pressing the trigger. It offers security to the door.

- **Hasp and Staple Bolt :** Similar operation as that of aldrop. Hasp is fixed to shutter and staple to the door frame. It facilitates padlocking. It is made of iron.

- **Espagnolette Bolt : Material :** Iron, steel, bronze. Extension bolt used for securing tall doors and casement windows the top of which can not be reached easily. Two long bolts, one which secures top and other securing bottom of the door are operated simultaneously by turning handle in the centre.

Locks

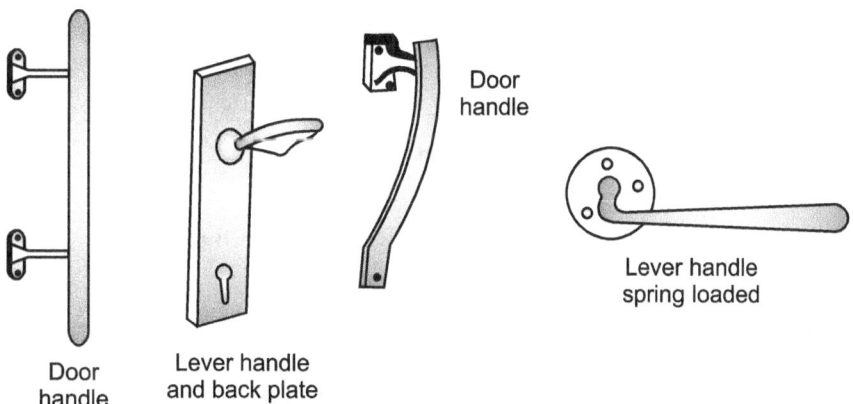

Fig. 8.4 : Various types of handles

- **Mortise Lock :** To be used when thickness is more than 5 cm. The lock is fixed in a mortise formed on the edge of door.

- **Cupboard Lock :** For securing doors of minor importance this is used.

- **Padlock :** Securing for entrance door or any other as per need.

- **Rim Lock :** It can be employed in case of thin doors. Fixed on edge with screw, such that it has projecting rim or flange.

- **Lever Handle :** Normally to be employed for interior doors.

Handles : For facilitating opening or closing of doors handles are provided.

Types : Bow handles, lever handles, wardoble handles.

It adds to the aesthetic of door. Different metals or materials are used for handles and they are made very attractive.

8.6 CLASSIFICATION OF DOORS AND WINDOWS

Doors are generally classified on the basis of :

(A) Functional :

- **Entrance Doors :** The door provided at the Principal entrances of a building are called **entrance doors**.
- **Ordinary Doors :** The main function of which is to permit passage of persons are called **ordinary doors or exterior and interior doors**.
- **Screen Doors :** The light doors which are provided in conjunction with main doors and mounted on the outside of the frames of exterior doors are called **screen doors**.
- **Fire Doors :** The doors specially designed to resist the passage of fire are called **fire doors**.
- **Wicket Doors :** A small size door provided within a large door to permit the passage without opening the large door.

(B) Operational :

- **Swinging Doors :** Shutters are hung to the door frame with hinges on one side and they swing about a vertical axis. Type - single swing or double swing.
- **Sliding Door :** Horizontal or vertical sliding action.
- **Folding or Accordian Door :** Shutter leaves fold on one or either side.
- **Revolving Door :** Door revolves around central pivot.
- **Rolling Door :** Vertical rolling of shutter.
- **Collapsible Door :** Door collapses on one side or on either side.

(C) Materials Used :

- Timber/Wooden doors.
- Plywood - Veneer - particle boards as types of timber.
- Glazed doors.
- Steel doors.
- Aluminium framed doors etc.

Classification of Windows :

(A) Functional :

- For admitting light only - fixed - glazed window.
- For admitting light and air - ordinary windows.
- For admitting air and maintaining privacy - louvered windows.

- Projecting windows - outward/inward projections.
- Ventilator - special category.

(B) Operational :
- Side hung - hinges on sides.
- Top hung - hinges on top.
- Bottom hung - hinges at bottom.
- Sliding - horizontal and vertical.
- Folding - normally on either side.
- Pivoted - horizontal and vertical pivots.

(C) Materials Used :
Wooden, Aluminium, Steel, Glazed etc.

8.7 TYPES OF DOORS   (Dec. 14, May 14, 16)

Following are the usual types observed in rural and urban areas in India.
- Battened and ledged doors.
- Battened, ledged and braced doors.
- Battened, ledged and framed doors.
- Battened, ledged, braced and framed doors.

(**Note :** Above types are becoming obsolete for many reasons such as - unpleasant elevation, scarcity of timber, it can be used only for narrow openings etc.)
- Framed and panelled doors.
- Glazed or sash doors.
- Sliding doors.
- Flush doors.
- Collapsible doors.
- Revolving doors.
- Swing doors.
- Rolling steel shutter doors.
- Louvered doors.
- Folding doors.
- Plastic doors.

(1) Framed and Panelled Doors :

Characteristics :
- These are commonly used as their appearance is pleasing and tendency of shrinkage is reduced. Also if the panel area is partially occupied by glazing it admits additional natural light inside the room.

- The ratio of glazed to panelled portion is 2 : 1. The styles run vertically for the whole height and are most important as all other parts are connected to it. If the width is more, then additional vertical member, mullion is also provided to give additional strength.

- Minimum number of rails is three i.e. top rail, lock rail and bottom rail. The available space between styles and rail is termed as panel. The minimum width of style is kept as 100 mm and for bottom and lock rail it is 150 mm.

- The thickness of shutter depends on various factors such as size of the door, type of work, position of door, number of panels, moulding size etc. Usually, it ranges from 30 mm to 50 mm. Internal edges are grooved to receive the panels and mortised-tenoned joint is preferred for framework.

- Total number and pattern of panel depends upon designer's aspect or owner's choice.

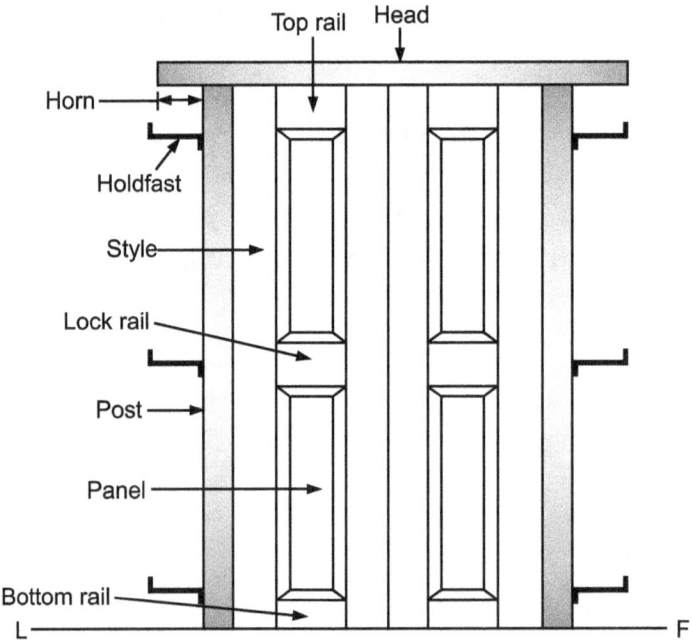

Fig. 8.5 : Doors frame and panelled shutters

(2) Glazed and Sash Doors

- If employed, this door gives very good effect, hence specially provided for private bungalows or in case of public buildings such as hospitals, colleges, libraries, showrooms etc.

- For fully glazed door, a single glass panel (plate glass) is received into the rebates along the inner edge of styles and secured by nails and putty or by wooden beads.

- Sometimes the glazed area is subdivided into number of small areas by providing sash bars. The glass panes are secured in the rebates of framework of sash bars.

- To increase the area of glazing, width of style above lock rail is sometimes reduced. These reduce dimensioned styles are known to be diminished or gunstock styles.

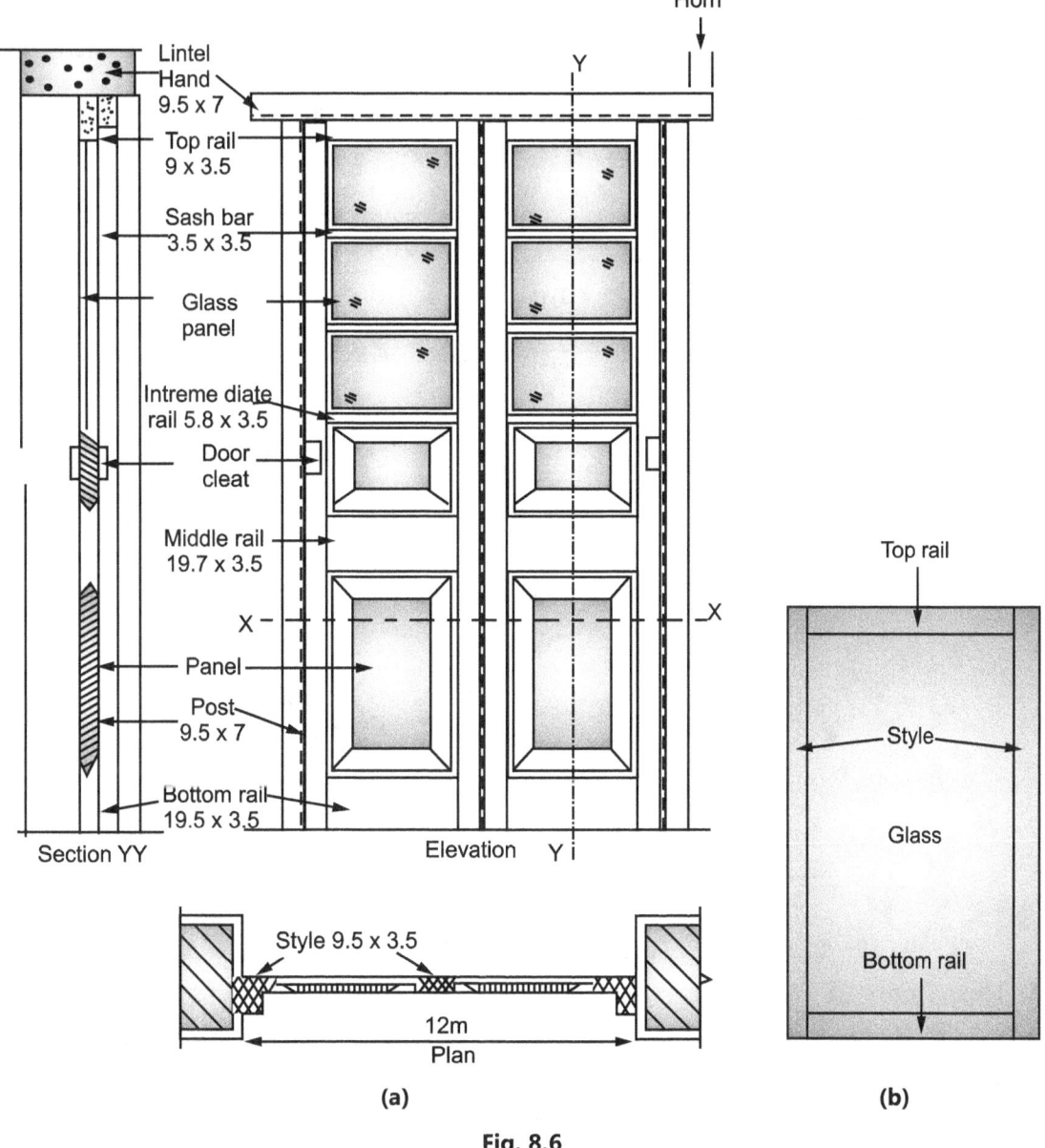

Fig. 8.6

(3) Sliding Doors

- The rotational movement about the hinges is completely avoided in this door as they are sliding parallel to the wall. They occupy less space as the support is provided at top and bottom.

- Through runners or guides, lateral movement of the door is restricted. These are used for entrances of godowns, sheds, shops, showrooms, offices and sometimes in residential buildings where the room area is less.

- The door may have more than one panel (leaf) and may have sliding tendency on one side or on either side as shown. (Ref. Fig. 8.7).

- For receiving the leaves either the cavities are provided in the thickness of the wall or the shutters lie against wall.

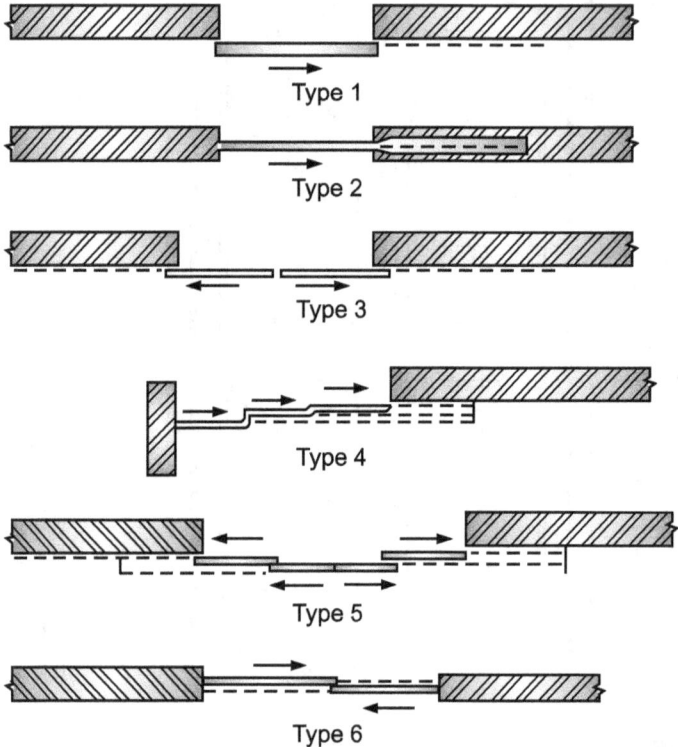

Fig. 8.7 : Plan showing arrangements of side sliding arrangement

(4) Flush Doors

- Use of plywood and block board increases the pleasing appearance of the flush door. Also it is simple to built or construct and has better weathering qualities.

- It provides plane surface for the shutter, hence economic, easy to clean, durable and less affected by moisture attack.

IS 2191 - 1962 and IS 2202 categories the flush door as :

- Solid core flush door.

- Cellular core flush door.

- Hollow core flush door.

(a) Solid Core Flush Door (Laminated Flush Door)

- As the name suggests, no hollow portion or space is left while forming the core thereby indicating heavy weight and consumption of more material.

- Core is made of strips of wood (laminee) glued together with width not less than 20 mm, under great pressure and placed edge to edge, within a framework of styles, top rail and bottom rail with width not less than 75 mm.

- For forming core, laminated strips can be replaced by particle board, block board or a combination of these two. Cross bands are laid with grains at right angles to the core, running on either face to the extreme edge of the shutter.

- Face veneer or plywood on either face is laid with grains perpendicular to the cross band. This placement or positioning of various layers make the door very strong and durable.

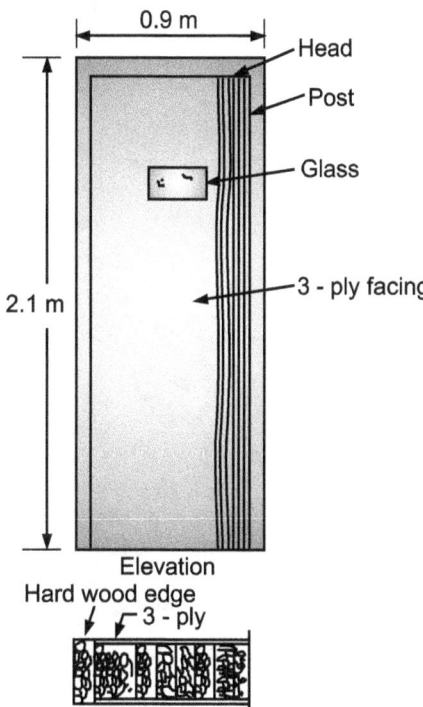

Fig. 8.8 : Solid flush door

(b) Cellular Core Flush Door

- The vertical and horizontal battens or ribs, not less than 25 mm wide, made up of strips of wood, plywood or blocks of compressed wood are so fixed that a grid of area not more than 25 sq. cm is formed with total void content not more than 40% of volume of core.

- Otherwise positioning of cross band and face ply is same as in case of solid core flush doors; with framework of style, top, intermediate and bottom rails.

Characteristics : Comparatively lighter, cheap and weaker in section.

(c) Hollow Core Flush Door

- A hollow core flush door consists of frame made up of styles, top and bottom rails and minimum two intermediate rails with width not less than 75 mm.
- The vertical battens with width not less than 25 mm are so placed such that they form void with area not more than 500 sq cm.
- Sometimes granulated cork is placed within the hollow portion. For free circulation of air ventilating holes are provided.

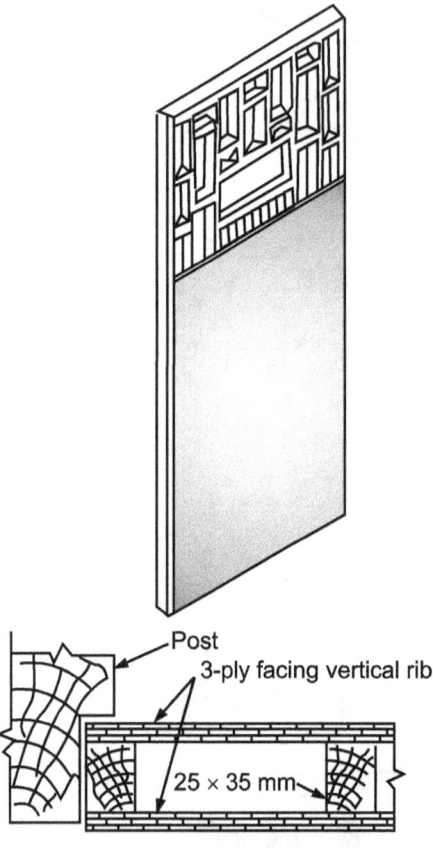

Post
3-ply facing vertical rib
25 × 35 mm

Fig. 8.9 : Hollow flush door

5. Collapsible Doors

- At the entrances for residential buildings, public buildings, sheds, workshops, godown etc. these doors are usually provided. These doors provide safety and are made up of single or double shutters, depending upon the width of the opening.
- It can be opened by giving a horizontal push to the shutter. The door is fabricated from vertical, double M.S. channels 16 mm to 20 mm wide (usual sizes being $18 \times 9 \times 3$mm, $20 \times 10 \times 2$ mm), joined together with hollows inside to form a vertical gap of 12 to 20 mm.

- These units are placed 100 to 120 mm centre to centre and joined together by means of iron flats 16 to 20 mm wide and 5 mm thick and placed diagonally. Diagonal allows the movement of assembled channels.

- Shutter rolls up horizontally and causes no obstruction to the motion. End channels are usually embedded in the masonry work leaving hollow space as it is or fixed to the wall. Two horizontal rails or runners are fixed at lintel and floor level. Lateral movement of the door is avoided.

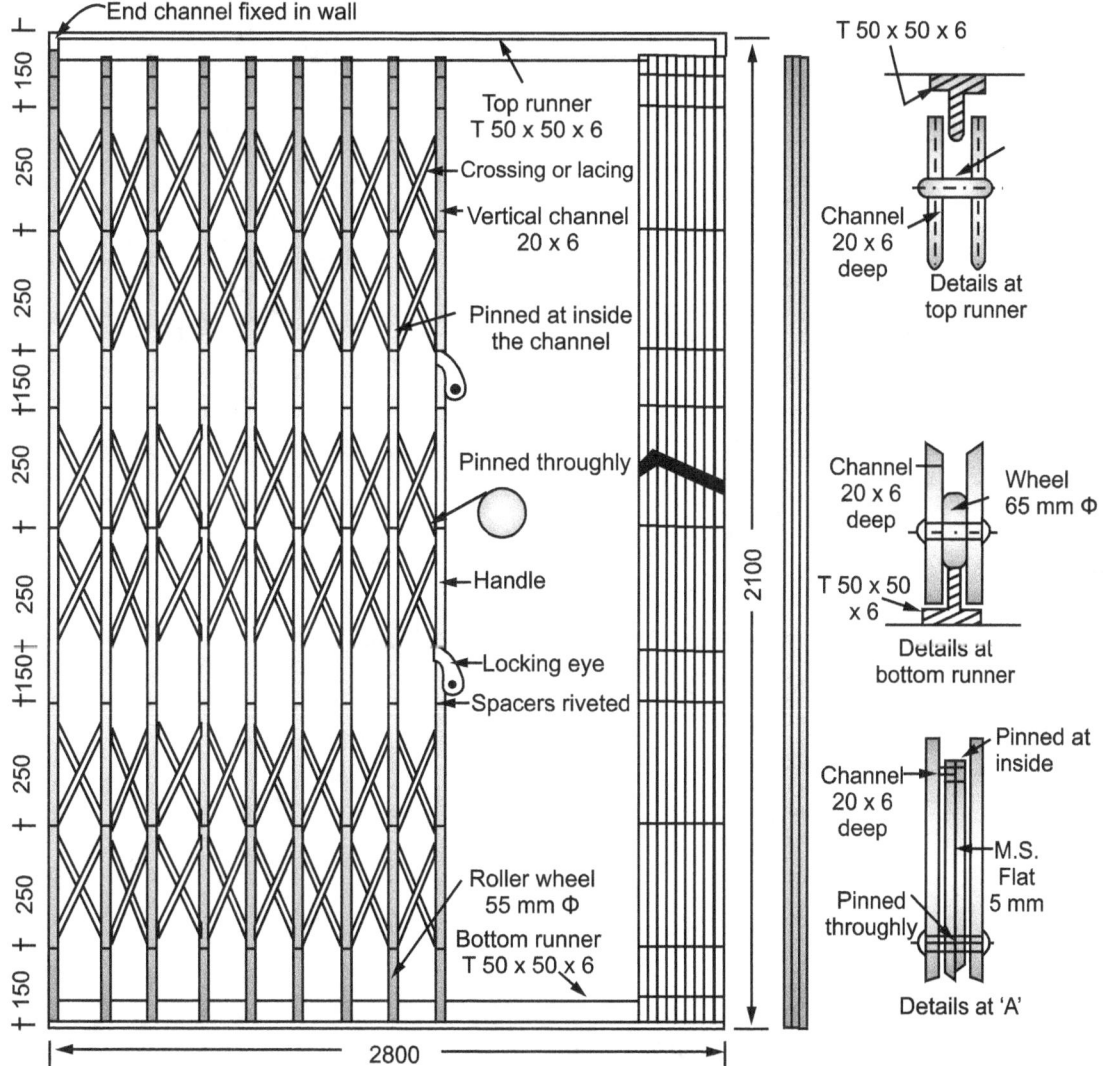

Fig. 8.10 : Collapsible door

6. Revolving Doors

- In case of some of public buildings, such as hospitals, big hotels, offices, banks etc. where predominant pedestrian traffic is utilizing the door way, revolving door proves to be most efficient as entry and exit is possible simultaneously.

- The door consists of a central pivot and four radiating shutters or leaves attached to central mullion, and which are fully panelled, fully glazed or partly panelled and partly glazed.
- The four rubbing ends of the shutters carry projecting pieces of rubber for preventing draught of air. When not in use, the door is automatically closed and during peak hours even the shutters or wings can be folded.

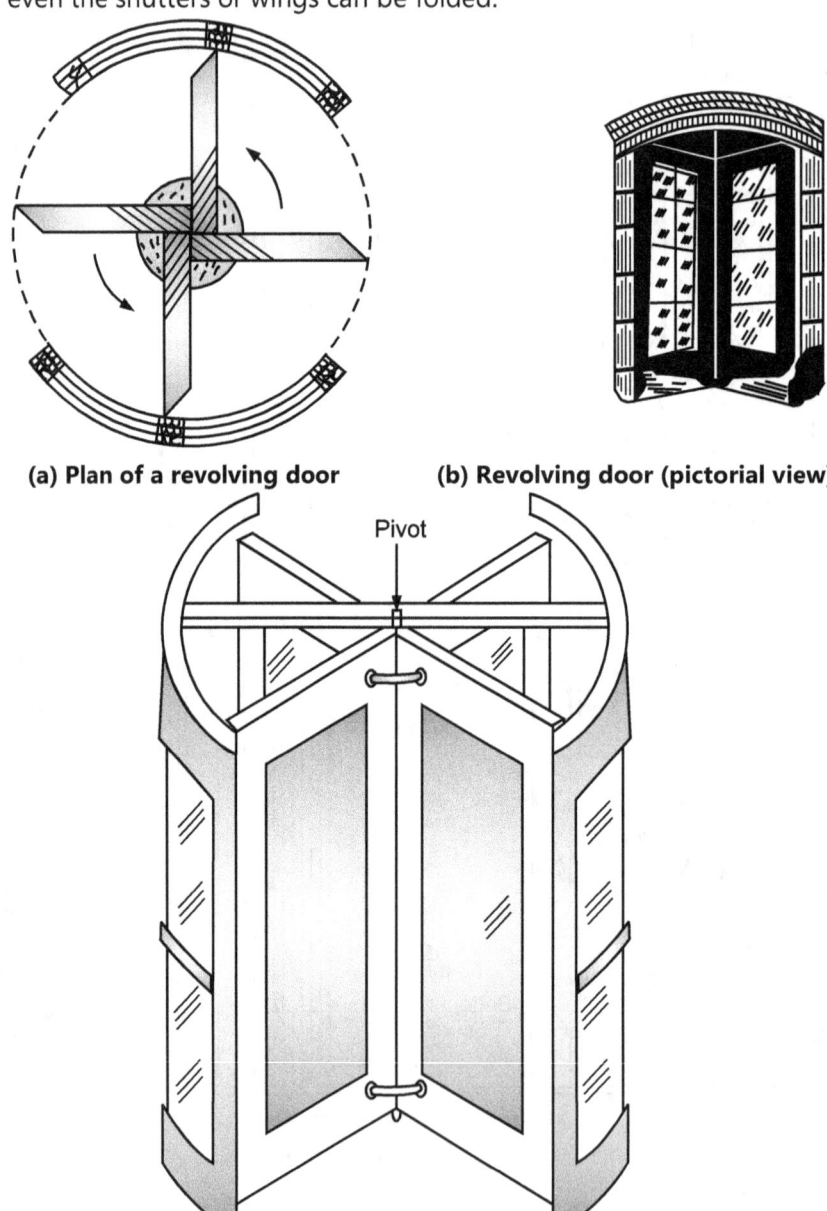

(a) Plan of a revolving door   **(b) Revolving door (pictorial view)**

(c) Isometric view of revolving door

Fig. 8.11

7. Swing Doors

It has single or double shutter arrangement with double action spring hinge provided for the fixation. A gentle push opens up the shutter and it returns back to its position with spring force. To avoid accident, partial glazing is provided to see the person pushing it for entry. The doors have meeting style without rebate.

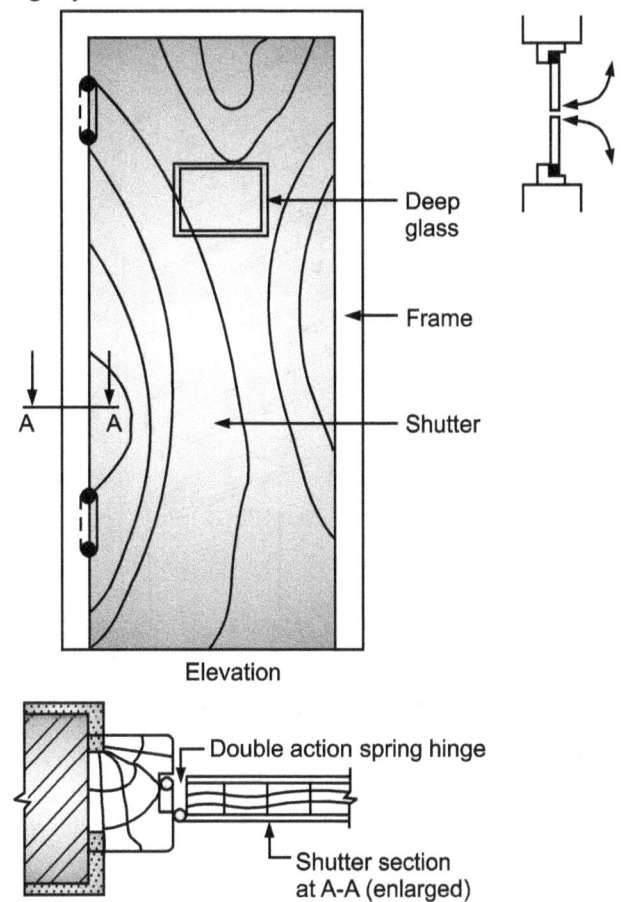

Fig. 8.12 : Swing doors

8. Rolling Steel Shutter Doors

Sufficiently strong, offering safety to the property, hence normally opted to secure big shops, godowns, garages, show windows etc.

Assembly for door consists of a frame, a drum and a shutter of thin steel plates (laths or slates) about 1 – 1.25 mm thick and interlocked together. Shutter moves within steel guides of the frame and coils around the drum (with diameter 200 to 300 mm).

Door is counter balanced by means of helical springs enclosed in drum. Hood of steel protects the drum. Size of rolling shutter is specified as W × H mm (clear opening).

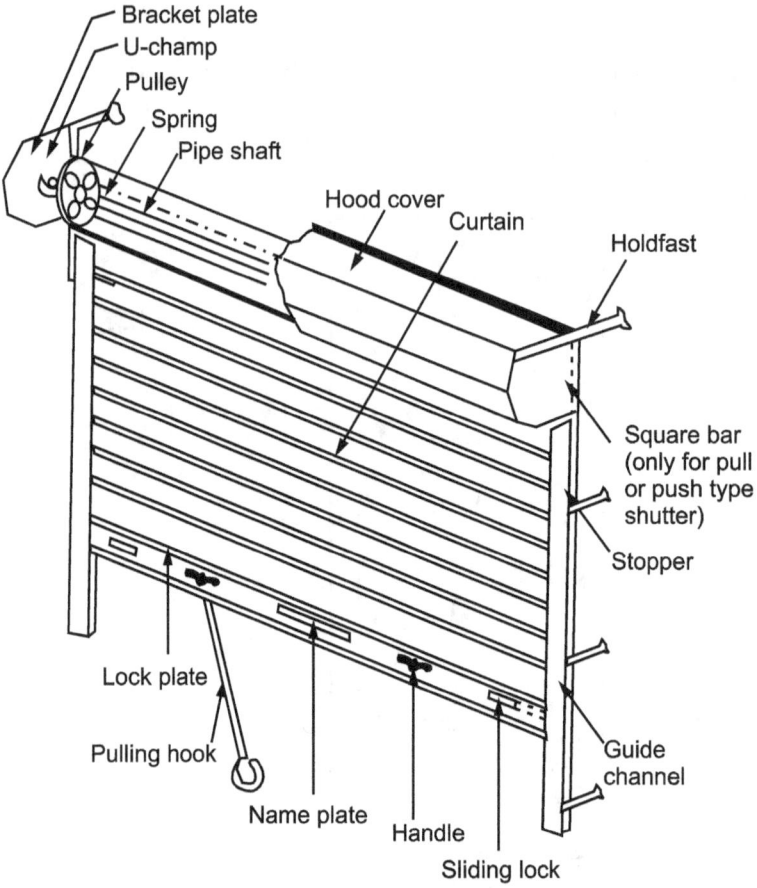

Fig. 8.13 : Component part of self coiling - rolling shutter

Operation of Door Shutter

- **Self coiling :** Pull-push force application is responsible for opening the shutter. The force can be applied manually, directly or indirectly by pulling hook. It shall be used for maximum 8 m² clear areas without ball bearing or 12 m² with ball bearings.

- **Gear operated - (Mechanical type) :** Ball bearing mounted shutter is operated by a bevel gear box and crank handle space (upto 25 m²) and with chain wheel and endless chain mounted on worm shaft (upto 35 m² area).

- **Electrically operated :** If the shutter area is more (of the order of 35 m² to 50 m²) then the shutter operation is carried out electrically.

9. Louvered Doors (Venetained Doors)

- These doors allow free passage of air when closed and are responsible for maintaining the privacy. Cleaning process is difficult as they harbour dust. However, at places like latrines, bathrooms of the buildings these may be suitably provided.

- Louvers may be for full height or partially and may be fixed or movable type. The arrangement is worked out at such an inclination that it obstructs horizontal vision.

Upper back edge of any louver is higher than lower front edge of the louver just above it.

- In case of movable type, the up - down motion is carried out by pivots. Louvers may be of timber or glass.

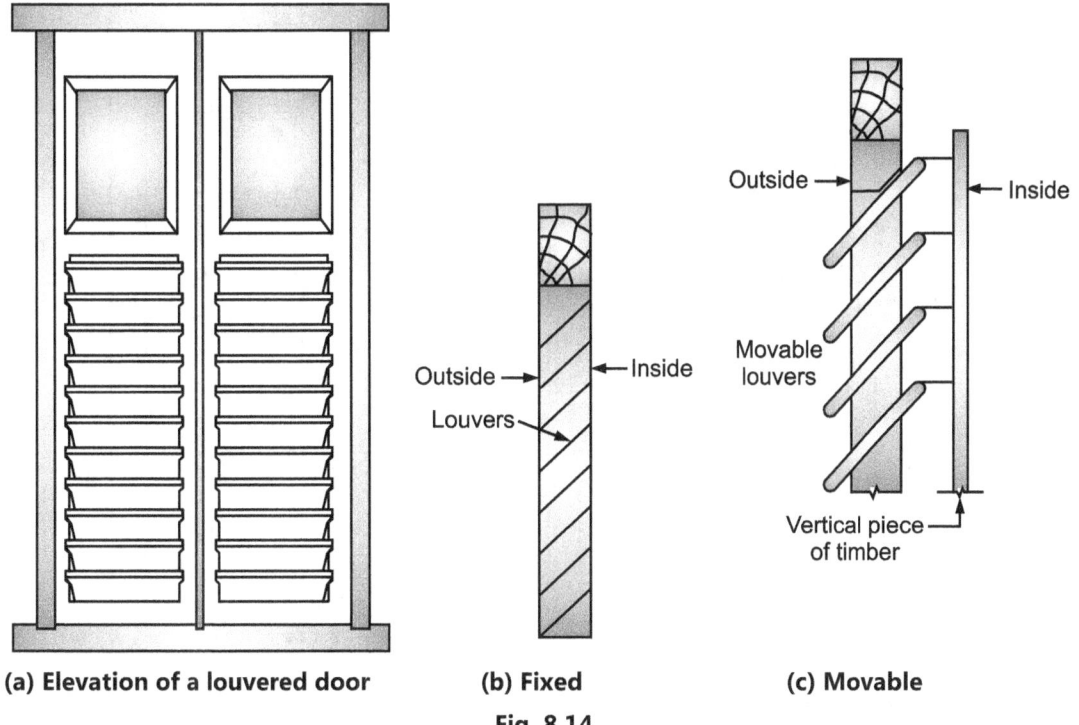

| (a) Elevation of a louvered door | (b) Fixed | (c) Movable |

Fig. 8.14

10. Wire-Gauged/Doors

- To avoid nuisance of flies, insects, mosquitoes etc. these doors are provided; specially in case of refreshment areas, kitchens, sweet shops, hotels etc.
- The shutter is made up of styles and rails and the galvanized, fine wire mesh is nailed to the frames with peripheral wood beading. This is the outer door in case of two door entry, and opens inside of the room.

11. Folding Doors

- The character differs according to the type of building. In case of public buildings such as educational institutes etc. larger entrance area is provided. Here the elevational treatment may not be that important, hence 4 folded shutters are provided, central two of which carries locking arrangement. 1st and 4th is joined to frame by hinges and 2nd and 3rd are hinged to them respectively.
- But in case of residential bungalows or lavish apartments elevation has got more importance, hence panelled door with 4 shutters may be fully glazed, fully panelled or partly glazed and partly panelled is provided to have access to attached terrace, garden or even these are located for main entrance.

Costlier in case of residential areas as special treatment is to be provided for enhancing the appearance.

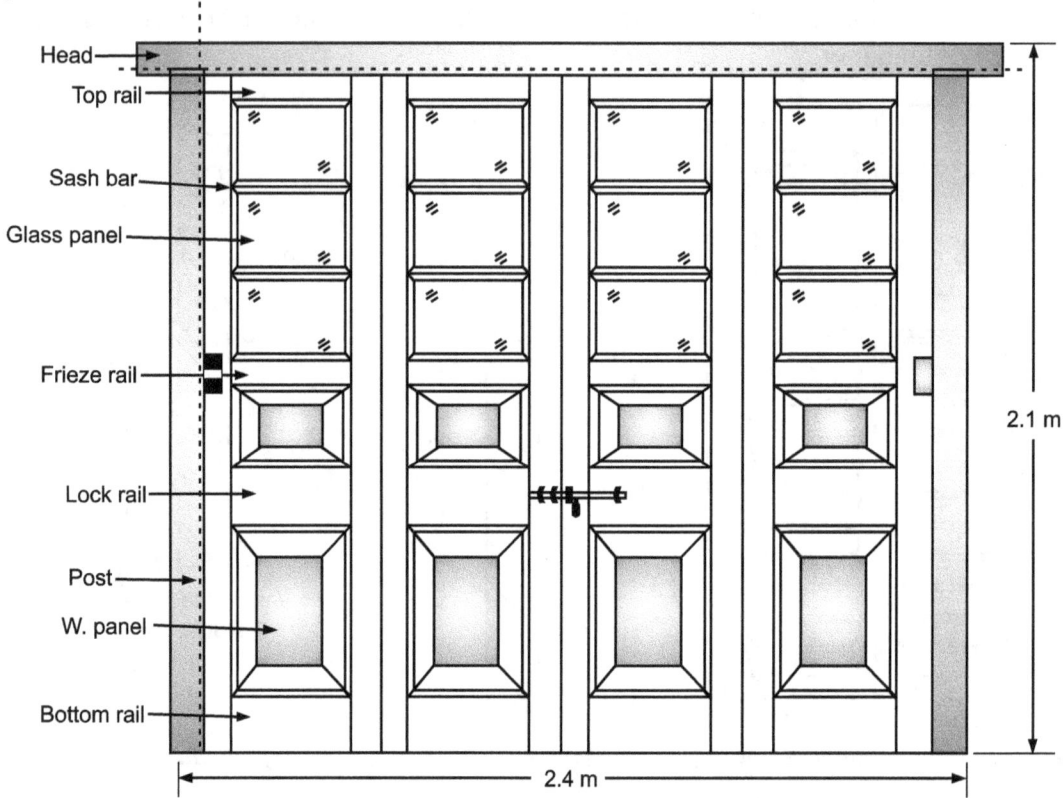

Fig. 8.15 : Detailed elevation of a folding door partly glazed and panelled

12. Plastic Doors

- Light in weight, ease in cleaning, water proof; hence these can be provided in case of bathrooms, toilets etc. for any type of building. The colour scheme of the area plays an important role in deciding the colour of plastic door.
- The durability depends upon the thickness of the door. Shutter is attached to the frames by means on nails built in with shutter.

8.8 WINDOWS   (Dec. 13, 14, May 14, 15, 16, 17 Nov. 15)

- Depending upon various natural agencies deciding the climatic pattern at a particular place the window area in % of floor area will vary with a minimum of $1/10^{th}$ (10%) of floor area.
- Continuous sash or one large window in a room gives better light distribution, than separated narrow windows.

The selection of size, shape, location and the number of windows in a room depends upon the following factors :

- Area to be ventilated and lighted.

- Location of the room.
- Utility of the room (Kitchen - Living - Bedrooms or otherwise).
- Direction to which window fronts.
- Direction of the wind.
- Other natural parameters like humidity, temperature etc.
- Exterior views (to be sighted or to hide).
- Architectural treatment for the exterior.

Terminology
- **Sash :** A single assembly of styles and rails made into a frame for holding glass, with or without dividing bars, may be glazed or unglazed.
- **Window :** Sash and the glass that fill an opening.
- **Styles :** Upright - vertical or border pieces.
- **Rails :** Cross-horizontal pieces.
- **Bar :** Member that extends in height and width of an opening to be ventilated.
- **Muntin :** A short light bar.
- **Mullion :** A vertical member dividing the window (Please refer other details with door section.)
- **Transom :** A horizontal dividing member.

Types of Window

1. Casement Windows

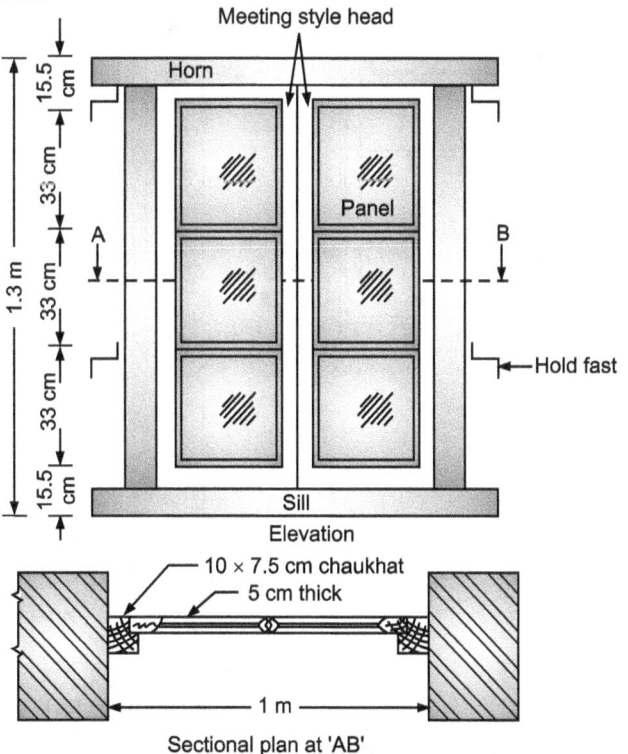

Fig. 8.16 : Casement window

Members : Shutter with styles, rails, sash bars, panels (glazed, unglazed or partially glazed). Frame with jambs, head, sill and sometimes with mullion and transomes.

Material : Timber, metal.

Sometimes a combination of door, window and ventilator is also provided specially at the entrance to enhance appearance and to check for unwanted entries.

Construction Method : Construction method is same as door, side hinged opening part of window with glass panes is known as casement and hence the name.

2. Double Hung Window : This window consists of a pair of shutters sliding vertically with upper shutter moving in downward direction and vice versa. They slide in two grooves made two posts. Two metallic weights are connected to each shutter by a cord or chain passing over pulleys. Chain is attached to style. When the weights are pulled, shutter can be opened to any extent half way in upward or downward direction.

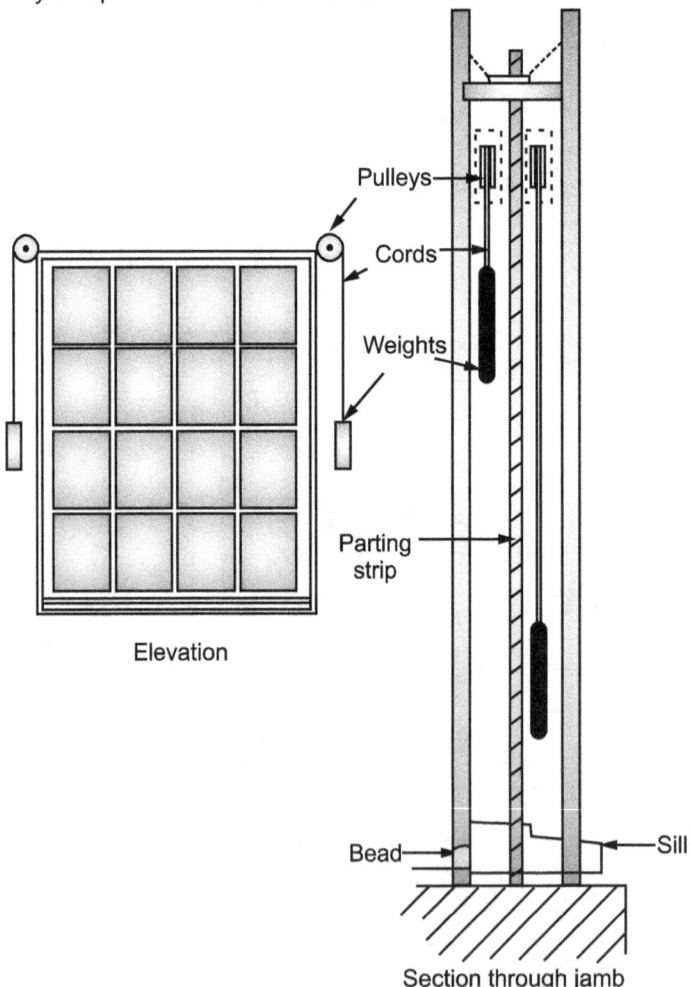

Fig. 8.17 : Double hang steel window

3. Pivoted Window : Shutters swing around the pivots provided either horizontally or vertically. Frame is without rebates.

Advantages : More light admittance, easy to clean but for security a special box type grill is to be provided additionally so as to facilitate rotation. Grills are not close to window frame.

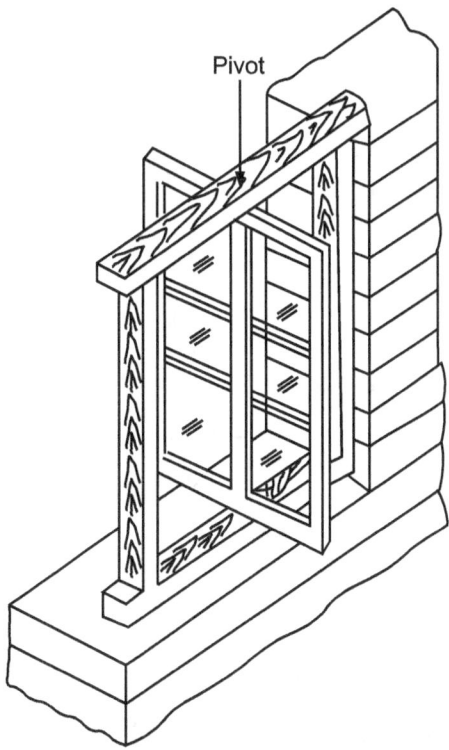

Fig. 8.18 : Pivoted window (vertical)

4. Sliding Window : Working or operational principle is exactly same as in case of sliding doors. Motion of shutters is either horizontal or vertical. The openings or grooves or cavities are provided in the frames or walls to receive the shutters. Usual occurrence - Buses, trains, shops, bank counters. Now-a-days aluminium sliding window with tinted glass pane and mosquito resistant jali is normally provided in residential buildings as well.

5. Louvered or Venetian Window : This provide free passage to air and sufficient light even when closed. The economical angle of inclination of the louvers is 45°C. The construction of this window is similar to louvered doors and as it also maintains privacy it is provided in W.C. rooms for all buildings with opaque glass louvers, timber or metal louvers. Sometimes, venetian shutters are provided with movable louvers.

6. Metal Window

Materials : Mild Steel (M.S.), Aluminium (Al), Bronze etc. are used for the purpose. Most commonly used in public buildings is M.S.; as it is cheapest with angle sections, channel sections, Z-sections (for frame) and T-sections (sash bars). A slight modifications may be adopted as per the requirement. Aluminium windows are rust proof, durable, hence very little maintenance is required and no paint is required.

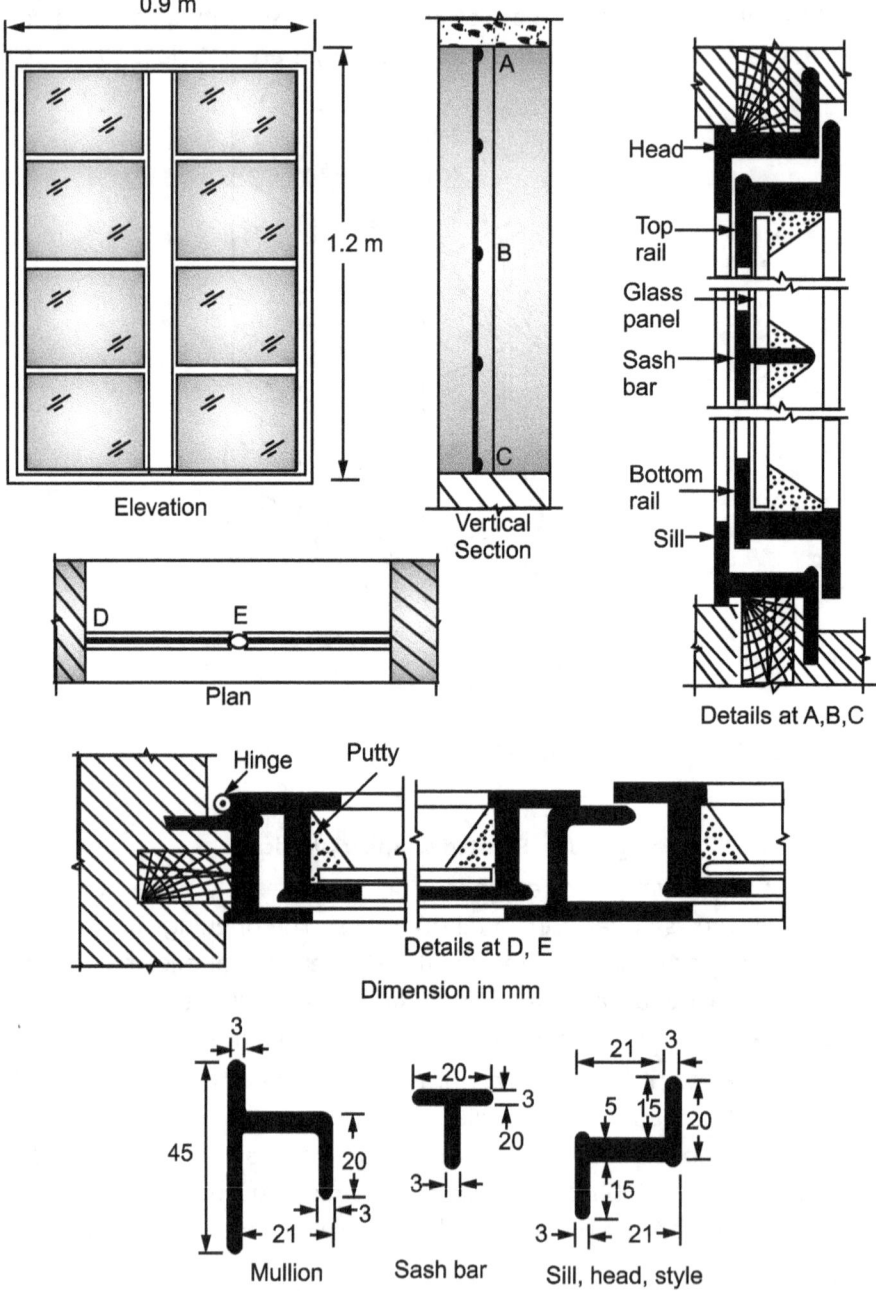

Fig. 8.19 : Elevation and other details of a steel window

During construction of any building window openings slightly more than frame size are left. Entire frame unit along with shutters can be fixed directly into the wall opening or through wooden frame. After the masonry work is over and lintels are casted above the openings, the framework is to be placed so as to ensure that no structural load is transferred onto the window frame.

Fixation Method

- If the frame is to be fitted directly in the brick or hollow concrete block masonry, the positions of fixing holes are marked on the jambs. Holes are cut in the masonry (5 cm sq. and 5 to 10 cm deep) and steel hold fasts or lugs are fixed in them tight with the help of cement concrete or otherwise.
- If the window is to be fixed in R.C.C. work or structural steel work, the holes for fixing the window are left in the correct position in the opening during construction work period.
- In case of window to be fixed in a wooden frame, the wooden frame is rebated to fix the steel window. Window unit is set within it with the help of wooden wedges and fixed to wooden frame with galvanized screws. One has to ensure that there is slight gap between actual opening and window frame.

The frames are made from light rolled steel sections. The glazing is fixed within the frame with the help of putty. First coat of primer should be applied to steel windows before they are installed at its place. Second coat is after fixing and a final coat is applied after the glazing is fixed.

Advantages :

- Manufactured in factories with great precision and better quality control.
- Elegant appearance.
- Stronger and durable.
- No contraction or expansion due to weather effects.
- Rot proof and termite proof.
- Fire resistant.
- Easy to maintain at negligible cost.

7. Sash or Glazed Window : Sash is a special type of frame of a lighter section designed for carrying the glass panes within styles and rails. Sometimes further division of shutter into small panels is achieved by providing transome, mullion as per the opening area. Categories under sash are casement window, double hung, sliding, pivoted. Horizontal and vertical sash bars are rebated to receive glass panes (with ribet width – 15 mm and depth – 5 mm). Fixation of glazing is achieved by putty, fillets or timber beads (known as glazing beads).

8. Bay Window : If the window is provided in the projected area of the room it is termed as Bay Window. It gives increased area of opening thereby admitting more light and provides more ventilation to a particular room area. It beautifies the elevation of the building.

The shape may be half square, splayed, (semi-hexagonal) semi-octagonal or semi-circular in shape. It is provided for full height from floor to lintel or from sill to lintel level.

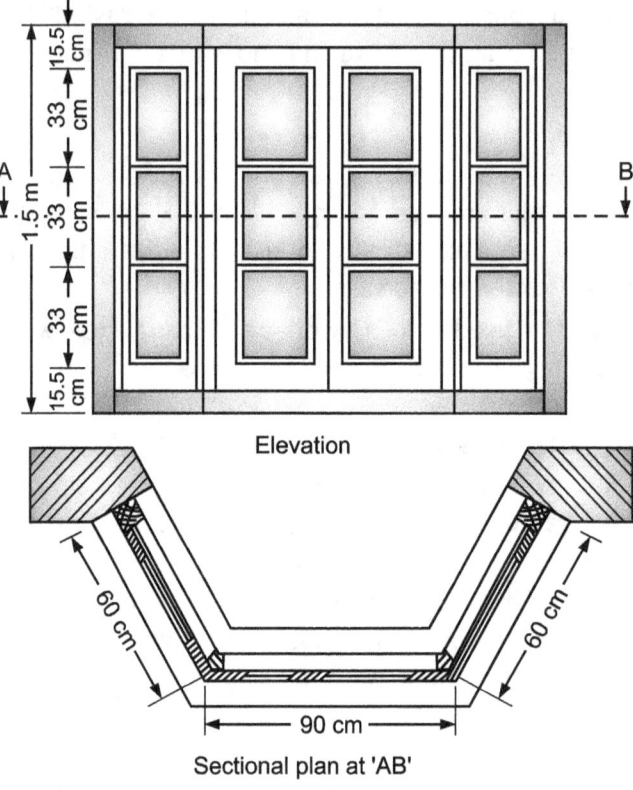

Fig. 8.20 : Bay window

9. Corner Window

- If the position of the window is in the corner of the room then it is known as Corner window. It admits light and ventilations from two sides at 90° to each other.

- It improves the elevation of the building. The central or corner jamb piece is heavier than the sides as it has to receive shutter from either side. Special lintel casting has to be carried out.

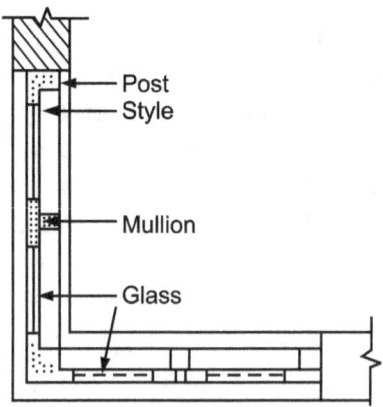

Fig. 8.21 : Corner window

10. Dormer Window : In case of old bungalows with sloping roofs or even Government buildings or quarters these dormer windows are seen, improving the elevation of the building. The vertical windows built on sloping sides of a pitched roof is known as Dormer Window. These are provided to admit light and air to the rooms or the enclosed space below the roof slopes.

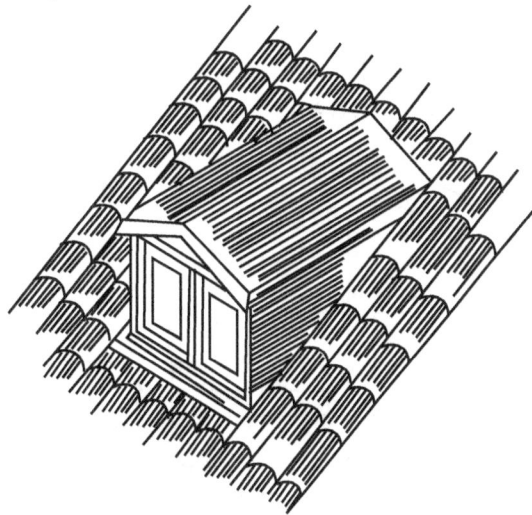

Fig. 8.22 : Dormer window

11. Gable Window : This serves the purpose of admitting light and ventilation from gable end of a pitched roof.

12. Skylight Window : A window i.e. provided in a sloping roof parallel to the pitch (means the angle of inclination) of the roof. Exclusively these are used to admit light, hence the panels are fixed-glazed panels.

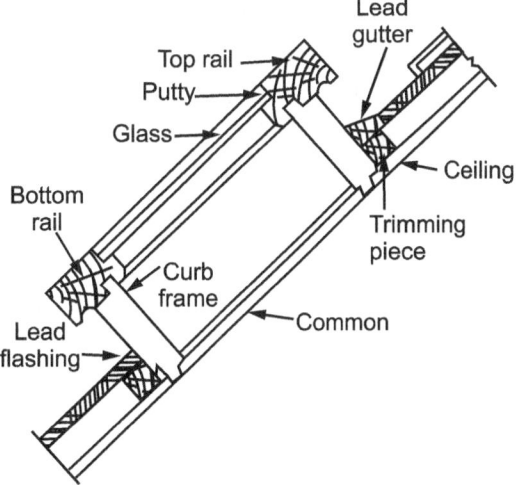

Fig. 8.23 : Skylight window

The framework supporting glass is made of trimming pieces, curb frame, top-bottom rails and lead flashings/gutters to ensure water proofing.

13. Circular Window : Following are the categories :

- The windows provided at greater heights, circular in elevation and providing light and ventilation when main windows are closed (horizontal pivots are usually provided).

- Full dimensioned circular window for improvising the elevation with framework of timber and some portion is fixed and glazed while the remaining is with openable shutters.

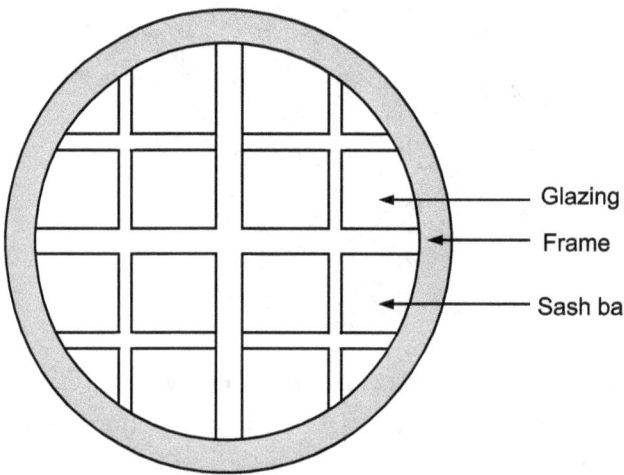

Fig. 8.24 : Circular window, Glazing - partially

14. Mosquito Proof Window/Wire Gauzed Window : Wire gauze is provided on fixed outer side whereas shutters will open on the inner side with parliamentary hinges. Now-a-days with the help of welcrow arrangement plastic-nylon nets are provided on the inner side as well if the window opens on the outerside.

15. Curtain Wall Window : A non-load bearing external wall is known as Curtain wall. Depending upon field installation methods walls are classified as :

- **Stick System :** Walls are installed piece by piece. Each principal framing member with windows and panes is assembled separately - hence more parts and joints are seen.

- **Mullion and Panel System :** Walls in which vertical members (mullions) are erected first and then wall units usually incorporating unglazed windows. A cover strip can be added to cap the vertical joint between units.

- **Panel Systems :** It consists of horizontal and vertical members.

Sometimes to have partial privacy a curtain wall is provided and there fixed glazed window admitting light partially is provided. Hence, it indicates a designer's view and owner's choice put together.

16. Clere-Storey Window : Horizontally pivoted window near top of main roof. Suitable for ventilation and light, if front verandah blocks the light/ventilation. Upper part of window opens inside whereas lower part opens on outer side.

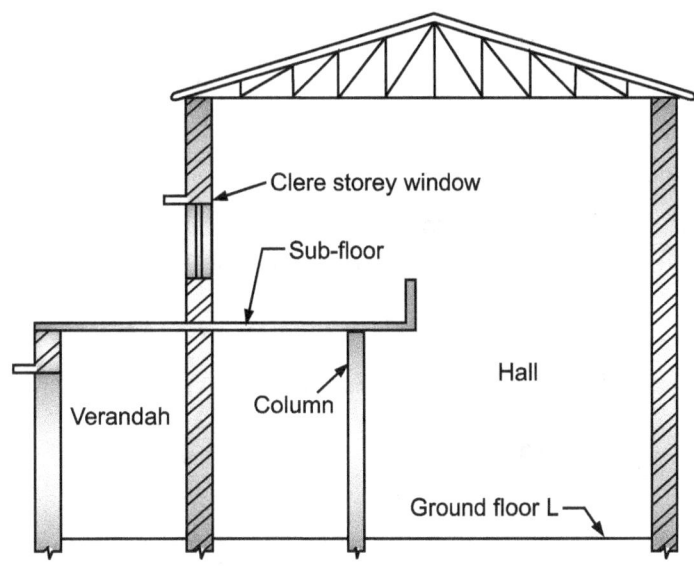

(a) Clere-storey window

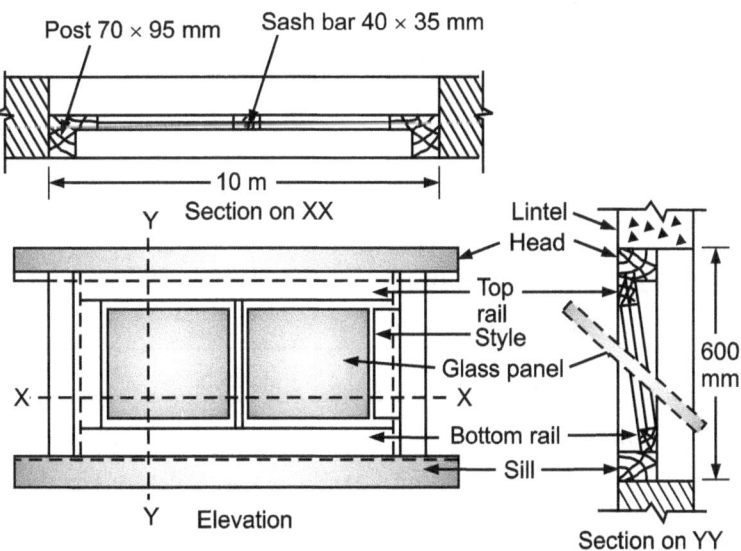

(b) Details of clere-storey window

Fig. 8.25

8.9 VENTILATORS   (Nov. 16)

- A ventilator represents a narrow window fixed at greater height than window, generally 30 to 50 cm below roof.

- A ventilator may be provided at the top of a door or a window. It consists of a frame and shutter assembly and the shutter may be horizontally pivoted or top hung.

- For ventilators sometimes wire gauze can also be suitably provided so as to avoid nuisance of mosquitoes, insects etc.

(a) Wall Ventilator (Horizontally Pivoted) : Top edge of the shutter opens inside and bottom edge of the shutter outside so as to avoid entry of rain water.

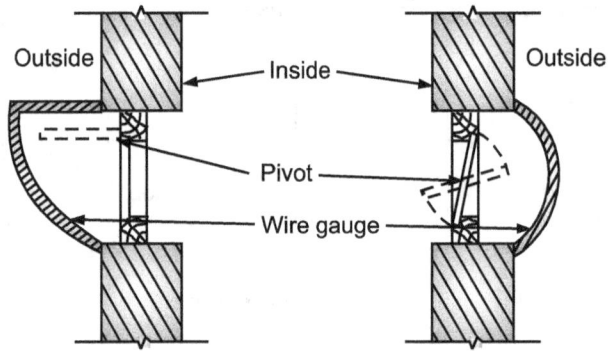

Fig. 8.26 : Mosquito-proofing of ventilators

(b) Roof Ventilators

- In industrial buildings to balance the ventilation rates of rising warmer air and incoming cooler air, these are located within roof.

- Factors affecting position are number of airflow cycles, difference between inner and outer temperature, pressure difference etc.

REVIEW QUESTIONS

1. Explain the designation 10 DT 20. Draw the sectional plan of above said door state advantages and limitations of different materials used for door frames and shutters.

2. Draw a labelled line sketch of a steel window for a wall opening of 1.50 × 1.20 m. Explain method of fixing glazing. Draw cross-sectional details plan. State different sections used for fabrication of steel window. State checks to be carried out for fabrication accuracy before installing window in position.

3. Draw labelled sketch of solid core flush door for opening of size 0.9 m × 2.0 m. Give dimensions of frame members and thickness of shutter. State all fixtures and fastening used for the flush door.

4. Explain with a neat sketch sliding, single shutter door management. State the situations favourable for type of door.

5. State different fixtures and fastenings used for doors and windows. Describe any two types of locks with neat sketches.

6. State different fixtures and fastenings used in doors and windows. Explain any four hinges with sketches.

7. Draw a detailed sketch of door and show the following terms :
   (a) Panel,   (b) Horn,
   (c) Hold fast,   (d) Meeting style,
   (e) Lock rail,   (f) Mullion,
   (g) Reveal.

8. Explain the sketches different types of hinges used in residential building.

9. Draw a neat sketch of a basement window having ventilators at the top to illustrate the different parts of a window.

10. Explain various fixtures and fastenings used for doors and windows.

11. Write note on : Location of doors and windows.

12. Describe collapsible door with labelled sketch.

13. Define door. Draw neat and labelled sketch of panelled door.

14. Draw neat and labelled sketch of panelled door. Give sizes of any four components.

15. Differentiate between : Bay window and dormer window.

SOLVED UNIVERSITY QUESTIONS

DEC. 2013

1. Explain the following with sketches: [6]
   (i) Nar – Madi. (ii) Horn. (iii) Dormer window.
   [**Ans.:** Refer Article 8.8. (10). 8.5]

MAY 2014

1. Enlist various types of windows and explain any one in detail.   [6]
   [**Ans.:** Refer Article 8.8.]

2. Draw a neat labeled sketch of panelled door. Show different parts of the same with dimensions. **[6]**

[**Ans.:** Refer Article 8.7. (1)]

DEC. 2014

1. Define the following with line sketches: **[6]**

    (i)   Door   (ii) Window

    [**Ans.:** Refer Article (i) 8.7 (ii) 8.8]

2. Explain the following with sketches **[6]**

    (i)   Corner window   (ii) Barrel bolt.

    [**Ans.:** Refer Article (i) 8.9(9) (ii) 8.5]

MAY 2015

1. Explain the following with sketches: **[6]**

    (i)   Dormer window   (ii) Meeting style   (iii) Barrel bolt.

    [**Ans.:** Refer Article (i) 8.8 (10) (iii) 8.5]

NOV. 2015

1. Write short notes on : Louvred window **[6]**

    [**Ans.:** Refer Article 8.5]

MAY 2016

1. Write short notes on : **[6]**

    (i)   Swing door   (ii) Dormer window.

    [**Ans.:** Refer Article (i) 8.7 (7) (ii) 8.8 (10)]

NOV. 2016

1. Explain with neat sketch the fixing details of wooden door frame installation. **[6]**

    [**Ans.:** Refer Article 8.3]

2. Explain the purpose and types of ventilators. **[6]**

    [**Ans.:** Refer Article 8.9]

MAY 2017

1. Draw a neat labeled sketch of paneled window with appropriate dimensions. **[6]**

    [**Ans.:** Refer Article 8.8]

◈ ◈ ◈

CHAPTER 9
ARCHES AND LINTELS

9.1 INTRODUCTION

- The openings for doors, windows, ventilators, cupboards, wardrobes etc. are invariably required in a wall. These openings are bridged by provision of either a lintel or an arch.
- Thus, both lintels as well as arch are structural members designed to support the loads of the portion of the wall situated above the openings and then transmit the load to the adjacent wall portions (Jambs) over which these are supported.

Fig. 9.1 : Example of arch

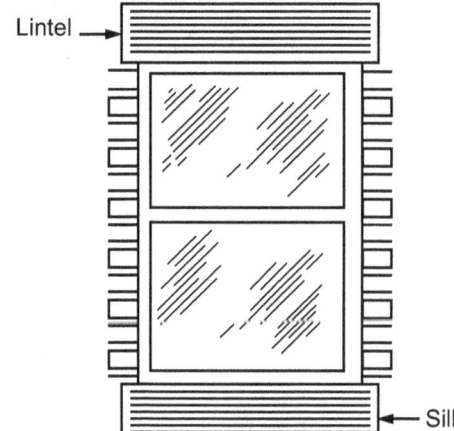

Fig. 9.2 : Lintel

The study of arches and lintels in this chapter will be made under the following sub-heads :

Part I : Arches

- Various terms related to openings
- Stability of arches
- Types of arches
- Method of construction of arches.

Part II : Lintels

- Types of lintels
- Details of R.C.C. lintel and chajja

9.2 DEFINITION OF ARCH   (Dec. 14)

- An arch may be defined as a mechanical arrangement of wedge - shaped units which mutually support each other and in turn, the entire arch is supported at the ends by piers or abutments.

- Wedge - shaped blocks are joined generally with rich cement or lime mortar. Arches of cement concrete, R.C.C. and steel are not built in wedge - shaped units but in form of a single unit.

9.3 TECHNICAL TERMS   (May 16)

Most of the technical terms used in connection with the arch work are illustrated in Fig. 9.3 and are described as follows :

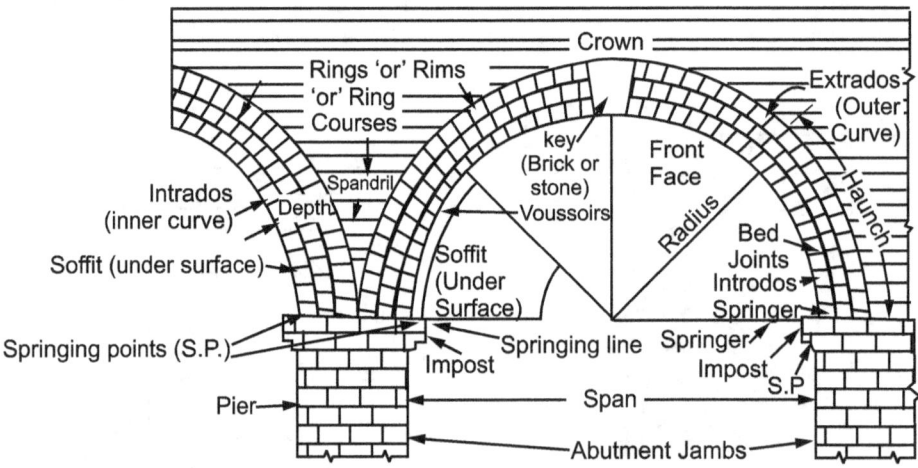

Fig. 9.3 : Semi-circular arch

- **Abutments :** These are outer most support of an arch, from which arch springs.
- **Piers :** These are intermediate supports of a series of arches or an arcade.
- **Arch Ring :** This is the curved ring of masonry forming the arch.
- **Voussoirs :** These are the wedge shaped or tapered units of bricks, stones or precast concrete blocks, forming the courses of an arch.
- **Arcade :** This is a series or row of arches supporting a wall above and being supported by piers.
- **Skew-backs :** These are the inclined or splayed surfaces of the abutments or piers, prepared to receive the arch. Arch work actually starts from skew back.
- **Springing Points :** These are the points of the intersection between the skew-backs and the intrados and from these points only, the curve of an arch springs are commences.
- **Springing Line :** This is the imaginary horizontal line joining the two springing points.

- **Intrados :** The inner curved surface of the arch is known as **intrados**.
- **Extrados :** Outer curved surface of the arch ring is known as **extrados**. It is also known as back of the arch.
- **Soffit or Bottom :** This is the inner or under surface of the arch. Soffit and Intrados terms indicate same thing.
- **Crown :** The highest point of extrados of arch.
- **Key Stone :** This is the uppermost or central voussoir of an arch. It is sometimes made prominent by making it larger and projecting it above and below the outline of an arch. This is inserted in the centre of many types of arches to improve the appearance but it does not carry structural significance.
- **Span :** Clear horizontal distance between the supports is known as **span of the arch**.
- **Depth or Height :** This is the perpendicular distance between the intrados and extrados.
- **Thickness (Breath of the Soffit) :** The horizontal distance measured perpendicular to the front and back faces of an arch is known as **breather thickness of soffit**.
- **Rise :** It is the clear vertical distance between the springing line and the highest point on the intrados.
- **Centre (or Striking Point) :** This is the geometrical centre point of the curve of an arch.
- **Springers :** These are the extreme or lowest voussoirs of an arch, which are placed at springing level on either side immediately adjacent to the skew-backs.
- **Haunch :** This is the lower half portion of the arch between the crown and the skew-back or springer.
- **Spandril :** This is the triangular space formed between the extrados and the horizontal line drawn through the crown.
- **Jambs :** These are the sides of the abutments or piers below the springing line.
- **Import :** The projecting course at the upper part of a piers or an abutment to stress the springing line.
- **Bed Joints :** These are the joints between the voussoirs which radiate from the centre.

9.4 STABILITY OF AN ARCH

An arch transmits the super-imposed load to the side walls (or abutments) through friction between the surfaces of voussoirs and the cohesion of mortar. Every element of arch remains in compression. It has also to bear transverse shear. An arch may therefore fail in the following four ways :

1. **The Crushing of the Arch Material :** In this case, the compressive stress or thrust exceeds the safe crushing strength of the materials and the arch fail due to crushing of the masonry. The measures to avoid failure of arch due to this reason are as follows :

- The material used for construction should be of adequate strength.

- The size of voussoirs should be properly designed to bear the thrust transmitted through them.

- The height of voussoirs should not be less than $1/12^{th}$ of the span or as below. (for brick work in cement mortar, 1 : 4)

- for span upto 1.5 m – 20 cm.

- between 1.5 to 4 m – 30 cm.

- between 4.0 to 7.5 m – 40 cm.

- For arch work, only first class blocks should be used, and in case of large spans the arches may be strengthened by steel reinforcement, so that safe crushing strength is not exceeded.

2. **Rotation or Overturning of some Joints about an Edge :** To prevent this following points are considered :

- The line of resistance or thrust at any section should be within the middle - third of the arch.

- The thickness of the arch and its curve are so designed that the line of resistance atleast falls within the section and crosses each joint away from the edge.

3. **Sliding of Voussoirs :** To safeguard against sliding of one voussoir or another, the following points are considered :

- All the bed joints should be perpendicular to the line of least resistance.

- The depth of voussoirs should be adequate to resist the tendency of the joints to open and slide upon the another.

4. **Uneven Settlement of Abutment or Pier :** The secondary stresses in the arch are developed due to the uneven settlement of the support of arch and to avoid such conditions, the following precautions should be taken.

- The arch should be symmetrical so that unequal settlement of the two abutments or abutment and pier are minimised.

- The supports should be strong enough to resist the thrust of the arch due to self weight and superimposed loads.

9.5 TYPES OF ARCHES   (Dec. 13. 14, May 15,)

An arch can be classified according to (1) Shape, (2) Number of centres, (3) Workmanship and (4) Materials of construction.

(I) Classification of Arches According to Shape :

According to shape, the arches are classified as follows :

- **Flat Arch (or Straight, Square or Camber Arch) :** In flat arch, the extrados is horizontal and the intrados is given a slight rise or camber of about 10 to 15 mm per metre width of the span. The angle of skew backs with the horizontal is usually 60°. Flat arches are not very strong and hence they should be limited to span upto 1.5 metres unless they are strengthened by steel reinforcement. (Fig. 9.4 (a)).

- **Segmental Arch (Fig. 9.4 (b)) :** This is the common type of arch used for buildings. The centre of arch lies below the springing line. The thrust transferred to the abutment is in an inclined direction.

- **Semi-circular Arch (Fig. 9.4 (c)) :** The shape of their arch soffit is a semi-circle and hence named as semi-circular arch. The centre of the arch lies on the springing line. The thrust transferred to the abutments is perfectly in vertical direction since the skewback is horizontal.

- **Horse shoe Arch (Fig. 9.4 (d)) :** The arch has the shape of a horse shoe, incorporating more than a semi-circle. Such type of arch is provided mainly from architectural considerations.

- **Pointed Arch (Fig. 9.4 (e)) :** This is also known as Gothic arch. It consists two arcs of circles meeting at the apex. The triangle formed may be equilateral or isosceles; in the latter case it is known as Lancet arch.

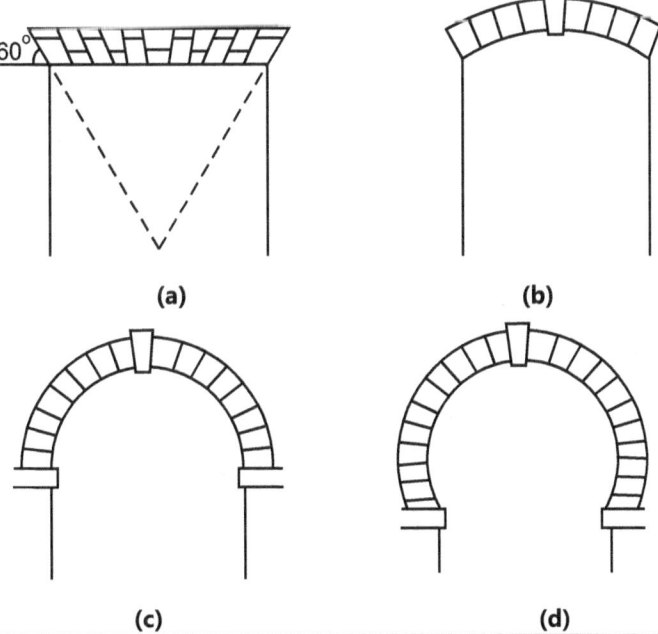

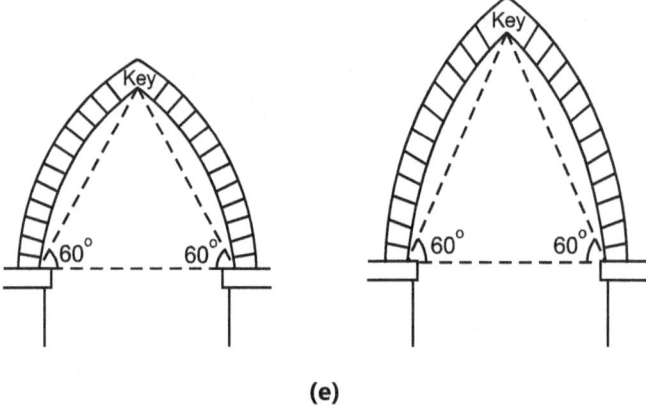

(e)

Fig. 9.4 : Types of arches

- **Venetian Arch (Fig. 9.5 (a)) :** This is another form of pointed arch which has deeper depth at crown than at springings. It has four centres, all located on the springing line.

- **Florentine Arch (Fig. 9.5 (b)) :** This is similar to venetian arch except that the intrados is a semicircle. The arch has, three centres, all located on the springing line.

- **Relieving Arch (Fig. 9.5 (c)) :** This arch is constructed either on a flat arch or on a wooden lintel to provide greater strength. The ends of the relieving arch should be carried sufficiently into the abutments. The relieving arch makes it possible to replace the decayed lintel later, without disturbing the stability of the structure.

- **Stilted Arch (Fig. 9.5 (d)) :** It consists of a semi-circular arch with two vertical portions at the springings. The centre of the arch lies on the horizontal line through the tops of the vertical portions.

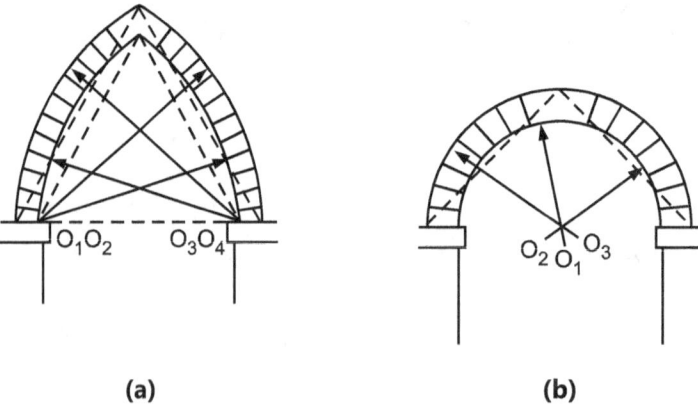

(a)   **(b)**

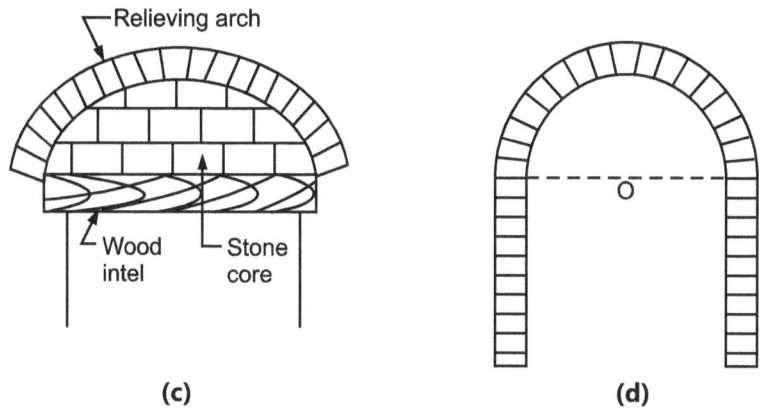

(c)	**(d)**

Fig. 9.5 : Types of arches

- **Semi-Elliptical Arch (Figs. 9.6 and 9.7) :** This type of arch has the shape of a semi-ellipse and may have either three centres or five centres.

(II) Classification Based on Number of Centres

The arches may be classified as

1. One-centered arch,
2. Two-centered arch,
3. Three-centered arch,
4. Four-centered arch and
5. Five-centered arch.

- **One-Centred Arches :** Segmental arches, semi-circular arches, flat arches, horse-shoe arch and stilted arches come under this category. Sometimes, a perfectly circular arch, known as bull's eye arch is provided for circular windows, as shown in Fig. 9.6.

Fig. 9.6

- **Two-Centred Arches :** Pointed arches, semi-eliptical arches and florentine arches come under this category.
- **Three-Centred Arches :** Eliptical arches come under this category. Fig. 9.7 shows a three-centered arch.

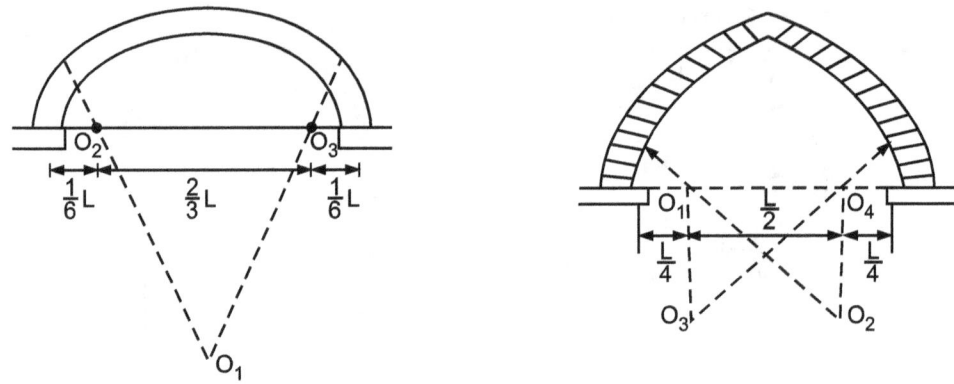

Fig. 9.7   **Fig. 9.8**

- **Four-Centred Arch :** It has four centres. Venetian arch is a typical example of this type. (Fig. 9.8)
- **Five-centred Arch :** This type of arch, having five centres, gives a good semi-eliptical shape. (Fig. 9.9)

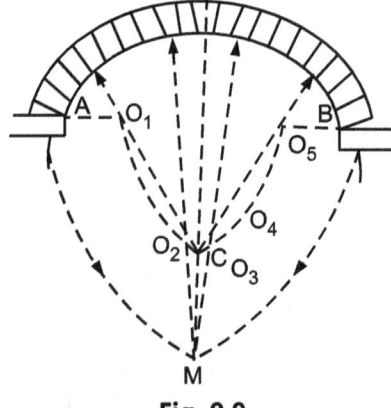

Fig. 9.9

(III) Classification Based on Material and Workmanship

On the basis of material of construction and workmanship, arches may be classified as follows :

1. **Stone Arches :**
   - Rubble arch
   - Ashlar arch
2. **Brick Arches :**
   - Rough arch
   - Axed or rough - cut arch
   - Gauged arch
   - Purpose made brick arch.

3. **Concrete Arches :**

   - Concrete block - units arch

   - Monolithic arch.

1. **Stone Arches :** These arches are constructed either in (i) Rubble arches or (ii) Ashlar masonry.

   - **Rubble Arches :** These arches are comparatively weak and is used for comparatively inferior work. These arches are made of rubble stones which are hammer dressed, roughly to shape and size of voussoirs of the arch and fixed in cement mortar. Rubble arches are used for limited span (upto 1.0 m). They are also used as relieving arches, over wooden lintels. Upto depth of 37.5 cm, these arches are constructed in one ring. For greater depths, rubble stones are laid in alternate course of header and stretchers.

   - **Ashlar Arches :** These are constructed of stones which have been properly cut and dressed to their true wedge shapes i.e. voussoirs. Upto depth of 60 cm, the voussoirs are made of full thickness of the arch. For determining the wedged shapes of voussoirs, it is preferable to set out the arch on a level platform, marking on it the keystone and voussoirs along with radial mortar joints. Fig. 9.8 shows some details of semicircular, segmental and flat arches of ashlar stones.

2. **Brick Arches :** Brick arches may be classified as rough brick arches, axed or rough cut brick arches, gauged brick arches and purpose made brick arches, depending upon the nature of workmanship and quality of bricks used.

   - **Rough Brick Arches :** These arches are constructed with ordinary bricks, without cutting these to the shape of voussoirs. In order to provide the arch curve, the joints are made wedge-shaped, with greater thickness at the extrados and smaller thickness in intrados. These types of arches, though cheap, yet lack in strength as well as appearance.

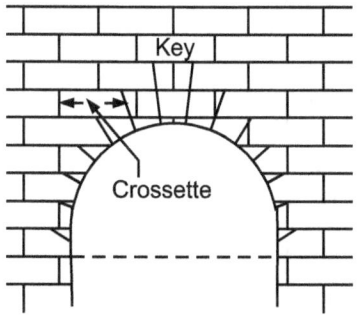

| **(a) Semi-circular arch** | **(b) Semi-circular arch** |

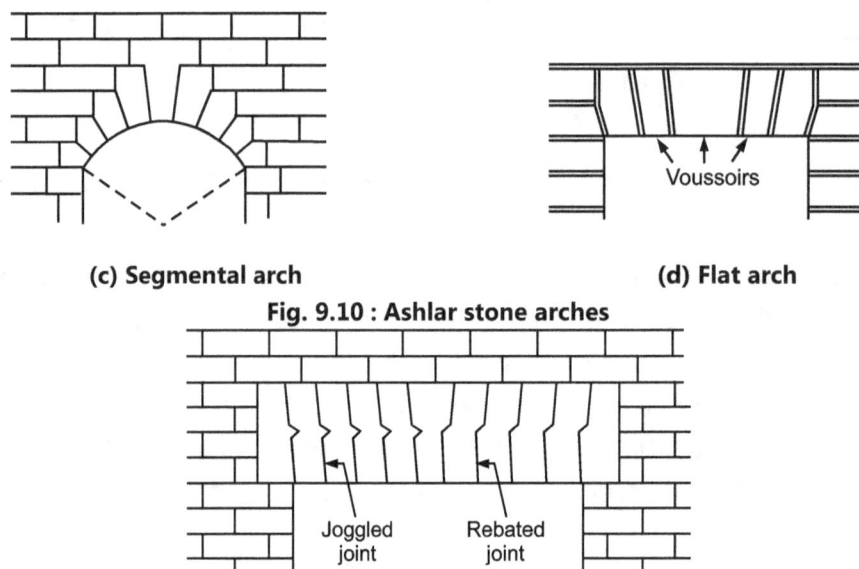

(c) Segmental arch　　　　　　　　　　**(d) Flat arch**

Fig. 9.10 : Ashlar stone arches

Fig. 9.11 : Joggled and rebated joints in flat arch of ashlar stones

- **Axed Brick Arches :** In this arch, the bricks are cut wedge-shaped with the help of brick axe. Due to this joints are of uniform thickness along the radial line. However, the appearance of the arch is not very pleasant because the bricks cut to wedge-shapes are not finely dressed.

- **Gauged Brick Arch :** This type of arch is constructed of bricks which are prepared to exact size and shape of voussoirs by cutting it by means of wire saw. For this, only soft bricks (called rubber bricks) are used. The joints formed in gauged bricks are the thin (1 to 1.5 mm) and truly radial. Lime putty is used for jointing. (Fig. 9.13 (a) and (b))

- **Purpose made Bricks Arch :** In this type of arch, the bricks are manufactured, matching with the exact shape and size of voussoirs, to get a very fine workmanship. Lime putty is used for jointing.

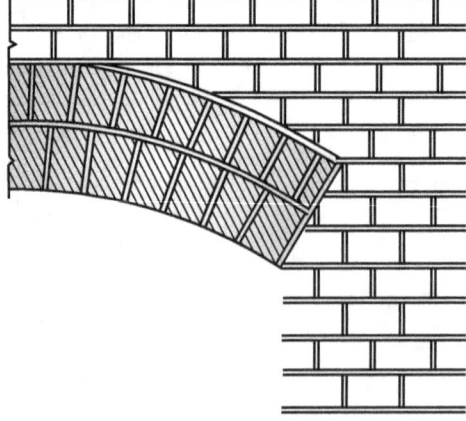

Fig. 9.12 : Segmental rough brick arch

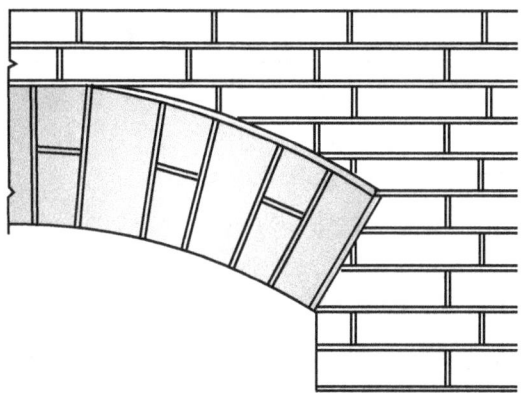

Fig. 9.13 : Axed brick arch

3. **Concrete Arches :** Concrete arches are of two types : (i) Precast concrete block arches and (ii) Monolithic concrete arches.

- **Precast Concrete Block Arches :** Such arches are made from precast concrete blocks, each block being cast in the mould to the exact shape and size of voussoirs. Special moulds are prepared for voussoirs, key block and skew-backs. Because of exact shape and size of blocks, good appearance of the arch is achieved. Also, joints, made of cement mortar are quite thin. However, casting of blocks is costly, and such work is economical only when the number of arches is quite large. Cement concrete of 1 : 2 : 4 mix is usually used.

- **Monolithic Concrete Arches :** Monolithic concrete arches are constructed from cast-in-situ concrete, either plain or reinforced, depending upon the span and magnitude of loading. These arches are quite suitable for larger span. The arch thickness is 15 cm for arches up to 3 m span. Form work is used for casting the arch, and is removed only when the concrete has sufficiently hardened and gained strength. Curing is done for 2 to 4 weeks.

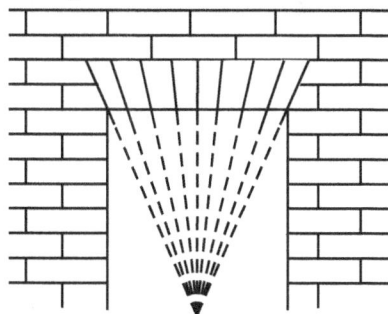

| (a) Flat arch | (b) Semi-circular arch |

Fig. 9.14 : Gauged brick arches

9.6 METHOD OF CONSTRUCTION OF ARCHES   (Nov. 16, May 17)

The complete construction of arches, whether of brick, stone or concrete, involves basically the following three steps :

1. Installation of centering or form work for arches,
2. Actual laying of arch - work or courses and
3. Striking or removal of centerings.

1. Installation of Centering for Arches

A temporary structure is required to support brick, stone or concrete arches during their construction. This is known as the centering which is usually of timber but may be of mild steel if so desired. The upper surface of the centering corresponds to the shape of intrados of the arch. Mild steel truss centering is used either for large spans or where large number of arches of similar nature is to be prepared.

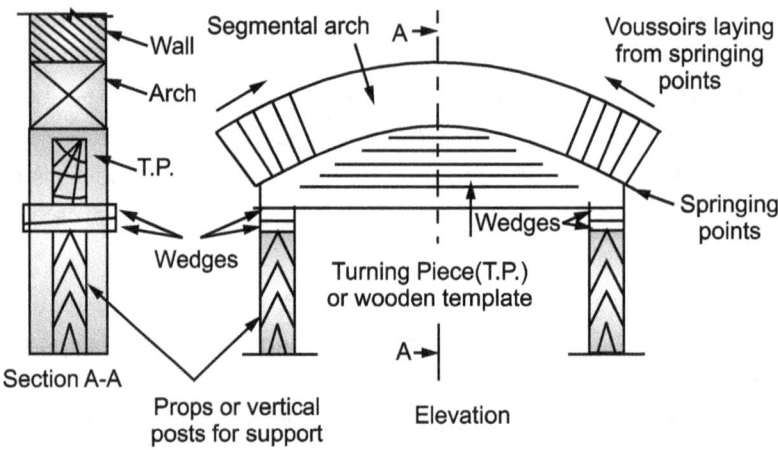

Fig. 9.15 : Centering for small spans and thinner soffit (upto 10 cm thickness) arches

- Timber centering is most common in arch construction as it is easy in installation and removal, and also economical.

- In simplest type of centering used for small spans with a thinner soffit (width = 10 cm) consists of a horizontal frame of timber known as "turning piece" or "wooden template".

Fig. 9.15 shows a thick wooden plank, with horizontal bottom and the upper surface shaped to the underside of the soffit.

- If the soffit is wider than 10 cm, two ribs, suitably spaced and suitably shaped at top may be used. These ribs may be connected by 4 × 2 cm wooden sections called laggings. At the ends the ribs are supported by bearers, wedges and posts as shown in Fig. 9.16.

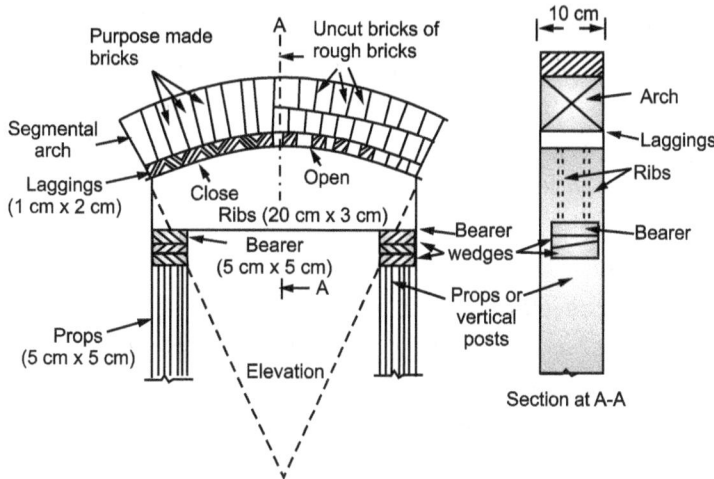

Fig. 9.16 : Centering for small spans but thicker soffit (more than 10 cm)
Arches (or simple Ribbed Centering)

- For wider soffits and for large span, a built up centering of cut wood ribs is used. The upper surface of the ribs is given the shape of soffit of the arch. Laggings are nailed across the ribs at close intervals to support the voussoirs at its top.

- The ribs (25 to 40 mm thick with width varying from 20 to 30 cm) are connected by braces and struts to strengthen them. The ribs are supported on bearers and a pair of folding wedges is provided at the top of each prop to tighten or loosen the centering. (Fig. 9.17)

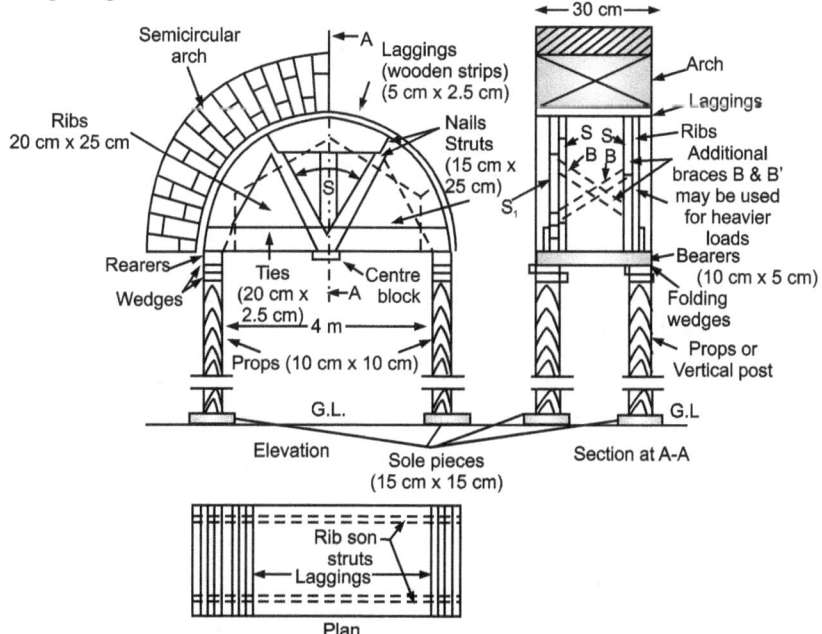

Fig. 9.17 : Centering for large spans and very wide soffits.
Semi-circular arches (or Ribbed - Truss Centering)

2. **Actual Laying of Arch Work**

- After the proper installation or erection of centering in position, skew backs are first prepared. Voussoirs are then arranged, starting from skew backs and proceeding towards the crown. Key stone is finally inserted to lock all the voussoirs in position.
- The voussoirs are bedded or laid in definite courses in sequence with radial joints to ensure stability and strength of the arch.

3. **Removal of Centering**

- When the arch has developed sufficient strength, the centering can be removed. The centering must be eased (i.e. slightly lowered) two days before its removal so that the voussoirs may close in and compress the mortar. No load should be placed on the arch unless the centering has been removed.
- For small spans, the removal of centering is done by slightly loosening the folding wedges. When the span is more than 7.5 m, sand box method can be used for loosening, so that shocks are avoided.
- A sand box, shown in Fig. 9.18 is placed below the prop. Sand is filled in the box with a plugged hole at its bottom. Prop rests on steel plate placed on the top of sand. In order to lower the centering, plug is taken out due to which the sand flows out and lowers the prop gradually.

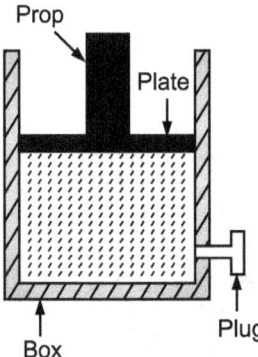

Fig. 9.18 : Sand box method

9.7 DEFINITION OF LINTEL   (Dec. 14, May 16)

- A lintel is a horizontal structural member which is placed across an opening viz. doors, windows, recesses etc. to support the portion of the structure above it.
- Though the lintels perform exactly the same function as arches, but they are preferred to arches due to the following reasons :
  - The arches require more head room to span the openings, like doors, windows, etc.
  - The arches require strong abutments (walls) to withstand the arch thrust.
  - Lintels are more stable as they support the load by beam action and transfer the loads vertically to the walls.
  - The lintels are simpler in construction.

The ends of lintels are built into the masonry and thus, the load carried by lintels is transferred to the masonry in jambs. In general, it should be seen that the bearing of lintel i.e. the distance upto which it is inserted in the supporting wall, should be the minimum of the following three considerations.

- 10 cm; or
- height of lintel; or
- one - tenth to one - twelfth of the span of lintel.

9.8 TYPES OF LINTELS   (Dec. 13, May 15)

On the basis of materials used in construction, the lintels are classified into the following types :

1. Wooden Lintels
2. Stone Lintels
3. Brick Lintels
4. Steel Lintels
5. Reinforced Concrete Lintels, and
6. Reinforced Brick Lintels.

1. Wood or Timber Lintels

- These lintels consists of pieces of timber which are placed across the opening. The timber lintels are the oldest type of lintels and they have become obsolete except in hilly areas or places where timber is easily available.
- Wooden lintels may either consist of a single piece of timber usually for small spans or may be of built-up sections of two or more pieces held together by bolts at suitable intervals as shown in Fig. 9.19.
- The bolts are provided through the packing pieces as shown. If the timber lintels are strengthened by provision of mild steel plates at their top and bottom, they are known as the flitched lintels.

The important features of wooden lintels are as follows

- Wooden lintels should be made of sound and hard timber, like teak wood, sal etc.
- The amount of bearing of lintel should be adequate (usually 15 to 20 cm) and lintel should rest on mortar to have a firm and uniform support.
- The depth of lintel should be $\frac{1}{12}$th of span or 8 cm, whichever is greater. The width of lintel is taken equal to the thickness of the opening.

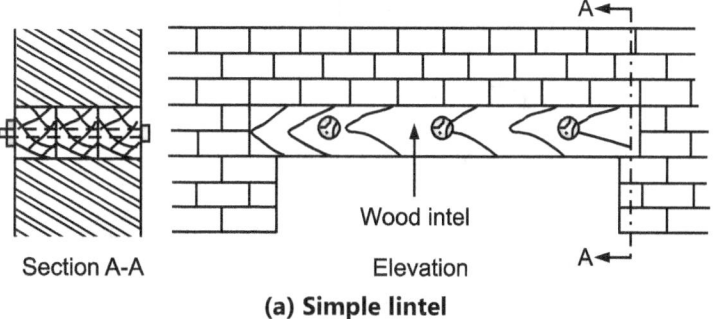

Section A-A   Wood intel

Elevation

(a) Simple lintel

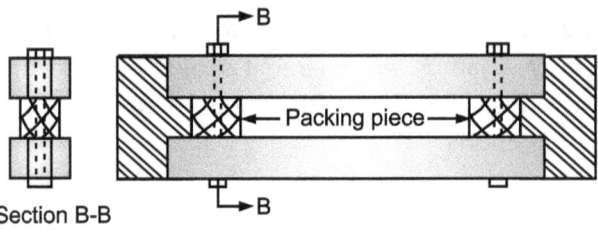

(b) Built-up Lintel
Fig. 9.19 : Wooden lintel

2. **Stone Lintels :** The use of stone lintels is recommended only in places where stone is available in abundance and the structure is made of stone masonry. These lintels consist of slabs of stones of sufficient length in single piece or combination of more pieces. The thickness of stone lintel should be 80 cm or 4 cm for every 30 cm of span, whichever is more.

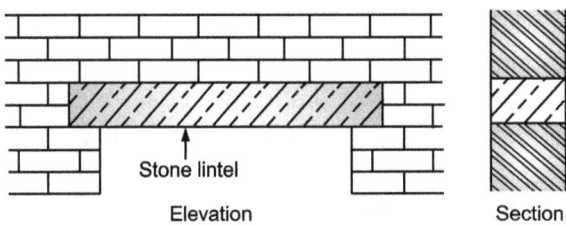

Fig. 9.20 : Stone lintel

The use of stone lintels in general is not recommended because of the following reasons :

- Stone, being poor in tensile strength, cannot withstand the transverse stresses.
- It is difficult to obtain the slabs of stones of sufficient length and depth, free from defects or flaws.

3. **Brick Lintels :** Brick lintels generally consist of bricks which are normally laid on end and occasionally on edge as shown in Fig. 9.21.

   The important features of brick lintels are as follows :

   - The bricks should be well burnt, hard, free from defects such as lumps, cracks, flaws etc. and with sharp and square edges.
   - A temporary wood support known as a turning piece, is used to construct a brick lintel.
   - In order to maintain the appearance of brick work, a brick lintel should have a depth equal to multiple of brick courses.
   - Brick lintels are used to span small openings (less than one metre) with light loading.

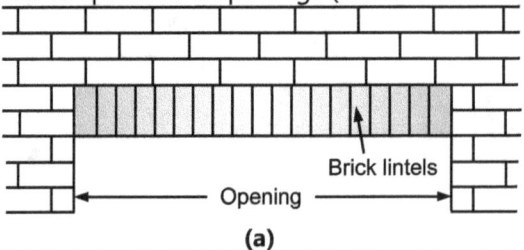

(a)

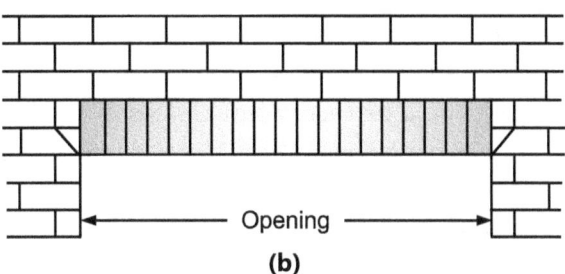

(b)

Fig. 9.21 : Brick lintel

4. **Steel Lintels :** These lintels consist of steel angles for small spans and light loading or rolled steel joints for large spans and heavy loading. A steel lintel becomes useful when there is no space available to accommodate the rise of an arch. The tube separators may be provided to keep the joints in position. The joints are embedded in concrete to protect the steel from corrosion and fire. (See Fig. 9.22)

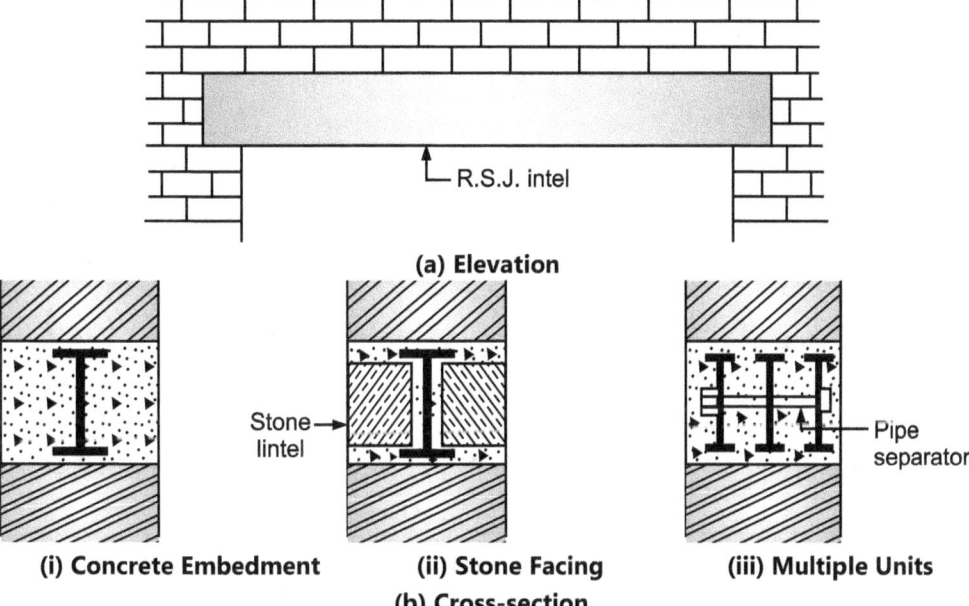

(a) Elevation

(i) Concrete Embedment   **(ii) Stone Facing**   **(iii) Multiple Units**

(b) Cross-section

Fig. 9.22 : Steel lintels

5. **Reinforced Cement Concrete Lintels**
    *   Reinforced concrete lintels are extensively used and practically R.C.C. has replaced all other materials used for lintels.
    *   The R.C.C. lintels are fire-proof, durable, strong, economical and easy to construct. No relieving arches are necessary when the R.C.C. lintels are adopted. R.C.C. lintels may be either precast or cast in-situ.
    *   Precast R.C.C. lintels are preferred for small span upto 2 metres or so, and they are economical as the same mould can be used to prepare a number of lintels.
    *   The precast R.C.C. lintels increase the speed of construction and allow sufficient time for the curing before fixing.

- One precaution to be taken in case of precast R.C.C. lintels is that the top of lintel should be properly marked with tar or paint.

For large spans, the lintels should be cast in-situ. Details of lintels are as follows :

(i) Depth of Lintel : For ordinary loads, adopt 15 cm depth for span upto 1.2 m and add another 2.5 cm for every additional 40 cm span.

(ii) Reinforcement in Lintels : As a rule, for thickness of wall 10 cm (half-brick), adopt 2 bars and for every additional 10 cm thickness, one main bar should be added. The diameter of bar varies with the span and is adopted as follows, as a general rule (Alternative central bars are bent up).

6 mm ϕ for spans upto 1 metre

8 mm ϕ for spans upto 1 to 1.5 metres

10 mm ϕ for spans upto 1.5 to 2.0 metres

12 mm ϕ for spans upto 20 to 30 metres

(iii) Concrete : The usual concrete mix for R.C.C. lintel is 1 : 2 : 4.

For cast in-situ, R.C.C. lintels, the centering is prepared, reinforcement is placed and concreting is done as usual.

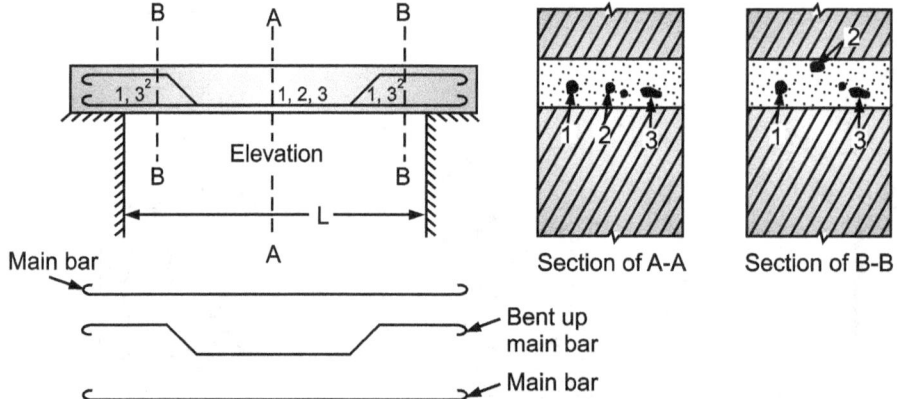

Fig. 9.23 : R.C.C. lintel - details for small spans (L < 2 metres)

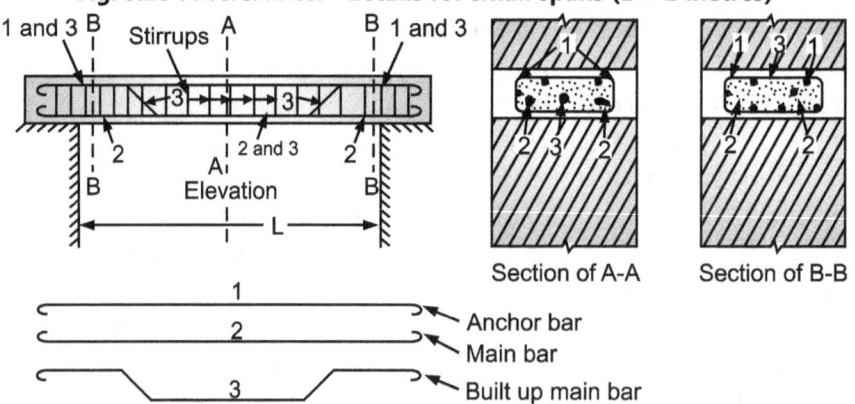

Fig. 9.24 : R.C.C. lintel - details for large spans (i.e. span > 2 metres)

The projection, in the form of weather shed Chajja can be easily taken out from R.C.C. Lintels, as shown in Fig. 9.25. The weather shed throws the rain water away from the wall.

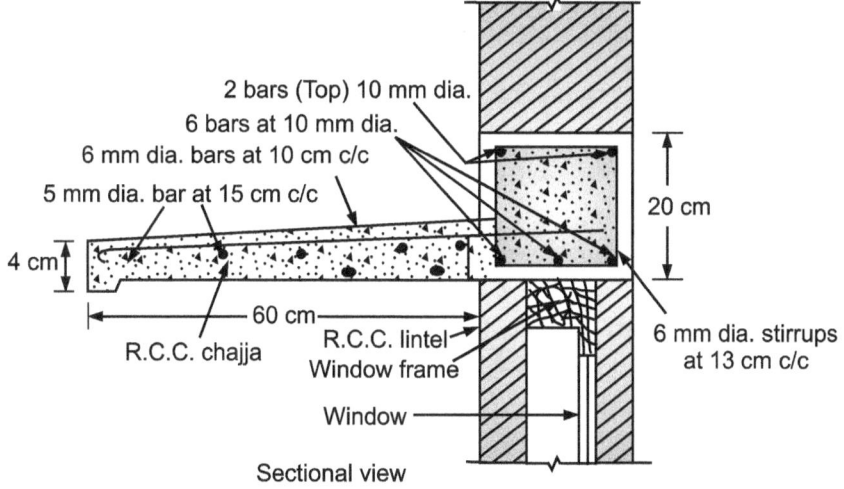

Fig. 9.25 : R.C.C. lintel with weather shed or chajja

6. Reinforced Brick Lintels :

- When brick lintels are required to be used over large spans, they are reinforced with steel bars. These lintels are constructed on the same principles as R.C.C. lintels, the only difference being good quality bricks are used instead of concrete.

- The bricks are so arranged in parallel rows that a 2 cm to 4 cm wide space is left lengthwise for inserting the reinforcements. These spaces with reinforcement are then filled with rich cement mortar or cement concrete.

-

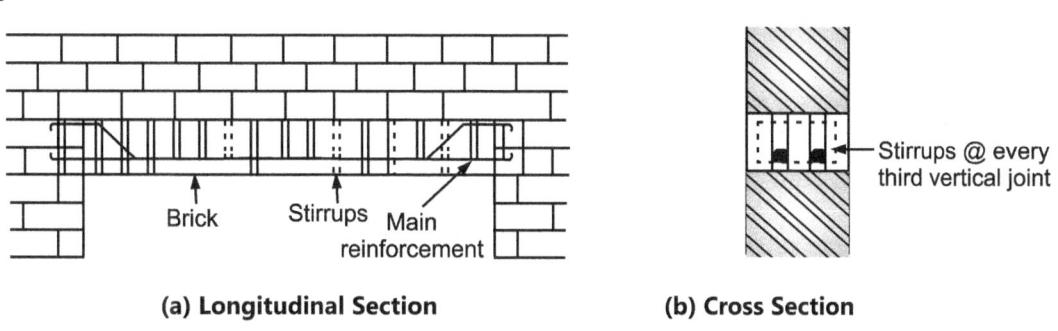

   (a) Longitudinal Section   **(b) Cross Section**

Fig. 9.26 : Reinforced brick lintel

REVIEW QUESTIONS

1. State the procedure of constructing a segmental arch for an opening of size 1.80 m × 2.40 m. Rise is one third of span.

2. Draw a labelled sketch of semi-circular arch and indicate the following :

   (a) Spring line,

   (b) Key stone,

   (c) Spandril,

   (d) Voussior,

   (e) Rise,

   (f) Extrados.

3. Write down the methods of construction of arches and describe how arch opening is constructed in residential building.

4. Differentiate between arch and lintel. Give detailed sketch of lintel with weather-shed.

5. What are the functions of arches and lintels ? Give relative merits of lintel over the arches.

6. Explain the detailed procedure of installation of centering for arches.

7. Differentiate between lintel and arches. Explain stability of an arch.

8. Explain the detailed procedure of construction of an arch in monumental building.

9. Write short notes on :

   (a) Types of lintels

   (b) Weather shade necessity and types

   (c) Lintel necessity and types.

10. Give a detailed sketch of lintel with weather shed. Write down its functions.

11. To maintain the stability of arches, which points will you consider ?

12. What are the functions of arches and lintels ? Give relative merits and lintels over the arches.

13. Differentiate between the following :

    (a) Extrados and Intrados

    (b) Spandril and Haunch

    (c) Axed Arch and Gauged Arch.

14. "In modern times, R.C.C. lintels have practically replaced all other materials use for lintels. Comment on the axiom.

SOLVED UNIVERSITY QUESTIONS

DEC. 2013

1. Write short notes on: **[6]**

    (i)   Arches in monumental building.

    [**Ans.:** Refer Article 9.5]

    (ii) Reinforced concrete lintels with sunshades.

    [**Ans.:** Refer Article 9.8 (5)]

DEC. 2014

1. Define the following with line sketches: **[6]**

    (iii) Arch

    (iv) Lintel.

    [**Ans.:** Refer Article (iii) 9.2]

    [**Ans.:** Refer Article (iv) 9.7]

2. Explain the following with sketches : Corbel Arch   **[6]**

    [**Ans.:** Refer Article 9.5]

MAY 2015

1. Draw a neat, labelled figured of semi-circular arch and name the various components.   **[6]**

    [**Ans.:** Refer Article 9.5]

2. Explain the types of Lintels and discuss about of two.   **[7]**

    [**Ans.:** Refer Article 9.8]

MAY 2016

1. Explain with neat sketch : (i)   Springing line (ii) Lintel.   **[6]**

    [**Ans.:** Refer Article 9.7]

Nov. 2016

1. Explain the method of Arch construction with neat sketch.   **[7]**

    [**Ans. :** Refer Article 9.6)

MAY 2017

1. Write a note on method of arch construction.   **[6]**

    [**Ans. :** Refer Article 9.6)

CHAPTER 10
VERTICAL CIRCULATION

10.1 INTRODUCTION

- A successful functioning of a multi-storey building needs circulation of traffic in normal use and in emergency requirement.
- For proper appreciation of building design, a due care should be required for selection of type of vertical circulation, their location, number of units required and design and arrangement.
- Vertical circulation is the means, by which building occupants access specific areas of a building, including: internal stairs. Internal ramps, elevators etc.
- A stair is a set of steps arranged for the purpose of connecting various floors and to provide means of ascent and descent between various floors of a building. Stairs can be made up of various materials such as wood, stones, bricks, steel, P.C.C., R.C.C. etc.
- The location of staircase in a building is very important. It should be located in such a way that, it should give maximum benefit to its user.

Fig. 10.1

10.2 TECHNICAL TERMS

- **Baluster :** It is vertical member of wood or any metal supporting the hand rail.
- **Balustrade :** The combined frame work of hand rail and baluster is known as balustrade.
- **Flight :** A series of steps without any platform, break or landing in their direction.
- **Step :** It is the portion of a stair which consists of riser and tread. This allows ascent and descent from one floor to another.

- **Tread :** It is the upper horizontal portion of each step on which the foot is placed while ascending or descending.
- **Rise :** This is a vertical distance between the upper surface of the two successive treads.
- **Going :** It is the width of the tread between two successive risers.
- **Landing :** It is the platform provided between two flights. It allows facility for change of direction and provides a resting place in between ascends and descends.
- **Nosing :** It is the projecting part of the tread beyond the face of the riser. It is generally rounded to give pleasing appearance.
- **Scotia :** It is a moulding provided under the nosing to improve the beauty of the step.
- **Soffit :** It is the under surface of a stair.
- **Winders :** These are tapering steps used for providing for change of the direction of a stair.
- **String :** It is the sloping member which supports the steps in a stair.
- **Newel Post :** It is the vertical post provided at the top and bottom ends of flights supporting the hand rails.
- **Head Room :** This is the minimum clear height from a tread to overhead construction.

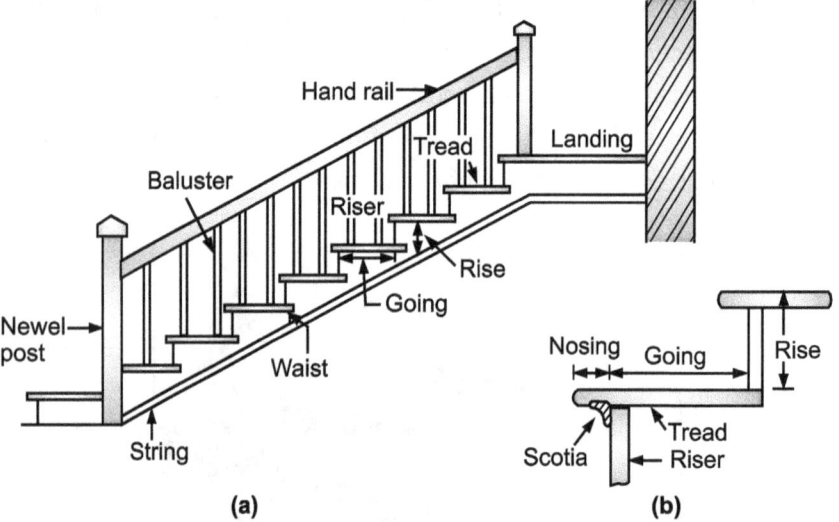

Fig. 10.2 : Terms used in stairs

10.3 REQUIREMENTS OF A GOOD STAIRCASE
(Dec. 14, Nov. 15, May 15, 16, 17)

- Stair should be so located as to provide easy access to the occupants, there should be proper light and ventilation directly from the exterior and it should be so located as to have approaches convenient and spacious approaches.
- It should have sufficient stair width to accommodate number of persons in peak hours. In residential building 90 cm wide stair is sufficient. While in public building 1.5 to 1.8 m width may be provided.

- The number of steps in a flight should generally be, maximum of 12 and minimum of 3 from comfort point of view.
- Sufficient head room should be provided to avoid head injury to tall people. At the same time it should give a feeling of spaciousness. Vertical clearance should not be less than 2.15 m.
- Risers and treads should generally be proportioned from comfort point of view. Treads should be 25 to 30 cm wide and rise should be 17.5 to 18.5 cm in height. Generally, the following thumb rules are used.
  (i) ($2 \times$ Rise in cm) + (Tread in cm) = 60.
  (ii) (Rise in cm) + (Tread in cm) = 40 to 45.
  (iii) (Rise in cm) $\times$ (Tread in cm) = 400 to 450.
- The minimum width of landing should be equal to the width of the stairs.
- The pitch of stair or slope of the stair should never exceed 45° and should not be flatter than 25°.
- The material used for the construction of stair should have sufficient strength and should be fire resistant.

10.4 TYPES OF STAIRS   (Dec. 13 Nov. 15, 16, May 15, 16.17)

Generally, stairs are of the following types :

(1) Straight stairs,   (2) Dog legged stairs,
(3) Open newel stairs,   (4) Geometrical stairs,
(5) Circular stairs,   (6) Bifurcated stairs,
(7) Open well stairs,   (8) Half turn stair,
(9) Quarter turn stair.

1. **Straight Stairs :**
   - These are the stairs which run straight between the two floors. These stairs are generally used for small houses where there is restriction for the width.
   - These stairs may consist of either single flight or more than one flights with a landing as shown in Fig. 10.3.

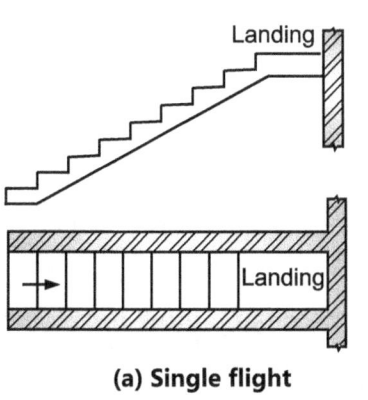

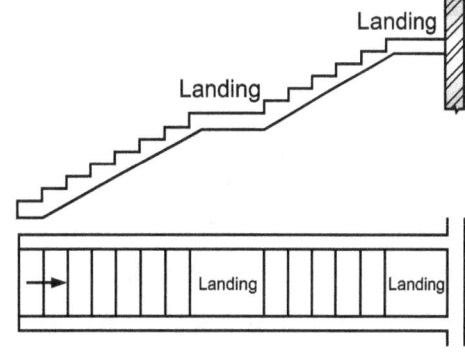

(a) **Single flight**   (b) **Two flights**

Fig. 10.3 : Straight stairs

2. **Dog Legged Stair:**
   - It consists of two straight flights of steps with abrupt 180° turn between them. In this type, a level landing is placed between the two flights at the change of direction.
   - This type of stair is useful where the width of the staircase hall is sufficient to accommodate two widths of stairs.

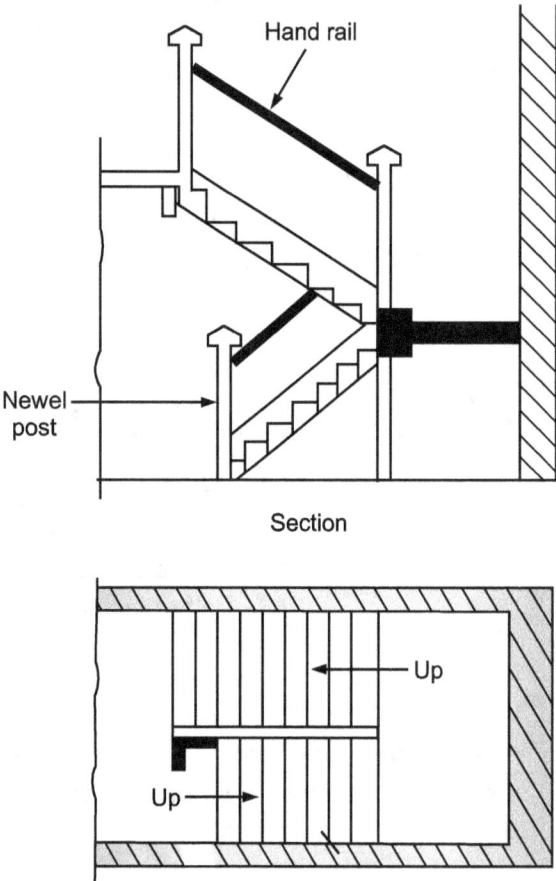

Fig. 10.4 : Dog legged

3. **Open Newel Stair/Open Well Stair :**
   - It has a space or well between the outer strings. It consists of two or more flights arranged in such a manner that a clear space known as well occurs between the backward and the forward flights.
   - When the width of the staircase hall is such that it becomes difficult to accommodate the number of steps in the two flights then a short flight of 3 to 6 steps may be provided along the width of the hall.

- In this, there are two type: one is open well half turn and second is open well stair with quarter space landing. Sometimes the width of well is so adjusted as to accommodate a lift in between.

Fig. 10.5

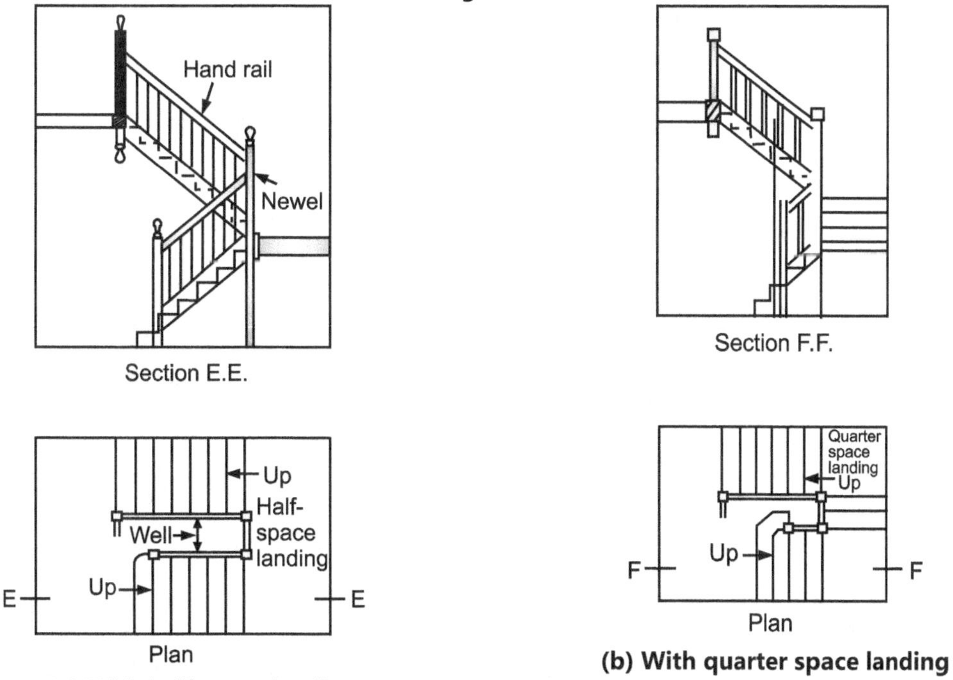

Section E.E.

Section F.F.

Hand rail

Newel

Plan

Up

Half-space landing

Well

Up

E   E

(a) With half space landing

Quarter space landing

Up

Up

F   F

Plan

(b) With quarter space landing

Fig. 10.6 : Open newel stair

4. Geometrical Stair :

- This is similar to the open well stair only the difference is that the shape of the open well between the forward and the backward flight is curved.

- In this type of stair, there is no landing and the change in direction is obtained by providing winders.

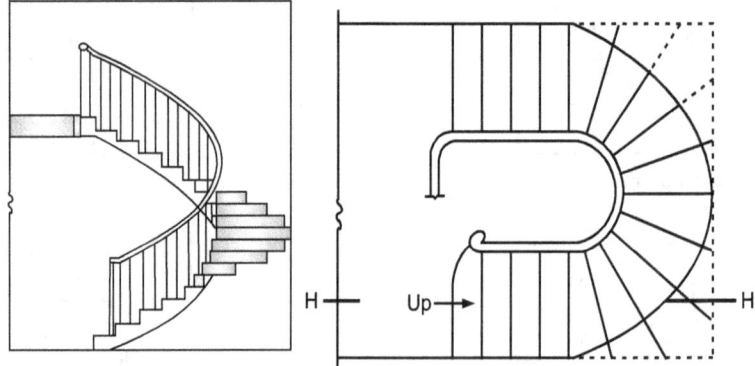

Fig. 10.7 : Geometrical stair

5. Circular Stair :

- Circular stair is usually constructed of R.C.C. or metal and is located at a location where there are space limitations.
- These stairs also used as emergency stairs and are provided at the back side of building. In this stair, all the steps radiate from a newel post or well hole, in the form of winders.

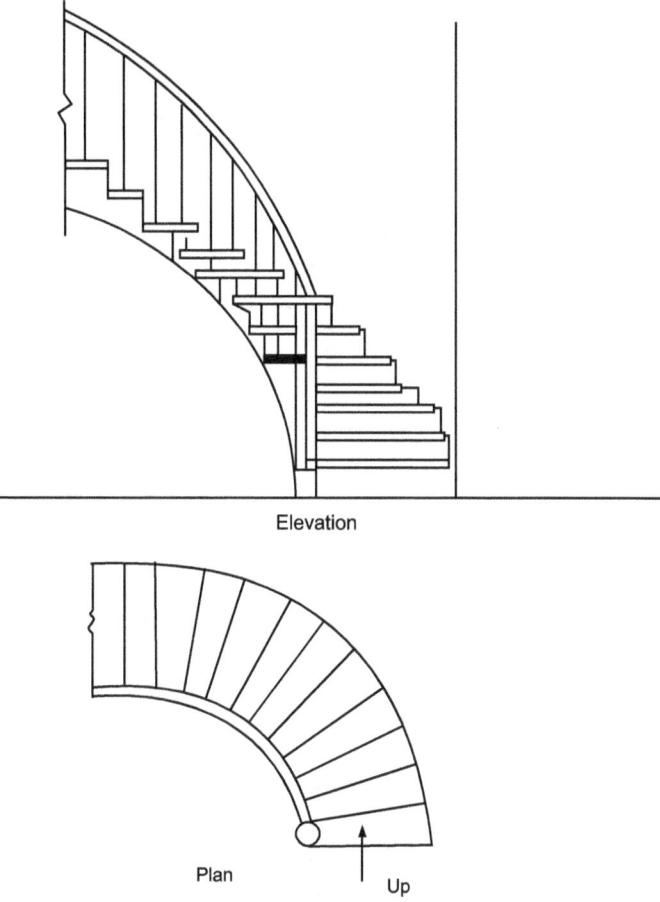

Elevation

Plan   Up

Fig. 10.8 : Circular stair

6. Bifurcated Stair :

- These stairs are so arranged that there is wide flight at the start which is sub-divided into narrow flights at the mid-landing.
- The two narrow flights start from either side of the mid-landing. This type of stair is commonly used in public building at the entrance.

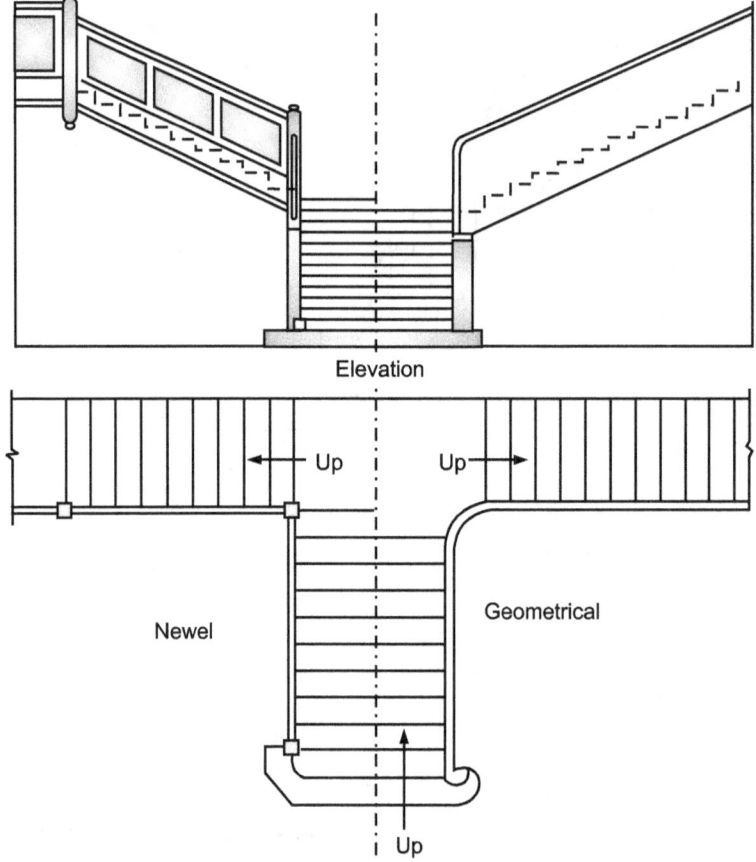

Fig. 10.9 : Bifurcated stair

7. **Turning Stairs :** Types of turning stairs are as follows:

   (a) Quarter Turn Stairs : In this type of stairs, flight changes its direction by 90°, either to the left, or to the right. At the quarter turn, either a quarter space landing may be provided or winders may be provided.

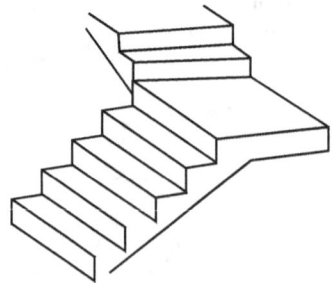

Fig. 10.10 : Quarter turn stairs

In a newel quarter turn stair, newel posts are provided at either end of each flight.

In geometrical quarter turn stairs, the stringer as well as the hand rail are continuous with no newel posts at the landings.

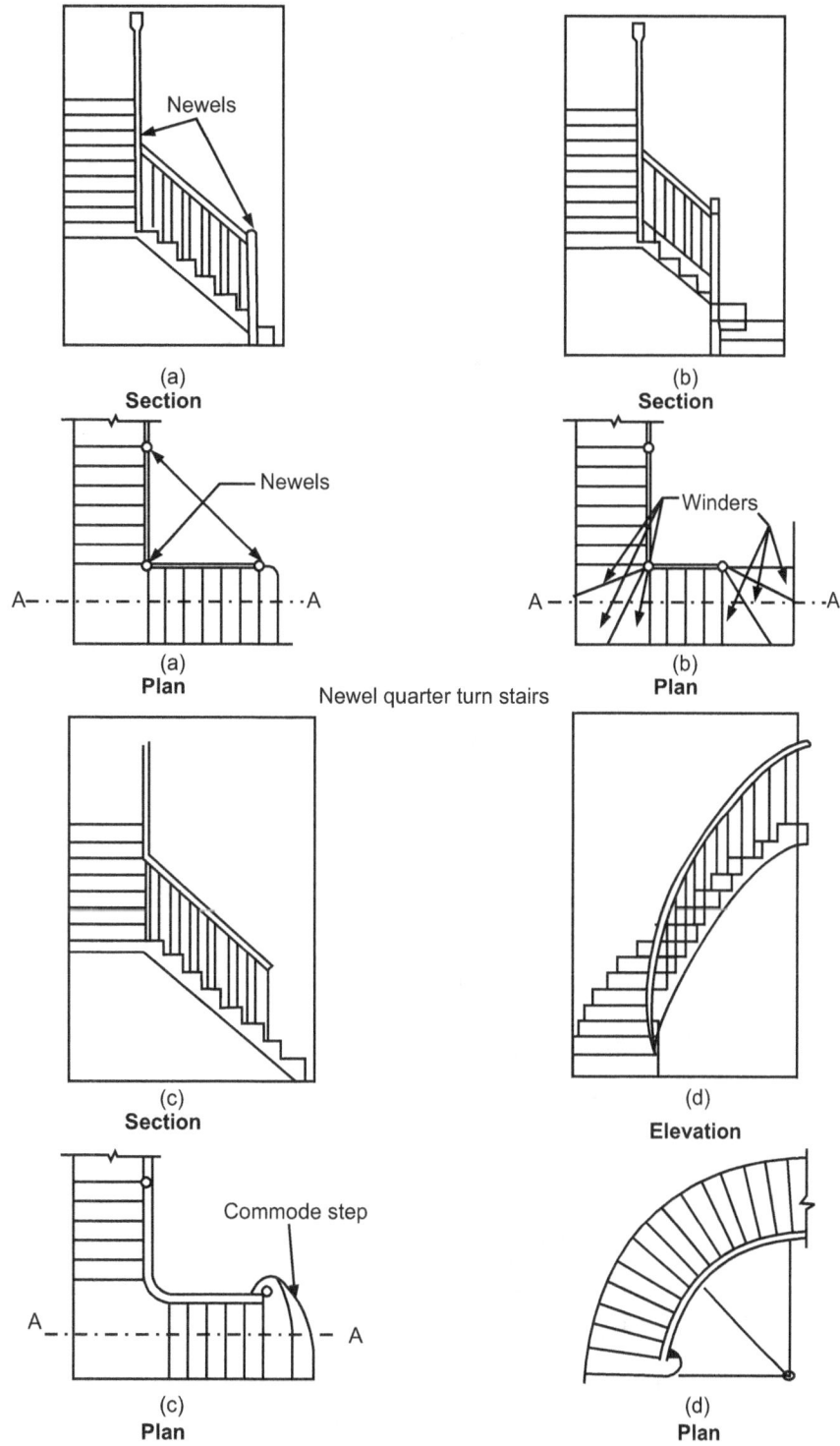

Fig. 10.11 : Geometrical quarter turn stairs

(b) Half Turn Stairs : In this type, the direction of succeeding flights is reversed. A dog legged staircase is a case of half turn stair in which there is no gap between the strings of the two flights.

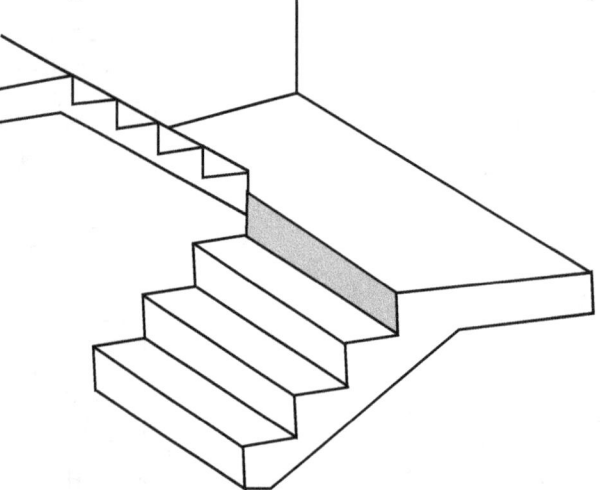

Fig. 10.12 : Half turn stair

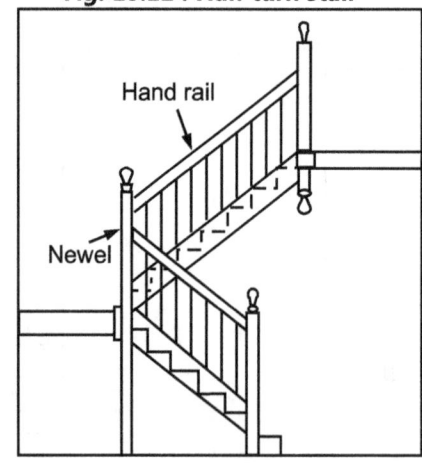

Section E.E.

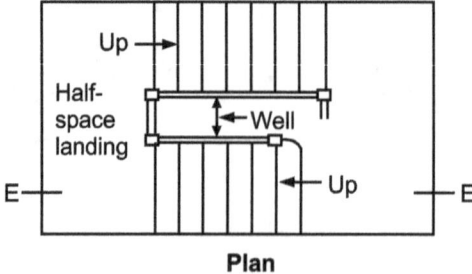

Plan

Fig. 10.13 : Open well with half space landing

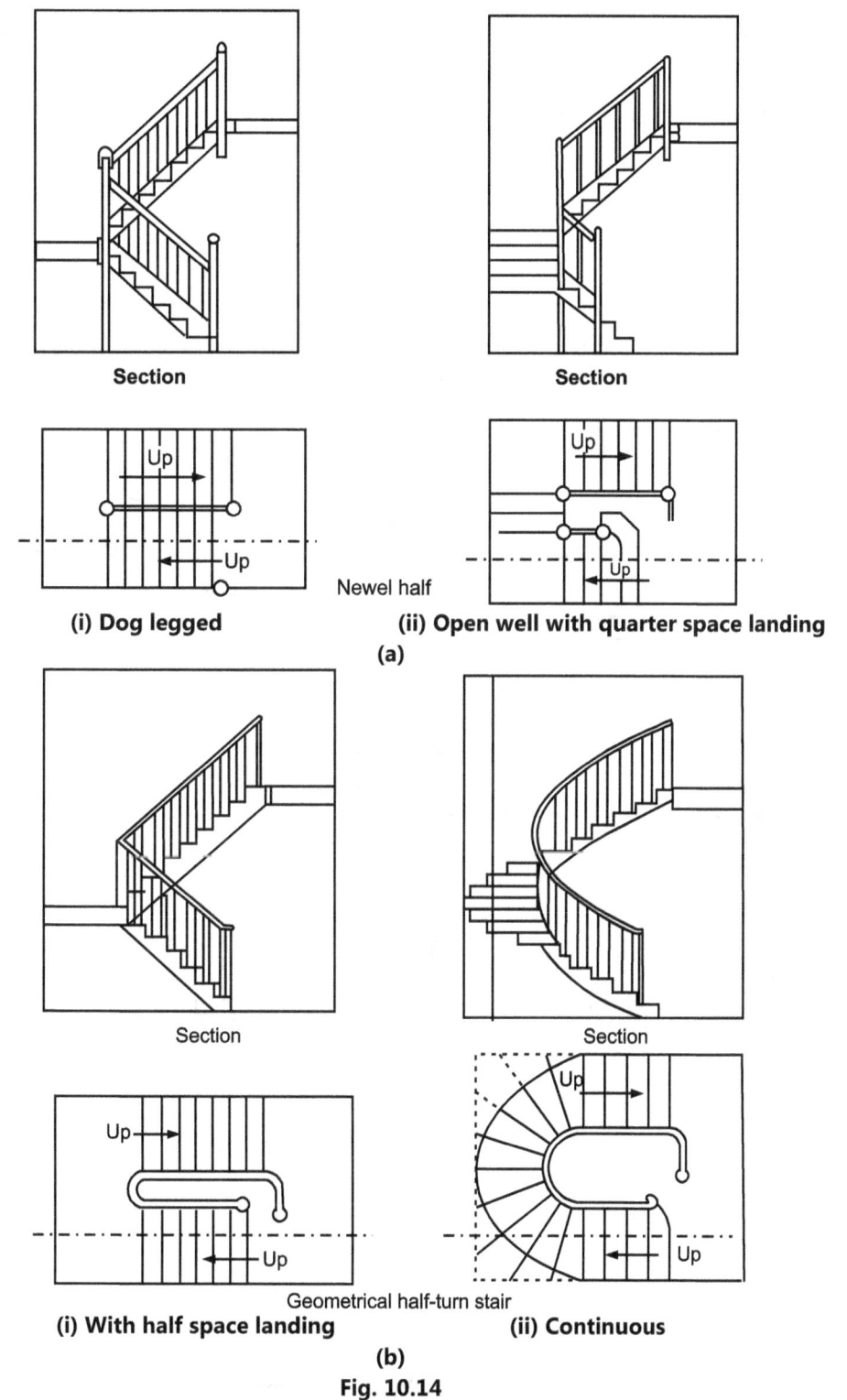

Section   Section

Newel half

(i) Dog legged   **(ii) Open well with quarter space landing**

(a)

Section   Section

Geometrical half-turn stair

(i) With half space landing   **(ii) Continuous**

(b)

Fig. 10.14

In an open newel half turn stair there is a rectangular well or an opening between the previous and the next flights. The landing between the two flights may be continuous, the gap between the two flights is more, then a few steps may be introduced on the narrow side of the well with two quarter space landing one on either side.

A geometrical half turn stair is one in which the stringer and the hand rail are continuous without any newels in between. The well hole is curved and there may be half space landing or winders radiating from the centre of curvature of the curve between the flights.

> **(c) Three Quarter Turn Stairs :** In this case, the direction of flight changes thrice with its upper flight crossing the bottom one.

> **(d) Bifurcated Stairs :** In this type, the bottom flight, which is wider, bifurcates into two upper flights of smaller widths, each flight being on either side of the bottom flight.

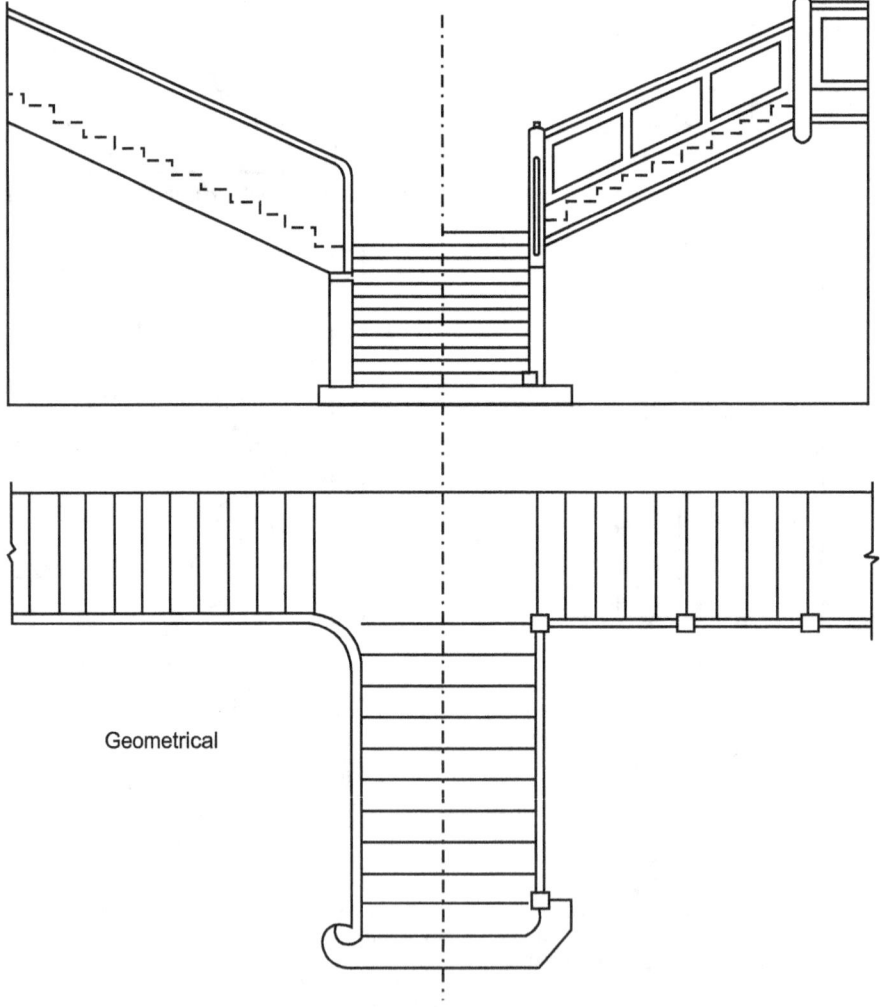

Geometrical

Fig. 10.15 : Bifurcated stair

(e) Spiral Stair : These do not have any landing and are therefore continuous type of stairs. Such staircases are normally of R.C.C. or steel. All steps are winders, hence not very convenient to use.

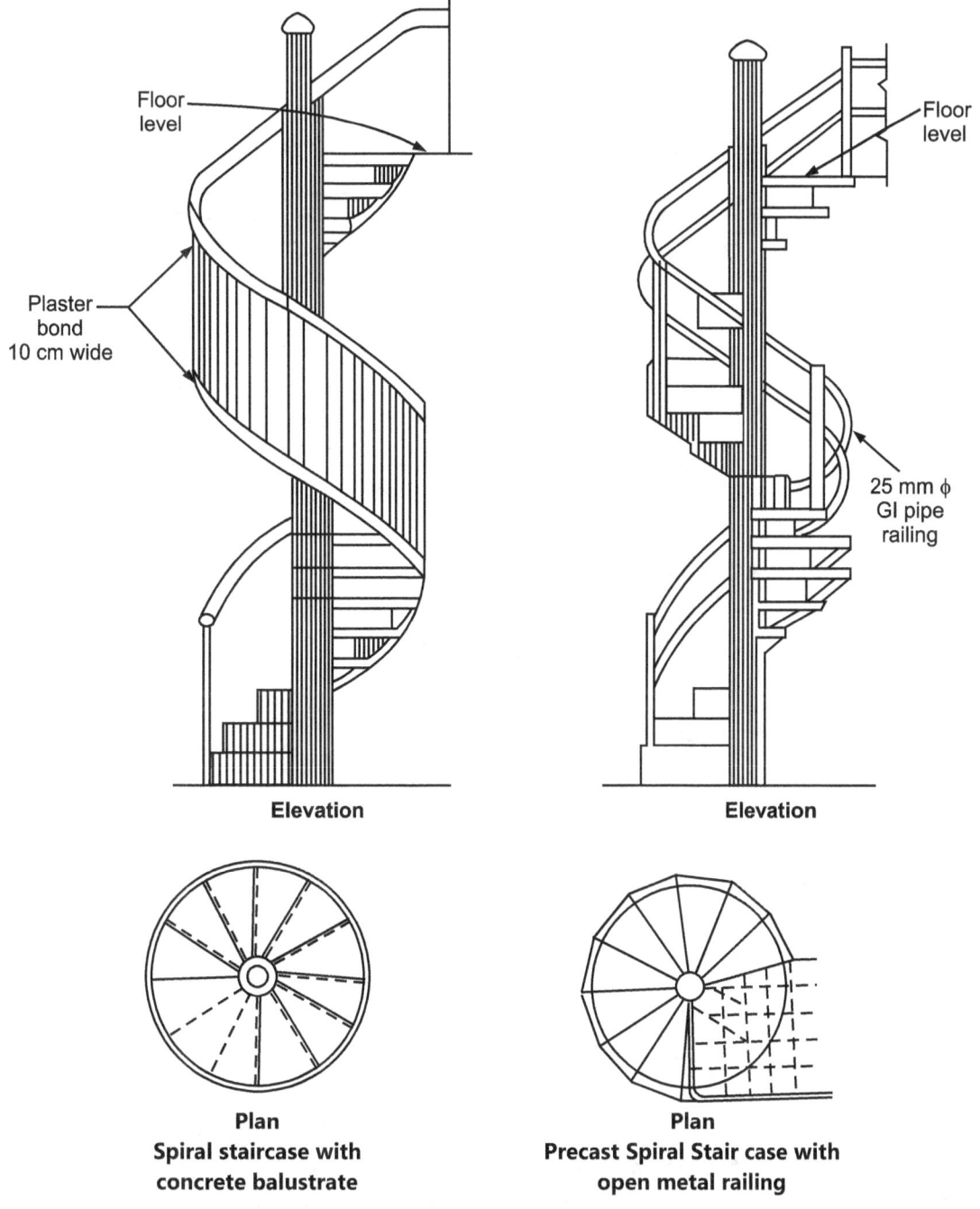

Fig. 10.16

10.5 MATERIALS USED FOR CONSTRUCTION OF STAIRS

The commonly used materials in the construction of stairs are wood, stone, steel cast-iron, plain cement concrete, reinforced cement concrete, precast concrete and bricks.

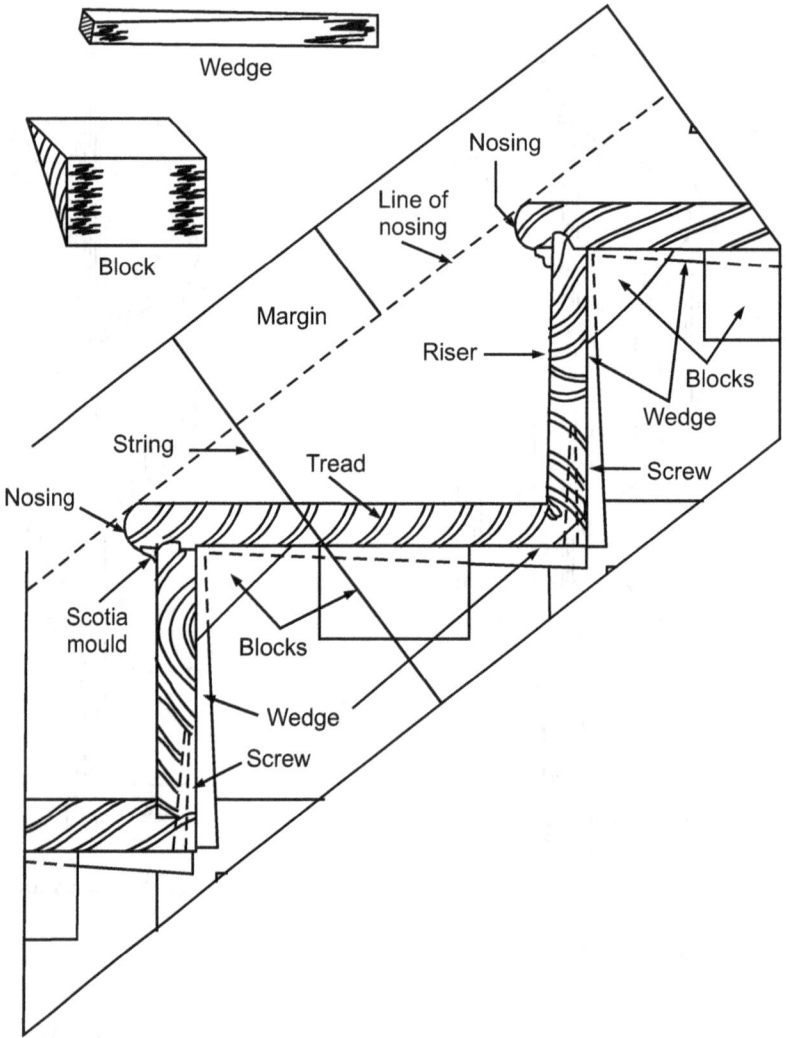

Fig. 10.17 : Wooden stair

1. **Timber or Wooden Stairs**
   - Timber stairs are light in weight and easy to construct, but they have very poor fire resistance.
   - These stairs are generally used for small residential buildings. Timber stairs are cheap, easy in construction and maintenance and light in weight.
   - These stairs are constructed from fire resisting hard wood such as oak, teak, mahogany, Babul, Neem etc.

- In wooden, stairs the thickness of tread should not be less than 32 mm and that of the riser as 25 mm. The risers and the treads are connected by tongue and grooved joints and the joints are nailed or screwed.
- The treads and risers are supported on one or more stringer beams. The upper edges of beams are cut to receive the riser and treads.
- Stringers are supported on transverse beam known as headers. To add rigidity, blocks are glued between the stringer and the treads and the treads and risers.

2. Stone Stairs

- Stone stairs are widely used at places where ashlar stone is abundantly available.
- Stone used for the construction of stairs should be hard, strong and resistant to wear. These stairs are commonly constructed in workshop, warehouses and other public buildings.
- In residential building, these stairs are generally restricted to outside stairs at the entrance. Being heavy in weight, stone stairs require stable support to avoid the danger of settlement of supporting walls.
- The main types of stone steps are described below :

(a) Rectangular steps

- These are the simplest type, prepared from solid stone into square or rectangular blocks of uniform size.
- In its simplest form, the steps are arranged with the front edge of one step resting on the upper back edge of the steps below.

(b) Built-up steps : These consists of treads and risers prepared from thin stone slabs. These are generally used as a facing for brick or concrete steps. The minimum thickness of tread, when supported at end is restricted to 5 cm.

(c) Spandril steps : In this, the steps are cut to give plain soffit. These steps are nearly triangular in shape except at the ends which are built into the wall.

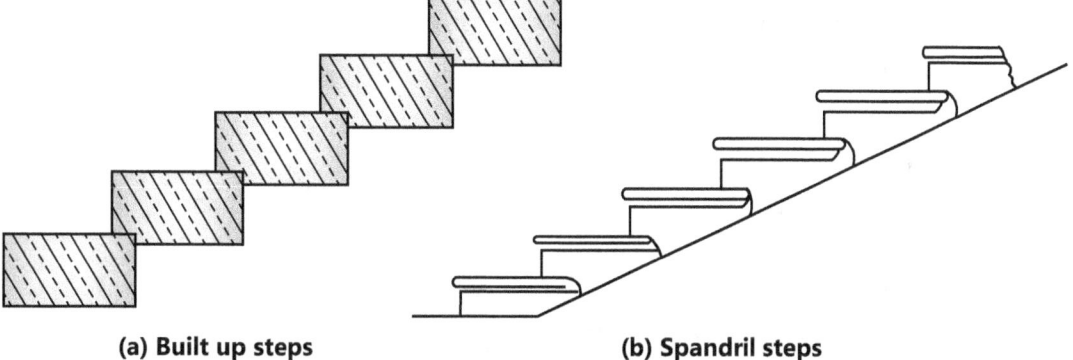

(a) Built up steps	**(b) Spandril steps**

Fig. 10.18 : Stone stair

3. **Brick Stairs**

   - Brick stairs are not very common, except at the entrance. Sometimes brick stairs of single flight are constructed in village houses.

   - These stairs may be built of solid masonry construction or arches and cupboards may be constructed in the lower portion which reduces masonry work and increases utility of underneath space.

   - These steps needs frequent maintenance. Hence, these may be faced with various types of stone slabs.

4. **Metal Stairs**

   - These stairs are made of mild steel or cast iron. These are generally used in factories, godowns, workshops etc.

   - In its simplest form, a steel stair consists of rolled steel stringers of channel section, to which angle sections are welded and steel plates are used as treads. Generally metal balusters with hand rails of pipe are used for these stairs.

5. **R.C.C. Stairs**

   - R.C.C. stairs predominate the stairs made from other materials. This is because of various advantages of R.C.C. over the other materials.

   - R.C.C. stairs are the one which are widely used for residential, public and industrial buildings. They are strong, hard wearing and fire resisting. These are usually cast in situ.

Advantages of R.C.C. Stairs

- R.C.C. stairs can be moulded in any desired shape to suit the requirement of the architect's design.

- These stairs are durable, strong, pleasing in appearance and non-slippery.

- These stairs can be designed for greater widths and longer spans.

- These stairs can be easily cleaned, and are fire resistant.

- The maintenance cost of these stairs is almost nil.

SOLVED EXAMPLES

Planning of Typical R.C.C. Stairs

Example 10.1 : Plan a dog legged stair for a building with the following data :

   (i) Vertical distance between the floors = 3.6 m.

   (ii) Size of stair hall 2.5 m × 5 m.

   (iii) Thickness of the floor slab = 140 mm.

   (iv) Thickness of the waist slab and landing slab = 100 mm.

Solution : Assume,   Rise = 150 mm

and   Tread = 250 mm

$$\text{Width of the flight} = \frac{2.5}{2} = 1.25 \text{ m}$$

$$\text{Height of each flight} = \frac{3.6}{2} = 1.8 \text{ m}$$

∴ $$\text{Number of risers required} = \frac{1.8 \times 1000}{150}$$

= 12 in each flight

Number of treads in each flight = 12 − 1 = 11

∴   Space required for treads = 11 × 250 = 2750 mm

∴   Space left for passage = 5 − 1.25 − 2.75 = 1.00 m

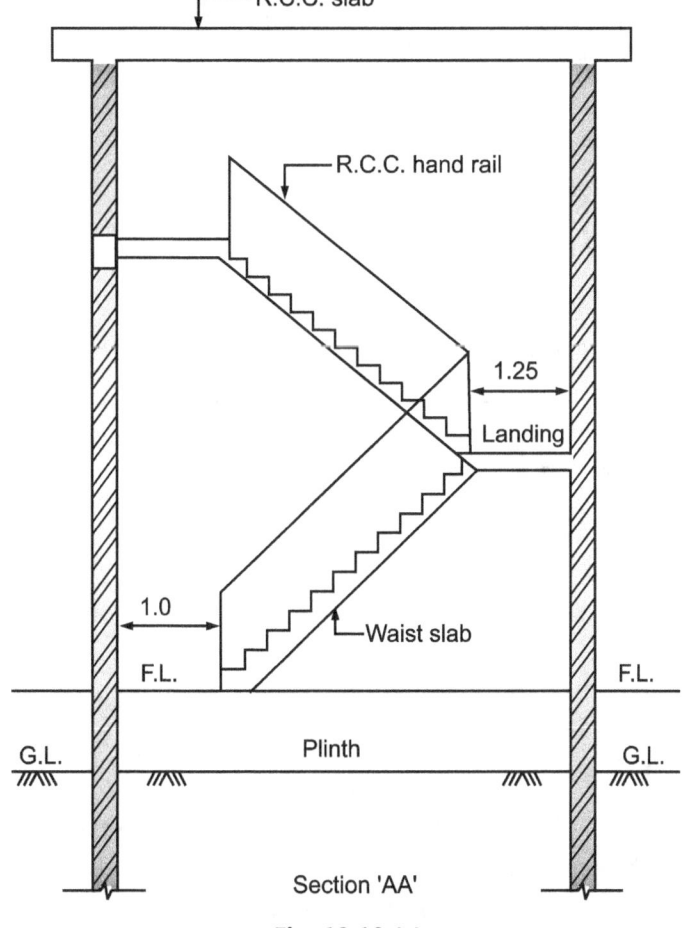

Fig. 10.19 (a)

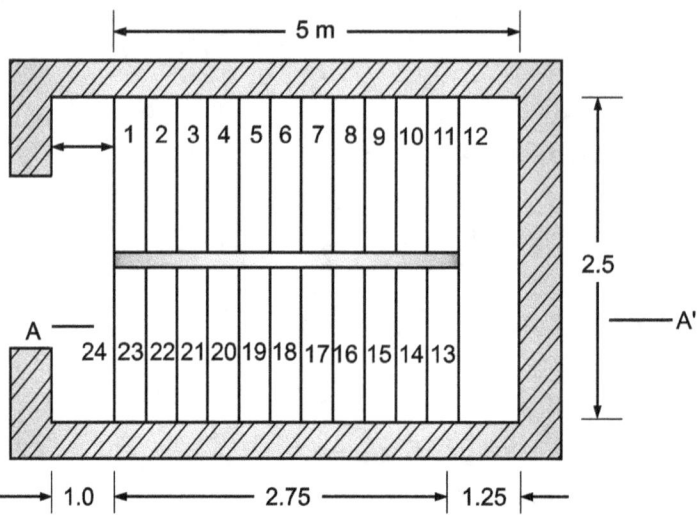

Fig. 10.19 (b): Arrangement of risers in stair case, when total risers are divisible by 4

Example 10.2 : Calculate numbers of risers and treads in each flight for dog legged stair, floor to floor height is 3.3 m and riser is 150 mm.

Solution : Given data :

$$\text{Floor to floor height} = 3.3 \text{ m}$$

$$\text{Riser} = 150 \text{ mm}$$

$$\therefore \quad \text{Total number of risers} = \frac{3300}{150} = 22$$

Assuming two flights, number of risers in each flight = 11 number and number of treads in each flight = 11 – 1 = 10 number.

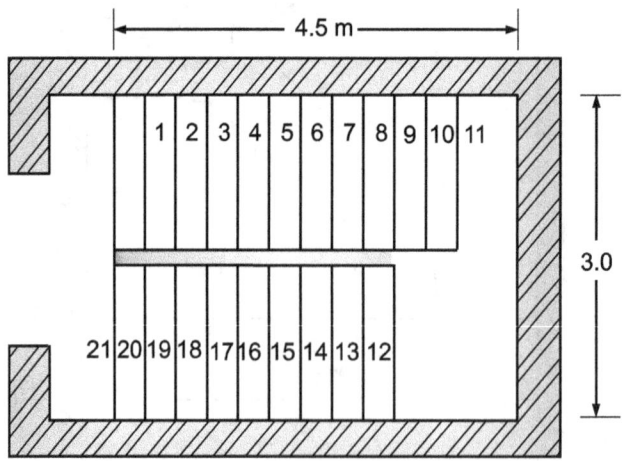

Fig. 10.20: Arrangement of risers in stair case, when total risers are even,
but not divisible by 4

Example 10.3 : Plan a staircase for a residential building in which the vertical distance between each floor is 3.36 m. The size of the stair hall is limited to 4.5 × 3 m.

Solution : Given data :

(i)   Floor to floor height = 3.36 m

    Let,   Width of landing = 1.5 m = Width of stairs.

    Assume,   Rise = 16 cm

$\therefore$ Total number of risers $= \dfrac{3.36 \times 100}{16} = 21$ risers $\Rightarrow$ 11 in first flight
 10 in second flight

Provide 11 risers in each flight.

$\therefore$ Number of treads in first flight = 11 − 1 = 10

                    in second flight = 10 − 1 = 9

10.6 ESCALATORS   (Dec. 13, May 14)

- A power driven, inclined, continuous stairs, used for ascending or descending, is known as an **Escalator**.

- It has continuous automatic operation, hence does not need any operator. Escalators are used when there is need to move more number of people from one floor to another. They have large capacity with low power consumption.

- The main components of an escalator are a steel trussed framework, hand rails and an endless belt with steps.

- The arrangement of escalators in each floor may be either parallel or criss-cross. Escalators are more preferable at places where movement of large number of people is involved e.g. Airports, Molls, Exhibition halls, Railway stations etc.

Fig. 10.21

Important points to be observed in an escalators :

- Angle of inclination should be between 30 to 32°.
- Tread should not be less than 40 cm, rise should not be more than 20 cm and width of steps should not be less than 45 cm and should not be more than 105 cm.
- The rate of movement of steps should not be 30 to 40 m/min.
- Escalators are generally installed in pair. One of them is used for carrying on upper floor people and the other for people moving down.

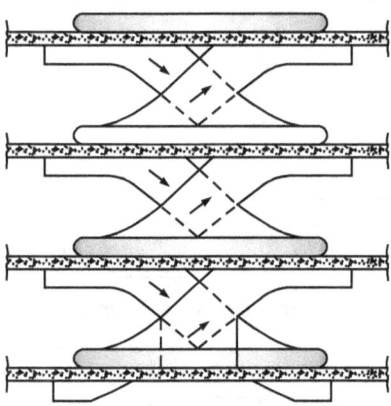   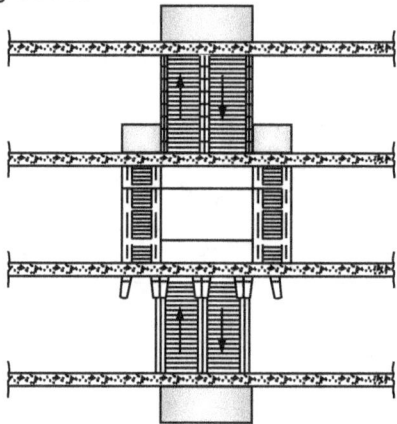

(a) Criss-cross arrangement of escalators   **(b) Parallel arrangement of escalators**

Fig. 10.22

10.7 RAMPS   (May 14)

- Ramps are the inclined surfaces used for the easy movement between different floors. These are essentially useful when more number of people or vehicles has to move from one floor to another.
- Ramps are usually provided in Hospitals, Garages, Railway station, Town halls, Stadiums, Office buildings, Exhibition halls, Schools of physically handicapped children etc. They must be constructed with a non-slip surfaces. They may be straight or curved.

Fig. 10.23

Some essential requirements for the construction of ramps :

- Slope for the ramp should be 10 to 15%.
- For pedestrian traffic minimum width of ramp should be 75 cm and maximum 2 m.
- For carrying vehicles and machinery, width of ramp should be 4 m to 8 m with slope of 10%.
- Hand rails must be provided on either side of ramp.
- For powered ramps, slope should be 8 to 11° and speed in between 47 to 60 m/min.

10.8 LIFT

- For multi-storeyed buildings, the installation of lift is must, to avoid fatigue in climbing up the stairs and for quick vertical circulation.
- Elevators or lifts are used in buildings having more than four storey height. The provision of lifts in the structure is a highly specialised job.
- Some provisions are required to be made in the building layout to accommodate lift and other accessories like operating devices.
- A vertical shaft with opening at the floor level is provided. The shaft is located at a suitable place such as by the side of the stair or within the open well of the stair.

Fig. 10.24

10.9 LADDER

- Ladders may be of fixed type or moveable type. They may be of wooden or cast iron. Pitch in ladder very from 75 to 85°, there is no hand rail provided to the ladder.

- Fixed ladders are similar to stairs except that they are usually of metal and are used as a means of access to roofs.
- Ladders are also used to have access to water tank, wells, sewer pipes, septic tanks, basements and mezanine floors.

Fig. 10.25

REVIEW QUESTIONS

1. Explain the situation in which the following means of vertical circulation are favoured :
   (a) Escalators
   (b) Ramps
   (c) Elevators
   (d) Spiral stairs

2. Explain the concept of head room and state its value. State normally used values of rise and treads for a commercial building.

3. State the requirements of good stair with respect to :
   (a) Pitch
   (b) Head room
   (c) Location
   (d) Rise and tread
   (e) Number of steps in a flight

(e) Width of stair.

4. Design a stair for stair case of size 2.40 m × 4.60 m. Floor to floor height is 3.15 m state number of risers, value of rise, width of landing, height of baluster, value of going and number of risers in each flight.

Hint: Assume riser of 15 cm. Therefore, total risers $= \dfrac{3.15}{0.15} = 21$. Proceed as per solved example 3. Fig. 10.18.

5. Draw a typical cross-section illustrating arrangements in a lift well. State the function of each component.

6. Write a short note on Escalators.

7. Write down the thumb rules used in design of stair. Explain the following terms with sketch :

   (a) String

   (b) Newel post

   (c) Rise

   (d) Riser

8. Write down types of stairs as per geometric design and describe any one in detail.

9. As a site incharge, if demolition of building in congested area is to be carried out, what preventive measures or precautions you will take ?

10. What is Elevators ? Explain important terms used in it.

11. Explain the following terms :

   (a) Baluster

   (b) Nosing

   (c) Head room

   (d) Pitch.

12. Design a suitable staircase for a residential building. Using the following data :

   (a) Size of the stair hall – 4.80 × 2.40.

   (b) Floor to floor height – 3.40 m.

   (c) Thickness of slab – 120 mm.

   Assume suitable data if necessary. Draw a detailed designed plan only.

Hint: Assume risers of 17 cm. Therefore, total risers $= \dfrac{3.40}{0.17} = 20$. Proceed as per solved example 1. Fig. 10.17.

13. Write down essential requirements for Escalators.

14. Give the plan of dog legged stair. Explain the design procedure for dog legged stair in detail.

15. Write short note on lift.

16. State the requirements of a good vertical circulation.

17. State the different types of stairs based on materials of construction. Explain any one in detail.

18. Explain the following :

    (a) Tread,

    (b) Going,

    (c) Riser,

    (d) Header,

    (e) Nosing,

    (f) Balustrade.

19. What is vertical transportation ? What are ramps and escalators.

20. What special consideration should be kept in view while designing stair cases.

21. State the different means of vertical circulations. Explain escalators in detail.

22. Name the different types of stair and draw a dog-legged stair.

23. Write notes on :

    (a) Steel stairs,

    (b) Bifurcated stair.

24. Design a R.C.C. dog-legged staircase and draw a detailed plan for an office building, a staircase room available is 3 m × 5 m with the outer wall thickness of 0.23 m. Height of the ceiling is 3.6 m. The thickness of R.C.C. slab is 0.10 m.

25. Write down the essential requirements of escalators.

26. Write a short note on ramps.

27. Discuss the various considerations that are made in planning of staircases. Illustrate the different types of staircases generally used, indicating their suitability for specific use.

28. What are the limitations on different types of staircase in regard to their rise and tread ? How would you choose them for :

    (a) House

    (b) School

    (c) Hospital

    (d) Railway Station

29. What shall happen –

(a) If the slope of the staircase is less than 25° and more than 40° with the horizontal ?

(b) If a straight flight stair is erected to reach first floor without any midlanding.

SOLVED UNIVERSITY QUESTIONS

DEC. 2013

1. Explain step by step procedure of design of dog-legged staircase.   **[6]**

   [**Ans. :** Refer Article 10.4(2)]

2. Define circulation. State different means of circulation. Explain Escalators in detail. **[6]**

   [**Ans. :** Refer Article 10.6]

MAY 2014

1. Write short notes on Ramps and Escalators.   **[8]**

   [**Ans. :** Refer Article 10.7, 10.6]

DEC. 2014

1. State ideal requirements of good stair. Explain defects in plastering.   **[7]**

   [**Ans. :** Refer Article 10.3]

MAY 2015

1. State the requirements of a good stair with respect to: **[7]**

   (i)   Pitch   (ii)   Head room   (iii)   Location

   (iv) Number of steps in a flight   (v)   Rise and Tread (vi) Width of stair.

   [**Ans. :** Refer Article 10.3]

2. Enlist types of stairs depending on the materials of construction. Explain any one in detail.   **[6]**

   [**Ans. :** Refer Article 10.4]

NOV. 2015

1. Explain ideal requirements of good stair.

   [**Ans. :** Refer Article 10.3]

2. Write short notes on : Quarter turn staircase   **[6]**

   [**Ans. :** Refer Article 10.4(9)]

MAY 2016

1. State and explain ideal requirements of good stair. Explain any one modern circulation mean. **[7]**

   [**Ans. :** Refer Article 10.3]

2. Explain step by step procedure of dog-legged staircase. Give sketch of dog-legged staircase. **[7]**

   [**Ans. :** Refer Article 10.4(2)]

Nov. 2016

1. Explain with suitable example the design of Dog-legged staircase. **[6]**

   [**Ans. :** Refer Article 10.4(2)]

MAY 2017

1. List any four types of staircases. Draw a Dogelgged stair. **[7]**

   [**Ans. :** Refer Article 10.4, 10.4(2)]

2. Explain the requirements of a good stairs with reference to the following : **[7]**

   (i)   Pitch

   (ii) Rise and Tread

   (iii) Headroom

   (iv) Width of stair

   (v)   Width of Landing

   (vi) Number of steps in a flight

   (vii) Location of a staircase.

   [**Ans. :** Refer Article 10.3)

CHAPTER 11
PROTECTIVE COATINGS

11.1 INTRODUCTION (May 16)

- Building finishes include plastering, pointing, white washing, colour washing, painting, varnishing, distempering etc.
- The main objective of finishing the surface is to protect surface from atmospheric agents like rain water, wind, temperature etc. and to improve the appearance of the surface.
- Various techniques are employed to cover the surface. These different types of building finishes are described in various articles of this chapter.

11.2 PLASTERING (Dec. 13, Nov. 15, 16, May 16,17)

- Plastering is the covering with material of various compositions applied either externally or internally to walls, partitions of ceiling etc. to cover rough walls and uneven surface of a building.
- Plastering is done by plastic mortar obtained by mixing some binding material with fine aggregate and water in suitable proportion. The binding material used may be lime, cement or mud.

Fig. 11.1 : Plastering

Objectives of Plastering

- To provide an even smooth, regular, clean and durable finished surface.
- To resist the atmospheric influences particularly the infiltration of rain.
- To conceal the defective workmanship.
- To fill the joints formed in masonry work.

- To cover inferior quality materials.
- The internal plaster provides a smooth surface which does not allow dust, dirt and vermin to lodge on it.
- To prepare satisfactory base for decorating the surface by the application of white or colour wash, distemper or paint.

The requirements of an ideal plaster are :

- It should be smooth, non-absorbent, reasonably sound deadening, flame retarding, washable and not affected by rise or fall in temperature.
- The plaster should not shrink while drying and setting.
- It should adhere firmly to the surface and should provide the surface with required decorative effect and durability.

Selection of Type of Plaster

The following factors affect the selection of plaster to be used :

- Availability of binding materials
- Desired durability
- Desired finishing
- Atmospheric conditions to which plaster is subjected.
- Whether the plaster is to be used on exterior surfaces or interior surfaces.

Types of Plaster

1. Mud plaster
2. Cement plaster
3. Lime plaster
4. Special type of plasters.

1. Mud Plaster

- This is the cheapest type of plaster which is generally used for construction in villages. Mud plaster consists of well tampered clay, cow dung, chopped straw and sand. The earth should be free from roots, grass, organic matter and stone pebbles.
- The earth is mixed with ample quantity of water and left to season for about a week. Chopped straw, hay or hemp is added to the prepared earth at the rate of about 30 kg/m^3. The mixture is converted into a homogeneous mass by working it up and down.
- The surface is prepared by knocking off projections, racking out joints, wetting with water etc. and then vertical screeds are formed so as to act as thickness gauges.
- Mud plaster is now applied between screeds by dashing the mortar against the prepared surface in a thickness of 12 mm. Before starting plastering, the surface to be plastered should be wetted thoroughly.
- Dashed mortar against the walls is then finished by means of a straight edge and wooden float. After 24 hours of setting, but before drying of the plaster of the first coat, the second coat is applied in thickness of 6 mm.

- The plaster is not cured but the surface is treated with fine white earth, cow dung and cement.

2. Cement Plaster

It is an ideal coating for external surfaces. It is suitable for damp conditions. The plastering includes two stages :

(i) Preparation of surface for plastering, ground work for plaster;

(ii) Application of cement mortar on surface.

(i) Preparation of Surface for Plastering

- For good plaster it is essential that plaster covering should have proper bond or adhesion with the surface of masonry to be plastered and therefore preparation of the background for plastering is very important.

   It is done in the following steps :

- All mortar joints of wall to be plastered are left rough and projecting which provide key or hold to the plaster.
- All the joints and surfaces are cleaned with wire brush. This process is very essential to obtain a good key of the plaster with the wall surfaces. Oil and grease spots should be removed either by brushing or scrapping.
- All cavities and holes in the surface to be plastered are filled up properly. The projections more than 12 mm on the surface are removed. The area to be plastered is washed and kept wet.

(ii) Ground Work for Plaster

- In order to maintain uniform thickness of the plaster, the screeds or bands are formed. On the prepared wall surface by fixing dots (patches of plaster 150 mm × 150 mm).
- These dots are applied horizontally and vertically at a distance of about 2 m over the surface to be plastered.
- The two dots lying in the vertical plane are checked for verticality by means of plumb bob. After fixing the dots the vertical strips of mortar are formed between the dots.
- These screeds act as gauges for maintaining even thickness of plaster being applied. Now the surface to be plastered is ready for applying plaster.

(iii) Application of Cement Mortar on Surface [Dec. 2005, May 2005] :

- Cement plaster consists of an uniform mixture of cement and clean coarse sand with suitable quantity of water.
- The proportion of cement to fine aggregate may vary according to the requirements of the plaster. But generally the ratio is 1 : 3 or 1 : 4.
- To produce mortar, these materials are thoroughly mixed in dry condition and water is added in the dry mix.
- In mortar, consistency of mix is very important. Cement plaster may be done in one coat or two coats as illustrated in Fig. 11.2.

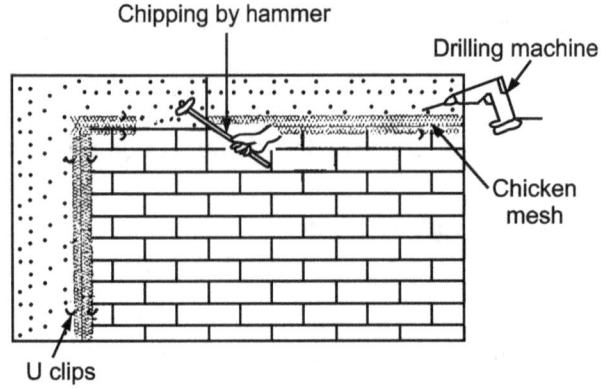

(1) It is essential to fix chicken mesh near the junction of concrete and stone/brick work before plastering to reduce cracks in plaster

(2) Prepare cement mortar of (1 : 4) mix and apply layer of cement mortar of 10 to 12 mm thickness

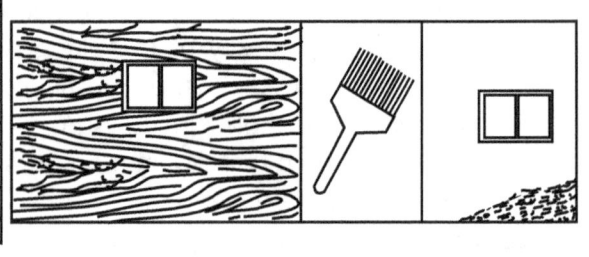

(3) Prior to plastering

(4) Make scratches over the plastered surface before it becomes too hard, so as to have good grip of the final coat over the previous coat

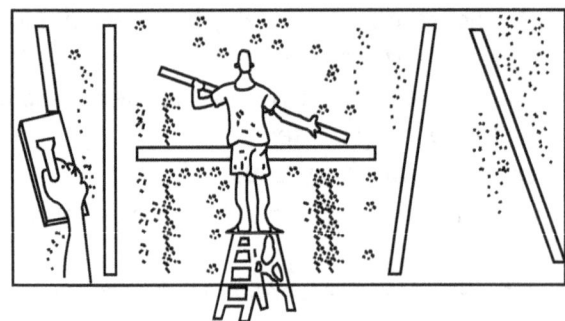

(6) Level with aluminium float

(7) Excess water present in mortar can be mopped by use of sponge

Fig. 11.2 : Procedure to be adopted while plastering

First Coat or Rough Coat

- Surface is well raked and cleaned off loose dust and well water before plastering. After preparing the surface as explained earlier and the mortar is dashed against the surface. Between the screeds, the surface of mortar when it is plastic, is levelled with the help of float and straight edges and finally finished with trowels.
- If second coat is to be applied, the surface of the first coat is not polished but roughened with scratching tool to produce key to the second coat of plaster. Second coat is applied after a lapse of 2 days. The thickness of second coat is normally 3 mm.
- The mortar that is used for second coat, consists of cement and very fine sand in proportion of 1 : 2. The finished plaster with one coat or two coats is cured by spraying water for atleast 7 days.

3. **Lime Plaster**

- Lime plastering is the process of covering the surface with lime mortar. In lime plaster, fat lime is normally used. Hydraulic lime slakes very slowly which results into blisters on the plaster surface.
- The lime mortar, generally, consists of lime and sand in the proportion of 1 : 1. The mixture is thoroughly ground in mortar mills to produce a uniform plaster mix. To improve the strength of the mortar, sometimes a small quantity of cement is added.
- The sand used is clean, coarse and free from deleterious matters. The plaster may be applied in one, two or more coats.
- The first coat has an average thickness of about 12 mm on brick or ashlar masonry and 20 mm on Rubble masonry. The first coat is applied by dashing the lime mortar between the screeds. It is then finished with the help of floats.
- The first coat is left exposed to air for a period of 2 days to set before applying the second coat.
- The second coat which is called as floating coat is applied after preparing the surface of the first coat. The surface is prepared by sweeping it clean off any dust or loose particles and spraying water.
- The second coat is spread uniformly with trowels. It is pressed and finished with straight edge to obtain the desired finish. The thickness of the second coat, generally, is kept between 6 - 9 mm.
- The third coat is applied after 5 - 6 days of the second coat. The mortar for finishing coat consists of cream of white or fat lime (NEERU) mixed with fine sand in the proportion of 1 : 2.
- The mortar is well rubbed with wooden float and finally finished with trovel to obtain desired surface. The surface is allowed to dry for 24 hrs. and then it is well watered for about a week. The thickness of the final coat is kept nearly 3 mm.

4. **Special Type of Plasters :** The special type of plasters are used to obtain a specific finish. Following are the details of some of the special plasters :

(i) Water Proof Plaster : This type of plastering is done with the help of mortar which is prepared by mixing one part of cement, two parts of sand and fine alum at the rate of 12 kg/m³ of sand. Water having 75 gm/lit. of soap is used as mixing water. The application of plaster is similar to that of lime or cement plaster.

(ii) Stucco Plaster

- This type of plaster is provided on external face and internal face of the wall. This is a decorative plaster which provides attractive surface. Stucco plastering is done in three coats and the total thickness is 25 mm

- The first coat which is called as scratch or rough coat, functions to bond with the wall. The second coat which is called as final coat or brown coat provides desired shape to the surface.

- The last coat which is known as finishing coat provides required texture, smoothness and decorative appearance to the surface.

- The composition of stucco plaster is different for interior and exterior surfaces.

Applications of Stucco Plastering

(a) For Exterior Walls

- In this case, the mortar for the first coat consists of 1 : 3 cement and sand to which about 10% of hydrated lime by weight is added.

- After preparing the surface in the usual manner, the first coat is applied in the thickness of 12 mm. After drying of first coat, second coat having thickness of 9 mm with same composition as the first coat is applied.

- After drying of second coat the third coat which is 3 mm in thickness is applied. The mortar used for the third coat is made up of cement and sand in proportion of 1 : 2 or $1 : 2\frac{1}{2}$.

- To give desired shade to the finish, white or coloured cement is used in place of gray cement.

(b) For Interior Walls

- For internal stucco plastering the first coat consists of ordinary lime plaster 13 mm thick.

- The second coat of lime plaster which is richer is applied in thickness of 9 mm. After drying of second coat the final coat is applied in thickness of 3 mm. The mortar consists of finest lime and well powdered white stone.

- The final coat is first polished with linen cloth containing moist chalk and then with oil and chalk. Finally, the surface is finished smooth and brightened by rubbing only with oil.

All the coats in the stucco plastering are cured for sufficient time to attain sufficient strength and hardness.

(c) Plaster of Paris

- It is obtained from gypsum which is a naturally occurring material. When gypsum is heated to a certain temperature, water of crystallization gets removed leaving behind a very fine powder of plaster of paris.

- When water is added in this powder, it sets immediately therefore, when plaster of paris is used for plastering purpose, the setting time is increased by adding certain salts, some burnt ash and fine sand.

- The dry mix of plaster of paris and sand is prepared on a platform. Small quantity of this mix is taken in a pan and suitable quantity of water is added. This plaster is applied within 5 minutes after addition of water.

- This type of plaster produces very good smooth finish with sharp edges and corners. This plaster is not used for external surfaces.

External finishes of plaster :

Depending upon the desired appearance, cost and degree of maintenance, the external walls are given different finishes.

Following are some of the commonly adopted external wall finishes :

- **Smooth Cast Finish :** This finish provides a levelled and smooth surface. The mortar used for final coat consists of 1 : 3 cement and fine sand. The plaster is worked with wooden float.

- **Rough Cast Finish :** In this type, the mortar is produced with 1 part of cement, $1\frac{1}{2}$ parts of fine sand and 3 parts of coarse sand with appropriate quantity of water.

  This mixture is dashed against prepared plaster surface with the help of large trovel and finished rough with wooden flat. Rough cast finish is waterproof, durable and resistant to cracking and crazing. This type of finish is used for buildings which are subjected to heavy rainfall and high winds.

- **Pebble Dash Finish :** In this type of finish, a coat of plaster having thickness 13 mm (with 1 : 3 cement and sand proportion) is applied. Clean pebbles of size varying from 10 - 20 mm are dashed on the first coat when it is plastic. On setting, dashed pebbles remain held in position. The pebbles are slightly tapped or pressed into the mortar with a wooden float. This type of finish is suitable for buildings which are subjected to heavy rainfall and high winds.

- **Sand Faced Finish or Sponge Finish :** This type of finishing is carried out in two coats, base coat and final coat. The base coat of cement mortar (1 cement : 4 coarse angular sand) is applied in a thickness not less than 12 mm. This coat is cured for a week and then second coat is applied. The thickness of second coat is about 8 mm and the mortar consists of cement and fine sand in the proportion of 1 : 1. The second coat, when it is still wet is worked with sponge so that equal and uniform sand grain appear on surface. The surface is cured for about two weeks.

- **Depeter Finish :** This is a kind of rough cast finish. In this type of finish, final coat of 13 mm thickness is applied as in the case of pebble dash finish. Over this coat, while it is still wet gravel or different coloured flints are pressed with hand. Therefore, it is possible to have beautiful patterns and design on the surface by selecting materials of different colours.

- **Scrapped Finish :** This type of finish is produced by allowing the final coat to stiffen for sometime and then scrapping so as to remove surface skin. Different types of scrapping tools are used to obtain different types of scrapped finishes. The final coat is 12 mm thick and thickness of 3 mm is scrapped by scrapping tools. Scrapping helps in exposing the aggregate inside the final coat. This scrapped surface presents a rough surface with exposed aggregate and texture depending upon the grading of aggregate used in final coat. This finish is not liable to crack.

- **Textured Finish :** In this type of finish, it is possible to produce various ornamental patterns and beautiful designs by working with suitable tools on freshly laid final coat of stucco plastering. This type of finish has advantages similar to rough cast finish.

11.3 POINTING   (May 15)

- The joints on the face of stone or brick masonry are roughly filled in, while the walls are being raised.
- Pointing is art of finishing the mortar joints in the exposed masonry with suitable cement or lime mortar, to protect the joints from weather effects and also to improve the appearance of building structure.
- Plastering involves use of mortar and labour and therefore it is costlier. The mortar joints are weak parts of the masonry and therefore they need protection from rain water, sunrays and snow.
- Pointing is comparatively a cheaper method of protecting the joints.

Mortar for Pointing : Pointing is done in lime mortar or cement mortar or sometimes in composite mortars.

Lime Mortar : The lime mortar for pointing is produced by grinding fat lime and sand in a mortar mill.

Cement Mortar : The cement mortar which is used for pointing is produced by mixing together cement and clean sand in the proportion of 1 : 2 or 1 : 3.

Composite Mortar : Composite mortar is produced by mixing cement, lime and sand in the proportion of 1 : 2 : 9 or 1 : 1 : 6.

Method of Pointing : Pointing is done in the following stages.

- All the mortar joints in the masonry are raked out to a depth of 10 - 15 mm with the help of pointing tools.
- Dust and loose mortars are thoroughly cleaned.

- The joints and the surface are washed with clean water and kept wet for sometime.
- Mortar is taken in small pans and the joints are filled up with small trowel by pressing it into the joints to form a close contact with the old mortar joints. The joints are left - flush, sunk or raised depending upon the requirements.
- Excess mortar is scrapped away.
- The finished work is cured for 3 - 4 days in case of lime mortar and for 10 days when cement mortar is used.

Types of Pointing

Pointing is classified according to the shape of finishing. The type of pointing is decided considering the type of masonry, nature of building structure and the desired effects of finish.

- **Flush Pointing :** In this type of pointing joints, are raked and they are finished flush with the face of the brick masonry. The edges are properly trimmed. It is the simplest type of pointing which is extensively used in masonry work. This pointing does not give good appearance but it is very durable and it does not allow dust, dirt or water to lodge over it.
- **Cut or Weathered or Struck Pointing :** In this pointing, the face of pointing is not kept vertical but it is kept inclined. The upper edge of pointing plaster is pressed inside the masonry by about 10 mm and lower edge is finished level with the face of masonry. This type of pointing is mostly used for brick work particularly for finishing horizontal joints.
- **Recessed Pointing :** In this type of pointing, finished face of pointing mortar is kept vertical but inside the wall surface with the help of suitable tool. This type of pointing is suitable for facing work of good texture bricks and superior quality mortar.
- **Keyed, Rubbed or Grooved Pointing :** In this type of pointing, the recked joints are filled up flush with the face of the wall and semi-circular notches are formed by a special tool. This type of pointing is commonly used as it improves the appearance of the wall.
- **Tuck Pointing :** In this type, the mortar is pressed in the joints and finished flush with the face of the wall. When the mortar is still wet a rectangular groove (5 mm width and 3 mm depth) is formed at the centre of joints. This groove is filled with white lime putty and small quantity of silver sand by keeping it slightly projecting outside the finished surface of the pointing plaster. This type of pointing gives attractive appearance but the fillet part is not very durable.
- **Vee Pointing :** In this type of pointing either 'V' - shaped grooves are engrooved in the finished surface of the pointing plaster when it is still green or by projecting the 'V' - shape of the pointing face outside the wall surface.
- **Beaded Pointing :** This type of pointing gives very good appearance but it is difficult to maintain. The raked joints are filled up with mortar and finished flush with the face of the wall and then bead is formed by a steel rod having concave edge in the middle of joints.

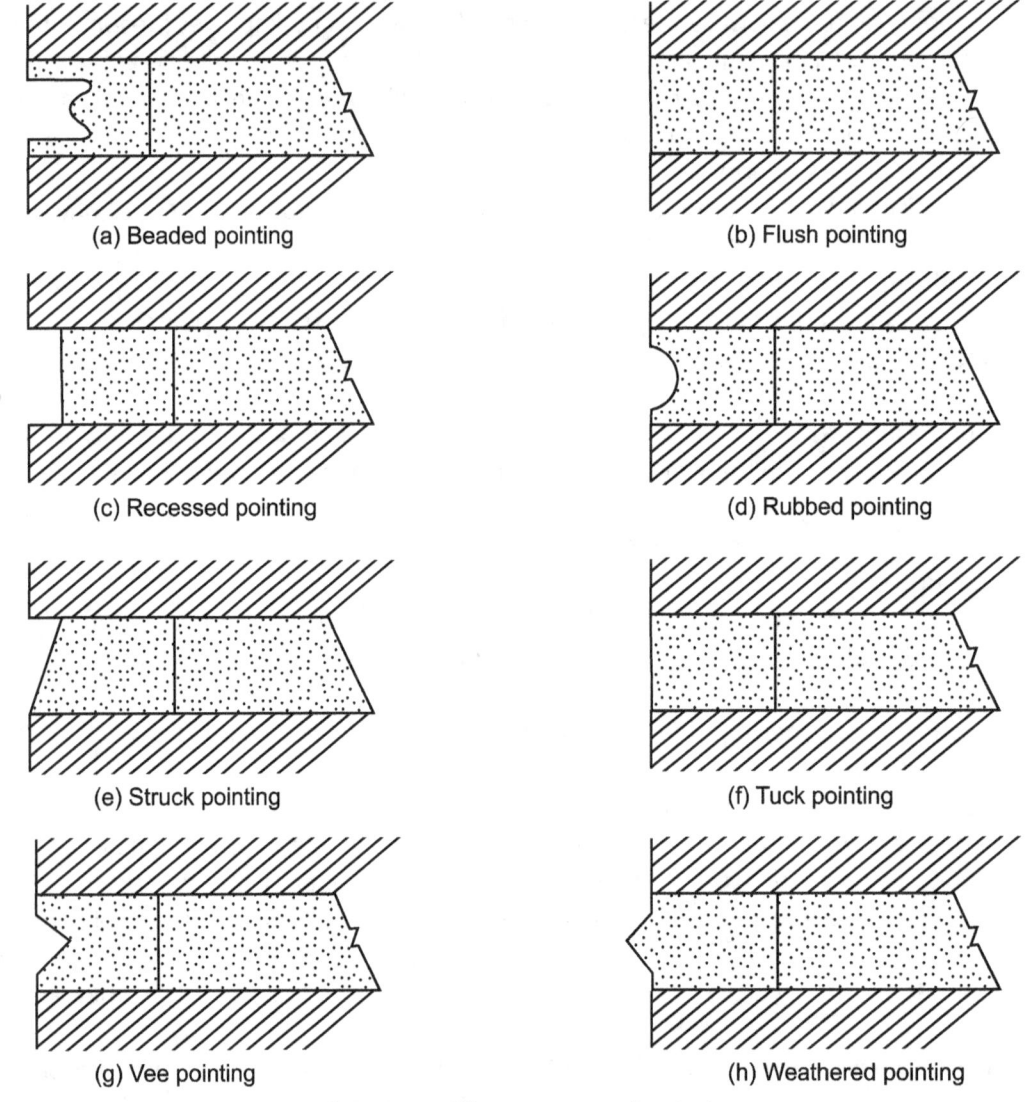

Fig. 11.3 : Different types of pointing

11.4 WHITE WASHING

- It is a process of giving wash covering to the plastered or pointed surface. In case of white washing a wash of slaked lime mixed with water is applied.
- Sometimes other ingredients like gum, rice water, common salt etc. are added to improve the properties of the lime.

White washing includes the following operations :

1. Preparation of white wash
2. Preparation of surface for white wash
3. Application of white wash.

1. Preparation of White Wash

- The material required for white washing is fat lime or shell lime. Unslaked lime lumps are mixed with water and the mixture is thoroughly stirred with the help of bamboo.
- The lime is allowed to get fully slaked for about 24 hrs. After 24 hrs. it is stirred up with a pole and additional water is added until it attains the consistency of thin cream.
- This mixture is then screened through a clean coarse cloth. Clean gum is dissolved in hot water at rate of 4 kg/m^3 of thin cream. The dissolved gum is added to the slaked lime solution.
- Sometimes alum, common salt or rice water are used in place of gum. To prevent the glare effect due to white wash sometimes copper sulphate at the rate of 4 kg/m^3 of thin cream is added.
- Gum or rice water is used to improve adhesive properties of white wash.

2. Preparation of Surface

- Before applying white wash, the surface to be white washed should be made thoroughly dry. If the surface is new, it should be thoroughly cleaned, brushed, and made free from mortar droppings or any other loose materials.
- If the surface is very smooth, the white wash will not stick to it and therefore, the surface should be rubbed with sand paper to ensure proper adhesion of white wash.
- In case of white washing the old surface again, all loose materials and scales should be scrapped off.
- The old loose white wash is removed by rubbing with sand paper. All holes in the wall, irregularities of surface should be filled with lime putty well in advance, so that the surface is dry before white washing.
- If there are oil or grease spot on the surface, they should be rubbed with sand paper and should be given a coat of mixture of rice water and sand, so that the white wash can stick to the surface.
- If the surface is discoloured because of smoke (as in case of kitchens) the surface should be washed with wood ash and water or Multani earth (yellow earth).

3. Application of White Wash

- After preparing the surface the white wash is applied in one coat, two coats or three coats. In case of new surfaces three coats of white wash are required and for old surfaces one or two coats of white wash are sufficient.
- The white washing is done with the help of a jute brush. For each coat one stroke is given from top to bottom and the other from bottom to top over the first stroke and one stroke from the right and other from left over the first stroke.

- Each successive stroke of brush should slightly overlap the preceeding stroke. If only one or two strokes of white wash are to be applied the last coat should be applied with horizontal strokes of the brush.
- Each coat should be allowed to dry before applying the next coat. The finished dry surface of white wash should be smooth and even and it should not come off readily on fingers when rubbed.

11.5 COLOUR WASHING

- The application of colour wash is similar to white wash.
- A colour wash is prepared by adding certain colouring pigments in suitable quantities in the prepared white wash to obtain desired shade of the finished colour wash.
- While using different types of coloured pigments it should be ensured that the colouring pigment is not affected by the presence of lime.
- Before applying colour wash on new surfaces, a coat of white wash should be applied. This coat acts as a primary coat.

Following Table 11.1 shows various types of colour wash and the materials required to be mixed in the white wash.

Table 11.1 : Showing types of colour wash and material mixed in white wash

Type of colour wash	Materials mixed in white wash
1. Buff colour wash	Multani mitti
2. Green colour wash	Solution of boiled mango bark and copper sulphate
3. Blue colour wash	Burnt coconut shells
4. Slate colour wash	Lamp black and copper sulphate
5. Yellow colour wash	Yellow earth
6. Pink colour wash	Vermillion

11.6 DISTEMPERING

- It is a process of applying wash on the surface. But the surface obtained by distempering is much more superior as compared to surface obtained by white washing or colour washing.
- The process of distempering is easy and less costly as compared to process of painting.

1. **The Composition of Distempers**
    - A distemper is composed of a base, glue or casein as binder water as carrier or thinner and suitable quantities of colouring pigments.
    - Distemper is termed as a water paint having whiting as base and water as carrier. Distempers are available in the market in a variety of shades under different trade names in the form of either powder or paste.
    - Distempers are required to be mixed with hot water before use.

Different forms of distempers are :

- White distempers
- Coloured distempers
- Oil bound distempers
- Casein paints.

All the manufacturers of distempers supply complete directions as how to use their products. These guidelines should be strictly followed to get the best results.

2. Process of Distempering

It includes :

- Preparation of surface
- Application of priming coat
- Application of coat of distemper.

(i) The Surface for Distempering is Prepared in the Following Manner

- If the receiving surface is rough, it should be made smooth by rubbing with sand papers.
- The surface should be perfectly dry before applying the distemper. If the surface is damp the distemper coat gets spoiled. If new plaster surface is to be distempered it should be allowed to dry for atleast 2 months.
- The newly lime plastered surface should be washed with a dilute sulphuric acid and left for 24 hrs. and then wall should be thoroughly washed with clean water.
- The new cement plaster surface should be washed with solution of zinc sulphate and should be allowed to dry. If the surface is having efflorescence patches they should be wiped clean with dry cloth before applying the prime coat.
- In case of distempering old surfaces all dust, loose materials, scales etc. are removed by wire brushes. Holes, patches, cracks and surface irregularities should be filled with lime putty or gypsum plaster and allowed to get hard before application of distemper.
- The surface should be thoroughly rubbed with sand paper, washed clean and allowed to dry befor applying the distemper.

(ii) Applying Prime Coat

- After preparation of the surface, a priming coat is applied and left to dry. This coat helps in ensuring good bond between the distemper coat and the surface.
- The prime coat may consists of materials as recommended by the manufacturer of the distemper or whiting in water or milk.

(iii) Application of Distemper

- After applying the prime coat, a coat of good quality distemper should be applied. The prime coat should be allowed to dry completely before distemper coat is applied.

- While applying the distempers the brush should be first applied horizontally and then vertically. Distempers can be applied with the help of spray pistols. On new lime plastered walls 2-3 coats are required over the priming coat. On old lime plastered walls one coat of distemper with priming coat is sufficient.
- Distempers which are used on cement concrete on the external surfaces are manufactured with weather resistant ingredients and therefore distempering coat lasts for longer period.

3. Properties of Distemper

- Distempers are available in the form of oil bound washable paints, washable oil free distempers, non-washable distempers etc. They are available in powder form and in the paste form. Powder distempers are called as dry distempers whereas distempers in the form of paste are known as oil bound distempers. Oil bound distempers are superior than dry distempers. Oil bound distempered surface is washable.
- Distempers are cheaper than paint and varnishes and also cheaper than cost of white wash in the long run. They are water paints and are easier to apply.
- Coating of distempers are comparatively thick and more brittle as compared to other types of water paints.
- The film of distemper is porous in nature and allows the water to pass through it. This property helps the new walls to dry out, without damaging the distemper film.
- Distempers are generally light in colour and provide a good reflective coating.
- They are less durable as compared to oil paints.
- Distempers are available in variety of shades, in powder and paste forms. They can be applied on cement plastered surface, lime plastered surface, brick work, insulating boards etc.
- On drying, the distemper film may lead to cracking and flaking due to shrinkage.
- Distempering gives poor results if the surface is damp.

11.7 PAINTS AND PAINTING   (Dec. 13, May 14, Nov. 15)

Paints are thick fluid materials which are applied over the surfaces of wood work, metal work etc. to provide a thin coating. The process of application of paints is called as painting.

Objects of Paintings

- To protect wood from decaying effects.
- To prevent corrosion in metals.
- To protect the surface from harmful effects of atmospheric agencies.
- To give decorative and attractive appearance to the surfaces and to make it pleasant.
- To render surfaces hygienically safe and clean.
- To provide healthy condition to live in.

Requirements of Good Paint

- It should have good spreading or covering power i.e. it should cover maximum area with minimum paint. The cost of painting depends upon covering power of the paint.

- It should have good consistency so that it can be applied easily and freely on the surface with the help of brush.
- It should be harmless to the user.
- The paint should be cheap.
- It should form a thin uniform film on the painted surface. The film should be hard and durable.
- It should adhere properly to the surface.
- The paint should dry within 24 hrs. after application, but should not dry too rapidly.
- The painted surface should not get affected by atmospheric agencies such as rain, heat, wind etc.
- The paint should give attractive, decorative and pleasant appearance to the surface.
- The colour of the paint should be retained for long time.
- After painting, paint should not show signs of brush marks, shrinkage marks or cracks on the painted surface.
- It should have good fire and moisture resistance.

Ingredients of a Paint

Following are the ingredients of a paint :

- A base
- An inert extender or filler
- A vehicle or carrier
- A drier
- A solvent or thinner
- A colouring pigment.

1. **Base :** A base is a solid substance of a metallic oxide in a fine state of division. It forms the main body of the paint and performs following functions.
   (i) To provide opaque coating which hides the surface to be painted.
   (ii) To make a coating film of paint resistant against abrasion and prevent formation of shrinkage cracks.

Sr. No.	Type of base	Properties and Uses
1.	White lead	Cheapest base and commonly used for ordinary painting work, forms base for lead paint, has great covering power, protective qualities and workability, very poisonous, available in powder and paste form, suitable for wood work painting but not recommended for painting iron work as it does not provide resistance against rusting
2.	Red lead	It is a oxide of lead which is base for lead paints, got excellent properties of rust prevention, toughness and durability. It is available in powder and paste form. Dries very fast and can be used as drier. Used for steel work and as a priming coat for wood work.

...Conti.

3.	Zinc white or Zinc oxide or Zinc sulphate	It is a base for zinc paint. It is non-poisonous transparent, smooth and does not get affected by sulphur fumes. It has got good binding and spreading properties. It is costlier than white lead and less durable and workable. The zinc white film is very hard, brittle and has tendency to crack.
4.	Iron oxide	It is the base for all iron paints. The tink of this base varies from yellowish to brown to black. It is used for the priming coat on structural steel work. It is very effective in preventing rusting of steel. It is cheap and durable and mixes rapidly with the vehicle oil.
5.	Titanium white	It is a oxide of titanium which is bright white in colour. It is non-poisonous and not affected by heat, light or chemicals. It forms opaque coating. It has high oil absorption capacity, high elasticity and great covering properties. It is used as under coat in case of enamel paints.
6.	Aluminium powder	It is the base for all aluminium paints. It is impervious and maintain moisture in the wood which reduces warping and cracking of wood. It is used as priming coat to new wood work.
7.	Lithopone	It is a white substance attained by mixing in equal quantities zinc sulphide and barium sulphate and processing under controlled condition. It is cheap and has good covering capacity. Since it changes colour when exposed to sunlight it is used as a priming coat for interior work.

2. **Vehicles :** It is a liquid substance which is used to keep solid ingredients in suspensions. It performs the following functions :
   - It imparts adhesive property to paint by acting as a binder for solid ingredients.
   - It helps the ingredients to spread evenly on the surface to be painted.
   - Because of vehicles, paint develops an elastic and protective film on the surface after drying.

Following are commonly used vehicles and their properties and uses.

Sr. No.	Type of vehicle	Properties and Uses
1.	Linseed oil	It is commonly used as a vehicle in all oil paints and is extracted from flax seeds. After oxidizing it gets thicker. Linseed oil is clear, pale, transparent, brilliant odourless. It is used in different forms as follows.
	(a) Raw linseed oil	It is thin, odourless, transparent and brilliant. It dries very slowly and therefore used for interior painting work.

...Conti.

	(b)	Boiled linseed oil	It is obtained by boiling the mixture of 10% drier like red lead or litharge and raw linseed oil. It is thicker and darker as compared to raw oil and dries rapidly. But has got lesser penetration power and elasticity. It is basically used for exterior painting work.
	(c)	Pale boiled linseed oil	It has got properties similar to boiled oil but it is not dark in colour. It can be used for light or white coloured paints. It is suitable for painting plastered surface and metal work.
	(d)	Double boiled linseed oil	It has quick drying properties but it is very thick and requires turpentine for thinning purpose. It is colourless and transparent. It is used for painting external work.
	(e)	Stand oil	It is obtained by heating linseed oil. It dries slowly, and gives clean, durable and shining finish.
2.		Tung oil	It is used for superior work as it has got properties superior than linseed oil.
3.		Poppy oil	It is obtained from poppy seeds. It dries very slowly. It is expensive. The colour lasts for longer period. Its raw quality is not suitable for painting work and is mixed with some other materials. It is used for making delicate, light coloured paints.
4.		Nut oil	It is obtained from ordinary walnuts. It is colourless, cheap, quick drying. But less durable. Hence, it is used for temporary painting work for white or light coloured paints.

3. **Extenders or Inert Filler or Adulterants :** These are the cheap inert materials used to alter properties of paints. Their functions are as follows :
- They reduce cost of the base and the cost of painting work.
- They keep other ingredients in suspension.
- They change weight of the paint and reduce rapid setting of paint.
- They increase durability of the paint.
- p They reduce shrinkage and cracking of paint.

The commonly used extenders are Baryte (barium sulphate), Silica, Lithopone, Whiting, Charcoal, Gypsum, Silicate of magnesia, Alumina etc. They should not be used in excess because in that case paint looses its original character and becomes weak.

4. **Drier :** It is a metallic compound and acts as a catalyte and accelerates the process of drying of the paint. It absorbs oxygen from atmosphere and oxidizes the vehicle to become thicker. It adversely affects colour and elasticity of the paints. It is not used in final coat of paints. Various patented driers are available in the market. They are either oil driers or paste driers. Types of oil driers are litharge, magnesium dioxide, magnesium

borates. Paste driers are compounds of lead, cobalt, manganese which are mixed in inert fillers and ground with linseed oil.

5. **Thinner or Solvent :** It is liquid which is added to the paint to obtain derived consistency so that the paint can be applied easily on the surface. It helps the paint to penetrate through the porous surface. It improves spreading properties of paint. It evaporates after application and surface becomes more even and smooth. For oil paints Turpentine is generally used as a thinner. It is inflammable, volatile and colourless liquid. It gets affected by weather and should be used for interior work. White spirit and naptha are also used as thinner in place of turpentine.

6. **Colouring Pigments :** It is added in white paints to get different shades of colour when the desired colour of paint is different from the colour of base. For white, black and other dark shades of paints are obtained by selecting base of specific colours. The other desired shade may be obtained by using single or combination of colouring pigments.

Table 11.2 : Colouring pigments for paints

Sr. No.	Desired colour of paint	Pigment used
1.	Blue	Indigo blue, pursian blue, cobalt blue, ultramarine blue
2.	Brown	Burnt umber, raw umber, burnt sienna
3.	Black	Lamp black, ivory black, graphite, vegetable black
4.	Green	Chrome green, copper sulphate, emerald green, green earth
5.	Yellow	Chrome yellow, raw sienna, yellow ochre, zinc chromate, barium chromate
6.	Red	Cormine, red lead, vermilion red, venetian red, Indian red.

Types of Paints

There are different types of paints available in the market in different forms and in different colour shades. The selection of the paint is governed by various factor such as nature of material required to be painted, nature of surface, properties of paints, climatic conditions etc. Following are the types of paints used for painting work :

1. **Aluminium Paint :** This type of paint is produced by mixing aluminium powder in quick drying spirit or slow drying oil. After application of paint spirit or oil evaporates leaving behind a coating of aluminium powder on the surface. Aluminium paint is used for painting wood work, metal work, hot water pipes, gas tanks, electricity poles, storage tanks etc.

It has got the following qualities :

- It protects iron and steel from corrosion.
- It has high electric resistance.
- It has good weather resisting and water proofing properties.

- Because of its shining colour it is visible in darkness.
- It has high spreading capacity.
- It offers resistance against effects of marine water.

2. **Anticorrosive Paints :** This type of paint is used to protect structural steel work against the adverse effects of weather, fumes, acids, corrosive chemicals etc. This paint is used for external work. It is very cheap, lasts for longer period and black in colour.

3. **Asbestos Paint :** This paint mainly consists of fibrous asbestos as one of the ingredients. It is used for stopping leakage of metal roofs and painting gutters, spouts, flashing etc. This paint is used as damp proof coat over the outer surface of the basement walls. This paint resists effects of water, acid and steam. This paint protects metal fittings from rusting.

4. **Bituminous Paint :** These paints are produced by dissolving bitumen or tar in naptha or petroleum. This paint is black in colour but colour can be modified by adding certain coloured pigments. These paints are alkali resistant and have high covering capacity. These paints are used for painting structural steel work under water.

5. **Bronze Paint :** This paint is produced by mixing aluminium bronze or copper bronze in suitable vehicle. This paint is reflective in nature hence used for painting radiators. The paint is used for painting internal and external metallic surfaces.

6. **Cellulose Paint :** It is prepared from celluloid sheets, nitro cotton and photographic films. This paint hardens by evaporation of thinner unlike other types of paint which get hardened by oxidation. This paint dries very quickly and provides flexible, hard and smooth surface. The painted surface can be washed and cleaned very easily. The paint remains unaffected under very hot and cold conditions and also when the surface comes in contact with hot water, smoke or acidic atmosphere. This paint is superior than other types of oil paints and therefore used for painting aeroplanes, cars and other superior work.

7. **Cement Paint :** The base of cement paint is white or coloured cement. This paint is available in various shades and in powder form. Cement paint has better water proofing qualities. It has good strength, hardness, density and durability. It offers excellent decorative appearance to the surface. This paint can be used for painting plastered surfaces, concrete surfaces, corrugated iron sheets etc.

8. **Emulsion Paint :** The main ingredient of this type of paint is a vehicle polyvenyl acetate or synthetic resins such as chlorinated rubber. This paint can be applied easily. It has got excellent alkali resistance. This paint dries very quickly and has good workability and high durability. The painted surface can be cleaned by washing with water.

9. **Enamel Paint :** This paint is obtained by mixing metallic oxide (white lead or zinc white) with petroleum spirit having resinous matter in solution form. Different colouring pigments are added to get desired colour. This paint dries slowly and produces a very hard, impervious, glossy, elastic, smooth and durable film over the surface being painted.

It is not affected by water, steam, acids, alkalies and other atmospheric agents. It can be used for external as well as internal surfaces.

10. **Plastic Paint :** This paint has various types of plastics as base material. Plastic paints are available in market in variety of shades and under different trade names. This paint is attractive, quick drying and has good covering power. This paint is used for painting commercially important buildings.

11. **Rubber Paint :** This paint is prepared by dissolving synthetic resins in suitable solvents. This paint dries quickly and little affected by moisture, atmosphere, sunlight, alkalies etc. This paint is cheap and can be used for painting cement or lime plastered surfaces.

12. **Silicate Paint :** It is produced by mixing calcium and finely ground silica with various materials. It produces a very hard and durable film on painted surface. It has good qualities of adhesion and there is no action of alkalies. It can be applied to brick work, plastered and concrete surfaces.

13. **Oil Paint :** These paints are made with one of the bases and pigments, described earlier, mixed with linseed oil. They are generally applied in three coats.

   - A thin coat of priming after the surface is prepared.
   - The second or undercoat is of the same material as used for finishing coat.
   - The final coat is usually of white zinc mixed with linseed oil and some pigment. A little turpentine is also added to accelerate drying of the paint. Each coat is applied only when the previous coat is fully dried.

11.8 VARNISHES   (May 14)

- The essential constituent of all varnishes is "resin" or rosin which is dissolved in oils, turpentine or alcohol. The liquid dries or evaporates and leaves a hard transparent, glossy film on the vanished surface.

- There are various types of varnishes obtainable in the market each suited to a specific work. The preparation of varnishes is a difficult matter, and it is best to purchase readymade.

- Varnish dries quickly and gives a hard and tough coating. Painted surfaces are also varnished to brighten them.

- *Water varnishes* are used for painting paper surfaces.

- *Oil varnishes are* used for interior or exterior works. Superfine Copal varnish is considered to be the best as it produces a higher gloss and smoother finish.

- Copal varnish is made from the fossil resins (the copals) which are found in several parts of the world and in many different grades of quality. English copal is considered to be the best. If the varnish is too thick, spirits of turpentine can be added.

- *Spirit varnishes:* Shellac varnish and French polish belong to this class.

- Resins used for preparation of varnishes are generally obtained from gums of various trees. The most common being Shellac, Gum, Arabic, Rosin, Amber.

11.9 WALL CLADDING   (Nov. 16, May 15,17)

- Wall tiling or cladding is a process of finishing the surface with tiles.
- They are fixed upto a height of 1.25 m above the floor level or upto ceiling, in passages, bath rooms, swimming pools, kitchens, staircases, boiler rooms, fire places and sometimes on exterior of building for decorative effect or protection from atmospheric agents. They make the wall non-absorbent and easy to clean.
- The tiles used are either of terra cotta, faience, china clay, natural stones like marble. Faience is similar to terra cotta but it is twice fired.
- These tiles are available in variety of colours and thicknesses. They are rectangular, square, rounded or corner type.
- For cladding, the surface of the wall is first plastered with cement mortar in usual manner and then the tiles, which are immersed in water for atleast one hour are covered with a paste of neat cement on back and laid flat against the wall surface true to line and plumb and pressed with light strokes of a wooden mallet. The joints should be as thin as possible.

Table 11.3 : Showing different materials and its uses in the content of wall claddings

Sr. No.	Description of wall finishes	Use
1.	Chettinad/brick tiles	Decorative for both interior and exterior walls.
2.	Clay/ceramic tiles	Doors in kitchen, wash areas and toilets, skirting in rooms with tiled floors.
3.	Mossaic tiles	Doors in kitchen, wash areas and toilets, skirting in rooms with tiled floors.
4.	FRP boards (Fibre Reinforced Plastic)	Maintenance fee, pre-painted boards for wall panelling.
5.	Glass tiles/sheets	Decorative finish for walls.
6.	Laminates	Decorative finish for wood and wood-based materials.
7.	Mirror	Reflective, decorative finish used to create an illusion of space and also used at corridor corners.
8.	Gypsum board	Bonded plaster board for interior walls.
9.	PVC sheets	Maintenance free, pre-painted wall panels, skirting and cladding.
10.	Natural stone cuddapah, granite, kotah.	Marble granite is used for interior wall as decorative finish. All natural stones can be used for external cladding.
11.	Reflective acrylic	It is used to create an illusion of space and at corridor corners.
12.	Rigid polyurethane panels	Panels available with several decorative facings for interior walls.

...Conti.

13.	Cork tiles/sheets	Decorative finish for wood/plastered wall. Good acoustic material.
14.	Coir mats, jute mats.	Fixed an wooden frame into interior walls.
15.	Wall fabrics velvet, suede.	Fixed with an adhesive.

11.10 WALL PAPERING   (Dec. 14)

- In this process, paper is pasted on internal surface and ceiling and aesthetics of the room is improved. The papers which are used for wall papering are (a) Satin paper, (b) Common or pulp paper, (c) Flock paper.
- While carrying out papering work, first the surface is cleaned and made smooth by rubbing the surface and scrapping it properly to remove dust, white wash and colour wash.
- Adhesive paste is prepared by mixing flour, glue and water. This paste is applied thoroughly and uniformly on back of the paper and the paper is pasted on the wall. The paper is finished smooth with a roller covered with clean flannel.

11.11 GLAZING WORK

- Glazing means fixing glass panels in frames of door and window made up of iron, steel or wood. A frame is an assembly of horizontal and vertical members which are placed at top, sides and bottom of an opening and form an enclosure to act as support for a door or a window.
- Glass panels which are cut to required dimensions are secured in place means of putty or wooden moulds. The glass panels are fixed in 15 mm rebate of the wooden frame leaving a gap of 1.5 mm all around for expansions.
- The putty is produced by mixing finely powdered whiting and linseed oil and kneading into a stiff paste. This putty is first applied on back side and glass panel is fixed in position with the help of small steel rails.
- Putty is then applied on the front side. It is pressed and finished properly to get a smooth surface. When large panels or plate glasses are required to be fixed, they are first placed in rebate by moulded wooden fillets all around with brass or nickel screws, inserting a strip of felt or rubber in the rebate under the glass which act as cushion.

Difference between Plastering and Painting

Plastering	Painting
1. It consists of application thin layer of mixture of binding material (such as lime, cement, mud), fine sand and water.	1. It consists of application of coating of fluid material on masonry wooden or metallic material.
2. Thickness of plaster ranges between 3 mm to 25 mm.	2. Thickness of paint is in microns.
3. After plastering curing is essential.	3. No curing is required.

REVIEW QUESTIONS

1. State step by step procedure for three coat sand faced plaster. Assume thickness of plaster is 25 mm. State specific thickness and care required for each coat.
2. State the types of defects in oil painting work and cause for the type of defect. Enlist types of paints used for metal surfaces.
3. State step by step procedure to provide three coat sand faced plaster to B.B. masonry.
4. State step by step procedure to apply paint on a new wood work.
5. Write down the objectives of plastering. What is ground work for plaster ?
6. State different market names of paints. Explain defects in painting.
7. What are the objectives of plastering ? Name the various types of plasters and mention the requirements of a good plaster.
8. Explain the various types of paints which are readily available in the market in various colours.
9. Write note on : Wax polishing,
10. Explain preparation of surface for plastering. Describe defects in painting.
11. State different materials used for wall cladding finishes. Write down the functions of base in a paint.
12. Describe the method of painting in detail. Explain defects in painting.
13. State different building finishes. Explain defects in plastering.
14. What is pointing ? Explain defects in plastering.
15. Differentiate between the following :
    (a) Plastering and painting,
    (b) Distempers and paints.
16. Describe the different tools used in plastering with sketches.
17. Explain "Wall cladding" with material used and method of fixing.
18. Enlist the types of plasters and explain cement plaster.
19. Write notes on :
    (a) Varnishing   (b) Wall papering

SOLVED UNIVERSITY QUESTIONS

DEC. 2013

1. State objectives of plastering and explain defects in painting.   [7]
   [**Ans.:** Refer Article 11.2, 11.7]
2. State market names of paints. Explain defects in plastering.   [7]
   [**Ans.:** Refer Article 11.7]

MAY 2014

1. Write a short note on Painting and Varnishing   [6]
   [**Ans.:** Refer Article 11.7, 11.8]

DEC. 2014

1. Write short notes on: [7]
   (i)   Wall papering   (ii) Quarter turn stair
   [**Ans.:** Refer Article (i) 11.10, (ii) 10.4(9)]

MAY 2015

1. Enlist types of pointing and explain any three types of pointing with figures.   [7]
   [**Ans.:** Refer Article 11.3]
2. Draw the figures showing different types of pointing.   [7]
   [**Ans.:** Refer Article 11.3]
3. Write a short note on Wall cladding.   [6]
   [**Ans.:** Refer Article 11.9]

NOV. 2015

1. State the objectives of plastering.   [4]
   [**Ans.:** Refer Article 11.2]
2. Write short notes on : Painting to new work   [6]
   [**Ans.:** Refer Article 11.7]
3. Explain the following : Defects in plastering   [6]
   [**Ans.:** Refer Article 11.2]

MAY 2016

1. Define protective coatings. Explain defects in plastering.   [6]
   [**Ans.:** Refer Article 11.1, 11.2]

NOV. 2016

1. Explain with neat sketch the defects in plastering.   [6]
   [**Ans.:** Refer Article 11.2]
2. Write a short note on : Wall cladding-materials and methods.   [6]
   [**Ans.:** Refer Article 11.9]

MAY 2017

1. Enlist various types of plastering and explain lime plaster in detail.   [6]
   [**Ans.:** Refer Article 11.2, 11.2 (3)]
2. Write a short note on wall cladding.   [6]
   [**Ans.:** Refer Article 11.9]

CHAPTER 12
MISCELLANEOUS MATERIALS

12.1 INTRODUCTION

- In previous units, some of the materials used in the construction are studied in detail viz. stone, bricks etc. along with characteristics, uses, occurrence etc.

- The present chapter will deal with miscellaneous materials, their properties, types and uses etc.

12.2 LIME

- It is a good-old cementing material the traces of which were found in ancient civilizations.

- In all historical constructions, prior to 20th century before advent of cement in 1852) such as Taj Mahal, Kutub Minar, many palaces and even in forts, lime had been used as binding material.

- Many big projects such as masonry dams, bridges were constructed using mortar with lime as its binding constituent.

12.2.1 Classification of Lime - is - 712 - 1984 (Third Revision)

Class	Uses
A – Eminently hydraulic uses	Structural work under water.
B – Semi-hydraulic	Superior masonry work.
C– Fat lime	Finishing coat, Plastering - white or colour washing.
D – Dolomite lime (magnesium)	Plaster - white wash.
E – Kankar lime	Masonry work.
F – Siliceous dolomite	Last and last but one finishing coat of plaster.

12.2.2 Manufacturing of Lime

(a) Calcination :

- Quick lime is the product of calcination i.e. heating to redness of limestone with major proportion of calcium carbonate ($CaCO_3$) and minor proportion of magnesium carbonate ($MgCO_3$).

- The calcination evaporates the water in the stone and after chemical dissociation CO_2 is liberated out; leaving oxides of calcium and magnesium. It is amorphous in nature, highly caustic and possesses great affinity to moisture.

(b) Slaking of Lime :

- *Slaked lime* or *hydrate of lime* is obtained by adding sufficient amount of water to quick lime. Quick lime cracks with hissing sound, swells and falls into the powder form and becomes calcium hydrate $Ca(OH)_2$.

- Considerable amount of heat is liberated during the process. In the same manner, as that of quick lime, it can be used as putty or paste but it does not require a long seasoning period.

(c) Artificial Hydraulic Lime : Hydraulic lime has more strength than pure lime but if it is unavailable then quick lime can be converted into hydraulic lime by :

1. Calcining Lime by Adding 20 to 30% of Clayey Matter :

- Pure lime, obtained as product of calcination of lime stone, is powdered and clayey matter in the range of 20 to 30% is added alongwith a minimum quantum of water.

- Balls of about 25 mm size made from above mixture and dried. These are calcined once again and calcium and aluminium silicates having hydraulic property are formed.

- The burnt balls of these twice kilned lime are ground into fine powder i.e. artificial hydraulic lime.

2. Addition of Pozzolanic Materials : Silicons and aluminous minerals on their own do not possess cementitious properties. But when mixed with lime, they react in presence of water and form calcium silicates and aluminates having hydraulic properties.

    (a) Natural pozzolans : Clays, shales, volcanic ash etc.

    (b) Artificial pozzolans : Surkhi, fly ash.

Properties of Pozzolans :

- Increase in workability and resistance to chemical attack.
- Reduction in shrinkage and heat of hydration.
- Quick setting and hardening.

(a) Surkhi :

- Extremely fine, burnt brick powder is known as Surkhi. When it is sieved through I.S. sieve no. 320, it must pass through the sieve. And minimum 50% of this passed material, should pass through I.S. sieve no. 160; so as to have control on percentage of sand.

- Surkhi from well burnt, over burnt and under burnt bricks is mixed with lime in same proportions to have three different grades. Balls of each designated mix are kept under water for gaining strength and then crushed, which will give the better judgement about surkhi.

- Surkhi and lime gives good strength to be mortar. The proportion 2 : 1 can be used for masonry work internal plaster etc.

(b) Fly Ash :
- Fine, light powder obtained as waste product of coal burning in thermal plant, rail locomotives, boilers etc. with rich content of Silica and Alumina.
- It is also to be sieved through I.S. 320. Mix proportion 3 : 1 to be used for internal plaster.

12.2.3 Characteristics of Classified Lime As Per is 712 - 1984

- **Class A :** Eminently hydraulic lime in hydrated form. Lime sand mortar in proportion 1 : 3 gives minimum compressive strength of 17.5 kgf/cm^2 and 28.0 kgf/cm^2 at the end of 14 days and 28 days, respectively.
- **Class B :** Semi-hydraulic lime, may be in the form of quick lime or hydrated form. Minimum strength in compression is 12.5 kgf/cm^2 and 17.5 kgf/cm^2 at 14 days and 28 days.
- **Class C :** Fat lime, can be supplied in both form i.e. quick lime or hydrated form can be used for producing artificial hydraulic mortars with surkhi.
- **Class D :** Dolomite lime, available in both forms.
- **Class E :** It is a kankar lime, available only in hydrated form.
- **Class F :** Silicous dolomite lime in both forms.

12.2.4 Uses

Civil Engineering and allied industries are using lime in many aspects such as :
- Mortar for brick and stone masonry.
- Lean lime - concrete mix in foundations and flooring.
- Plastering and white washing.
- In manufacturing of cement, paint, artificial stone, sand - lime bricks, tiles etc.
- Stabilization of soil etc.

Also lime is popularly used by other industries in many ways as :
- For metal processing works etc.
- As a refractory material it is used in kilns.
- As a chemical in petroleum refining, sugar industry, water - sewage treatment plants etc.

12.2.5 Properties

Chemical and Physical properties of lime :

Table 12.1

	Class A Hydraulic	Class B Semi-hydraulic	Class C Fat Lime	Class D Magnesium Lime	Class E Kankar Lime	Cement
(A) Chemical Properties :						
(1) Max. % of CaO and MgO	60%	70%	85%	85%	85%	63% + 2.5%

...Conti.

(2)	Impurity % (silica, alumina and ferric oxides - min.	25%	15%				22 + 6 + 3%
(3)	Insoluble matter	5% max.	5% max.	5% max.	5% min.	5% max.	< 4%
(B)	**Physical Properties :**						
(1)	Fineness Test :						
•	Residue on 850 micron IS sieve	Σ 5%	Σ 5%	Nil on IS 300	$\geq$ 5%	Σ 5%	Σ 10% on IS 90
•	Passing through IS 850 retained on 300	Σ 10%	Σ 10%	Nil	< 5%	Nil	
(2)	Setting :						
•	In presence of	Water	Water	Air	Air	Water	Water
•	Initial setting time	< 2 hrs.		–	–	> 2 hrs.	© 30 min.
•	Final setting time	Σ 2 days	7 days	–	–	Σ 2 days	Σ 10 hrs.
(3)	Transverse strength	Modulus of rupture on 25 × 25 × 100 mm sample in kgf/cm^2 at the age of 28 days.					
		© 10.5	© 7	–	–	© 7	–
(4)	Min. compressive strength 1 : 3 - lime mortar cubes 28 days (kgf/cm^2)	28	17.5	–	–	17.5	160 at 3 days
(5)	Soundness	Expansion measured on the Le-Chateliers's apparatus.					
		Σ 10 mm	Σ 10 mm	–	–	Σ 10 mm	Σ 10 mm
(6)	• Slaking	Difficultly	Slowly	–	Vigorously	Slowly	
•	Heat and noise	Nil	Little	–	Much heat and noise	–	More
•	Increase in volume	Slight	Slight	–	2 to 3 times	–	Less

The synonymous terms Plastic and Synthetic Resins denote synthetic organic high Polymers.

"The process in which a large number of small molecules (monomers) linking together to form a large molecule (polymer) under specific conditions of temperature, pressure and catalyst is known as polymerization".

12.3 PLASTIC/POLYMERS   (Nov. 16)

- It is an organic material of high molecular weight which is plastic at some particular stage of their manufacture, hence can be moulded into required shape.
- Natural substances like coal, petroleum, cellulose are the major constituents and binders are resins or cellulose derivatives.
- The chemical process of manufacturing is condensation or polymerization whereas physical processes worked out are - moulding (compression, injection, transfer and cold moulding), extruding, laminating, blowing, machining and cementing.
- Compounds used are binders, fillers, plasticizer, solvents/catalysts, pigments, lubricants etc.

Broad Classification :

1. **Thermoplastics :** These are softened under application of heat and regain the original properties during solidification, without any chemical change. Hence, moulding and remoulding by applying pressure is possible.
2. **Thermosetting Plastics :** When heated, chemical changes occur and solidify even when hot. Not possible to reshape them as no appreciable softening is seen on heating.

Following **Thermoplastic Resins** have different applications in building construction industry:

Sr. No.	Name	Properties	Applications
1.	Acrylics	Clarity, transparency, softer than glass, optimum combination of flexibility and rigidity, can have any colour combination, readily formed into any shape.	Transparent windows, parts of lighting equipments, decorative panels.
2.	Acrylonitrile Butadiene Styrene (ABS)	Tough, hard, chemically resistant resins.	Pipes and fittings.
3.	Polycarbonate	Excellent transparency, high resistance to impact, good resistance to weathering.	Safety glazing, (with interlayer of polyvinyl butyral) general illumination.
4.	Polyethylene	Flexible, waxy, translucent, partly crystalline.	Insulating material for wires, corrosion proof lining for tanks.
5.	Polypropylene	Harder, stronger, more temperature resistant.	Water cisterns for water closets.

...Conti.

6.	Polyvinyl Fluoride	Inertness to chemical attack, weathering.	Thin film overlays for exposed building boards.
7.	Polyvinyl Formal Resins	Tough, water resistant.	Insulating enamel for electric wires.
8.	Vinyl Chloride Polymers and Copolymers	Hard, rigid but can be plasticized, abrasion resistance.	Insulation, floor coverings (i.e. tiles), tubing, pipes.
9.	Vinylidene Chloride	Highly resistant to inorganic chemicals, organic solvents, impervious to water on prolonged immersion.	Where less impact, shock resistance is required.
10.	Polystyrene	Light weight, ease in moulding, less expensive, good dimensional stability, negligible water absorption, resistance to chemicals.	Light weight concrete.
11.	Thermoplastic Resins	With marble chips and similar aggregate for decorating elements.	Finish, protective coat.
12.	Polyimide	Impact, abrasion resistance, chemical resistant.	Coating to wires.

Cellulose Derivatives : It is naturally occurring polymer in woody plant tissues, cotton etc. Oldest plastic is cellulose nitrate.

Sr. No.	Name	Properties	Applications
1.	Cellulose Acetate (C.A.)	Provides basis of safety films, may be hard - rigid and soft - flexible.	For temporary enclosures of buildings during construction (when reinforced with wire mesh).
2.	Cellulose Acetate Butyrate	Softer and flexible than cellular acetate but has good impact resistant.	Tubing is used as irrigation and gas lines.
3.	Ethyl Cellulose	High impact, toughness.	Same as in case of C.A.
4.	Cellulose Nitrate	Tough, high impact strength.	Commercial photographic film, commercial leaquer for furniture.

Thermosetting Plastics : Following thermosetting plastics have different aplications in construction industry.

Sr. No.	Name	Properties	Applications
1.	Polyster Resins	Water resistant.	Thermosetting concrete with other fillers like gravel, quartz, stone dust, fly ash etc.
2.	Phenol Formaldehyde	Hard rigid, glossy surface, does not burn readily and does not support combustion, light weight.	Electrical field, decoration, thermal applications.

3.	Epoxy and Polyster Resins	Resistance to thermal and mechanical shocks. Adhesion to various materials.	Combinations with copper, brass, steel, aluminium, are used at appropriate places and for concrete is in (1).
4.	Polyster Moulding Materials	Compounded with fibres (like glass).	Putties and premixes.
5.	Melamine Formaldehyde Materials	Unaffected by organic solvents, oils, weak acids and alkalies, less water absorption, flame resistant.	Electrical accessories.
6.	Polyurethane	Thermal insulation, occupancy in irregular shapes.	Clear or colour coatings and finishes for floors, walls, furniture, its rubber form is employed for sprayed or troweled on roofing.
7.	Alkyds - (Alongwith Fillers)	High impact strength.	Electrical appliances.
8.	Urea Formaldehyde	Opaque colour, light fastness, resistance to organic solvents, mild acid and alkalies.	Not recommended for continuous water exposures.
9.	Silicons	Inert, durable, difficult to mould, low water absorption.	Moisture resistance to walls, base for paints.

Typical Applications of Composites :

- **Fibre Reinforced Polymer Plastics :** Made from fibre glass reinforced plastics.
  Characteristics : High strength, light weight, weather resistant, fire resistant, opaque, hence they compete with wood products.
- **Aluminium Plastic - Paper Composite Boards :**
  Characteristics : High strength, ease in installation and maintenance, excellent heat insulation, impact resistance etc.
  Applications : In case of exterior applications and to have light weight for structures.
- **Coir Polymer Composite :**
  Characteristics : Made from coir fibre, strong, rigid, flame retardant, eco-friendly, economic, flexible, ease in working, easy nailing etc.
  Applications : Substitute for wooden furniture decor, masonry etc.
- **Jute Fibre Polyster Composite :**
  Characteristics : Adequate tensile strength, impact strength, weather resistance etc.
  Applications : Tiles, shutter, sanitary units.
- **Unplasticized PVC Pipes :**
  Characteristics : Ecofriendly i.e. recycling is possible, adequate acid/alkali resistance.
  Applications : Bath/W.C. pipe, pipe fittings etc.

- **Fibre Reinforced Polymer (Plastics) :**
  Characteristics : Energy efficient, mouldable, highly aesthetics, strong, weather resistant.
  Applications : External cladding, roofing, ceiling, flooring etc.
- **Non-conventional Concretes :**
  Polymer cement concrete : Polymer fills up gaps/voids in concrete and makes it dense. Imparts more compressive strength, fatigue resistance, impact resistance, acid alkali resistant.
- **Polymer Impregnated Concrete :** Obtained by impregnating precast cured hydrated concrete with low viscosity monomer (methyl methecrylate) and polymerized in situ. Creep reduces almost to zero value and elastic modulus is twice that of ordinary concrete. Used for beams, prestressed members, slabs, sewers, pipes etc.

12.4 MASTIC GROUP

Mastic gum (pistacia lentiscus) is a large irregular evergreen shrub grown as patio tree and hedge. Mastic may be used for waterproofing, foundation treatments or caulking compounds.

Glazing and Caulking Compounds (Mastic) : The compounds used for sealing are caulking compounds and the compounds used to seal glass are glazing compounds (one of the representative caulking compounds).

Asphalt, mastic, vegetable impregnated tar are used for the said purpose.

Properties for Caulking/Glazing Group :

- Adherence to surface, workability under considerable range of temperature, tough, elastic, good movement capability, ability to recover, low sensitivity to water, good service performance.
- The mastic group includes linseed oil putty, mastic glazing compounds, asphalt and polybutene caulking compounds.
- Mastics have recovery of 0 to 10% whereas electromastics (butyl caulks) have recovery of 10 to 49%.
- Linseed oil putty is made by mixing very finely ground calcium carbonate with raw linseed oil. It hardens easily. Its life can be extended by priming the sash before glazing and frequent painting. It has no practical elongation value.
- Some additions are responsible to have longer elastic life for mastic compound such as drying and non-drying oils, drier, solvent, mineral stabilizer, filler etc.

12.5 GYPSUM   (Dec. 14)

- A hydrated calcium sulphate ($CaSO_4 \cdot 2H_2O$) which is crystalline in nature with colourless transparent crystals.
- When finely ground gypsum is heated at temperature of about 165°C, it loses about 14.7% (Total 21%) of its water content and the product thus obtained is plaster of paris which is semi-hydrate of calcium sulphate. Again after adding water it solidifies within three to four minutes.

This Gypsum plaster is used for various purposes :

- As fire resisting material.
- Insulator of heat and sound.
- False ceiling.
- Internal lining of walls.
- Phospho-gypsum tiles.
- Decorative articles.
- As raw material in manufacturing of cement (to control its setting time).
- Manufacturing of blocks.

12.6 CLAY TILES

Clay or Pottery Tiled Floor : Available in many forms i.e. square, hexagonal or any other shape, size, thickness. Employed for any type of building with pleasing appearance, durability, ease in maintenance as inherent qualities.

Clay Tiles : Ecofriendly, fire resistant, uniform, durable, cheap, low weight are the characteristics of clay tiles. Use of locally available clay for production is a money generative aspect for skilled/unskilled labours. These are preferred for roofing with proper overlap so also for flooring. (Refer other types in same chapter).

- **Merits :** Decorative, non-absorbent, quick installation.
- **Demerits :** Initial cost is more, slippery surface.

12.7 GLAZED WARE

Many categories lie under this but most important in buildings are glazed tiles.

Glazed Tiles : The tile shall confirm to all specifications as per IS 777 – 1970.

Characteristics : Flat, free from cracks, crazy spots, chipped edges and corners. The appearance is glossy or matt finished with uniform colour shade or decor pattern.

Normal Sizes : 150 × 150, 100 × 100, 200 × 100 mm etc. Tolerance limit ± 1 mm for facial dimension and for thickness (5 to 6 mm), it is ± 0.5 mm.

Application : Dado in W.C., bath, kitchen etc.

12.8 TIMBER   (Dec. 14, Nov. 15, 16, May 17)

- Timber is a natural, good old material suitable for building, carpentary or other engineering purposes.
- As per old English it means "to construct or build". At many locations it can be appropriately used such as beams, trusses, rafters, joists in floors, door-window shutters and frames, staircases, poles, piles, columns, partition, furniture etc.
- The natural wood-timber as a living tree is known as **standing timber**. The timber obtained after falling a tree is known as **rough timber** and the one which is sawn and cut to suit the need is known as **converted timber**.

- Day-by-day, its use is decreasing due to scarcity, high cost of labour and timber and availability of relatively cheaper and stronger material.

Classification of Timber : Timber is classified according to :

(a) Growth of Tree :

- *Exogeneous* i.e. outward growing trees. Distinct consecutive rings are formed in the horizontal section of such trees known as annual rings. Further, it can be divided into two categories conifers and deciduous, Soft - Chir, Deodar, Fir, Pine, Spruce etc. Hard - Babul, Oak, Sal, Teak, Mahagony etc.
- Endogeneous or inward growing trees, such as palms, canes and bamboos.

(b) Durability : Indicative average life of group of trees.

(c) Strength :

(d) Refractiveness : Indicating resistance to defects during seasoning.

12.8.1 I.S. 399 - 1963 Classification

1. **Zonal :** Depending upon the zonal division of India i.e. North, South, East, West, Central.

2. **Uses :** Depending upon classification for timber uses are as follows.

   - Construction,
   - Furniture and cabinet making,
   - Light packing cases,
   - Heavy packing cases,
   - Agricultural implements and tools,
   - Turnery articles and toys,
   - Veneers and plywoods.

3. **Availability :** Depending upon the quantum available per year the classification is as under :

   - X – Most common with quantity $\geq$ 1000 tonnes/yr.
   - Y – Common with quantity 250 to 1000 tonnes/yr.
   - Z – Less common with quantity < 250 tonnes/yr.

4. **Durability and Strength :** If the trees are susceptible to various actions due to fungi, insects, chemicals, physical and mechanical agencies then the strength is less, there by it will indicate a less durable tree.

   - Class I   – average life $\geq$ 120 months.
   - Class II   – average life 60 to 119 months.
   - Class III – average life < 60 months.

Table 11.2 : Safe working stresses and other properties for Indian Timbers
Commonly used : Standard grade

Trade Name	Ave. Wt. kg/m³	Modulus of Elasticity T/cm² All grades	Bending and tension along grain extreme fibre stress			Shear stress all locations		Compressive stress Parallel to grain			Compressive stress Perpendicular grain			Durability Grade or Class
			Inside Location	Outside Location	Wet Location	Horizontal	Along grain	Location	Out-side Location	Wet Location	Inside Location	Out-side Location	Wet Location	
1. Babul or Kikar	835	108	182	154	124	15.4	22.2	112	102	80	65.5	50.5	41.5	III
2. Benteak	675	110	138	112	92	9.2	13.0	88	78	64	41.5	32.5	26.0	I
3. Blue Pine	515	68	66	56	50	5.6	8.0	52	46	38	17.0	13.5	10.5	III
4. Chir	575	98	84	70	60	6.4	9.2	64	56	46	22.5	17.5	14.0	III
5. Deodar	560	95	102	88	70	7.0	10.2	78	70	56	26.5	23.0	17.0	I
6. Fir, Partal	465	94	78	66	56	6.0	8.4	60	52	42	16.0	12.5	10.5	III
7. Haldir	675	91	138	112	92	9.4	13.4	84	74	64	36.5	28.0	23.0	III
8. Kail	515	68	66	56	50	5.6	8.0	52	46	38	17.0	13.5	10.5	III
9. Sal	800	127	168	140	112	9.4	13.4	106	94	78	45.5	35.0	29.0	I
10. Spruce	480	92	78	66	52	6.0	8.4	56	50	42	17.0	13.7	10.5	III
11. Teak	625	96	140	116	94	9.8	14.0	88	78	64	40.0	31.0	25.5	I
12. Walnut	575	91	116	94	78	8.4	12.0	66	70	50	23.0	18.5	15.0	III

5. **Refractiveness :** It indicates resistance to defects during seasoning of timber.

   (a) Class A (Highly Refractive) : Timber which while air seasoning is not prone for development of any defect, fall under this category.

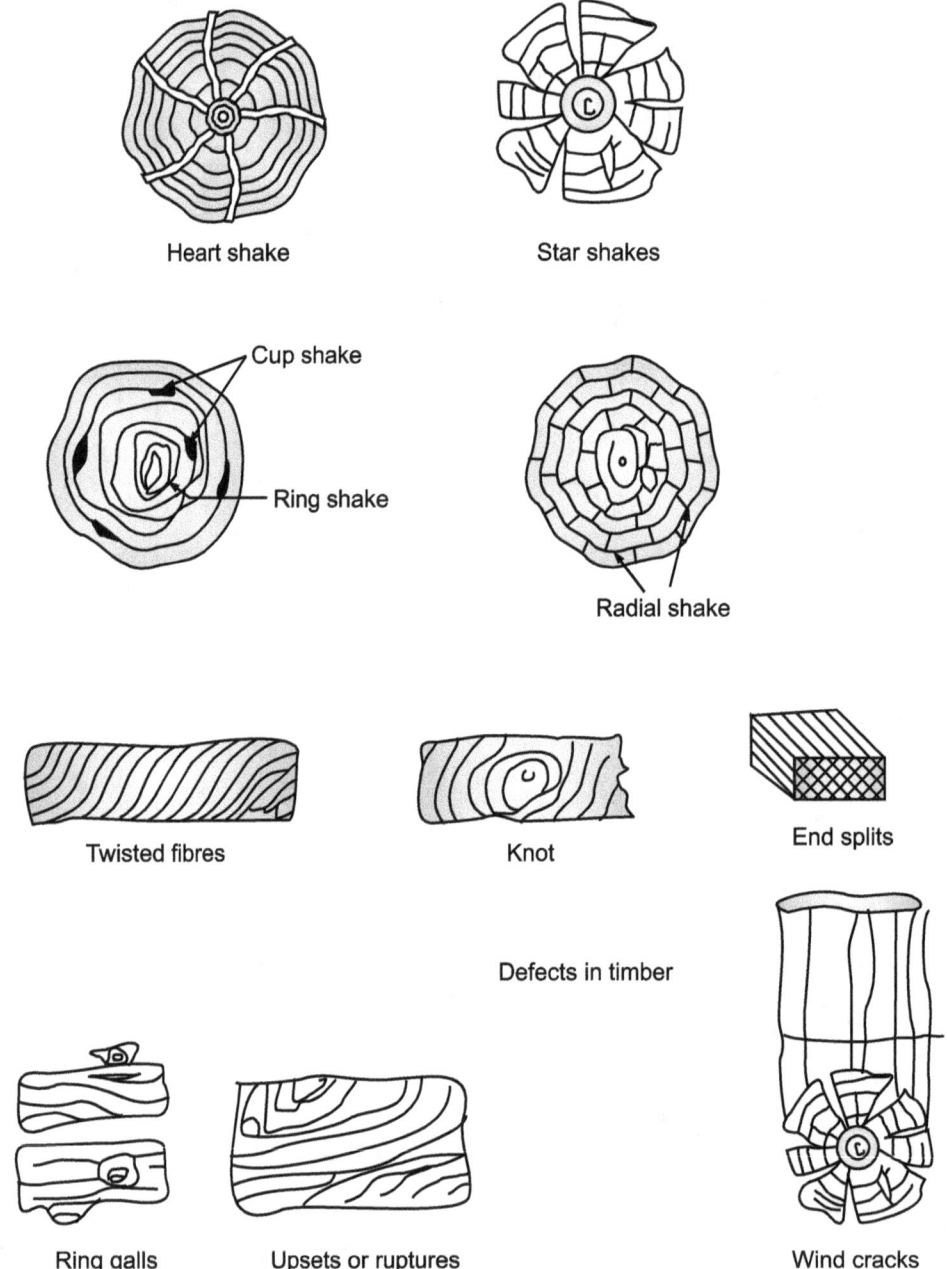

Fig. 12.1 : Defects - Diseases - Decay of timber

   (b) Class B (Moderately Refractive) : Timbers under this class can be seasoned with appropriate precautions against rapid drying; e.g. Teak, Sheesam etc.

(c) Class C (Low Refractive) : These require special precautions during seasoning.

In general for a good timber, it must exhibit following properties viz. strength, durability, weather resistance, fire resistance, elasticity, workability, toughness and resistance to wear, sufficient weight, uniform structure, hardness, compact, dark colour, straight fibres, shiny appearance, sweet smell, good sound when struck etc.

12.8.2 Defects - Diseases - Decay of Timber   (Dec. 14, Nov. 15, May 15,16)

Depending upon soil texture, fertility and climate some natural defects are observed. As far as possible during conversion these defects are to be removed, for use.

Following are the defects which are normally observed :

*   **Heart Shake :** Observed in case of over matured trees or quick drying of central part of a tree nearing maturity, indicating shrinkage of heart wood. Cracks are wider at centre and go on reducing along medullary rays. (This is permissible if it does not go beyond 25 to 55 mm from nearest edge.)
*   **Star Shakes :** Cracks or splits extending from bark towards sap wood and are caused when tree is subjected to extreme heat or frost. Width narrows towards the centre.
*   **Cup Shakes and Ring Shakes :** Rupture of tissues in circular direction, across the cross-section of a log (partially - cup, nearly all along the circumference - ring). Defect is caused due to unequal growth or sudden contraction.
*   **Radial Shakes :** Similar to star shakes, occur due to exposure to sun, of felled timber undergoing seasoning. Cracks are fine, irregular and numerous. Going from bark to centre, following annular ring, finally reaching centre radially.
*   **Rind Galls :** These are peculiar curved swellings found on living or dead tree. Usually, caused by growth of layers over the wounds left after branches have been imperfectly cut off or removed.
*   **Upsets or Ruptures :** Ruptures of fibres of wood caused due to some sort of impact, injury, pressure, unskillful felling, violent wind effect.
*   **Twisted Fibre or Wandering Hearts :** Caused due to unidirectional twist of wind by the force of prevalent wind.
*   **Wind Cracks :** Shakes or splits on the sides of a bark of timber due to shrinkage of exterior surface exposed to sun, wind etc.
*   **Knots :** Knots are indication of bases of small branches of trees may be live or dead and break the continuity of fibres.

Type	Diameter
Nail knot	$d < 6$ mm
Small knot	$6.5 \le d \le 20$ mm
Medium knot	$20 \le d \le 40$ mm
Large knot	$d > 40$ mm

Maximum permissible diameter – 75 to 600 mm depending upon edge or central location of knot.

Many large knots or continuous peripheral small knots are harmful.

- **End Splits :** Reduction in tensile strength is observed. Cracks extending from one face to another.
- **Druxiness :** Early decay of healthy wood is indicated by whitish spot because of access to fungi.
- **Dead Wood :** Timber obtained from dead standing tree, which is light in weight with less strength.
- **Wane :** Lack of wood or bark because of any cause at edge or corner of piece.

Grade of Timber	Permissible fraction of width of face occupied by width of wane
Grade I timber	1/8th of width
Grade II timber	1/6th of width
Grade III timber	1/4th of width

- **Slope of Grain :** Strength is reduced if the cross-section indicates slope of grain.

Grade	Permissible
I	1 in 20
II	1 in 15
III	1 in 10

- **Bow and Cupping :** Converted timber bends along the direction of length indicating bow. (Prohibited defect) cupping - Distortion of board in which face is convex or concave.

      Grade   I – Non coniferous can be prohibited

               II – Maximum 5 mm for any width.

Diseases :

At places which are subjected to alternate dry and wet conditions or in the areas with dampness, unventilated areas, prevailing dark conditions etc. then the timber use within such areas gives birth to common diseases like dry rot and wet rot.

- **Dry Rot :** Growth of fungus is promoted due to lack of ventilation. Fungi eats up the fibres of timber and reduces to dry powder. This disease may be observed in case of seasoned timber as well. Sound test on timber detects this disease.
- **Wet Rot :** Alternate wet-dry conditions decomposes the timber. It may be observed in dead or live timber.

Decay of Timber :

'Decayed timber' is a deteriorated timber to such an extent that it loses its value as an engineering material. Deterioration is in both ways, i.e. Aesthetics and strength.

Causes : Defects, diseases, improper stacking, improper seasoning, unpreserved timber usage, improper handling and positioning, natural agencies etc.

12.8.3 Seasoning of Timber   (Dec. 14, Nov. 15, May 15,16)

It is "the process of drying out the timber to a moisture content approximately equal to average humidity of situation where it is to be used".

Advantages :

- Decrease in volume and weight is in turn making the timber easy for handling and reducing cost of transport.
- Strength, hardness and stiffness are increased.
- Increased resistance to fungus or insects attacks.
- Improved working qualities of timber.
- Size and shape retaining qualities are observed even after finishing the work.
- Ability to take special treatments like paints, preservatives, varnishes is increased.
- Reduction in tendency to crack, wrap, bend, shrink etc.
- Fueling quality is enhanced.

Preparing Timber for Seasoning :

- **Girdling :** Prior to felling, 5 to 8 cm deep and 15 cm wide cuts are made at bottom of timber peripherally. The felling of tree is observed after two or three years when tree dries.
- Thick sections liable to end splitting are coated with thick layers of moisture proof substances such as paraffin wax, bitumen paint, coal tar etc.
- **Water Seasoning :** Entire log is submerged fully in running water for a fortnight so as to wash away sap. Then moisture content is brought down to 40% and further processed for seasoning.

Methods of Seasoning :

(a) Natural or Air Seasoning :

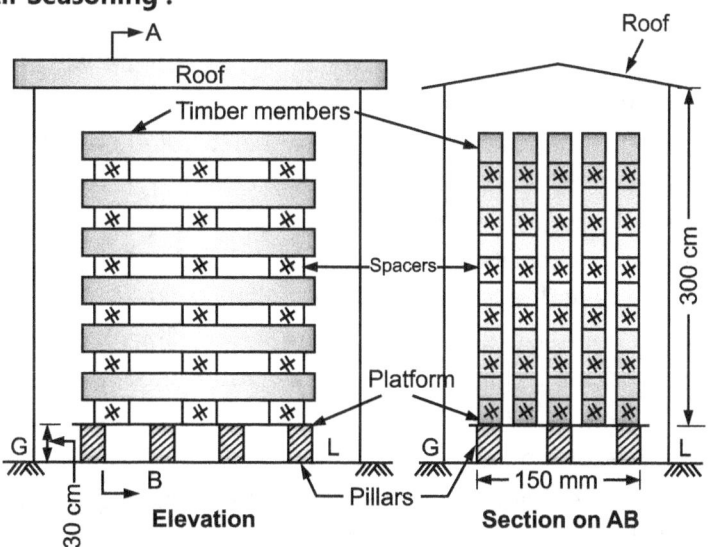

Fig. 12.2 : Horizontal stack for air seasoning

- It is a good old method of seasoning. Removal of sap and moisture takes place in a natural way with the help of air movement.
- Logs of timber are stacked in layers, first layer being at a distance of 30 to 45 cm from ground. The area where timber is to be placed is elevated, dried with free access to air. Alternate layers are arranged in such a way that they are at 90°, to each other.
- Normal duration in case of soft wood for every 25 cm thickness is of 2 to 3 months whereas in case of hard wood of same dimensional aspect it is around 12 months.
- Hence, softwood is seasoned or stacked for seasoning during summer and hardwood in winter.

Advantages :
- Simple, cheap and less supervised method.
- It renders a good quality timber.
- Low cost

Disadvantages :
- Longer duration for the completion of process. More area and capital is blocked.
- Moisture content reduction is about 20% and hence where less moisture content is required this cannot be used.
- As the total time is more and area is open; timber is likely to be attacked by fungi and insects.
- No effective control on moisture content reduction is observed.

(b) Kiln Seasoning or Hot Air Seasoning :
- This is a very quick method of seasoning. As it is very costly, normally it is applied to every good quality of timber.
- Timber is cut to the required sizes, stacked on rail mounted trolleys and placed inside closed air tight chamber. The kiln chamber is lined with refractory lining to reduce loss of heat.
- Heating system is arranged in such a way that the temperature can be raised to maximum and lowered to minimum smoothly.
- Sufficient humidity is also maintained. Fans are arranged in such a way so as to ensure uniform air circulation with sufficient velocity and air can be changed or controlled. Short period, less space and no capital blockage are the advantages.
- Stationary or progressive kilns suitably are responsible for seasoning. This is an expensive method and requires skilled labour. Also without a proper control timber is liable to end split or warping.

(c) Boiling or Steam Seasoning :
In this method, timber is first immersed in water and then water is boiled for 3 to 4 hours. Then timber is exposed to action of steam spray thus dried out and seasoned. It is a quick method, comparatively and reduces shrinkage but affects strength and elasticity of timber.

(d) Chemical Seasoning :

Timber is soaked in a solution of sodium chloride, sodium nitrate or urea before subjected to kiln. These chemicals absorb the moisture content from inside of timber and because of this phenomenon the surface cracks are not developed (i.e. shrinkage is avoided).

(e) Electric Seasoning :

A green timber offers less resistance to flow of current; as resistance to current is inversely proportional to the moisture content in timber. High frequency alternating currents producing heat are used to dry out the timber. It is the most rapid method but very costly, hence cannot be used for seasoning of timber on a large scale.

(f) Smoke Drying :

Timber is dried out over a fire of straw or twig. Application of heat is to be carried out carefully to prevent splitting. Hardeneds, more durable and worm proof production of timber is the output of this method. This method is generally used for bending planks in boat building.

(g) Charring or Scorching : Ends of timber piles or posts (to be used under water or ground) are burnt by charcoal to remove moisture content. But green timber may be subjected to dry rot.

Preservation of Timber :

It is the process of protecting timber from the attack of destroying agencies such as moisture, dry rot, internal decay, fungus attack etc. This ensures increased life of timber.

Preservatives :

1. **Oil preservatives :** Oil paints, Solignum paints, Coal tar etc.
2. **Water soluble preservatives :** Zinc chloride, Boric acid, Sodium fluoride etc.

Industrial Timber :

The timber which is manufactured scientifically in a factory to suit the need and to serve the desired purpose is known as industrial timber; such as veneers, plywood, particle board etc.

1. Veneers : These are superior quality thin sheets or slices of timber obtained by rotary cutting, peeling of logs or slicing. Large veneers are produced by rotary cut whereas attractive decorative veneer is obtained by slicing on radial face of woods of teak, walnut, rose wood, sheesam etc. The thickness of veneer varies from 0.4 mm to 0.6 mm or more.

2. Plywood : These are thin board formed by gluing together thin sheets of veneer. (Odd in number) under pressure (70 – 150 kg/cm^2). Placement of sheets is carried out in such a manner that grains of one layer are at right angles to the other. This offers greater resistance to cracking and splitting.

Advantages : Same strength in both directions and uniform but very less shrinkage in both directions. Inner veneers with grains parallel to face veneer are known as core whereas the one with grains at right angles are called cross bands. Adhesives used for gluing are synthetic resins.

Superior quality veneers are placed as outermost veneers on either faces to ensure the plywood for better polish.

3. Fibre Board : Manufacturing of fibre board involves pressing of pieces of wood of about 20 mm, cane, wood fibres, saw dust etc. The matter is initially boiled in water. Then passed to an autoclave where steam pressure of about 2300 kN/m^2 for about half minute and 7000 kN/m^2 for few seconds is applied and released. During this trapped water is vapourised to steam and wooden particles teared apart; producing fibres. The fibres are then spread on woven wire belt in the form of mat, subjected to heat and hydraulic pressure to form dry sheets. Thickness varies between 3 mm to 15 mm. (Normal sheet length 1.2 – 5.5 m, width – 1.2 m).

They are good heat and sound insulators, sturdy, give smooth finish after suitable coat and used for form work and partitions as well.

Sr. No.	Category	Density	Use
1.	Low density or Semi-hard Board	480 – 800 kg/m^3	Ceiling, soft wall decor
2.	Hard board	800 – 1000 kg/m^3	Painted exterior cladding
3.	High density (for superior works)	> 1000 kg/m^3	Where more strength is required

4. Particle Board : Particles or chips are randomly mixed with strong adhesives and subjected to high pressures. Random orientation of particle indicates that the strength will depend upon quality of adhesive and shape of particles. This is weaker than plywood. Long thin chip during orientation will depict more overlap, hence give better strength. Cuboidal particles involving end grain joints in larger proportion results in weaker board.

Three layers with middle layer of longer chips and outer of small particles for better finish are pressed together to give final product.

5. Veneer Faced Boards : Thin veneers are used on either faces and are glued to the core. Veneer will give better look. Grains of veneer are at right angles to that of core.

Depending upon core material further classification is :

Sr. No.	Name	Description	Uses
1.	Batten Boards	Core with about 8 cm wide strips i.e. battens.	Partitions, packing cases, furniture, ceiling decor etc., but liable to crack or split.
2.	Block Boards	Strip width is less than 2.5 cm.	Same as above.
3.	Laminated Board	Width is not more than 8 mm, hence the name. Cross band or Core may be continuous or cut and joint type. Stronger than block board. Thickness is 1 cm to 5 cm.	For interiors.

Category of Work	Used Indian Timber
Chaukhat - Frame	Sal, Teak, Deodar, Jamun, Chir, Kail etc.
Door - Window shutters	Teak, Jamun, Deodar, Kail, Chir etc.
Piles or posts	Sal, Sheesam, Jamun
Rail sleepers	Teak, Sal, Deodar, Chir
Handles and Cart wheel	Babul, Sheesam etc.

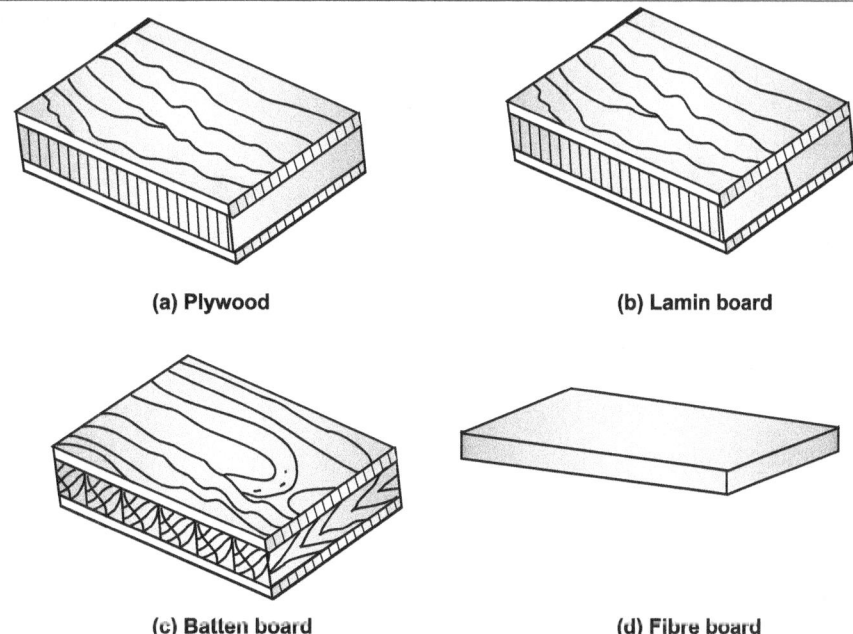

(a) Plywood   (b) Lamin board

(c) Batten board   (d) Fibre board

Fig. 12.3 : Plywood and allied products

12.9 ALUMINIUM AND ALLOYS   (Dec. 13, Nov. 15,16)

The most popular non-ferrous metal is Aluminium. Other non-ferrous metals are lead, copper magnesium nickel, tin, zinc etc.

Main ore for aluminium is bauxite. Bluish-silver white lustrous metal i.e. aluminium is obtained from it. The necessary provision for extracting aluminium from its ore is continuous abundant electric supply. This is the main drawback in commercial exploitation of rich bauxite deposites in India.

Aluminium Plants	States in India (With Hydroelectric Power Supply)
Belgaum	Karnataka
Mettur	Tamil Nadu
Koyana	Maharashtra
Renukoot	U.P.

Procedure : Crushed ore is treated with caustic soda forming sodium aluminate. This is separated by filteration and converted into Aluminate hydrate by precipitation. Finally, after calcination what is obtained is aluminium oxide called alumina. Alumina thus obtained is deoxidised by electrolysis of molten solution. Further, subjected to purification which give 99.5% pure aluminium.

Properties of Aluminium :

- It is soft, ductile, light in weight (specific gravity 2.7), malleable metal with high luster, corrosion resistant (due to formation of tough adherent oxide film when exposed to air).
- It melts at 658°C and is a good conductor of heat and electricity.
- The tensile strength of aluminium is about 100 N/mm^2 for pure metal but for alloys it can reach to 500 N/mm^2.
- During cold work strength goes to 150 N/mm^2 but there is considerable loss of ductility.

Uses :

- Production of utensils, electric wires, machine parts etc.
- Structural load bearing members.
- Construction of aeroplanes.
- Roofing sheets.
- Post-panels-balustrade formation.
- Door-window frames etc.
- Aluminium paints, glazing bars, rods etc.
- Bathroom fittings, surgical instruments, explosive manufacturing, precession survey etc.
- Flash bulbs for photography.
- Self lubricated sintered aluminium bearing (improved corrosion resistance, high thermal conductivity, greater oil retention and stability, less frictional coefficient).

Alloys of Aluminium :

Pure metal does not satisfy all requirements of an engineering structure. The properties exhibiting in case of pure metal can be improved by adding one or more element to it; thereby forming an alloy.

Alloy Preparation : First, metal with highest melting point is heated upto that point in fire clay crucible. Subsequently to this molten metal, other metal/metals with decreasing melting points are added in molten state. Homogeneous mixture is obtained by continuous stirring, agitation, which is poured into suitable moulds and cooled to solidify.

Aluminium alloys find uses in structural applications because strength to weight ratio is often more favourable than that of other materials. This also requires minimum maintenance since aluminium stabilizes in most varied atmospheric conditions.

Aluminium forms alloys after adding one or more elements such as : (1) Copper, (2) Silicon, (3) Iron , (4) Magnesium, (5) Nickel, (6) Manganese etc. Out of different alloys widely used alloys are : Duralium, Aldural, Y-alloy etc.

Sr. No.	Composition Elements	Duralium		Aldural	Y-alloy
1.	Aluminium		94%	10%	92.5%
2.	Copper	4% average,	2 to 6%	90%	4%
3.	Magnesium	Max.	0.5%	–	1.5%
4.	Manganese	Max.	0.4%	–	–
5.	Silicon	Max.	0.5%	–	–
6.	Iron	Max.	0.5%	–	–
7.	Nickel	Max.	0.5%	–	2%

(a) Duralium :

- Slightly heavier than Al, with specific gravity 2.85 and as strong as steel.

- It can be forged and machined, hence applications are wide such as reciprocating pistons, air crafts, I.C. engines, with less weight for moving parts.

- It can take high polish, hence can substitute german, silver, brass, copper.

- After heat treatment (heating and quenching), it acquires strength in 2 - 3 days because of its ageing property and it offers more resistance to corrosion.

(b) Aldural : It can be produced in rolled form and consists of duralium with coating of purest Al. More corrosion resistance than duralium.

(c) Y-alloy : Similar to duralium, possesses high strength at high temperature. It can be forged and machined. Being a good conductor of heat suitable for gear boxes, propellers, engine pistons etc.

REVIEW QUESTIONS

1. State the advantages and limitations of the Polymer.

2. State any six plastic building components and state which property of plastic makes it more suitable for the particular application.

3. State three building products which can be made by using ferrocrete technology. Explain step by step procedure to produce any one product.

4. What is seasoning of timber ? Explain defects in timber.

5. What are the characteristics of a good timber ?

6. Write explanatory notes on :

   (a) Glazed earthen ware tiles

   (b) Lime and its types.

7. Write down minimum two building components where each of the following building materials is used.

   (a) Aluminium,

   (b) Plastic, (iii) Plaster of Paris, (iv) Polymers, (v) Timber.

8. What is seasoning of timber ? Enlist methods of seasoning and explain one method in detail.

9. Compare thermoplastic materials and thermosetting materials.

10. What is seasoning. Enlist methods of seasoning and what are the relative advantages of each method.

11. State the advantages and limitations of the following materials :

   (a) Ferrocrete,

   (b) Glazed ware.

12. Mention the properties and uses of the following :

   (a)   Aluminium,

   (b)   Gypsum,

   (c)   Clay,

   (d)   Ferrous metals.

13. What is meant by preservation of timber ? Describe one method briefly adopted for the preservation of timber.

14. Enlist the types of lime and explain fat lime.

15. What is seasoning of timber ? What are the methods of seasoning ?

16. Write a note on eco-friendly materials.

17. Write down the advantages and disadvantages of the following materials.

    (a) Glass

    (b) Ferrocrete

18. Write a short note on Plaster of Paris.

19. What are the properties of plastics in general ? Discuss their uses and the future of plastics for use in building industry.

20. What is meant by preservation of timber ? Describe briefly the various methods adopted for the preservation of timber.

21. Mention the properties and uses of the following :

    (a) Aluminium

    (b) Gypsum

    (c) Mastic

SOLVED UNIVERSITY QUESTIONS

DEC. 2014

1. Define seasoning of timber. Explain defects in timber.   **[6]**

   [**Ans. :** Refer Article 12.8.2, 12.8.3]

2. Write short notes on: Gypsum   **[7]**

   [**Ans. :** Refer Article 12.5]

3. Write down engineering properties of: Timber   **[7]**

   [**Ans. :** Refer Article 12.8]

MAY 2015

1. Define seasoning of timber. Explain defects in timber.   **[6]**

   [**Ans. :** Refer Article 12.8.2, 12.8.3]

NOV. 2015

1. Define timber. State defects in timber. Explain any one.   **[6]**

   [**Ans. :** Refer Article 12.8, 12.8.2]

2. Define seasoning. Explain any two methods of seasoning of timber.   **[6]**

   [**Ans. :** Refer Article 12.8.3]

3. Write short notes on : (i) Aluminium (ii) Ceramic product   **[7]**

   [**Ans. :** Refer Article (i) 12.9 (ii) 13.4]

MAY 2016

1. State the defects in timber. Explain any one in detail.   **[6]**

    [**Ans. :** Refer Article 12.8.2]

2. Define seasoning of timber. Explain any two methods of seasoning of   timber.   **[6]**

    [**Ans. :** Refer Article 12.8.3]

NOV. 2016

1. Enlist the engineering properties of the following :   **[6]**

    (i)   Timber

    (ii)   Aluminum.

    [**Ans. :** Refer Article 12.8, 12.9]

2. Write short note on :   **[7]**

    (i)   Fiber reinforced polymers

    (ii)   Eco-friendly materials.

    [**Ans. :** Refer Article 12.3]

MAY 2017

1. Write short notes on: **[7]**

    (i)   Characteristics of good timber

    (ii)   Types of Glass and their properties used in construction

    [**Ans. :** Refer Article 12.8]

CHAPTER 13
GLASS

13.1 INTRODUCTION (May 14)

- Glass is a non-crystalline amorphous solid that is often transparent and has widespread practical, technological, and decorative usage.
- It is an important engineering material and it has many applications in construction industry.

Manufacturing Process :

- It is an amorphous, transparent or translucent, coloured or colourless material which is obtained by fusing a mixture of pure sand (SiO^2), soda (NaOH or KOH) and chalk ($CaCO^3$) with some quantity of broken glass.
- These ingredients are grounded to fine powder and are melted and fused in a furnace known as Tank Furnace at about 800 to 950°C. The molten mass is poured into moulds of required shape.
- Many varieties of glass have been developed so far and it is possible to make glass lighter than cork, softer than cotton or stronger than steel.

13.2 TYPES OF GLASSES (Dec. 14, Nov. 16, May 14, 17)

1. **Crown Glass (Soda Ash Glass) :** Major constituents are 75 parts silica, 12.5 parts soda, alumina and cullet (pieces of glass). It represents cheapest quality and used for window panes, bottles, bulbs etc.

2. **Sheet Glass (Window Glass) :**
    - Transparent, thin (2 to 6 mm), glossy, apparently smooth surface (with some wavy texture visible at an acute angle or in reflected rays).
    - Transmits light rays of visible portion (85 to 90%) and blocks ultraviolet rays. Properties like density, strength, thermal conductivity are similar to that of soda - lime - silica glass. Used for glazing, interior doors, skylights and if thickness > 3 mm then employed for multiple glass units, exterior doors, shop windows, showcases etc.

3. **Flint Glass :**
    - Major constituents are 100 parts (by weight) of sand or silica, 70 parts of lead, 33 parts of potash, 100 parts of cullet.
    - It is a very fine variety of glass and is used for making glassware, art glass, radio valves. Very fine polished surface can be obtained for this variety.

4. **Ground Glass :**
   - It is semi-transparent or translucent variety, hence to be used in situations where light transmission without transparency is essential.
   - One of the surface is made rough either by grinding or by melting powdered glass over it.

5. **Pyrex Glass :** Very much heat resistant variety. Sand 90 parts, lime 36, borax 0.5, feldspar 0.5 and cullet 90 parts by weight. Used for laboratory apparatus, cooking utensils, electric insulators etc.

6. **Plate Glass :**
   - Thickness ranges within 5 mm to 25 mm and is available in larger sheets (upto 4.5 m × 3.5 m).
   - There is no distortion of vision at any angle of observation. It is obtained by mechanical grinding and polishing or by floating molten glass on surface of molten tin contained in tank.
   - Manufactured glass is usually flat. It has very high compressive strength (about 1200 MPa). Bending and impact strength can be improved by tempering, ion exchange or alike methods.
   - As light transmission is good (around 87%), it is used for shopping glass window, showcases, mirrors, furniture etc. Also in case of public building fenestration it is employed.

7. **Tempered Glass :**
   - Tempering dates back to 17th century but commercial production began in 1930s. It has high mechanical strength and heat resistance.
   - Manufactured by heating thick sheets (thickness > 5 mm) to a temperature of 700 to 900°C and then subjected to rapid but uniform cooling with a stream of air or a liquid (By immersion, spraying or hosing).
   - Glass products to be tempered are fully shaped in advance as tempered glass cannot be cut, ground, drilled etc. Bending strength is 5 to 6 times and resistance to heat is twice as that of ordinary annealed glass.
   - Used for shop windows, public building fenestrations, flush doors etc. and where impact load is predominantly to be resisted.

8. **Wired Glass :**
   - It is an ordinary plate glass 5 to 6 mm thick with wire mesh reinforcement. Like tempered glass, it constitutes no hazard when shattered.
   - It is more heat resistant as steel wires are good conductor of heat.

9. **Glass Blocks :**
   - These are hollow or solid, translucent masonry units made from structural glass annealed to withstand the stresses. Available in various sizes 140 × 140 × 100, 190 × 190 × 100 or 194 × 194 × 98, 244 × 244 × 98 mm (depending upon the partition wall thickness appropriate use is expected).

- Block units are formed by fusing two sections at a high temperature which are casted separately. They may have one or two air cells. Partial vacuum in the interior improves heat insulation capacity.
- The joining edges are painted internally and sanded externally to form a key to mortar and front and back faces are decorative or plain.
- Blocks are laid in cement lime mortar 1 : 1 : 4. If the height is upto 150 mm then expanded metal strip reinforcement is placed in every third or fourth course, however if the height is more than 250, it is to be provided in every course.
- Provision for thermal expansion is made along jambs and heads of each panel. Glass bricks are also casted with joggles and end grooves to form glass wall; glass claddings.

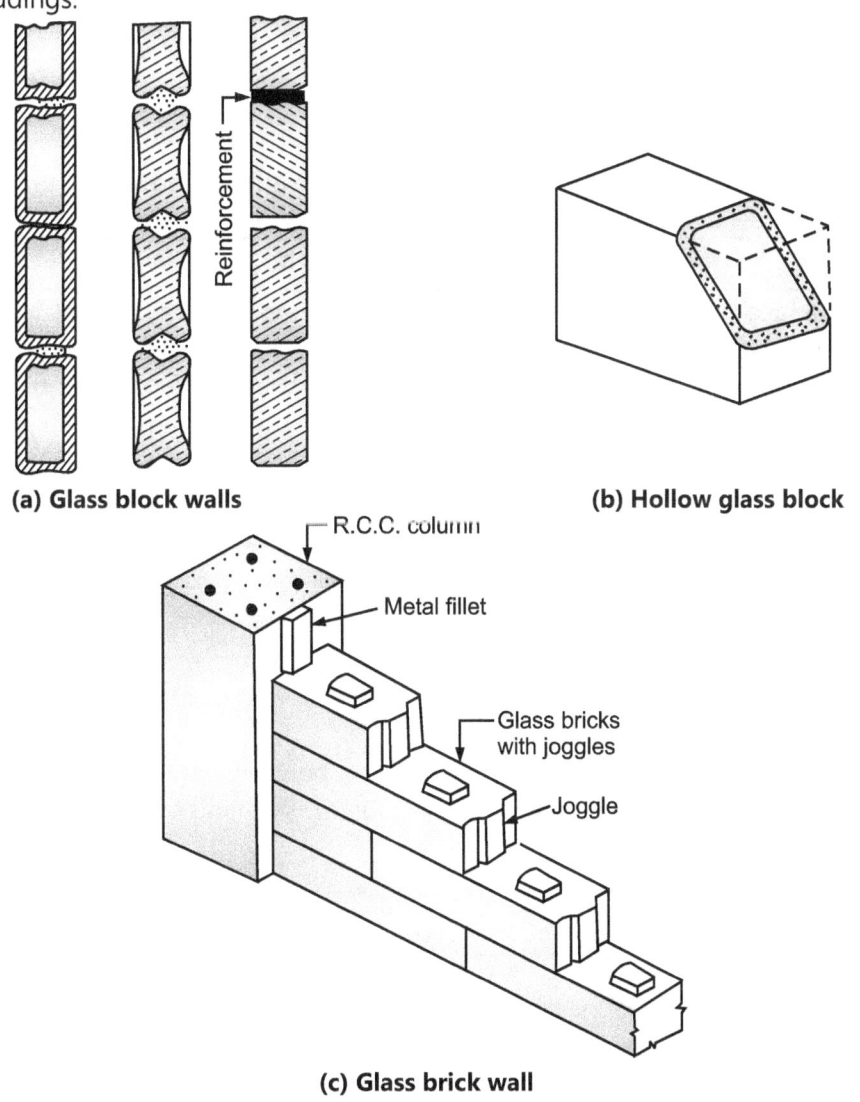

(a) Glass block walls   **(b) Hollow glass block**

(c) Glass brick wall

Fig. 13.1 : Glass block and glass brick

Properties :
- Compressive strength   – 1.5 MPa (min)
- Toughness   – 0.8 joule
- Light transmission   – 30 to 50%
- Thermal conductivity   – 0.5 W/machine
- Fire resistance   – upto 2.4 hrs.

Uses : Exterior claddings, external walls, partitions, windows or in combination with concrete, masonry work, roofing where concrete members serve as a skeleton.

Advantages :
- Non-porous, impervious, non-absorbent of moisture.
- Diffused light admittance, at desired tinge of colour, pleasing to eye.
- As the surface is smooth, less catch to dirt/dust.
- Does not allow condensation on the internal surface.
- Provides good architectural effect.
- Sound proof, fire proof, heat proof to some extent.
- If used as external cladding, no necessity to provide windows, at the same time admittance is less and diffused, hence partial privacy is maintained.

13.3 GLASS AND ALUMINIUM CLADDING

- All the mega cities in the world are adopting a modern international look, for their residential and commercial projects.
- For improving the exterior facades of any building whether old or new; techniques like cladding are adopted. The material used for cladding is glass, aluminium, tiles etc.

13.3.1 Aluminium Composite Panel Cladding   (May 16)

It is basically a typical metal curtain wall system. Its application include Exterior claddings, Column covers, In-fill panels, Fascias-Canopies, Clean rooms, Interior walls and partition panels, Sunshades, Cornices etc.

Characteristics :
- Light in weight, modern finish, available in many colours, ease in installation, weather proof coats, colour consistency, flatness, can take various forms of bends and curves, recyclable, non-toxic etc.
- It consists of 3 mm thick flame resistant polyethylene compound sandwiched between 0.5 mm thick aluminium foil facings with coating of polyvinyledene fluoride for one of them with thickness 0.25 microns.

13.3.2 Glass Cladding

- Realizing the fact that glass can be transparent or translucents, wider applications of glass are observed.
- Glass cladding fulfills functional requirements of building such as lighting, heat retention etc. with visual impact creation.

Characteristics: Total safe, aesthetical, recyclable, energy saver, time saver (constructional aspect), no flaws of plaster and paint, attractive colours, can take any shape etc.

- **Tempered Safety Glass:** (Plain or coloured) It is easy in cleaning and maintenance can be used for cladding. Tempered glass also provides resistance to pressure, temperature variations and impact loads.
- **Ceramic or Vitrified Glass :** Stable, available in wide colour - range/varieties, abrasion resistance, virtually any pattern can be screen printed, enhanced solar control performance, covers spandrel panels.
- **Spandrel Panels** are the areas between the floors which has concrete, pipings, floor slabs, ceilings etc.

13.4 CERAMICS   (Dec. 14, Nov. 15, May 14, 16)

- Materials whose melting points are very high relative to room temperature are called refractories, may be metallic or non-metallic (i.e. ceramics).
- Their absolute maximum service temperatures may be as high as 90% of their absolute melting temperatures.
- Various types of ceramic products are used in construction industry.

13.4.1 Ceramic Tiles

- For areas not subjected to heavy traffic, concentrated loads or excessive amount of water, organic adhesive is used for fixation or cement mortar usually.
- Appearance and resistance to wear make ceramic tiles suitable for use in kitchens and bathrooms, roof etc., available in various colours and cheap.

Types : Glazed, unglazed mosaic, marble, granite, laminated, vitrified etc.

Kitchen sinks or laboratory sinks. Ceramic.

Rectangular Hollow Receptacles : One piece with or without rim, drainer board; sloping towards the waste outlet. Height of top is around 90 cm.

Kitchen sinks	–	$600 \times 450 \times 150$ mm
	–	$600 \times 450 \times 250$ mm
	–	$750 \times 450 \times 250$ mm
Laboratory sinks	–	$400 \times 250 \times 150$ mm
		$450 \times 300 \times 150$ mm
		$500 \times 350 \times 150$ mm
		$600 \times 400 \times 200$ mm

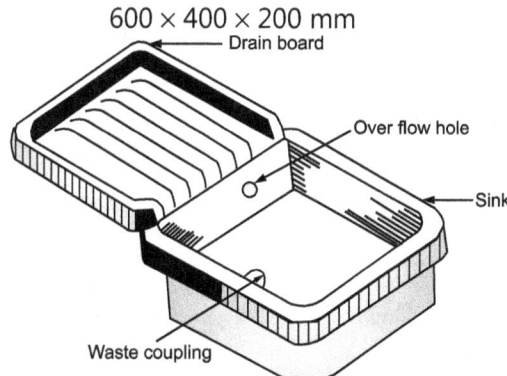

Fig. 13.2 : Kitchen sink

13.4.2 Ceramic Water Closets

Responsible to flush out human excreta to soil pipe.

1. Squatting Type or Indian Type : Manufactured in two different pieces; (a) squatting pan, (b) trap. Pan is provided with flushing rim. On the inner side sufficient slope is provided and appearance is glazy so as to make it easy for cleaning. The top of the trap is connected to antisiphon or vent pipe.

Three Categories : Rural (L = 425 mm), Long pan (L = 450, 580, 680 mm), Orissa pan (L = 580, 630, 680 mm).

All the ceramic varieties are glossy in appearance, easy to clean and available in many colours in local market.

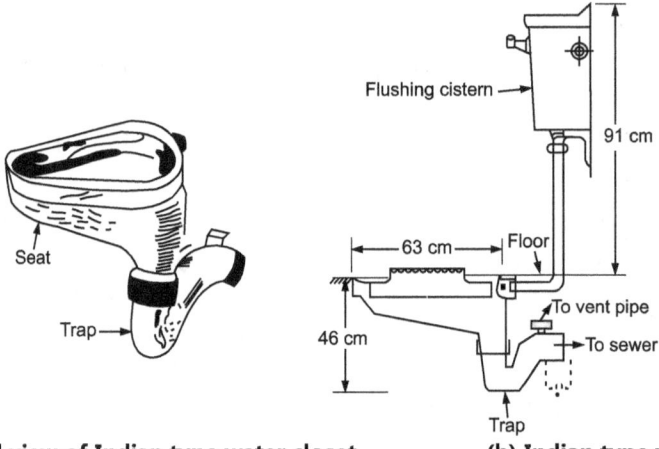

(a) Pictorial view of Indian type water closet	**(b) Indian type water closet**

Fig. 13.3

2. Wash Down : Pedestal or European Type : One piece construction of pan and trap. It is provided with wide flushing rim and 5 cm trap. These W.Cs. required less space than squatting type and cistern may be at low level. Popularly used in high class buildings.

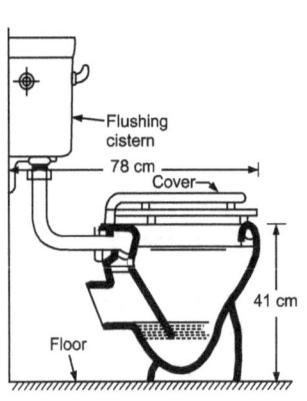 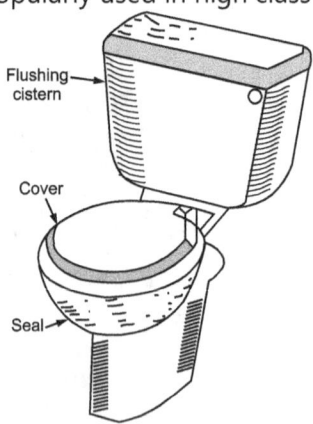

(a) Section through a wash down type water closet	**(b) Isometric view of a European type water closet**

Fig. 13.4

13.4.3 Urinals

Bowl Shaped : Used in gents toilet.

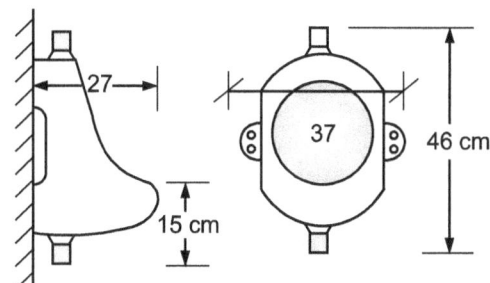

Fig. 13.5 : Bowl type urinal

Types :   Flat back – 430 × 260 × 350 mm (min.)

Angle back – 340 × 430 × 265 mm

One piece, with two holes for fixation to wall. Outlet horn connects it to trap. Inner surface is smooth to facilitate cleaning and flushing, provided with sufficient slope.

Slab and Stall : Used in public places as cinema houses, restaurants, stations etc.

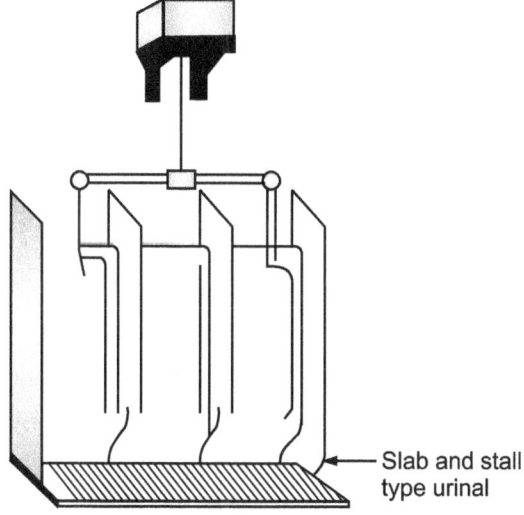

Fig. 13.6 : Slab and stall type urinal

Squatting Plate Urinals : Used in ladies lavatories, one piece construction with outlet horn, towards trap, 450 to 600 mm in length and 350 mm wide.

13.4.4 Wash Basins

- **Flat Back Mounting on Walls :** One piece construction with one or two tap holes. They have over flow slotted hole and the curve set in such a manner that it facilitates cleaning. Soap holder is an integrated part of the basin.

- **Angle Back :** Similar to that of flat back except that it is provided at the junction of two walls. Normally, the dimension is very less to fit in the corner.

- **Pedestal Type :** Larger dimensioned (640 × 480 mm) with a pedestal at bottom which covers the drain pipe. Hence, preferred in HIG societies, big hotels etc. It has one or two tap holes and may facilitate hot - cold mix system.

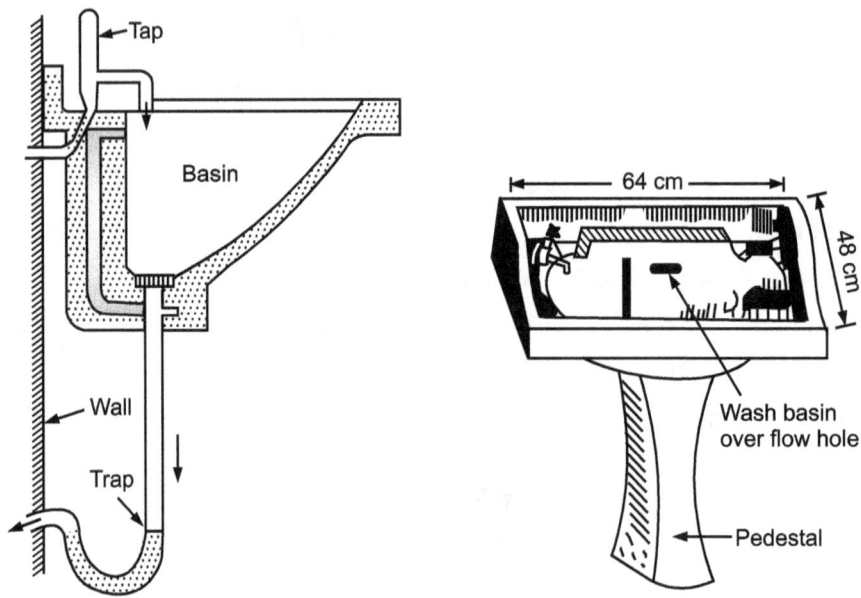

(a) Sectional view of wash basin   **(b) Isometric view of wash basin**

Fig. 13.7

13.4.5 Bath Tub

Depth near waste pipe is about 45 cm. Square type – 900 × 900 mm (can be modified), rectangular type 750 × 1650, 975 × 1950, 675 × 1350 mm (approximately).

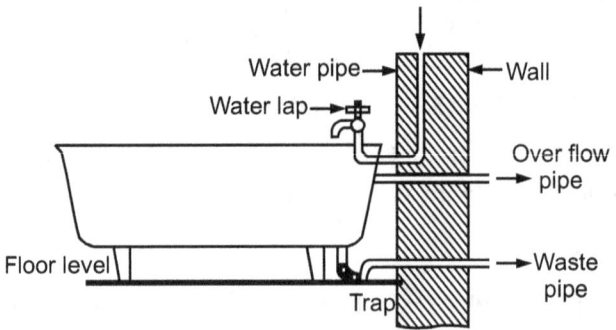

Fig. 13.8 : Section through a bath tub

13.4.6 Pipes and Fittings

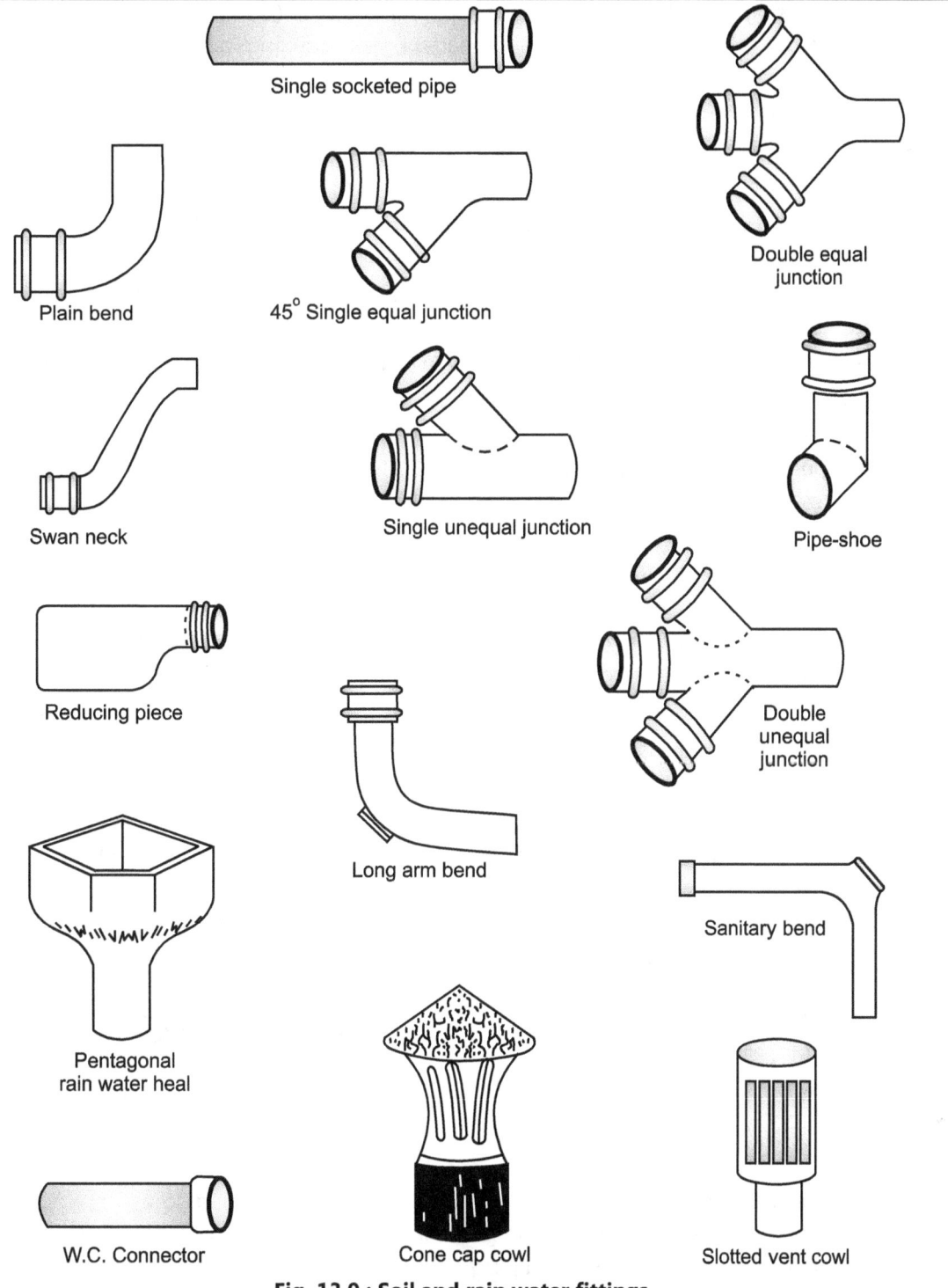

Fig. 13.9 : Soil and rain water fittings

Plumbing System:

- Plumbing system includes the water supply and distribution pipes, plumbing fixtures and taps, soil waste, vent, antisiphonage pipes, building drains - sewers etc. For storage of water tanks of cast iron, wrought iron, galvanized M.S. plates or R.C.C. are kept usually on roof of building with inlet, outlet and overflow pipes.
- The fittings for soil and rain water are detailed in Fig. 13.9 (which is self explanatory).

For supply of water and drainage system following types of pipes are commonly used :

- **Cast Iron Pipes : Types :** Horizontal, vertical, centrifugal. These are extensively used for water distribution.
- **Steel Pipes :** Used for mains where water pressure is high. These should be properly treated before use.
- **Galvanized Iron Pipes :** Made up of wrought iron with zinc coating. Used for plumbing services and are connected to other pipes by socket joints - T, elbow, bends, cross, reducer etc.
- **Copper Pipes :** Used to supply hot water. Not so common in our country. They possess high tensile strength, can be bent very easily.
- **P.V.C. Pipes :** Light in weight, non-corrosive, do not require threading for connection. Used to supply cold water.

Traps : These are the devices used to stop the escape of foul gases. Traps generally consists of a bend tube which provides a water seal between the atmosphere and the sewer gas. Deeper the water seal, more effective will be the trap. [Refer Fig. 13.10 (a), (b), (c), (d), (e)]

Types of Traps : P, Q, S traps, gully traps, intercepting trap, anti-D trap, antisiponage traps.

1. **P, Q, S Traps :** Consists of bent tube which retains water seal and the shape of tube resembles P or Q or S.
2. **Gully Traps :** Waste water from sinks, bath enters through back inlet and unfoul water from sweeping of room from top, where a coarser screen grating in fitted.

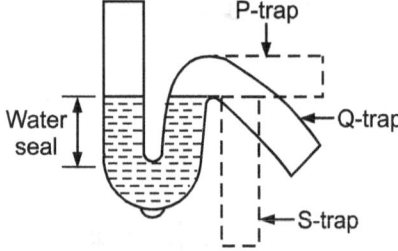

Fig. 13.10 (a) : P, Q and S traps

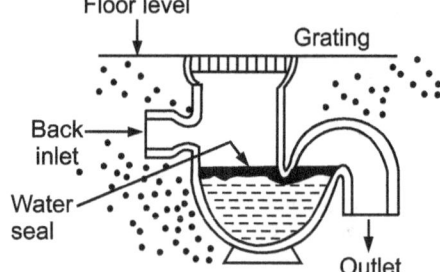

Fig. 13.10 (b) : Gully trap

3. **Intercepting Trap :** Foul gases from street sewers are trapped so as to avoid entry into house drains. This trap is installed in inspection chamber outside the house. It is provided with a cleaning eye and plug.

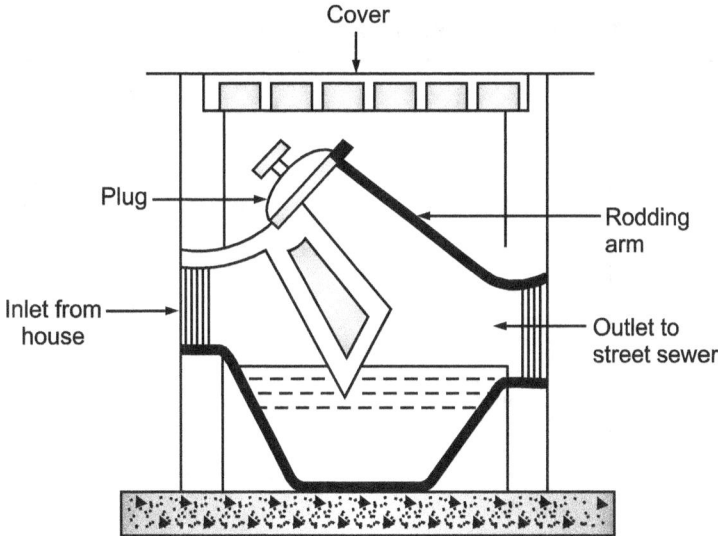

Fig. 13.10 (c) : An intercepting trap

4. **Anti-D Trap :** Improvement of P, Q, S with shaping the trap with its outlet as square in cross-section and larger than inlet. Thus, inlet water way is reduced which ensures removal of refuse and larger outlet prevents the pipe from filling full.

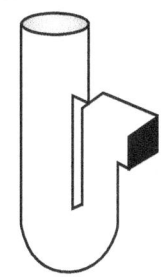

Fig. 13.10 (d) : Anti-D trap

5. **Anti-Siphon Trap :** (Resealing trap) : These avoid connection to vent pipe and reduce expensive work. Water seal when subjected to siphonic action, heavier atmospheric pressure on the inlet side presses the water down and the air can pass from by-pass tube B (Fig. 13.10 (e)) and water is stored in section C of the pipe and when there is balance in pressure; water levels in inlet, B and C are same.

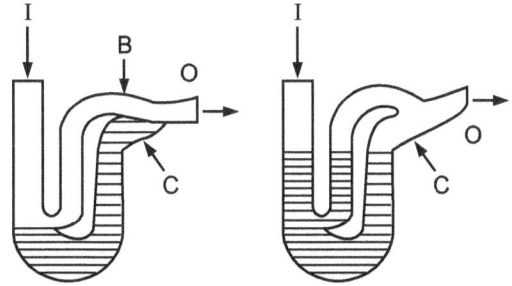

Fig. 13.10 (e) : Anti-siphon trap

13.4.7 Fixing and Jointing Pipes and Accessories

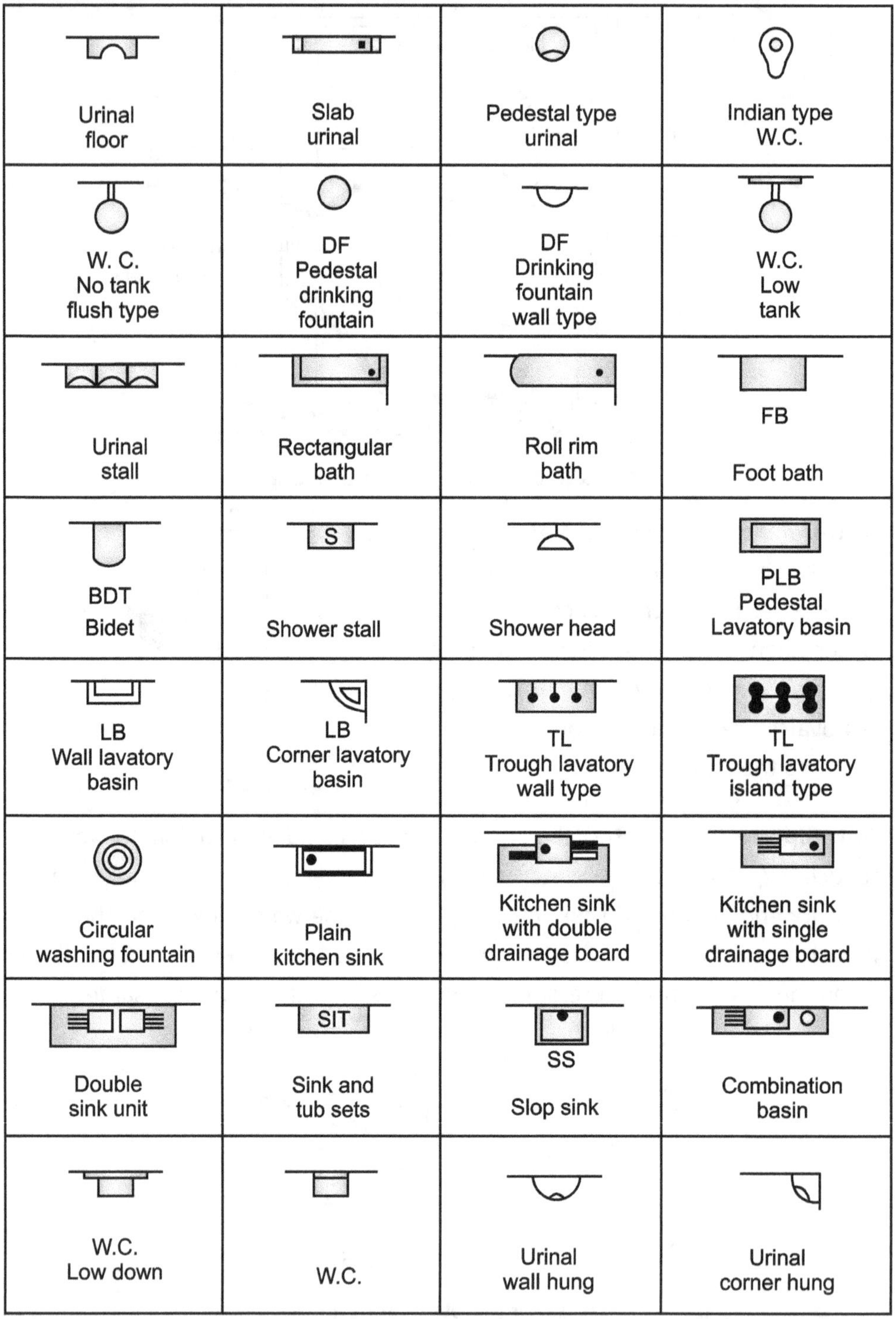

Urinal floor	Slab urinal	Pedestal type urinal	Indian type W.C.
W. C. No tank flush type	DF Pedestal drinking fountain	DF Drinking fountain wall type	W.C. Low tank
Urinal stall	Rectangular bath	Roll rim bath	FB Foot bath
BDT Bidet	Shower stall	Shower head	PLB Pedestal Lavatory basin
LB Wall lavatory basin	LB Corner lavatory basin	TL Trough lavatory wall type	TL Trough lavatory island type
Circular washing fountain	Plain kitchen sink	Kitchen sink with double drainage board	Kitchen sink with single drainage board
Double sink unit	Sink and tub sets	SS Slop sink	Combination basin
W.C. Low down	W.C.	Urinal wall hung	Urinal corner hung

Fig. 13.11 (a) : Symbols for sanitary installations as per IS : 962 - 1967

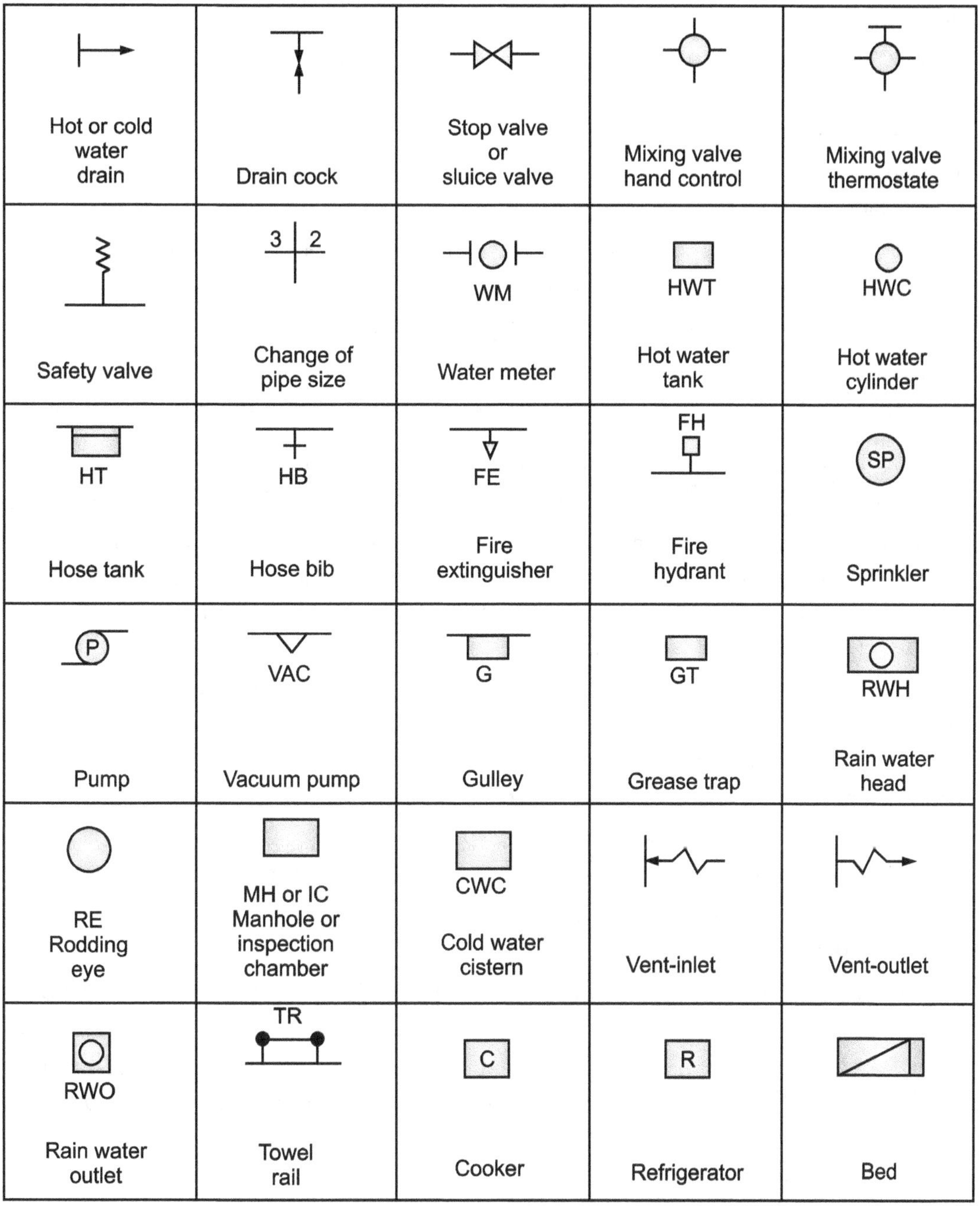

Hot or cold water drain	Drain cock	Stop valve or sluice valve	Mixing valve hand control	Mixing valve thermostate
Safety valve	Change of pipe size	Water meter WM	Hot water tank HWT	Hot water cylinder HWC
Hose tank HT	Hose bib HB	Fire extinguisher FE	Fire hydrant FH	Sprinkler SP
Pump P	Vacuum pump VAC	Gulley G	Grease trap GT	Rain water head RWH
RE Rodding eye	MH or IC Manhole or inspection chamber	Cold water cistern CWC	Vent-inlet	Vent-outlet
Rain water outlet RWO	Towel rail TR	Cooker C	Refrigerator R	Bed

Fig. 13.11 (b) : Fitment symbols as per IS : 962

Normally to have ease in maintaining the pipe lines, the pipes are fixed on outside of wall. Most common type is aluminium painted clips used as brackets for fitting the pipes. These clips fit closely round the pipes and have ears for securing to the face of the structure.

The jointing of pipes and accessories is employed with bituminous compound caulking. The space between the collar and plain end is grouted by stiff cement mortar.

Pipe Joints :

- **Spigot and Socket :** Used in case of C.I. pipes.
- **Expansion Joint :** If length of pipe line is too large, this joint is provided for expansion of pipe.
- **Ball and Socket Joint :** Takes care of settlement of pipes, hence suitably provided at places where settlement is possible.
- **Flanged Joint :** To be employed for pipes with flanges.
- **Collar Joint :** To connect R.C.C. pipes through cement mortar collar.
- **Screwed Joint :** Pipes are screwed together by socket. Normally in case of small diameter pipes.

13.5 ECOFRIENDLY MATERIALS   (Nov. 15, 16, May 16,17)

- Ecofriendly housing or natural building is nothing new. It is as old as the paper wasps who construct insulated hives out of chewed wood fibre, aquatic caddies fly larvae who make protective shells by cementing together grains of sand and the Chimpanzees who build rain shelters out of leaves and sticks.
- Our own species followed the same track for building the shelters out of locally available material.
- It is not a secret that the global ecosystem is ill and modern housing technology is a major contributor to the problem. Every material used in a typical modern building is the product of energy intensive processing.
- It is impossible to build a house without environmental impact but it is our responsibility to minimize and localize the damage.

What is an Ecofriendly Material?

- Dictionary describes "a product that has been designed to do the least possible damage to environment.
- US EPA-Epp "products or services that have a lesser or reduced effect on human health and the environment when compared with competing products or services that serve the same purpose".

Why Ecofriendly Materials?

- As they have very less impact on environment, recyclable and less energy consumer, use of these materials for various aspects or features of the building is increasing to have sustainable approach for construction.
- Use of these materials has emerged as a response to an increasing concern for our built environment.

Following are few examples of ecofriendly materials:

13.5.1 Ecofriendly Decorating Materials

From good old days the houses are decorated to give a feeling of aesthetics, warmth, coziness. Selection of ecofriendly materials for the same is an indication that we prefer to stay close to nature.

For example :

- **Clay Tiles:** Ecofriendly, fire resistant, uniform, durable, cheap, low weight are the characteristics of clay tiles. Use of locally available clay for production is a money generative aspect for skilled/unskilled labours. These are preferred for roofing with proper overlap so also for flooring. (Refer other types in same chapter).

- **Bamboo Board Flooring :** A good alternative to wood, less in weight, renewable, cost effective with adequate toughness and elegance.

- **Door Shutter and Panels :**

    (a) **Red Mud Based Composite :** A waste from Al industry, natural fibre and polymer.

       Stronger than wood, durable, corrosion resistant, termite, fungus, fire resistant. These characters makes it comparable with other product.

    (b) **Coir Boards :** Light in weight, cheap, sound insulator, low thermal conductivity, low water absorption.

    (c) **Bamboo Mat Boards :** Used for wall finish, door, ceilings door, prefabricated houses. Less cost, less weight, use of renewable resource.

- **Pipes and Pipe Fittings :** Unplasticized PVC pipes are stiff, strong, acid-alkali resistant, cheap, flame retardant, transparent. Timber product, jute product, ceramic and clay products do fall under decorative category.

13.5.2 Ecofriendly Flooring   (May 14)

Using renewable raw material, ecofriendly tiles are manufactured which are energy efficient, less costly, also some of the varieties are disaster resistant. (See Linoleum, Cork for detail description).

Bamboo Board Flooring :

   Characteristics : Elegant, tough, enough water resistance, ease in installation.

   Availability : Various shades and sizes with interlocking arrangement.

Terrazzo Flooring :

Terrazzo topping i.e. terrazzo mix of broken marble chips, stones, ceramic articles is laid on concrete sub-base. Cement and epoxy resins are used as binders. Normally, it can be used anywhere in residential, public buildings as the look is effective. It also takes high polish and seamless laying of the mix makes the layer water proof.

   Thickness of topping – 6 mm with marble chips 3 to 6 mm.

Jute Tiles: Characteristics of jute fibre (obtained from stem of sisal, banana etc.) are adequate tensile strength, reinforcing ability, impact strength etc. Other assets of jute are low cost and low energy requirements, hence composites of jute can be used for tiles, shower - bath units, pipes, false ceilings etc., also can be effectively used in disaster prone areas because easily erected and laid to suit the need.

Adobe :

- These are sun dried mud bricks representing a thermal mass to modulate temperatures (i.e. during day absorption of heat and slow release during night.)
- These bricks are used everywhere around the world in traditional earthen buildings and even for vaulted and domed structures.
- Manufacturing of adobe bricks consists of moulding the saturated mix of clay, sand, straw etc. After partial drying the bricks are removed.
- Adobe can take any desired shape. Several days are required for drying. Mud mortar or cement lime mortar may also be used for jointing.
- Adobe must be given special treatments to secure them against heavy rains etc. Wide eaves may serve the purpose, gutters are used to prevent splashing and foundations are to be protected from moisture penetration towards adobe walls.

Cob :

- It is also a similar technique as in case of adobe, only difference that it is rediscovered technique of building monolithic walls of moist earth and straw.
- The process of building with cob includes mixing local subsoil with sand and clay (depends upon base earth composition), straw, other fibrous material to form a stiff mud which is formed into small loaves (Cobs). This cob can be tossed or forked as a mass on the wall in layers.
- Technique is extremely economical for owner - builder but time consuming. Five hundred years old houses are still in perfect condition in England.

Ice : In Arctic zone or any other, where abundant snow is available, ice is the only cheapest material e.g. Igloos.

- In modern days big hotels totally made of ice are constructed. e.g. Ice Hotel - Sweden.
- The snow from Torne river is sprayed on steel forms and allowed to freeze. After a couple of days forms are removed and free standing corridors of ice formed. Dividing walls are built in for rooms and suit formation.
- Every year the hotel shapes to take a different form and around 4000 tonnes of ice is required.

Asphalt Mastic Flooring :

- One of the types, of asphalt flooring with mix proportion of sand and asphalt in the ratio of 2 : 1, mixed hot and laid in continuous sheets. Cold laying is also possible by mixing mineral oil and asbestos.

- Thickness may be about 25 mm for ordinary works with base of cement concrete. Spreading and levelling is achieved by trovels. Joints for successive bays are to be lapped so as to avoid penetration of water.

Mud Flooring:

- Particularly in villages mud floors are provided. They prove to be economical, hard, fairly impervious, easy in construction and maintenance with good thermal insulation property.

- A 25 cm thick layer of selected moist earth is laid on prepared base and rammed to 15 cm depth. Chopped straw is mixed before ramming. A wash of cow dung slurry is to be applied once or twice a week.

Clay or Pottery Tiled Floor : Available in many forms i.e. square, hexagonal or any other shape, size, thickness. Employed for any type of building with pleasing appearance, durability, ease in maintenance as inherent qualities.

- **Merits :** Decorative, non-absorbent, quick installation.
- **Demerits :** Initial cost is more, slippery surface.

1. **Thatch :**
   - Thatch allows us to create a roof without ecological compromise. Warm in the winter and cool in the summer; thatched roofs provide responsive shelter and offers sustainable, insulating, non-polluting and durable alternative which may be treated with fire resisting solution before laying.

   - It is the cheapest type of roof covering, simple in construction, mainly observed in case of rural areas.

   - Supporting framework may consists of simple trusses alongwith network of battens over which the thatch could be tied. Rafters may be made up of strong bamboos or wooden bullies.

   - Thatch covering should be at least 15 cm thick and should have a slope of at least 45° to provide adequate resistance against penetration of rain. Also thatch should be strong and straight. Thatch bundles are to be placed in such a way so as to have sufficient overlap.

Roofing Material : Straw, palm leaves, reed etc.

Rise Husk Board : Recyclable Agro waste, cost effective, different patterns and columns with elegant look, termite resistant, fire resistant, nailing ability, abrasion resistance are the qualities of RHB. It has wide range application and better substitute for wood in decor. It can be used for wall panels, doors, window, furniture, false ceiling roofing. Partioning floorings etc. specially in low cost techniques.

2. **Bamboo :** Bamboo is believed to have originated in Asia. The tree grows in wild - all around most parts of India.

- **Composition :** It is a perpetual tree which grows upto a height of 12 m, with its trunk width 8 to 15 cm in diameter. Every year (July and October), new shoot germinate at the base of trees which are always found in bunches. Stem is round, even, hollow with many nodes.
- **Leaves :** Plain, glittery, skinny, polished, dark green.
- **Flowers :** In bunches.
- **Chemical Composition :** 88.8% moisture, 3.9% protein, 0.5% fat, 1.1% minerals, 5.7% carbohydrates in 100 gm of its eatable solution.
- The characteristic features which make bamboo as a potential building material are its high tensile strength and very good weight to strength ratio. It is thus resisting even high velocity winds and earthquake forces as well. It is a renewable raw material with reasonable life of about 30 to 40 years.

Species used in Construction :

Bambusa Balcocoa, Bambusa Bamboos, Bambusa Tulda etc.

Use of Bamboo Based Products :
- Bamboo Mat Corrugated Sheets (BMCS) - durable, strong water proof, decay - insect and fire resistants.
- Treated bamboo for columns and beams.
- Treated bamboo for rafters, trusses, purlins.
- Bamboo Mat Board for door shutters, furniture etc.
- IPS flooring.
- Bamboo reinforcement.

2. **Linoleum :**
- It is made up from oxidised linseed oil, pulverised cork, wood floor, saw dust (i.e. oil, natural or synthetic resins, filler and pigments).
- The paste thus formed is backed by canvas, gunny sheets or rag felt. These sheets are available finally in plain or printed format and in rolls (2 to 4 m wide and thickness 1.6 to 6.7 mm) or tiles in the market.
- The backing is susceptible to moisture and fungus attack, hence it should be laid on dry surface or residential or commercial buildings.
- It can be glued to concrete base or wooden floors in different pattern. It is less affected by weak acids, hence cleaning is possible easily, hence preferred in hospitals, canteens, industrial buildings as well, being attractive, resilient, durable and cheap.

Linoleum covering is laid on wooden or concrete base by the following three ways :
- Tiles/carpets are laid loose on dry base.
- Attached to the base by a suitable adhesive.
- In case of prepared wooden base (resin bonded plywood) covering is nailed down at the ends in order to prevent tearing due to timber movement.

1. Cork : **(May 14)**

- Natural, flame retardant, made from bark of cork oak tree (bark being peeled after every 9 to 14 years with average life of 500 years).
- The flooring do not react to any fluid, supple under your feet but with a drawback that impact load creates a depression mark on it.
- The other characteristics of cork are as follows :
- Insect repellent, scratch resistant, fire resistant, sound absorbent, heat insulation qualities, non-slippery. The cork tile or carpet is made by heating or baking cork granules with linseed oil, phenolic or other resin binders under pressure.
- Sizes of tiles available are 10 cm × 10 cm to 30 cm × 90 cm and thickness ranging between 5 to 15 mm. Cork tile with natural finish should be sanded, sealed and waxed immediately after installation.
- Cork floors must be maintained with sealers and protective coatings to prevent soiling.

Applications : Libraries, Theatres, Art galleries, Broadcasting stations etc.

Constructional Aspect of Flooring : Sub-floor or sub-base made up of 3 : 1 or 4 : 1 sand cement is screed finished with a wooden float and then the laying is same as in case of linoleum flooring.

REVIEW QUESTIONS

1. State the market names of glass. Write down advantages and disadvantages of glass as a building material.
2. Mention the properties and uses of the following :
   (a) Aluminium,   (b) Glass,   (iii) Bronze.
3. Explain various types of alloys, their properties and uses.
4. Differentiate between Glass Cladding and Aluminium Cladding.
5. What are the outstanding qualities of glass ? Discuss various varieties of glass and their use in building industry.
6. Write notes on : (a) Glass claddings   (b) Eco-friendly materials

SOLVED UNIVERSITY QUESTIONS

DEC. 2013

1. Write down engineering properties of : [7]
   (i)   Aluminium (ii) Glass   (iii) Ceramic Product.
   [**Ans.:** Refer Article (i) 12.9 (ii) 13.1 (iii) 13.4]

MAY 2014

1. Write short notes on : [8]
   (i) Ceramic products used in construction (ii) Glass used in construction
   [**Ans.:** Refer Article (i) 13.4 (ii) 13.1, 13.2]

2. Write a note on Bamboo and cork as Eco-friendly materials [6]
   [**Ans.:** Refer Article 13.5.2]

DEC. 2014

1. Write short notes on: Ceramic products [7]
   [**Ans.:** Refer Article 13.4]
2. Write down engineering properties of: [7]
   (i)   Glass   (ii)   Ceramic products
   [**Ans.:** Refer Article (i) 13.2 (ii) 13.4]

NOV. 2015

1. Write short notes on : Eco-friendly materials [7]
   [**Ans.:** Refer Article 13.5]

MAY 2016

1. Write short notes on : [7]
   (i)   Ecofriendly building materials
   [**Ans.:** Refer Article 13.5]
   (ii)   Ceramic product
   [**Ans.:** Refer Article 13.4]
   (iii)   Aluminium in cladding.
   [**Ans.:** Refer Article 13.3.1]

NOV. 2016

1. Write short note on : [7]
   (i)   Fiber reinforced polymers
   (ii)   Eco-friendly materials.
   [**Ans.:** Refer Article (ii) 13.5]
2. Write a short note on Glass-uses, types and properties. [6]
   [**Ans.:** Refer Article 13.2]

MAY 2017

1. Write a note on Eco-friendly materials in construction. [6]
   [**Ans.:** Refer Article 13.5]
8. **(a)** Write short notes on: [7]
   (i)   Characteristics of good timber
   (ii) Types of Glass and their properties used in construction
   [**Ans.:** Refer Article 13.2]

◈ ◈ ◈

CHAPTER 14
SAFETY IN CONSTRUCTION

14.1 INTRODUCTION

- There are many factors which may contribute to an accident prone environment.
- There may be a lack of proper safety equipment at work sites; workers may be ignorant about use of any safety gear in the absence of any training; the design of the structure etc.
- Poor living conditions, lack of experience and motivation are other governing factors. Added to all these is the occasional insensitive attitude of some contractors towards human lives.
- Therefore, the vital requirements for any successful construction enterprise is designing and constructing safe structures and providing safe work environment to the personnel engaged in construction.
- The concern for safety starts with the conceptual and design stage and continues through the construction process. It does not end even after the facility has been handed over to the user.
- It continues further throughout the use and maintenance and repair of the structure.

14.2 ASPECTS OF SAFETY   (Nov. 15)

14.2.1 Planning

- For timely, economical and smooth completion of any project, it is necessary for the owner to adopt a systematic approach, right from the beginning of the project.
- Planning will include planning for the various agencies required for designing and building of structures or part thereof, appropriate scheduling of fire prevention measures and fire protection facilities, timely procurement of construction materials and equipment and proper stacking, storage and handling of construction materials at site.
- Modern techniques of management such as Programme Evaluation and Review Technique [PERT] and Critical Path Method [CPM] may be used in planning for more efficient control over the entire project.
- All new work or alteration should be planned, designed and supervised by licensed personnel, namely, town planner, architect, engineer etc.
- For the quality of materials used, even though procured by the contractor, the owner has to take responsibility, unless a licensed architect or engineer has been engaged to supervise and will be responsible for these technical aspects.

14.2.2 Storage and Handling of Materials

- Materials should be stored, stacked and handled in such a manner as to prevent deterioration or intrusion of foreign matter and to ensure the preservation of their quality and fitness for the work.
- Materials should be stacked on well drained, firm and unyielding surface. Materials should not be stacked in a manner which may impose any undue stresses on walls or other structures, nor in a manner as to constitute a hazard to passersby.
- At such places, the stacks shall have suitable warning signs in day time and red lights on and around them at night.
- Stairways, passageways and gangways should not get obstructed by storage of building materials, tools or accumulated rubbish.

Methods of Storage of Some Construction Materials :

[a] Cement :

- Cement should be stored at the work site in a building or a shed which is dry, leak proof and damp proof.
- The building of shed for a storage should have minimum number of windows and close fitting doors and these should be kept closed as far as possible.
- Cement bags should be stacked off the floor on wooden planks in such a way as to keep them 150 to 200 mm clear from the floor and a space of 450 mm minimum shall be left around between the exterior walls and the stacks.
- In the stacks, the cement bags should be kept as close together as possible to reduce air circulation between them. The height of stack should not be more than 15 bags to prevent the possibility of lumping up under pressure.
- The width of the stack should not be more than 4 bags length or 3 m. In stacks, more than 8 bags high, the cement bags should be arranged alternately lengthwise and crosswise so as to tie the stacks together and minimize the danger of toppling over.
- During monsoon or when the cement is expected to stored for an usually long period, the stack should be completely covered by a water proofing membrane such as polyethylene, which will close on top of the stack.
- Care should be taken to see that this membrane is not damaged any time during use.
- Drums or other heavy containers of cement should not be stacked more than two layers high.
- The manner of storage should facilitate the requirement that lots of cement received are removed and used more or less in the order in which they are received.

[b] Aggregate :

- Aggregates should be stored on the site on a hard dry and level patch of ground.
- If such a surface is not available, a platform of planks or old corrugated iron sheets, or a floor of bricks, or a thin layer of lean concrete should be made so as to prevent the admixture of clay, dust, vegetable and other foreign matter.

- Stacks of fine and coarse aggregate should be kept in separate stockpiles sufficiently separated from each other to prevent the materials from getting intermixed.
- Fine aggregate should be stacked in a place where loss due to the effect of wind is minimum.

[c] Steel :

- Steel reinforcement should be stored in a way as to prevent distortion and corrosion.
- It is desirable to coat reinforcement with cement wash before stacking to prevent scaling and rusting.
- Bars of different classification, sizes and lengths should be stored separately to facilitate issues in such sizes and lengths as to minimize wastage in cut from standard lengths.
- Structural steel of different sections, sizes and lengths should be stored separately, above ground level by at least 15 cm upon platforms, skids or any other suitable supports to avoid distortion of sections.
- For each classification of steel, separate areas should be earmarked. Ends of bars and sections of each class should be painted with separate nominated colours.
- Tag lines should be used to control the load in handling reinforcements or structural steel when a crane is employed.
- Heavy steel sections and bundles should be lifted and carried with the help of slings and tackles and should not be carried on the shoulders of the workmen.

[d] Masonry Units :
Bricks :

- Bricks should not be dumped at site. They should be stacked on dry firm ground in regular tiers directly as they are unloaded to minimize breakage and defacement of bricks.
- For proper inspection of quality and ease in counting, the sacks should be 50 bricks long and 10 bricks high the bricks being placed on edge, and preferably, the width of each stack shall be two bricks. Clear distance between adjacent stacks should not be as far as possible, less than 0.8 m.
- In case of bricks made from clays containing lime KANKAR, the bricks in stack should thoroughly soaked in water to prevent lime bursting. Bricks of different types and classification should be stacked separately.

Bricks : Concrete blocks, stone blocks, etc. should be stored in stacks of such height as will not damage the blocks in the lower layers not there be fear of toppling of stack.

[e] Timber :

- Timber should be stored in stacks upon well treated and even surfaced beams, sleepers or brick pillars so as to be above ground level by at least 150 mm to ensure that timber will not be affected by accumulation of water under it.

- Various members should preferably be stored separately in different lengths and materials of equal lengths should be piled together in layers with wooden battens, called crossers, separating one layer from the other.
- In any layer, an air space of about 25 mm should be provided between adjacent members. The longer pieces should be placed in the bottom layers and shorter pieces in the top layers but one end of the stack should be in true vertical alignment.
- The crossers in different layers should be in vertical alignment. The most suitable width and height of a stack are about 1.5 m and 2 m, distance between adjacent stacks being atleast 450 mm.
- The stacks should be well protected from fire, hot dry winds, direct sun and rain. Care must be taken that workmen are not injured by rails, straps, etc., attached to the used timber. This applies particularly to planks and form work for shuttering.

[f] Doors, Windows and Ventilators :

- Metal doors, windows and ventilators should be stacked upright on their sills on level ground preferably on wooden battens and should not come in contact with dirt or ashes. If received in creates, they should be stacked according to manufacturer's instructors and removed from the creates as and when required for the work.
- Metal frames of doors, windows and ventilators should be stacked upside down with the thick plates at the top.
- During the period of storage, aluminium doors, windows and ventilators should be protected from loose cement and mortar by suitable covering, such as tarpaulin.
- Wooden frames and shutters should be stored in a dry and clean, covered space, away from infestation. The frames should be stacked one over the other in vertical stacks with cross battens at regular distances to keep the stack vertical and straight. The door shutters should be stacked in the form of clean vertical stacks one over the other and atleast 80 mm above the ground on pallets or suitable beams to ensure that they will not be affected by accumulation of water under them. The top of stacks should be covered by protective cover and weighted down by suitable weights.
- Precast concrete doors and window frames should be stored in upright position adopting suitable measures against risk of subsidence of soil or support.

Paints, varnishes, lacquers, thinners and other flammable materials should be kept in properly sealed or closed containers.

The containers should be kept in a well ventilated location, free from excessive heat, smoke, sparks or flame.

Care should be taken not to use any naked flame inside the paint store. Buckets containing sand should be kept ready for use in case of fire.

Each workman handling lead based paints should be issued $\frac{1}{2}$ litre milk per day for his personal consumption.

[h] Water :

Water to be stored for construction purposes should be stored in proper tanks to prevent any organic impurities.

14.2.3 Safety in Execution of Building Works   (Nov. 16, May 17)

Following are some of the causes of accidents in Civil Engineering :

- Persons falling from a height or into excavated pits.
- Persons being struck or trapped by objects in motion.
- Persons stepping on or striking against objects.
- Persons handling objects in such a way so as to cause injuries.
- Persons using hand tools in an improper way.
- Electrical shocks.
- Fires.
- Misuse of power tools, plant, machinery and transport.

A few of the construction operations are discussed below, where safety measures are of paramount importance :

[a] Excavation :

- Deep excavation especially in loose soils and black cotton soils poses a potential danger to workers. Adequate precautions, depending upon the type of strata met with during excavation shall be taken to protect the workmen during excavation.
- Excavating machinery and tools required for excavation should be kept well away from the excavation trench.
- Excavated material should be dumped sufficiently away from the edge of the excavated trench to avoid slipping of the excavated earth or caving in, causing injury to workers.
- During any excavation, sufficient slopes to excavated sides should be provided by way of steps or gradual slopes to ensure the safety of men and machines working in the area.
- Deep excavations beyond 3 m depth should be properly fenced to prevent workers and members of public from falling in.
- Warning signals, red danger light should be displayed prominently near excavated sites.

  When occupations are being done on roads, diversion of the roads shall be provided with adequate notice boards and lights indicating the diversion well ahead. Where necessary, a watchman should be appointed, to prevent accident to the general public, especially during hours of darkness.
- Where gases or fumes are likely to be present in trenches, sufficient mechanical ventilation should be provided to protect the health and safety of persons working there.

If necessary, the personnel working should be provided with respiratory protective equipment when work in such unhealthy conditions has to be carried out.

- Blasting operations of rock must be handled by qualified experts with prior permission from a competent authority.

  Before blasting, prior inspection for the stability of slopes should be carried out. After blasting, overhangs or loose boulders should be cleared by expert workers carrying out blasting, prior to continuation of occupation by normal working parties.

[b] Scaffolding :

- Scaffolding should be properly designed and constructed by competent persons. It should be made of sound material, free from any defects. After the initial construction of the scaffolding, frequent inspections are necessary to ensure that no damage has occurred to the scaffolding, which would endanger workmen.
- The platforms, gangways and runways provided on the scaffoldings should be of sufficient strength and width to ensure safe passage for the workmen working on the scaffolding. Where necessary, cross bars should be provided to the full width of gangway or runway to facilitate safe walking.
- Loose materials should not be allowed to remain on the gangways. Workers should not be allowed to work on the scaffolding during bad weather and high winds.

[c] Walls :

- Depending on the type of wall to be constructed the height of construction per day should be restricted to ensure that the newly constructed wall does not come down due to lack of strength in the lower layers. Similarly, in long walls, adequate expansion/crumple joints should be provided to ensure safety.
- Whenever, an opening in the existing wall is to be made, adequate supports against the collapse or cracking of the wall portion above or roof or adjoining walls should be provided.
- All wall openings and holes should be properly guarded by barriers.
- Whenever projection cantilever out of the walls, temporary form work should be provided for such projections.

[d] Roofing :

- Prevention of accidental falling of workmen during construction of roofs should be ensured by providing platforms, catch ropes etc.
- If the materials are to be hoisted from the ground level to the roof level, adequate precautions should be taken by way of correct technique of handling and hoisting.
- While working with asbestos cement sheets, workers should not be allowed to walk on them but should be provided with walking boards.
- It should be ensured that joints of corrugated galvanized iron or asbestos cement sheets are kept secured in position and do not slip, causing injury to workmen.

- While working with tiles, loose tiles should not be kept on the sloping roof resulting in falling of tiles on workmen in lower area.
- If any glasswork is to be carried out, it should be ensured that injury to passer by due to breaking of glass is prevented. Workers should not be allowed to work on the sloping sections during wet conditions.
- In case of flat roof construction any form work provided should be inspected frequently for possible damage which may result in the collapse of the slab causing serious injuries to workmen.

[e] Flooring :

- Every temporary floor opening should have railings or should have a floor hole cover of adequate strength.
- In the absence of a cover, the floor hole should be constantly attended by someone or adequate warning signs should be put up all around it.
- Similarly, every stairway floor opening must be protected by a railing on all exposed sides except at the entrance to the stairway.

[f] Machinery :

All machines and equipment at work sites should be used by properly trained workmen.

- Mixers used on the site should be properly checked and a trial run should be made to remove defects if any.

  All cables, clamps, hooks, wire ropes, gears and clutches, etc. of the mixer should be checked, cleaned, oiled and greased and serviced once a week.

- Cranes should be operated by trained personnel only. A crane must be used to lift only the designed load and must be operated within the safe reach of the crane as specified by the manufacturer. Cranes should not be operated in dangerous proximity to live overhead power lines.

  Cranes should not be used at a speed which causes the beam to swing. No person should be lifted or transported by the crane on its hook or boom.

  A standard code of hand signals should be adopted in controlling the movements of the crane and both the operator and the person signaling should be thoroughly familiar with the signals.

- **Trucks :** There are many hazards associated with operation of vehicles at construction sites. Wherever possible, a loop road should be provided to permit continuous operation of vehicles and to eliminate their backing. If this is not possible, then backing operations should be properly carried out with the help of a signal man who will guide the driver while backing. Many a time, these vehicles knock down parts of building or scaffolding / ladders etc. during difficult backing operations, causing serious injuries.

[g] Form Work :

- Form work should be designed after taking into consideration spans, setting temperature of concrete, dead load and working load to be supported and safety factor for the materials used for form work.

- All timber form work should be carefully inspected before use and members having cracks and excessive knots should be discarded.

- Tubular steel centering should be used in accordance with the manufacturer's instructions.

- A thorough inspection of tubular steel centering is necessary before its erection. Buckled or broken members should be replaced and care should be taken that locking devices are in good working order.

- Centering layout should be made by a qualified engineer and should be strictly followed. The bearing capacity of the soil should be taken into account for every centering job.

- Forms should not be removed earlier than as laid down in the specifications and until it is certain that the concrete has developed sufficient strength to support itself and all loads that will be imposed on it.

- Those engaged in removing the form work should wear helmets, gloves and heavy solid shoes and approved safety belts if adequate footing is not provided above 2 m level.

- While cutting any tying wires in tension, care should be taken to prevent backlash which might hit a workman.

[h] Safety Against Fire :

- Fire extinguishing equipment should be provided and conventionally located within the building under construction or on the building site, as required by the authority.

- All fire extinguishers should be maintained in a serviceable condition at all times.

- It should be ensured that all workmen and supervisory staff are fully conversant with the correct operation and use of fire extinguishers provided at the construction site.

[i] Safety in Demolition of Buildings :

- Before beginning the actual work of demolition, a proper plan of demolition should be worked out.

- Prominent danger signs should be posted all round the property and all openings giving access to the structures should be kept barricaded or manned except during the actual passage of workman or equipment.

- During night, warning lights should be placed on or above all barricade safety distances to ensure safety of the public should be clearly marked and prominately sign posted.

- Prior to commencement of work, all material of fragile nature like glass should be removed.
- Dust should be controlled by suitable means to prevent harm to workmen.
- Stacking of material or debris should be within safe limits of the structural member.
- Adequate natural or artificial lighting and ventilation should be provided for the workmen.
- Safety devices like industrial safety helmets conforming to the accepted standards and goggles made of celluloid lens, should be issued to the worker.
- Foreman-in-charge of the work area should ensure that all the workmen are wearing the safety devices before commencing any work.
- While demolishing RCC, steel structures, etc., gloves of suitable material should be worn by workmen.

14.3 ADDITION AND ALTERATION

It is a method of providing new foundation below the existing foundation without damaging the stability of existing structure to meet the following requirements :

- If deep foundation is to be constructed adjoining to a building having shallow foundation; the shallow foundation may face some problems and may need strengthening.
- If height of existing building is to be increased, and existing foundation, if, unable to bear increased load, may require strengthening.
- If basement is to be provided to the existing building and if depth and strength of existing foundation is insufficient, then existing foundation may need strengthening.

Methods of Addition and Alteration :

Of the various methods, the following methods are commonly used for Addition and Alteration :

- Alternate pit method
- Cantilever beam method
- Micropile method.

(a) Alternate Pit Method (Ref. Fig. 14.1 (a)) :

- Pits of size 1.2 × 1.2 m or 1.5 × 1.5 m and to a depth greater than the depth of existing foundation, are excavated on either side of the existing wall.
- To start with, pits are excavated at mid length of wall; and further pits are excavated in alternate bays spaced at 3 to 4 m c/c.
- Holes are made in the existing wall at desired level, so that, steel joists (RSJ) called as needle beam with bearing plate on the top can be inserted. Bottom and top of the hole is levelled and RSJ with bearing plate is inserted and RSJ is supported at either ends. With this arrangement, load of wall above the needle beam is transferred on

needle beam, and no damage will be caused for a short period, if soil below the existing foundation is removed.

As soon as soil below the foundation is removed it is replaced by new, stronger foundation on an unyielding strata.

- Same process is continued in alternate bays; and new foundation is provided using rich cement concrete.
- Later on balance pits are excavated and new foundation is provided in similar manner.
- Needle beams and vertical supports are removed, and load is transferred to the new foundation.

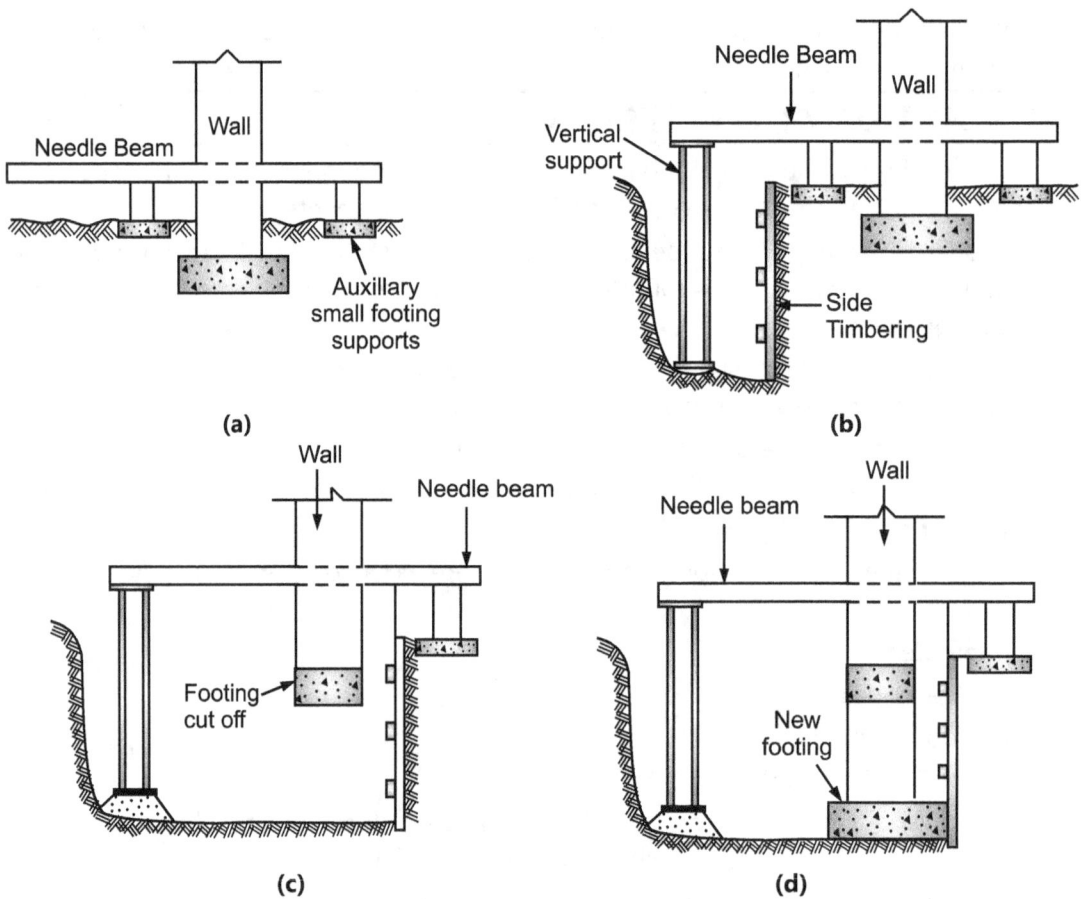

Fig. 14.1 : Alternate pit method

[b] Cantiliver Needle Beam Method (Ref. Fig. 14.2) :

If sufficient space is not available to support the needle beams, outside the existing building, then, the needle beam is supported on a fulcrum inside building. At the end of needle beam, load is placed on the needle beam. Due to cantiliver action, load of the wall is transferred on the needle beam; and soil below existing foundation can be removed without causing any damage to existing building and new stronger foundation can be *provided*.

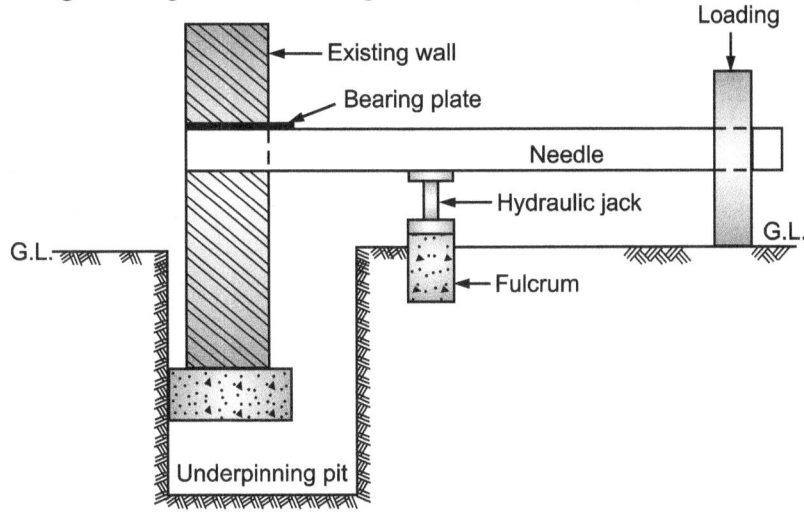

Support by cantiliver needles

Fig. 14.2 : Cantiliver needle beam method

[c] Pile method (Ref. Fig. 14.3) :

Pit method is used with strong strata at a shallow depth and without any ground water problem pits can be excavated. However, if ground water table is met at shallow depth and unyielding strata is available at greater depth, then bored piles are provided on either side of existing wall; and the piles are interconnected by providing pile cap through existing wall.

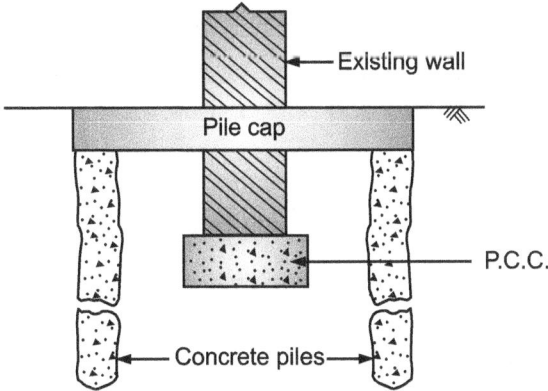

Fig. 14.3 : Pile method

14.4 SHORING AND STRUTTING   (May 14,17)

- Term scaffolding is used for the arrangement made to facilitate construction of new walls or repairing and maintenance of old walls, whereas term shoring is used in connection with arrangements made to give support to a damaged wall, so as to prevent it from further damage / collapse.

- Shoring is provided to a structure under the following circumstances :
- When a structure has become / or is likely to become unsafe due to differential settlement, or negligence of maintenance, bad workmanship, unequal settlement due to excessive de-watering or vibrations in adjoining area.
- More skill, care and factor of safety is required while providing shoring. Shores are generally made of timber, but for heavier loads, steel beams are adopted.
- Shores may also be made of concrete or masonry. Support may be given externally or internally or both externally and internally.

Types of Shoring :

Support to be provided may be (i) Inclined, (ii) Horizontal or (iii) Vertical. Based on the characteristics of the support, shorings are classified as :

- Raking or Inclined Shoring
- Flying or Horizontal Shoring
- Dead or Vertical Shoring.

[a] Raking Shores :

- These consist of providing inclined timber called as *raker*, one end of which rests against a defective wall through wall plate and other end rests against *sole plate* which is embedded in ground at an inclination, [preferably at right angles to raker] to distribute load uniformly.
- Wall plate is a thick wooden plank [of about 30 cm in width] placed against defective wall and is secured to the wall by means of needles.
- Wall plate is provided to distribute the load. Rakers are inter connected by braces and are tied at bottom by iron dog or hoop iron.

Following precautions should be taken while providing rakers :

- In order to maintain equilibrium, the following three forces must meet at a point and form a triangle of forces.

   Vertical load from wall, over turning forces from floors or roofs and resisting inclined. *For this purpose, centre line of raker and centre line of wall must meet at floor level.*
- Higher the inclination of raker, lesser will be its horizontal component. i.e. its resistance to outward movement of wall reduces. Hence, inclination of top raker should not be more than 75°.
- Rakers should not be fixed by providing wedges as it is likely to damage the building.
- There is greater uncertainty about magnitude of destabilising forces. Hence, higher factor of safety should be provided.
- Provisions made in local bye laws, etc. should be taken into account.

R.C.C. shore in the form of R.C.C. frame may be used to resist unstable tall retaining wall. Similarly, R.C.C. shore connected to pile cap on top of raker pile can resist destabilising forces effectively.

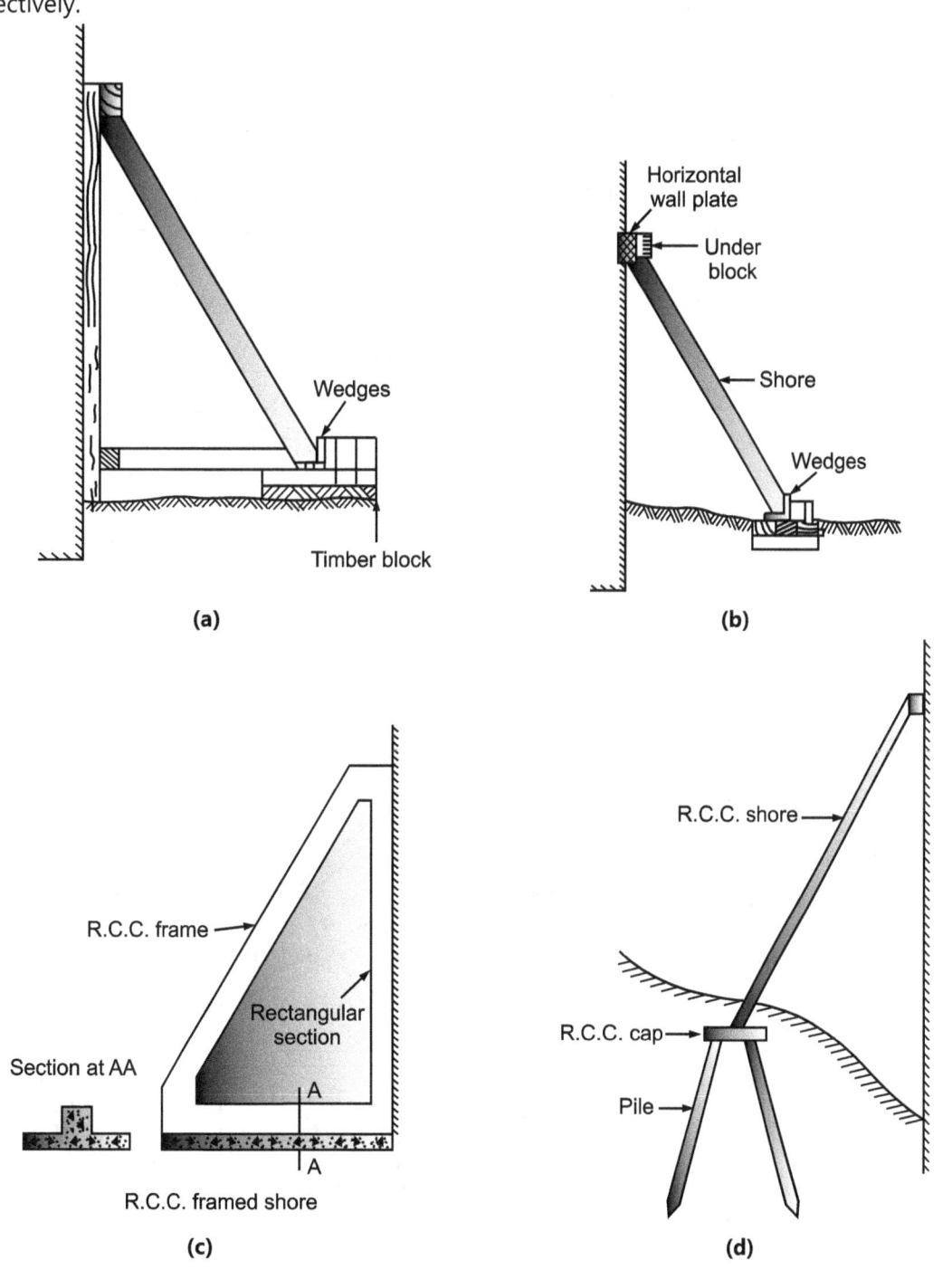

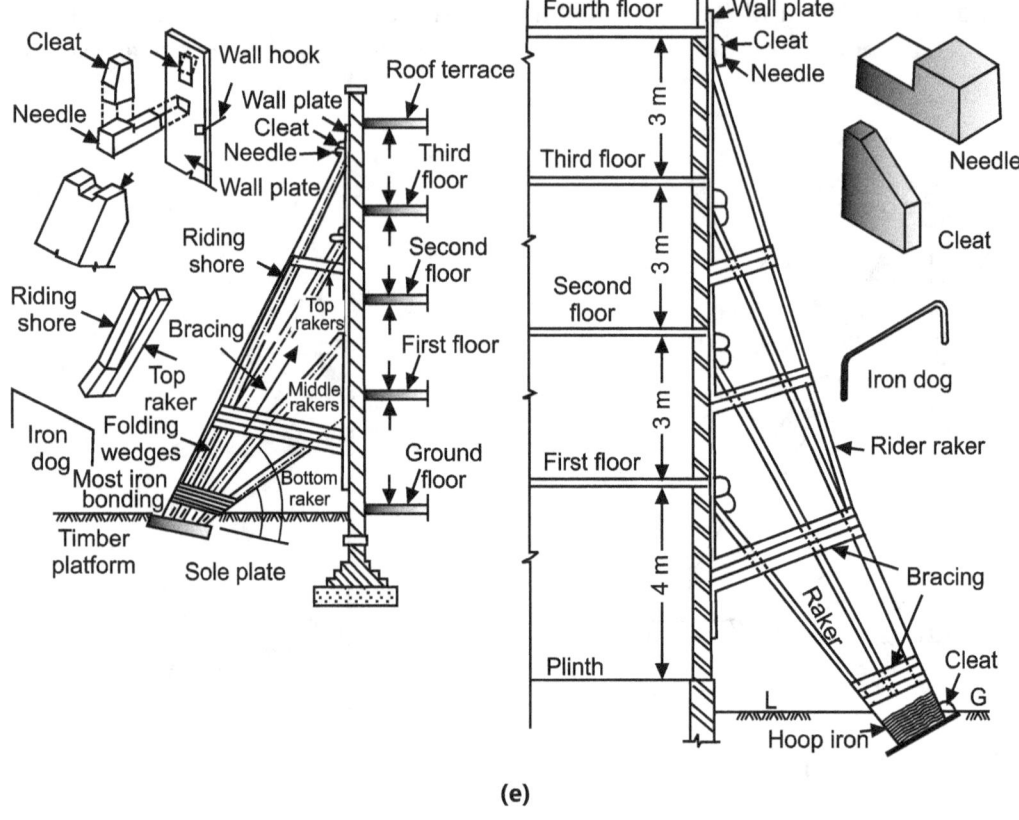

(e)

Fig. 14.4 : Types of raking shores

[b] Flying Shores or Horizontal Shores (Ref. Fig. 14.5) :

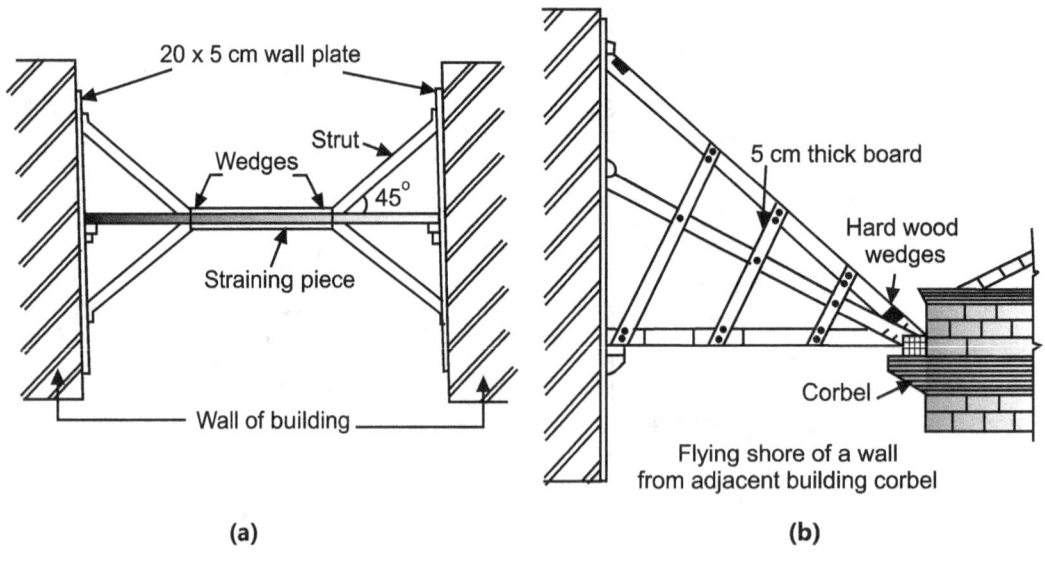

Fig. 14.5

- Horizontal shores called as flying shores are the ideal shores to resist horizontal component of destabilising force. This type of shoring is provided when, parallel walls to provide support at a reasonable distance [< 10 m] is available.

- Centre line of horizontal shore and centre line of wall should meet at floor level. Similarly, centre line of strut, and centre line of wall should meet at floor level. Wedges are driven in between straining piece and strut.

- Angle of the inclination of the strut should be between 45° to 60°. When the distance between the two parallel walls is more than 10 m but less than 15 m, then double flying shore as shown in Fig. 14.5 is provided.

- Flying shores are provided when damaged building is being removed. Flying shores temporarily take up the position of dismantled building and is kept in position till new building is constructed to sufficient height to provide required stability.

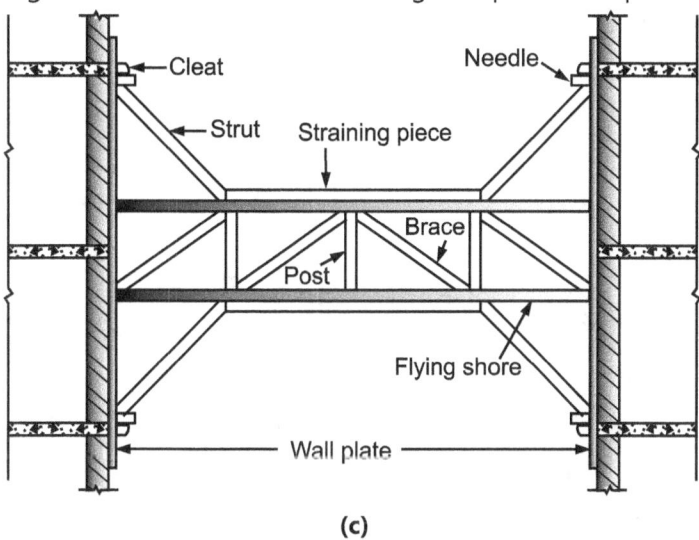

(c)

Fig. 14.5 : Flying stores

[c] Vertical Shore or Dead Shore (Ref. Fig. 14.6) :

This type of shoring is provided, when,

- It is required to strengthen or replace existing unsafe foundation.
- To remove and rebuild a part of defective load bearing wall or
- To provide larger doors, windows or openings in existing walls.

Comparatively, nature, quantity and location of forces acting are known in this type of shoring, than in case of raker shoring. As such, risk involved is comparatively less. Following steps are taken while providing the shoring :

- Those doors, windows and other opening floors and other parts of structure, which are likely to be effected by removal of defective wall or demolition of wall, are properly strutted or supported.

- Small openings of size just enough to insert wooden beams or steel joists are made in wall above the portion of wall which is required to be removed.
- Top and bottom portion of the opening is levelled and steel joist / wooden beam is inserted in the hole. If required, slightly wider wooden plank or steel plate is provided over top of the beam to distribute load evenly over large area.
- The projected ends of beams are supported by heavy vertical strut called as dead shore. As shown in Fig. 14.6, head piece or sole plates are provided so that load is transferred on the dead shore correctly.
- Once again, whether all struts provided in all openings are properly fixed or not is checked and then defective portion is gradually removed.
- Defective portion of wall / foundation is replaced properly.
- Shoring is removed in the following sequence only.
  (a) First needle beams are removed.
  (b) Struts from windows, doors etc. are then removed.
  (c) Finally, struts of floors are removed.

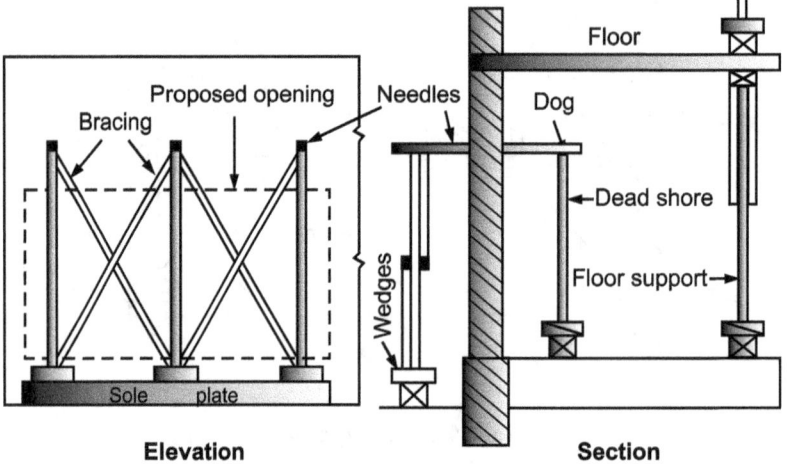

Fig. 14.6 : Dead or vertical shores

Distinction between Scaffolding and Shoring :

- Both shoring and scaffolding are temporary structures, but comparatively shoring is required for a longer period than scaffolding.
- Scaffolding is subjected to lesser loads viz. load of construction materials and workmen working on the platform, and nature of load can be estimated fairly accurately. In shoring it is not possible to precisely determine load acting on shore.
- More care, skill and factor of safety is required for providing shoring than for providing scaffolding.
- Prior permission/approval of local municipal bodies may be required while providing shoring, whereas no such prior approval is required in case of scaffolding.
- Scaffolding is intended to serve as work platform.

REVIEW QUESTIONS

1. Explain the term shoring. State important points to be observed in case of ranking shores.

2. Explain the method of supporting load bearing structure while creating opening at ground floor level of multi-storeyed structure. State the sequence of removal of components.

3. State six important personal protective equipments used on civil engineering sites.

4. State the situations where shoring is needed. State four important points to be observed while installing any shoring.

5. State six important precautions to avoid accidents due to storage or handing of materials on civil engineering site.

6. Draw a labelled sketch of flying shore. State the preferred location and position of flying shores and strut.

7. What is shoring ? Mention the situation where shoring is needed.

8. State the safety precaution to be observed during the excavation work.

9. Write down the safety precautions to be observed in demolition of building.

10. Write short note on Addition and Alteration.

11. Enumerate the benefit of safety to employers, employees and customers.

12. Discuss the different factors leading to accidents in construction project.

13. What is shoring ? Explain one type in detail.

14. Describe in detail the essential components of raking shore showing neat sketches to illustrate your statement.

15. What is Addition and Alteration ? Explain cantilever needle beam method of addition and alteration.

16. What are the important aspects of shoring of construction materials ?

17. What is strutting ? Under what situations the use of strutting is warranted ?

18. Write notes on : (a) Shoring, (b) Strutting, (c) Safety on site.

19. State the safety precautions to be observed during the excavation work.

20. How to prevent the accidents on site ?

21. Describe in detail essential components of raking shore.

22. State six important safety precautions to be observed on building site.

23. Explain the term 'Shoring'. State important points to be observed in case of raking shores.

24. Describe briefly the five resisting properties of common building materials.

SOLVED UNIVERSITY QUESTIONS

MAY 2014

1. Write a note on strutting and shoring   **[5]**
    [**Ans. :** Refer Article 14.4]

NOV. 2015

1. Write short notes on : Repair and maintenance   **[7]**
    [**Ans. :** Refer Article 14.2]

NOV. 2016

1. Enlist the seven safety precautions you will take on construction site.   **[7]**
    [**Ans. :** Refer Article 14.2.3]

MAY 2017

1. Explain the precautions to be taken for safety of workers on site.   **[7]**
    [**Ans. :** Refer Article 14.2.3]

2. Explain the term Shoring. State the situations where shoring is required. **[6]**
    [**Ans. :** Refer Article 14.4]

SAMPLE QUESTION PAPER

End Sem (Theory) Examination

Time : 2 Hour   **Max. Marks : 50**

Instructions to the candidates :

   (1)   Answer all questions.

   (2)   Neat diagrams must be drawn wherever necessary.

   (3)   Figures to the right indicate full marks.

   (4)   Your answers will be valued as a whole.

   (4)   Assume suitable data, if necessary.

1. (a)   Define masonry. Explain Ashlars and Rubble Stone Masonry.   **[6]**

   (b)   With an appropriate figure any two types of Shallow Foundation and their suitability.   **[6]**

OR

2. (a)   With an appropriate figure any two types of Deep Foundation and their suitability.   **[6]**

   (b)   Explain the construction procedure for Reinforced Brick Masonry.   **[6]**

3. (a)   State functional requirements of flooring. Draw sketch of King post truss.   **[6]**

   (b)   Define the following with line sketches: **[6]**

       (i)   Door

       (ii)   Window

       (iii) Arch

       (iv)   Lintel.

OR

4. (a)   State four market names of flooring tiles. Draw sketch of Queen-post truss.   **[6]**

   (b)   Explain the following with sketches   **[6]**

       (i)   Corner window

       (ii)   Corbel Arch

       (iii) Barrel bolt.

5. (a)   Explain the following with sketches: **[6]**

       (i)   Baluster

       (ii)   Scotia

       (iii) Landing.

   (b)   Explain the types of Lintels and discuss about of two.   **[7]**

OR

6. (a) State the requirements of a good stair with respect to: **[7]**

    (i)   Pitch

    (ii)   Head room

    (iii) Location

    (iv)   Number of steps in a flight

    (v)   Rise and Tread

    (vi)   Width of stair.

    (b) Enlist types of stairs depending on the materials of construction. Explain any one in detail.   **[6]**

7. (a) Define timber. State defects in timber. Explain any one.   **[6]**

    (b) Write short notes on   **[7]**

    (i)   Repair and maintenance

    (ii)   Eco-friendly materials.

OR

8. (a) Define seasoning. Explain any two methods of seasoning of timber.   **[6]**

    (b) Write short notes on   **[7]**

    (i)   Aluminium

    (ii)   Ceramic product

    (iii) Safety measures

    (iv)   Road excavation.

www.ingramcontent.com/pod-product-compliance
Lightning Source LLC
Chambersburg PA
CBHW081141020726
47504CB00009B/1956